Stranger in the Mirror

For a moment, I thought I was looking through transparent metal—a window of some kind. Then the man "outside" moved when I moved.

I was looking at my own reflection in a Gandalaran mirror—except that the face I saw in it was *not* my face. At least, it was not the face of Ricardo Carillo.

The supraorbital ridges were quite pronounced, making a semicircle of bone that hooded the eyes. The brow was high, and short dark-blond hair swept down from the scalp in a sharp widow's peak.

I looked down to the mouth. Firm and large, perhaps a bit too thin-lipped, but a very pleasant mouth—a mouth I could live with. I smiled, and great white canines showed.

I smiled wider, accepting the incredible truth. What I saw in the mirror was *my* face. I was behind it, looking out. I controlled it. It belonged to me—and yet it didn't. . . .

Bantam Spectra Books by Randall Garett and Vicki Ann Heydron
Ask your bookseller for the titles you have missed.

THE GANDALARA CYCLE I:
The Steel of Raithskar
The Glass of Dyskornis
The Bronze of Eddarta
THE GANDALARA CYCLE II:
The Well of Darkness
Return to Eddarta
The Search for Kä
THE RIVER WALL

The Gandalara Cycle: Volume 1

Randall Garrett and Vicki Ann Heydron

BANTAM BOOKS
TORONTO • NEW YORK • LONDON • SYDNEY • AUCKLAND

THE GANDALARA CYCLE: VOLUME I

A Bantam Spectra Book / May 1986

This book was first published in three separate volumes:
The Steel of Raithskar, The Glass of Dyskornis, *and*
The Bronze of Eddarta.

Map by Robert J. Sabuda.

ISBN 0-553-25942-3

Published simultaneously in the United States and Canada

Bantam Books are published by Bantam Books, Inc. Its trademark, consisting of the words "Bantam Books" and the portrayal of a rooster, is Registered in U.S. Patent and Trademark Office and in other countries. Marca Registrada. Bantam Books, Inc., 666 Fifth Avenue, New York, New York 10103.

PRINTED IN THE UNITED STATES OF AMERICA

O 0 9 8 7 6 5

Contents

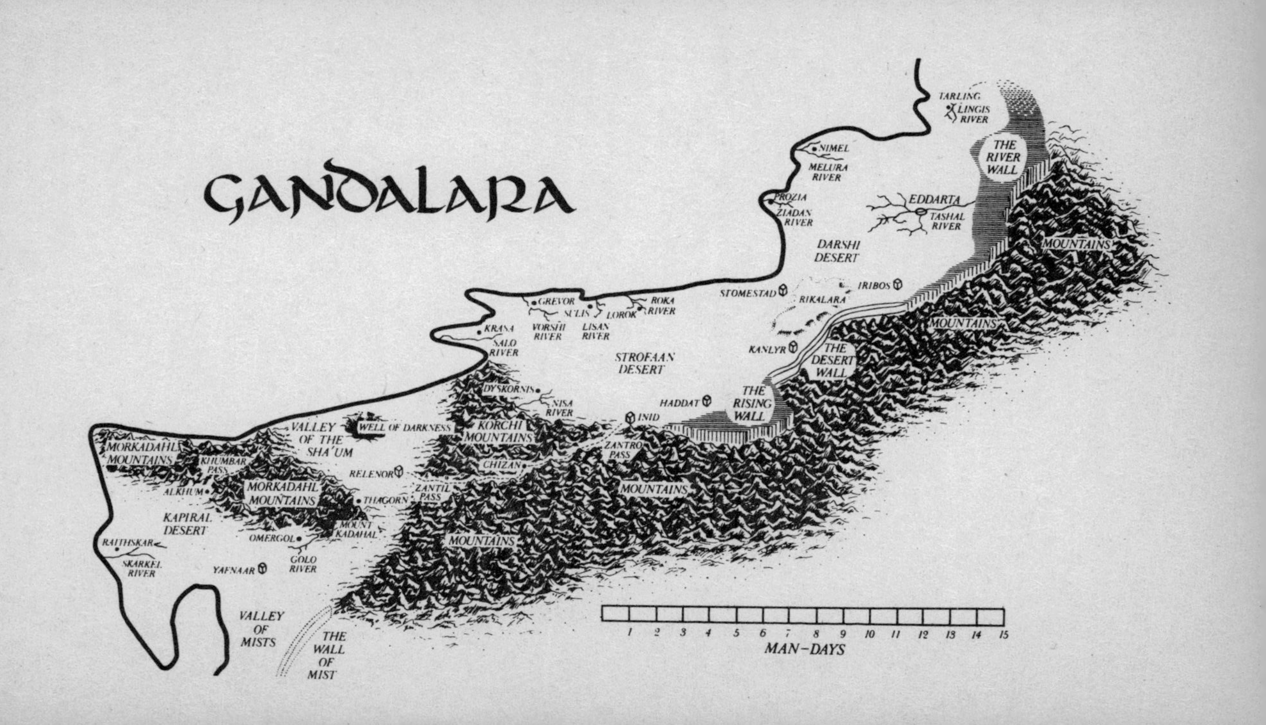
GANDALARA
TARLING
LINGIS RIVER
THE RIVER WALL
NIMEL
MELURA RIVER
PROZIA
ZIADAN RIVER
EDDARTA
TASHAL RIVER
DARSHI DESERT
MOUNTAINS
IRIBOS
STOMESTAD
RIKALARA
GREVOR
SULIS
LOROK
ROKA RIVER
KRANA
VORSHI RIVER
LISAN RIVER
SALO RIVER
MOUNTAINS
KANLYR
THE DESERT WALL
STROFAAN DESERT
DYSKORNIS
NISA RIVER
HADDAT
THE RISING WALL
INID
VALLEY OF THE SHA'UM
WELL OF DARKNESS
KORCHI MOUNTAINS
MORKADAHL MOUNTAINS
KHUMBAR PASS
ZANTRO PASS
CHIZAN
RELENOR
ZANTIL PASS
ALKHUM
MORKADAHL MOUNTAINS
THAGORN
MOUNTAINS
KAPIRAL DESERT
MOUNT KADAHAL
OMERGOL
RAITHSKAR
MOUNTAINS
SKARKEL RIVER
YAFNAAR
GOLO RIVER
VALLEY OF MISTS
THE WALL OF MIST
1 2 3 4 5 6 7 8 9 10 11 12 13 14 15
MAN-DAYS

The Steel of Raithskar

PRELIMINARY PROCEEDINGS:

INPUT SESSION ONE

—You understand what you must do. You have undertaken and completed your training for this task. You know that what you are about to do is of the utmost necessity for the further continuance of the well-being, and perhaps the existence, of our descendants. Are you in agreement with that concept?

—I am, Recorder.

—Good. What goes into the Record must be of the highest quality. No truth can be absolute, but the truth of the Record must be as close to absolute as it is possible for us to make it. Do you understand and believe that?

—I understand and believe it, Recorder.

—Then you know that every detail, down to the slightest, should go into the Record. Every impression, no matter how fleeting; every nuance of thought and emotion; every memory that can be made available must be brought forth.

For all that the work will be purely mental, and not physical, you will find it the hardest labor you have ever undertaken in your life. Do you willingly undertake this labor?

—I do willingly undertake it, Recorder.

—Are you ready, then, to begin this Recording?

—I am ready, Recorder.

—Then make your mind one with mine, as I have made mine one with the All-Mind . . .

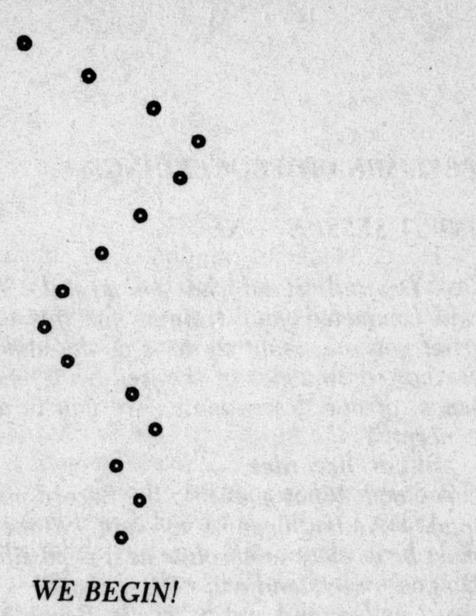

WE BEGIN!

1

Heat, pain, and blinding light, burning through my skin and my eyelids. And the taste of bitter salt in my mouth.

The sensations filled me, rooted me in consciousness while that part of my mind which *could* think floated away and returned. Among the jumble of wandering thoughts, one came clearly:

The fireball killed me. This is what Hell feels like.

But it had no real meaning and it ebbed away into a blankness which seemed eternal.

At last I became aware of directional sensation. The incredible heat surrounded me, but under my fingers as I moved them weakly, pressing against my left cheek, scattered in my eyes and mouth, there was a grittiness that was somehow familiar. Rationality was returning. It was sand.

I was lying on the ground somewhere, on gritty, salty sand.

I lifted my head and tried to spit out the sand, but my mouth was too dry and all I could do was push the sand out with my tongue. With one hand I brushed grit from my eyes and opened them.

I groaned, and lurched up into a sitting position. I sat there with my hands covering my eyes and wept away the savage sting of salt.

When I could open my eyes again, I did so very cautiously, shading them with my hands. At first I thought that I had been blinded in a reverse way, that instead of blackness I was destined always to see only a brilliant white glare. Slowly the light grew tolerable, and the whiteness resolved itself into understandable divisions.

Above me a thin cloud layer diffused the sun's light, but had no discernible dimming effect on it. Light and heat beat down on a fierce white desert, which amplified and reflected them. I had never believed that *anything* could be that hot.

As I turned my head to look around, the pain in my body focused sharply. A lump on my head, above and behind my right ear, was throbbing mightily. And my neck was so stiff that I was forced to wonder how long I had been lying here, slowly frying on the floor of this desert.

What I saw around me was a broad vista of nothing. Or almost nothing. In the flat, nearly featureless desert, two things stood out.

One was nearby. A few yards to my right lay a man, perfectly still, with his face turned away from me. The bright yellow and green of his clothes was oddly comforting, a single spot of color in the gray-white desert.

The other was distant. Toward every horizon but one, the desert flowed unevenly. Here and there were short bushes, spreading almost flat just above the ground. In the sand, crawling around me, were small, pale ants. Yet all this life was a part of the vast, deadly desert, blending smoothly into the endless panorama of nothingness.

Except in one direction.

The land rose slowly to touch the white cloud layer of the sky, and in the far distance a strip of blue, parallel to the horizon, marked their meeting. I had no way of knowing what that line of blue meant, but it was far more attractive than the grayness which surrounded me. It was the only way out of the desert, and I knew I had to move in that direction.

That desperate need carried me clumsily to my feet, and I was instantly grateful that I had managed to stand. My clothes had been crumpled and pressed against my body, but the movement jarred them loose, and, as they fell away from my skin, the heat became almost bearable.

A weight dragged on my right shoulder. I looked at my clothes, touched my chest, and discovered a folded strip of sturdy tan fabric supporting that weight. A baldric—and a sword?

The sword was too heavy for my trembling hands to hold it up for examination, but behind it was hanging a small pouch. At the thought that it might contain food, I was suddenly very hungry. But when I opened it, I found only five large golden coins.

Perhaps the other man had some food . . .

The other man!

I staggered over to him and fell to my knees. I hadn't the faintest notion who he was, but if he were still alive . . .

He wasn't. The stiffness of the corpse as I rolled him over

told me he had been dead for long. And the blood-caked shreds of his tunic made it obvious that he had not died of thirst. He was an ugly sight.

The dry heat had desiccated what could never have been a handsome face. The supraorbital ridges were prominent beneath a high brow. The nose had a pushed-in look, like that of a gorilla, so that the nostrils showed. The chin was massive and squarish.

The dead mouth was open. Cracked and shrunken lips had shriveled back from large, even teeth; the canines were unusually long. Ants were crawling in and out of the open mouth.

I looked away quickly.

But I searched the body thoroughly, hoping to find a bottle of water or some food. All I could come up with was a sword I took to be like the one I was wearing, and another pouch. This one was filled with smaller coins of different sizes, and, without thinking, I poured them out of his pouch and into mine. Some of the coins spilled over my shaking hand. I didn't pick them out of the sand; it was just too much trouble to try.

I stood up then, and looked around again. There was still nothing that promised change except the tantalizing blue ridge at the edge of the visible world. I started to walk toward it, but something drew me back to the dead man. His sword.

Clumsily I pulled the baldric off the body and tried to lift it over my head—but I hadn't the strength to lift the sword. So I set off toward the horizon, holding the baldric and dragging the heavy sword behind me. I didn't know why, but I knew I didn't want to leave the sword out in the desert.

For an endless time I stumbled across the desert floor. My feet slipped in the sand; I tripped over low bushes I was too tired to avoid; sometimes my legs just let me fall. Tiny, sharp-edged rocks, concealed by the sand, cut my hands and face. Each time I fell, the salty sand ground into my raw wounds, until my skin was on fire.

I kept moving. The only *real* thing in the world was the faint line of blue, always ahead of me but never any nearer. I knew I had to keep walking to reach it, so walk I did. One foot in front of the other, struggling back to my feet when I fell, I forced my way across the desert.

I realized dimly that I must be moving north. The sharp glare in the sky which must be the sun above the cloud layer was behind me and moving toward my left. But it didn't matter. Nothing mattered.

I stopped once with a feeling of surprise. Why couldn't I move? I traced the problem to my left arm—something was pulling at it. I looked down and saw that I still held the loop of the baldric in my hand. Somehow the sword had become too heavy to move. Why was I dragging it, anyway?

I had no answer. I let go the baldric and almost fell. I started walking again, with a feeling of satisfaction that I had solved an immense problem.

I was suddenly convinced that I was being followed. I whirled around, the violence of the turn making me stagger, and looked for the follower. Nothing. As far as I could see, the desert was empty except for me. But the sensation persisted: I was not alone.

Now my steady, straight-ahead plodding became a zigzag course. I walked a few yards, then jumped around to try to catch whoever or whatever was trailing me. There was never anything: no movement, no sound. So I turned back and walked on—not quite in the same direction I had been going.

So, for a time, I forgot about the blue line. My attention was behind me, and almost as if it were a game, I walked and turned, walked and turned.

My strength failed. My legs suddenly quit, and I slammed heavily into the salt-thick ground. I simply lay there. I knew I could not stand up again.

Could I move at all? Yes. I could crawl.

The shock of this last fall had knocked some sense back into me. Forget the whatever-it-is that's following; *blue* means salvation. I sighted the line of blue and aimed for it again, began to drag myself through the sand.

I heard a rumbling noise behind me. I was too weak to turn around, so I rolled over on my back and dug my elbows into the sand to lift my head. I wasn't afraid; rather, I was glad to find the answer to the mystery.

A few yards away from me stood the biggest damned cat I had ever seen.

No wonder I hadn't been able to spot him. He was covered with a grayish pale tan fur that blended almost perfectly with the drab surroundings. The low coughing sound came from his throat as he paced restlessly back and forth.

He began to walk a spiral, moving slowly around me and coming gradually closer.

I was sure that the cat's shoulders would have brushed my chin if I were standing. He—I had never thought of him as "it" after I saw him, and as he prowled around me, his maleness was obvious—was built like a tiger, with a powerful chest and a long, agile body. When he growled I could see well-developed canines in his mouth. The image of a sabertooth came to me, but these teeth were nothing like the exaggerated knives of that animal.

I watched the cat watching me. He came in closer, sniffing. I became aware of *his* odor: vaguely muskish, not unpleasant, and somehow familiar.

My neck was getting tired, following the cat's circling. Suddenly he stopped and looked directly at me.

I couldn't defend myself against a kitten, I thought at him. *You might as well come eat me. It's better than dying of thirst.*

The cat didn't move.

Come ahead, I urged. *You're welcome.*

As though he had heard my thoughts, the cat let out a roar that literally shook the ground, and bounded eagerly toward me.

I knew that I had invited him. I was even willing to let him eat me, in a tentative sort of way. But the sight of that great cat closing in for the kill drained away my remaining strength. I collapsed back into the sand and my mind slipped away from me.

2

Water!

It was dripping on my lips, and I licked at it weakly. More drops fell. I licked again.

"Not too much at first," said a voice. "When a man has been too long without water, it is a strong shock to his system to give him too much."

The voice was that of a man, but he spoke with an odd, faintly guttural accent that I couldn't place. I was fully awake now. But I didn't open my eyes. I was perfectly content to lie there licking the water as it dripped on my lips.

"More, Respected Father?" The voice of either a woman or a young boy. The accent was the same.

Drip. Lick. Drip. Lick. Nothing in my life had ever tasted quite that good. It seemed that the water even *smelled* good. Drip. Lick.

I was flat on my back, resting on something noticeably cooler than the desert floor. The air around me and the delicious water were cool and fresh. Suddenly the dripping seemed too slow. I wanted a *drink* of water. I opened my mouth.

"See." The man's voice. "He responds. A little more now, Lamothet. Not too much."

When my mouth felt moist enough to talk, I said: "Has Keeshah water?"

"The sha'um will take it only from you, Rider."

I knew what I had said, and I understood what had been said to me. But it had no meaning. I blinked and sat up. What the hell were we talking about? My mind seemed fuzzy, as if it were slightly out of focus.

The room I was in was cool because it was protected from the desert heat by thick walls made of huge translucent blocks. Sunlight penetrated the walls and suffused the room with a soft light, which was a welcome change from the painful glare I had first seen.

More of the large, regular blocks stood free around the room as furniture. On some of these, and hanging on the walls, were finely woven cloths, richly embroidered. One served as a pad for the man-sized block on which I had awakened.

There were three other people in the room with me. A young boy—Lamothet, I presumed—was holding a small, delicate cup, adorned with tiny geometric designs. There was a strong-looking man who could only be "Respected Father", and another man not quite as young as Lamothet. The older man wore authority with the same ease that he wore his long, clean, white tunic.

My voice sounded as strange as theirs when I spoke.

"Where am I?" I asked. "How did I get here?"

"You are in the Refreshment House of Yafnaar, and are most welcome, Rider," said the elder. He put gentle hands on my shoulders and pressed me back. "As for how you got here, why, you came on the back of your sha'um, of course." He unstoppered a small-mouthed jar that matched the cup's design, took the cup from the boy, and filled it. He lifted my shoulders and helped me drink.

"You must rest a while longer."

I lay back and looked closely at the man's face, and realized with a start that he could be related to the corpse I had left out in the desert. He was by no means as ugly, but he had the same high forehead, jutting brows, and pug nose, all a little less pronounced. Even the canines. They weren't the pointed fangs of a movie vampire, but wide, strong teeth, more like short tusks than fangs. The other two had that same look—a family resemblance?

I decided not to mention the corpse. If these were his family, they might think I had killed him. And it troubled me in an unknown way that I had left his sword out on the desert.

I closed my eyes to a wave of weakness, and again an unfamiliar word came naturally to my lips. "Keeshah?"

"You may tend your sha'um when you are more rested. He is strong—stronger than you. Relax."

My sha'um. Funny word. *Shah-oom.* With a glottal stop.

I remembered.

The big cat looming over me, not attacking but nuzzling in an urgent way. Trying to get his huge head under my unmov-

ing bulk. I understood at last, and put my arms around his neck. He surged upward, lifting me to my knees, then lay down on the sand in front of me. I fell across his back, managed to turn my body to straddle him, and again locked my arms around his neck. Then he carried me across the desert in long, loping strides. The last thing I could remember before waking here was the regular, comforting motion of the strong body beneath me.

Yes, Keeshah was stronger than I could ever hope to be. He was a sha'um.

Sha'um. Great cat. Or, literally: cat great. This language put the adjective after the noun, as the Romance languages did.

What? I started from my half-doze. *What the hell is going on in my head?* It suddenly became very important for me to find out who I was.

I tried to sit up and ask my new friends, but I couldn't. That last cup of water must have been drugged. I gave in and relaxed again. *I think I'm better,* I told myself with crazy logic. *At least I know now that I don't know who I am.*

I dozed off, still puzzling over a language I understood perfectly, and at the same time knew damned well I had never heard before.

I dreamed a dream.

"The Mediterranean is beautiful on a moonlit night, is it not?" said a voice at my elbow. A woman's voice, huskier than contralto, a voice that suited the evening. Her Italian sounded Milanese.

I turned to look at her, sure before I saw her of what I would see. I had just been thinking of her, remembering the happy laugh I had heard across the dining room, wishing that during this cruise I might meet her on deck and share just such a lovely night with her. If I have learned anything in my long life, it is that wishes occasionally come true.

She was tall, five feet seven or so—she would have said 170 centimeters—with the blonde hair and the svelte figure of the Lombard. Her gracefully and delectably low-cut gown had the unmistakable, expensive look of Alderuccio of Rome.

"It is made even more beautiful by your presence, Contessa," I said. A man of sixty can afford to be gallant, especially if it's the truth.

Her lovely laugh rang out. "I am not the Contessa, signore."

"You must be, my dear. At dinner this evening, the gentleman next to me—Colonello Gucci—distinctly said to me, 'Dottore, you see that most beautiful woman sitting a few places down from the end, at the Captain's table? That is the Contessa di Falco.' Since you were the most beautiful woman at that table—indeed, on the ship—I concluded he meant you."

"No." She shook her head and made the silver-set dangles at her ears wink in the moonlight. "That is my sister, who was sitting next to me. I am Antonia Alderuccio."

I gestured at the dress. "You are Alderuccio of Rome?"

"Wrong again, signore. That is my uncle." She moved closer to the railing, and the breeze brought the light scent of her perfume past me. "I am sorry, signore, that no one pointed out to me such a distinguished man as yourself. You are Dottore . . . ?"

"Ricardo Carillo, at your service, signorina."

She turned to face me. The surprise on her face was a fine compliment. "You are Spanish? You speak Italian perfectly!"

"Thank you, but I am Spanish only by ancestry. I am an American."

"Naturalized, then?"

"No, native born. My ancestors were living in California before the English ever heard of the place."

"How wonderful! I have seen the cinema films of the early Californians." She drew up the skirt of her gown, assumed the en garde, *and attacked me with an invisible rapier in her right hand. "Zorro! So! Zzzt-zzzt-zzzt!"*

She stopped. I looked at her in astonishment, then laughed as I had not laughed in years. She dropped her pose and laughed with me.

I was grateful to her. She was young enough to be my granddaughter, yet with her exuberance, she had not so much flaunted her own youth as reminded me of mine. We were closer now; friends.

When we could speak again, she said: "But that still does not explain how you speak Italian so well."

"The truth is dull, I'm afraid. I have the honor to be a Professor of Romance Languages, University of California at Santa Barbara."

"But I think of professores always as intense and stoop-

shouldered, wearing glasses and not quite looking at one." She looked at me critically. "You look more like a military man."

Her zaniness was infectious. I snapped to attention and saluted crisply.

"Master Sergeant Ricardo Carillo, United States Marine Corps, Retired; at your service, signorina." I relaxed and added, "Actually, I only made corporal in the regulars; the six stripes came from reserve time."

"I know the reputation of the Marines of the United States—they are the finest fighting force in the world. How brave you must be!" Was she laughing at me? A little, perhaps, but not entirely. I had indeed impressed her; knowing that I could impressed me.

"Not brave, signorina. Cautious. The Corps has a saying: 'There are old Marines, and there are bold Marines, but there are no old, bold Marines.' It's funnier in English, I'm afraid."

"But it makes sense in any language," she said seriously. "Why are you sailing the Mediterranean on a cruise ship, Ricardo?" The sound of my first name was very special in her voice. It was a gentle intimacy between us.

"I'm taking a sabbatical leave, Antonia. I've been to Europe before—often, in fact. But always on business. Linguistics research, conferences, and other such mundane activities which didn't allow me to appreciate *the countries I saw. This time it's just for fun: a pleasure trip."*

I told her only what she needed to know of the truth. Could I tell her that my health was bad, that diabetes and kidney infection and just plain old age had caught up with me? I don't think the knowledge would have driven Antonia away, but I was afraid that it would drive her closer, which, under these circumstances, would have been even more repellent to me. Besides, the deck of a cruise ship, surrounded by the shimmering, restive Mediterranean, was no place to speak of death.

"Oh, look, Ricardo. Look!*" She had been watching the sky with that thoughtful look that is so appealing in young women, but now she pointed upward, completely alert. "That star! It is getting brighter and brighter."*

I did look. There was a pinpoint of light in the sky, unmoving, which was indeed growing brighter second by second.

"Is that what the astronomers call a nova?" she asked. There was excitement in her voice.

I watched the light closely; it changed color. It was orange, then yellow, finally white. And still it grew brighter.

"I'm afraid that's not in my line, Antonia," I told her. "But I'd say it has to be at least a supernova."

I tried to keep the fear from my voice. But now it was a small ball of fire, visibly growing, which did not seem to move. I thought I knew what it was.

A meteor, *I thought*. It's coming straight at us.

A falling star, a boloid, a great hunk of rock or iron—it wasn't my field, as I'd told Antonia, but I knew enough to be frightened. It was a huge mass of space debris, coming in from the sky at a velocity measurable only in miles per second. To say "thirty-six thousand miles an hour" doesn't mean anything unless you think about it, and we had no time to think.

But I had time to feel. *I had come to terms, more or less, with my own death long ago. I had half expected to die before I got home; only the manner of it was an incredible surprise. But I felt a totally irrational guilt, as though this disaster were my fault, and because of me, everyone on the ship would die, too.*

And Antonia. I was angry on her behalf. So young . . . Too young . . .

I didn't tell her what I knew. I didn't even try to give an alarm, because I knew there was no time. We simply stood together and watched it grow in eerie silence—it was moving far faster than the speed of sound. From the time she had first seen it until it struck could not have been more than ten or twelve seconds.

Brighter and brighter . . . larger . . . closer . . .

It became a great ball of unbearable light . . .

I woke up screaming.

3

I opened my eyes. The soft light around me, diffused through the frosty walls, told me that day had come again. I sat up slowly, surprised to find that I was feeling quite well.

The young man was seated on a nearby white block, padded, as mine was, with colorful tapestry. He stood up with the silent grace cultivated by those who tend the sick, and smiled at me tentatively.

"You had a bad night last night," he said. "Are you better this morning?"

"Much better," I assured him. "I'm sorry if I worried you. I had a—a dream." As I said it, I knew it hadn't been *precisely* a dream.

"You screamed," he said. There was a look of consternation on his face, as though he wanted to ask me why, but hesitated. He compromised. "Were you sent a portent of disaster?"

"No. A . . . memory of a past one." I smiled at him; I didn't want more questions right now. "Don't disturb yourself, please. It was nothing."

The worry fell away from his face. "Good. I am Keddan of the Fa'aldu. I think you will have more water, then we will bring you a porridge. These things must not be done too swiftly, or you will be sick at your stomach and waste much water."

I watched him as he unstoppered the decorated pitcher and poured water into two of the fragile cups. He moved with studied care and spilled not a single drop. He was wearing the same kind of long white tunic as the "Respected Father" had worn, and I wondered briefly if the white robes were a uniform of some kind. I put the thought aside as Keddan brought the two cups over to me.

He offered both of them, unmistakably inviting me to choose one for myself. I understood the gesture; he was assuring me that *this* drink was not drugged. And it wasn't until he dismissed it in this way that I realized the suspicion had been in my mind. Gratefully, I took one of the cups and drank thirstily—though I was careful not to spill any.

The water was cool and had a pleasant flavor which I didn't recognize at first. I realized as I finished the cup that it was brackish. There was salt in the water—enough, at least, to taste it.

The well must contain a trace of salt, I decided; that would hardly be surprising out here in the desert.

"I will go now to prepare your breakfast," Keddan said, when he had placed pitcher and cups in a narrow recess cut from one of the blocks that formed an inside wall. "Is there any other service you desire?"

"No, thank you, Keddan. May I sit here and rest a little?"

"That would be good, Rider. When you are ready to water your sha'um, you have but to ask." He pushed aside a tapestry which concealed a doorway and was gone.

I was glad to be alone. I had a lot to think about. And I was infinitely glad to be *able* to think again. The day before had been a jumble of confusion and exhaustion; an incoherent desperation had driven me across the desert. Yesterday I had only wanted to survive.

Today I wanted answers. *What the hell has happened to me? Where am I? Oh, I know,* I told myself impatiently, *in the Refreshment House of Yafnaar, among the Fa'aldu. And where does that get me?*

Today, at least, I had a rational mind. I had defined the problem and could approach it logically. The first step: assemble all the facts I had—the facts, that is, as I understood them.

FACT ONE: My name was Ricardo Emilio Carillo, lately of California. *All right, face the toughest one first. Do you mean "lately" or simply "late"?* Yesterday I had considered with utter detachment the possibility that I had died and arrived in Hell. Certainly I had believed, when the fireball was coming toward me, that I was about to die.

I had never thought much about the character of Hell—or, for that matter, of Heaven. But I had always assumed, I realized as I thought about it now, that I would *feel* very different. Whatever the place was like—either one—I should not feel as . . . well, as *alive*.

And right now, with my head still dully throbbing, the hardness of the block beneath me intangible even through the thin padding, the pleasant salty taste of the water lingering in my mouth, I felt very much alive.

I made up my mind, then, to set aside the question of my death in another life. In *this* life, in *this* world, I was alive; and the world around me was absolutely real.

It occurred to me that my decision followed classic lines of thought: the nature of reality *a la* Bishop George Berkeley, and the Cartesian *cogito ergo sum.* Whatever it was based on, having made the decision made me feel much better. And it led me to examine the next fact.

FACT TWO: This place did not exist on the Earth as I knew it. It had similarities to Death Valley in California, the great salt flats of Utah, and the desert areas around the Dead Sea. But I had been to all three places; I knew for a certainty that this desert was different. Nor could it be the Sahara or the Gobi, which I *hadn't* seen; I knew they had nothing like the salty quality of this place.

Could I be on an entirely different planet? Only, I decided, if it weren't in Earth's planetary system. Even *I* knew that there were no planets except Earth in the Solar System with breathable atmosphere.

I didn't have enough information to settle this question at the moment. I set it aside.

FACT THREE: I had studied languages all my life, specializing in the Romance languages, but along the way acquiring a nodding friendship with most of the languages of my world. I had never even heard of this language. Where, when, and how did I acquire such an automatic command of Gandaresh?

There! It happened again! A word I need pops out of nowhere—a word I know, and yet I don't.

Gandaresh: people-talk.

The word was there in my mind as though it had always been there. With it was another one: *Gandalara.* People-place. I had one of the answers I had been searching for. Where was I? Why, in Gandalara, of course.

But where, damn it, is *Gandalara?*

No answer.

So I had a memory I hadn't had before, but it was limited to things of this world, the Gandalaran world. It would be no help in solving the puzzle of my presence here. *But,* I thought with relief, *it's going to be a hell of a lot of help in getting along here!*

FACT FOUR: I had a very painful bump on the right side of my head, just above and behind the ear. What was *that* contributing to my state of mind?

It didn't matter, I decided. I had done all the logical thinking I could or wanted to do. I'd relax a while and simply accept things as they came.

I got up from the padded stone and stretched experimentally. I could feel an annoying sting here and there on my hide—and winced at the memory of my trek across the desert. Looking back, it was almost as though I had *bounced* across it: up on my feet, flat on my face, up on my feet, slam to the ground . . .

All in all, it was remarkable that I felt so good. Abrasions all over my body, of course, and the palms of my hands felt very tender. I was a little stiff, but the stretching helped that. It could have been worse. Very much worse. By comparison to the condition I might have been in, I felt terrific.

I walked a few steps around the room, intending to look at everything, but I was first drawn to the wall of the house. Its translucent stone intrigued me; it was like no building material I had ever seen before. It had a random crystalline quality: it was generally more translucent than alabaster, but in some places it was as transparent as glass, in others as opaque as fine white marble. The closest familiar comparison I could make was to rock crystal—quartz.

The engineering problem seemed enormous. It took precision and skill and *lots* of power to mine and shape that hard mineral, and the impression these people had given me had no suggestion of that kind of power. How on Earth—*try to think like a native: how in Gandalara?*—could they mine and handle blocks about the size and shape of a case of beer?

Faen. Beer. *Thank you, memory*. It was nice to know that fermentation was practiced here. Oh, a beer—how I wanted an ice cold beer!

I withdrew from that line of thought as fast I could. I had to concentrate on learning about *this* world, not waste time in longing for the one I had lost.

Still fascinated by the stone, I ran my dry palms over the wall. It was smoother than I had suspected. In fact, it seemed too smooth to be a natural mineral. Could it be some kind of cast glass? No; the crystalline structure was quite apparent. As I stared thoughtfully into the block which was at my eye level, I began to see something familiar in it. Distorted as they were, the crystals seemed cubic and they reminded me of *something* . . .

It came to me. To confirm it, I wet one forefinger with my tongue, rubbed it on the wall, and tasted it.

Son of a bitch! I thought. *The place is made of rock salt.*

Now here was knowledge I could use. It meant, of course, that rock salt was readily available to the Fa'aldu, but besides that: One, it hadn't rained here since this house was built; and Two, rain must have been unknown here for a long time *before* they built it. Surely nobody would go to the trouble to build a house like this if he expected it to be washed away at any moment. Building materials have to suit the environment. Adobe works fine, for instance, in the arid Southwest United States, but try building a 'dobe *hacienda* on the coast of Maine.

I moved over to the draped doorway through which Keddan had gone. The heavy curtain seemed to have been woven of several different thicknesses of yarn. Some were merely thin threads, as smooth as tanned leather, but others were three times as thick, some of them fuzzy and bristly, like fat twine.

They were all different tones of the same medium blue, except for a wide strand so much lighter than the rest that it stood out from the blue background. It formed no pattern that I could see this close to it, so I stepped back a pace—

—and caught my breath.

The overall effect of the thing was a sheet of water—cascading from ceiling to floor.

An indoor waterfall in the middle of the desert! It was incredibly beautiful—even cooling.

I wondered, suddenly, if one of the people I had met had crafted that amazing tapestry.

As I looked around the room for more wonders, I caught sight of a polished bronze plaque set shoulder-high in the outer wall. I was seeing it from a shallow angle which should have made visible anything etched on its surface, and I could see nothing there. Curious, I walked over to stand directly in front of it.

For a moment, I thought I was looking through transparent metal—a window of some kind. Through it I saw, looking in, another member of that same family of heavy-browed, pug-nosed people. Embarrassed by the confrontation, I opened my mouth to speak—I don't know what, a greeting, an apology—but I never said anything.

The man "outside" moved when I moved.

I was looking at my own reflection in a Gandalaran mirror—except that the face I saw in it was *not* my face. At least, it was not the face of Ricardo Carillo.

I stared into the eyes of a face I had never seen before, and they began to look terribly frightened. I looked away and examined the rest of the face instead. I was wearing it, after all; I should get to know it.

The supraorbital ridges were quite pronounced, making a semicircle of bone that hooded the eyes. The eyebrows were faint and sparse, composed of fine dark-blond hairs that followed the bony ridges across the top of the nose, around, and down to the corners of the eyes.

Above the supraorbital ridges, the brow was high, and short dark-blond hair swept down from the scalp in a sharp widow's peak. I reached up with my left hand and touched it. It was short all over, like a crew cut, but it lay nearly flat against the skull. It was fine and soft, almost like fur.

I followed the line between the eyes down to the nose, and as I watched it, it wrinkled with distaste. Pug. Not as flat as that of the corpse in the desert, but most definitely a pug nose, and I have never been fond of them. They offend me for some reason—maybe because I don't care to be looking up people's nostrils.

I looked down to the mouth. Firm and large, perhaps a little too thin-lipped, but a very pleasant mouth—a mouth I could live with.

I smiled at the mirror image, just a little. Only the great canines showed. I smiled wider.

Look at those beautiful teeth!

Strong and white, even those tusks were gorgeous. I made faces into the mirror, trying to see all the way inside my mouth. Not a single cavity that I could see. I grabbed my upper teeth with the fingers of both hands and shook them until my head wobbled. They didn't budge. They were rock-solid in this new mouth of mine.

No more dentures and their problems: Would my teeth click at the faculty meeting? Let's see—no, I'd better not have a cob of corn. Trying surreptitiously to get a seed out from under my lower plate. No more of that now.

My own teeth again. *Hot damn!*

I liked the chin, too. It was wide and strong and well-formed. So far, it was the most familiar part of the face; I fancied it was much like the Carillo chin.

The ears were a bit on the small side; they lay almost flat against the side of my head. Not bad ears at all.

The skin was dark, like a heavy tan on an Amerindian. Much darker than the skin of Ricardo Carillo. That was all right, too—I hadn't had a decent tan in years.

Now I could look into the eyes of my new face, and I was pleased to find that, aside from their frame, they were very much like the eyes I had always known. Darker brown, perhaps, and clearer around the iris.

I stepped back to take a look at the face as a whole. Not bad, actually, once one got used to it.

I accepted the incredible truth: what I saw in the mirror was *my* face.

I was *behind* it, looking out. I controlled it. It blinked or smiled when I told it to. It *belonged* to me—and yet it didn't. I reminded myself that the English "face" and the French *façade* are cognates. Yes, I told myself, it *is* my face.

Now: *Who am I?*

A few minutes before, I could have answered without hesitation: Ricardo Emilio Carillo. But that was before I saw myself. Coupled with the odd, unearned memory that popped up now and then, my new appearance changed everything.

As I groped for understanding, it occurred to me that sometimes amnesia acted this way. A concussion destroyed a man's memories, and he had to start life over again. Years later a second blow on the head restored his memories of the early life and wiped away the years immediately past.

It wasn't a true model for my situation, of course. But it helped me think things through. For me it was as though the "second blow" had called up only vague memories of that early time. I was still consciously Ricardo Carillo, but I was also someone else—someone whose memories were not quite available to me.

I wondered with a flash of panic if they would ever be entirely mine. I had to live in *his* world; without knowing who he was, without understanding this Gandalaran as well as I did Ricardo (which, after all, was little to ask—do we ever really know ourselves?), I would never make this world *my* world.

The amnesia model fell apart when I considered the physical change which had taken place. At that point in my thinking, I looked down at my new body. A man is more than his face.

I undid the drawstring and dropped the loose blue trousers I was wearing. Were these the same ones I had worn across the desert? I couldn't tell. Then I removed a loosely-woven undergarment that was very much like boxer shorts with a drawstring.

I stood back far enough from the mirror to see my whole body, and I was very pleased with what I saw.

My neck was short, thick, and muscular, like that of a wrestler. My shoulders and chest were broad and well-muscled. They tapered slightly to a waistline fuller than the one I remembered, but flat and harder even than mine had been in my youth.

My genitals seemed quite adequate and appropriate for my size and weight. I would have to see how they stood up to the ultimate test if the opportunity arose.

My legs were muscle-corded, and ended in feet which looked quite ordinary. The toes were a little longer, I thought, but when I flexed them, they worked fine. What more can you ask of toes?

I looked at my hands then, wondering how it was that I had not noticed the difference before now. Ricardo Carillo's hands were not in any sense delicate, but these made them look weak. The fingers were long and fine, full of strength. The hands themselves were large, though not massively so. With the corded wrists that held them, they were appropriate to the long, thickly muscled arms.

The dark-blond hair of my head grew downy-fine along my forearms and over the backs of my hands, more coarsely on my chest, on the back of my neck, and around my genitals.

I turned and posed in front of the mirror, getting acquainted with my body as I had with my face.

As Ricardo Carillo, I had been tall and reasonably strong; my muscles had remained firm until only a few years ago. The height of this Gandalaran I couldn't judge until I compared it to others, but he was unquestionably strong. "Rider," they had called me. I could well see that clinging to the back of that cat for any length of time would develop every muscle you could find.

Whoever it was who shared this body with me, he had taken very good care of it, considering the short time he'd had to develop it . . .

It hit me then, with more of a shock than looking in the mirror. This was the body of a *young* man.

I'm young again!

I had been ready to die. In the only way I could reckon it, less than two days ago I had come to terms with the fact that I would be dead within a year. To face such a truth, to let it penetrate down to the core of your being, demands incredible effort and indescribable pain. No matter how much life you've had, you want more. There are things undone, words unsaid, potentials unexplored. You know you could have done more with your life, and you beg fate, or whatever god you believe in, to give you more time. You know in your heart that another entire lifetime would not be sufficient, yet you pray for just a few more years. You've been goofing off, you think; please, just an extra year or two to finish all those abandoned projects!

But you know it can't be done. Your time has come, and there's no changing it.

So then you look back and count what you *have* done. And, all in all, the balance is really in your favor.

I looked back and realized that I had spent most of my adult life doing exactly what I wanted to do; exposing younger minds to the variety and the history of the world that I had discovered through languages. Some of my students had taken the time to tell me how much I had changed them. Their viewpoints had broadened, their lives had felt richer. They were aware of themselves as individual units in the composite of civilization. And those words of thanks were precious trophies.

There had been personal relationships, friendships I remembered warmly. Coming back from the war to find "my girl" married to someone else had been a blessing in disguise. I was left free to study all over the world, and to make friends wherever I went. Many of them were women, and some were very special. We shared our lives for a time. It was always—at least for me—very satisfying, and it ended naturally and without bitterness. Yes, I could say to my credit that I had never made a friend, man or woman, who was not still my friend.

So I had accepted, at last, that my life had been full, and well worth living. I had contributed what I could to the lives of other people; hopefully, through them and their memory of me, to the human race as a whole. An extended pleasure trip, to see the places I'd always traveled *between*—that was what I had wanted to do with what remained of my life.

I had made that adjustment. Painfully. Finally. I had been prepared to die.

And now I am alive in another world, young *in another world, with another lifetime of experiences—new experiences—ahead of me.*

I stood motionless for some time, taking it in. Letting the silent raging joy wash away the musty taste of death. And giving thanks in an incoherent, inexpressible way. I knew that I might never know why or how this had happened. But, *Oh, God!* was I glad!

A grumbling roar that I remembered well sounded from outside and brought me back into focus. I dressed again quickly; Keddan would be back soon with my breakfast. And then . . .

I would have to go out and face that monster cat.

4

The door curtain was swept aside, and the older of the two men came in, followed by Keddan, who was carrying a bowl. I glanced quickly from it to the recess where the stoppered pitcher stood. Yes, it was the same pattern. These people appreciated fine craftsmanship, if they did not, in fact, create these lovely things themselves.

They stopped a few paces from where I stood and Keddan, still in the background, said in formal tones: "Rider, I present the Respected Elder Balgokh."

Help! I thought. *What am I supposed to do? What are the customs?* No answer was forthcoming, so I followed my instincts; I bowed slightly and spoke, relieved to find that the words, at least, were there.

"Greeting, Respected One."

"Greeting, Rider." He did not return my bow, but he showed no offense. In fact he smiled, and waved Keddan forward. "We bring you breakfast. You seem to have recovered well. How do you feel?"

"Remarkably well, all things considered," I said. I accepted the good-smelling bowl of food from Keddan and smiled at him. "Thank you."

A quick smile lit Keddan's face, then he left the room. I looked at the imposing figure of Balgokh in his floor-length white robe. He was older than I had first thought, but that did not affect the attitude of accustomed authority which emanated from him. He was a little taller than I, his hair darker and sparser, his hands thinner. He moved them in a gesture of invitation.

"Sit, Rider, and eat," Balgokh said.

I sat down and took up the eating implement which was partially imbedded in the contents of the bowl. It was ceramic, shaped very much like a spoon, except there were two slots in the end, which formed three fork-like tines. It matched the other pieces of the serving set, and said something about basic values in Gandalara: graceful utility.

The bowl contained what appeared to be finely chopped vegetables and chunks of meat. I scooped a small bite into my mouth, braced for anything. It was pleasantly warm, and tasted something like oatmeal with bits of lamb—a distant relative of haggis.

"This is delicious," I said, meaning it. Balgokh bowed slightly, accepting the compliment.

"We offer the best fare we can to those who pass through our compound. Please, eat. We will talk when you have finished."

As I ate—I was intensely hungry, and had to try not to wolf down the food—I considered what they had called me: "Rider." It was a title, not a name.

The bowl of food was quickly gone and, surprisingly, I was quite satisfied. When I finished, Keddan came back in to take away the bowl and fork-spoon. Had he been watching through the curtained doorway?

When he had gone, Balgokh reached into his flowing robe and took out a small pouch and handed it to me. "Your money, Rider. Your sword will be returned when you are ready to leave."

I accepted the purse with new misgivings. Hesitantly, I asked, "Do I owe you for your hospitality?"

Oops.

The tall man stiffened, and his voice lost the note of familiarity that had been present earlier. "We sell water to the caravans," he said with deadly formality, "for that is the living of the Fa'aldu. But we demand nothing of the distressed, and we *never* accept coin."

Hurriedly I stood up and bowed with what I hoped was formal grace. "I ask your pardon, Respected One."

Boy, do I need more information about this culture—for that matter, about the person I'm supposed to be. But how the hell can I ask questions about things which are absolutely obvious to other people? A man wandering around California asking questions like "What are grapes?" or "Who is the president of the United States?" is going to be suspect as a mental case. If I don't want to head straight for the local equivalent of a twitch bin, I'd better think about everything *I say before I say it. Unless. . .*

I decided to tell part of the truth.

I touched the side of my head gently. "This blow on my head has left me confused, Respected One. My memory is addled."

To say the least.

He thawed instantly, and looked so concerned that I felt a twinge of guilt. "I have heard of such cases," he said. "I saw one, myself, many years ago, when I was an apprentice. An unfortunate man. He was a caravan driver, who had been kicked in the head by one of the vleks. He did not know his name or where he came from."

"What happened to him?" I asked, glad to hear Balgokh's voice lose its frostiness.

"He died." Then, at what must have been a look of utter shock on my face, he added quickly, "But he was in much worse shape than you. It was a miracle that he lived the three days he spent with us."

I laughed a little. "I'm not going to die." The words held infinite meaning for me. "But I admit I can't remember my own name."

He grinned broadly. I was interested to see that, old as Balgokh was, he, too, still had all his own teeth. I was getting used to the large canines; Balgokh's smiling face was not what I could yet call handsome, but I was beginning to like it. Especially when Balgokh said:

"I am delighted to be of help to you in that respect. Four days ago, the caravan of Gharlas stopped by, trading food and cloth for water. You were with them as a mercenary guard—at least, so Gharlas said." His grin faded, and a look passed across his face which I couldn't read. It might have been dislike, or wry humor. "He confided to me—not at my request, I assure you—that he intended to bypass Thagorn in order to save that portion of his freight which would go as duty to the Sharith."

Sharith. Catfolk. There was something about the carefully neutral tone in which Balgokh spoke that word that worried me.

"You said 'so Gharlas said'?" I prompted him.

"Yes." He began to walk around the room. There was too much dignity in the slow movement to call it pacing. It dawned on me that he was embarrassed, and I recalled Keddan's reluctance to ask personal questions.

It must be a code of privacy, I decided. *Or self-preservation. The Fa'aldu don't get involved with their clientele. But I'm a mystery he couldn't resist thinking about. Could he be afraid of offending me with his opinions?*

"Respected Elder," I said, and he stopped. He turned to look at me. "Do you know my name?"

"Your name was given to me as Lakad."

Nice phrasing, I thought. The name meant nothing at all to me. "But who am I, really?"

Balgokh sighed, and seemed to make a decision. "My first thought," he said, "when you returned as a Rider, was to believe that you had been a Sharith agent, planted on the caravan. But after we had cared for you, and I considered carefully, I wondered why your sha'um hadn't taken you directly to Thagorn, given the time you must have been exposed on the desert.

"If you were not Sharith, as I had begun to suspect, your identity was obvious. I know of only one Rider in this part of Gandalara who does not reside in Thagorn. He and his sha'um live in Raithskar. When you named this one Keeshah, the proof was complete." He paused for emphasis.

"You are Markasset, son of Thanasset."

"Thank you, Respected One," was all I said. I had to push the words through a chilling rush of associations too tangled and jumbled for me to read them yet. "My mind is still clouded, but at least I know my name. You have been a great help."

Markasset. Yes, it was my name. It *felt* like my name. But it wasn't. Not quite. Not completely. I still felt like Ricardo Carillo, too.

Thanasset. My father. As I thought of his name, I could see his face quite clearly. I would recognize him when I met him. But how would I feel about him? There was no emotion connected with the memory. A picture only—a face much like mine, but older and etched with lines. A good face, but only that. Like a photograph.

But instead of solving everything, my new knowledge only led to more questions. If I had been with a caravan, how did I wind up alone in the desert with a dead man? Why was I traveling under an alias? What happened to the rest of the caravan? The old man was looking at me speculatively. I assumed he was thinking those same questions. But I was wrong.

"I am not a Recorder, Rider Markasset," he said gently, "but it has been said of me that the All-Mind has touched me with the power to read men. And I tell you now that you have changed greatly since you came through here four days ago. Has some Ancestor given you wisdom?"

"Changed?" I asked, avoiding his last question because it made no sense to me at all. "How have I changed, Respected One?"

"As I said, I did not speak to you. But I observed you, and heard what you said to others—in the caravan and here in the compound. Let me say only that now you are . . . less prideful. Less arrogant. And yet, you seem much more sure of yourself."

If I'm more sure of myself now, I thought, *I must have been* really *confused four days ago*.

"If I was disrespectful to the Fa'aldu, I am shamed, Respected One," I said. And meant it. The Fa'aldu and their water meant survival in the desert, Markasset's memory told me. Only a fool would offend these desert-dwellers.

Balgokh came a little closer to me, and looked intently into my face. "There is honesty there," he said, then nodded sharply. "Yes, I believe an Ancestor has touched you with wisdom." He bowed gracefully. "You are most fortunate, Rider Markasset."

"Thank you, Respected Elder Balgokh." What else could I say?

From outside I heard again the low roar of the huge cat, and I glanced toward the outer door. When I looked back, Balgokh was staring at me.

"I only hope," he said, "that you are not too changed for your sha'um. If you have been too radically altered by your contact with the All-Mind, your mount will not recognize or obey you. If that is so, we are all in danger."

"Danger? What danger threatens the Fa'aldu?"

Balgokh almost laughed as he gestured to the door—obviously beyond the door to the animal we had heard. "Perhaps you do not consider the rage of a sha'um dangerous? At the moment he is only restless and unsettled, waiting for you to come to him again. So far, he has done nothing, but he prowls incessantly. Our women and children are staying behind bolted doors. If you do not take command soon . . . If you *cannot* take command . . ."

I know, now, about the sha'um. A Rider and his sha'um are together from the time the boy is twelve and the sha'um is a year-cub. And it's strictly a one-to-one relationship; one man, one cat. If Markasset had died in the desert, Keeshah would have returned to the wild, grieving. But Keeshah had accepted that confused, exhausted wretch in the desert as his master and had brought him here for help.

If he doesn't recognize Markasset in me, I thought, *he'll blame the Fa'aldu for changing me—or, rather, for causing Markasset to disappear. And he'll avenge "me." Probably starting with* me.

As though I were seeing it again, I remembered the way the corpse had looked in the desert. I had noticed, then, only that his clothes were torn. As I looked back now, they seemed to have been shredded by some giant animal's claws. Keeshah?

Damn! I wish I could understand this whole thing. I have Markasset's memory, I can remember—not dependably, either, damn it again—what he knows. But I don't remember being *Markasset. And if I have no real sense of the identity of his master, how can I expect Keeshah to have any? To recognize me now that I* know *I'm strange?*

"I will take care of Keeshah," I said. "If I am too changed, my own death will be enough for him."

I was more scared when I said that than I had ever been in my life. But, what the hell; you only live once.

In the back of my mind an impish voice said, "*Oh, yeah?*" and I answered, *Yeah! I'm not fool enough to try to parlay miracles*.

"May it not be so," Balgokh said. There was sincerity in his voice. "We have a haunch of glith for him, and plenty of water. *Keddan!*"

Keddan brought in a hunk of raw meat that seemed to be the rump and one hind leg of a sheep-sized animal, and a tanned skin that might have been the hide of the same animal. The skin was tightly sewn where the legs should have been, and thick twine tied the neck. It was stretched taut with the weight of the water inside it.

I slung the haunch of meat over one bare shoulder and tucked the skin under my other arm. I looked a wordless, hopeful farewell at Balgokh and Keddan, and went out into the blistering heat of the compound.

Keeshah wasn't there.

Far from being disappointed, I was relieved to have a moment to get my bearings. The Fa'aldu compound was a large rectangle marked at either end by a man-high wall of rock salt blocks. There were openings in the walls to permit the passing of caravans, but these were covered now with thickly-woven cloths tied through holes carefully drilled near the edges of the top and bottom blocks. They were not designed, obviously, as defensive barriers. But they were a symbol that entrance to the Refreshment House of Yafnaar required the consent of Balgokh, as eldest of his family. And they were sufficient, once a caravan had entered, to keep the contrary and exceptionally stupid vleks from wandering out into the desert.

The sides of the rectangle were formed by seemingly identical rows of buildings, individual units sharing one side wall with its neighbor, each one opening onto the compound through a small square-cornered doorway. Markasset knew that the doors I faced across the compound led only to cubicles lined with sleeping blocks which were padded with the plainest possible pallets.

The room I had left, however, was only the beginning of the larger compound which was the living area of the Fa'aldu. From somewhere in its private interior, the Fa'aldu brought the water. I searched Markasset's memory as closely as I could; he had no idea how the Fa'aldu drew water from the wasteland of the desert. He did know about wells, it seemed, and was certain that they were not used here. It was a generations-old secret among the Fa'aldu clans.

Wondering about it was pointless—and it was putting off the inevitable.

I walked out to the watering troughs in the center of the large yard. There were three of them, the larger two almost exactly twice and three times the length of the smallest. They were made of large, semi-cylindrical tiles laid with the rounded side down and supported by short walls of brick-shaped salt blocks. The smallest trough contained only one tile, flanged at both ends and fitted with half-discs of tile. It was a darkish brown in color, and glazed to be watertight.

The longer troughs were made of two and three of these tiles, the edge of one fitted exactly within the flanged lip of the next, the extreme edges sealed as this one was.

I set the meat down on the edge of the trough, and untied the knot at the neck of the waterskin, carefully holding the opening closed until I had the skin in position over the trough. Then I let some of the water run out, feeling my arm indent the lower surface of the skin. I re-tied the opening, set the skin on the ground, and took a deep breath.

"Keeshah!" I called.

As though he had been waiting for that summons, the sha'um came easily, gracefully, over the high wall to my right. As he had done out on the desert, he kept his distance, padding back and forth along the wall, watching me and making growling noises in his throat.

"I have brought you water, Keeshah. Come and drink."

He stopped pacing and came a few steps nearer, stretching

out his head to sniff in my direction. Then, with a roar, he shook his head and sidled off.

Does the water smell bad, Keeshah? I thought. *Or is it me? Scratch that—it's a silly question.*

It had never occurred to me that the cat might accept me simply because I *looked* like the Markasset he knew. Even in the world of Ricardo Carillo, domestic cats were sensitive to personality changes and moods in the humans they chose to live with. No, Keeshah knew I was different. He had proved it already by hanging back for so long while I made my way across the desert. And if he had been confused then, when I wasn't sure who I was, he must be even more skittish now that I had a strong conviction of an identity which was alien to him.

I watched the huge cat pacing, and fear gave way to admiration. I had never seen such a powerful animal. His muzzle was a broader wedge than that of a tiger, the mouth cut deeper into it and, I thought, lined with even more teeth. Ridges of muscle flowed from the powerful jaw along his smooth throat to help form the wide shield of pectorals that rippled across his chest as he paced about.

His legs were thick, his paws easily the size of my head; their claws, retracted now, must be proportionately large. His long body looked lean, but I remembered how it had felt beneath me: wide, supportive, secure.

Markasset?

At first I didn't know what it was. A pulsing from somewhere inside me, familiar, compelling. A warm touch directly to my mind—friendly, yet wary.

Of course: Keeshah.

Markasset? came the thought again. It wasn't really the name, simply an identifying thought and a sense of question. Uncertainty.

I understood many things then. The special bond between a Rider and a sha'um was a telepathic link. The huge cats could not verbalize or think in exactly the same way that a man can, but they were intelligent in a feline way, and they had a low-powered type of telepathy. They could communicate with men.

That is, *one* sha'um chose to link with *one* man. And the basis for that link was mutual loyalty, a friendship which went deeper than human friendships. When Markasset turned twelve, he had gone to live for a season in the Valley of the Sha'um. The cats had accepted him as their own; a huge gray female had allowed Markasset to take with him his "brother," her only cub—Keeshah.

Markasset had passed the judgment of the sha'um. That gave me a deeper impression of him than anything I had yet learned about him. Now I had to face that same judgment, and there could be no deception in this mind-to-mind relationship.

The question came again: **Markasset?** With a growl of impatience.

I walked toward the sha'um, and as I moved, he grew still. Only the tip of his great tail moved, barely twitching.

I was still afraid. Not of death under the teeth and claws of a huge, dangerous cat. But of failing to win Keeshah's trust. In Markasset's body—*as Markasset*—I had shared the special, wonderful friendship of the sha'um. I was desperately afraid . . . that I might lose Keeshah.

I stopped directly in front of the sha'um and looked up into his face. Even his eyes were gray, flecked with silver, and as unreadable as any cat's. He made no move, though he was tensed to leap in any direction.

No longer Markasset, I spoke to him in a way that was automatic, a way I didn't understand. **Not the Markasset who brought you from the Valley.**

The big head moved then, up and down my body, sniffing.

Same smell. Different. Who?

I answered the most honest way I could. **Myself.**

Not Markasset? Keeshah relaxed a little, sat in the classic cat pose. His tail curled around his feet, and its tip still twitched restively. He tilted his head and wrinkled his mouth and regarded me with a perfect look of puzzlement.

Suddenly I laughed: a loud, raucous sound that filled the courtyard as Keeshah's roar had done. The cat laid back its ears and fled in startled confusion. He stopped a few feet away, turned in an incredibly small circle, and crouched to the ground, watching me.

"I don't blame you for being mixed up, Keeshah," I said aloud, conscious that I could choose to speak at the same time I was projecting to him mentally. I walked toward him slowly and muscles rippled along his side as he crouched even lower. The claws on his hind feet were out, digging into the sand for better traction.

Who? he asked again.

**Myself, Keeshah. Someone who is neither Markasset nor Ricardo Carillo. Someone who is both. Myself. I have had a hard time accepting it; I know the change puzzles you.*

But I am certain of this, Keeshah. I knelt in the sand and looked levelly into the cat's solemn gray eyes. **I need you as Markasset did. More. Already you have helped me. And I think you—and only you—understand how strange I feel. How alone.*

Not Markasset, Keeshah. Markasset is gone. Please let me take his place.

For a moment, the cat gazed at me steadily. Then his head darted forward in a light nudge to my midsection. I fell over and rolled several feet, once more tasting salty sand.

Not Markasset, he said as he rose to his feet. A single bound and he was looming over me. His mouth opened, and my breath dried in my throat. The razor-sharp teeth closed gently on my shoulder. **But same friend. Keeshah's friend.**

He released me, and rubbed his great soft-furred head against my chest; his whiskers tickled my abdomen. I laughed and grabbed the huge head with both arms, burying my face in the fur on his wide forehead.

Keeshah lifted me from the ground as he had done out in the desert. I released him and we walked without touching toward the water trough. I dipped my hand in the water and held it to his muzzle.

While among men, a sha'um always eats or drinks first from the hand of his Rider.

5

The caravan trail led north across the salt wastes, toward the base of the Great Wall, where Raithskar lay. The Respected Elder had offered me simple directions, as well as a pouch of dried meat and a small leather canteen of water, assuring me that it was but three days' trip for a sha'um. I soon found that directions were unnecessary; once Keeshah knew where we were going, he knew the way. I lay my head upon the wide back and dozed as he moved with long, seemingly effortless strides across the desolate land. He did not gallop headlong, as I fuzzily remembered him doing in his urgency to bring me to the Refreshment House, but fell into an easy lope which ate up distance without tiring him. An easy, rhythmic, soothing motion—I drifted in and out of sleep as the distance passed.

At first I had been hesitant about riding the sha'um. Especially was I hesitant about mounting him. I remembered the scorn I had felt as a kid, watching a cowboy comedy and laughing as the greenhorn tried to swing into the saddle from the horse's right. There was no one watching, as by custom I would not ride my sha'um within the walls of the Refreshment House. But Keeshah was there, and I most certainly didn't want to make a fool of myself in front of *him*.

There was no saddle to give me a clue. The sha'um is the only animal in Gandalara big enough for a man to ride, and the great cats would not have put up with a saddle. Even the cargo-carrying vlek, with hardly enough mind to get mad, threw a fit every time a pack-harness was tightened around its low-slung belly. It could carry only as much weight as that of a ten-year-old child, but it was untrustworthy as a child's pet. So there was no such thing in Gandalara as a riding saddle.

But I need not have worried. My body behaved in an almost automatic fashion. Keeshah lay upon the ground, and

I sat astride his back, seating myself near the base of his spine. Then I lay forward, drew my knees up against his sides, and reached up with my hands to grasp his huge shoulders. My knees were just below his rib cage, my feet tucked up just forward of his thighs. I could direct him with slight pressure from my hands or my knees—but, as I have said, Keeshah needed no directing.

We traveled for some hours across the desert, the only sound in that vastness the *pad-pad-pad* of Keeshah's thickly calloused paws against the hard-baked bed beneath us. Occasionally I would hear the cry of a bird, and look up to see a flash of wings, or a distant, almost stationary soaring form. But there seemed to be nothing larger than the sand-ants alive on the desert floor except for Keeshah and me.

I had accepted the leather canteen of water from Balgokh with formal thanks and unspoken skepticism. Keeshah would need no water in that time—he could go for several days without it. But the canteen contained, at a guess, somewhat less than a pint of water, four or five hundred milliliters. Hardly enough for a man for three days in the desert. I felt it wouldn't be politic to ask for more; I decided I would have to make it last.

I soon found that it would be plenty. In the first place, I didn't feel thirsty very often—not nearly as often as I should have in this heat. In the second place . . .

I was a water saver.

We had been on the road for some hours when I noticed a pressure in my lower abdomen which indicated a need that should be taken care of. **Stop,** I directed Keeshah, and when he did, I sat up and swung my right leg over his back, sliding down to the ground. I walked a few paces from the smoothly worn area that was the road and urinated.

I passed very little liquid. As it touched the dry, hot desert floor, the dark urine crystallized rapidly, leaving a little heap of yellow crystals. I stared at them for so long that Keeshah walked over and nosed my back, anxious to get going again.

Wait, I told him. **Just a little while.** Absently I rubbed his jaw and moved my hand up to his ear to scratch lightly. He agreed with some impatience, and lay down by the side of the road.

You find truth in the oddest places, I was thinking to

myself. The concentration of organic and inorganic salts in that urine solution must have been *high*. *Very* high! Like the kangaroo rat of the American southwest, my kidneys were designed to save every possible drop of water.

With a concentration like that, a human being would have died of kidney stones or other renal failure long since. And here was the truth I had found in a simple, natural act.

I am not Homo sapiens. *Whatever I am, wherever Gandalara is, I am not a man as I knew men.*

Keeshah growled, and obediently, almost in a daze, I mounted him and we set off again. For a long time I simply clung tightly to his back—as though he were my own humanity and I wanted to hold it as long as possible. I pressed my face into his fur and closed my eyes and tried not to think. But by the time I detected Keeshah's complaining thought—I was pinching his shoulders, and he could sense my distress and was worried—I had accepted it.

I was not human.

I apologized to Keeshah and rode more lightly, turning things over in my mind. The whole situation made less and less sense. And this last twist was cruel. The problem wasn't so much that I knew I wasn't human, but that I was so damned *nearly* human. I had already speculated that Gandalara might be, fantastically, on some world that orbited Alpha Centauri or Procyon. If that were true, I wouldn't really expect to be human—but it was far less likely that I would *look* human.

Parallel evolution was a little too much to swallow. Look at the wide and wild variety of life that had evolved on Earth during two or three thousand million years. The notion that a water-oxygen world much like Earth would necessarily evolve a dominant, human-shaped, intelligent species was nonsense on the face of it. The Earthly dolphin has a brain as fully evolved as the human.

I don't think I'd have gotten as much pleasure out of waking as, say, a highly intelligent, good-natured spider, I speculated. *But after the first shock, it might have been philosophically easier to accept*. *And I'd have known, positively, that I wasn't on Earth*.

I think.

Information, damn it! I need more data before I can place myself in the "grand scheme of things."

For the rest of that day, I tried to keep my mind a blank. I failed, of course. The questions kept circling and spinning, seemingly in rhythm with Keeshah's powerful movement under me.

The cloud layer diffused the diminishing rays of sunlight as night approached, so that the light dimmed only gradually. When the sun finally set, the world was plunged into darkness with startling suddenness. I called Keeshah to a halt, slid wearily off his back, and was asleep almost before I touched the ground.

It was full light when I woke again, and I realized that I was not fully recovered from the desert ordeal yet. I ate a light meal and drank sparingly of the water, still surprised by the tiny amount which satisfied me. Then I mounted Keeshah and we were on our way again. I rested my head on his furred back and dozed as he carried me.

Keeshah angled toward the left, and I raised my head from his back to see what had caused the slight change in direction. The caravan trail had turned, and Keeshah was following it. If we had continued straight ahead, we would have had to cross an area of the desert that had a strangely smooth and shiny look about it.

I caught a picture from Keeshah: anyone stepping onto that shiny area would break through the crust and sink. It was a bog of some kind. Though I had known, intellectually, there was more to Gandalara than the dry waste of the desert, the sight of anything wet surprised the hell out of me.

I sat up a little and looked around, glad to have a new puzzle to distract me. In the distance I could see things growing in the marsh. Farther ahead, thicker now as we approached it, was the line of blue that had drawn me through the desert. I knew now that it was the Great Wall, at the foot of which lay Markasset's home city of Raithskar.

The city has to get its water from somewhere, I decided. *This bog is the end of the line for whatever source feeds the city.*

It had to be a river which flowed down from the mountains, through or beside the city, and picked up more and more salt as it ran south into the desert. Here the intense heat caused such rapid evaporation that the water simply disappeared. Some of it might soak into the ground, but I'd bet money that the hot, dry air sucked up most of it.

At the final edge, the brine concentration was so great that nothing could live in it except some stubborn algae and bacteria. Farther upriver, less hardy plants could live with water that was merely brackish. But this bog contained a saturated salt solution, into which no more salt could dissolve. It was thick, stagnant water covered by a mush of salt crystals which formed a thin, shiny crust.

Keeshah was right; it would not be a good place to walk over.

By noon, the marshy area was dotted with clumps of reeds and an occasional sickly-looking tree. Keeshah slowed, stopped.

Too hot. Rest.

I was willing. Riding a sha'um is less work than being one, but it was no picnic.

I ate a bit of food from the pouch and leaned up against Keeshah's heaving side.

"I don't wonder you're pooped," I told him, and he turned his head to look at me. I poured a little of the precious water into my hand and offered it. He lapped it up carefully, the big raspy tongue flipping it *under* itself and into his mouth. Then, deliberately, he licked across the palm of my hand, lightly enough that he didn't quite scrape off hide.

For a while we sat in companionable silence, staring at the Great Wall. I glanced at Keeshah, and smiled. He looked for all the world like a sphinx in informal dress. I leaned up against his shoulder and scratched under his chin absently as I surveyed the wall.

It looked like a range of mountains stretching to the horizon on the east and west. There didn't seem to be any high peaks or deep valleys, though; the top edge was a little uneven but, all things considered, remarkably smooth. I'd never heard of any such long, *high* wall as that, anywhere on Earth. China's Great Wall might be as long or longer, but it was certainly not so incredibly high.

Keeshah's eyes were closing, and finally he shoved me aside so he could stretch out. I lay down against his back and fell asleep in the shadow of his body.

I woke to a nearly inaudible whining noise and a very definite nudge. As I started to complain, Keeshah's urgent thought reached me.

Silence. Danger. Hide.

I woke up fast.

We crept quietly away from the road and lay flat behind a shallow rise. It was dotted with scraggly bushes that wouldn't have hidden a jackrabbit in the daytime—but it was the best cover available.

It was already night—the sun must have set some time ago. In the east there was a white glow that was the moon shining beyond the thin overcast. It spread an eerie silver radiance over the bleak landscape.

Soon I could hear what had alerted Keeshah. Carrying over the flatland came the sounds of a group of men moving toward us. The low murmurs of men's voices. The muffled pacing of many feet. An occasional sharper voice calling commands. An organized group of men, coming at a fast march from the north.

It was several minutes before I could see their shadowy figures moving along the caravan trail in the veiled moonlight. Their voices became clear before their bodies resolved from the shadowy silver of the night.

"Might as well be chasing a wild thaka!" grumbled a deep voice. "I say the stone's somewhere in the city."

"Aw, you been singing that fleabitten tune for hours, Devok. It don't matter *what* you think. Orders is orders. Anyway, Klareth's group is still searching the city."

A third voice added, "Yeah, Devok, and if the fleabitten thing *did* get shipped out with the caravan, we'd best catch it now. If they get to Chizan or Dyskornis with it, we'll *never* get it back."

I could see them clearly now: a dozen men, each leading a pack-vlek.

"What we ought to have done is arrest the fleabitten old man and persuade him to tell us all about it."

"Arrest a City Supervisor with no evidence? You're crazy, Devok. Shut up and march. We want to make it to Yafnaar before sundown tomorrow."

They marched in silence for a while, drawing nearer. Then I heard a new voice.

"What *I* can't figure is why anybody'd try to steal the Ra'ira. It'd ruin its value to cut it up, and if you leave it like it is, anybody in Gandalara would know what it was and whose it was."

"Not if it was kept hid for a while." That sounded like the first voice which had replied to Devok.

"How's that? What good would that do?"

An exaggerated sigh. "One of these days, Mord, you ought to go to a Recorder and pick up a little education. That's how *we* got the fleabitten jewel."

"Awww. That thing has been in Raithskar for hundreds of hundreds of years."

Another voice. "Not that long. Several tens or hundreds, maybe. But he's right, I've heard the story myself. Tell him, Ganneth."

"Serkajon himself stole it from Kä," Ganneth supplied. "Brought it to Raithskar and set up the Council."

"Didn't know that!" said a voice down the line.

"Dummy!" came another voice, disgusted. "Whatcha think Commemoration Day is all about?"

The words brought a flash of memory. Parades and celebration, the statue of a man riding a sha'um carried through the city, and his image miniaturized and multiplied in banners displayed everywhere. In one large building, encased in glass so that it might be viewed and appreciated by the public during that annual celebration, a pale blue stone about the size of a glass doorknob. Its surface was unfaceted, but the blue color darkened as one looked deeply into it, and hinted at an imperceptible crystalline structure.

The Ra'ira.

"Him?" another voice bantered. "Give him free faen and he'd drink to his mother-in-law!"

Laughter, then Devok's voice again, challenging. "So what? Kä's been long deserted; nobody even knows where it is, anymore. And that was a long time ago. Way I hear it, we never even got a complaint from Kä when Serkajon ran off with it. But you can bet we'll raise a holler if some other city has heisted it from us! Raithskar ain't deserted by a long ways.

"Naw, no other city'd have the nerve to swipe the Ra'ira; I still say it's inside Raithskar!"

"Not again!"

"Knock it off, will you Devok?"

"Yeah, ain't it bad enough we gotta march—"

The straggly column was abreast of us. I hadn't noticed that there was a slight breeze . . . until it changed direction. The vleks caught Keeshah's scent, and all hell broke loose.

I've never heard any sound that can compare with the harsh bawling of a frightened vlek. The pack animals screamed and stamped, straining against their leads and doing their best to trample anybody who got in their way.

Two or three of the vleks seemed to be carrying live cargo of some sort. A horrendous, terrified clacking rose from the woven-reed cages and drove the vleks into an even higher frenzy.

Beside me, Keeshah was tense as coiled wire. I tried to see what was in his mind, but it was seething and unreadable. Anger and contempt for the vleks mingled with predatory desire, frustration and a flash of . . . guilt? If a sha'um could swear, the silver night around us would have been tinged with blue.

It's all right, I tried to reassure him. **How could you have known the wind would shift?** No response. He moved his hind legs, getting ready to lunge into the melee. Eagerly.

No, Keeshah! I ordered sharply. **They don't know we're here. Keep still; they may yet pass us by.**

He didn't move. But he didn't relax.

For that matter, neither did I. My hand was on the hilt of my sword.

They were beginning to make sense of the chaos. I could hear Gandalaran voices above the vleks braying.

"Settle down, you fleabitten . . ."

"Hey! Ganneth tripped! Get him out from under . . ."

The wind shifted again, and the frenzied animals calmed almost instantly. There was a moment of stunned silence, broken by the now familiar voice of Devok.

"Didn't I tell you we shoulda never left—"

"WILL YOU SHUT UP!" roared a voice I hadn't heard before. "Now, anybody know what set 'em off?"

"I dunno," someone answered. I knew they must be peering into the shadows on either side of the trail—I pressed my face into the hard ground, willing myself to disappear.

"There's nothin' out there," someone said disgustedly. "Almost anything will spook these fleabitten animals. We should just be glad it's over and nobody's hurt."

"Whaddya mean, nobody. My foot . . ."

"Didn't hurt you none . . ."

"AWRIGHT!"

When a muttering quiet had set in: "Your jabbering probably set 'em on edge. It sure as Gandalara was makin' *me* nervous.

"Let's get moving again. And this time do less talkin' and faster walkin'. We've wasted enough time, and you'll need your breath before dawn. Let's go."

They moved away in silence. Only when the sound of their feet on the hard-worn trail had faded completely did I dare to breathe again. I let what I judged to be another twenty minutes go by before I remounted a restless Keeshah and we were on our way.

From what I'd heard, it sounded as though the cops were out in force tonight. I didn't know what instinct had driven Keeshah to conceal us from them—a natural wariness of the unidentified, probably—but I was glad he had done so. In my travels, I have learned that even a respectable university professor is wise to steer clear of the police if he doesn't know what all the laws are.

6

Raithskar was itself a jewel.

It sprawled uphill, following the slope that had risen gradually from the salt bogs. Now the slope steepened swiftly to merge at last into the majesty of the Great Wall, some miles beyond the city.

We had stopped several yards distant from the huge main gate, over Keeshah's anxious protests. I needed time to get reacquainted with this city.

Through the gates I could see a portion of the wide boulevard which led into the city, and I could *hear* the marketplace that filled the boulevard. Voices haggling over prices. The squealing of children forced to tag along on a shopping trip. The clinking of coins.

I could smell it, too—the tang of blood from the butcheries, sweet fruits, sharp spices, perfumes I could not quite identify.

Raithskar seemed familiar to me in many ways. The smells, the sounds, the look of the place made me feel I had been here before—yet I did not recognize it in the sense of *knowing* it. And it called up Earthly memories. The clustered roofs climbing the slope in a riot of color made me think of San Francisco before skyscrapers spoiled the natural line that was so beautiful when viewed from the bay. Some of the roofs had small interlaced tiles like the one which had formed Yafnaar's watering trough. They were dark brown in color, but otherwise much like the Spanish-style roofing that had been a feature of Santa Barbara.

Raithskar gleamed and glittered in the early morning light. In different ways, it made both Ricardo and Markasset homesick.

I found my gaze drawn to the Great Wall, four or five miles away. It stretched clear to the sky and disappeared in the clouds. How tall was it, I wondered? A mile? Two miles? Maybe three? There was no way to know for sure, but I'd have said at least two.

And directly behind Raithskar was a sight I had never expected to see. From out of the mists at the top of the great escarpment, water cascaded down the almost sheer face of the cliff. At its base was a rainbow-crowned lake which foamed continuously as the tons of water thundered into it. The lake narrowed to a river, which rushed down the slope and through the city.

This had to be the source that wound up miles later as a treacherous salt bog. The Skarkel Falls—the name surfaced from my memory.

The base of the falls was shrouded in mist—the water, falling from such a height, virtually pulverized the lake, sending up an endless spray of water vapor.

I could see then why Raithskar glittered so in the sunlight. Even this far from the falls, there was *moisture* in the air, cooling off the fearsome heat of the desert. Invisible droplets coated the roofs of the city, causing them to shine as though they were polished.

After the hot, dry journey, the coolness of the city called out to me.

* * *

Keeshah and I had traveled through the night. From his back I had watched the dimly-lit countryside change around us. The vegetation in the swamp had grown denser, the mucky ground gradually solidifying to support short grasses and bushes. I saw trees more frequently, and they seemed taller and healthier—although I had seen larger manzanita bushes in California. Just as the land began to look all overgrown, with fields of grass and shadowy clumps of growth that might almost have been wooded areas, the moon set.

The blackness was complete; it was as though I had been suddenly blinded. The cloud layer had diffused and distributed what little moonlight remained, so that I hadn't noticed the gradual dimming.

Frightened in the abrupt blackness, I ordered Keeshah to stop. He did, but he protested.

*_Soon there,_’ he said.

Can you see through this darkness?

No. Follow road smell. He was panting heavily; he had been running for hours without a break.

We'll wait till dawn, I told him.

I slid off his back, and when I moved away from him he was completely invisible. But we were still together. He was a large warm presence in my mind, and I was no longer frightened of the dark.

Rest, Keeshah.

He agreed—not with reluctance, but with some puzzlement. I heard him moving around in the bushes, settling to the ground. I lay on my back in the tart-smelling grass and looked up into the darkness.

As though the sky had been waiting for me, the clouds broke apart and I was looking at the stars.

But not _my_ stars.

I had spent enough romantic moonlit nights gazing into the sky to know that for sure. There wasn't a single constellation up there that I recognized. And there was one bright configuration that I knew I had _never_ seen. Then the clouds swept together and left me again in darkness.

I'd had enough of questions today. So the stars were different—I listed that among things to think about and sort out later. It was another datum, only that.

I was emotionally drained, tired past the point of sleeping, afraid that if I slept, I would dream of unfinished puzzles, mazes with no end and no beginning, paths that led only into other paths. So I listened to the night.

Riding with my head on Keeshah's body, the soft sound of his paws striking the ground had blocked out all other aural input. I had noticed the landscape changing visually; now I became aware of the different sound of it.

The desert had been so quiet. The cry of a bird had been an intrusion out there. Now I could hear the flutter of wings all around me, and the soft rustling of small animals moving through the grass and bushes. Skittering sounds made me think of squirrels and their nervous, rush-and-stop zigzags.

What did these night creatures look like? Would I ever see them clearly in the daytime? I could well understand that even here, where the desert was fading, the cooler night was more inviting than the day. And I wondered then whether the vast savage desert, so desolate in the heat of day, had its own sort of night life.

As I lay there listening in a sort of sleep-daze, it occurred to me that I believed dawn was imminent because on Earth it would be so. I'd had no evidence so far that I *was* still on Earth. It might be hours before dawn.

I was too relaxed to move right then. But eventually I summoned the energy to sit up, to tell Keeshah it was time to get started. I looked for and found him nestled into some scratchy-looking bushes . . .

Looked? Bushes?

It was gray and dim, but the dawn had already begun. A few minutes later, the red glow of the rising sun spread through the thin clouds in the east, flushing the sky. I stood up and stretched, and watched while Keeshah yawned and *stre-e-e-etched*. I ate a little food, and we shared what was left of the water. Then I mounted and we were on our way again.

The land began to change quickly, the open area giving way to cultivated fields. There were waist-high, grass-like plants that had to be some kind of grain. Evenly spaced humps of vines or low bushes—what they produced I could only guess.

Smaller tracks crossed the caravan road, and as the morning brightened we passed Gandalarans on the road. Some carried wood-handled, bronze-headed tools toward the fields. Others were leading laden vleks in to the market.

I sat up on Keeshah's back and moved forward to ride just behind his shoulders, asking him to slow to a walk. The people who passed us greeted me politely and edged carefully past Keeshah with looks of mingled fear and curiosity on their faces. Those who led vleks simply stood still until we had passed, holding tightly to the looped halters so that the beasts would not stamp around and spill their cargo.

And so we had come to Raithskar at last, and I had paused a moment to absorb my first impressions of the place which was to be my home now.

I yielded to Keeshah's impatience and urged him on; he ran eagerly toward the gate, then stopped.

Well?* I asked him. **I thought you were in a hurry?

He twisted his neck to look back at me.

City,* he explained. **Get off.

Oh, sure. Sorry.

It was logical. Balgokh had said that Markasset was the only Rider not connected with the Sharith. Therefore I was the only man in Raithskar who could ride instead of walk. Common courtesy demanded that I shouldn't flaunt it. I dismounted and walked into the city beside Keeshah with my hand resting lightly behind his left ear. That, too, was at Keeshah's direction—a ritual gesture to assure the people in the china shop that the bull was under control.

The bustling marketplace reminded me strongly of the older sections of Fez and Marrakesh. The streets here were wider and much cleaner, but the noise and the confusion were the same. There was color everywhere, as though the town itself was rejecting the uniform paleness of the desert. Most of the shoppers wore long- or short-sleeved tunics of lengths which varied from very short for the children to ground-sweeping for some of the women.

Here and there a man was dressed, like me, for the desert: loose trousers tied at waist and ankles, long-sleeved tunic slit to the waist for leg freedom, soft leather boots calf-high under the trouser legs, a piece of cloth tied so that its loose edge hung down the back. More commonly, however, and almost as a rule for the vendors seated in the shade of the selling stalls, the men wore only the loose, comfortable trousers.

No one made any attempt to blend colors or find compatible combinations, and all the colors were bright. A green tunic was belted round with red; yellow trousers screamed against a rich purple tunic; a worn blue tunic was patched neatly at the shoulder with lurid orange.

I blinked at the vivid display, but soon found that the unplanned, fluid melange of colors cheered me. Unmistakably, I had left the desert behind me.

The only *pattern* of color to be seen was in the fabric awnings under which the merchants sat. Each one was a square of canvas supported and stretched by a framework of wooden poles. In places there were several of the same pattern grouped together. Markasset's memory told me that the weave of the fabric identified the merchant, much like a Scottish tartan identified a clan.

Merchandise was arranged in the same neat, hollow squares under each awning. They were spaced so that a customer could walk all the way around them. The merchant or his man sat in the center of the square, calling out the value of his goods and hawking business like a carny talker. A customer could touch, look at and, within reason, test any merchandise as long as he remained standing or kneeling. When he'd found something he wanted, he literally "settled down" to dicker, seating himself beside his choice. Then the merchant turned to him and they began to haggle over price.

The bright, busy stalls lined the boulevard three deep on each side of the wide, hard-surfaced street. The thronging pedestrians were polite and cautious, avoiding collisions with studied care, laughing and smiling. As Keeshah and I threaded our way through them, I felt my spirits lifting. The touch of light mist on my face, the gay color all around me, people who were happy and ordinary, though they might not be human—and an unforced feeling of having come home.

We moved out of the busiest area of the marketplace, where the out-of-town merchants conducted business under their temporary shelters, and into the city's own trade district. Neat, stone-walled buildings crowded together and narrowed the street slightly, offering for sale those things which the townsfolk would regularly need. From the aromas here, as richly confused as the colors of the bazaar, I guessed we were in the food-selling district.

Keeshah and I stopped at the same time. We were outside a meat shop which was a cross between a delicatessen and a butcher shop, and featured both cooked and fresh meat. The roast had stopped me; the raw had stopped Keeshah.

Eat? The quasi-question hung in his mind, and it echoed through mine.

"Markasset!"

I turned toward the high-pitched, slightly breathless voice. A woman was hurrying toward me.

Though there were not consistent or obvious style differences between what I had seen men and women wearing as I walked through the marketplace, the sexual dimorphism in this race was more pronounced, and I had been having no trouble differentiating the sexes. Nor did I now. There was no doubt in my mind that this was a woman. Or that she knew me.

I tried to keep my expression pleasant but noncommittal. I had a faint memory of having met her before, but no name would come to mind. She rushed up to me, smiling eagerly, golden, fur-like hair, no longer than mine, coated with mist and winking in the sun. Her canine teeth were as well-developed as mine. Somehow, they looked even better on her.

"What are you doing back in town?" she asked a little breathlessly. I could hear concern in her voice. "You told me you'd taken a job with Gharlas the merchant!"

I opened my mouth to say something—damned if I knew what. Luckily I didn't get a chance.

"Darling," she rushed on, "once you were gone, you should have *stayed* gone! Worfit is furious because you left town still owing him money, and he probably already knows you're back. Why didn't you leave Keeshah outside the city, so fewer people would recognize you?"

"Well, I—"

"Did you hear that the Ra'ira has been *stolen?* And Zaddorn has been asking me questions about you." She stopped for breath, looked around almost furtively, stepped closer and lowered her voice. Like most of the women I had seen, she was small and delicately boned; I had to bend my head to her to catch her words.

"I told him that what's between you and me is none of his business, but he says that the Chief of Peace and Security has the right to ask anyone questions in a case like this. What with Worfit and Zaddorn both looking for you—darling, coming home right now was *terrible* timing!"

I was trying to put together what I had learned from her with what I had overheard from the police squad on the road the night before. I didn't much like what I came up with.

"Do you mean," I asked, "that somebody thinks *I* stole the—uh—Ra'ira?"

"Oh, you know Zaddorn—he's always been jealous of you. He thinks if he could discredit you, I would turn to him. It hasn't even been officially announced that the Ra'ira is gone, but there are rumors everywhere. I don't know if he really thinks you did it, or is just trying to make *me* think you did. I don't. I know you'd never do such a thing, especially when it was in your father's care."

"Thanks," I said, but I couldn't help wondering about the "especially" qualification. What sort of man *was* Markasset?

"You'd better get home fast," she was saying. She was looking around again as though she expected to be caught at any moment. "Before Zaddorn hears you're back. Your father can give you protection."

"Keeshah needs food," I told her. As Keeshah had been telling *me* during the entire conversation. "I'll get a side of glith for him, then I'll go straight home." The look she gave me was unreadable. "I promise," I added.

"You can't take Keeshah in a meat shop! And you can't leave him out here!"

"I know," I covered rapidly. "I was going to ask you to go in and get it for me, if you would."

I had another reason for asking; I hadn't the least idea of how much glith meat was worth, nor how much the coins in my purse were worth. I handed her the pouch. She looked impatient, but she glanced over at Keeshah and finally agreed.

"Oh, all right. If it will get you off the streets sooner. You want a whole side? Wait here and I'll have the meatmonger bring it. I'll be right back." She went into the meat shop.

I stood quietly, scratching Keeshah's ear and trying to digest this new, gratuitous information. There was plenty of it, and I *didn't* like it.

ONE: Markasset apparently was engaged to marry this talkative wench—but we (Markasset and Ricardo) couldn't remember her name.

TWO: A certain Zaddorn, who seemed to be the equivalent of the Chief of Police, was also (?) in love with her and was jealous of Markasset. And maybe not above using his position to ace out a rival.

THREE: Worfit—now *that* name rang a loud bell. A money-lender of the shadier kind, unhandsome, powerful, dangerous. Little Caesar with fat teeth. Markasset owed him a rather large sum of money—I didn't know exactly how much, but I had an impression that it was a gambling debt, and not his first.

FOUR: If Zaddorn had been telling the girl the truth, Markasset might really be suspected as a jewel thief.

None of this spoke well for Markasset. I had the feeling that he—*I*—had not been the most reputable of young men-about-town.

Keeshah rubbed his cheek against my chest, reminding me that I had stopped rubbing behind his ear.

I had to laugh at this huge, dangerous cat that wanted to be petted like a kitten.

I guess if* you *liked Markasset, Keeshah, I told him, **he can't be as bad as all that.**

7

I was distracted suddenly from my own problems. Two monsters were walking down the street.

Part of my mind told me that they were only a couple of working vineh. Nothing remarkable. Nothing to worry about. But I couldn't help feeling like the lead idiot in a Friday night Creature Feature—who hadn't had a chance yet to read the script.

At first, I thought they were blond gorillas. They were taller and wider than I, but on closer inspection I could see that their legs were longer and their arms shorter than those of *Gorilla gorilla*, and they held themselves more naturally erect.

Their faces were definitely apelike. The head sloped back steeply from the supraorbital ridge, leaving little room for prefrontal lobes. The lower jaw was massive and muscular, and the great canines made my own look ridiculously small. Their faces and bodies were covered with short, curly fleece, as though they had grown pubic hair all over. It was a light tan in color, not much darker than Keeshah's fur. But where Keeshah carried his pale bulk with grace, these lumbering brutes were even uglier for their pallor.

To add to their grotesqueness, they were wearing gray-brown shorts and were wielding push-brooms. And as I watched, a third one followed them from the crowd; he was pushing a wheelbarrow-like cart.

No one else was in the least disturbed by their presence or their appearance. Shoppers stepped out of their way automatically as they passed. Apparently they were a normal sight on the streets of Raithskar, a simple street-cleaning detail, sweeping up sand and leaves, and leftovers from passing vleks.

Then one of the broom-pushers caught the cart-pusher in the side with the end of the broom handle. It was purely accidental, a miscalculated backstroke. But Cart-pusher roared, spun the cart out of his way and cuffed Broom-pusher on the side of the head from behind. Broom-pusher swung around, his broom cutting a wide arc and knocking the wind out of Cart-pusher.

The Gandalaran pedestrians were paying attention now, scattering away from the fight. The two vineh were literally at each other's throats, grappling and snarling and trying with single-minded determination to kill each other. The second broom-pusher turned and looked, crouched and eager to join the brawl. I had the feeling that the only thing that stopped him was having to decide which side to join.

A man in a yellow tunic, whom I had seen near the vineh but hadn't really noticed, pushed against the outward tide of people and ran toward the fray, shouting with authority. "Break it up!" he ordered the struggling vineh, who paid him no attention. The third ugly took a step toward the other two, but stopped in confusion when the man yelled, "Gooloo, you stay out of this!"

He was carrying a thick baton nearly as long as his arm. He thrust it between the two fighters, but they ignored it.

"Stop it, you fleabitten filth-heads! Stop, I say!" They pulled out of their clinch for a second, and, with a quick flick of his wrist, the man gave each one of the pair a painful smack on the nose.

Both vineh roared their indignation, forgot their quarrel, and turned on the man, who backpedaled quickly. "Back! Back! Stay back!" he ordered. But the note of authority in his voice had been replaced by one of terror. He was the one who was backing, trying to hold the brutes off by jabbing with his baton like an inept fencer.

His heel caught in an irregularity in the hard clay surface of the street and he went down, flat on his back. The two vineh who had been fighting were close now, and the third was converging on them. This decision, obviously, was easier to make. It was going to be a slaughter.

I had to do something. Without my even thinking about it, my bronze sword was suddenly in my hand, and I was sprinting toward the fallen man, who was still poking upward with his baton to ward off the beasts. One of them grabbed, jerked, and took it away from him. I tried to put on more speed.

But before I could reach them, the attack stopped as quickly as it had begun.

The vineh who had grabbed the baton dropped it, looked stupidly around, and went back to pick up his broom. The other went back to the cart. He was limping slightly, and both of them were bleeding slowly from gashes and bites. I marveled at the toughness of their hides. They picked up their equipment and continued along the street as though nothing at all had happened. The third, who had been halfway to the scene of the fight, recovered his own broom and joined them.

The man picked himself up and grabbed his baton. He ran a few steps after the vineh, but stopped when he saw me. I could see him relaxing, the anger and terror going out of him.

"Thanks," he said. "I'm glad you were here. But I don't think they'll make any more trouble."

Someone in the crowd called out: "You ought to have better control over your vineh than that, Foreman; someone might have been hurt!"

The foreman smiled and nodded, but I, standing next to him, heard him mutter, "Fleabite you, townsman."

"You hurt?" I asked, sheathing my sword.

"No. I'll be all right." He smiled at me. "Thanks again." He moved off, following his charges, who were once again calmly sweeping the street.

I turned to go back to the shop, and found Keeshah beside me. Together we walked to where the girl was waiting anxiously. Beside her stood the meatmonger, holding a wrapped bundle half the size of a goat.

"Markasset, what is the *matter* with you? Are you crazy?" She glanced at the meatmonger and refrained from reminding me that news of the fight—and my almost-participation—was sure to reach Zaddorn. "Why didn't you stay out of it?"

I was shocked. "And let a man get killed?"

"Don't be silly. Whoever heard of a vineh killing anyone? He would have been all right. He *was* all right, wasn't he? You didn't do any good by going out there, brandishing your sword, and making a spectacle of yourself."

"I don't know," the meatmonger spoke up for me. "I never saw *two* of 'em gang up on a man before. It could have been nasty."

She gave him a look that might have quick-frozen the meat he held, so hurriedly did he hand it to me. "Here's your side of glith, townsman—er—Rider." Then he disappeared back into the shop.

I laid the bundle across Keeshah's shoulders.

Eat?

When we get home.

The girl handed back my pouch, but came close to whisper to me. "Markasset, why are you carrying around so much money? Do you realize that you have *five* twenty-dozak pieces in here?" I did now. "Why, you might be robbed!"

"With Keeshah around? A thief wouldn't get very far," I said. There was a short silence which was, for me at least, very awkward. Did she expect an explanation for the money? If so, I couldn't help her. "Well," I said at last, "if I hurry, I can get home before Zaddorn gets the word I'm back." I hesitated, then asked, "Are you coming?"

"Oh, no," she said. "I can't come with you now, darling. Mother gave me definite instructions. 'Get your shopping done and come right back,' she said. 'I need that cloth right away.' " The girl sighed.

She looked up at me, and for a moment there was a look on her face that spoke more than all her words. Beneath the chattering, the nagging, the impatience, she was really frightened for me. She cared.

"I'll come by your house later, darling. And if I see Zaddorn I'll try to send him in the wrong direction. Just hurry now and—take care of yourself." And she was gone.

I remembered her name now. Illia.

Keeshah knew the way home, and I followed him through streets which narrowed and twisted as we approached the residential district. The homes reminded me of the Spanish Colonial style—mostly stone and sun-baked clay, plastered over and finished with pastel-pigmented whitewash.

Thanasset's house was larger than most, a sprawling two-story building. On the side facing the street, there were windows only in the upper story, and the front wall continued away from the house to enclose a large yard area. There were two massive parquet doors: one directly into the house; the other one, through which Keeshah and I passed, into the patio garden. It was carefully arranged and tended, patterns of green broken up with colorful and fragrant flowers. A cool and pleasant place.

A broad pathway, inlaid with large flat stones, led through the garden and split. Half of it led to the back of the house on my left. Keeshah and I followed the other half, which took us to the end of the large enclosure. Here there were small storage buildings and a large stone structure that was Keeshah's home. Double doors made of heavy wood stood open, braced against the outer walls on either side of the archway. Inside was a big square room with a roof twice as tall as a man.

Against the rear wall, a broad ledge had been built of stone and laid over with grasses and leaves. In one corner, there was a wide pit filled with sand; in the opposite corner, a stone trough had been built against the wall and lined, as at Yafnaar, with tile. The walls had been built with a pattern of openings in lieu of windows; it was well ventilated, but it had the cool semi-gloom of a cave.

Keeshah, glad to be home at last, went directly to a thick round post, in the center of the room, that I had taken to be a roof support. But Keeshah put first one front paw, then another against it and stretched upward, then back, clawing it joyfully with claws as long as my fingers. It was the trunk of a tree larger than any I had yet seen—and it had been hauled in and placed there as a scratching post for Keeshah.

I unwrapped the meat, and Keeshah, his homecoming ritual complete, attacked it hungrily. I brought water for him from a cistern beside one of the storage buildings, moving automatically and not stopping to wonder how I knew where things were.

Soon I was walking up the stone pathway to the rear of the house. There were lots of windows back here on both floors, letting plenty of light into the interior. They were made of lozenge-shaped panes only as large as my hand, joined together with thin strips of wood. Even the three doors had wood-latticed windows in them.

I came to the central door and stopped, frozen. What was I doing?

Up to this point, I had been merely following a logical line. It had seemed the most natural thing in the world to come here to "my" home, where "I" had always lived. I had begun to accept this world, to feel almost comfortable in it. But all familiarity vanished now in a wave of alienness.

I was Ricardo Emilio Carillo, elderly American gentleman, walking around in what some might regard as a stolen body. I had been about to walk, without invitation or by-your-leave, into the house of a stranger, a man whom I had never seen before. This wasn't *my* home at all. It was the home of a near-human, *not*-human being, a native of an alien world who spoke a language I had never heard before. The mores, laws, customs, and civilization of this world were unknown to me. *I* was the stranger here.

What the hell had I been thinking of?

I wanted desperately to turn and run—but there was no place to run to. Only danger waited beyond the walls which surrounded me. A man named Worfit who might slit my throat for welching on a debt. One Zaddorn who might throw me into prison, or worse, because of some sacred bauble I knew nothing about—or because of his jealousy over a woman. And the woman herself, a promised marriage to a girl who, though she seemed sincere enough, was hardly a rock of strength.

No, I didn't want to stay here, but where else could I go? What could I do? How could I live? Illia seemed to think I had a lot of money with me, but how long would that last, especially when I couldn't tell if I was being cheated? I had strong doubts about the existence of unemployment offices, welfare checks, and food stamps in this world. How could I support myself and Keeshah?

For I knew that I could not leave the great cat behind me if I fled. And the thought increased my despair. I would be instantly recognized anywhere with Keeshah in tow. And that would lead all the dangerous people directly to me.

I had to stay here. I was safe here—for the moment. But I just *couldn't* walk into this house and face a man who was supposed to be my father. What would I say to him? How would I act? He was sure to see through me, to realize that, although I looked just like Markasset, I was *not* the person who had grown up in his house.

In that moment, torn by fear, unable to make any decision, paralyzed by the whole situation, I came as close to total panic as I ever have in my life.

Then the door opened, and the man who had opened it said: "Don't just stand there, son. Come on in."

8

For a moment I just stared at him stupidly. The only clear thought in my mind was a question: how had he known I was out here?

This was the man whose face had flashed through my memory when Balgokh had first told me who I was. It was a strong face, the brows a little more prominent than mine and a faint white scar running from forehead to cheek beside his left eye. The hair on his head had thinned and darkened with age, and fine lines rayed out from his eye-corners and along his mouth.

The tone of his invitation had been neither welcoming nor

rude. His voice had held only exasperation. I had a sudden intuition that some of those lines had been put there by Markasset—that Thanasset disapproved of his son in some ways, but still loved him. Very much. I was beginning to like Markasset less and less.

"I don't know why you're back so soon," the old man continued, in a somewhat lowered voice. "I suppose you'll tell me when you feel like it. But have the courtesy to keep your tongue civil until we're alone. There is a guest in the house."

He turned on his heel and walked before me into the house. He was taller than I, with wide shoulders and a brisk stride. He was wearing a sleeveless green tunic that reached to his thighs and his body, though thinning, was still muscular and strong.

We had gone only a few steps when Thanasset turned and looked at me coldly. I stopped hastily, just in time to keep myself from colliding with him. *Have I already goofed?* I asked myself, and the answer was quick in coming.

"As long as you are a son of this house, Markasset, you will not bear arms under its roof!"

"Oh, of course," I said in confusion, and pulled the baldric off over my head. I dislodged the scarf tied around my head, which fluttered to the floor. I bent and retrieved it and stood there with the scarf in one hand and the baldric in the other, feeling utterly foolish.

Finally, Thanasset took the baldric from me and walked back to the door to hang it from a rack mounted on the wall. I took the moment to look around the room, and I was impressed.

Everything about the room bespoke wealth. Not ostentation, but quality. The floor and the walls were finished with fine parquetry in a light, richly grained wood. The floor, highly polished, was a regular pattern of small diamonds, but the walls were random mosaics. Each piece of wood had been cut and matched by hand by some brilliant craftsman.

The room in which we stood was like a wide hallway that led straight through the house. Across from me were the doors I had passed in the street before reaching the garden entrance. Directly to my left was a short, narrow hallway leading to a small door and to a flight of stairs; the outer door at the rear of the house which I had passed opened at the foot of the stairs. On my right were two doorways and, against the front wall of the house, a second staircase.

The walls were decorated with sketches and small tapestries, most of which depicted animals. There was one, quite good, of a sha'um—not Keeshah; its markings were different. On the right wall, between the doors, the mosaic pattern seemed to be less random than elsewhere, but it was not until Thanasset passed me again and led me toward the front of the house that I could see what it was.

Standing opposite that wall, the pattern plainly was the outline of a sha'um. Darker woods had been used here to emphasize a line or to suggest a fur marking. Nothing had been placed on the wall to cover that exquisite mosaic portrait, but mounted above it was a sword—not bronze, like the one I had been wearing, but a gleaming gray-white metal. Steel.

I had time for only a brief glance, then we were walking through an open double-doorway on our left. This room held a comfortable array of armchairs and small tables of different shapes. Their surfaces, too, were parquetry, some of the fitted wood pieces mere slivers. Wood, I thought, must be very precious here; every smallest fragment seemed to find use.

In here, the stone of the walls had been left unfinished. A ledge that served as a bench ran the length of the room along the outside wall, beneath two tall, latticed windows that admitted both daylight and the beauty of the garden. And my earlier question was answered: the windows looked out on the pathway where it entered the garden. Thanasset, sitting in this room with his guest, had seen me as I passed by. When I hadn't come in after a natural interval, he had gone to the back door to find me standing there uncertainly.

Thanasset's guest was a man a little older than my father, a small man with laughter around his eyes. The smile he gave me in greeting wreathed his face in wrinkles.

"Chief Supervisor Ferrathyn," said Thanasset, "I present my son, Markasset."

Chief Supervisor? The old man made no move toward me, so I bowed as I had done to Balgokh and said what seemed right. "Our house is honored by your visit."

Thanasset flashed me a strange look, then turned away to fetch a stoppered glass pitcher with a dark liquid in it.

"Come, come, my boy—you needn't be so formal," said the Chief Supervisor. "Sit down, please, and tell us—what news? What rumors reached you in the marketplace?"

Thanasset refilled Ferrathyn's glass, then his own. Then he brought a third from the stone-and-glass shelves that formed one wall of the room, filled it and handed it to me.

I sat down and took a sip, then a deep draught. This, I realized, must be faen. Good it was, too, but not like beer as I knew it. For one thing, it wasn't carbonated. It reminded me of Japanese *sake* lightly mixed with Mount Vernon rye whiskey—but it was cool and tasted much better than such a mixture would have tasted.

Besides liking the stuff, I was stalling for time, trying to think. Was I or wasn't I supposed to know about the theft of the Ra'ira? Illia said that Zaddorn suspected me. Did my father and Ferrathyn know of his suspicions? And what did *they* think?

A frightening realization swept over me, almost causing me to choke on the faen. I don't know myself whether I—Markasset—was guilty or not!

I set my glass down on the small square table beside my chair. "The marketplace is churning with rumors," I told them. "It is said that the Ra'ira is missing, and that the Peace and Security Department is looking all over for it."

Ferrathyn looked at Thanasset. "I knew we could not keep it quiet for very long, old friend. We'll have to make an official announcement soon." He looked back at me. "Is that all? No mention of how it was stolen, or by whom?"

I hesitated, then said, "No. Not that I know of, sir." That was technically true. Illia had said that everyone seemed to know of the theft, but Zaddorn had spoken to her privately when he mentioned his suspicion of me.

I thought to myself, *If it's all that secret, and I've been out of the city* . . . I took a chance. "May I be told what happened?" I asked them. They glanced at each other, and Ferrathyn nodded.

"Please do tell him, Thanasset. Perhaps, after he has heard everything, he may be able to help us."

"Very well," Thanasset sighed, and took a long drink from

his glass. Then he spoke directly to me. Ferrathyn, obviously, had heard the story before.

"It happened on the night you left—Kryfer before last." *Kryfer. Day Two*, Markasset's memory said. "As you know, I had Guardian Duty that night, beginning at midnight. I went to the Council Hall, relieved Ferrathyn, and formally took custody of the Ra'ira."

I *didn't* know. I tried to dig a memory of that day or night out of Markasset's storehouse, but with no success. Thanasset might have been reading *Little Red Riding Hood* for all the personal connection I felt to what he was saying.

"Ferrathyn left me in charge," Thanasset continued, "and I locked the Security Room. I was there alone with the stone.

"About an hour into the watch, the door opened, and two men came in."

He looked at me, waiting for me to bring up the discrepancy I had already noticed.

"Through a locked door?" I asked.

Ferrathyn sighed, but said nothing.

Thanasset stood up and began to pace the room, making little noise on the green carpet that almost covered the floor. "That's the whole trouble," he said. "I distinctly remember locking that door. But they came in as though it had never been locked." He threw open his arms in a very human gesture of hopelessness. "I can't explain it."

"Can't it be unlocked from the outside?" I asked, and instantly wondered if I should already know the answer.

"No," Ferrathyn supplied. "That is part of the whole security program. It is unlocked *by the Supervisor on duty* when the next man arrives. The shift changes every third-of-a-day, and the new man re-locks the door."

"As I did!" Thanasset almost shouted. "For fifteen years, I have *never* failed to lock that door. And yet they came in!"

"Go on with your story, old friend," the Chief Supervisor said in a kindly manner. "We will worry about the locked door later."

Thanasset came back to his seat, and refilled our glasses. "Well—as I said, two men came in. They were armed with truncheons, not swords, and both of them were wearing hoods with eyeholes. I couldn't identify them if I saw them again, except that one of them had the little finger of his left hand missing.

"Neither of them said a word. One came at me, and the other went to the desk where the jewel was resting on its pedestal." His hands clenched and trembled with recalled frustration. "I fought them, of course. I would have given my life to protect the Ra'ira. But even that small dignity was denied me. I was knocked senseless. I lay unconscious on the floor of the Security Room until Supervisor Noddaran came to relieve me at the end of my shift. He found the door ajar, the Ra'ira gone, and me . . . asleep." He took a deep breath and lifted his glass again. "That's all. That's exactly what happened."

"Are you well now, Father?" I asked. He looked strong enough, but I knew what it was like to wake up from a clobbering like that. And his body was older than mine.

Thanasset looked at me so long that I lowered my gaze in embarrassment. "Yes," he said then. "Yes, Markasset, I'm fine now." A short, awkward pause. "Thank you for asking, son."

I tried to bring the conversation back to the point. I remembered a scrap of the discussion I'd heard among the cops on the trail south the night before. I decided it was worth quoting. "Why would anyone steal the Ra'ira?" I asked them. "Its value would be destroyed if it were cut up, and, if left intact, it would be recognized anywhere for what it is."

"Prestige, for one thing," Ferrathyn answered, and sipped from his glass. "Are you aware of its history?"

"Only vaguely," I said, and blessed the talkative flatfeet who had passed me that night. "I know it came from Kä originally."

Ferrathyn shook his head. "Not originally. Many tens of hundreds—perhaps a hundred of hundred—years ago, it was found here at Raithskar, in our own precious metal mines. At that time, the Kings of Gandalara at Kä held sway over the whole of the land between the Walls of the World. The jewel was sent as tribute to either King Beykoth or King Veytoth—the Record is unclear on that point—and remained there for tens of hundreds of years, until the fall of the Kings and the sacking of Kä."

"When Serkajon brought it back," I contributed.

"Yes," Thanasset put in. "Our esteemed ancestor returned it to its rightful home, and for tens of hundreds of years it has been the symbol of the power and authority of the Council of Supervisors of Raithskar."

Our ancestor, I thought. *Markasset comes from good stock. Or does he? After all, to the Kings of Gandalara, Serkajon must have been a thief.* I turned away from that line of thought, only to realize that what Ferrathyn was saying brought me back to it.

"The descendants of the Kings went to Eddarta when they escaped from the sacking, and they rule that city yet. They have long claimed that the Ra'ira is rightfully theirs—with some justice on their side. The Lords of Eddarta claim that since the stone was freely given to the ancient kings, it is theirs by family right."

"Our reply," Thanasset added, "is that the gem was given to the Kings of *Gandalara.* Since there are no such kings anymore, the rights of the stone revert to us." He chuckled—a deep, warm sound. "Besides, we are—or *were*—in possession of it."

Nine points of the law, I thought. Aloud, I said, "Then you think that the Lords of Eddarta are behind this robbery?"

"It's one possibility," Ferrathyn said. "Possession of the Ra'ira would certainly increase the prestige of the Lords of Eddarta—except, of course, in Raithskar." His face acquired a troubled look. "They might well try to re-create the kingdom and rule from Eddarta rather than lost Kä. Some of the cities near them, already dependent on their rich harvests and busy marketplace, might even support them in their claim."

"But many others would not," Thanasset said in a quiet voice. "There would be such fighting as has not been seen since the First King united the Walled World. There would be no safety for caravans—no trade—very little water sharing."

"It would disrupt *everything.*" Ferrathyn was leaning forward in his chair, as though he were trying to impress me with the importance of what he said. "We can't allow it to happen; we *must* get the Ra'ira back!"

I was duly impressed. Even a little frightened by the man's intensity. And puzzled. The men on the trail had treated the whole affair like an ordinary jewel theft—a very special jewel, to be sure, but a simple robbery. It was their job to find the thieves. And their pride was at stake; that someone had stolen *their city's* treasure was galling.

But I had heard nothing in those rough voices to compare with the passion concealed in the quiet tones of these two men. The Ra'ira had a significance for them that went beyond anything the townsfolk had ever thought of. Listening to them, I felt as though Archduke Ferdinand had just been assassinated.

"Are you sure Eddarta is behind the theft?" I asked.

Ferrathyn relaxed back in his chair as Thanasset refilled his glass. He took a hefty drink before answering. "As a matter of fact, we're not certain of anything. When the robbery was first discovered, we tried to keep it quiet for two reasons. First, we saw no need to excite the townsfolk. And second . . . well . . ."

"We thought that someone local must have taken it," Thanasset finished. "The manner and method of its keeping are not widely known. Whoever planned the theft needed accurate information. So we asked Zaddorn to search the city."

"House by house?" I asked, astonished. "Respectfully, that's no way to keep it quiet!"

They laughed, and I was glad to feel the tension in the room ebb away.

"Nothing so obvious," Ferrathyn said. "Zaddorn and his men have contacts—sources of information—that know about everything that goes on in Raithskar."

So even this world has an underworld, I thought to myself, and a name attached itself to the thought. *Worfit. And Markasset? How closely was he involved with them?*

"I hate to ask the same question twice," I said, "but again: why? Why would anyone *in* Raithskar want to steal the Ra'ira?"

"Ransom," said Thanasset shortly, then shrugged. "At least, that was Zaddorn's theory. What other reason would there be? It's the only practical way to make money from the theft."

"*Was* his theory?" I asked. "What changed his mind?"

"A quarter-moon passed with no message from the thieves, and all of Zaddorn's digging brought up exactly nothing," Ferrathyn said. "Either it's the most tightly-held secret in Raithskar's long history, or the rogueworld really does know nothing about it."

"And so he blames Eddarta now," I said, and refrained from mentioning the posse I had seen.

"Yes," Farrathyn agreed. "It was actually my idea that sparked the new theory. When he could learn nothing, Zaddorn came to us—" he gestured to include Thanasset "—in desperation for any clue. He seized on my suggestion of city rivalry and, with his usual sharp understanding, quickly determined that if the Ra'ira left Raithskar, it must have traveled with the caravan of Gharlas."

"Which is where you come in, son."

Here it was at last. I held out my glass for a refill, surprised that my hand wasn't shaking.

"That girl, Illia, delivered the note you left for me. When Gharlas was suspected, I confided in Ferrathyn that you had signed on with his caravan. Naturally, seeing you back home so soon, Ferrathyn and I wondered . . ."

You wondered? I thought at him. *You should be on this side of things!*

"Did you see or hear anything, Markasset," Ferrathyn asked me, "that might suggest to you that our thieves rode with your caravan?"

How the hell could I answer them? Yet answer them I must, and I had only seconds to decide what to say. The truth? *"Sorry, folks, I'm a stranger here myself."* I had a strong hunch I'd get a lengthy tour of the local equivalent of the madhouse. Would they believe me if I told them I was Ricardo Emilio Carillo, and that, in some fashion I did not understand, I had been loaned the use of Markasset's faultless body and faulty memories? I thought not.

But I couldn't lie, either. Not from any compunction over lying to "my" father—though I did feel a reluctance—but from the sheer impracticality of it. A good lie has to be based on a sound knowledge of the truth, or it won't fit in, even for a moment.

Even a censored version of the truth wouldn't work. If I said, "I don't remember," I'd sound like a *Capo Mafioso* testifying to a Congressional committee.

But I had to talk, and *talk fast!*

"I'm sorry, sir, but I can't help you there. I don't recall any suspicious or peculiar behavior on the part of anyone in the caravan."

I waited for more questions, but Ferrathyn only nodded. "Good enough. But—" I had taken a mouthful of faen in my relief; it turned bitter and I had to struggle to swallow it. "—then why did you return early to Raithskar?"

I looked at him directly and brought out my most sincere voices. "Sir, with all due respect, that is a personal matter. I assure you it had nothing whatever to do with the Ra'ira."

Was I lying? Or telling the truth? I didn't know. No wave of guilt surged up from Markasset's memory, but I couldn't count on that to mean he wasn't involved in some way.

The Chief Supervisor gazed at me for a long two seconds. He looked kindly, puzzled, and just a little sad. "I see," he said, and sighed. "Well, we'll know for certain before too long. Yesterday Zaddorn sent out a special squad with only food and water. They can travel half again as fast as a heavy-laden caravan—but even so, we cannot expect them back for more than a moon yet. We shall just have to be patient."

A moon, I thought to myself. *It will be much longer than that. The caravan had a nine-day head start. That means Zaddorn's squad won't catch up with them for . . . um . . . eighteen days, and then it will take them at least that long again to get back . . .*

My chain of reasoning was cut off sharply by the realization that I didn't know just how long a time period a "moon" was in Gandalara. On my Earth, it was twenty-nine and a half days, but if I were on some planet circling Deneb or Fomalhaut, its moon could have an entirely different period.

"If it can be found," Thanasset said, "we can trust Zaddorn to find it eventually. He's tough and he's smart."

Ferrathyn nodded. "He is that. And he hates to give up." Suddenly he chuckled. "He may yet find the Ra'ira here in the city." The chuckle became a laugh and the old face crinkled up with merriment. "Oh," he gasped. "I can see it now. The squad reports back, exhausted, dejected, drained by the heat of the desert, and its leader reports sadly to Zaddorn: 'Sir, we have found no trace of the Ra'ira.' "

"And Zaddorn," added Thanasset, laughing with his friend, "looks up from his desk with that absent expression he has when his mind's on something else, and says: 'Oh, that! We found that thirty days ago!' He'd certainly have twelve very unhappy men on his hands!"

"And it would be my fault," Ferrathyn said, "since it was my idea that sent them after the caravan!" He chuckled again, shaking his head. "And I can't say I'd be sorry for it, either. Zaddorn is a fine man, but his independent ways have given me headaches enough in the past." He drained his glass and stood up. "Well, I must be going. I'll see you in the morning, Thanasset?" It was only half a question.

"Of course," Thanasset replied, standing up and walking with Ferrathyn to the door of the room. "I'll have to see to Tailor's Street first thing; it hasn't been resurfaced in eight moons, and the ruts are getting bad. I received a note on it yesterday. And *then* I'll try to get to the threescore other matters waiting for me. This whole business has thoroughly disrupted my routine."

"I know," Ferrathyn said feelingly. "You should see my desk." He turned to me and smiled. "It's been a pleasure to meet you at last, young Markasset."

I stood up and bowed as I had earlier. "You honor me, Chief Supervisor."

Both men left the room then, and I collapsed back into my chair. I could hear the soft whisper of their sandals as they crossed the polished wood floor toward the door which opened into the street. And I could hear their voices.

"A well-spoken lad," Ferrathyn said softly. "He is a credit to you, old friend."

"Thank you," Thanasset said, and I heard the heavy door swish open. "Until tomorrow, then."

"Yes. Good fortune until then."

Thanasset came back into the room and silently refilled his glass, then mine. But he didn't drink his. He just sat there, across from me, and stared moodily at the surface of the faen, tipping the glass slightly and watching the shifting liquid. The tip of his tongue worried his right tusk in about the same spirit as I might drum my fingers on the table. He was thinking. He was worried.

And so was I—and for the first time since I had awakened on the desert, not just about myself. I liked this man. Whether that was a carryover from Markasset I couldn't tell, but the fact remained that I felt a strong liking for him. I remembered what that cop on the trail had said: something about arresting "that fleabitten old man" and persuading him to tell them all about it. They had meant Thanasset, of course—the Ra'ira had been stolen from him. Did they think . . .

"Father, are you in trouble?" I asked softly.

He looked up at me with the same expression I had seen on his face when he introduced me to Ferrathyn. He seemed about to say something, then apparently decided against it. At last he said, "I don't know, son. Maybe. I'm not suspected of the theft, of course, but—I may be open to a charge of criminal negligence."

"The door," I said, and he nodded. "*Did* you leave that door unlocked?"

"*No!*" He slammed the flat of his palm on the top of the table beside his chair. Ferrathyn's glass, which had been left there, jumped clear off the table. Even with the thick green rug covering the parquet floor, it would have shattered when it landed. With a reflex speed I didn't know I had, I leaned out of my chair and caught it in midair. Thanasset barely noticed. "I locked that door when Ferrathyn left!" he said. "My honor on it!"

I took the glass and set it on the shelf where the pitcher stood. "I believe you, Father. The question is, how *did* the robbers get in? It definitely can't be unlocked from the outside?"

"Absolutely not."

I thought for a minute. If that room was *always* occupied by a Supervisor, it was unlikely that visitors, even the son of one of the Supervisors, would be admitted. It seemed like a safe bet that Markasset didn't know any more about the room itself than Ricardo did, and I could ask questions freely.

"What would happen if the Supervisor on duty suddenly became ill or dropped dead? How would the others get the door open?"

Thanasset's eyebrows tried to crawl up over his jutting supraorbital ridges. "That would never happen. A man that ill would never be allowed to take the duty!"

"Not if anybody knew he was ill—of course not," I agreed. "But if something happened unexpectedly? Suppose . . . his heart just stopped?" There was no way to say "coronary thrombosis" in Gandaresh.

His face cleared of its puzzled look. "Oh, I see! You're proposing a purely hypothetical case: that for some reason a man's inner awareness failed to tell him of the possibility of an oncoming malfunction."

Inner awareness? I wondered.

"I've never heard of such a case. But, assuming such a thing *could* happen, I suppose we'd just have to take an axe to the door."

I managed to keep my face straight, but inside I was gawping at him like an idiot. The Guardian shift was a third of a day—eight hours—and Thanasset had *never heard* of a case where a man hadn't *known* of a fatal malfunction *at least eight hours before his death*.

No doctors, I thought, stunned. *No lab tests, no outside opinions. Just "inner awareness." I must have it, too. Perhaps I would have the rare privilege of* twice *knowing beforehand that I'm about to die!*

But, I reminded myself, *that only works for interior failings. My "inner awareness" is giving me no messages about whether or not I'll be executed for the theft of the Ra'ira!*

"How does the lock work?" I asked, to cover my surprise and confusion.

Thanasset shrugged. "It is not a thing generally known outside the Council, but I see no harm in telling you now that there is nothing to protect. The building is very old, and the lock on that door has never been changed. But it lacks nothing because of its antiquity—it's the strongest door and most secure lock I've ever seen. The door is a pace wide and half a hand thick, solid wood, reinforced and nailed with rakor."

Rakor. Markasset's memory came through. The word meant "most precious metal"—but the English equivalent was "steel." Evidently iron mines were far from common in Gandalara.

"There is a set of five steel brackets," he continued, "two on the door itself, two on the wall on the opening side, on the left, and one on the wall on the hinge side, on the right. A heavy wooden bolt slides in the brackets. When the door is unlocked, the bolt is pushed clear of the door, to the left. To lock it, you slide it to the right until it rests in the bracket on the hinge side. There's a hole in the bolt that matches a hole in the bracket, and there's a steel pin as thick as your thumb that goes in there. The bolt won't slide until that pin is removed."

"And you put the pin in?"

"I did. I remember it distinctly."

I believed him. And not just because I liked him. It didn't

make sense to think he had left that door unlocked on purpose and expected to get away with it. He was not a stupid man, nor an irresponsible one. That the Ra'ira had been stolen from *his* care troubled him deeply, and his anxiety for the stone's return was compounded by his bewilderment over this business about the lock.

Somehow, that door had been unlocked by the robbers themselves. But how? I had no better answers than Thanasset did. I'd read plenty of locked-room mysteries, but this was the first *un*locked-room mystery I'd come across.

"I'd like to take a look at that room," I said.

"As I said before, there's no harm now. Yes, we'll go there tomorrow. I have this day off, and I need the rest." He eyed me, and smiled wryly. "And *you* need a bath. You're all over salt and dust." We both stood up. "Bathe and change your clothes. Lunch will be ready by the time you're through."

A bath and some food! Suddenly nothing was more important.

9

I remembered where "my" room was. I rushed up the stairs that led upward from the street entrance. They were made of wood, but the stepping surfaces had been covered with rough-surfaced tiles—for safety, I presumed, and to protect the precious wood. A hallway led off to my right when I reached the top of the stairs, and the second door on the left side was my room.

Another of the tall, latticed windows in the far wall overlooked the neighboring garden. A cloth hanging was mounted above the window, and would cover it if it were allowed to drape naturally. But now its folds were gathered and drawn to the side of the window, held there by a long wooden peg mortared into the stone of the wall.

Beneath the window was a man-sized woven pad much like the ones I had seen in the Refreshment House. This one seemed larger and thicker, and it lay upon the floor of the room. A light, soft blanket was neatly folded beside the pad. This was to be my bed, and it looked comfortable enough.

I turned to one of the side walls, which was covered completely with narrow bronze-hinged wooden doors. When I pulled at the two handles in the middle of the wall, the doors folded apart, exposing room-length shelves spaced about two feet apart from floor to ceiling.

Wow, I thought, looking at the contents. *Markasset does know how to dress!*

Arranged on the shelves was an enormous wardrobe of brightly-colored tunics, trousers, and belts. And boots and headscarves. And sandals. And pins and rings and metal chains that were either belts or necklaces.

I picked up a bright yellow tunic and shook it out. It had long sleeves and a high neck, and reached to mid-thigh on me. I looked back at the stack of clothes and found a bright green sleeveless jacket about the same length. It was heavier and elaborately embroidered and bordered with yellow—they made a beautiful match.

But I put them back. For one thing, the fact that their colors were deliberately coordinated set them apart from the ordinary street wear I had seen so far. They must be Gandalaran formal dress. For another, though I admired them and longed to wear them, they were a little too . . . obtrusive for me yet. I was learning more and more about this world, but I was still a stranger here. Best, I thought, to attract as little notice as possible.

So I selected a relatively plain blue tunic and set it out on the woven pad with some sandals. Then, with relief, I stripped off the clothes I had found myself in when I woke up in the desert. They had been carefully washed by the Fa'aldu at the Refreshment House of Yafnaar, but three days on the trail had thoroughly dusted them up again. The boots I shook off and placed on the floor of the closet with the other footwear. The clothes I dropped in a pile in the corner.

On one of the shelves was a short robe of a soft, thick fabric. It was well-worn, and obviously designed as a bathrobe. I put it on and went downstairs, the rough tile pleasant against my bare feet.

I went out the back door and along the path I had followed

before, toward the back buildings. I looked in on Keeshah and smiled. He was sound asleep on the floor, lying on his side and twisted just enough so that one huge foreleg was suspended in mid-air. I had a strong impulse to go in and scratch the lighter fur of his chest, but I knew it would disturb him.

Rest well, Keeshah, I thought at him. *You deserve it.*

As though my thought had reached him dimly, he moved in his sleep, lowered the hovering paw, and curled around to rest his head on one extended hind leg. I left him then, and hunted for the bath-house.

It was only two doors down in a long series of outbuildings that formed the rear wall of the estate. It wasn't large, just a squarish room with a rectangular sunken pool long enough for a man to lie down in, and about as deep as the tubs I was used to. The tub was lined and bordered with pale gray tiles, each one decorated with fine blue traceries in an intricate design.

A ceramic pipe a couple of inches in diameter led down from the ceiling, evidently from a cistern on the roof. *No problem pumping water up there*, I thought. *The lake at the foot of Skarkel Falls is higher up the slope than the city—there would be plenty of pressure. And the water standing in the cistern would be sun-warmed.*

There was a rope hanging beside the pipe. I pulled it tentatively and was rewarded by a flow of water into the tub. On a ledge in the corner was a stack of scratchy-looking towels and several bars of soap. I took one—its scent was odd but pleasant—and climbed down into the tub. The water was comfortably warm, and I slid down the smooth tile until only my head was above water. I simply soaked for a while, really relaxing for the first time since I had awakened in the desert. I let my mind wander.

It was apparent that the firm of Thanasset & Son were in a jam. Thanasset was suspected, at least in some quarters, of aiding and abetting in the theft of the Ra'ira. At the very least he had, apparently, been negligent in his care of it, thereby contributing to the felony. And one person—one very important Chief of Police Zaddorn—suspected Markasset of complicity in the same crime. Markasset could even be said to have a motive: a certain rogueworld character named Worfit was very anxious to have a large loan repaid.

Markasset was better off than his father in one way: all he had to do was get on his sha'um and ride off to another city. To my mind, that was exactly what he had been trying to do when he took up the job with the caravan—though he had obviously had sense enough to travel incognito, with Keeshah following downwind.

Had Markasset been involved with the jewel theft? I just couldn't make up my mind about that. All the evidence I had seen assured me that Markasset had been a pretty wild young man—but I didn't want to believe that he'd pull off a robbery for which his own father would be blamed.

Besides, if he *had* been in on it, that meant that his job with the caravan had been part of the plan, and that the stone *was* going to Eddarta. That was more than robbery; that was treason. And I didn't believe that treason was in Markasset's character.

Or, no—*wait a. minute! Suppose Markasset had helped steal the thing for ransom and then the crooks double-crossed him? If they had threatened him, that would explain his flight with the caravan.*

No. There hadn't been a ransom request. And anyway, I didn't want to believe that Markasset would run away from a fight.

But it seems certain that he was running away from a debt. What's the difference?

I couldn't tell. I was infuriatingly close to Markasset, but I still didn't know him. But something—maybe, I had to admit, my own hopes—told me that no matter how it looked, Markasset hadn't really been running away.

Could he have been chasing the stolen gem? I wondered suddenly, then instantly rejected the idea. *No, the only way he could have known it was gone was to be involved in the theft himself.*

And what about Worfit? Could he have demanded the Ra'ira as payment for Markasset's debt? Or is he somebody else altogether, unconnected with this whole mess?

After chasing everything I knew through my brain at least ten times, I gave up. My sole knowledge of detective work came from extensive reading of detective stories, which is something like trying to learn the Latin language by reading *Quo Vadis?*, *Spartacus*, and *Ben Hur*. That won't get you to *amo-amas-amat*.

I considered myself a rational, reasoning person with greater than average intelligence, and better than half a century of training in using my brain. It had been a long time since my undergraduate courses in logic, but some of it stuck with me. *All A is B; no B is C;* ergo *no A is C*. Perfectly true, but no help if you don't know what *A*, *B*, and *C* are. It's *impossible* to construct a chain of syllogisms when you don't know the subjects or the operators.

It all boiled down to the same thing which had been plaguing me since I came to in Gandalara. Lack of information. Except this particular information was absolutely necessary for my survival and Thanasset's. *Damn!*

Thanasset couldn't run from Raithskar the way Markasset could. The boy had been fairly footloose. But Thanasset's business, his career, his friends, his life were all here in Raithskar.

And I couldn't leave him.

I knew, then, that I had already made a commitment. Just when it had happened, I wasn't sure about. Probably when I first met Thanasset. But I knew now that, however I had arrived in Gandalara, I was here. Raithskar was my home now, and I had a life to live. I would sure as hell live it as honorably as I had lived my life before. That meant sticking it out with Thanasset, come hell or damnation.

I sat up in the tub, scrubbed myself down, and rinsed off. Then I climbed out, and while the tub was draining I reached for one of the towels. They were fuzzy and stiff, and they scratched away the water, rather than absorbing it. They left my skin tingling. I put on the bathrobe and returned to my room.

While I was dressing, I heard voices from below. One of them was Thanasset's, I was sure, but the others were higher-pitched. I couldn't make out the words. One of the higher voices said very little, then stopped altogether while the other went on talking to Thanasset.

Then there was a rap on my door, and the voice which had stopped downstairs said, "Are you dressed, young man? I'm coming in." I was startled—the voice might have belonged to my own father's mother, Gra'mama Maria Constanza!

"Dressed," I said, unnecessarily. She was already coming through the door.

For a moment, I froze. The thing that had come into my room was a creature out of nightmare.

The apish head was bald except for a black fringe around the edges, and the grayish skin was incredibly wrinkled. The deep-set eyes seemed to glitter evilly. The tusks in the half-open mouth gleamed whitely in the diffused sunlight from the window. An amalgamation of the Mummy and Dracula had somehow stepped down from the screen and into my presence.

The wizened horror spoke. "What ails you, boy? You sick?"

And the spell was broken. Ricardo's mind had been receiving that startling first impression. As Markasset's memories came flooding in, it was as though I turned from an image in a distorted mirror back to the original. And the person who faced me was a softly aging lady with a sweet, puzzled smile on her face. *Lavender and lace*, I thought, and smiled at her in real welcome.

"Milda, darling!" I heard myself say. "You startled me!" And I held out my arms.

She came forward in three quick steps and hugged me with a fierce strength. She was half a head shorter than I; she pressed her cheek to my shoulder as she very nearly squeezed the breath out of me.

"Oh, Markasset!" she said. "It's so good to see you again! I thought you'd be gone for moons—maybe years!"

"But I'm back now, as you can see!" I laughed, hugging her around her shoulders.

She pushed me away and tried to look stern. But the gentle old mouth still trembled on the edge of a smile. "Your father says to come down to the table as soon as possible. And *behave yourself*," she added. "We have company."

"Anybody I know?"

"I should hope to ride a sha'um! That girl Illia is here, and—for all her dizziness—she seems to be properly worried about you. Your father asked her to stay for lunch." She stopped, hesitated, and finally asked, "Nephew, you know I don't pry—" *That's true; she doesn't, bless her*, I drew out of Markasset's memory—"but . . . does that scatter-brained girl have any real reason to worry?"

I told her the truth. "I'm not sure—no, I'm not trying to put you off, darling," I added, as her face took on a look of hurt, "I really don't know. Maybe, after we've talked at lunch, I'll be more certain." I smiled at her again. "I'll let you know when to start worrying."

"Oh, *you!*" She said, and gave me another quick hug, then went to the door. "Hurry down now," she said. The door closed behind her, then reopened and she stuck her head back in. "I'm truly glad you're home again, Markasset." Then she was gone.

She was, I knew, my mother's father's sister. My great-aunt Milda. Or, rather, Markasset's great-aunt. *Will I ever get used to these double references?* I thought. *I'll have to work at keeping my two sets of relatives straight!*

But I knew that in Milda's case it didn't matter. She was such a dear old lady that Ricardo loved her already as much as Markasset did. In that moment, Milda became *my* Milda.

I went down the front stairs and into the room that opened from the midhall across from the parlor where Thanasset, Ferrathyn, and I had been sitting. This room was very light; the tall, narrow windows filled the wall that was the side of the house. There was a large square table in the center of the room that was set with china dishes finer, if possible, than the cups and pitcher I had seen at Yafnaar. They were worked in an intertwining blue and green pattern, with touches of yellow that seemed to suit the brightness of the room.

Thanasset and Illia were already seated at the table.

"Of course, I don't know if he really thinks that," Illia was saying earnestly, "or if he's only jealous of Markasset."

"What cause might Zaddorn have to envy Markasset?"

"Why—" she stammered, astonishment clear in her voice, "why, *me*, of course. I have told him that Markasset and I will marry soon, and he might—well, do *anything* to stop us!"

"Oh. I see," said Thanasset.

I wish I did, I thought. Then I said out loud, to announce my arrival in the room, "I see you've been filling in my father about Zaddorn's suspicions."

"Yes," Thanasset said drily. "And about your wedding plans."

I looked at the girl uncertainly. *I* hadn't heard anything about wedding plans, but I couldn't be sure what Markasset had said to her or agreed to. And I was a little annoyed that she had mentioned Zaddorn to Thanasset. She had seemed to regard his suspicions as a secret; I saw no need to worry the old man with them. *Or maybe*, I conceded, *I'm afraid they're right and wanted to spare him the truth.*

Illia was talking again, in a rush. She seemed to sense my displeasure. "I'm sorry, darl—Markasset. Perhaps I shouldn't have said anything, but I thought your father should know."

"About Zaddorn?" I asked her. "Or about our 'wedding plans'."

She looked very uncomfortable, and Thanasset was looking from her to me. *He's wondering the same thing I am*, I realized. *Am I really going to marry this girl?*

"Zaddorn, of course, silly," she said. "The other—well, he had to know sometime. Is it my fault you hadn't told him yourself before this?"

Now there she had me. If Thanasset were really as surprised—and not altogether pleased, I thought—as he seemed to be, why *hadn't* Markasset told him?

I sat down at the table and expressed my most fervent wish. "Father . . . Illia . . . I've had a long ride back, and I'm so hungry I could eat this table. Would you mind if we didn't talk about Zaddorn, or weddings, or *anything* while we have lunch?"

Illia opened her mouth to say something, but Thanasset interrupted smoothly and enthusiastically. "A fine idea." He beamed at me. "Milda!"

She came through a hinged door from the back of the house, carrying an enormous tray piled with food. She set it down in the center of the table, and we served ourselves. There was a large bowl of stew very much like the porridge I'd been served at the Refreshment House. We had each been given a utensil like the one I had seen at Yafnaar; we dipped our servings out of the large bowl into the small bowls before us, and filled our plates from an assortment of fruits. There was a fine-textured bread and a sharp butter-like spread. Milda filled three tall glasses with cool water, put the stoppered pitcher on the table, surreptitiously squeezed my shoulder, and disappeared back into the kitchen.

I didn't worry about manners. I really *was* hungry, and it was a great relief not to think for a while. The food was delicious, and I put away an enormous amount of it. At last I became aware that Thanasset and Illia had both finished eating and were watching me. Illia looked concerned; Thanasset seemed amused.

"It seems like ages since I've tasted Milda's cooking," I said, by way of explanation.

Thanasset laughed. "Milda will be pleased to hear that you noticed, Markasset. She did prepare the rafel herself in honor of your return. For my part, I'm glad to see that this business with Zaddorn hasn't dulled your appetite!"

There it was again, as though I hadn't put it off while we were eating. *I can't handle this*, I thought. *Not Illia and Thanasset together, with so many unknowns to deal with.*

"I feel like stretching my legs a little," I said. "Illia, will you walk in the garden with me? You will excuse us, won't you, Father?"

Thanasset caught on. He smiled. "Of course, son. Enjoy your walk."

We walked in silence. The garden was really a small park, with a stone-laid path leading from the house to the end of the row of outbuildings that formed the back boundary of the estate, along in front of the buildings and then back up to the house along the side wall. The area enclosed by the functional pathway was beautifully landscaped with slender, twisting trees, and flowering bushes which added fragrance to the cool, slightly misty air. Smaller stone pathways were part of the landscaping. It was a place to walk and be at peace.

We followed one of the narrow paths until it curved around a clump of trees and we were screened from the house. Then Illia stopped. Without a word, she put her arms around my neck and kissed me.

I was a full head taller than Illia; I could have resisted that kiss easily. But it was the most natural thing in the world for me to bend down to her and put my arms around her. Her mouth parted lightly under mine. I ran my tongue over her smooth, rounded tusks, expecting them to feel strange. But they seemed delicate in her mouth, perfect and erotic.

"Thank goodness!" she said, when she finally pushed me away. "The way you acted in front of your father, I was afraid . . . Markasset, I *am* sorry if I made trouble for you by telling Thanasset about . . . our plans."

"Plans?" I said stupidly, trying not to show her how shaken I was. She couldn't know how many years it had been since I had been kissed in just that way—but I hadn't forgotten what a lover's kiss felt like.

Along with the new awareness of the relationship between Illia and Markasset, I had to deal with Markasset's physical response to the girl. Or mine. It was very confused. Under . . . less uncertain circumstances, I would have been delighted. But as it was, I tried to clear my head and think straight.

"Yes, plans!" she said. We walked over to a stone bench and sat down. "You haven't forgotten what you said to me—" she lowered her gaze to the ground "*—that night*, have you?"

That's just the point, I thought desperately. *I* have *forgotten. What did I say to you?*

I couldn't ask her. I was convinced that she loved Markasset, and that he might have returned her love. Looking at her here in the garden, with shade dappling the smooth golden fur on her head and her dark eyes shining in the fine-boned, alien face, I felt a physical echo of what must have happened on "that night." When I had accepted *being* Markasset, I had also accepted responsibility for anything he had done before I somehow acquired his body. That meant, I decided, accepting his promise to this girl. But not right away.

"Illia," I began—then found I didn't have the words.

She reached out and took my hand. "I know you're in trouble, darling, and this really isn't the time. But . . . I know Thanasset doesn't like me very much."

I started to object politely, but stopped myself. I thought she was right. Thanasset *didn't* like—or at least didn't approve of—Illia.

"All I want is—some assurance from you, Markasset," she said with dignity. "I know very well we can't marry before this nonsense with Worfit and Zaddorn is straightened out."

"Will it ever be?" I asked. "Oh, I'll pay Worfit what I owe him, that's no real problem. But Zaddorn is a powerful man, and rumor lasts a lot longer than the truth." *What* is *the truth, damn it!* "Are you sure you want to be married to the man who *might* have stolen the Ra'ira?"

"Is that what you're worried about?" She laughed and looked relieved. "Darling, you know very well that one day you'll be a Supervisor like your father. Nothing in your past can outweigh *that* honor." She moved closer and put her head on my shoulder. "And I'll be the *wife* of a Supervisor." Suddenly she sat up and looked at me squarely. "Won't I?"

Markasset had let her think so. Maybe it had been only a

good line, and it had obviously worked. But a promise—even an implied one—was a promise.

"Yes," I answered her.

After a while we walked back into the midhall of the house. Thanasset was standing in front of the sha'um portrait in wood parquetry, staring thoughtfully up at the sword mounted on the wall. He turned when we entered, and smiled.

"Well, there you are, children. Isn't the garden pleasant today?"

"It's lovely, sir," Illia replied. "It must be the most beautiful garden in Raithskar."

He turned and walked with us to the huge street door. "I'd like to think so, yes," he said. He opened the door for her. "Thank you for your visit, Illia."

"Thank you for your hospitality, sir." She turned to me and smiled radiantly. "Goodbye for now, Markasset." She started to leave, but turned back to face Thanasset. "Take care of him, sir. He's—" she looked my way with a slight smile "—not quite himself. I'm afraid that Zaddorn's suspicions have upset him more than we know."

"Rest assured I will see to his good health, my dear," Thanasset said. He closed the door behind her with a sigh. Then he linked his arm through mine and drew me back to where he had been standing.

Again he looked up at the sword and he said, almost offhandedly, "A nice girl, I suppose—but not terribly perceptive, is she?"

"I—I don't know what you mean, Father," I said. But I was afraid that I did know.

He moved to face me, and looked at me keenly from under his ridged brow.

"You're not my son," he said. "Just who *are* you?"

10

Surprisingly enough, I did not panic.

For one thing, there was no hostility in his manner or his voice. Wariness, yes. Curiosity. And something else—was it *respect?*

And I felt linked to Thanasset, committed to him. I was in his world, and in this world he had become *my* father. Somewhere along the line since I met him, I had realized I would have to confide in him eventually. But this soon? I wasn't ready.

Don't kid yourself. You'll never be ready, I told myself honestly.

Thanasset was watching me, reading the hesitation that must have shown on my face. "If you don't wish to tell me, I won't ask it of you," he said, with that oddly disturbing note of respect clearer now in his voice. "Any Visitor from the All-Mind is welcome. But . . ." He let his voice trail off.

"I do wish to tell you," I said, and knew it was true. It would be a tremendous relief to share even a little of this confusion with someone I could trust. And I *did* trust Thanasset. "I simply don't know where to start. Uh," I stalled, "could we sit down?"

"Certainly." He led the way back into the light, comfortable room where I had met Ferrathyn—was it only earlier that same day?

When we were comfortably seated with glasses of faen, "Who," I asked carefully, "do you think I am?"

"An Ancestor," he said, without hesitation. "A Visitor from the All-Mind who has chosen to grace the body of my son, Markasset."

I thought about that. Hell, for all I knew, I might be just that. Whatever it was.

Balgokh had said something similar—what had it been? *He said I had been touched with wisdom by an Ancestor*. I remembered. *And even he, who had seen Markasset for only a few minutes, had noticed the change.*

"Am I so different from your son?" I asked Thanasset.

He smiled at me, a little sadly. "Yes. You are courteous, well-mannered. You have a bearing of . . . confidence that Markasset lacked. He is a good man at heart, but rash and thoughtless, not given to thinking things through. He sometimes does foolish things."

Like helping to steal the Ra'ira? I wondered. *No, he doesn't even think that. He said "foolish"—not "criminal."*

Thanasset got up and walked over to the window. For a few seconds he stood there, looking out over the garden. At last he turned back to me, and what he said confirmed the brief impression I had received when I met him for the first time.

"I confess that I do not always *like* my son. But he is my only son, and I love him more dearly than my own life." His voice deepened, and for the first time I could see through his outward calmness to a core of grief and fear. "You need not reveal your identity to me," he said, with a dignity I admired more for having had a glimpse of its shaky foundation. "I have seen enough of you to be well content that your presence honors the body of my son. But I ask you, as a father, to tell me this: when will Markasset return?"

My brain seemed to freeze. *Return?*

Great God in Heaven!

The thought had simply not occurred to me before. I had accepted the fact that I had possession of a body that belonged to someone else. I felt no guilt for taking it over—certainly without its owner's permission. It had just happened. I hadn't planned it—hell and damnation, I had never even dreamed that something like this *could* happen.

That's not to say that I believed that reincarnation was impossible. As a child I had had the concepts of Heaven, Hell, and Purgatory (and Limbo, which didn't concern me since I had been baptized) drilled into me. As I grew older, I began to question the truth of those teachings, and to consider other alternatives. Philosophically, Nirvana and the Final Blackout were equally unappealing to me. Reincarnation—well, it seemed like wishful thinking to me. The defining factor for my entire attitude toward an afterlife of any kind was the total absence of objective evidence. I decided fairly early to suspend belief. "Wait and see" was my personal policy with regard to eschatology.

And now, what I had seen fit none of the alternatives I had considered. Even reincarnation was supposed to be an entirely new beginning—not an interruption of someone else's life.

I had lived through a dizzying displacement. I had come to accept the change. I was prepared, after traumatic adjustments I haven't been able to describe adequately, to assume the identity of Markasset. And with his identity, his responsibilities. For Thanasset. For his possible involvement with the theft of the Ra'ira. For his obligation—one which Ricardo had never undertaken in his own life—to Illia. For his wonderful bond with Keeshah.

I had accepted Markasset's life. *The rest of Markasset's life.*

It had never occurred to me that I might only have borrowed it.

I felt suddenly like some indigent old drunk who has awakened from a rotgut binge to find himself in a fine house with no idea how he got there. He takes advantage of it, enjoys himself—clean silk sheets, caviar, and champagne—and then realizes suddenly that the owner may come back at any moment and throw him out. Or worse.

"When will Markasset return?" Thanasset's words echoed in my brain, stirring up a maelstrom of emotion. Not panic. Panic is unreasoning and unreasonable. It was logical, possible, even, I had to admit, *just* that Markasset might reclaim the place I had unwillingly taken from him. What I felt was a thundering, horrible fear.

Not fear of death. I had felt that before: when the doctor gave me the bad news, when I watched the meteor approach, when Keeshah rushed toward me out in the desert. This was far worse. It wasn't only that after having been given a second chance at life, it might be snatched away from me. It was . . .

The closest thing I had felt to it before was beginning a really entertaining mystery novel and misplacing the book. It's a poor simile, and only a shallow imitation of what I felt now, but it shared the sense of . . . leaving something important, something worthwhile unfinished.

I *cared* about this old man, about the town, about the

Ra'ira. It terrified me to think that Markasset might return before I could straighten out the mess he had left behind!

I realized that Thanasset had said something to me.

I fought down the surge of fear, got it under control, and searched my short-term memory for Thanasset's words.

"Is something wrong?" came the playback. He was standing beside my chair, his hand on my shoulder. I was stiff and cramped, and I realized that I was clutching the arms of the chair as though holding on to life itself. Which I had been trying to do. With an effort, I relaxed my arms and reached for the glass beside the table. My hand was still shaking.

Thanasset picked it up before I could reach it. "I'll refill your glass," he said.

While his back was turned, I sat up straighter, shook my head to clear it. It would do no good to think of the future right now. I had to face a man who wanted to know about an intruder who had taken his son's place. I needed all my wits to be honest with him without frightening or alienating him.

Thanasset brought back my glass and sat down again across from me, obviously expecting an answer to his question. I looked at him directly.

"I don't know, Thanasset. Please believe me, I would tell you if I knew, but I don't."

His shoulders sagged, and I saw a brief struggle in his face. Then he smiled.

"A fair answer. Then—can you tell me about yourself? Who are you?"

Here, I knew, I needed caution. One of the things that had led me to be skeptical about reincarnation had been a uniform quality of silliness in the Westerners I had met who professed to "remember" past lives. The Hindu or the Buddhist of eastern Asia bears his belief with dignity. It is part of a religion. To so many Westerners, it was a topic for discussion at cocktail parties.

The "remembered" lives had always been exciting and ended in murder, execution, or dramatic suicide. Not one of them had been a potato farmer who died quietly in his bed after seventy years of monotonous hard work. I had heard the argument that only violent personalities survived intact, but I frankly saw more late-night television than actual memory in the "past lives" I heard retold. No, I had kept an open mind about reincarnation—in spite of those people, not because of them.

But if I had been unwilling to believe such stories about a world and a time within my experience, if even as history, what would Thanasset think of a man who claimed to have fought his way through the South Pacific in World War Two, had written fourteen well-received books on linguistics and three detective novels, and had died four days ago by being hit by a huge meteor?

My world had oceans, an abundance of wood and iron, horses instead of sha'um . . . Thanasset wouldn't even believe the world I had lived in—much less the role I had played in it. So what *could* I tell him?

Carefully, I said, "Before I tell you that, Thanasset, I—well, let me put it this way: I'm more than a little confused, myself. What do you know about . . . this kind of thing? Have you met cases like this before?"

"I?" he answered with surprise. "No, it happens but rarely. Maybe once in a generation in all of Gandalara. But I have read the accounts of most—if not all—of the Visitations. If I can help you at all, I'd be glad to try."

"I hope you can." *You don't know how much I hope you can!* "It's my memory, you see. It's . . . unreliable. I can 'remember' things that did not happen to *me*. I have some of Markasset's memories, but not all of them, by any means." I smiled at him. "I remember you well, and Milda."

"And Illia? Is my son really planning to marry her?"

"That's one of the blank spots, I'm afraid. I didn't remember her at all at first. No one else I have met even strikes a bell." That wasn't quite true. I remembered Worfit all too clearly. But I didn't want to bring the outside story, so to speak, into this conversation.

He nodded. "According to the Recordings, that is not at all unusual for a Visitor. Enough memories remain of the displaced one to allow the Visitor to adjust."

"Well, yes, I appreciate what I have. But I still feel I'm missing some important pieces. That I don't know a lot of things I should."

"Such as?"

"Well . . . this All-Mind you mentioned. If I'm visiting from it I ought to know what it is. But . . ." My voice trailed off weakly when I looked at his face. "I—I don't."

He might have turned to stone, but his eyes widened. He stared at me with the same expression a devout Christian might wear if a radiant being with golden wings and a halo had said to him, "Pardon me, but who is this Jesus fellow you're talking about?"

After a moment, he relaxed. "I'm sorry," he said. "Your . . . ignorance startled me. But it was foolish of me to suspect you as one of the Nine." *Nine what?* "Even if I believed my son open to such evil—and he is not; he may be wild but he is basically good—the fact that Keeshah brought you home is perfect evidence of your worth.

"But . . ." he shook his head, obviously concerned, "not to know of the All-Mind? It's—well, it's like not knowing of the sky or the air."

"The knowledge may have been removed from my mind for a purpose," I said carefully. "Perhaps it is something I must learn . . . from you."

He looked up sharply, suddenly excited. "Yes, that may be it! Markasset had almost no conscious mind-link, and it was a source of bitter argument between us. I always contended that if he could bond with Keeshah, the other skills were there. I said he simply didn't want to try—" He shrugged and sighed. "Perhaps I was being unfair. But it seemed like a willful failing to me, and symbolic, somehow, of the other ways in which he hadn't become the son I wanted him to be. It was the main reason why I told him that I would not recommend him to the Council, should a vacancy occur."

"You *wouldn't?* Did he have a chance without your support?" I wasn't sure what the election process was for the Supervisors, but I was fairly sure of Thanasset's answer before he said it.

"Not the slightest. And he would have been the first son of the house of Serkajon to fail to qualify for the Council. He always seemed rather unimpressed with our family history—but I believe that he realized it, and felt a little shame over it."

"How long ago did you tell him this?" I asked. *The night before he left with Gharlas?* I wondered. *Have you just given me the true motive for Markasset's involvement—revenge?*

"Several moons ago. Our relations have not been . . . peaceful ever since." A wry smile touched the corners of his mouth. "You're thinking of Illia, aren't you? He didn't tell her."

"Maybe he didn't believe you'd really bar him from the Council."

"Maybe. But I prefer to think that it finally dawned on him that his future position meant a great deal to his romance with that girl, and telling her would diminish her interest in him rather drastically."

I think he's underrating her. Though she did say specifically "wife of a Supervisor." In any case, it explains Thanasset's disapproval of their relationship.

"But to get back to your suggestion of the purpose for your Visitation—I hope you're right. If I can help you understand about the All-Mind, perhaps Markasset will also learn. Then, when—if—he returns to me . . ."

Thanasset stood up, taking a small key from the pouch at his belt. He strode over to a wall cabinet, unlocked it, and took out a curiously-wrought bottle and two glasses. Special refreshments, obviously.

I was ready for it.

I felt a deep sense of relief that at last I would be able to discuss the situation, even in limited terms, with someone I could trust. And I was glad to notice that in Thanasset's attitude there was no trace of religious fear or awe. Respect, yes. But no more than that. For him, my situation was an individualized repetition of something that had happened before. I began to hope he might really help me to understand.

I couldn't help contrasting the present circumstance with the way such a thing would be treated in California. If a person I believed to be St. Michael or St. Francis came to my home, could I carry it off so naturally? Would I have offered him a shot of even my *best* booze?

That was, indeed, what Thanasset was pouring into the glasses. It smelled wonderful.

"Can you tell me something of yourself?" Thanasset asked as he handed me my glass. "What were your lifeskills?"

"When I was young," I said, choosing my words with much care, "I was trained as a fighting man. I was no great champion, but I learned to survive. In later life, I became a scholar and a teacher, adequate, but not famous beyond my own academic circles. I was not, I fear, a very distinguished person."

"A commendably modest answer." He sat down and looked me over critically, as though trying to see the mind inside his son's body. "Still, there must be *some* special quality about you, or the All-Mind would not have sent you to us."

"If there is, I don't know what it is," I said, honestly. "I am not even aware of what the All-Mind might have had in mind." He chuckled, and I realized what I had said. "Sorry; I didn't mean that to sound flippant."

"I understand." He waved a hand in the air. "You know, it's an odd feeling talking to someone you know, and yet you don't. I keep trying to call you Markasset, and reminding myself that you're someone different. It would help—may I ask your name?"

In Gandaresh, I knew, men's names always ended with a consonant, women's names with a vowel sound. I adjusted my own given name and gave it to Thanasset: "Rikardon."

"Rikardon," he repeated, thinking about it. "Rikardon. A very old kind of name. *He who leads upward.* A good name. But I confess that I have never heard it before."

I shrugged. "I told you I was not particularly distinguished." *Especially in Gandalaran history,* I thought. *I'd be very surprised if they had heard of me here.*

"Mmmm." He picked up his glass and sipped. I had been waiting for his opening; now I picked up my own glass eagerly.

The glasses were small; I could barely have fitted my thumb in one. After one sip, I could see why. The stuff had a rich flavor without being sweet, and an aroma that invaded the nose like a whiff of mint—but it was not mint. And there was power there. It wouldn't take very many slugs of that stuff to put a man flat on his face.

I liked it.

I learned later that it was *barut*, made by the Fa'aldu of the desert from a secret mixture of herbs and fruits. An old family recipe, as it were, handed down through the generations. It was part of their trading stock, less plentiful but more lucrative than water. Ounce for ounce, its selling price was a hundred times more than that of water. How terribly, foolishly *human!*

The drinking customs were strong in Markasset's memory. After Thanasset and I had each sipped from our glasses, he lifted his glass to me and said: "Wisdom!"

I answered him, the words coming automatically, but I meant them: "And good health!"

We tossed off the remaining liquid in the little glasses in one swallow, and Thanasset went to refill them while I enjoyed the warm tingling which flowed gently through my whole body.

"There is so much to explain," Thanasset said while he poured from the bottle on the shelf. "I'm not sure where to begin."

He didn't even have a chance.

There was a sharp series of raps at the front door. Demanding. Authoritative. I looked over at Thanasset, the question plain on my face. He sighed and scowled.

"That's Zaddorn. I'd recognize that knock of his anywhere, anytime."

11

Thanasset replaced the bottle on the shelf and set down the glass he had been about to fill. He went through the doorway of the room and walked over to the large double doors that were the street entrance into the house. I followed him part of the way, and as he reached the door, he turned back. I thought he meant to say something to me, but the knock sounded again. He shrugged and opened the door.

The man who came through the door was dressed unlike any Gandalaran I had yet seen. He wore a long gray cloak of what seemed to be oiled linen, and on his head was a broad-brimmed gray hat of stiffened felt. He strode through the door and with a graceful, elaborate motion swirled the cloak from his shoulders and deposited it on a hook beside the door. Then his hat came off, and was placed on the same hook. Both were damp from the heavy mist outside, caused by the roaring falls behind the city. He had done all this silently and with an unconsciously theatrical flair, as though announcing his right to be welcome. But now he hesitated slightly, and I felt his cold, dark gaze on me—first on my face, then inspecting my waist. Then he lifted over his head the richly embroidered baldric which carried his sword.

He checked to see if I was armed! I realized, and I felt a stirring of anger that was partly Markasset's long-held rivalry, partly my own indignation. *In my father's house—does he think I would wear a sword here?*

Now I understood Thanasset's anger when I had, in ignorance, walked into his home wearing a sword.

"Good afternoon, Supervisor Thanasset," he said at last. "I must request a few minutes of your time." Again he glanced at me. "And of your son's."

"Certainly, Zaddorn. We were just having a drink. Won't you join us?" He bowed slightly and led the way back into the sunlit, high-windowed room. Zaddorn followed him and I followed Zaddorn, wishing that I had decided to wear the green-and-yellow suit I had found in the closet. For Zaddorn was wearing an embroidered gray tunic with a high collar and matching gray trousers. Somehow I knew that it was not a uniform, but merely his own conception of what the Supervisor of Peace and Security *ought* to wear. Fancy dress for daytime, perhaps, but not for a community leader who needed to be set apart from the crowd.

And I had to admit he cut an impressive figure. He was tall and broad-shouldered, and the belted tunic emphasized his muscular chest and arms. His voice was deep even when he spoke softly, as he had done to Thanasset. Yet I could imagine that, raised in command, it would stop a mad vlek in its tracks.

I found myself wondering what it was that Illia saw in Markasset.

Thanasset went directly to the shelf, but Zaddorn shook his head. "Ah, no. I thank you, Supervisor Thanasset, but barut is too heady for a man who needs all his wits about him. Please do not let me keep you from your pleasure, however."

Thanasset filled his glass, and brought it to me. Standing, we made the toast. "Wisdom!"

"Wisdom!"

"And good health!"

Thanasset replaced the bottle and glasses—apparently they were used only for barut, and were thus self-sterilizing—locked the cabinet, and we sat down. Zaddorn wasted no time in coming to the point.

"I came here because I heard you had returned to Raithskar, Markasset. I presume," he said, glancing at Thanasset, "that you have learned of our loss?"

Zaddorn had a thinner, flatter face than most Gandalarans, with a longer, more normal-looking (to Ricardo) nose. But his eyes were still shadowed by the brow ridge, and they were dark and piercing. I could sense the intelligence behind them—and the subtle menace of an honest cop determined to solve a crime.

Perhaps it was his manner, smooth and deadly as a sword, which irritated me. Or perhaps it was some remnant of bad feeling between Zaddorn and Markasset. But I wanted more than anything to shake him out of his self-satisfied composure.

"Chief Supervisor Ferrathyn mentioned it when I arrived," I told him. "But it wasn't news by then." Zaddorn blinked, and I waited just until he was ready to say something before I went on. "There were rumors of it all through the marketplace."

Zaddorn was cool, but I had seen the well-controlled flashes of expression on his face. Eagerness, thinking it was going to be easy, after all. Disappointment when I didn't admit anything. And finally, awareness that I had staged it that way on purpose. A glimpse of anger then, before his face closed into a granite-hard expression of mild interest. I wouldn't be able to break through again—but I was delighted to have done it once.

"They must have upset you terribly," he said, "for you to have drawn your sword in Vendor Street."

"If you know about that," I countered, "you know why I did it."

He waved a hand negligently, as if to brush aside the reason. "I heard that there was a disturbance. Something about a couple of vineh attacking their foreman."

Zaddorn and I both heard Thanasset's sharp intake of breath. But we didn't take our eyes off one another. Beneath our normal-toned conversation was a declaration of private war, a contest of wills we both knew had not begun here, nor would it end now.

"I discounted it," Zaddorn continued. "Vineh do not behave in that fashion. They are never fierce."

"They certainly gave that appearance," I said.

"Perhaps. But I think it more likely that both you and the

foreman misapprehended their motives. The theft of the Ra'ira is a most serious thing, and if—as you have assured me—everyone knows about it, it has created a general tenseness in the city, ready to be set off by anything unusual. You both panicked; that's all. And you drew your sword.

"You realize," he added, "that I could arrest you right now for waving a naked blade in the streets."

"Isn't it more important," interrupted Thanasset, "to find the Ra'ira? May I ask what progress you've made?"

Zaddorn looked at Thanasset, then back at me. We had been leaning forward in our chairs; now we both sighed and settled back—a temporary truce, a break before the next round.

"We are fairly certain that the gem has left the city. There is no trace or rumor of it in the city's rogueworld. It is my personal opinion that it left the city in the caravan of Gharlas. I have sent a guard command group after them, but it will be some time before that group returns with any information."

Again his eyes met mine, and I knew that this was the real reason he was here.

"I am in hope, Markasset," he said, "that since you have—ah, left your position with the caravan and returned early, you may have some useful news for us."

"I have already discussed this with the Chief Supervisor," I said, keeping my voice steady. Ferrathyn had merely been interested; this Zaddorn was out for blood. His voice slipped out of its impersonal tone into a deeper one which almost rang around the room.

"Well, you're discussing it with *me* now, Markasset. Why should I trouble the Chief Supervisor for second-hand information when I have the original source right here? Now tell me what you know about the theft of the Ra'ira!"

"There's nothing to tell, Zaddorn," I said. "During my time with the caravan, I neither saw nor heard anything that I can remember that would make me think there was anything odd going on."

"Why did you leave the caravan?"

"Personal reasons," I answered, and I couldn't keep all the anger out of my voice. "They have nothing to do with the theft of the Ra'ira. In fact, they're no business of yours whatever!"

He sat back with a smile and I realized, too late, that he had wanted to provoke me—and he had succeeded.

"No?" he said, all smooth steel again. "Perhaps not. But one can theorize, eh? I have been informed by usually reliable sources that you owe a certain Worfit some seven hundred zaks—a gambling debt, I believe. Is that correct?"

"I don't see how my personal finances are any of your business, either."

"You'd be surprised how little bits of unrelated information often come together at unlikely times," he said coolly. "For instance, I happen to know that you left town still owing him the money. He was quite put out to learn about it, according to my sources."

"He'll be paid," I said. He was getting at something, I could tell. And it worried me.

"Oh, I'm sure of it, since other—ah, sources tell me that you returned to town with enough and more to repay him. More, I daresay, than you would have earned from Caravan Master Gharlas, even had you completed the journey with him." He stood up, walked over to the window and looked out into the garden for a few seconds. Then he came back to his chair, placed his hands on its back, and leaned across it toward me. "*Where did you get that money?*"

I couldn't answer him for several reasons. First, I really didn't have the least idea where the large coins—twenty-dozak pieces, had Illia called them?—had come from. Second, I *knew* that the small coins had come from the money pouch of a man who had died horribly in the desert. And last, there was only one way Zaddorn could have learned about the money at all. Dear little Illia did not confine her confidences to me alone.

I was trying to digest the shock and come up with some kind of answer when my father said calmly, "My son is carrying twelve hundred zaks in the form of five golden twenty-dozak pieces. I gave them to him the night before he left. He told me about the debt, and I gave him enough to cover it and to provide him some spending money during his journey."

"But you still have all that money," Zaddorn said, still looking at me. "And Worfit is still looking for you. Why didn't you pay him, if you had the money before you left?"

Good question. C'mon, Markasset, tell me why, I thought, searching the elusive memory of the Gandalaran. To my surprise, he told me.

"I couldn't find him!" I answered, and I'm sure Thanasset and Zaddorn were both startled by the sound of triumph in my voice. "That kind of debt you repay in person, and . . ." I almost laughed, "he had been arrested by one of your agents."

For the first time since he had arrived, Zaddorn's dignity slipped. He stood up and cleared his throat. I'm sure that, if he had been wearing the kind of necktie Ricardo was familiar with, Zaddorn would have adjusted it slightly at that moment.

"Yes," he said finally. "I had forgotten—Worfit was being questioned that night about another matter entirely." He gave Thanasset a long, hard look. "I can see that I'll get no more information here—but there are other lines of inquiry open to me. Perhaps they will prove more fruitful."

He strode out through the doorway, and we stood up and followed him. He was putting on his baldric and sword by the time we reached the door. He swirled the cloak to his shoulders with the same grace he had used in removing it and then, hat in his hand, he turned to Thanasset.

"Thank you for your time, Supervisor Thanasset. Markasset." He opened the door, then turned partway back. "I'm sure I'll see you both later." Then he put his hat on and was gone.

"Well, that's that," I said as Thanasset closed the door with a sigh. "There's no question that he thinks I stole the Ra'ira from you."

Thanasset shook his head. "You're only half right," he told me. "What he thinks is that you and I conspired to steal it."

"*What?* Where would he get such a foolish idea?"

Thanasset smiled at me with a tenderness that touched my heart. "Thank you for your faith in me, Rikardon. But Zaddorn reads people very skillfully. He knows that I lied about giving you—Markasset—the five gold pieces."

"Huh?" We were walking back into the "drinking room," as I had begun to think of it, with no help from Markasset. But the time had come for serious talk, and Thanasset did not offer, nor did I want, anything which might cloud our minds.

"Yes," he said as we sat down. "Markasset did tell me about his debt to Worfit. We both knew that thought of Keeshah would prevent Worfit from applying physical violence. We talked—no, argued, is a better word—on the evening before the theft, a few hours before I went to the Council Hall for Guardian Duty. I refused him the money, told him that I was tired of his irresponsible behavior, that this was one scrape he could get himself out of without my help." He had been looking at the floor; now he looked up at me.

"Don't think too harshly of me, Rikardon. I—I was angry. I would have given it to him the next day, probably. I guess I just wanted him to be frightened for a time, to teach him a lesson. When I read his note, I . . ." His voice trailed off.

I thought that the old man had done exactly the right thing—or it would have been exactly right if the complication of the theft hadn't come up. But I wasn't about to offer a personal judgment of how a father handled his son. Instead I asked the question that the new information raised.

"If you didn't give Markasset the money, why *do* I have twelve hundred zaks in my pouch?"

"It is the money I didn't give to Markasset. A few minutes after I went on duty, Markasset came to the Council Hall and went into my office. He carried his own key—which he left behind after he took the five gold pieces out of my cabinet."

"He left his key?"

"Yes." Thanasset smiled. "To show that he had taken it—he would not have wished that someone else be blamed for it. I have tried to explain—Markasset is an honest man, in his own way."

"I think I understand." And I was relieved. I wanted very much to think the best I could of Markasset. "It was more a forced loan than a theft."

"Exactly."

"And when did you learn about it?"

"After the excitement had died down a little over the *real* theft. I returned to my office, found the key there and the money missing."

"He took your money. Do you think he might also have been involved with the men who stole the Ra'ira?"

"NO!"

At last, the question I had dreaded had been asked, and answered. Thanasset's response was so immediate that I knew he had felt it hanging between us ever since I admitted that I knew little of Markasset's life.

"I do not entirely understand my son," Thanasset said, "but I know him. He would never betray me or Raithskar."

Another great weight had lifted from me. I didn't know much about Markasset, but I trusted his father. "I believe you," I told him, and relief and gratitude showed in his strong, craggy face. "Who *did* take it?"

He shrugged. "You have heard all that I know. Ferrathyn's theory about the Lords of Eddarta seems likely to me. But they would have needed information only available in Raithskar—someone here must have helped them. That is, if they really *did* take the Ra'ira to help support their claim as the heirs of the ancient Kings of Gandalara."

"Tell me about them," I said. "The Kings of Gandalara." Thanasset's face took on a look of complete astonishment. I must have had the same look on my face as he suddenly stood up and bowed deeply before me.

"I am fortunate," he said. "If you know nothing of the Kings, you are one of the Very Ancients. And if you have no knowledge of Kä, then—" he paused, "you must not know about Steel."

I knew about "steel" in my world—but "Steel" in Gandalara was a mystery, especially as it was spoken by Thanasset. I could hear the capital "S" in his voice. I shook my head, though what he said had not been a question.

"Come with me," he said, and led the way out into the large central room. We walked over to the inlaid wall with the beautifully intricate sha'um pattern, and he pointed to the sword mounted on the wall above it.

"That is Steel," he said. "Its name is—" He stopped suddenly, and turned toward me. His voice was almost a whisper. "I should have known. Its name is *Rika*. Upwards."

I said nothing as he looked back at the sword and stared at it thoughtfully for several seconds.

"That sword was forged for Serkajon. It is one of the few swords in the world made of the Most Precious Metal." It was another Gandalaran term for Steel. "They stay strong and sharp for lifetimes of men, and they carry an imprint of the men who have wielded them.

"Serkajon was the first to hold *Rika*. In the generations since his death, it has been the duty of each father to judge whether his son was worthy to carry it. There have been only five, since Serkajon, strong enough in body and spirit that their touch on the hilt would not dishonor his memory." He smiled. "You will be the sixth."

Who, me? But . . .

Thanasset had turned away from the wall and was pacing slowly around the large room. I followed him, trying to think of something to say. But he was talking again.

"The Most Precious Metal came to Gandalara with the skybolt." He raised his heavy brows as he glanced at me. "Even as ancient as you are, you must know the legend. Back, far back, long before the first *written* history, a starbolt struck down from the sky, blinding everyone near it, killing many of our ancestors."

I bit my tongue; I had been about to remind him that if they had died, there was a strong possibility they *hadn't* been his ancestors. And besides, the image he had given me recalled one of my own. A starbolt? A meteor, certainly. What else could it be? And I, Ricardo, had been killed by a meteor—or my body had. Yet that was in a different world. Why did it seem to me that the two events were linked?

"Yes," I told Thanasset. "I know of the starbolt."

He nodded. "I thought you would. The memory of it remains in the All-Mind, though dimly now. For it happened in the unthinkably remote past—a hundred hundred centuries ago."

A million years, I calculated. *And the All-Mind, whatever it is, still remembers it!*

"It struck here," he said, swinging one arm generally in the direction of the waterfall behind the city, "in what is now Raithskar. Some theorists believe that it brought the Most Precious Metal with it. Others say that the metal is a transformation product of its power. In either case," he shrugged, "it remains the only known deposit of Steel in all Gandalara." It seemed that the term for the finished metal was also applied to its main and indispensable ingredient: a chunk of nickel-iron meteor.

"Our Ancestors at that time were little more than animals, barely aware of their latent ability to think rationally and to anticipate the future. After the skybolt struck, those who survived began to use that ability. The trend was magnified threefold in their children, and, within two generations, the All-Mind had become fully aware."

It all made sense.

A huge chrome-nickel-iron meteor had come smashing in through the atmosphere in the distant past at somewhere between ten and twenty miles per second. At those velocities, plenty of hard radiation is given off during the time it takes to go through the atmosphere—between ten seconds and two minutes, depending on the speed and the angle at which it struck. That radiation would be lethal to those creatures near enough to barely survive the impact, and disabling to those who caught a smaller dose. And it was certain to produce mutations—most of them probably unfavorable.

But at least one favorable mutation had survived, and its descendants mined and worked the very fabric of their beginnings when they forged swords like *Rika* from the Steel of Raithskar.

"And the All-Mind?" I asked. "You were going to tell me about it, just before Zaddorn arrived."

"Yes, I was," Thanasset agreed, then hesitated. Suddenly he chuckled. "You'll have to forgive me, Rikardon. The All-Mind is so much a part of us now—I hardly know where to begin. But I'll try."

And so he did. We walked slowly around the beautiful parquet floor of the midhall as he talked, and I listened attentively, trying very hard to understand. But it was difficult. The meteor was a physical phenomenon which my world and Thanasset's, no matter how far apart, could share. But there was nothing in Ricardo's experience to help me now.

The concepts and vocabulary were strange to me—some of the terms Thanasset used simply had no equivalent meaning, and they were apparently so second-nature to Markasset that I got no help from his unreliable memory.

Besides, I don't believe that Markasset understood the All-Mind. And Thanasset, who was trying his very best to explain it to me in simple, logical language, didn't completely understand it, either. But both of them *accepted* it. For them, it was a basic fact of life.

But Ricardo Carillo had lived in a civilization where such notions were discounted by a large percentage of the intelligent population. Even those who did not discount them could not prove them. They could not even agree among themselves on terminology or basic theory.

But in spite of all the impediments to understanding, by the time Thanasset had finished, I did have a conception—my own, certainly, which probably didn't match Thanasset's—of what the All-Mind is.

12

The All-Mind is a *linkage* between Gandalarans. It is not precisely telepathic, but it seems to have some properties closely akin to telepathy. The Gandalarans believe that the All-Mind is the collective mind of all Gandalarans, both living and dead, with only a few exceptions.

They believe that each person is a new individual when he is born, but while he lives, and after he dies, his soul-mind (my word, not theirs) is part of the All-Mind, linked with it irrevocably, and so linked with every other Gandalaran, both living and dead. The webwork of those linkages, throughout the total four-dimensional space-time matrix which is the lifetime of the *race*, comprises the All-Mind.

I was surprised to find that Thanasset's attitude toward the All-Mind was respectful, but not quite reverent. Certainly it was implicit in what he told me that he believed in the survival of the individual soul-mind after death through its linkage with the All-Mind. Yet the All-Mind was not a god to Thanasset.

The Gandalarans have no temples, no rites or ceremonies, nothing even faintly resembling what I would call "worship" directed to the All-Mind. Each Gandalaran admires and honors it above all entities which are alive in his world, for he knows that the All-Mind is a greater entity, and that he is a part of it. Thanasset admitted, with a look of mild disapproval, that some radical thinkers believed that the personality—what I would call the soul—of the individual died with his body, and that only the integrated memories remained linked to the All-Mind. But whatever the actual nature of the survival, all Gandalarans are certain of their place in the history of their world. They will be remembered.

I have no opinion to offer as to which theory is correct. But I do understand why, though their regard for the All-Mind is the closest thing Gandalarans have to a religion, they do not worship it.

Thanasset didn't think of the All-Mind in the way I had been taught to think of God. I think it was Graham Greene who said something to the effect that he could not worship a God he could understand.

Gandalarans think they understand the All-Mind pretty well. They do not worship it, fear it, or try to win its favor. They do not even have faith in it or believe in it. It does not need faith or belief; it is merely a fact.

It is accessible.

Everyone is in continuous contact with the All-Mind. With most of them, however, that contact is largely subconscious. The few who can regularly operate that contact have a special duty in Gandalara. They are called Recorders, and it is their job to put explicit, carefully indexed knowledge into the memory of the All-Mind. And to tap it for stored knowledge.

In some ways the All-Mind functions like a giant computer-recorder. A non-Recorder can go to a Recorder to get information—history, law, customs, economics, and the like. From what Thanasset said, I got the impression that either the Recorder could establish his or her link and search out the information directly, or the inquirer could be put into something like an hypnotic state and his or her subconscious link could be raised to the conscious level.

Either way, it seemed, the answers weren't always there. Either nobody knew it to begin with, or for some reason it just isn't available.

In that one way, at least, the All-Mind resembles most of the deities I have ever heard of. It sees all, knows all, and tells what it damn well pleases.

When I said earlier that it was hard to understand what Thanasset was saying about the All-Mind, I omitted one large factor—part of the time I just wasn't listening. My skepticism was functioning in high gear, and while it stewed over one point, Thanasset covered two more.

Which just goes to show the stubbornness of the human mind. Here was I, who should be dead, living out of my own time and world, in the body of another being who wasn't even human—and I was discounting half of what Thanasset was saying because it seemed like the same sort of occult mysticism crap I'd laughed at all my life.

But if I gained little true understanding of the All-Mind from our discussion, at least I did realize at last why Thanasset treated me with such respect. To him, I was someone who had died long ago and had been an intimate part of the All-Mind—for how long?—and had come back or been returned by the All-Mind to a particular body for a particular purpose.

And that contributed to my skepticism, too. Because I couldn't buy Thanasset's theory about me. Rick Carillo of California, U.S.A., didn't fit into the matrix of the All-Mind in any way, shape or form. No matter how logical, well-reasoned, self-evident, or even *true* Thanasset's explanation had been up until that point, *I* tore a glaring hole in them.

What I believed, however, was far less important than what Thanasset believed. And that, at least, I could comprehend.

"If you know nothing of the Kings of Gandalara," Thanasset was saying, "it indicates that your own life-span antedated them. Do you know anything of the City of Kä?"

"Nothing," I admitted honestly. I didn't feel that the conversation I had heard, crouching behind a bush out in the desert in the middle of the night, could even be counted.

"What do you remember of the Great *Pleth?*"

Pleth? Markasset's memories refused to translate it.

"I'm afraid I don't know the word. Perhaps if you'd define it . . ."

"Ah, of course. It is little used these last twenty centuries. It is an extensive body of water. The Great Pleth was *very* extensive."

Oh sure, I thought. *A sea!* I was relieved to be able to say, for once, "Yes, I understand now. The—uh, Pleth was quite extensive in my day." I tried to frame a sentence which would say that I had even sailed the "pleth," but the vocabulary would not come to mind. Apparently there was no Gandaresh word for "sail" or "boat."

"Then you must come from some five hundred centuries in the past," he said, with a touch of awe in his voice. "This must be a completely different world for you!"

"Oh, it's all of that," I agreed wholeheartedly. Then I paused and thought about it for a few seconds. "Yet it is much the same in many ways. People still live and die, love and hate, succeed and fail. And the reasons behind the actions of men—motivation, emotion—are the same here as in my world."

Thanasset smiled sadly. "Do we progress so slowly, then? Are folk no more noble now than they were in your day?"

I realized that I had been speaking, thoughtlessly, of Ricardo's world; yet Thanasset interpreted my words as applying to his own history. And that brought the point home sharply to me.

We weren't so different, after all, Thanasset and I. And he was trying to understand me in the terms of my own world, even as I had needed to know about the All-Mind to understand Thanasset better.

I resolved to be as honest with Thanasset as I could. I had to mislead him, at least to the extent of allowing him to believe that my world *was* a part of his history. But I wanted his friendship, and I wanted that friendship to be based on truth. As much of the truth as he could accept.

"I received my training as a fighter because I had to oppose a group of people who intended to conquer all the existing territory."

"And did you succeed in preventing that conquest?" Thanasset asked.

"That one, yes. But fighting continued for most of my life, for various reasons and in different areas. I took a less active role in these later wars, training other fighters and making sure our own borders were well defended."

Thanasset was nodding. "Yes, that agrees with the few records I have found of the time before the Kings. In spite of later abuse of the power he claimed, Zanek is often given credit for ending a period of continual, debilitating conflict between neighboring territories."

"Zanek was the first King of Gandalara?" I asked.

"Yes, it was he who united the Walled World. Led by the Riders, his armies reached out from the shores of the Great Pleth and first demanded, then won, the tribute and allegiance of city after city, until all of Kä was ruled by Zanek.

"For a long time Gandalara rested in peace. Zanek and his

sons ruled wisely. But life became harder as the years passed and the Great Pleth diminished. The Kings began to demand greater tribute as their own fields failed to support Kä."

"Was that when Raithskar sent the Ra'ira to Kä?"

Thanasset looked at me sharply, but what he said was, "Yes. And it was shortly after we sent that single great prize to Kä that the Kings began to demand a different kind of tribute—slaves.

"Raithskar was spared that degradation because we had a more important gift—water. Our craftsmen built a carrier pipe to transport our clear, pure water to the great city, and that was considered tribute enough.

"But from everywhere else in Gandalara, slaves poured into Kä. They worked a few years—some only a few months—and then they died from the hardship and were replaced."

"That must have been shortly before the kingdom fell."

"Why do you say that?" Thanasset asked me.

"Because in my—time, men could not bear to be slaves. And any ruler who was dependent on slaves eventually became so weak that the slaves could break free of his rule. Did that not happen at Kä?"

"No," said Thanasset, with an odd flat note in his voice. "The slaves did not resist."

"Then—?"

"It was one of the Riders, the King's own elite guard, who destroyed Kä."

"Serkajon."

"Yes. The Riders were honorable men who served the Kings with absolute loyalty as long as they believed that their rule was good for all of Gandalara. But Serkajon knew—" Thanasset hesitated, searching for words—"he realized that the Kings were no longer ruling Gandalara; they were exploiting it. So he took the Ra'ira."

"Which had become a symbol of power?"

"Yes," agreed Thanasset. "When he brought it out of Kä, home to Raithskar, the Kingdom collapsed. The Riders came after Serkajon, of course. But he talked to them, explained what he had done and why, and they never returned to Kä. Instead they settled in Thagorn and kept their own traditions, in the hope that they might someday serve another king worthy of their loyalty."

"The Sharith," I said, remembering the conversation with Balgokh at Yafnaar. "Something was said about a 'duty' that is paid by the caravans."

Thanasset sighed. "They claim the right of tribute. To them, they are still the King's Guard, and entitled to a measure of support from the rest of Gandalara—even though there is no king, and hasn't been for hundreds of years. If it's not paid willingly . . ."

"They attack? That must be why Gharlas was hiring guards. Balgokh said that Gharlas planned to bypass Thagorn."

"Did he?" Thanasset asked, eyebrows raised.

"I don't know," I told him. "I woke alone in the desert. I don't know what happened to the caravan." I wasn't counting the corpse.

"Well. I regret what has happened to the Sharith. The Riders had a high and noble purpose when they settled in Thagorn. They deserted Harthim, the last King, because he used Gandalara for his own profit. Yet now—it seems to me they are doing the same thing."

"Is there no connection at all," I asked, "between the Sharith and the house of the man who once led them?"

"No. And I believe that Serkajon knew it would be this way when he elected to stay in Raithskar. It has been a kind of exile, really, though there was purpose in his choice, too. Yet every generation since Serkajon has contained a Rider, in spite of the expense of maintaining a sha'um in the city."

"Were the Riders also the Supervisors?" I asked.

"Often," Thanasset answered. "But not always. In some generations there were two and three sons. Only one boy in a generation felt the call of the Valley of the Sha'um, and it happened sometimes that the other sons had the skills necessary to act as a Supervisor."

"So the family of Serkajon has continued to lead—in Raithskar, if not in Thagorn."

"True, and I have never doubted Serkajon's choice. But I wonder what the Sharith would be today if Serkajon had gone to Thagorn. I have a strong memory of what they were. I mourn greatly for what they have become."

"They still ride," I said. I realized how important Keeshah had become to me. Even then, standing here and talking to Thanasset, the great cat was a comforting presence in the back of my mind.

Thanasset smiled at me. "True. It is a great honor to be chosen by the sha'um. Since they are still being chosen, there is still value in them."

He sighed, and went on more briskly. "I have answered my own question. We have not progressed. In Eddarta, those who claim the kingdom also claim the rights of kings. They keep slaves there still, starving and terrified tribute from the nearby provinces, which need Eddarta's water."

When Thanasset spoke of slavery, I thought about the vineh. My first impulse was to think of them as slaves, but as I remembered how they had looked, one moment docile and the next fierce, and how they had all three attacked their—what would you call it, their "keeper"? When I remembered the entire incident, I was glad that I hadn't mentioned the vineh in connection with Thanasset's discussion of slavery. They might be dressed like people, but I was sure they were not. They were work animals that happened to look like people.

"And we may not have 'wars'," Thanasset was saying, "but we honor and maintain the martial tradition. A man's sword is part of his family's history, to be passed on to his son at the proper age. The bronze sword you were wearing has been in our family for generations. Twice, when it became too damaged to be useful, it was melted and reforged."

I was beginning to understand why I felt guilty about leaving the dead man's sword out in the desert. I resolved to retrieve it someday, if I had the chance.

"Boys learn to fight more eagerly than to read, and compete regularly in training games. As men, they carry swords daily, with the implied purpose of defending their cities against attack.

"Granted, Raithskar has more reason than most cities to need such a force of fighting men—for the few times when the vineh have gotten out of hand, and,"—he barked a laugh—"for the protection of the Ra'ira. But I always thought it pointless and backward-looking, especially since I considered the Council sufficient security for Raithskar's treasure.

"That was another problem between my son and myself. He excelled in the games, especially in personal combat, and I could never appreciate that as much as he would have liked."

Thanasset looked at the sword on the wall. "When I was a boy, I learned fighting skills because it was required, but I never struggled to be the best. *My* father told me that in all other ways I was worthy of Serkajon's Steel, but my lack of interest in our fighting traditions made him withhold it from me." He reached out a hand to trace the outline of the portrait. "And it was Markasset's enthusiasm for that, above all else, that made me feel *he* was unworthy."

He stood there for a moment, lost in thought, then abruptly shrugged off the mood.

"Well, back to the subject. No 'wars', as I said, but personal frailty and violence still exist. Every city has its rogueworld and its share of dishonest merchants, murderers," —he made a wry face—"and thieves. No, we haven't really progressed. How very sad."

"If you really believe that, Thanasset," I said, "you're wrong."

"What do you mean?"

"Only that you shouldn't believe that it's a sad thing. It's a natural thing. People are like that. The trick is to learn to handle things so that the sort of people who want to take advantage of others have to work at it.

"Raithskar took the first step when Serkajon brought back the Ra'ira. Now, there may still be slavery in Eddarta and forced tribute to the Sharith, but here in Raithskar you live peacefully with only the violence of individuals to contend with. And it seems to me that Zaddorn has that pretty well under control.

"*My* world was torn with war and full of fear." Suddenly I wanted to stop talking. My throat tightened up, but I went on, saying things I had always known but had never spoken. "Terrorism and greed were the watchwords of my time. The world had learned to be cynical. To be trusting was to be a victim. To be fair was to be foolish. Virtue and corruption were at constant odds. Honorable men had to fight to be recognized, and still were doubted by other honorable men.

"I am not saying that I was personally unhappy in my world, Thanasset. I wasn't. But in Raithskar I don't feel so pressured and defensive. Sure, Zaddorn may believe that you and I have committed a dishonest act. But he suspects that only because something—mistakenly—leads him to believe it, not because he naturally suspects everybody's motives. And when we prove him wrong, he will accept that proof and trust us as much as he did before all this happened.

"You asked if people had 'progressed' since my time, Thanasset. I can't really judge that. But I will tell you this—I believe that people are more naturally honest in Raithskar than in my world.

"I have never met a more honorable man than you are. Whatever brought me into Markasset's body, I am proud to be known as your son."

13

Thanasset stared at me, no less astonished than I at what I had said. I have never been one to confuse sentiment with emotion, and I know that that moment might have been one of the most emotional of my two lives.

But it was interrupted.

There was a loud banging on the door, followed just a bit too soon by Milda literally running down the front stairway to open the door. Illia fell through, sobbing, and Milda caught her around the shoulders. Illia reached out toward me, saying "Markasset" over and over again, until Milda shook her into silence.

"Now," Milda said, when Illia was under control, "I saw you running up the street as though Keeshah were after you. If you've got something to say, say it!" This was not the sweet old lady I had met earlier and loved almost instantly—this was a woman made of iron! And I still loved her.

Illia looked over at me. "They're coming after Markasset."

"What?" asked Thanasset. "Who is coming after him?"

"Zaddorn," she wailed, and I noticed that though she had all the human reactions of weeping, there were no tears. They would have been a waste of water.

"What *happened*, girl?" Thanasset demanded.

Illia calmed down, and twisted gently out of Milda's grip to walk across the floor of the large room toward us.

"Zaddorn sent a guard command group out after Gharlas's caravan."

"It couldn't have gotten back already!" I said. My computation of their travel time wasn't completely accurate, of course, but given the caravan's head start . . .

"How did you know about them?" Illia asked, looking at me sharply.

"The Chief Supervisor told me earlier today," I answered. "Anyway, does it matter?"

"It matters," she said. "A maufa just arrived with a message for Zaddorn. The guard group didn't catch up with the caravan—they met it on its way back to Raithskar. Or, rather, they met what was left of it. Two men and a vlek. The Sharith got the rest."

Maufa? I was asking myself, then a memory surfaced. *A trainable bird, like a pigeon, that carries messages! That must be what I heard in those cages when the posse passed me. Why didn't you tell me this sooner, Markasset?*

Thanasset grabbed Illia and turned her toward him. "What are you implying about my son?"

"*I'm* not implying anything, sir. But the men from the caravan said that when the Sharith attacked, Markasset—not by that name, of course, but Zaddorn figured out who it was—was nowhere to be seen. They're saying that your son was a Sharith agent, but now Zaddorn has some complicated theory about Markasset and the Ra'ira." She turned to me, her eyes pleading. "I know you didn't steal anything, Markasset. But your position as guard—why weren't you there when the Sharith attacked?"

She was hoping for a reasonable explanation. So was I. I was thankful when Thanasset interrupted again.

"What is Zaddorn going to do?"

"He's on his way here right now," Illia said. "He has legal grounds for putting Markasset into confinement on a charge of failing to perform a contracted service. But I know he's convinced that Markasset stole the Ra'ira."

O boy. And if I'm in the hoosegow . . .

"Father, I have to go."

Thanasset nodded. "I know, son. But not like that," he added, indicating my pantless blue tunic. "Take the time to dress properly."

"Where are you going?" Illia asked.

"To Thagorn. If the Ra'ira was on the caravan, it's in the hands of the Sharith now. Whether or not they were involved in the theft—" I glanced at Thanasset, who shrugged. It had occurred to both of us, I was sure, that the Sharith could have the same motives we had early attributed to Eddarta. "I couldn't say. But the trail leads there, and I can't follow it if Zaddorn is sitting on me."

"You didn't answer my question," she said softly.

I put my arms around her and drew her close. She wasn't soft and yielding as she had been in the garden that afternoon. Her body was stiff, and she kept her arms between us.

"I promise you, Illia, when I get back to Raithskar, everything will be clear. But now I must go. Thank you for coming to warn me."

I lowered my head and kissed her cheek lightly, then released her and ran upstairs. I dressed quickly in the same sort of outfit I had been wearing when I woke up in this world. Then I ran downstairs to find the three of them still standing in the middle of the room. But Milda was holding a pair of leather bags tied together with three lengths of strong rope, and Thanasset was putting something into one side of the—they could only be saddlebags.

When they saw me, Thanasset said, "Be careful on your way to Thagorn," in an *almost* natural tone of voice. For an instant I was puzzled, then I knew what was happening. Thanasset was trying to tell me, without revealing to Illia that I didn't know a damn thing about Gandalara, where to find the Sharith. He must have been putting a map into the pack.

You're a smart old dodger, Thanasset! I thought to myself. Aloud I said, "Thank you, Father. I'll be as careful and as quick as I can." Without thinking, I stuck out my right hand. There was barely a moment's hesitation before Thanasset reached out and gripped my hand in both his own.

"Goodbye, son."

I turned to Illia, who was staring at the floor. I lifted her face with my hand and kissed her lightly on the lips. "Don't worry, Illia. Soon I'll be back and you'll know the whole truth."

"Why won't you tell me now?" she asked. "What are you hiding from me, Markasset?"

I couldn't say "nothing" because it wasn't true. I shook my head. "I am sorry, Illia. I just can't tell you now. But please believe me, it's not because I don't trust you. I—I simply can't tell you, that's all."

With a sob she fell toward me, and for a moment I held her.

"Hurry back, Markasset," she whispered. "Come back to me safe."

I released her and turned to Milda, who handed me the rope-linked packs, then tied a belt around my waist which had several small waterskins attached. They were already filled.

"There's enough food to last you for several days," she said. "And the water should go further, if you're careful with it. Markasset," she asked suddenly, looking up at my face and touching my cheek with one age-soft hand, "is it time to start worrying?"

Just then there was a knock at the door. A distinctive, emphatic knock. I had only heard it twice, but I recognized it now—Zaddorn!

"Never mind, nephew," Aunt Milda said. "There's my answer."

"Go now, son," Thanasset said. "I'll delay him as long as I can."

I ran to the back door and shifted the heavy packs to one arm. I grabbed my sword and baldric off the peg by the door and awkwardly drew it over my head. Then, with a last look into the room where Thanasset was standing beside the front door now—as I watched, the knock sounded again—I flung open the rear door, took two steps out, and stopped.

There were three men waiting for me with their swords already drawn. And from the worn look of their brown leather baldrics, I could guess that they knew how to use those swords. I could read that in their faces, too, in the scar along one man's right cheek, and in the looks they gave me. They were measuring, appraising me as only a fighting man looks at an opponent.

I was surprised. Not because Zaddorn had thought to place a rear guard, but that he had risked it with Keeshah in the yard. I glanced down the length of the yard. Even over the low mounds of the garden, I could see Keeshah's house. The heavy wooden doors which had stood open when we arrived were now closed and bolted shut with a length of bronze slipped through rungs on the outside of both doors.

Now that sounds like Zaddorn's planning, I decided.

"That's him," the man in the middle was saying. "That's Markasset. Grab him. The Chief says he has it on him."

I dropped the bags and drew my sword. They advanced slowly, and I tried to cover all of them at once.

I sent out an anxious thought. **Keeshah!**

I am here.

Can you break out?

No need. I heard them coming. I am up on the roof. I wait.

These men want to take me prisoner.

So far they hadn't really tried. They were circling, watching me, gauging me.

I kill, came Keeshah's thought, calm, with no anger.

No! I ordered. These were Zaddorn's men. **No, Keeshah, don't kill them. But—frighten them.**

They will shit.

In their place, I know that I would have. For Keeshah let out a roar that seemed to shake the ground beneath our feet. The three men whipped around to look at the cat house, where they thought the sha'um safely locked away, and saw the tall, lithe cat standing on the roof, his head lifted in that gut-wrenching roar.

Then he turned directly toward us, and fixed his gaze on the three men. He crouched down to the edge of the roof, and behind him we could see the tip of his tail, slowly lashing. He moved slightly, gathering himself, but even at a distance of some twenty meters, we could see that the pale golden eyes never blinked.

For a long moment—even I was holding my breath—Keeshah was absolutely still. Then he came down off that roof in a graceful leap that brought him five yards closer to us, and he was already running.

He stopped just short of the armed trio, snarling. He made feints at the men, leaping in and then back, staying just out of range of their swordpoints. Two of them were almost hysterical with fear, but they were holding their own. The middle one, whom I thought of as their leader, had more nerve than the other two—he turned his back on Keeshah.

"You guys take care of that fleabitten sha'um!" he ordered in his growling voice. "I'll take care of this filth."

He came at me with a high overhand cut.

Fencing with a broadsword is very different from fencing with a foil, a smallsword, or even a rapier. There is a lot more edgework and less pointwork. Besides, bronze is both heavier and softer than steel, so the blade can't be as long on a bronze sword.

Briefly, I wished I had grabbed the steel sword from the wall. But only briefly. Thanasset had said its name was *Rika*, but I had the feeling it was really Excalibur. I had enough troubles.

Right in front of me, trying to cleave me in two, was my biggest immediate trouble. I had learned broadsword work in Berkeley under Master Paul Edwin Zimmer, and I—that is, Ricardo—had never been anywhere near as good as my teacher. But it was not Ricardo who handled that sword now.

Markasset took over. Not his mind—I was still Ricardo Carillo—but his body. Markasset had been a far better swordsman than Ricardo could ever have hoped to be. He had been trained thoroughly. And his body remembered. In an emergency, reflexes take over. I was grateful to have Markasset's reflexes.

I parried the leader at *forte*, and as his blade slid off my quillon to my right, I swung around for a cut at his midsection.

My opponent leaped back to avoid my cut and started to lunge in with his point as my blade went by him. He barely parried me in time.

I was doing the fighting; I was in control. But it was a control the like of which I had never experienced before. My blade was placed with precision in space; my timing was accurate to the millisecond; my footwork was as beautiful and as automatic as that of a trained dancer.

I fought steadily, warily, waiting for an opening. I never took my eyes off my opponent, but I could sense Keeshah behind him, still keeping the other two busy, even enjoying the game.

At last my opponent let his blade drop just a fraction of an inch too low. I aimed a slash at his chest, knowing he would have to parry me by knocking my blade upward and to his right. He tried, but too weakly and too late. As his blade struck mine, I stopped the cut and lunged. If he had responded as I had expected, that lunge would have allowed the point of my sword to graze his right shoulder, and disable him enough for me to make my escape.

He had lifted my blade, but not deflected it. To my horror its point went deep into his throat. Blood spurted over bronze.

I withdrew and stepped back as he collapsed.

The other two were too busy with Keeshah to notice. Their backs were toward me. With two quick swings, I slapped each of them alongside the head with the flat of my blade. I didn't want to kill them.

Hell, I hadn't wanted to kill the first man.

I gathered up the pack I had dropped, and leaped onto Keeshah's back. I slung the rope between the bags across Keeshah's back, then crouched into position, lifting the heavy rope until it rested on my cloth-protected thighs rather than Keeshah's skin.

Over the wall, Keeshah.

But he had anticipated me, and was already running toward the nearest wall, which joined Thanasset's yard to his neighbor's. An eight-foot wall is nothing to a six-foot cat, even with a man on his back. I felt his muscles bunch and release like steel springs, and we were on the roofs of the neighbor's outbuildings.

There were people out in the yard—they must have heard the racket Keeshah and the swords had been making. When they saw Keeshah jump down from their bath-house, they ran off in every direction. Keeshah ran through the yard, carefully avoiding trampling the infant who had been forgotten, and jumped the far fence. The next fence brought us to the corner, and now we were out in the street.

To the city gates, I urged him. **Don't stop for anything.**

We made quite a sight, the huge cat and his clinging rider, streaking through streets that had never before been ridden. It was almost dusk, and there were people out for strolls, walking through the warm early evening. We startled some of them, frightened others. Some laughed and pointed at us. Some watched us pass in silence, their eyes shining, and I knew they wanted to be where I was.

The gates of the city stood open as they had when we had entered that morning. It was incredible to me that only a day had passed since then!

The men at the gates had not been expecting us. Four of them, wearing gray baldrics like Zaddorn's, were standing close together, talking. Their attention seemed to be directed out the gate toward a group of farmers bringing in vleks laden with vegetables for the early morning market.

On the street, Keeshah's padded paws made hardly any sound, and while some people stared and others jumped back, nobody screamed. I was past the guards and out the gate before any one of them could get a sword out.

Keeshah went off the road to get around the small group of laden vleks. They became skittish, but their masters managed to keep them under control, for which I was thankful. No need in making matters any worse by dumping innocent folk's food all over the highway. We kept on going.

Soon there was no one on the road to be seen, and Raithskar was behind us, flowing slowly away as night descended around us.

I laughed aloud and hugged Keeshah's neck. I got a warm answering flow from his mind. We were safe for the moment, and together. I wanted to put plenty of distance between us and the city, and I knew Keeshah could do it.

After a mile or so, however, the flush of our success in escaping began to seep out of me, and a feeling of desolation began to creep in. I had just begun to realize that I could not return to Raithskar now unless I were willing to sacrifice my freedom, even my life, in order to prove Thanasset's innocence.

Was I willing? Yes. I knew that I would have to return. That commitment had been made a long time ago. Whatever it cost, I would prove the old man's honor.

If I had the time.

That's what bothered me—I was a fugitive now, in unfamiliar territory. If I didn't make all the right moves, I stood a good chance of being captured and prevented from finding the proof I needed. Keeshah was fast, but there could be delays.

And I had no doubt at all that I would be followed. As soon and as fast as possible. These people were not *homo sapiens*, strickly speaking, but they were utterly human. And throughout the human history of my world, no police force had ever given up on a cop-killer.

14

We stopped to rest a couple of hours before sunrise. I didn't wonder, this time, how I knew the night was almost over. Thanasset had explained that Gandalarans had a highly efficient internal warning system. It seemed logical that Markasset's internal awareness extended to his body's diurnal rhythms, so that I simply knew what time it was within fifteen minutes or so. They must use sandglasses or waterclocks in the cities for accurate timing, but they wouldn't be worth a damn on sha'um-back. So every Gandalaran in the desert conveniently carried a reasonably accurate clock inside himself.

I slept a little, stretched beside Keeshah on the salty desert floor. But I woke just before dawn, and I was facing east when the sun came up.

I have witnessed sunrises in most of the deserts of the southwestern U.S. I had never seen anything so beautiful.

I never saw the sun. The soft, mist-like cloud layer overhead began to glow with rich color. The same dramatic colors of any sunrise in Ricardo's world, but not as sharply defined. Red, orange, bright yellows in a random, shifting pattern, with no distinct break between them. The sky was filled with a gorgeous color show. The clouds seemed to absorb the colors from the east and diffuse them across all of Gandalara. The floor of the desert echoed the changing pattern of the sky, and I laughed to see Keeshah's face ripple from red to yellow to violet.

It was like watching a rainbow before it had been called to attention.

All too soon the sun tired of its coloring game and got on with its business of creating day out of night. As the desert grew swiftly lighter, I pulled out the map Thanasset had given me. I spread it out on the sand very carefully.

And saw absolute gibberish.

The big piece of glith-skin parchment was covered with a

maze of red lines and black lines. Some were big scrawls of curves and wiggles, others were peculiar little angular squiggles that looked like a cartoonist's lightning bolts tied in a sailor's knots.

If that is a map, I thought, *I am Chesty Puller's maiden aunt*.

I turned the sheet of parchment slowly around, trying to figure out which way was up. The one obvious line on the thing was a firm black border line which ran along one side and off two sides of the square parchment. Obviously this was a map of only a portion of Gandalara, which could be matched up to others in the set for an overall map.

I looked around me and tried to orient the map. *That huge wall behind Raithskar should logically be this bold border line*. I turned to face Raithskar. *And there are mountains on my right. Yes, these markings might represent mountains . . .*

Suddenly a little group of the angular figures near the bold border line jumped out at me. There were only six of them in a row, but they read:

Raithskar.

After that, the whole thing suddenly made sense. It had simply taken a little time for Markasset's memory to come up with the reading skills necessary to understand the Gandalaran conventions of mapmaking. They weren't all that different, it seemed. North was the top of the map—once Markasset translated the squiggle-code for me, the rest was easy.

The bold line of the Great Wall ran irregularly on either side of Raithskar. It flowed to the southwest until it ran out of map. On the other side, it moved directly east until it made a sharp curve to southeast by south, then it disappeared off the edge.

Beyond the Great Wall, no landmarks were shown. The Sharkel Falls, which gave the city its water, were shown—but no source was even postulated, much less named.

There was indeed a range of mountains shown on the map. They were east of me and ran south by west from the Great Wall, making a sort of peninsula of high ground—the Mokardahl Mountains. At their southern tip was nestled a city marked by symbols:

Thagorn.

I studied the map carefully. Distances were marked in

"days"—which meant the distance a man could walk in a day without killing himself. I figured that a sha'um could cover roughly three times that distance in a day—probably more.

I recalculated all the distances into sha'um-days. If we tried to go directly across the desert to the southern tip of the mountain range, it would take us three days. The Refreshment House of Yafnaar lay directly along that route, but I thought it best not to stop there. Zaddorn would be likely to check there, and, though he'd be several days behind, he'd then have definite proof of which direction I had taken.

No, we'd have to go straight across, if we chose the desert. And we'd be three days with too little water and—more importantly—no food for Keeshah.

I decided our best bet was to head southeast by east to the little town of Alkhum shown at the foot of the nearby mountains. Then we could travel almost due south past another little town called Omergol, to the southern tip of the Mokardahls. From there it was a straight shot—or so it looked on the map—east to Thagorn. It would be twice as long a trip as crossing the desert, and more dangerous in terms of being spotted along the way—but we'd have food and water, and our full strength when we reached Thagorn.

Sound all right to you, Keeshah? I asked. Keeshah had been right behind me, looking over my shoulder at the map. I didn't believe that he could read the map, but I was sure he had been following my thoughts. He dropped his chin to my shoulder and I pulled gently at one of his ears, scratching behind it.

Good, came his approving thought, but for a moment I wondered if he meant my plan or my scratching. He followed it immediately with an image and a sense of appetite. It seemed there was game in that area that Keeshah remembered fondly. There was no name identified with the singularly unattractive animal—that sort of thing doesn't occur to a sha'um. I got only the briefest glimpse of it in Keeshah's mind, and it was more than I wanted. It was built something like a wild boar, but it had long, curving tusks and it looked trimmer and faster than any I had ever seen photographed. As a matter of fact, it looked mean and rather tough, but Keeshah remembered its taste with keen anticipation.

**If that's what you want—at least I won't have to carry a*

*side of glith slung nonchalantly over my shoulder when I leave town.**

I mounted Keeshah and we set off for Alkhum.

I was relieved to know that Keeshah could find food easily for himself. Once I had formed the plan of following the mountains southward, I had immediately rejected the idea of riding or leading Keeshah into town, for the same reason I would not have stopped at Yafnaar if we had decided to cross the desert.

The people of a town might or might not remember a man traveling on foot. They would remember a man who left town with a huge hunk of meat slung over one shoulder—but they might not think it worth mentioning when Zaddorn came to call.

But a man on a sha'um would be a topic of conversation for days, and when Zaddorn asked about me—I could almost hear it:

"You see a stranger on a big golden palomino tiger?"

"Shore did, Sheriff. He went thataway."

So, when we reached the general area of Alkhum two days later, I cautioned Keeshah again about being seen.

Do not worry. What I do not eat, I will bury.

Like all the big carnivores in my world, Keeshah needed a regular supply of food. He seemed to have an internal system for processing food energy as efficiently as water usage. Nothing else could account for his tremendous endurance and the relative infrequency of his need for fuel. But his storage tank, as it were, had to be maintained at a minimum level and topped off now and then.

Right now, he was hungry. He had been looking forward to the imminent hunt with single-minded anticipation. And I had shared his thoughts until I was about ready to eat one of those evil-looking beasts myself.

I untied the rope that laced the packs together, stood up on Keeshah's back and hung one of the packs and my sword and baldric over the gnarled branch of a tree. Then I jumped down, told him that I would meet him back here, and watched him disappear into the forest. I turned eastward to where I figured the town should be, and started walking.

It was an odd sort of forest. It had grown up around us as we had climbed into the low hills that sloped toward the steep, craggy mountains still some distance away. There had been grass—real green grass, not the grayish, fluffy stuff that grew on the desert floor—and then scattered bushes, and finally this wooded area.

There were no tall trees such as Ricardo remembered from the California mountains. The tallest were no higher than three yards, and more than once in the last few hours, I had been forced to press myself to Keeshah's back to keep my head lower than the highest branches. To someone who might be standing on a hill, the head of a man jogging along at treetop level would be a remarkable sight indeed.

There were a variety of trees in the forest, but their one common feature solved a minor puzzle for me. I had thought, from the intricate parquetry in Thanasset's house, that there was a wood shortage. The forest proved me wrong—it was simply that there was no *straight* wood to be had, or at least it was rare in this part of Gandalara. I wondered, in passing, where Keeshah's scratching post had come from.

One of the common trees—Markasset's memory obligingly supplied the name *dakathrenil*—had a trunk which would have been twice as long if straight. But it twisted and curved, zigzagged upward in a ragged spiral until it was as tall as a Gandalaran. Then the trunk disappeared into a slightly mounded webwork of branches, forming a wide, flat umbrella. Its leaves were long and thin, and a rich deep green in color. They grew in clusters directly from the branches, spaced so that not a leaf missed the sunlight, and very little sunlight got past the leaves.

So dense was the shade cast by these trees that the ground underneath them was clear of any growth except the hardy grass which seemed to carpet these hills. Several times Keeshah and I had traveled almost in darkness through groves of dakathrenil trees. Their spacing had been so exact that I thought of them as orchards—as indeed they were. The tree in which I had concealed my pack and sword had been in full bloom with dozens of tiny blue flowers. The air around me was thick with their fragrance—a sweet pungence that reminded me of one of the fruits I had eaten at Thanasset's table.

I reflected, as I walked along, that I might be tramping through someone's apple orchard, and I wondered how the owner would feel about that. I decided not to let it worry me—I had plenty of other things to think about.

I wasn't sure what I would find in Alkhum—but I hadn't expected *not to find* Alkhum. The map had shown it located at the mouth of a pass—the Khumber Pass—and I had somehow expected a busy trade city at least the size of Raithskar.

When I finally came out into a clear area and saw the brick wall of Alkhum, I saw the reason why it had been hard to find. The "pass" rose behind the city in great craggy steps. It was clearly not easily negotiable for a man, much less a caravan. So I walked through the unguarded city gates into a sleepy farm town. It might still have been a trade center, I thought to myself, if Yafnaar didn't provide a comfortable stopover along the shorter desert route.

Obviously there was some foot traffic through the city, because no one I saw on the streets paid any attention to me. They lounged in front of stores or pursued their normal work. Just inside the gate, a man was molding the cupped tiles that seemed to be a universal roofing material. Women with bundles walked along, chatting together, and at the far end of what seemed to be the only street in the town, vlek-drawn carts were being unloaded. Baskets of greenish-brown grain were handed into a doorway by a line of men. Past them at another door, carts were being loaded with bulky sacks—a grain mill.

No one I saw was wearing a sword, and I congratulated myself on having had the foresight to leave mine behind.

I didn't need a sign to lead me to an eatery—a mouth-watering aroma was coming from an open door on my left. I went directly there, and stepped out of the bright sun into a cool dimness.

"Welcome to the house of Nasin, traveler," a raspy, friendly voice greeted me. My eyes adjusted quickly, and I saw the man who had spoken as he came out from behind a square window at the back of the room. He was the oldest Gandalaran I had yet seen. The top of his head was entirely free of fur, and the skin had darkened over his skull and clear down around his eyes until he looked as though he were wearing a close-fitting black mask and hood. He smiled at me broadly and without embarrassment, even though most of his front teeth were missing. The skin had wrinkled and shrunken in around his mouth, so that his one gleaming tusk, still solid and straight, hung outside his lower lip when he talked.

"A thirsty day out, sir. A glass of faen?"

"Yes, please. And some food."

"Right away." He went back through a doorway and appeared in the window again. I was just wondering if I should sit down at one of the small tables when he called out, "Here you are, sir." I walked over to the window. Its sill served as a counter—there was a rough clay bowl of delicious smelling stew and a glass of faen. I reached for my pouch, but the quick old man shook his head. "No, sir, thank you. You can pay me when you're through—you might be hungrier than you think!"

"If this stew tastes as good as it smells, you may be right!" I told him.

"The best to be had anywhere, sir! I make it myself."

I threw my pack under the nearest table and sat down with the dishes. The stew was indeed delicious, and both the glass and the bowl were refilled before I was finally satisfied.

"It's a pleasure to see a man appreciate good cooking!" rasped the old man. "Tell you what, I'll only charge you for the first bowl—that will be a zak six."

I opened my pouch and went cold all over. I had forgotten that Illia had bought a side of glith for me—she had used almost all of the smaller coins. Feeling like a man offering a hundred dollar bill to pay for a candy bar, I pulled out one of the large gold pieces. I said, "I'm afraid this is all I have."

The old man stared at me in surprise, tried twice before he was able to speak. "I couldn't change that for you, sir. Even if I charged you for the second bowl. Have you nothing smaller?"

"Only these," I said, and showed him the three quarter-zak coins Illia had left. The old man shook his head.

"That'd be only half your debt, sir. I hate to put you to the trouble, sir, but Lorbin the goldsmith has his shop just across the street. He'll be able to change that gold piece for you—at a fee, of course." The squinty gaze dropped quickly to my pack, where it still lay on the floor, and then back to my face. "You go on over, sir. I trust you to bring me my due."

"You're very kind," I said, and went out the door—leaving my pack.

Lorbin was a short Gandalaran, not fat but round-faced and sleek. His voice was smooth and rich.

"Ah, young man!" he said the moment I walked through his doorway. "How may I help you?"

"The proprietor at Nasin's can't change a twenty-dozak piece," I told him. "He said you could help me."

"Certainly, certainly." I handed it to him and he looked it over, measured it with a pair of calipers, and weighed it on a small balance. "Raithskar coinage—workmanship second only to Eddarta. Are you from Raithskar, young man?" He began counting out bronze and silver coins, still talking. "We get a little news here, and I've heard rumors of some trouble back there."

"I'm sorry I can't help you," I managed to get out, then went on with what glibness I could muster. "I am from Raithskar originally, but I've been away for a few years."

"Ah, yes, restless youth. Wanted to see more of the world."

"Yes—but I always knew I'd come home someday. That's why I've saved this coin through the years—for the trip home."

"Well," he said, stacking the coins on the counter between us and counting them again, this time toward me, "don't be troubled by what I said. Rumors are only rumors, after all.

"And Raithskar's a nice city. I've been there more than once—I'd be tempted to set up business there, myself, if the folk here didn't need me so much. But that's life, eh? Find yourself a niche and make the most of it."

He pushed the neatly stacked coins across the counter to me. "There you are, young man. Eighteen dozaks in silver, twenty-four zaks in bronze." I glanced over them. They were stacked by sixes, and easily countable.

"Correct," I confirmed. "And your commission?"

He carefully lifted two bronze coins off the top of a stack. "Quite right. Less two zaks for my trouble."

Less than one percent commission for money-changing? "A fair price. A pleasure to do business with you, sir."

"A smooth trip home to you, young man," he said, smiling. "And a happy homecoming."

I thanked him and went back to Nasin's to pay my bill and collect my pack. I insisted, because of the delay, on paying him for the second bowl of stew. And, since he knew I wasn't on my last dozak, he accepted, and wished me a happy day. I filled my waterskins at the well, and headed out of the village.

That's a great way to travel incognito, I said to myself. *Play the classic rich bum. Get a man to offer you sympathy and undercharge you, then flash a wad that would choke a vlek.*

Zaddorn knows I have those gold pieces. And Lorbin will remember me. He believed that homecoming story—but will Zaddorn? Sure he will—when Keeshah rides a vlek.

I had calmed down a little by the time I reached the tree where my other pack and my sword were hidden. Even if I had thought about those gold pieces earlier, what could I have done about it? There had been no time for moneychanging in Thanasset's house, and no opportunity between there and here.

Keeshah was waiting for me, radiating contentment. He sent me a welcoming thought and indicated that he was ready to move on again.

Not right away, Keeshah. Let's rest a little, and let our lunch settle.

Again I felt a sense of surprise from him. **Thank you.**

He allowed me to stand on his back to retrieve my things from the treebranch, then he wandered off into a shaded area, curled up and was instantly asleep. The way a cat sleeps, with one ear open.

I pulled the map out of the pack and studied it. If I were Zaddorn, what would I do? What would I think of Markasset? Where would I think he would go?

I thought back to the fight in Thanasset's garden. The cop I had ended up killing had said: "*The Chief says he has it on him.*"

That seemed to mean that Zaddorn believed I had stolen the Ra'ira and was still carrying it around. Did he think I had taken it with me on the caravan and then brought it back to Raithskar, only to take it out of the city again? Going where? *Chizan*, and eventually Eddarta?

Neither city was on the map, but Markasset's memory told me that *Chizan* was ten days east southeast of Thagorn, and Eddarta some thirty-five days beyond *Chizan*, east and south of it.

No, Zaddorn was no fool and he knew Markasset wasn't one, either. But he might believe—*that's it!* I thought. *He must think that I stole the gem and hid it in Thanasset's house, then left on the caravan to make him think it was already out of the city. He probably thinks I did betray the caravan to the Sharith—to cover my tracks. I went back to Raithskar expecting him to believe that the Ra'ira had been lost with the caravan, so that I could stay home without being suspected.*

And do what with the Ra'ira? Pay off Worfit? And what would he do with it?

What does it matter? I asked myself. *If you're writing a fairy tale, don't quibble over talking bears.*

Why I would be confident of not being suspected, I couldn't imagine. Zaddorn might reason that I expected the entire caravan to be wiped out, and the two escapees had ruined my plan, making it necessary for me to grab the jewel and hightail it out of town.

But where? I thought irritably. *Damn it, where does he think I'm going? Where will he go in order to catch up to me in the shortest time possible? He knows I'm days ahead of him already, riding Keeshah. What the hell is the man thinking right now?*

He could have decided that I would head west—the map didn't show me what lay in that direction, and Markasset's memory was not cooperating. But I couldn't count on that. I'd have to assume he figured I would head southeast. And whether I was going to Eddarta to turn the Ra'ira over to some Lord who had paid me to steal it or whether—and this was a new possibility—I was going to collect it from the Sharith, whom I had paid to steal it—whichever he thought it was, I would have to go through Thagorn.

So Zaddorn is heading for Thagorn, too, I decided. *And he'd take the quickest route with the best chance of finding definite traces of my passing, knowing that he can't hope to catch up with me until I stop somewhere—maybe in Thagorn itself.*

I drew my finger across the map from Raithskar to the Refreshment House at Yafnaar. *He'd go there first, looking for me. If he doesn't find news of me there—which he won't—would he go directly to Thagorn?*

No, I decided. *Because he still wouldn't have any* proof *that I'm heading for Thagorn. He'll know that if I don't stop at Yafnaar I'll follow the mountains down to Thagorn. But he won't bother to backtrack to Alkhum—he'll cut across the Omergol and look for me there.*

I did some quick calculation. Ten days for Zaddorn to travel from Raithskar to Omergol. I had been two days on the road, so that made it . . . eight days from now, Zaddorn would reach Omergol.

Keeshah, I called. He was instantly on his feet and trotting toward me.

I replaced the maps and retied the packs, mounted Keeshah, and slung the packs across my lap as I had done before. As we started southward, I was thinking:

Zaddorn will be in Omergol eight days from now, and I'll be there tomorrow. That gives me a clear seven-day lead on him.

So why am I still worried?

The answer to that was readily summed up in one word.

Zaddorn.

15

I might have made better time if I'd been able to use the road that ran along within a few miles of the towering cliffs, but I didn't dare. The next town of any size was Omergol, a good day's ride on sha'um back, and four days by shank's mare. Any traffic I met would remember me. There were disadvantages to being partners with a sha'um, though the advantages outweighed them by twenty to one.

Like the ancient Roman roads of Europe, the highways of Gandalara don't need repair very often, and when they do, the job is fairly easy and the materials close at hand. They're built of rock salt, which is just about as hard as marble. In some places, I found out later, the road is simply a smoothed ribbon over a natural bed of rock salt. In a place where it never rains—*never*—there was no need for the ancient road-builders to take drainage or seepage into account.

There should be an old saying here, "There's only two

kinds of weather in Gandalara—hot and dry." There should be, but there isn't. There is no word for "weather" in the language. The concept doesn't even exist, because the condition doesn't exist. Climate, yes; weather, no.

Does a fish ever talk about humidity?

The most widely-traveled roads are those that run near the Great Wall, where the water is. So when a rut or a pothole develops in the surface of a road, the locals get a few buckets of sludge from the edge of the nearest salt swamp and fill the defect carefully. When it dries, you have rock salt again.

Since it is only the roads and the caravans that keep trade going, and since only the roads will take wheeled vehicles, the local folk do a pretty conscientious job of keeping them in repair.

Near dusk of the second day the sounds on the highway grew more frequent, and the cheerful voices of men greeting friends blended with the inane bawling of the vleks. I rode low on Keeshah's back, and we moved carefully through the trees, watchful for the occasional cottage. We had reached the outskirts of Omergol, and it was obviously far different from the sleepy farm village of Alkhum. From the amount of traffic flowing from it, I decided it must be a good-sized city, and I was overcome with a need for a hot meal and a cold beer and a night's rest on something softer than the salty earth. Surely one more traveler would not be noticed.

I dropped my saddlebags over a nearby limb then slipped off Keeshah's back.

Stay out of sight, I warned him, and received an answering flow of scorn—did I think he was stupid? I laughed and scratched his forehead in apology.

Back when? he asked.

Tomorrow. Dawn—no, I hesitated. I wasn't sure, after all, how far away the city was and how long it would take me to get back here on foot. And Milda's pack of supplies was running low—it might be a good idea to wait until the shops opened and replenish my food rations before I left Omergol.

Tomorrow noon, I decided.

Here?

Yes. Feed well.

I watched his tawny form move silently through the trees away from the road. Then I set out on foot, still following the road, but some distance from it.

That is, I thought I was moving parallel to the road—until I almost stepped right out on it. I caught myself in time and made sure I was screened from the flow of traffic while I took some time to think.

This was a wide and busy highway, with traffic moving at a steady pace going both ways. To my left—toward the city, which was hidden from me by the trees—groups of men moved on foot, laughing and talking. They were dressed in the same kind of coordinated outfits I had seen in Markasset's closet—not as rich, perhaps, but obviously these were young men all set for a night on the town. Carts traveled in that direction, too, mostly farm carts laden with produce, and men dressed in simple clothing who looked as eager for the city as their better dressed counterparts. But, as I watched, a dusty caravan groaned and waddled by, weighed down with cargo well-wrapped against the dryness of the desert. I thought I recognized in the colored cloth covering the carts one of the merchant banners I had seen in Raithskar.

That's what gave me the clue that solved the puzzle. When I had looked at Thanasset's map, I had judged that Zaddorn would cut straight across the desert from Yafnaar to Omergol. It hadn't occurred to me, then, that the same route might be used as an alternative to the hot, dry march across the desert from the south. The road I was watching was not the one I had been following, but one which intersected it at Omergol.

Any caravans which took this route must follow the Great Wall south—through Thagorn? Under the noses of a band of Riders who raided the desert travelers to collect their just "tribute"?

Tribute—of course. The Sharith probably charged these caravans a high toll for safe passage near Thagorn. And they would pay it—for the privilege of a more comfortable trip, for the safety of the remainder of their goods, and for the assurance of getting to their destinations alive. The Sharith probably regarded anyone who dared the desert route as traitors trying to evade their taxes.

But as I said, I had seen only one caravan going *toward* Omergol, and its role as a trade route stopover would not account for the high volume of traffic. The city itself must have some attraction of its own.

One thing more I learned, watching the traffic moving by.

Nine out of ten men on that road going in either direction were wearing swords. And the rest wore long knives at their belts. Well, when in Rome . . .

I wore my sword. I stepped out from behind the bushes as though I had stepped behind them for personal reasons, and joined the parade. Nobody looked twice at me. I returned the courtesy.

But I did glance at the carts coming from Omergol. They were larger and sturdier than the farm carts, which were wood frames mounted on a single axle with wooden spoke-wheels rimmed with bronze. All the carts I had seen up until now had beds and sides of interlaced rope, which had seemed eminently reasonable to me, considering the time and expense it must have taken just to laminate the long bars of wood together which make up the cart frame, axle, wheels, and tongue.

The carts coming from Omergol were wagons, really, with double axles and beds strengthened with long slats of wood interwoven with rope. It took four vleks to pull the ones I saw, and they were *working* at it. I was finding myself more and more curious about what Omergol produced that had to be hauled away with so much effort.

The road turned a slight corner, and I had my answer. Boy, did I have my answer.

I was looking into the intersection of the two roads, and past that through the gates of the city straight up its throat. I say "up" because Omergol climbed the foot of the Great Wall in huge terraces. I could distinguish five levels, and straight through the center of the city ran a continuation of the wide highway on which I was standing. Stairsteps as wide as the broad avenue climbed between each level.

To the right of the city, further up the slope, which was gentler here than behind Raithskar, I could see a fine mist which meant a river. I could hear it, too, and it was not falling, as the Sharkel did, but rushing down the side of the mountain.

To the left of the city was a huge pit, which had climbed the hillside at about the same rate as the city. A stream of men and women was flowing from that worksite back into Omergol.

And between the pit and the river gleamed the beautiful city of Omergol.

I was to learn later that Omergol was primarily a mining town, digging and polishing semi-precious stones from underground mines further up the slope of the Wall. But it had a second interest which had to be hauled away in double-axle wagons, and which it flaunted. Between its high-demand goods and its place along the trade route, Omergol was a rich city—and it wore its wealth proudly in a mantle of pale green marble.

It took all the control I had not to stop in the middle of the road and just stare at it. Every building, large and small, was faced with smooth, polished marble. The westering sun cast soft shadows into the streets and across the lower buildings. The murmur of the river in the background added to the whole effect. The city looked clean and cool; its wide avenue was an open invitation; and the crowds of people moving along that avenue amid peals of laughter made me conscious of being alone and very tired.

It was hard to keep my eyes on the road, but I tried. I didn't want to draw attention to myself for looking like a classic case of hickdom. But I needn't have worried—the city had the same effect on the people around me. In tacit agreement we all began to move a little faster.

As I watched the city draw nearer, I wondered about the odd color of the marble. I decided that there must be a vein of copper in those hills somewhere. Basic copper carbonate, in adequate quantity, might account for the soothing pastel green of Omergol's walls.

Had the first builders of this city planned to build it of the beautiful marble they found nearby? Or had some Gandalaran analog of Augustus Caesar found a wooden city and transformed it into this cool green elegance? As I passed through the gates, I felt again that sense of antiquity I had experienced when Thanasset and I had too briefly discussed the history of Gandalara.

The wall and gate had been recently refinished with a fresh surface of marble, but just inside, the buildings wore their original faces, which in some places were scarred and rounded by erosion. In rainless Gandalara, only the wind could have accomplished that slight damage. And, even throwing a duststorm or two every year, my mind simply couldn't grasp the enormous amount of time these buildings had been standing.

To either side of the wide avenue just inside the city wall were open areas which served as the city's marketplace. Beyond them the stairs began their ascent, and the wide avenue was edged with open doorways. From them came the savory smell of cooking meat and fresh-baked bread, and a heady mixture of sound. The clatter of dishes and coins and the wooden rectangles used for gaming spilled from the doorways. Music from string and wood instruments, here in a light tune, there offering steady, stirring rhythms, and occasionally acting as accompaniment for voices. Other voices, men's and women's, were laughing and talking, in one case, at least, quarreling. In that one case I managed to dodge past the doorway just before two young Gandalarans, farmhands by their dress, and smelling strongly of faen, fell out into the avenue and rolled, struggling together, down the stairway. Several people followed them, shouting with excitement. Roughly half, I guessed, were trying to stop the fight. The other half were betting on their choice to win. From somewhere appeared another group of men with the efficient look of cops.

I had been trying to decide where to stop for the meal and rest I wanted so badly. At that point I decided to move on; the neighborhood seemed a little rough, and the last thing I needed in Omergol was trouble.

So I mounted the rest of that flight of stairs, ignoring my clamoring belly. The second level of the city was less crowded and somewhat quieter. I considered going further up, but rejected the idea. The higher levels were undoubtedly the newest; the business districts would be more expensive and a common traveler would be more conspicuous there.

Just about then I saw it. It was on the other side of the street, its open door inviting me. And above the door, carved in bas relief out of the deepest green marble I had yet seen, was a large and somewhat stylized image of a sha'um. It was passing to the left, but its head was turned out toward the avenue, and it looked quite fierce. Under the carving, set in gold lettering, were Gandalaran characters: The Green Sha'um Inn. It looked like just the place I wanted.

I walked through the door into a narrow lobby. Stairs led upward on my right; a door opened on my left and I hesitated at the cheerful sound of voices and the unmistakable aroma of a bar. First things first, I told myself.

A man was seated at a desk just beyond the beginning of the stairway. As I started toward the desk, he stood up and bowed. "How may I help you sir?" he asked.

"I need a room for the night," I said.

"There is a room available," he replied. "The charge will be ten zaks."

I did some quick figuring and decided that it was a reasonable sum for a night's lodging. I fished a dozak piece out of my pouch and put it on the desk.

He didn't take the money immediately. Instead, he brought a huge register book from somewhere behind the desk, a thin brush, and an inkwell. My throat went suddenly dry as I realized that I had never written a Gandalaran word. But my fear passed as the man opened the register book, dipped the pen in ink, and looked up at me. "Your name and home, sir?" he asked, poising the brush above the page.

I was ready for that. I hoped my relief didn't show as I gave him the alias: "Lakad, Mildak's son, of *Chizan*."

He wrote. Then he took the coin, put it somewhere in the desk, and gave me two zaks change.

"I hope you enjoy your stay with us, sir." He handed me a key. "Room eight; up the stairs and to your right."

"Thank you. I-uh-sure need a bath." Did the rooms come with one? I suspected they didn't, but I didn't want to come right out and ask a stupid question.

"Ah. Koreddon's Bath-house is just around the corner to the east—almost behind us. You can't miss it. But they're closed for the dinner hour. Won't open for a while yet. Why not have a bite yourself, while you're waiting? Or a nice cool drink?" I looked at him and he knew he'd made a sale and smiled. "The Onyx Room," he nodded toward the doorway I had passed as I entered, "is always open. Welcome to Omergol."

"Thanks."

The Onyx Room ran the length of the building back from the street. To my right, as I entered, a bar of shiny black marble stretched along the far wall. Behind it were two burly bartenders, each serving half a dozen people of both sexes. I hadn't realized just how thirsty I was until I saw one of the bartenders serving up a mug of faen. He caught my look and grinned. He was missing a couple of lower teeth, a silent testament to the hazards of tending bar in a neighborhood that could turn rough. I guessed he must have served his apprenticeship on the first level of the city.

He poured a mug of faen and handed it across the bar to me. I took a deep drink. "Thanks. Can I get some dinner?"

"The best in town," he answered, and the smoothness of his voice was a surprise. "Make yourself comfortable and I'll inform the kitchen the dinner crowd is starting to arrive."

The room was fairly wide, with tables and chairs scattered across the marble-tiled floor. Against the wall opposite the bar was a regular pattern of tables and high-backed benches which created a booth-like effect. The tables had mosaic surfaces of green and black marble shavings, the visual effect very similar, though more dramatic, to the wood parquetry I had seen in Raithskar.

I drained the mug and handed it back for a refill before I walked over to a small booth and sat down. I was facing the rear of the large room, and I watched the bartender go to the far end of the bar, open a door and say something, then return to his work. He grinned at me again and said my dinner would be ready soon. I nodded and smiled my thanks, but I could feel my mind drifting. Whether it was fatigue or the faen I had downed so quickly, I couldn't tell, but I suddenly felt completely relaxed and free of worry.

For the first time since I had left Raithskar I began to wonder, in a comfortably detached sort of way, what I would do when I did reach the stronghold of the Sharith. I had little doubt that arriving unseen would be impossible. From all I had heard, they were too well-trained to forego an effective sentry system. And if it were somehow possible for me to slip through the "human" guards, how could I elude the sense of smell of their sha'um?

I floated in a sort of limbo, separate from the noise of the growing crowd in the bar, aware of my surroundings, but only peripherally, as if they did not concern me at all. I thanked the bartender, who personally brought my dinner, and I was not too detached to enjoy a well-cooked glith steak and a rich assortment of fruits.

At times I watched the people around me, and I was vaguely surprised to see that not everyone was enjoying the same meal I had been served. In fact, now that the crowd had arrived, there were waiters and waitresses taking orders for specific dishes. The bartender, obviously, had chosen my meal for me. I was somehow deeply flattered that he considered me a steak-and-potatoes type.

I had several more glasses of faen, and I took my time over the meal. The entirety of my experiences in Gandalara wandered through my thoughts. Yafnaar. Keeshah. Thanasset. Zaddorn. Illia. Keeshah. The Ra'ira. The Sharith. Kä. Milda. And always Keeshah.

People came and went around me; I overheard scraps of conversation and was comforted by their triviality. I was nursing what I had decided must be my final glass of faen when there was a general movement in the room. People standing up, chairs and benches scraping. At first I thought, *There must be a very specific dinner hour here, and it's over*. But that was disproved by the voice of my bartender friend, speaking in the doorway behind me.

"Good evening, gentlemen. Where will you be seated?"

But it was a small mystery and not worth my attention. I stared into my faen and thought about the greater mystery. What had happened to the Ra'ira?

The room had grown quiet, but I assumed that most of the people had left. I was thinking that I, too, should be going, when a deep voice sounded at my shoulder, crashing through my preoccupation.

"I think we will sit *here*," it said.

I looked up, then. Two men were standing next to me. They were dressed in a manner I had not yet seen in Gandalara. Their trousers and tunics were a finely-woven fabric exactly the color of the desert sands. Their boots and wide-brimmed hats were a darker tan, and tied around their waists were long sashes of a pale yellow muslin. They wore baldrics, swords, and an arrogant manner.

To one side of them stood the bartender, looking at me, his expression one I could not read.

16

I blinked up at them, trying to will away the fog. I was bewildered by the fact that the room hadn't cleared, after all. It was still full, but everyone was standing up, away from their tables. Everyone except me.

As I struggled to grasp the significance of that fact, the newcomers glared at me. One of them put a hand to his chin and slid a wooden bead down a slim string. Then he thumbed his hat back from his forehead and it slid off to hang from his shoulders, held around his neck by the string. It was a curious hat, stiff-brimmed with a rounded top.

If it were red instead of tan, I thought crazily, *that hat would do a nineteenth-century cardinal proud.*

"Well?" the stranger asked.

"Well?" I repeated, feeling as though I had just awakened. I was confused. I was beginning to be frightened.

"Stand up, you son of a flea!" he yelled. Both of them took a step backward, and they drew their swords.

Suddenly everything seemed crystal clear to me.

Those are uniforms! They must be local cops. How the hell did Zaddorn get word here so fast?

The effects of the faen and the calmness of my brief reverie faded away from me. I was back in focus, sharply alert, and there was one driving thought uppermost in my mind.

I can't let them take me now—not when I've come this far. Thanasset's future depends on my getting to Thagorn and finding the truth.

I've already killed a cop. They can't hang me twice . . . and I can't go back to Raithskar without some answers.

The glass of faen was in my right hand, still half full. I tossed it into the face of the nearest man—the one who was still wearing his hat. At the same time, I stood up and launched my empty dinner plate at the other one. He ducked.

I had knocked over my bench and the one behind it. I kicked them away from me, and drew my sword.

The bartender moved then. He went behind the bar and with steady, practiced movements, began pulling breakables down from the shelves.

Some of the customers left hurriedly out of whichever door was nearest. Most of them just pressed back away from the three of us, me and the two hats. They looked on with great interest.

I decided I had misjudged the bartender. He needn't have worked the lower level of the city to have earned those broken teeth.

As the two uniformed men squared against me, my perception shifted the same way it had done when Milda had come into my room the first time I saw her. In one timeless instant, it was as though the flim of life had stopped and I was looking at a single frame frozen on the screen.

The title of the film should have been *Tarzan on the Planet of the Apes*.

I was faced by a couple of mad bull apes clad in comic khaki uniforms. The one on my left, who had pushed his hat back, had a snarl on his face that revealed a snaggled right tusk that somehow looked more dangerous than the normal one.

The one on my right had a neat scar that ran down his right cheek from the inner corner of his eye to a point about an inch from the corner of his mouth. You might have called what he was doing a smile—if you were feeling generous.

The film started moving again.

Snaggletooth came in with an overhand cut that was meant to cleave me from guggle to zatch. Scarface came in with an underhand thrust to my belly. These two boys knew how to work together.

I brought my own sword up from my left in a backhand slash that slammed Snaggletooth's sword aside and brought its edge dangerously close to his partner's nose. Instinctively, Scarface leaped backward, and his thrust missed me by inches.

As Scarface's sword arced upward without meeting any resistance, I reversed my own slash and slammed my blade against his. The weapon spun free of his hand and looped to my left, spinning. It clanged point-down on a tabletop, fell over, and skittered off the edge.

That marble surface can't have been any good for the point of the bronze sword, I was thinking. *In fact, I hope he'd have trouble roasting a marshmallow with it now.*

Snaggletooth recovered from the deflection of his overhand chop and moved in to protect the disarmed Scarface. For a few seconds it was cut, parry, thrust, and parry while Scarface ducked around behind his partner and snatched up his sword.

I was beginning to tire, and I knew that I couldn't handle both of them for long; I had to put one of them out of commission, and fast.

I picked on Snaggletooth because he was closer, and because he was doing his very best to slice off whatever of my body he could get at. I backed him a little, waited for an opening, and aimed a thrust at his midsection. As he was recovering from that, I whipped the sword up in a backhand slash at his head. His blade came up in time to deflect mine a little. My wrist turned—instead of the cutting edge, the flat of my blade slammed against Snaggletooth's temple.

He dropped his sword and crumpled to the floor.

I whirled to find Scarface aiming a low, shallow slash at my legs. I jumped the swinging sword and chopped down with my sword, drawing blood from a gash on his forearm.

He stepped back toward his partner, watching me. Snaggletooth was rousing; he rolled and started to get up from the floor. Scarface misjudged the distance, collided with his partner, and fell over him, knocking Snaggletooth back to the floor.

I suppose I could have killed both of them right there, but it didn't occur to me. Ricardo had done his share of scrapping, but always in self-defense. So I retreated down the room, moving backward to keep both of them in sight while I caught my breath.

I glanced behind me; the kitchen door at the end of the bar was blocked by spectators. The two sand-uniformed men were between me and the front door, and they were recovering fast. Snaggletooth seemed groggy still, and Scarface had shifted his sword from his bleeding right arm into his left hand. But they were getting to their feet and they looked, if possible, even less friendly than before.

I was about to make up my mind to try a surprise dash between them when the front door was blocked.

An angry sha'um squeezed through the man-sized door and

filled up that end of the room. He padded toward us, and another one came in after him. They knocked aside tables and ranged themselves on either side of the uniformed men. Then, almost in unison, they let out snarling roars and started across the littered floor for me.

I suddenly felt sorry for the men who had faced Keeshah in Thanasset's garden.

Nobody was more surprised than I was when they stopped. The men walked forward and stood beside their cats, glancing from them to me and back again.

They sheathed their swords.

"We have other business, stranger," said Scarface.

"But we will see you again," said Snaggletooth. "Next time save yourself some trouble—show the proper respect."

The big cats got themselves turned around and padded softly back out the front door. One of them looked back at me one last time. It had eyes the color of gold, and they shone with hatred. It growled softly—*That's a promise if I ever heard one*—then went on out.

Before the men could follow their sha'um, the bartender moved his bulk to block the doorway.

"What about the damage to my place?" he asked.

Scarface jerked his hat in my direction.

He never lost his hat! I noticed. *Shades of Roy Rogers!*

"He started it," he said, and now he was holding his right forearm with his left hand, applying pressure to stop the bleeding. The right leg of his trousers was decorated with vertical red streaks. "Let him pay."

"He's a stranger here," defended the bartender. "And he didn't draw the first blade." He smiled. "Though he did draw the first blood."

Scarface would have backhanded him for that, but Snaggletooth grabbed his shoulder and squeezed. Then he opened his pouch and drew out some coins. "This cover it?" he asked, and dropped them into the bartender's hand.

The bartender hefted the coins thoughtfully, then stepped aside. "That's fine. Come again anytime."

The two men glared at him and walked out. There was a heartbeat or two of stunned silence, then the crowd descended on me in a rush of noise. I was backslapped and congratulated and bought more faen than I could have drunk. I caught fragments of conversation:

"Never saw anyone better with a sword."

"Standing up to them alone. Imagine! *And* their sha'um. That takes real guts."

"Stupid, if you ask me."

I agree with you, buddy. I just wish I'd had a choice.

"Maybe they'll learn they can't push everybody around, the arrogant . . ."

"They'll be back, and he'll be gone. What then? I'll tell you what," the voice rose in pitch, "they'll take it out on us, that's what."

"Worth it, I say, just to see them taken down a notch or two . . ."

In the end—and it didn't take very long—they all wandered away to spread the legend I had fumbled into being. All at once I was almost alone with the bartender.

I looked around the wrecked room and said, "I'm sorry for all this."

"Don't be," he grinned his gap-toothed grin. "You've made me famous."

Yeah. Great way to travel incognito. I sure as hell hope I'm a good long way ahead of Zaddorn. He's not going to have any trouble at all following this trail.

I reached for my pouch. "How much do I owe you for that delicious dinner?"

He waved his hands. "Forget it. What they paid will cover your tab, too." He shook his head. "Beats me what happened. I'm not complaining, mind you. But that's the first time I ever saw any of the Sharith walk away from a fight."

"I can't help you," I told him. "I figured it was all over when those sha'um showed up."

The bartender looked at me sharply. "You didn't know they were Sharith? That explains a lot."

"The man at the desk said something about a bath-house," I changed the subject.

"Koreddon's?" I nodded. "Out the front door to your left. At the end of the stair level there is a side street that comes around back of the inn. Koreddon's is the third door on the opposite side of the street."

"Thanks."

He grinned again, and I decided that, on him, the missing teeth had a certain charm. "My pleasure."

I found Koreddon's with no trouble, and I was delighted to learn that it had some of the qualities of a Japanese bathhouse. It was run by a large family. The youngest boy brought me towels and soap and filled a marble-lined tub in a large, ornate room. As I soaked, I listened to some beautiful minor-toned strains produced by a mature woman I took to be Mrs. Koreddon from what looked like a rectangular harp.

And when I was clean, an almost toothless old man dried and massaged me with iron-strong hands.

So that's what the Sharith are like, I was thinking. *Not very appealing, are they? But not foolish, either. Their cats brought a message about something more important than an upstart stranger who didn't know enough to offer his seat to the Riders, and they listened.*

At least Zaddorn didn't send them. I still have some time. What happened today could cause trouble in Thagorn—but I'll face that when I come to it.

I feel as though I should be worrying about Zaddorn, I thought as I relaxed under the old man's soothing fingers. *But I'm too tired to do any more worrying.*

The old man had to wake me when he was finished. He solemnly accepted the extra zak I offered him when I settled the bill. From the boy I got a shy smile of thanks.

I went up to my room and settled down on a fluffy floor mat such as I had seen in my room at Raithskar. It had been a long, eventful, confusing day, and I was pooped. I reached out with my mind to touch Keeshah's—he was already asleep, but he responded to the contact with the mental equivalent of **Mmph?**

Nothing, Keeshah. Sleep well. I'll see you in the morning.

Mmph, he agreed.

Still lightly linked with Keeshah, I dropped gratefully into sleep.

17

I woke well after dawn, feeling refreshed and eager to see Keeshah again. I ate breakfast in the Onyx Room, and was surprised when the bartender from the night before brought out two plates of food and sat down to join me.

His name, as it turned out, was Grallen. Throughout the delicious breakfast, I was entertained by stories about the bar's regular clientele and the odd and sometimes funny confrontations between different types of people which occur in hotels.

When we were finished, he gathered up the dishes and seemed to be ready to leave.

"Going off duty now?" I asked him. "You work a long shift."

"Have to," he said. "It's my place."

For a moment I thought he was referring to class status of some sort, and I had to struggle to fit such a self-effacing statement into the frontal-assault personality I had already observed. Then it hit me.

"You mean you *own* the Onyx Room?"

"And the Green Sha'um Inn. And a good chunk of real estate on this side of the street." He grinned. "Surprised?"

"Yes," I said, laughing. "Sorry, but you sure *look* like a bartender."

"Not at all strange, since that's what I am. But I figured out early on that there's no profit in pouring someone else's faen." He settled back into his chair and devoted a few seconds of concentration to scraping and stacking the plates. "I don't usually make any noise about having a little money and some weight to throw around."

"Why are you telling me?" I asked him.

"Last night."

"You mean the two Riders?"

He nodded. "Let's just say I owe the Sharith a little aggravation, and I feel as though you've paid part of that debt. It's a service I won't soon forget."

He looked *into* me with dark, knowing eyes. I wondered how I could have missed seeing the wisdom behind the battered face.

"I know people, my friend. You're not just an ordinary stranger. I don't care what you're up to. I just want you to know that Grallen's behind you if you ever need help. And I thought you should know the value of the help I could offer.

"Breakfast," he finished briskly, "is on the house."

He stood up, and so did I.

"Thank you." It was all I could think of to say, and he understood that I wasn't just referring to the free breakfast.

Grallen carried the dishes back into the kitchen, and I walked out into the morning.

I made my way slowly down the central stairway toward the city gates. I stepped into several shops along the way to make small purchases: cured strips of meat, fresh and dried fruits, and a tasty loaf of coarse-grain bread that looked as though it would keep well. I also bought a few sweet bakery treats and I munched them happily as I walked out of Omergol.

Instead of retracing my steps exactly, I turned right as I left the city and walked north along the road which followed the foothills. The morning smelled fresh and new, and the people I passed greeted me with cheerful good humor. After last night's massage, my body felt loose and strong and ready for anything.

A suspicion nibbled at the back of my mind. *You shouldn't be feeling this good,* it warned me. I slapped it down and told it to shut up. *Feeling good feels wonderful for a change!*

When I had walked about as far north as I had traveled south the day before, I stepped off the road and headed west. I hadn't gone far when that annoying suspicion sat up and said *I told you so*.

I saw them at the same moment Keeshah's warning sprang into my mind.

Markasset. Sha'um. I am close. I come.

"Them" was Snaggletooth. Riding the mean-looking, golden-eyed sha'um. I heard a soft sound behind me. I didn't have to turn around to know that Scarface and the other sha'um were back there.

No, Keeshah, I ordered, and grappled with my own fear

so that I could better control the cat. **Are you downwind? Do they know you're nearby?**

Yes. No. He sounded puzzled.

Snaggletooth slid off his sha'um's back and walked slowly toward me.

Keeshah, stay away unless I call. Please. If they see you, they'll know who I am. These guys could be my ticket into Thagorn—don't spoil it. Please stay hidden. I promise I'll call if I need help.

I felt Keeshah hesitate, wonder, grumble. He was primed for a fight; I sensed his conflict as he tried to obey my wishes above his own instincts.

Yes, he agreed at last, then added: **Don't like it.**

I didn't have time to thank him because Snaggletooth's bruised face was only inches away from mine. It was no more attractive from such a close view.

"We got a score to settle," he said. His tone told me that there would be no reprieve this time—the score *would* be settled.

I wasn't quite sure how these two men could help get me into Thagorn. The possibility had only occurred to me when they had shown up just now. But I had already settled on step one of the unknown plan: *Don't get yourself killed.*

"So now you're going to let your sha'um finish the job you couldn't do yourselves?" I asked. Snaggletooth's face turned dark.

It was an old trick, a challenge of honor by ridicule. Like when an unarmed man challenges a man with a gun to a fist-fight. *Yeah,* I thought uncomfortably, *and the man with the gun laughs in the other guy's face and blows his head off.*

Either it worked in this case or they had never had any intention of letting their sha'um interfere. Because Snaggletooth waved his hand and the sha'um ahead of me moved back and lay down. I heard Scarface slip down from his cat's back, and that cat, too, move away. Scarface appeared at my right elbow. I took a step backward as they drew their swords. Scarface was using his left hand now; his right forearm was tightly wrapped with a length of linen.

I drew my sword. "Two against one?" I asked hopefully. But that honorable they weren't going to be.

"Same odds as last night," Scarface said. And they came at me in a double rush.

I ran through a short, wordless prayer to Markasset.

We were standing in a young grove of dakathrenil trees. They had grown taller than our heads, but their umbrellas of branches were still narrow and lacy enough to admit a lot of light.

I dodged to my left, evading Scarface's overhand slash and blocking Snaggletooth's thrust. Scarface turned and deftly shifted the momentum of his chop into a vicious two-handed swing at my midsection. I jumped backward and the edge of his sword whacked a good inch into a tree trunk on my left. Snaggletooth had anticipated the move. He grabbed the tree and swung around it to my left.

He very nearly skewered me. I saw him just in time, twisted to get my sword between us and deflect his aim; the edge of his blade dragged a long, stinging cut across my chest.

Markasset hurt, came Keeshah's raging thought. **I come now.**

No, not yet.

Please.

No. Stay downwind.

I could feel him seething, eager to join the fight. The fire I sensed in him seemed to flow into me until I felt stronger, quicker, more alert.

Snaggletooth roared at the sight of my blood and began to press me back. I needed all Markasset's skill and more to keep his bronze blade away from my skin.

Through the clanging of our swords, I heard the soft snicking sound of Scarface's blade being drawn out of the treetrunk. I looked over Snaggletooth's shoulder; Scarface had disappeared.

I began to worry about where he was.

Snaggletooth leaped forward with a grin of triumph. Had I retreated, as he expected, I'd have been chopped in two by Scarface's sword. But I smelled him behind me and jumped, instead, to the right. Snaggletooth had to pull up short to keep from catching Scarface on the point of his sword.

They were beginning to stink of frustration, and I knew they would start taking chances. So I stayed close to the trunk of a tree, using it for a shield. The lowest branches were eye-ridge level, but I always knew exactly where they were. The other two weren't as lucky, and several times narrowly missed knocking themselves out.

Finally Scarface used his bandaged arm to swing around the treetrunk as the other one had done earlier. He aimed low, and he had a lot of momentum in his thrust.

I knocked the point of his sword into the ground and brought my knee up under his chin. He went down.

Snaggletooth was behind me. I jumped over Scarface and ran for another tree, Snaggletooth following me. From the sound of his heavy breathing, I judged the distance. I whipped around the tree to face him, leaped to catch the highest branch I could, and swung my weight on the springy tree, legs extended. Both feet connected with Snaggletooth's midriff.

He dropped his sword and doubled over, gasping for air. I landed on the ground, sheathed my sword, and walked up close to him. Ricardo delivered a sharp, satisfying right cross and Snaggletooth collapsed in a heap.

The two sha'um came up roaring, and I backed off. They didn't come after me, but stood guard over the unconscious men, now and then nuzzling and licking. I was reminded of Keeshah and me out in the desert.

Keeshah. I could feel him fading, and for the first time I realized what had happened.

You were with me, weren't you Keeshah? I could smell and hear better. You did help me fight this battle, after all, didn't you?

Tried, he answered. *_Hurt?_*

I looked down at the blood on my tunic, pulled it away to examine the cut. It was a bad place and might take a while to heal, but it wasn't deep. I was suffering more from the fading link with Keeshah, and I realized that his splendid fighting spirit had kept me going far past the point of my own endurance. I felt let down and shaky now, and I leaned against the tree I had swung on, because I didn't trust my legs.

I'm all right, I told Keeshah. *_That's a very special trick. You and Markasset must have made quite a fighting team._*

_No._

What?

First time.

I didn't have a chance to wonder about that. Scarface and Snaggletooth were coming to.

Scarface's arms came up around the great wedge of his cat's

head and held it, stroking and soothing the sha'um's concern for its master. Snaggletooth woke up choking and holding his gut; his cat lay down beside him, watching me with its golden eyes. Snaggletooth recovered enough to throw an arm up around the cat's neck. The sha'um stood up slowly, helping Snaggletooth first to sit, then to stand up.

Maybe these two wanted to kill me a few minutes ago, I was thinking. *But as Thanasset said to me in different words not too long ago, anybody a sha'um loves can't be all bad.*

I stood up straight and came out from under the tree. I was tense until I was sure neither one of them would reach for his sword.

Scarface moved to stand beside Snaggletooth. They touched their cats, who roared and complained, then quieted and sidled off unhappily.

If that means what I think it does . . .

It did. Snaggletooth worked his mouth, spat out a tooth, and spoke with a quiet dignity that I wouldn't have expected—but which somehow suited him.

"They won't hurt you now."

"I don't want your lives," I said, understanding and impressed by what he had meant. "I do want some information. First your names."

"I am Bareff," said Snaggletooth, "and he is Liden."

"Why did you quit so suddenly last night?"

They glanced at each other. Scarface—that is, Liden—answered.

"We thought you were one of us."

"Sharith?" I was beginning to see, but it wouldn't do to understand too easily. "What made you think so?"

"When our sha'um came in, they said you smelled of sha'um," explained Bareff.

I did, I thought. *But I bathed and had my clothes washed. And I haven't touched Keeshah yet this morning. I'll bet their cats are confused.*

"Then why all this hassle today?" I asked them.

Liden spoke up. "We're supposed to be told where our agents are, so that this doesn't happen. We sent a message to Thagorn last night, and the answer arrived this morning."

Handy things, those maufa, I thought. *Fast, too.*

"The Lieutenant told us we didn't have a man in Omergol,"

said Bareff. "He said to bring you in just to see what was going on."

"Then you weren't supposed to kill me?" I asked them.

Scarface rubbed his swelling jaw. "Not that it wouldn't have been a pleasure."

I laughed then, and I caught a facial twitch from Snaggletooth that might have been the start of a smile. Or maybe not.

"Well, Bareff and Liden," I said finally, "I demand that you never raise sword to me again. But that's all I demand. Your lives are restored to you; the debt is settled."

They looked at each other, waiting for the catch. I let them stew for a few seconds, then I laid it on them:

"I need to go to Thagorn." I just let it hang there.

"Why?" asked Bareff. He bent over and picked up his sword: Liden walked back a few paces to retrieve his. They both looked at me thoughtfully before they sheathed the bronze blades.

"A personal matter," I said. "It's important to me that I have a chance to talk to—" What had they called their leader? "—the Lieutenant."

"The Lieutenant don't talk to groundwalkers," sneered Bareff.

"You'd have taken me back to Thagorn as a prisoner, right?"

Liden nodded, the scar showing white against the bruise flowing upward from his chin.

"If I had wanted it, I could have taken you back as my prisoners, right?"

Another nod. I didn't need their facial expressions to tell me that every member of the Sharith would have despised me for doing it. I, too, was a Rider. I'd have felt the same way.

"Neither way suits me. Your Lieutenant—he might talk to me if I came to him in the company of two of his best men." That wasn't flattery; I was sure they were exactly that. "Not as prisoner or master—but as a friend."

They chewed that over, staring at me. Finally Bareff said: "I've never met a groundwalker I'd call friend."

I felt a temptation to call in Keeshah, to prove my kinship to them and end this bickering. But Balgokh had said that Markasset was the only Rider not connected with the Sharith. They already knew that I wasn't one of their own. Seeing

Keeshah would identify me positively—and I was still plagued by Markasset's lack of knowledge about the Sharith. They might welcome me as a long-lost brother. Or they might think me a traitor, a maverick, and refuse to have anything to do with me. I couldn't take the chance.

I felt Keeshah in the distance, getting ready to come in as he sensed my almost-invitation.

Sorry, Keeshah, I told him. **Stay where you are.**

To the two Sharith I said: "I'd say most groundwalkers feel the same about Riders. But I've had a taste of your honor—" I waved vaguely at the sha'um "—and of your swords."

I waited. Ricardo had been a military man for a large portion of his life. As a Marine, I'd had the occasion to convince a few wetfeet that mudsluggers were worth something, too. I was hoping I'd just taught the same kind of lesson to these two members of the Gandalaran cavalry.

"Well," said Liden. His sha'um came up to him, and he put out a hand to stroke the smooth brow. "Well, let's get moving, then."

I sighed.

It's not hail-fellow-well-met, I decided, *but it's a start.*

18

The two sha'um knelt beside their masters. Liden mounted; his cat stood up and ambled a short distance southward. Bareff swung his leg over the cat's broad back, then turned to me and grinned. There was a gap in his lower left jaw.

"Come on, groundwalker. See how it feels to Ride."

I just stood there, looking at the flattish, dark-furred head of the kneeling sha'um. It was watching me, hating me.

"Or have you changed your mind about going to Thagorn?"

Bareff's voice sounded dimly in my ears. I could spare no attention for him or for his cat. I was paralyzed by the icy rage that swept through me from Keeshah's mind.

YOU RIDE ONLY KEESHAH!

I could barely breathe through the onslaught of emotion.

Keeshah's anger, yes—but my own reactions, as well. Love for the great cat. Awareness of our unique partnership, guilt over this necessary betrayal. I knew he was coming closer and was ready to attack Bareff's sha'um. I was desperate to stop him for Thanasset's sake. I was desperate to make him understand the need for this ugly deception, to win his forgiveness and cooperation.

Wordlessly, I reached out to him. I pushed against the violent waves of disappointment and pain and outrage and fury. I seemed to push *through* a barrier—and we were linked as we had been during the fight. Only now I shared his perceptions more completely. I could see the trees passing, feel the ground thudding by underneath me/him.

I pushed further, and another barrier yielded. I felt Keeshah slow and stop. I had touched the center of Keeshah.

It was not a union, precisely. We were each aware of ourselves and of the other as separate entities. But in that intense moment of contact, we shared something more than communication, something far more intimate and revealing. The best term I can find for it is *understanding*.

It lasted a bare instant, a closeness so pure and complete, a joy so sharp that we could endure it only briefly. Then we slipped back to the less complete, but more comfortable, communication pattern we had always shared.

You must go, Keeshah agreed reluctantly. **I will follow.**

No, I told him gently. **There are too many sha'um in Thagorn. You couldn't hide from all of them. Will you wait here for me? A few days?**

Yes.

Keeshah. I felt I had to say it. **This one I ride means nothing to me.**

I know. A rumble of impatience. **Go.**

Keeshah's presence left me abruptly, and I felt empty and vulnerable. But my sight cleared and I looked at Bareff, who was enjoying what he took to be my hesitation.

"*Have* you changed your mind, groundwalker?" he asked.

The cat's golden gaze had never left me.

"Your sha'um doesn't like me much," I told Bareff as I finally moved toward the pair.

He uttered a short, scornful laugh. "He hates your tusks, groundwalker. But he'll put up with you for my sake. Hurry up."

"My name is Rickardon," I told him as I swung a leg over the cat's back behind Bareff. I didn't have to pretend to be awkward. The sha'um surged upward before I had my balance, nearly dumping me off on my keister.

I grabbed at Bareff's tunic for support. The sudden movement jerked open the cut on my chest, and it started to sting and bleed again. I hauled myself into position and held on, suffering the laughter of the men without comment.

It was a nightmare ride.

Bareff occupied the space I would have taken on Keeshah, lying along the big cat's back and moving with its rhythm. But I was riding almost on the cat's hindquarters. Even though I lay forward as far as I could over Bareff's back, I was still almost sitting up.

My spine jarred with the cat's every step, and its pelvis ground painfully into my inner thighs. I couldn't help thinking that it wasn't very comfortable for the cat, either. So I pulled on Bareff's hips with my hands and used what pressure I could from my legs to ride more lightly.

It wasn't until we stopped for a light meal that I remembered the parcel of groceries I had dropped when the fight started. Not that they were needed: while I had been fighting Keeshah's jealousy and mounting Bareff's sha'um, Liden had retrieved their saddlebags from somewhere nearby, and they were well-stocked. I recognized some of the items from the same shops where I had bought my purchases—except that the Sharith had the finest the shops could offer, and I'd have bet my shirt they never paid a cent for any of it.

We traveled south for the rest of the day, stopping frequently to let me shift from one cat to the other. The sha'um hunted while we slept that night, and in the morning were fresh again. At midday we rounded the southernmost point of the Mokadahl range, marked by a sheer, looming cliff, then headed eastward.

We had been following the road from Omergol, through semi-cultivated areas dotted with grainfields and orchards. When we turned east, the ground began to rise and go wild. The curly-trunked trees I had seen so often on the way south had been cultivated and trained to their upright stance and umbrella of branches. Here the same trees covered the hillsides, twisting closer to the ground and all overgrown with branches.

The low trees, tall grass, and other types of brush made the hillsides ideal for the concealment of small animals. As the sha'um passed by, the creatures concealed near the road panicked and fled, and I amused myself by trying to classify the types I saw.

None of them were identical to the animals Ricardo had known, though there were similar body configurations. I asked Markasset's memories for the names of the animals I saw; it gave me a few, but not many. I gave up fairly quickly and simply watched the activity and listened to the hoorah stirred by the passing cats. There seemed to be a huge bird population in these foothills, and some of them had very musical voices.

A poet might say I was watching a living symphony. But I'd have to be more truthful and admit it sounded more like Spike Jones' band tuning up. In a hurry. Loudly.

But it made the day pass quickly, and I was surprised, that afternoon, when the cats reached the top of a long slope and stopped to catch their breath.

I slid off the cat's back—Liden's—and stretched as I looked up at a fortified wall made of stone and packed with earth. It had been built as a dam is built, filling a narrow depression between two steep hillsides. It was perhaps a hundred feet long, and at the deepest point of the valley it stood at least thirty feet high.

There were men stationed at intervals along the level top edge of the wall, but just now their attention was focused on the gate at the center of the wall. A caravan master was supervising the payment of his toll fee. He was talking to a man wearing the same type of uniform as Bareff and Liden, except that the sash tied around his waist was red. They conferred over a list and checked things off as items were laid on a low stone shelf that had been built, apparently, as part of the wall.

It was a noisy scene. The caravan vleks were hysterical with the smell of sha'um all around them. Those men who weren't actually unloading goods were busy swearing at the vleks, trying to control them. The actual appearance of Bareff's and Liden's sha'um was hardly noticed by the frenzied animals.

So this is Thagorn, I thought. *The wall must guard a sheltered valley—a strong defense position. Even if you dis-*

count the cats, it's easy to see why nobody wants to take on the Sharith.

I just hope I can find some answers, get out of here with my skin intact, and get that skin back past Zaddorn.

I looked up at Bareff and Liden, who were still mounted. The heads of the cats were turned toward me, nodding slightly with their heavy breathing. Was it my imagination, or had the gleam of hatred I had seen in the eyes of Bareff's sha'um faded somewhat?

He's just tired, I decided. *And he deserves to be. It wasn't an easy trip for them, either.*

"Your sha'um," I asked the men, "what are their names?"

"Their names?" Liden sounded surprised. His jaw had returned to normal size, but the bruise had turned so black that the white of his scar looked like an open wound. He reached forward and stroked his hand along the cat's right jaw. "Cheral."

I looked at Bareff.

He made the same gesture and said: "Poltar."

I moved to stand in front of the two huge cats. Poltar was much darker and shorter than Keeshah; Cheral had a rangy look, and splashes of slightly varying shades of tan, giving his fur an indistinct color. They were standing, still carrying their Riders, and I had to look up into their faces.

I raised my hands to my waist level, palms upward.

"Poltar, and Cheral—thank you."

The two great heads lowered, and my upturned palms felt the very lightest touch of their furred muzzles.

I turned away and started walking toward the gates, trying to clear a tightness from my throat. I would have given everything, at that moment, to have Keeshah with me to ride through those gates as the unquestioned equal of the Sharith. But if I couldn't ride Keeshah, I'd walk.

I had taken only a few steps when I discovered that I had company: Bareff and Liden on either side of me, Poltar and Cheral following them. I glanced quickly at their battered faces, but they stared straight ahead and didn't look at me. So I turned my eyes forward and the three of us marched abreast toward the city gates.

We approached the man with the red sash, stopped, and waited. He glanced up at us, his face almost hidden by the brim of the hat which shaded his eyes, and nodded slightly to acknowledge our presence. Then he gave his attention back to the caravan master and his tally sheet.

The man with the sash seemed satisfied, and he signed one of his men to hand over a colored cloth, which was tied to the pack of the leading vlek. Then he turned to us.

"Bareff. Liden." He didn't even look at me. "Come inside the gate; the fleabitten vleks will not pass while your sha'um wait out here. And though Shaben is one of the few who pay their fair duty willingly, I have had enough of caravaners for one day."

We walked through the gate, and I had another surprise. I had not yet seen any city gate in Gandalara closed, even at night—but the heavy wood-and-bronze gates of Thagorn swung shut behind us.

Now he looked at me. I couldn't see his eyes, but the hat brim moved up and down in my direction. "Is this the man you sent the message about?"

"Yes," answered Bareff.

"He wants to talk to the Lieutenant," added Liden.

I was relieved to learn that red-sash wasn't the Lieutenant. I hadn't gotten a clear look at his face, but I was sure he was fairly young. Something in his slimness or the slight swagger in his walk, the effort audible in his speech to make his light baritone voice convey authority.

"*He* wants to talk, does he? Well, talk, groundwalker."

"To the Lieutenant," I said quietly.

The boy took a deep breath—to calm himself or to swell his chest, probably a little of both.

"I am Thymas, Dharak's son. Anything you have to say—"

"He'll say to the Lieutenant," Bareff interrupted. "After he's had a chance to get cleaned up."

"And what say do you have in this?" the boy asked, seething. "He's a common groundwalker—"

"He's not a *common* groundwalker, Thymas," Liden said, "and he's here as our guest."

"Tell your father that *we* need to talk to him. Tonight, if possible. We'll come to the Hall after supper," said Bareff. He nudged me and the three of us, followed by the cats, started off toward some large buildings to the right.

Behind us, we heard a sword leave its scabbard. "You need a lesson in manners, Bareff," said the boy's voice, shaking with anger. "I am the Lieutenant's son; no one gives me orders!"

Bareff stopped and turned slightly, talking over his shoulder. "You make me draw my sword, I'll have to kill you, boy. Now no groundwalker, even an *uncommon* one, is worth this kind of fuss. Ask Dharak. Let him decide. *But ask him.*" We started forward again. My back itched until I heard Thymas put away his sword and move off in the opposite direction.

I also heard muffled laughter and whispering from the ramparts of the wall. *Public humiliation,* I thought, *is no way to make a friend of the boss's son.*

The large buildings turned out to be barracks, with a dining area and individual, fairly comfortable apartments. Bareff pulled out some of his own clothes for me—"civvies," I was relieved to note, instead of a tan uniform—and directed me to the common bath-house near the river which bisected the valley. Then he and Liden went off to attend to their cats. They joined me later; we returned to the barracks and were served a flavorful rafel by a girl of an age equivalent to thirteen or fourteen human years. Then we walked back to the main thoroughfare which led from the gate, crossed it, and climbed a gentle hill toward a big square building which topped it.

I had expected an ornate audience hall such as I had seen in European palaces. Instead, we went through one of many sha'um-sized doors into a HALL.

It had a high ceiling, walls of wood parquetry polished to a high glow, and a floor inlaid with thousands of small marble tiles that must have come from Omergol. It was the size of half a football field, and in its exact center a huge block of pale green marble served as a speaking and review platform.

There were two men standing on the platform. One was the boy who had met us at the gate. He wasn't wearing his hat now, and the light from oil lamps suspended from the ceiling washed over a head of pale golden hair, lighter even than Illia's.

And the halo seemed drab compared to the white crown the other man wore. While the boy seemed only to be waiting for us, the man beside him was compelling us, drawing us across the marble floor toward him like a magnet.

He was wearing tunic and trousers of desert tan like the others, but the cloth was a tighter, finer weave. The tunic draped softly, and was cinched to the large man's trim, muscular waist with a blue sash of a material that resembled shiny brocade. The trousers were tucked into the tops of sueded leather boots, and the upper edges of the boots were reinforced and trimmed with leather stitching on the outer edges.

He was an elegant, commanding figure: the Lieutenant.

Bareff and Liden and I had marched, shoulder to shoulder, in silence across the huge room. There had been only the whisper of cloth against cloth and the reassuring swish of my sword against my pantleg as we walked. I had dared only one quick glance at the other two: the rough, marginally sloppy men I had encountered in a bar in Omergol had been transformed into soldiers.

As we halted neatly in front of the dais, I called up my own military training. I needed every inch of it to stand at attention under the penetrating eyes of the Lieutenant.

"Why is a groundwalker brought before me armed?" he said at last. His voice was rich and deep, resonant in the empty Hall. If there had been a thousand troops around us, every last one of them could have heard him clearly.

Beside me, Bareff spoke up. "His name is Rikardon." There was respect in his voice, but no fear or tension. "He won our life-debts, and freely gave them back. He said he needed to talk to you."

"And you think I should listen?" the Lieutenant asked. "What do you say, Liden?"

"I say he's not afraid of sha'um. By the time we got here, he was riding second place with respectable skill. Poltar was carrying him willingly."

"Cheral, too, Lieutenant. I don't know what he wants with you," Bareff said, "but I'll stand for him while he's in Thagorn."

"So will I," added Liden.

The Lieutenant stepped down from the dais to stand in front of me. Thymas moved to the edge of the platform, his hand on the hilt of his sword.

"Rikardon," the Lieutenant said, nodding slightly at me. He was taller than I, with a narrow face well-lined with age. The bristling shock of snow-white fur which swept back from his prominent forehead seemed anomalous to me—everywhere I had been so far, age had darkened the Gandalaran brow.

"Dharak," I said, and nodded back at him.

For a few seconds we just stared at one another.

"You bring a high recommendation, Rikardon," he said at last. "Say what you have to say. I'll listen."

19

"Someone I care about is unfairly accused as a thief, Lieutenant," I said. "I believe that the stolen article was on the caravan of Gharlas and I know that the Sharith—un—*acquired* the goods on that caravan. May I look through them?"

"The goods we—uh—*acquired,*" he said with the hint of a smile, "have already been distributed among the families. Perhaps if you'll tell us what you're looking for . . . ?"

I cupped my hands close together and called up Markasset's memory. The men around me faded and I spoke to them through a vision of the Ra'ira resting in its glass case. "A gem about this size, Lieutenant. Irregular, clear blue if you look through the edge, darker and twisting toward the center—"

"The Ra'ira!" Thymas shouted, startling all of us. "Father, if the Ra'ira has left Raithskar—"

Dharak whirled toward his son, and Thymas's voice choked in his throat. "Bareff, Liden," said the Lieutenant as he turned back to us, "you've done well, bringing Rikardon to me. I understand I owe you, Bareff, another vote of thanks for not taking Thymas up on his challenge this afternoon."

"Father!"

The Lieutenant went on as if he hadn't heard the furious outcry. "If you wish it, Thymas will apologize publicly for his rude treament of your guest and his disrespect to you."

"I'll do it when Eddarta frees the slaves!" The boy jumped down from the platform and started to draw his sword.

Dharak caught Thymas's sword hand in one of his, and forced the sword back. They stood there, eye to eye, a tableau of the struggle between generations. Then Thymas relaxed, lowered his gaze, and stepped back a pace. The muscles along his neck stood out with the force of his anger.

The old man seemed outwardly calm, but the torchlight reflected from his eyes with an odd shine.

"The boy needn't apologize," said Bareff. "It's all past the gate now, anyway."

"Thank you," said Dharak. "Again. You're training the cubs tomorrow morning, aren't you?"

Bareff nodded.

"Then I'll let you get on with your preparations. You brought Rikardon here, left him, and didn't hear a word he had to say. Understood?"

Liden and Bareff both nodded, then turned to me. "I hope someday we find out what this was all about," said Liden.

"I don't know all the answers, myself," I told them. "Thanks for your help."

Bareff barked a short laugh. "Sure. Anytime you need more help, just kick our teeth out again."

He slapped me on the shoulder, and he and Liden started back toward the door through which we had entered. The Lieutenant waved at me, and he and I, followed by Thymas, walked around the dais toward a door in the opposite wall.

"As you can guess, we would have recognized the Ra'ira if it had been with the caravan," the Lieutenant told me. "No man or woman of the Sharith would keep it from its rightful place in Raithskar. That would be breaking the pledge made by the first Lieutenant to Serkajon during the time of the Last King."

We had reached the door, and we stepped outside to find it already dark. Thymas and Dharak reached to either side of the doorway for torches, and I looked out over the valley of Thagorn.

Across the stream which divided the long valley, single-family homes had been built in clusters of six, with a community cooking area in the center of each. I had noticed that much as we had climbed to the Hall. At night each cluster cast a soft glow upward into the blackness, the inner walls of the homes reflecting and channeling the cheerful light of the cookfires.

It looked as though someone had lit giant candles and placed them with pleasing randomness on the floor and around the edge of the valley.

Through the silence surrounding the empty Hall, we could hear distant laughter, and catch strains of music from a stringed instrument. Children screeched and were hushed. Sha'um roared and were quieted. The sounds came to us clearly, if faintly, from across the stream.

It was so beautiful that I wanted to share it. I reached out for Keeshah.

Yes, came the acknowledgement instantly, eagerly. The touch of that warm and familiar link made the beauty of the night complete.

Can you see, Keeshah? Through me? Can you see this?

There was a moment of silence, then a question so wistful that I felt my chest tighten with physical pain.

I come there?

Not now, Keeshah, I told him. *_What I'm doing here is too important to my father. But one day we'll come back together. I can't promise,_* I told him, thinking about the horrible moment when the point of my sword sank into a man's throat, *_but if it's possible at all, we'll return to Thagorn together one day._*

Light sparked beside me and I jumped, breaking the contact with Keeshah. Thymas had lit a torch with a small contraption that looked like a pair of tongs. The arms were twisted as well as curved, so that their tips would pass one another. In the tips were mounted a piece of flint and a very small piece of steel. This, I reflected, must be Gandalara's primary use of Raithskar's rakor. No wonder a _sword_ made of steel was so rare and highly prized.

We turned away from the peaceful scene on the other side of the stream and went back down the hill toward one of the barracks buildings.

"Some of the caravan people are still with us, waiting for the arrival of Eumin, the slave trader from Eddarta," explained the Lieutenant. "Perhaps one of them has information which will help you find the Ra'ira."

A recent memory crossed my mind. "Is there among them, by any chance, a man with four fingers on his left hand? The smallest finger missing?"

"I have seen too little of them to know," said Dharak. "Thymas? Have you seen such a man?"

"Yes, Father," said Thymas, who had remained strictly silent after the confrontation with his father. There was a note of controlled excitement underneath the subdued tone he used now. "A man called Hural. He has been very quiet since his capture, hardly eating."

"We'll soon find out what he knows about this," the Lieutenant assured me grimly. "I blame myself in part; I should have known that Gharlas, flea though he is, wouldn't have come to us just for the reasons he gave me. He—"

Just then a shout of laughter rang out from the guards on the wall, which lay now to our right. We had reached the main avenue and had clear sight of the gate area, which was ablaze with light activity. Four men on each side swung open the huge doors of the gate, and two men rode through it. A shapeless bundle was suspended between them in what looked like a rope net; the supporting lines for that cargo net were looped around the men's hips so that they, and not their cats, would bear the chafing.

The bundle was moving and shouting. I felt every single hair on my head stand at attention.

It was Zaddorn's voice.

There flashed through my mind, finally, that memory of Markasset's which had been warning me vaguely but eluding me as to specifics. It was the end of a foot race, an annual event by the size of the crowd cheering as Zaddorn was awarded the cash prize. He looked much younger in the memory, and Markasset felt much younger—and exhausted. He had come in a poor second to Zaddorn, who wasn't even breathing heavily.

In a world where most people traveled on foot, Zaddorn was an endurance runner. The memory gave me another piece of information, too. Clearly through the years came the special smirk of triumph Zaddorn flashed to Markasset from the awards area. Their rivalry had not begun with Illia.

The Lieutenant called to the two Riders, and they swerved toward the sound of his voice. Their cats stopped barely two yards away from us and sidled closer together so that the bundle slapped to the ground; they released brass catches at their hips to loosen the carrying ropes.

I felt a sweeping relief. Had things happened differently, I was certain that I'd have arrived in Thagorn in exactly this manner.

Zaddorn quieted until he had been unrolled and untangled from the net. One of the Riders leaned down to help him up; Zaddorn grabbed one of the man's legs and jerked him off balance, delivering a knee into his midsection as the man fell. Zaddorn twisted on the ground to face the other Rider, but stopped dead still. The point of a bronze sword hovered just above his throat.

"You put your groundloving feet in the dirt and stand up, you," the Rider said. He moved his head toward us, and I stepped back a pace, out of the torchlight. "This is Dharak, Lieutenant of the Sharith, and his son, Thymas. Show some respect or I'll gladly give your blood to the ground."

Instantly the snarling, fighting animal who had been hauled into this place as a potential slave was transformed into the elegant city official I had met in Thanasset's house. He stood up and bowed gracefully to the Lieutenant, then a little less deeply to Thymas.

His clothes were dusty and torn, and his handsome face was swollen along one side of the jaw. His skin was abraded from the friction of the rope; one muscular shoulder was completely bare, crusted with blood.

"Gentlemen," he said. I could almost see the soft gray of his suit, the swirl of his cape. "May I introduce myself? I am Zaddorn, Chief of Peace and Security for the City of Raithskar. I have come in friendship, seeking only information. I am looking for—"

I had been quiet long enough. "The same thing I am," I said, interrupting and stepping forward. Zaddorn wasn't surprised to see me; rather, he smiled with satisfaction. "A man with four fingers on his left hand."

Zaddorn stared at me, considering. It was obvious he knew I hadn't told the Lieutenant who I was, and that identifying me would prove me a liar. I was standing, armed, in the company of the leader of the Sharith and he had been dragged into Thagorn like a load of glith skins. He wanted to expose me; I could see it in the way his jaw tensed.

But his jaw relaxed. *You're a good cop, Zaddorn,* I thought at him. *The crime—or the mystery—comes before your personal feelings. Thanks.*

"Have you found him?" he asked.

"Not yet," I answered, and gestured vaguely toward the barracks buildings. "But he's here. A man named Hural."

The Lieutenant had been following our exchange, looking from me to Zaddorn.

"Is this man a friend of yours?" Dharak asked me.

In the silence that followed, I watched Zaddorn. We both knew what the situation was. In Raithskar, I was a suspect in a robbery and a possible candidate for the Gandalaran equivalent of second degree murder—of a cop, no less—and his main rival for an attractive woman. In Thagorn, he knew he needed me. And how he *hated* it.

I'm no saint. I let him worry for a few seconds. I even enjoyed it a little.

"He is not my friend, Lieutenant. But he's telling you the truth. He's an officer of the government of Raithskar." I remembered the phrase Bareff had used. "I'll stand for him while he's here."

"Good enough," said Dharak, and waved away the guards.

"My sword—" began Zaddorn.

"Will be returned to you when you leave," said Dharak. "Now listen well. Rikardon has given his life as bond for your good behavior."

Is that what it means? Holy—!

"In Thagorn, that means silence except when you're spoken to," Dharak continued. "Understand?"

Zaddorn nodded, and Dharak grinned.

"All right. Thymas, go find this Hural and bring him here."

There were several people sitting and standing around the cookfire near the barracks. Thymas went over to them, spoke to one of them, then approached a dark bundle lying against the wall of the building. He said something, grew impatient, then leaned over and dragged a small man to his feet. The man coughed raspily, jerked his arm out of Thymas's grasp, and staggered toward us. He came into the circle of our torchlight; I was holding the torch Thymas had carried down from the Hall. When he saw me, he lurched forward and peered up into my face. His breath smelled foul.

"You," he whispered, and spluttered through a choking cough. "You were supposed to guard the fleabitten caravan! Where were you when the Sharith attacked?" His eyes narrowed. He laughed insanely, his voice rising, then gurgling into another racking cough.

"That's enough out here," said Dharak. "Let's go inside. Bring him, Thymas."

Dharak led the way into another barracks, this one apparently empty. He lit a lamp and placed it on the largest dining table, and we sat down around it. The little man had worked himself into a regular fit, and he lay half across the table, coughing and gasping for breath.

I was glad of the short break. I could almost hear Zaddorn thinking it, and my own mind echoed his question: *That's right, Markasset, where were you when the Sharith attacked? And what is your connection with Gharlas?*

20

The lamp was a thick, smokeless candle placed inside a beautifully faceted glass chimney. It cast a remarkable amount of illumination over the faces of the others at the table: Hural and Thymas across from me and Zaddorn, Dharak at one end of the table.

"Awright," said the four-fingered man at last. "Whattaya want with me?" His words were slurred and hurried, as though they were being chased by a cough.

"Answers," I said. "You helped Gharlas steal the Ra'ira. How did you get into the security room? Where has Gharlas taken the gem?"

"You'll ride a thaka before I tell you anything, you filthy, sneaking—"

Thymas caught the man by the back of his neck and nearly lifted him from the chair. "Show the proper respect," he grated, "or you'll be missing more fingers."

He let Hural down. The little man rubbed his neck and looked hatefully at Thymas, then over at me. For the first time, he noticed Zaddorn. "Hey, ain't you the Chief of Security from Raithskar?"

"I am Zaddorn, yes," he answered.

"Keeping low company, ain't ya?" he sneered.

"That will be enough," said Dharak, the command in his voice making Hural cringe back from him. "Answer the questions."

"Why should I? You gonna give me my freedom and make me healthy again? Eh? What you got to offer?"

"Revenge," said the Lieutenant. "You've no need to keep

silent out of loyalty to Gharlas. Rikardon, here, did not betray the caravan to us. Gharlas paid us handsomely—not only to raid the caravan but to kill everyone on it."

"Kill—?" Hural assimilated it rapidly, and his face stiffened. "Then why didn't you?"

"It seemed wasteful. Obviously Gharlas never wanted to see you and the others again. We could accomplish that as effectively by assuring your presence in Eddarta's copper mines as by destroying you. And make a tidy profit."

"Why?" I asked. "Did Gharlas tell you why he wanted this?"

The Lieutenant frowned. "As I said before, I blame myself for not seeing through him at once. He gave me a complicated story about the trip having been funded by a man he hated. It would be an amusing vengeance, he told me, to use his rival's money to pay for his rival's ruin." Dharak shrugged. "It sounds patently stupid repeated like that. All I can say is that Gharlas in person is a very persuasive man. I agreed to it, though I couldn't tell you, at this instant, why I did."

"I'll tell you why," spoke up Hural, and there was bitterness in his hurried whisper. "You said he's persuasive. He's all of that and more. Gharlas has the ancient power—he can control minds!" This last was almost shrieked, and set off another bout of coughing. When he had recovered somewhat, he stared across at me.

"Yes, I'll tell you; why not? You asked about the security room. Gharlas used his power to make the old man *believe* he locked the door—he didn't. We walked right in!" A shrill giggle, choked off by fear of more coughing.

"Why did Gharlas want the Ra'ira?" asked Zaddorn, and Dharak and Thymas were too interested to rebuke him for speaking out of turn.

"Now that's the weird part. I been overseeing Gharlas's caravans for a long time. I've known he's not quite right up here." He tapped his temple with a finger of his mangled left hand. "I've always thought it pretty strange that he always—and I mean *always*—got his way around people.

"This trip seemed pretty ordinary until we got to Raithskar. We stopped here, paid the tribute, Gharlas worked his deal—but I didn't know about that. After we've set up in Raithskar, he calls me to his room one night and confesses that he is—get this!—*the rightful King of Gandalara*. And he's going to prove it by taking the Ra'ira back to Eddarta with him.

"I ask him how he plans to get away with that, and he gives me the news about this power he's had all along. His eyes are shining and strange and I *know* he's gone over the Wall."

Hural stopped, cleared his throat, and spat on the floor—to the obvious disgust of the Lieutenant and Thymas.

"But—you know—we been together a long time. And he scares me with that power stuff—maybe he was using it on me, I don't know. But anyway, I went along; I helped him steal the filthy thing."

"How was this man involved?" Zaddorn asked, pointing at me.

"Him?" The little man grinned. "What was it you called him? 'Rikardon'? Well, that's not the name he gives me. He tells me he's—"

My body went completely tense; I could feel a similar movement in Zaddorn beside me.

"—Lakad. Says he's from *Chizan*."

That's why the alias I used in Omergol came so easily, I thought. *I—Markasset—had used it before.*

"He comes to me the night before we're scheduled to leave and wants to hire on as a guard. Well, I already know there's going to be a special, important cargo this trip, and he looks strong enough, so I says yes. But the next morning, when we're packing and this guy shows up for duty—at the last minute, so late I'd given up on him—Gharlas has a regular fit! He don't say anything to you, but to me he says plenty. Don't I know Sharith agents are everywhere? Didn't I have more sense than to hire on a stranger? And so on. And later, when the Riders came in without any warning, and you had been on guard duty, I figured Gharlas was right."

"What happened to Gharlas?" I asked. "Where was he when the Sharith attacked?"

"Didn't see him. Figured at the time that he was one of the lucky ones to escape," he said wryly. "Now I guess he just left us during the night—some old friend, eh?"

The cough had been suppressed long enough, and now it shook him again. The thin shoulders jumped violently as he doubled over the table. When he sat up, still panting heavily, there were flecks of blood on the table and around his mouth. He looked at me with eyes that were glazed with pain.

"Cheated two kinds of fate," he said, and allowed himself a thin, gasping laugh. "First the Riders don't kill me like Gharlas wanted, then they don't get to sell me, either."

"What do you mean?" I asked, but I was all too sure what he meant.

"I'm dying," he said. "Known it since this morning. Wanted it." He looked up at the Lieutenant. "Lost finger same place I picked up this nuisance cough—copper mines of Eddarta. Cough goes away if I eat right. Stopped eating when I came here. *Never going back to those mines*." He said it with such force that he began to gasp. He was too weak now even to cough. Thymas had an arm around his back, supporting him.

"Please, Hural," I asked him, horrified by what was happening but desperate for some answers at last, "where is the Ra'ira? What happened to it?"

His eyes turned to me, focused with great effort.

"Gharlas . . . has . . . it," he said.

It was the last thing he said.

Some hours later, I was standing outside the door of the Lieutenant's richly appointed home. It was situated on a rise near the river, the only single-family dwelling on the barracks side. I had been there for several minutes, watching the candle-flames of the cookfires dwindle, one by one, and die down.

We had turned Hural's body over to the Sharith guards, and had come here. A gracefully aging, smiling woman had greeted her huband and son with warm affection, and had served us faen as we sat around a tile-topped table. The conversation had remained neutral until Shola excused herself, which she had done as soon as she had realized we were all thinking about something else.

"Do you believe what he said?" I had asked Zaddorn as soon as she had left. "About the mind-power Gharlas claims to have?"

Thymas had spoken up before Zaddorn could answer. "Such power exists," he said excitedly. "We have seen it used."

"Indeed?" Zaddorn had inquired. "By Gharlas, you mean?"

"No, I don't mean Gharlas," Thymas had said impatiently. "I'm talking about Tarani."

"An illusionist with a traveling show who stops by here now and then," Dharak had explained. "The illusions are so perfect that no other conclusion is possible. And Tarani admits to holding the power, tells us in every show that it is being used, and challenges us to see through the illusions. We can't.

"Yes, I must agree that the kind of power Hural described is possible. There is no evil in the illusions cast by Tarani for our entertainment. But the idea of Gharlas with such power and, if Hural again is to be believed, with such ambition—" He had shuddered. "The old words are true: 'To crave power is to be ruled by madness.' Surely Gharlas *must* be mind-ill."

"Oh, I wouldn't argue that point at all," Zaddorn had agreed. "But what *Rikardon* wants to know is whether I believe that Gharlas has that power and used it to steal the Ra'ira." He had looked at me thoughtfully for a long moment, fair repayment for the few seconds I had let him squirm before I spoke up for him to Dharak.

"Yes," he had said at last, "I believe him. He was dying; he had no reason to lie. And it explains some puzzling things: how he learned about the security system, for instance, as well as how he got into a supposedly locked room—without the aid of the Supervisor on duty.

"I believe him," he had repeated, "and that's what I'll tell the Council of Supervisors when we get back to Raithskar."

I had let out a sigh of pure relief. Thanasset was safe.

The Lieutenant, too, had seemed to relax from the edge of tension. Thymas, however, had reared back indignantly.

"Back to Raithskar?" he had repeated incredulously. "Aren't you going after Gharlas, to get the Ra'ira back?"

"My duty is in Raithskar," Zaddorn had explained quietly, stifling a yawn. "I'll send discreet messages to the security people in the other cities; I'll be notified when Gharlas turns up. We'll get it back, don't worry."

"Don't worry?" Thymas had repeated again. "The Ra'ira *belongs* in Raithskar. You can't just—"

"That will be enough, Thymas," Dharak had cut him off abruptly. "For the second time today," he had said to Zaddorn, "I must apologize for my son's manners." Zaddorn had nodded; the boy glared at his father but had said nothing. "It's getting late," Dharak had said then, "and we all need some rest. You'll want to leave for Raithskar tomorrow, of course."

And the group had separated. Zaddorn and I had excused ourselves and left father and son together to talk things over.

Zaddorn had accepted an earlier offer of the use of Dharak's private bath-house, and I had stepped outside to be alone with my thoughts for a few minutes.

Thanasset was in the clear at last—that was the most important thing. I thought about the man I had killed and regretted it, sharply, again. Not because of the possible consequences now, but because I hadn't wanted it to happen. And because I knew Thanasset well enough to know that a death in his service must have grieved him.

I let my thoughts wander through the time I had spent in Gandalara. Idly I counted the days and was astonished to realize that it had been less than two weeks. I felt a strong life-investment here. I had met people I respected, some of whom I also loved. I had begun to get a feel for Markasset, though I still didn't know him. Hural's information hadn't explicitly cleared Markasset of any involvement—I still didn't know how he wound up in the desert, or who the dead man . . .

I had been leaning against the wall of Dharak's home. Now I stood up straight, startled.

Could that have been Gharlas? I wondered. *I searched him thoroughly and he didn't have the stone. Can it be that the precious Ra'ira is wandering out in that desert right now, riding Gharlas' masterless vlek?*

I was so occupied with this new line of thought that I barely noticed a young boy run up to the front door to my left, knock, and go in.

Come on, Markasset, I pleaded silently. *What did Gharlas look like? Was he that dead body? It will look queer for me to ask about a man it's been proven I knew—but if I have to, I will.*

I was distracted, then, by the appearance of Dharak through his front door. He looked first to his left, then turned to his right and saw me. He was holding a strip of cloth in his hand.

"Oh, there you are, Markasset. I have news."

"News?" I asked. Then it hit me. "You—you called me—"

"I've known all along who you are," he said calmly. "Come, step away from the house and I'll explain."

We walked down the hill toward the river, which made a constant rushing noise—not loud, but soothing. Away from the lighted windows of the house, it was pitch black. Only the sound of Dharak's voice told me where he was.

"It's quite true that we Sharith have 'agents everywhere', as it is whispered in every marketplace," he said, laughing lightly. "They are people who owe us loyalty for one reason or another. And they do not, as most people seem to think, merely spy out the caravans which do not pay their proper portion to the Sharith.

"We are isolated here in this valley," he continued. "By choice, it is true, a choice made long ago, a bond sworn and kept by generation after generation. But isolated, none the less. Our agents tell us what is going on in the world.

"Naturally, as soon as the Ra'ira was stolen, we heard about it."

"But Thymas—your son seemed surprised," I said.

"He was. All communications come directly to me. I was the only one who read that one, and I didn't tell Thymas about it. For that matter, I didn't tell anyone."

"Why is the Ra'ira so important to him?"

Dharak sighed. "It is important to all of us. You, of all people, must know the story of Serkajon."

"That he took the Ra'ira back to Raithskar, that the King's guard followed him there for vengeance, but instead abandoned the King and settled here in Thagorn."

"That's essentially it. Serkajon convinced the first Lieutenant that the Ra'ira was a symbol of power, and that the Kings had outlived their right to power. That first Lieutenant had sworn loyalty to Serkajon and to his purpose: to keep the Ra'ira surrounded with honorable men so that no single man could ever use its beauty to call to himself power over other men."

I was beginning to understand. I thought of the gemstones in Ricardo's world which had carried "curses" of ill luck and evil fates. All of them that I could recall had been coveted for their beauty as well as for their value. The Ra'ira was a compellingly beautiful stone, the kind to attract legend. Originally a symbol of a city's loyalty to its King, it had changed hands again during the social upheaval associated with the end of a monarchy. It may have been only coincidence; it may not. But certainly, if it had not already acquired its reputation when Kä fell apart, that event, following so closely the removal of the Ra'ira, had stamped a mystic aura of power on the beautiful gem.

"I am merely the Lieutenant. Because Thanasset no longer

rides, you are, by right of heritage, the Captain. Originally, I kept silence out of a sense of duty to your family.

"Among the Sharith, rank must be earned. The messages said only that you had fled, but I refused to prejudge you as a coward. When you *walked* into Thagorn, you proved several things to me. First, it took a great fighter to win the respect of Bareff and Liden. Second, it took a great commitment of loyalty to deny yourself the companionship of your sha'um for any man's sake. Third, Zaddorn didn't race out here merely after the information Hural had; he was chasing you. Yet you have treated him with honor, and you will return with him to Raithskar to set straight whatever he holds against you.

"So, after I had the chance to know you, I kept silence still out of a sense of duty—to you. As far as I'm concerned, you *are* the new Captain, and in spite of Thymas's impatience, I will await your orders about the Ra'ira."

I began to breathe again as Dharak continued talking, a disembodied voice in the darkness saying incredible things. *Not me,* I was thinking frantically. *No Captain here, I'm just an NCO. Don't call me "sir"!*

"Of course, you must settle things in Raithskar first, and that brings me to the news," he was saying. "Rumors about the theft have spread widely through Raithskar until there has been a general demand for answers. Tonight's message tells me that the Chief Supervisor has had to yield to public pressure and suspend Thanasset from the Council."

"*What?*" I was jolted from my momentary panic. "Thanasset suspended? When?"

"Only today. But the message says things are getting ugly. The public has begun to believe that Thanasset did cooperate with the thieves. They are calling him a traitor and asking for the forfeit of his property."

I felt a chill crawl up my spine. "A mob."

"I'm afraid so. From what I've seen of Zaddorn, I'd say he could control them, but he's not there now." He hesitated. I could almost hear him deciding whether or not to tell me what I had already guessed. "You and Zaddorn need your rest tonight, Markasset—but tomorrow, I suggest haste. The people are asking for more than Thanasset's rank—

"They are demanding his life."

21

I was glad to find Zaddorn already asleep in the room we were to share. I lay down on the fluffy pallet on my side of the room, called Keeshah and arranged for a meeting place the next day, and tried to blank out my mind. I thought it would be impossible—but it seemed only a moment later that I woke to sunlight streaming in through the latticed window.

Zaddorn and I said our farewells at the gate of Thagorn. Thymas was still sour and resentful, but his words were courteous enough. Bareff and Liden grinned and waved at me from a distance; I called to them to say goodbye to their sha'um for me. The Lieutenant exchanged a few polite words with Zaddorn, then turned to me.

"I have no doubt you will return to Thagorn soon, Rikardon. It will be my pleasure then to greet you personally, and show you more of the life of the Sharith."

"I'd like that very much, Lieutenant," I said, ignoring Thymas's startled look as best I could. I fell back on Ricardo's customs once more and offered my hand. "I can't promise I'll be back, but I'll try. I'd like to get to know you and your people better."

Dharak hesitated only briefly, then gripped my hand so strongly that I felt a sudden surge of affection for him. I knew I wasn't the man he thought I was—but just for a moment I wanted to be. He carried a tremendous burden of leadership.

He and Thanasset should meet, I decided at that moment. *They'd understand each other. They both have slightly inappropriate sons.*

I was warmed, then, by a feeling of kinship with Thymas, and impulsively I offered him my hand, too. He looked surprised, then took it. Dharak smiled at the look of puzzlement on his face.

Then Zaddorn and I set out at a jog for the place where I had asked Keeshah to meet me this morning, the stream which had been my last stop on the trip to Thagorn. I had given Zaddorn the news about the developments in Raithskar. He had agreed, grimly, that we had to hurry back. But he had been quietly noncommittal when I assured him that Keeshah could carry us both.

So we traveled in silence, expending all our energy in covering distance. It suited us both, I think—as I had told Dharak, we weren't friends. As Gra'mama Maria Constanza would have said, if you can't say something nice . . .

Shortly before noon we left the road and headed for the appointed spot. Keeshah was already there, and he could wait no longer. He came running to meet me. He was still some distance away when we could hear him crashing through some thick brush. Zaddorn stopped, but I paid no attention. The trees were taller here, and the ground generally less overgrown, than was usual in this area; I caught a glimpse of Keeshah's tawny head and I started running, too.

The one with you? Keeshah asked. **Friend?**

Yes, I called. **Thank you for being patient.**

It was hard, he told me, not griping or boasting, just stating the truth.

I know. I've missed you, too.

When we were about three yards apart, I caught the glimmer of joyous mischief from him—it wasn't enough warning.

Keeshah came straight at me, bent his neck downward, and rammed me in the stomach with his forehead, knocking me off my feet. Still running, he lifted his head and flipped me up and over his back in a dizzy somersault. I crashed into a tall cluster of the curly trees and grabbed desperately at branches as I fell. I managed not to break my skull when I hit the ground.

That's where I stayed, because Keeshah was right on top of me, grinding his muzzle into my chest. I grabbed his head and twisted, trying to wrestle him down to the ground. He roared and began to scoot backwards, shaking his head to dislodge me. He dragged me a good, scratchy ten yards before I gave up.

"Enough, Keeshah," I gasped out loud, out of breath from laughing.

He nudged my chest again, this time almost tenderly.

Together, he said. **Glad.**

Then he lay down beside me, panting a little from the run

and the playful struggle, and rested his chin on my outstretched arm. A few minutes later, Zaddorn's voice penetrated our peaceful communion.

"I couldn't see what was happening," he said, "but that *sounded* like a lot of fun."

"It was," I said, ignoring his sarcasm, and stood up.

Home now? Keeshah asked me.

Yes, I told him. **All three of us must go, Keeshah. I know it will be hard for you to carry two all that way, but it's important.**

I can do it, he said, almost scornfully. **I won't. Not him. You don't like him.**

I felt a deep sense of sympathy for Bareff. But if he could convince his sha'um to carry a man who had beaten him senseless . . .

As I had done then, to convince Keeshah of an urgent need, I reached out to him now. I felt his mind quiet expectantly, and this time it was easier to achieve that intimate bond that conveyed understanding without the need to compose communication symbols.

And Keeshah agreed to carry Zaddorn.

He will mount first, I said to Keeshah, and forestalled his objection. **It will be easier for you; I have learned to ride second.**

Zaddorn had been watching us quietly for the few seconds required for the exchange. Now I turned to Zaddorn and said: "Watch." I sat on Keeshah's back and slid into riding position, then sat up and got off again. "Like that. I'll mount behind you."

Zaddorn didn't move.

"Well?" I said impatiently. "You know how important time is. Get on!"

"I—" It was the first time I had seen Zaddorn lose his composure. There had been a certain style even in the way he had come up fighting from the cargo net in Thagorn. Yet now his face, thinner than ever from the long run across the desert, was ashen white. His dark eyes reminded me of something . . .

"I don't think I can do that."

That's the way I looked in the mirror at Yafnaar, I realized. *Scared right down to my toenails. It's not just that Keeshah's a big, dangerous cat. Zaddorn has spent all his life with both feet on the ground. At least I was accustomed to the idea of riding an animal—he has never even considered it.*

I was learning something else about the relationship between Zaddorn and Markasset. No matter what other triumphs Zaddorn had scored, Markasset held the ace: he had Keeshah.

Well, sympathy won't help him now, I decided.

"Either you get on Keeshah's back," I said aloud, "or he'll carry you through the gates of Raithskar by the seat of your trousers."

The challenge stirred him up, as I had hoped. Zaddorn glared at me, then the muscles along his still-pale jaw twitched with determination. He walked up to Keeshah, sat down on his back as I had done and slid into an approximation of the position I had shown him. I checked both sides, moved his hands a little higher on Keeshah's shoulders, then mounted behind him. He was stiff as a salt block.

He's terrified, I explained, and I had to smile at Keeshah's disgusted agreement. **Stand up slowly and walk around. Let him get used to you.**

There was no direct response from Keeshah, but I felt him getting impatient and stubborn. I had just barely enough time to warn Zaddorn.

"Close your eyes and don't pinch Keeshah's shoulders," I shouted as Keeshah leaped up and set off at full run. He found the road and headed for Raithskar. I was very glad that I couldn't read Zaddorn's mind.

Keeshah tired quickly, of course, and gradually Zaddorn thawed out. We followed the mountain trail, the route by which Keeshah and I had made the trip out. It would have been faster to cross the desert, but Keeshah needed food to sustain him through the trip. There was game for him along the hills.

But we used the same travel pattern Zaddorn had adopted for the sake of speed: travel four hours, rest for one. We took a longer rest occasionally, to allow Keeshah to feed and rest more thoroughly. Zaddorn didn't complain—in fact, our tacit agreement to silence held except for the purely mechanical communication relating to food and rest stops—but I knew he was approaching the end of his endurance by the end of the second day. He had worn himself thin on the way *to* Thagorn, and this constant application of a different kind of strength was telling on him quickly.

For all our sakes, I called a halt near a stream in the late afternoon. I didn't wake him on time, but let him sleep an extra three hours. Keeshah, too, accepted the extra resting time. But though I tried to sleep, I found I couldn't. My head was buzzing with thoughts of Thanasset—what was happening to him? A mob—would they even listen when we got there? Always assuming we would get there on time?

"You let me oversleep," Zaddorn's voice spoke to me from the dark.

"You needed it," I said, then called "Keeshah!" We heard him stand up, stretch and shake himself. "And I need you."

After we had all taken care of some necessary body functions, Keeshah knelt and I waited for Zaddorn to mount.

"You take the front position for a while," he said. "Fair trade for the extra sleep."

"You'll be sorry," I told him, and asked Keeshah to let me know if he were too uncomfortable with Zaddorn riding second.

"Probably," he agreed drily, and we mounted.

It's all right, Keeshah told me after a few minutes. **He learns.**

Gratefully I gave up my weight and my troubled mind to Keeshah's soothing rhythm. I slept clear to the next stop.

After that, we traded positions every time we stopped. Zaddorn, too, learned to nap while Keeshah carried us.

It was noon of the fourth day since we left Thagorn that we rode up to the gates of Raithskar. The last leg had been a long one, Keeshah as eager as we to get back. He pulled up short, snarling, as a cordon of armed men flowed out the gate and surrounded us.

I slid off Keeshah's hindquarters, lifting my hands to show that I had no intention of drawing my sword. Zaddorn sat up, still on Keeshah's back, and the effect on the men was electrifying.

"Zaddorn?" said one of the men, stepping forward and dropping the point of his sword. "We didn't expect you back for another week." He grabbed his gray baldric with one hand and replaced his sword in its sheath. His face said plainly what he wouldn't put into words—certainly they didn't expect Zaddorn to arrive on the back of a sha'um.

Want home, Keeshah told me. He was panting heavily. **Rest. Want home.**

As soon as possible, Keeshah. I promise.

Zaddorn swung his right leg over Keeshah's back and slid to the ground with his characteristic grace. "Well, I'm here now, Klareth. What's the situation?"

"You know about—?"

"Thanasset, yes. Now answer me, man!"

"It's bad, Zaddorn. We've had to put the Supervisor into custody in his own home. The tension had been building ever since he—" he nodded in my direction "—rode out of here. The people took that as an admission of guilt for him and for the Supervisor." His voice dropped almost to a whisper. "I've never seen the people this stirred up about *anything,* Chief. Things could get very nasty any minute now."

"Let's go," Zaddorn said, and started for the gate. I followed him, my hand on Keeshah's neck. The cordon of men fell in around us in a double rank.

There was a lot of whispering in the marketplace as we passed, but nobody challenged us. The crowds got thicker as we approached Thanasset's house, and I felt a coldness in the pit of my stomach.

The street in front of Thanasset's door was packed solid with people. Word of our coming had been shouted ahead, and the crowd turned its attention in our direction.

"There he is," someone yelled, "the traitor's son! How dare he come back to Raithskar?"

"Zaddorn, too!" someone else called. "Zaddorn's with him."

"What news?"

"It's the traitor Markasset!"

The tide of people swept toward us, tumultuous, curious, demanding, abusive. The noise was incredible; even those who merely wanted information wouldn't have been able to hear us. The cordon of men was pressed back by the sheer weight of people until Keeshah—though he wouldn't have phrased it this way—was beginning to feel like a furry sardine.

Home close! he told me impatiently. **I go.**

"I can't hold him back much longer," I shouted in Zaddorn's ear.

"Let him go," he yelled back. "He'll get us some room."

I let him go. By then I didn't have any choice.

Try not to kill anybody!

He shouldered his way between two of the guards and announced to the crowd that *he wanted to move*. A climbing wail of panic began around him and rippled outward. His claws and teeth damaged the nearest people, but the far reaches of the crowd still didn't know what was going on. Many more people were hurt by being crunched between the edge of the mob, still pressing inward, and the center of it trying to get away from Keeshah.

Zaddorn and I followed Keeshah closely, with four men around us guarding our rear. The rest of the cordon got separated and swallowed in the crowd. There were guards around the house shoulder to shoulder, all of them standing tense and quiet until we got close to the garden gate. Then they came forward and formed a protective V around us until the gate was opened and we got through.

I have never felt a sense of relief quite like I felt when that gate had closed behind us.

Keeshah started off for his house, but Zaddorn said: "Call him back. Only for a minute."

I did, and he came grumbling.

"We can't leave that crowd without some information; they'll tear down the house," Zaddorn told me. "Ask Keeshah if I might mount him once more and climb to the top of the wall."

Keeshah knelt for us at my request, and in a few seconds we were both standing on top of the garden wall, a tapering structure of gray brick. The edge was narrow; Zaddorn overbalanced and I caught his arm to steady him. It trembled slightly.

He's about ready to collapse, I thought.

But once he had his balance again, he stood rock-still and waited while the crowd noticed us and roared, realized slowly that Zaddorn was waiting for quiet so he could speak, and, more slowly still, gave him what he wanted. We stood above the silence for a full two minutes, looking over the mass of jutting-browed faces.

Young, old, and in between—they all carried that same terrifying expression. The look of an individual who had discovered the power of many. These groundwalkers were riding now, riding a high sense of strength, and to support that insidious addiction they joined each with his neighbor to keep the power directed. Some of them, I knew, didn't even care *where* the mob's energy was directed; they only wanted to be part of it, to maintain that heady sensation of a current of power flowing through them.

Enough of them had been legitimately concerned—at least originally—that the target for their threatened violence was still what it had been: Thanasset's house. They were quiet, now, waiting. But they could be set off at any moment, and there were far too few of Zaddorn's men to control them.

We need riot guns and tear gas, I thought desperately. Then: *The hell we do! Didn't I tell Thanasset that I liked his world better, where violence was a personal matter rather than a group activity? I'll be damned if I'll let this crowd of misguided fools prove me wrong!*

They had quieted to listen to Zaddorn. But they heard from me first.

"How many of you," I asked, using my best drill-sergeant voice, "know what this is all about?" I didn't wait for an answer, but went right on. "I'd be willing to bet that most of you were on your way to the market, or to school, or back to work, when you saw a crowd starting here and came on over to see what was happening. Some people are angry, they say that a crime is going unpunished—maybe the people you talk to are *strangers,* even, and yet you accept their word for what has happened, and join in, adding to the noise and confusion.

"Well, I want you to *think,* now, about what you're trying to accomplish. Does any of you, individually, want to kill me or my father?" There was a rumble, a couple of affirmative shouts that died when the shouters didn't get immediate support from the people around them. "Then why," I asked them, "would all of you want to do such a thing?

"Oh, you don't want our deaths, you say?" I began to walk along the narrow rim of the wall. "All you want is justice? Fair punishment for whoever stole the Ra'ira? Well, *who made you the judges?*" I shouted at them.

"The theft of the Ra'ira is a crime against Raithskar. It's especially a crime against the Council, and because Thanasset is *under suspicion,* the Council has suspended him until his involvement could be proved or disproved.

"This man," I pointed back to where Zaddorn stood. He had placed himself with a hand against the wall of the house for stability when I started pacing. "This man has worn himself out looking for that proof. He has it. But he doesn't owe it to *you*. You're not concerned citizens of Raithskar—you're a howling, mindless mob! Let him give his evidence to the Council, and let the Council judge us. Raithskar has thrived for generation after generation under the administration of the Council—give them your trust again. Let them decide."

There was a restless movement and a murmur as they became people again instead of a crowd.

Then someone shouted: "Fine words from a man who turned a sha'um loose on us!" He had a point, and the crowd could see it. "And who will it be good for if we turn away now? *Him*, that's who! He wants to save himself and his father. The Council will never rule against them! He said it himself—Thanasset's been a Supervisor too long!"

"That's where you're wrong," said a voice from my right. The door of the house had opened quietly and Ferrathyn stood in front of it now, his slight old body clothed with dignity. The small porch was a couple of steps up from the street level; the crowd could see who it was.

"The Council will judge fairly, with the interest of Raithskar at heart. You know that Thanasset is an old and valued friend to me, but that would not stand in the way of any action, should be Council decide he is in any way to blame for the theft. If you have no faith of your own in the Council, then will you accept my personal guarantee that the matter will be decided according to the evidence, no matter what it may show?"

He's got them, I cheered to myself. *He's turned the tide in our favor!*

"I did not send Keeshah against you," I said quietly. "You pressured him until he couldn't be controlled. And surely, after seeing what he can do, you can have no doubt that I have returned to Raithskar willingly. I mean to stand beside my father as we face the Council's judgment."

"Now," Zaddorn said at last, "all of you go on about your business. And be glad no one was seriously hurt. As soon as anything is decided, an official announcement will be made in the square. Now stop blocking up this street!"

They started to move. Zaddorn and I jumped down into the garden. Keeshah had long since gone into his house.

"You go in and join the others," I told Zaddorn, who

looked ready to fall over. "I'll draw some water for Keeshah and come right in."

He nodded wordlessly; we walked toward the back of the house and he turned left while I continued on toward the back buildings. Keeshah was already sound asleep on his ledge. I drew some water for him and spent a few seconds just standing near him. Then I went up to the back door of the house, comparing how I felt now with the way I had felt that first time.

I had been confused then, frightened of a world I didn't understand, uncertain of my future here. I had a lot to learn, but I was gaining a feel for this world. Ricardo had made his own connections with the people Markasset knew; he had made *Ricardo's* presence mean something in Gandalara.

I paused at the door, assimilating the way things had changed since that other time. While I hesitated, the door opened. Thanasset stood there, smiling a true welcome—for me, and not for Markasset. I was so touched that I couldn't say a word.

But Thanasset, too, had seen the parallel.

"Don't just stand there, son," he said. "Come on in."

22

With exaggerated care, I removed my baldric and hung it on one of the pegs beside the door. Thanasset laughed and slapped me hard on the back, then somehow he was hugging me, quick and hard.

I turned from him to the others, who were all standing in the great hall. Milda said, "Oh, Markasset!" and ran over to me. I wrapped my arms around her and lifted, swinging her around until she was breathless with laughter. Then I set her down and opened my arms to Illia.

"We've been so worried, darling!" she said, and rushed into my arms. Zaddorn or no Zaddorn, I let myself enjoy that kiss. Then, with one arm around the girl, I walked over to where Ferrathyn and Zaddorn were tactfully not watching us.

"Your timing was perfect, sir," I told Ferrathyn. "Thanks."

"Don't thank me, young man," he said, a smile wreathing his face with more wrinkles. "You displayed a gift for oratory your father tells me he never suspected. Without your groundwork, my words would have had no effect.

"Zaddorn has just been giving me the evidence you spoke of. I have no doubts that the Council will reinstate your father with full pay for his missed time." He shook his head. "It's a frightening thing, the reappearance of mind-power in an ambitious man. Gharlas could make trouble for all of Gandalara."

"What's this?" asked Thanasset. "What about mind-power and Gharlas?"

Zaddorn repeated what Hural had told us for the others, who had been busy greeting me while he reported to the Chief Supervisor. Thanasset was horrified.

"And it was used on me? Without my knowledge? Great Serkajon, Ferrathyn, Gharlas must be impossibly strong." He was pale. "You know, now that I know the truth, I almost wish I *had* forgotten to lock the filthy door!"

"You mustn't feel that way, Fa—Thanasset," Illia corrected hurriedly. "After all, this clears you of any blame. And it proves Markasset wasn't involved, too, doesn't it, Zaddorn? Doesn't it?" she repeated when he didn't answer immediately.

"Yes, Illia," he said tenderly, and sighed. "I'd still give a week's pay to find out just what did happen—where he got the money, why he was on the caravan in the first place (and under an alias at that), and why he wasn't around by the time the Sharith attacked. But I've learned enough, about the theft and about our friend," he said, waving a hand at me, "to convince me that he wasn't involved in the theft. Unfortunately, that makes the rest of it none of my business. Oh, he might be chargeable for leaving his post on the caravan, but I doubt that Gharlas will be willing to confront him according to the law.

"So—yes, as far as the office of Peace and Security is concerned, Markasset's name is clear."

"Of involvement with the theft," I corrected him.

"Isn't that what I just said?" he asked.

"I *killed* a man on the way out of Raithskar," I said, thinking: *If they've forgotten, don't remind them! Keep your mouth shut!* But I was too surprised to follow my own advice. "One of your officers."

"One of my—" Zaddorn began. "You mean the man out back, don't you?" He walked over and stood eye to eye with me. "Those men worked for Worfit." He said it quietly, then waited a few seconds, staring at me closely. His words and his attitude were good news and bad news. I waited for the other shoe to drop.

"Markasset would know that all peace officers wear gray baldrics. Who are you?"

"Why—why, he's Markasset, of course!" Illia said and tried to squeeze herself between us, defensively facing Zaddorn. I took her shoulders, stepped back a pace and turned her to face me.

"Illia, I'm sorry you had to find out about this so abruptly, but Zaddorn's right. I'm not Markasset." She put a hand to her mouth and began shaking her head, her dark eyes wide.

I heard a gasp behind her and I looked out at the others. Zaddorn had a calculating look on his face. Milda had made the sound: Thanasset had moved over to her and put an arm around her shoulders. He'd had some time to get used to the idea.

Ferrathyn's face was so gray with shock that I was alarmed. But his sharp mind had worked it all out in a flash, and had come to the same conclusion Thanasset had reached. Only he had gone a step farther, and chosen a logical candidate for the alleged Visitor.

"Are—are you Serkajon?" he whispered.

"No!" I said hastily. "Oh, no." *Don't call me "sir"*, I thought again. "I'm—well, I'm nobody special."

"Rikardon," said Zaddorn. "The name you used in Thagorn?"

I nodded.

"Rikardon?" repeated Illia. "Then w-what happened to Markasset?"

"Please tell us," begged Milda. "I know the boy had his problems, but—but his heart w-was good." She looked tiny and frail in the circle of Thanasset's arm.

I let go of Illia and walked over to take Milda's hands. "Milda darling," I said, and she made a little sobbing sound. "I have some of Markasset's memories—not all. But some of the strongest and happiest concern you." I reached down into Markasset's memories and tried to separate the warm feeling for Milda into separate images. "The sound of your voice singing over the cookstove. The neat way you stitch when you're mending things." I smiled at a memory. "And you never complained when he teased you—did he really unravel your weaving every night for a half a moon?"

"Yes, he did, the scoundrel!" she said with a giggle. She glanced up at Thanasset and said, "I never told you about that, Thanasset—I was afraid you'd really get after the boy. But he unraveled *most* of what I'd done during the day. I went to the loom next day convinced I was crazy because I remembered doing more than I really had done. And once I caught him, I told him he could just learn to do what he'd undone. Your sleeping pallet was woven by your son!" She said it with such triumph that we all laughed and for a moment the tension was broken. Then she looked at me seriously again.

"Thank you for bringing back those happy memories, young man. I want to say that I have no fault to find with you—you've done a great thing for our family, and I'm grateful. But I—will Markasset—is he—?"

"I don't know, Milda," I said gently. "I don't understand what has happened; it might *un*happen at any time and it might not.

"But I want you to believe something. I know how much Markasset loved you, and I love you, too."

"Th-thank you," she said in a shaking voice. I released her hands and she turned her face to Thanasset's shoulder.

"What did happen?" Zaddorn asked.

I shrugged. "I woke up out in the desert with a lump on my head. Everything I know about Markasset—except, as I said, a few scattered memories—I've learned since then."

"So you don't have the answers either?"

"No. I can't remember anything about the night the caravan left, or the night Gharlas disappeared. I can't even remember what Gharlas looks like!"

"And were you," Zaddorn asked in a low, tight voice, "going to marry Illia in Markasset's place?"

"I felt an obligation to complete Markasset's life, since I had somehow borrowed his body. That included keeping his promises."

I walked back over to Illia, who was looking wildly from me to Zaddorn.

"But it's different, now, dear," I told her. "I expected to have to hide behind Markasset when we talked in the garden that day. It's really better this way. I'd like to think that I'd have told you before the wedding, anyway, to give you a fair choice. Let's just leave things for a while so you can get to know the person I really am. And take my advice—give Zaddorn another chance, too. We've been through a lot together these past few days. He's a man I'd trust my back to."

"I—oh, I'm so confused!" she wailed. She looked at Zaddorn steadily for a moment, then turned her dark eyes up to mine. "In the garden that day, and just now—it was *you* kissing me, not Markasset, wasn't it?"

"Yes," I admitted. "I'll admit I appreciate Markasset's taste, and maybe I took advantage just a little. But I don't *know* you yet, and you don't know me. Give it some time. Please."

"Yes," she said at last. "All right."

"Thank you," Zaddorn said, and came toward us, holding out his right hand. "This is your custom, but it's one I like. Welcome to Raithskar, Rikardon." I took his hand gratefully. "I hold nothing of Markasset against you," he said. "And for what it's worth, I think you'll be rougher competition than he was." He glanced at Illia, who lowered her eyes in sudden embarrassment. "But I'll be trying harder."

"Friends," Thanasset drew our attention to him. He came over to me and put an arm around my shoulders. "I'm glad that there is no need of deception among us any longer. I have known about Rikardon since the day he returned to Raithskar from the desert. I saw no need to worry you, Milda," he added.

"I regret the loss of my son," he said, and had to pause for a second or two. "But in Rikardon I have found qualities Markasset lacked: steadiness, confidence, a strong feeling for what is right and the conviction to stand by it. Whatever brought him here, he awoke into a mess not of his own making. He accepted and fulfilled Markasset's obligations.

"We cannot tell if Markasset will ever be returned to us; we must accept Rikardon in his place." He walked over to the portrait of the sha'um, stretched up and brought down the sword of Serkajon. I realized, suddenly, what he was going to do. I would have objected if my voice had worked, but I was trying to swallow a tennis ball.

He faced me, holding the long, gleaming sword across his body. It had been recently polished.

"Rikardon, few men of our family have carried the Steel of Serkajon. It has been the tradition for father to judge son; I found Markasset lacking, a fact which did nothing to draw us together. But I must change that judgment now." He offered me the hilt of the sword.

"Please accept from my hands not only the great sword of Serkajon, but the love and respect I would feel for Markasset, could he be here. Whatever he might have asked of me is now yours."

There were a lot of things I wanted to say. I looked at Thanasset and I knew *he* understood. I could explain to the others later, when that tennis ball finally moved.

I gripped the hilt of the sword and lifted it from Thanasset's hands.

I felt a strange sensation, like the jarring crawl of an electric shock, but without any pain. There was a sweep of images through my mind, so swift and varied that I felt myself reeling.

Thanasset was there, as a younger man, riding the sha'um whose portrait decorated the wall. Laughing. And Milda, too, was younger, softly sad over the death of a man she had loved.

She changed into Gra'mama Maria Constanza, who patted my hand and dried my tears over a torn book page. And there was Julie, the first time we were together—sweet and wonderful. The war marched by and there she was again, weeping in shame because she hadn't had the strength to wait for me. I kissed her and shook her husband's hand and walked away. . . .

Illia was there, near me, naked, eager. Zaddorn, a boy, losing a sword trial to me. Illia was watching, Zaddorn was angry, I was laughing.

Two lives paraded through my mind and mingled. A wall had dissolved and the stacked-up contents of two rooms crashed together and bounced around.

Ricardo's life moved quickly through. School, reserves, students, summers, women . . . the doctor . . . the meteor. I viewed them lightly, as though I were watching an old movie so familiar that I could quote the next line at any given time.

I tried to cling to Markasset's memories, to absorb them,

make them part of me. But they, too, slipped by, one by one, giving me barely time enough to recognize the people in the images. I learned to let them go easily, sure now that I could call them back when I wished. I lived through Markasset's life up to a night not long past . . .

Then I remembered the night the Ra'ira was stolen.

23

"It's only seven hundred zaks, Father!" I pleaded desperately, hating him because I knew he was right. "I promise it's the last time, and I'll pay it back."

"How?" he demanded. "You've applied yourself to the mondea tables, but to nothing else. You might have been a scholar, a teacher, an administrator. You might have learned a craft. Never mind this debt; how will you support Keeshah after I'm gone? Will you go and live in the wilds and share the game he kills?"

"Don't start that old argument up again," I warned him. "We're talking about a single debt—my last gambling debt. I'll find a way to pay it back. But Worfit wants his money, Father. And I do owe it to him."

"Now you've hit the right word," he said grimly. "You *owe it to him.* So you *pay him."*

"It's the last time!" I repeated again, appalled that he didn't believe me. I meant it. I'd never made that promise before: I meant it now. Why wouldn't he believe me?

"It's one time too often!"

I left, then, slamming the back door hard enough, I hoped, to break the latticed glass panel. I sat with Keeshah in his house, rubbing his stomach and thinking.

Father was right about one thing: I had no way to earn that money myself.

Or had I?

"I do have one skill," I told Keeshah. He looked at me with one eye still closed and told me to keep rubbing. "I can fight. I'll hire on as a caravan guard."

The more I thought of it, the better it sounded. It would get me out of Raithskar, and out of Worfit's reach for a while. If the caravan went far enough, and was rich enough, and if I caught another caravan back, I could pay Worfit off completely. That would show the old man I could pay my own debts, make my own way.

And the promise was still good, I decided. I'd never gamble again. I didn't have a hope in the world of becoming a Supervisor until I quit the rogueworld and really tried to study city administration. And I'd been letting Illia think that Dad would put me up for it next opening, which would probably be when Ferrathyn fell over at last. So—when I got back from wherever it was, NO MORE GAMBLING.

I gave Keeshah's chest a final scratch and headed for the marketplace. On the way I revised the plan a little. I had been going to hire out me and *Keeshah, then find Worfit and tell him what I'd done, promise him his money as soon as I got back. But I had a better idea—I'd hire on as a footguard, and use a phony name. Nobody'd get hurt; Worfit would get his money; and meanwhile, Markasset would just mysteriously disappear. The only bad thing was not riding Keeshah—but he could follow the caravan, and I could see him every night. He wouldn't like it, but he'd do it.*

I was in luck when I reached the marketplace. A big caravan, owned by a man named Gharlas, was leaving the next morning and going all the way to Eddarta. I hadn't really wanted to go that far; the little man with only four fingers on his left hand said if I'd go as far as Chitzan, that would get the caravan past the raiding territory of the Sharith. They didn't expect trouble; they'd paid their duty on the way in; but it didn't hurt to be extra careful. If I wanted the job, I had it.

I took it.

It was dark by then. I thought about going home. Father would still be there, since he wouldn't go on duty tonight until dayend. I thought I should tell him I was going, then decided just to let him worry. It was his fault I had to go. But if I went home, we'd only argue again.

So I went to say goodbye to Illia.

She came to the second-floor window when the pebbles hit it. "I can't come out now, Markasset!" she whispered. "Mama's in the front room; she'd see me and we'd fuss over me going out this late."

"Jump down from there," I told her. "That slim waist of yours will fit through. I'll catch you."

There wasn't much light except what fell from her room. She stared down, deciding. "Are you sure you can catch me?"

"Yes, you don't weigh anything! Jump!"

"All right," she said, a little breathlessly. "Here I come!"

And she jumped. I felt a twisting in my chest. Illia believed in me completely. If I said I could do a thing, I could do it. She trusted me.

She nearly pulled my arms off when I caught her, but I kept on my feet. I could tell I had impressed her, but for once I didn't care about that. I had realized, for the first time, how good it felt to be trusted.

"Put me down," she said, but I kissed her instead. She was wearing her sleeping shift, and her body was soft and warm underneath it. Her breathing quickened to match mine, and I carried her out into her father's garden. There was a place, near the bath-house, that was blocked from the house but open to the sky. The song of the Skarkel Falls seemed especially beautiful right there.

We had made that place our own. That's where I took her to say goodbye.

"You really ought to tell your father where you're going," Illia said later. "He'll worry something fierce."

"You're right,"I said. "But if I see him again, we'll only yell at each other over this, too."

"Write him a note," she suggested. "I'll take it to him tomorrow." Her parents had gone to sleep by then, not even missing their daughter. She went quietly into the house, brought out brush and parchment, and I did write a note. "Leaving this morning on caravan to earn money for Worfit. Back when I get here. M."

"That's not much of a note," she said when she read it.

"It's all he'll get. Listen—I'm going to miss you."

"I'll miss you, too, Markasset. Terribly. Hurry back."

"When I get back, you'll see, love. I'll dig in, and I'll be ready to be a Supervisor in no time. And then—"

"Yes?"

"Will you marry me, Illia! After I'm a Supervisor?"

"You know I will."

When I left her, it was less than an hour before dawn, the time set for the caravan to depart. I realized that I hadn't planned things too well—I had no extra clothes, and no money to buy extra food for Keeshah on the off chance that he couldn't find game in the hills while we crawled across the desert at vlek pace.

So I stopped by Dad's office. It was closer than going home, and he had never objected when I used my own key to the drawer where he kept extra money. That is, he hadn't started to complain until I started gambling against money not yet in hand, and began losing. He had forbidden my use of that money, but hadn't asked for my key back.

Well, this wasn't for gambling, so I went into the building and up the stairs to Dad's office. He would be in the security room now; it was some four hours into his scheduled shift. I unlocked the drawer—and found five twenty-dozak pieces.

It was the money Dad had had at home, in the wall niche. He had brought it down here and locked it up—why? Because he knew I knew there was never much money here. And he also knew I knew he had that money at home. He had been afraid I'd steal the money from him to pay Worfit!

If that was all he thought of me, so be it!

I reached in and took the money. I'd pay off Worfit before I left, I'd take the rest for travel expenses, and I'd come back when I was good and ready, not before. I'd come back to Illia.

I threw the key down on top of the desk. I wouldn't be needing it again.

I went to Worfit's largest gaming house, where he usually spent his dust-to-dawn office hours. Marnen, his one-eyed assistant, told me that Zaddorn had ordered Worfit's testament about a disturbance in another of his houses the night before—a "scuffle" that had resulted in two dead men.

"I can't wait," I told Marnen. "Tell Worfit that I've got his money, but I have to leave town for a while. As soon as I get back, I'll pay him what I owe him."

Marnen nodded. "Sure, Markasset. You always been good for it before. A little slower than usual this time, maybe. You'll be back when?"

"I can't say for certain. Two moons, on the outside."

The one-eyed man shook his head. "He won't like that."

"Tell him if he kept better security in his places, he'd have been a richer man tonight."

Marnen hooted with laughter. "I ain't gonna tell the Chief that, not me!" He wouldn't try to stop me; he understood the peculiar code of honor that demands personal payment of gambling debts. "See you soon, Markasset."

I had to leave with the caravan in only a few minutes—I had *signed a contract. As I hurried through the streets toward the marketplace, I considered this new twist of events.*

The effect would be the same, I decided. I'd just keep the money until I got back, then pay off Worfit. If he got impatient meanwhile, maybe he'd go directly to Dad and show him what it's like to owe money to the rogueworld. They wouldn't hurt him any more than they'd hurt me—because of Keeshah. But they could annoy him a lot.

I reported to the caravan and the little man—Hural—yelled at me for being late. He introduced me quickly to Gharlas, a tall, thin man with a piercing stare that made me uncomfortable. Then we were on our way.

I let the first few days of the caravan flow through my mind. The caravan passed through Yafnaar, and I understood Balgokh's comment about the "change" in Markasset. He was unhappy with the choices he'd made, and he was curt and aloof from the people on the caravan. I skipped along to the caravan's last night on the trail. . . .

It was shortly after moonrise. As usual, I had met Keeshah a goodly distance from the caravan to keep his scent away from the vleks. The wind tonight was southerly, so we were out ahead of the caravan.

Keeshah warned me someone was near, and we flattened out on top of a mound to see who it was. Gharlas! Leading a well-packed vlek. What was he up to?

I had watched him a lot since the caravan started, and I had met many men I liked more. There was something odd about him—that piercing stare, the way he sometimes went all vacant, as though he were living in a dream world. He had been snappish and unpleasant the entire time; I'd come to the conclusion he was nervous about something.

And now he was sneaking off in the middle of the night?

"I'm going to follow him," I told Keeshah. "You keep out of sight and be sure to stay downwind of that vlek."

I did follow him. For about half an hour. Then there was a blinding, crashing pain in my head. . . .

"Markasset is dead," I told the others. "Touching the sword—I remember now." I looked at Thanasset and Milda. "I'm sorry." Then I turned to Zaddorn. "I remember what happened that night—"

I told them the bare facts of what I had relived in the few short seconds it had taken for the memories to march by. And while I talked, all sorts of pieces, scattered and out of sequence, fitted together.

I had been with Illia at the time of the robbery. But I couldn't remember that, and no one had thought to ask her. If they had asked her, without telling her why, she would probably have fudged the time and circumstances so that, if her folks found out, they wouldn't be too angry.

The men in Thanasset's back yard had said: "The Chief says he's got it on him." I had thought that meant Zaddorn suspected me of carrying the Ra'ira. But no—one of Worfit's informants must have told him I was back in town.

What I "had on me" was enough money to pay my debt to him.

And one more piece of information was pertinent.

"There's something I haven't told you," I said. "When I woke up out in the desert, there was a dead man nearby. I've been concerned, ever since we found out that Gharlas took the Ra'ira, that it was his body, and that his vlek was wandering around loose somewhere, carrying the stone. But I know now, definitely, that it wasn't Gharlas."

"Who was it?" Zaddorn asked.

"One of the other men on the caravan," I said. "I never knew his name."

"What happened to Gharlas?" Ferrathyn asked me.

"I wish I knew. It's a blank between the last of Markasset and the beginning of Rikardon."

"How did the man die?" Thanasset asked softly.

"I can't be sure—but I think Keeshah killed him."

Thanasset nodded. "I'd have thought so. That man must have been my son's murderer. Why don't you ask Keeshah where Gharlas is."

I did, rousing him from a deep sleep. He didn't quite

understand until I stopped using the name and tried to picture the man and his vlek, walking away.

He left, Keeshah said.

You didn't want to kill him, too?

Why? I kill the one who hurt Markasset. Then you came.

"He doesn't know," I told the others. "He revenged Markasset, then grieved for him until I surprised him by standing up."

"Well, we know where he's heading," Zaddorn said. "I'll alert every peace officer between here and Eddarta. We'll get the Ra'ira back."

"I certainly hope so," said Thanasset fervently, then he smiled at me. "Meanwhile, I have the pleasant task ahead of me of getting reacquainted with my son." His face clouded. "Are you uncomfortable being called Markasset?"

"A little," I admitted. "I am not Markasset. His memories are accessible to me now—not yet assimilated in the sense that they are truly a part of my personality, but available on demand." *And I'm no longer Ricardo,* I admitted to myself. *I am too completely a part of Gandalara now. I'm someone new.*

"It is an ancient custom to give a boy a new name when he first carries a sword," Thanasset was saying. "I don't think anyone will be too surprised if I invoke the old custom on the occasion of awarding Serkajon's steel sword to my son. It will take a little while for word to get around everywhere, but it will eventually. Will that suit you, Rikardon?"

"Yes. Thank you."

Thanasset looked around at the others. "Of course, I don't need to say that no one here will reveal your secret. Now," he said, grimacing at me, "I think it's high time you had a bath. You, too, Zaddorn."

That night I lay in my own bed for the first time since I had awakened in Gandalara. In spite of being dead tired, my mind kept buzzing. I'd long since given up recriminating over not having asked Illia or Keeshah a long time ago to help fill in the gaps of my memory. They hadn't had all the answers in any case, and, until I touched that sword, I couldn't have asked the right questions to draw out the few they had.

The sword lay beside me, unsheathed. I reached out and

touched the cool metal of the blade. The sword of Serkajon. I wouldn't even make a guess as to why it was the catalyst that unified Ricardo and Markasset. But the sword had felt just right in my hand. It seemed in its proper place, lying beside my sleeping pallet.

Gandalara—a strange world only a few weeks ago. Now it was my home, and I wanted no other. I belonged here. I thought of the people, now dispersed, who had been in this house today. My family: Thanasset, with his straight back and tiny scar and his infinite understanding even through his own pain; Milda, dear and kind and fragile, and stronger sometimes than the steel beside me. And my friends: Illia, special and exciting, trusting and loyal; Zaddorn, stubborn and proud and devoted to his job; and Ferrathyn, full of quiet, supportive strength. What I knew of them would change as they got to know me; we would forge new relationships, and I hoped I could heal some of the wounds Markasset had caused.

I thought, too, of Worfit. Thanasset had insisted that I use the stolen gold pieces to repay Markasset's debt. I would meet Worfit at last tomorrow because, as Markasset—that half of me which had been Markasset—had understood, that kind of debt must be paid in person.

Ricardo owed Worfit something, too. In fear and ignorance and error, Ricardo had killed one of Worfit's men. By law the death was self-defense, and unpunishable. But Worfit deserved an explanation, an apology.

Rikardon would honor both debts to Worfit, then end the association.

Last—deliberately so—I thought of Keeshah.

In the moment I had taken Serkajon's sword into my hand, one of the flashing memories had been particularly strong. I had been a young Markasset, just turned twelve, already tall and strong for my age, eager for the test of crossing the Khumber Pass into the Valley of the Sha'um. Eager at first, then weary, and finally moving along in an odd past echo of my desert awakening.

I dragged my trembling limbs a few feet at a time through the thin air at the top of the pass. My chest was on fire, my body felt almost useless, my eyes couldn't focus, my head was reeling. Purpose forgotten, I kept going out of sheer stubborn inertia.

I discovered gradually that I could breathe again, and the burning pain in my chest was abating. I had made it past the crest. There was no path on the other side of the mountain, only the hard-baked rock and a few scrubby bushes, and an occasional treacherous patch of loose shale. My coordination was gone. I had lost my pack of food and was shamefully weak. I stumbled and rolled down the steep hillside, finally crashing into a bed of vines tangled around a fallen tree. The sweet, cloying smell of the disturbed earth was my last memory for a long while.

I woke to a sharp pain in my left foot. It took a moment to remember where I was, then the pain increased as the foot was pulled against the weight of my body, dragging it a few inches through the vines. I yelled, thrashed my arms, sat up.

A sha'um, a yearling cub the size of a grown tiger, jumped away, crouched down and considered me. His ears lay back against his head; his mouth was ready to snarl.

He thought I was dead, Markasset was thinking. He thought I was food. He still thinks so.

As if to prove it, the cub chose that moment to spring forward, knocking me backward again, reaching for my throat with his jaws. I slammed my forearm against his head, diverting the deadly teeth and calling forth a high-pitched roar. He swung his head back toward my neck and I grabbed handfulls of fur and skin behind his cheeks and strained to keep his teeth away from my skin. We weren't badly matched for strength, and I began to feel some hope of winning. He was furious now, roaring and lunging down, then back, trying to break my hold. When he began to press down steadily again, his jaws snapping, I shifted my position and let his own weight and strength push him off to my side. I let go my stranglehold on the sides of his neck, sat up and straddled his back, pressing him to the ground with my weight. I caught the hold again, this time from behind him. He couldn't move now, and I felt a glow of triumph, even though I knew I could not keep the hold for long. Already my arms were trembling from the strain and my hands were cramping.

Hurt me.

The message came from the cat beneath me, and it brought a flash of joy. So that's what it's like! My hands loosened, and I felt the muscles in the cat's sides ripple in anticipation. I grabbed again, more tightly, and tried to speak to the cat.

I am Markasset,* I told it. *I want to stay in the Valley with you for a season. I will not hurt you again, and you will not let the other cats hurt me. Agreed?

There was no message; I tightened my fingers in the fur, and the cat made a whimpering sound that made me want to let go. But I held on until I felt the cat's mind struggling to speak to me again.

Yes.

I let go then, and stood up. The cat leaped up and out of reach, then turned to look at me. I walked toward him and put out my hand. His ears went back and his head jerked away, but he held his ground and I stayed still, waiting. Then I moved my hand again, slowly bringing it closer to his head. He eyed it with a sidelong glance, growling nervously, but he didn't move away this time. I touched the place on his neck where I had pinched him so badly. I rubbed it lightly, then brought my hand forward to stroke the soft fur under his chin. His eyes closed and his ears twitched.

**I'm sorry I had to hurt you,* I said, savoring the special kind of speech.*

**Fair,* he said, and reached down to lick the blood from my foot.*

The memory had cleared up one more puzzle for me. The forest in which Markasset had wrestled with the sha'um cub had been full of straight, tall trees. It was the only place, I had learned, where such trees grew, and they were effectively guarded from potential lumber barons by the presence of the sha'um.

Now I understood, too, Keeshah's puzzlement from time to time since Ricardo's arrival in his world. There were subtle differences between his relationships with Markasset and Ricardo. His meeting with Markasset had set the tone for their relationship; although there was an unbreakable bond of affection between them, Markasset was always the master, demanding of Keeshah everything he was willing to give.

So the small things I had done out of simple consideration—sharing the last of my water, letting him rest simply for his own comfort and not because he could go no further—these things had been new to him. And we had communicated in a different way.

That had been Ricardo. Would Keeshah need to adjust again to the new combined form? I knew, this time, that he would accept the change—even as he had accepted a confused wretch in the middle of a salty desert.

Suddenly I needed Keeshah. He had slept through the afternoon and was still sleeping lightly. I reached out for him, and his mind roused to my touch.

Thank you for helping me, Keeshah. Before anybody else, you knew I was changed, but you trusted me. I appreciate it—more than I can say. . . .

As it had happened before in times of stress, it happened now in the name of friendship. Keeshah and I merged. I could feel the comforting solidity of the stone ledge, smell the fresh grass. And this time the understanding flowed both ways. With conflicting pride and humility, I felt Keeshah's commitment to me, whole-hearted and without reservations. He was not surprised by the change in me, only mildly curious. Though he didn't care about other people, he sensed that I was unique among the people of this world, and there was pride—no, not pride; *smugness*—that he was associated with me.

We couldn't hold the meld for long, and as it faded, I sensed Keeshah falling back into sleep.

Good night, Keeshah, I said softly, not expecting him to hear me. But he roused again and answered me sleepily.

Good night . . . Rikardon.

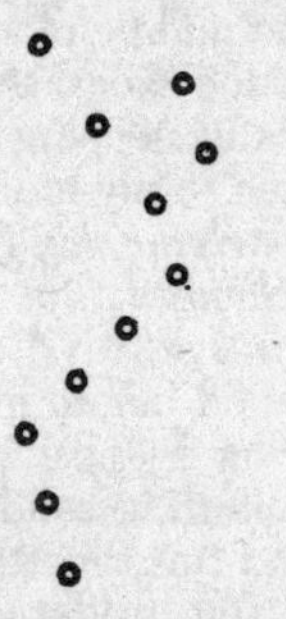

END PROCEEDINGS:

INPUT SESSION ONE

—Enough, you are tiring. We will withdraw together from the All-Mind. . . .

The Recording is complete for now. I will detach my mind from yours. . . .

How do you feel?

—I am exhausted.

—As it should be for the work you have done.

—There is more.

—When you have rested, we will Record again. For now, sleep. . . .

The Glass of Dyskornis

PRELIMINARY PROCEEDINGS:

INPUT SESSION TWO

—Ah, you have awakened. And eaten well, I see. Do you feel well enough refreshed to begin again?

—Yes, Recorder. I am ready.

—Good. Before we start, let me review the material already entered into the Record of the All-Mind. Then you may continue. Agreed?

—Agreed, Recorder.

—You have told of your previous identity outside our world of Gandalara. Your name was Ricardo Carillo. You were an instructor of languages, sixty years of age, a veteran of your world's wars. You had been told you would die soon of internal disorders. You were . . . "sailing"? Is the word correct?

—Yes. I was traveling in a structure which floated on a large body of water, the Mediterranean Sea.

—Sailing then, in the company of a woman named Antonia Alderuccio, when you saw a bright light in the sky which seemed to fall directly toward you. You thought it was a skybolt, is that not true?

—My word for that is meteor. I thought it was a meteor.

—When the bright light struck, you were unconscious for a time. Then you awoke in Gandalara, wearing the body of a native named Markasset, alone except for a dead man and Markasset's sha'um, Keeshah. There was a creature in your own world like Keeshah, it was called . . .

—A cat. But there was nothing in my world quite like the Gandalaran sha'um. Most of our cats weren't half big enough. There was a prehistoric breed, the sabertooth, that might have come close to Keeshah's size. All the mammals in Gandalara, including the men and women, have enlarged canine teeth, but Keeshah's tusks do not resemble the outsize fangs of earth's sabertooth.

May I ask you a question, Recorder?

—Yes.

—You seem uncertain of the material already recorded.

—The All-Mind has perfect memory. I do not. May I go on?

—Of course. My apologies.

—You awoke in the Kapiral desert, and Keeshah saved your life by carrying you to a Refreshment House. There you learned of your new identity, and first heard the name of Thanasset, Markasset's father.

Later, you discovered that Thanasset and his son were implicated in the theft of the Ra'ira, a beautiful jewel which had become a symbol of power in Gandalara. It had played a role in the destruction of the ancient Kingdom, had it not?

—In a way. The Ra'ira had been sent from Raithskar to one of the Kings as tribute. It had become a symbol of authority for the rulers of Gandalara.

As the sea called the Great Pleth had diminished, other cities had sent tribute in the form of slaves to work the fields and fight a losing battle against the salty desert that was closing in on Kä. Raithskar's contribution to Kä's support was water.

Markasset's ancestor, Serkajon, realized that the Kings had ceased to rule Gandalara, and were merely exploiting it.

—So Serkajon stole the symbol of their power.

—Yes, Recorder. He took the Ra'ira back to Raithskar. The King's Guard followed him and demanded the return of the Ra'ira. But he persuaded them that he was right. They abandoned the last King of Gandalara and took a vow to support their Captain's plan to keep the jewel surrounded and protected by honest men.

The protective system Serkajon set up, a ruling Council of twelve Supervisors, continued until Gharlas stole the gem.

—Gharlas was the master of the caravan which had departed Raithskar the day of the theft.

After an attack by the Sharith, the sha'um riders descended from the King's Guard, the remnants of the caravan told the Chief of Peace and Security that Markasset (under the name he had given) had left his guard post on the night before the attack occurred—which gave Zaddorn good cause to confine you for questioning.

—It was fortunate, for me, that Illia had time to warn me. I couldn't help Thanasset by staying in Raithskar, and I truly didn't know where Markasset had been when the Sharith

attacked. If the Ra'ira had been with the caravan, and if the Sharith had attacked the caravan . . .

—So you set out for Thagorn, killing a man, during your escape, whom you thought to be one of Zaddorn's officers. You entered Thagorn in disguise, and met Dharak, the Lieutenant of the Sharith, and his son, Thymas.

Gharlas had arranged for the attack, requesting that everyone on the caravan be killed. The Lieutenant had decided, instead, to sell the survivors to an Eddartan slaver. One of the prisoners, Hural, had been involved in the theft, and he answered your questions.

—Don't forget that Zaddorn was present, too. He had made the trip to Thagorn in record time, the last few miles in the uncomfortable cargo net of a Sharith patrol. When he realized that I was about to uncover some information, he didn't reveal my identity to the Lieutenant.

—And his presence was a good thing, because Hural died, of his own wish, at the end of his testimony. He described the madness of Gharlas, who believed obsessively that he should be King of Gandalara. Hural said that Gharlas carried a power, long rare, to read and to influence men's minds. Gharlas had compelled Thanasset to believe he had locked the door of the Ra'ira's vault when, in truth, he had left it quite open.

Dharak and Thymas assured Zaddorn that such power was possible. An illusionist, Tarani, claimed and used that power for the entertainment of the Sharith. Zaddorn was convinced of Thanasset's innocence.

—Dharak had known who I was, the moment I had walked into Thagorn. He told me, privately, that as Serkajon's descendant—and because my loyalty to Thanasset had proved something to him—he regarded me as the new Captain of the Sharith, and would await my orders about the Ra'ira.

—You sound as though this disturbed you.

—It did. I had accepted Markasset's responsibilities toward his father, and his engagement to Illia, but my only interest in the Ra'ira lay in proving that Thanasset didn't steal it. I hated to disillusion Dharak, who had been more than fair with me, but I would have told him "no" right then, if he hadn't also told me that Thanasset was in danger.

—So you and Zaddorn returned to Raithskar, after persuading Keeshah to accept Zaddorn as a second rider.

—And after persuading Zaddorn to ride him. That was the hard part.

—When you reached the city, Ferrathyn heard Zaddorn's story, and assured you that the Council would clear Thanasset of all involvement with the theft. But you inquired about the penalty for killing a peace officer, thereby alerting Zaddorn to the change in you.

—I really should have known, Recorder, that all peace officers in Raithskar wore gray baldrics. But, as I explained earlier, Markasset's memories were not totally accessible to me. So I told everyone present what I had told Thanasset earlier. I said I was not Markasset.

—Who was present at that time?

—Zaddorn, Illia, and Ferrathyn; Markasset's great-aunt Milda; and, of course, Thanasset and myself. Illia agreed to postpone any wedding plans until she could get to know me better. Milda was most troubled by the fact that I didn't know what had happened to Markasset, or if he would ever return.

—Which he wouldn't, as you found out when Thanasset presented you with the great treasure of his house, Serkajon's sword. Markasset's memories came to you and you knew that he had died in the desert, as he followed Gharlas away from the caravan, the night before the Sharith attack.

—I assume that the third member of the team of thieves killed Markasset by hitting his head with a rock, thrown or slung from a distance.

Keeshah killed him, Markasset's murderer, but Gharlas simply went on his way, with the Ra'ira.

It was . . . difficult to tell Thanasset that his son was dead. But he accepted it well, and even offered to invoke the ancient custom of awarding a new name with the sword, so that I could be called by the more familiar name, Rikardon.

—I believe that sums up your first entry into the Record. Has anything been ommitted?

—Yes, two things.

—And these are . . . ?

—First, the All-Mind. My understanding of it is imperfect, and somewhat different from the native Gandalaran's viewpoint.

—Then describe it in your own words, so that it may be clear in your mind before we begin this session.

—Thanasset tried to explain it to me. I understood it to be a sort of group consciousness, accessible in different degrees to all Gandalarans. Two lines of thought prevail in Gandalara about the All-Mind: first, that it is composed of the surviving personalities of all men and women who have ever lived; and second, that only their memories have survived. In either case, the All-Mind is accepted as natural and useful, respected but not worshiped.

—Thanasset explained your appearance within this framework, did he not?

—He tried, and I thought it best to let him believe something he could accept. He said I was a Visitor, a personality of someone long dead, whom the All-Mind had sent into Markasset's body for some purpose which I might not even know. Such Visitations had occurred before, though rarely. He thought it an honor to Markasset, and I believe it brought some ease to the pain of losing his son. I could not take that from him.

—Ferrathyn suggested that you might be Serkajon. A logical choice, certainly, since you were of his house, and were to carry his sword.

—He did suggest it, but I told him he was wrong. As I said regarding the conversation with Dharak, Markasset's responsibilities were quite enough for me to handle.

—There was another point overlooked?

—Keeshah. You have mentioned him as an animal which carried Markasset, but you have not discussed the special bond between him and Markasset, and between him and me.

—The nature of the telepathic link between sha'um and rider is well understood in the All-Mind.

—But you asked me, in the first session, to tell everything as it happened, in the greatest detail possible, leaving nothing out. The bond may be routine in Gandalara, but it was new and wonderful to me, a sharing such as I had never known in my world. When he accepted me in Markasset's place, Keeshah became my first and strongest tie to Gandalara.

Together, we created a new bond, a deeper touching. We were more than sha'um and rider, we were friends and partners.

—You are right to include that in the review, since Keeshah was so important to you. Please accept my apology for being

impatient. Is there anything more upon which we haven't touched?

—I don't think so. . . . No, wait! Worfit has been left out.

—Ah, yes, the roguelord. It was his man you killed on your way out of Raithskar. Markasset owed him a large sum of money.

—Seven hundred zaks. It was that debt which led to Markasset's contracting for the guard position with Gharlas's caravan, and to all the later events. I had not yet met Worfit, but I had resolved to pay him off and be rid of him as soon as possible. The continuation of the story must begin with him.

—Are you ready, then, to continue?

—I am ready, Recorder.

—Then make your mind one with mine, as I have made mine one with the All-Mind . . .

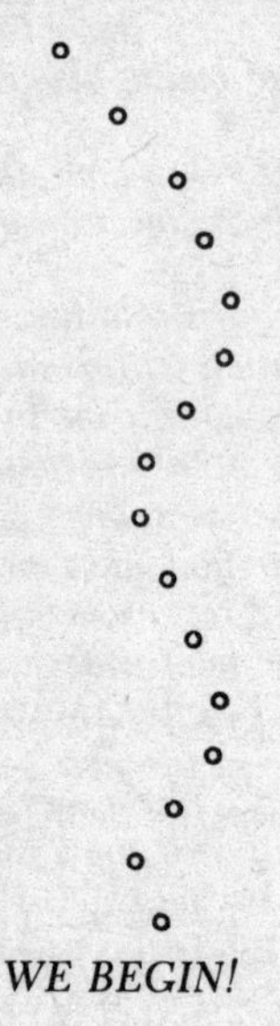

WE BEGIN!

1

Nobody, not even another Gandalaran, would call Worfit handsome. But nobody would tell him the truth, either. For one thing, he sat behind a big marble-topped desk and in front of two tough-looking characters whose expressions said: "Make the Chief mad and I'll break your face." For another, he had a certain personal trait which would make the most talkative person taciturn. In a word, that trait was *meanness*.

It glittered in the pinpoint eyes which lurked underneath extra-prominent supraorbital ridges. It could be seen in the way he used his thick-fingered hands. They lay still until they were needed. They didn't tap tables or crack knuckles. And when they moved, they moved fast, grasping at things as though each item were an enemy's throat.

Just now, his right hand lay on the desk before him, palm upward. On that palm were stacked the twenty-four coins which, in sum, repaid Markasset's debt to this man. With a sudden movement, Worfit flipped his hand over, scattering the smaller bronze and silver coins and slapping the two gold twenty-dozak pieces to the desk top.

"You owe me more than this, Markasset," he said. His voice was high-pitched, soft, menacing.

I knew what he meant, of course. I had killed one of his men. But his manner throttled the gracious apology I had planned.

"Seven hundred zaks is the *exact* amount of the debt," I said. "Enjoy it. It's the last money you'll see from me."

Worfit's head pulled back a little. He looked at me the way a dog might regard a rabbit who barked.

"You've said that before, Markasset, but I think you mean it this time. Don't tell me this hoorah over the Ra'ira has finally turned you into daddy's good little boy."

How could Markasset stand this creep? I wondered, with an unreasonable feeling of betrayal. Relying on Markasset's memory of Worfit as a "gentleman gamester" with a high sense of honor, I had made the difficult choice to come to his office unarmed. Now my hand itched to hold Serkajon's sword.

Keeshah, resting in his house in Thanasset's back yard, sensed my uneasiness.

Need me? came his thought. I could feel his eagerness. But there had been a number of armed men lounging around the closed gambling salon I had crossed a few minutes ago. I had the definite feeling that Worfit had expected my visit—and possibly one from Keeshah.

Thank you, I told the cat. **I can handle this.**

I hope, I added to myself. The exchange had taken only a fraction of a second, and Worfit was still staring at me with contempt plain on his face.

"Everybody changes sometime, Worfit," I said. "Look at you. You used to be a lot nicer."

He grinned.

I'd like to stuff those coins, one by one, through his digestive system in reverse, I thought.

"That was when you were a good customer, and paying on time. You've just said you're quitting the tables, and I believe you. That means you aren't worth being nice to any more."

DANGER! Keeshah's mind screamed the warning as, linked with me, he heard the soft step behind me.

I ducked to the right. A double-fisted blow that might have knocked my head off struck the top of my left shoulder and spun me around. I caught my balance and faced the man who had swung at me, a big, muscular man with a patch on one eye. Marnen, Worfit's assistant and bouncer.

"I been waiting for this a long time, Markasset. Let's see how far your uppity manners get you now." He spread his arms and came toward me. "Like the Chief said, I don't have to be nice."

At least he's not armed, I thought. *Thank goodness for grudges. He wants to tear me apart, piece by piece.*

He'll do it, too, if I don't get moving.

I bent over and lunged head-first at his midriff, which was hard as rock. But I did knock him backward, so that there wasn't much punch to the two-handed blow he landed on my spine. We crashed against the wall near the office door. I grabbed his ankles and pulled. He sat down heavily.

His big hands caught my tunic and jerked me toward him, and I didn't resist. When my head was near his chest, I braced my hands on the wall on either side of him, and snapped my head up under his chin. The back of his head slammed into the wall.

His grip relaxed.

My head hurt.

Oh, boy, did my head hurt.

Headaches seem to be a way of life with Markasset, I grumbled to myself as I staggered to my feet. Somewhat less than gracefully, I turned to face the desk, expecting the two plug-uglies behind Worfit to join in the fight. But they were right where they had been. One of them was even smiling.

Not too popular with the troops, are you, Marnen?

Hurt? came Keeshah's anxious thought. *I come there.*

No, Keeshah, I'm all right. I'd be dead by now if that's what Worfit wanted. I'm safe.

Slowly, Worfit stood up. He was short, his head barely clearing my shoulder. But he was heavy and solid, with wide shoulders and a barrel chest. He came around the desk, and I tensed again, certain that Worfit would be harder to handle than Marnen. But he only came up to me and pushed a stubby finger into my chest.

"You owe me, Markasset," he said. "For the irritation and inconvenience of Zaddorn's close interest in my affairs because of that fleabitten Ra'ira. Maybe that wasn't your fault, but it feels that way to me.

"And you killed one of my men. *You owe me a life.*

"I won't kill you today, Markasset. Not for years, yet, maybe. But I collect all the debts I'm owed. Remember that, and keep looking over your shoulder. Don't make it easy for me."

His eyes were gleaming, and his mouth was stretched in an ugly smile. His large canine tusks looked eager.

He hates Markasset, I realized. *He has always hated him. Because of Keeshah, Worfit never had the complete power over the boy that a life-threat brings. And Worfit wouldn't dare strike at Thanasset, because then boy and cat would come looking for him. So Worfit had to do a certain amount of play-acting to keep Markasset's respect—and his business.*

Now he hates me, too, because I don't have Markasset's gambling fever. He's lost the little power he had. A few hundred zaks was nothing to Worfit. But now he figures it's worth it to put time and energy into finding a way to get to me. Just to prove he can do it.

He can. He's doing it right now, damn it.

I pushed his hand away, then I shoved Marnen with my foot to get him clear of the door. Before I could get through it, Worfit spoke again in that sneering voice.

"Watch your back, Markasset."

This ugly little man had belittled, threatened, and intimidated me. Worst of all, he knew he'd gotten to me, that I believed his threat. I wanted—*badly*—to wipe away his self-satisfied smirk.

"Markasset isn't my name," I said. "Call me Rikardon. Thanasset renamed me. When he gave me Serkajon's sword."

I left then, with a warm memory of Worfit's unpleasant features beginning to register shock. My gloating lasted about ten paces past the outer door of the gaming house.

How stupid can you get? I asked myself, then added: *Don't test it out.*

Sure, you impressed Worfit. He knows about Markasset's family history. He knows what Thanasset thinks of his son, to give him Serkajon's sword.

So now he'll be careful not to underestimate you.

That's good?

And you gave him another reason to want you dead—that damned sword is valuable.

When Thanasset had presented the steel sword to me, I had been intrigued by its history and touched by the high regard implicit in the old man's gesture. It wasn't until I had all of Markasset's memories that I realized that it was a treasure beyond price. Markasset did not know of another steel sword which existed in Gandalara. Rika, as the sword was called, was unique.

Iron was amazingly scarce in this world. Raithskar had the only known deposit of it, and its mining was a community affair, closely supervised by the Council. Steel was forged, sold, and traded at premium prices in minute quantities. Its most common use was in the scissor-like sparkers, bronze tongs with cupped tips set with pieces of flint and steel for striking fires.

In the language of Gandalara, Gandaresh, the word for both steel and its basic material, iron, was *rakor*. Besides the sparkers, rakor was used for other, very special purposes.

The lock mechanism of the chamber from which the Ra'ira had been stolen was a strong bar of wood with brackets and a locking pin made of rakor. That seemed to me to be another measure of the esteem in which the Council of Supervisors held the beautiful gem.

Serkajon's sword, because of its history as well as its composition, was the second most valuable article in Raithskar. Telling Worfit I had it had been like dangling a carrot in front of a donkey.

Except it's hard to tell which one of us is the jackass, I thought gloomily.

The thing to do, I decided, *is not let it get under your skin. Worfit wants you to sweat a little. He won't do anything for a while, at least. So cheer up, have some breakfast, take a look at the city. Do you realize this is the first chance you've had to relax? Enjoy it!*

I had stepped out into an open court, one of four good-sized plazas which surrounded the huge central meeting area of the city. Though all these courts were square in shape, when a Raithskarian spoke of "the Square", he meant the big one, with stone terraces stepping down to meet an elevated stage. The announcement of the Council's judgment had been made there last night, clearing Thanasset and Markasset of any blame in the Ra'ira incident.

This plaza was smaller and level, but it, too, was paved with hand-fitted stone. Benches were placed in attractive groups, often in combination with a planting of trees and shrubs which grew tall enough to shade the benches. Although there was a specific district in the city for restaurants, a few were allowed to operate facing each plaza, for the convenience of the workers of the surrounding districts.

I followed my nose into a pastry shop, and came out with two meat pies and an earthenware drinking bowl filled with a strong herb tea.

It was still early morning, as I had timed my arrival at Worfit's offices for just after the dawn curfew for gaming houses. I took my time over breakfast, enjoying the food, and letting the faint mist from the Skarkel Falls dampen my clothes. The three other plazas would be bustling with people on their way to work, but this one was nearly deserted at this time of day. It lay in the center of the night district, and the "rush hour" home had happened earlier, probably while I had been with Worfit.

One of the few people crossing the court was a young woman. Her golden head fur winked with a sheen of mist. It reminded me of walking in Thanasset's garden with Illia, and I thought: *What better relaxation is there than the company of a lady?*

I returned the drinking bowl to the restaurant, got back my deposit, and started northward. I had no trouble finding Illia's house, and she answered the door on the first knock. A smile of welcome froze and turned shy, and her mother appeared from a doorway somewhere.

"Who is it, Illia? . . . Oh." She nodded a greeting to me, even while she was speaking to her daughter. "Don't be too long, dear, I do need your help." Illia's mother went back through the doorway—into the kitchen, I presumed. Both women were wearing long aprons heavily stained with a pinkish fruit juice.

"I'm sorry if I've come at a bad time," I said. "I only wanted to ask—will you have dinner with me tonight?"

"I'd like that very much," she said softly. "What time?"

We set a time, and I turned to go.

"Rikardon?" she called me back. "Thank you for asking."

Her smile thawed a little, and I left, feeling a keen anticipation of the evening. Breakfast, the walk, and the prospective dinner date had finally done away with the headache.

I walked through Raithskar, seeing it twice. Once with Markasset's familiarity, again with Ricardo's objectivity. I passed a party of vineh spreading a fresh coating of dark clay mud over a worn street. Markasset wouldn't have noticed them at all, but they sent Rikardon searching through the Gandalaran's memory for facts relating to the man-like animals.

Gandalarans aren't human physically, though they are mammalian humanoids. They are water savers, like the kangaroo rat of the American southwest. Socially and psychologically, they are so similar to humans that identifying them as men and women is no insult to Ricardo's humanity.

If the Gandalarans are the men of their world, then the vineh are the apes. Though the people of Raithskar had trained the beasts to perform simple tasks under close supervision, in their natural state they exhibited more ferocity than intelligence. Vineh are bigger than the men of Gandalara, and their stance is more erect than that of the apes of Ricardo's world. They are covered with a coarse and curly fleece, light tan in color.

In Raithskar, they wore shorts.

The first time I had seen vineh, I had assumed that the shorts were meant to respect the modesty of the people of Raithskar. That had seemed foolish to me, but on recalling a crusade during my former lifetime to put human-style clothes on the animals in zoos, I wasn't about to criticize.

In any case, I had been wrong. The only surefire, ironclad, indisputable reason for one male vineh to beat the living tar out of another one is the fact that the other is male, and might someday be competition for the attentions of a female. Obscuring sight of a rival's genitalia removed his identity as a rival.

Don't ask me why.

The men of Raithskar had discovered this quirk, collected a colony of vineh, and put the males to work. The females were always in some breeding phase, producing three males for every female. Whether this created the fierce rivalry, or was a natural compensation for the high murder rate among males, was a "chicken or egg" problem that didn't rate much analysis.

Beyond those facts, Markasset hadn't known a whole lot about the vineh. Having his memory accessible to me wasn't the blessing I had first thought it would be. For one thing, I had his *understanding* of facts and his *impression* of the events he remembered. For another, I needed always to be setting him aside to view things more objectively. Whenever I looked at anything within Markasset's experience, it stimulated a natural search for associations that I had come to think of as Markasset's "echo." Worst of all, Markasset took this world, these people, this city for granted. A lot of the things I wanted to know, he had never bothered to learn.

2

It was almost noon by the time I reached home. The meat pies had worn off, and I was looking forward to lunch.

Hungry too, Keeshah told me, as I started in the front door of the big stone house. He had been given an entire side of glith the evening before, but I could well believe he needed more food. He had carried two men almost six hundred miles in just over four days. Even though he had hunted and fed during that time, his reserves had to be just about gone.

Right after lunch, I told him. *I promise.*

Lunch, as it happened, was going to be delayed.

Thanasset came out of the sitting room to the right of the midhall as soon as I opened the door. He was taller than I, and his head fur was beginning to darken with age. But he always gave an impression of vigorous health and great dignity. Just now he looked relieved.

"We were beginning to wonder if something had happened to you," he said. He didn't mention Worfit.

" 'We'?" I asked.

"Yes, Ferrathyn has been here most of the morning, waiting to see you."

I hurried into the sitting room, where the slight old man was sipping a glass of *faen,* the Gandalaran equivalent of beer.

"It's good to see you again, Chief Supervisor," I said. "I'm sorry you had to wait. If I had known . . ."

He waved his hand and shook his head. "Not at all, not at all. One of the few good things that has come from losing the Ra'ira has been my frequent visits to Thanasset's house. He and I have spent the morning renewing a friendship long neglected.

"Anyway, it happens that I have nothing else to do. Seeing you is my assignment from the Council."

Uh-oh, something's up, I thought. It didn't take much

deduction. Ferrathyn was smiling up at me, wrinkles wreathing his face. And Thanasset was beaming, but not looking at me, as though I might read the secret in his eyes.

"I am empowered to invite you, Rikardon, to join the Council of Raithskar as its thirteenth member," Ferrathyn said. "There are normally certain—uh—character tests to be passed, but these have been waived in your case, largely because the Council feels you have already proven yourself to be of excellent character. The Council will have a general meeting tomorrow, just after the luncheon hour. Please attend, and deliver your decision in person."

He stood up and sighed. "Now that I've completed my mission, I must be on my way. I don't think I need to say, Rikardon, that I hope you will decide to join us. Good day." He turned to Thanasset. "Thank you for the refreshments and the conversation, old friend. I'll see myself out," he added, with a chuckle, after looking at me. "You'll be needed to answer questions."

"There have *never* been more than twelve members of the Council!" I said to Thanasset as the street door closed behind Ferrathyn.

"The Council created this position just for you," Thanasset said, and I could see he was proud of it. "I didn't attend last night's meeting—technically, I was still under suspension until I was cleared—but Ferrathyn told me about it. The Council was very impressed with your command of the crowd outside the house. We all have so much work that there is little communication between the Council and the people. You are to be—well, a liaison, a communications link."

A PR man, I translated. *Right up there in the public eye. Where Wofit will always know where I am.*

Maybe he'd be less likely to attack a public official? It sounds like the job might be interesting. And I guess it's time I looked for a way to make a living. Guarding caravans is not *a possible choice.*

What else is Markasset trained to do? Trained . . . the boy was a fine swordsman. Maybe I could use that skill to become an instructor?

Thanasset watched me thinking about it, and his pleased expression was replaced by one of unbelief. "Don't tell me you are thinking of refusing the Council's offer? It is an unprecedented honor."

"I realize that, sir," I said.

Should I tell him about Worfit? No, he'll only send Zaddorn to harrass him again, which is partly what started this in the first place.

"It's a little sudden," I told Thanasset. "I'm glad they've given me a day to get used to the idea. I just want to think about it for a while."

"Rikardon, I wish you *would* accept the position," he said seriously. "As a Supervisor, you could learn . . . so much about Raithskar, so quickly. I have the feeling that you may need information that Markasset didn't have."

Your intuition is right on the money, Thanasset, I thought. *And that's a point well worth considering.*

I smiled and tried to put him at ease. "I do appreciate the honor of being asked, Father, and I want to accept, but I can't say yes or no right now."

Someone knocked at the street door, and Thanasset went to answer it. I poured myself some faen and had the glass halfway to my mouth when Thanasset called to me. I put the glass down on the stone-and-glass shelf and went out to the door. A man in a gray baldric was standing there, and I felt my neck hairs rise.

You were cleared of all charges, I reminded myself. *There's no reason to be nervous just because a cop comes to your door.*

"Zaddorn's apologies for not calling in person, Rikardon," said the man in the street. "He asks if you will join him at his offices as soon as possible."

Asks?

Zaddorn?

That's a laugh.

"Of course." I lifted my own baldric from the peg beside the door and slipped it over my head. I felt better with the weight of Serkajon's sword at my left side. "Father, we'll talk again before the Council meeting." Thanasset nodded, and I stepped out to the small porch beside Zaddorn's officer. "Let's go."

The center of the government district—which was very close to Thanasset's house—was marked by another plaza. The largest building in Raithskar was located here, a three-story structure that held the offices and meeting room for members of the Council. There was also a large open room which took up most of the first floor. On Commemoration Day, the holiday which honored Serkajon's return to Raithskar, the Ra'ira had been on display in that room, mounted in a special case. The vault where the gem had been kept at all other times was located on the top floor.

Across the plaza was a long, single-story building which was Raithskar's jail, and headquarters for the Peace and Security Department. Zaddorn's office was all the way at one end of the building, with a private outside entrance. The officer led me to that door, knocked, and opened the door for me at the sound of Zaddorn's voice, oddly muffled: "Enter."

I walked in to find him sitting at a huge desk that was covered with paper, some of it punched and bound into sheafs, some of it in neatly tied rolls, a lot of it just lying around loose. There was one small clear space right in front of Zaddorn, and in it was an empty bowl. The lingering aroma told me his lunch had been *rafel*, a meat and vegetable porridge I had grown to like a lot. Zaddorn was swallowing the last mouthful as I entered, and my stomach growled with envy.

"You're looking better," I told him. He had lost the look of pale weariness he'd had for the last two days of our trip back from Thagorn. "What can I do for you?" Without waiting for an invitation, I dropped into one of three chairs facing his desk.

Zaddorn finished his glass of faen and took the empty dishes to the inside door of his office, where someone was waiting to take them. He came back to his desk, sat down, and leaned his elbows on the clear spot.

"You can come work for me," he said. "I've had the funding for an assistant for the past three years, but I've never found anyone I could trust, or wanted to work with."

"You called me down here to offer me a job?" I asked. "There's a lot of that going around."

"Oh? Who else, if it isn't prying?"

"Ferrathyn," I said, and watched his eyebrows go up. "And the Council. They've decided to create a thirteenth Supervisor, and they want me to be it."

He was trying hard not to be impressed.

"You haven't accepted yet, have you?" he asked.

"No, I'm to attend a Council meeting tomorrow and give my answer then. I got the impression from Ferrathyn, however, that he regards it as a formality. I think *he's* sure I'll do it."

"There's not the slightest doubt of that," Zaddorn said with a grimace. "It is becoming increasingly difficult for the Chief Supervisor to conceive of anyone opposing him." Then he smiled. "You've given me another reason to hope that you'll choose to work for the Peace and Security Department."

"Ferrathyn once said something to me about your providing him with a lot of headaches."

Zaddorn laughed out loud. "Did he now? I'm delighted to hear it." He looked at my face and laughed again. "You're shocked. Beleive me, I show Ferrathyn all the proper respect. But since he has been Chief Supervisor—he moved up when Bromer died, shortly before I took this job—he has become increasingly insistent on having his own way. Maybe it's his age. But on principle, I oppose pampering anyone, even our most important citizen. So I get in his way when I can."

I see one reason why Markasset wasn't fond of Zaddorn, I thought. *He's so sure of himself, so secure. And he's graceful, both physically and socially. Markasset had a way of starting off on the wrong foot with people. I'll bet that's why Illia was so important to him—she didn't see his social clumsiness as a handicap. Worfit took some pains to make Markasset feel like a high-class person, and the boy was probably subconsciously grateful. That would have become associated with his love of gambling, and reinforced it.*

And speaking of Worfit, working for Zaddorn would be no more self-concealing than being a Supervisor.

I feel like a frayed rope in a three-way tug-of-war. I'm getting out of here.

I stood up.

"You'll have my answer tomorrow."

Zaddorn walked over to the door with me. "Good enough. All I ask is that when you think about this, you remember the way my desk looks right now. The Council already has twelve people, but I'm only one man."

Outside, I took a deep breath. *Why can't I just sit around this world for a while?* I complained to myself. The answer was already there. *Because that's what Markasset was doing. Everybody who knows about me expects me to be different.*

And I am, I guess. I'd like to do something useful here. But I was expecting some time off, first!

I still had the feeling that had brought me out of Zaddorn's office, the need to get away from the pressure, be by myself and think things out.

Not quite by myself, I amended.

Keeshah, how would you like to go on a picnic?

The reference escaped him, but he got the general idea.

Food?

And solitude, I told him. **We'll go for a run outside the city and have our lunch under a tree somewhere. Does that suit you?**

I halfway expected his reaction to be "as long as there's food, whatever you want is OK by me." But I received a sense of complete agreement from him, as though he were as eager as I to get away from the city for a while, even though we had only returned to Raithskar yesterday.

I walked down to the market area and arranged to pick up a side of *glith* and a roast fowl. Then I went back home to get Keeshah.

I walked through the big double gate and followed the garden pathway to the outbuildings at the rear of Thanasset's property. One of these was huge and square, its stone walls spattered with small openings for ventilation. Heavy bronze doors stood open to the garden.

Two grayish-tan paws appeared out of the shadows in the doorway. Claws as long as my fingers dug into the ground, and in a moment the wide wedge of Keeshah's head appeared. His tapering ears were laid back and his mouth wide open in a stupendous yawn. His tusks glistened. He took a few short steps forward, stretching his hind legs and arching his tail, until he was all the way out in the sunlight. I could see the muscles rippling under his skin when he stretched. He was big. Powerful. Beautiful. He was part of me.

Sleepyhead, I teased him. **You almost missed lunch—hey, wait, no fooling around now . . .**

He had jumped toward me at exactly the same moment I had caught a flash of his intention, and he was too fast for me. One forepaw whipped out and slapped my legs out from under me. Even before I hit the ground, Keeshah had my left ankle in his jaws and was dragging me toward his house.

Have you for lunch, he said.

I grabbed the trunk of a big bush, pulled against it, and snatched my foot away. He let me go, of course. By now boot and foot would have been a total loss, if he'd been the least bit serious.

Come on, you big pussycat, I said, grabbing his head and hauling myself to my feet. I ruffled the fur around his ears. **Let's get going. I'm hungry.**

I knelt down by the bush, which was tilted crazily, and tried to repack the soil around the disturbed roots. I whispered an apology to Thanasset, who had planned and planted this landscaped garden himself. Then Keeshah and I went out into the street and headed for the main avenue.

The meatmonger saw us coming, and brought out my order. The roast *thaka* was packed in a draw-string bag of oiled canvas. I tied it to my belt and slung the glith carcass, about thirty pounds of meat and bone, across Keeshah's shoulders. With my hand resting behind the sha'um's left ear, we walked down the broad, packed-clay street that led directly from the Square at the center of the city to the gates in Raithskar's ancient stone wall.

Keeshah would have had no trouble meeting me at the gates or at the meatmonger's shop. But the riders of the house of Serkajon had always taken pains to make it clear that their sha'um were under control. When Keeshah was in Raithskar, he stayed home unless I was with him.

We walked through the caravan market area that lay just within the city gates. It was bustling with people, but everyone made sure we had plenty of room to pass through.

As soon as we were out of the city, Keeshah crouched down and I sat on his back. I tucked my feet up just ahead of his hindquarters and held down the glith carcass with the weight of my body. The sha'um stood up, moving slowly because he knew I wasn't as securely attached to him as I usually was.

Where? he asked me.

Somewhere peaceful, Keeshah. You choose.

He set off at an easy run, following the city wall westward. We crossed the Skarkel River on a jiggling pontoon bridge that made me so queasy that I had to close my eyes. Then he turned northward, following the river on its western bank. Past the city, the eastern bank was crowded with buildings. Grain mills, refineries, a big building that housed the

Raithskarian mint—the river's power assisted most of Raithskar's industry.

The western side of the river boasted more agriculture than industry, though we did pass a grain mill or two. When the ground began to rise toward the Wall, cultivated fields gave way to wilder country, lush grassy growth, and thick groves of the short Gandalaran trees.

The Great Wall of Gandalara was a sheer escarpment, so high that its upper edge was obscured by the ever-present cloud layer. When I had awakened, dazed and irrational, in the middle of a salty desert, I had seen the Great Wall as a faded blue line in an otherwise featureless vista. I had scrambled toward it desperately, until Keeshah had decided, finally, that I was worth saving.

The Wall ran roughly east to west, several miles north of Raithskar. Ahead of us now, striking up the thunder that had been growing louder with Keeshah's every step, were the Sharkel Falls. A massive sheet of water poured down the rock face from the clouds above. The spray it cast around the lake at the base of the Wall formed a new, ground-hugging cloud in the hot Gandalaran air. If we had gone further north, we would have run into the misty cloud. As it was, beads of moisture were already collecting in Keeshah's fur.

The sha'um turned aside to climb a short, steep slope that was crowned with several of the curly-trunked *dakathrenil* trees. These seemed to be part of an abandoned orchard, for they had been trained, at one time, to stand upright and form an umbrella-like topknot. Now branches twisted downward, intertwined between the trees, and created a perfect backrest for a man sitting on that knoll and looking out over the mist-shrouded lake.

Picnic? Keeshah repeated the strange image.

It's perfect, Keeshah. Let's eat.

3

What should I do, Keeshah? I asked the sha'um. We had finished our food and drunk the water I had brought in a pouch from home. Keeshah was stretched out on his side, and I was sitting propped up against his back, shredding stalks of a hardy, thick-bladed weed.

Scratch between shoulders, he suggested. I laughed and complied, enjoying the way his thick fur whispered through my fingers.

I mean, which job should I take? Or should I pass up both of them? What should I do about Worfit?

I kill?

No. At least, not unless you have to, OK?

He agreed, with the mental equivalent of a shrug. Unless Worfit actually caused me harm, or I gave Keeshah specific orders regarding him, the little roguelord meant absolutely nothing to the great cat.

You don't want jobs, Keeshah volunteered.

Yes, I . . . You're right, as usual, Keeshah. Both jobs need doing, but I'm not the one to do them. At least, not yet. Still—I have to do something to make a living for us. The idea of teaching kids to use a sword doesn't strike me well, either.

With his stomach full and his back being scratched, Keeshah had almost fallen asleep. I assumed that I was talking to myself. But a thought from Keeshah reached me, sounding slow and sleepy in my mind.

Need time. Rest.

You or me, Keeshah?

Both.

Hadn't I had the same thought earlier? That I needed some leave time before I could settle down to—well, to whatever career I chose in this world? And even then, I hadn't considered Keeshah's needs, assuming that just lying still after all that running would constitute rest for him.

I realized now that it didn't work that way. He could always sense unhappiness or anxiety in me. As long as I couldn't relax, neither could he.

I'm sorry I haven't asked you before this, I said to him. **Is there something you would like to do?**

Yes.

He stopped there, and I sensed a reluctance in him, as though he wasn't sure whether I'd approve of what he wanted.

Tell me, I urged.

Hard to say, he explained, and I felt his mind groping for the close bond we had shared on other occasions. As he had done for me then, I stilled my mind and waited for what he wanted to tell me.

An image formed slowly, at once familiar and all new. It was the nighttime scene at Thagorn which had moved me so much that I had reached for Keeshah to share it. The river which cut the valley in half was murmuring nearby. Across it, dying cookfires cast glows like candle flames into the night sky. There was music, and the sound of children playing. Through Keeshah's perception, odors I had not even noticed were distinct and plentiful.

And there was the sound of sha'um.

What I had felt when I looked at that scene paled to insignificance beside the emotions it had stirred in Keeshah. I had heard growling and rumbling and roaring from the sha'um. Keeshah had heard music far more potent than the flute and harp and voice which had charmed me. He had heard the song of his own heritage, and it had stimulated long-ago memories and unrecognized needs.

The vision lasted only a short while, for this kind of sharing was both a joy and a tremendous strain for both of us. When Keeshah withdrew, he waited silently for my response, lifting his head to look over his shoulder at me.

How could it hurt me to know that you are lonely for your own kind? I asked him gently. **I felt something like that, too—a kinship with those people who understood the partnership between a man and his sha'um. And I do remember saying to you that we would go back to Thagorn together someday, if it were possible. That's what you want to do, isn't it?**

Yes. We go?

I don't know, Keeshah. There's a job waiting there for me, too. And I know I don't want that one.

You don't want job, he agreed, staring at me with unblinking gray eyes. **You do want to go. Say when.** With that, he lowered his head to the ground and slipped into a light sleep.

It's an unsettling experience, having a cat tell you what you're thinking. Especially when you're not sure, yourself, about something. But it's useful.

I do want to go back to Thagorn, I realized, as I lay down beside Keeshah and looked up through pointed leaves at the cloud-masked sky. *I like Dharak a lot, and it seems unfair to let him believe I'm going to come back and take over the burden he's carried all these years. If I could get there, and talk to him alone before he makes anything official . . .*

Boy, I would like to spend some time with the Sharith. Get to know their routine. Share the experience of riding. Relax. Be myself.

Markasset never set foot in Thagorn. I don't believe he ever thought very much about the Sharith and their connection with his family. In Thagorn, I could be free of his "echo" for a while, and get acquainted with this world on my own.

Zaddorn doesn't have lines of people waiting for that job. He'd accept a short delay before I stepped into it. He wouldn't like it, but he'd let me do it. He wouldn't have much choice.

What about Ferrathyn and the Council? I can't know for sure, of course, but I suspect they'll want a definite answer tomorrow. They might accept the delay if I could be confirmed, or sworn in, or whatever, before I left. But that would still require a decision right now, which is what I'm trying to avoid.

And here's the sixty-four dollar question: if I leave Raithskar and get out of his reach, will Worfit take out his anger on the people close to me? Would I be justified in taking away their protection?

Puzzles! Always puzzles! I complained. *I'm not getting anywhere.*

Gharlas is responsible for all this, I thought. *If he hadn't stolen that fool gemstone, Zaddorn wouldn't have harrassed Worfit into threatening me.*

But then, I'd never have gone to Thagorn. For that matter, Markasset would have had no reason to follow Gharlas away from the caravan in the middle of the night and get himself killed.

Would I be here if Markasset were still alive? I wondered. *And if both our personalities were intact, in the same body, which one would dominate? Unimportant, since it didn't happen that way, but as an intellectual exercise, I'd have to say the native, because of his familiarity with the world and the way his body worked.*

I can't buy Thanasset's explanation of me. I'm not part of this world, wherever it is. Or I wasn't, until I died in my own. And if there was some purpose in my coming here, as Thanasset thinks, it's my guess that I've already accomplished it by getting the old man off the hook over the Ra'ira's theft. So the rest of this life is mine, and I do want it to be worthwhile. All I have to do is decide how to support myself . . .

I drifted off to sleep.

I woke late in the afternoon, alarmed to think I might be late meeting Illia. Keeshah was instantly alert and, as he had already buried the remains of his meal, we took off running.

I clung to his back with hands, elbows, and thighs, trying to make myself an extension of Keeshah. I closed my eyes against the wind, and reached out to form a light linkage with Keeshah's mind. He loved to run, to stretch himself and drive the ground along underneath him. I let my problems drift away as I shared that total, physical joy with the great cat.

We stopped at the gate of the city, and I walked Keeshah home, all the way to the semi-dark house at the back of Thanasset's yard. As I left him, I realized that he hadn't brought up Thagorn again. I supposed he had considered his last words sufficient.

I went to the back door of the house and found it off its latch, swinging wide open. A shiver crept up my spine.

"Milda! Thanasset!" I shouted, as I ran into the house.

The midhall was a mess. Dishes had been brought from the dining room and shattered against the fine parquet walls. The portraits and sketches which had decorated one wall had been pulled down and thrown around; not one glass frame was intact. The beautiful parquet was marred, and the floor was littered with broken crockery.

"Markasset?" The voice was old and thin, and it sounded from the dining room.

"Milda!" I ran in to find her bending over the dining table, rubbing a dark and glistening oil into white scars that criss-crossed its polished surface. "Are you all right, darling?" I asked her. I put my arm around her shoulders and turned her face toward me, pulling her gaze away from the table. Her eyes looked through me at first, then began to focus.

"Markasset!" This time, her voice carried awareness. She moved to hug me, then drew back. "Oh, I forgot. You're not . . ."

"It doesn't matter, Milda," I said, and pulled her into my arms. The top of her bald head barely reached my shoulder. "Please tell me you're all right."

With a little sob, she put her arms around me and hugged me with all her strength. Gandalarans don't weep tears except to cleanse their eyes of foreign matter; emotional tears would be a waste of water. They do have physical reactions similar to the human expression of grief. For a few seconds, Milda gasped and choked and clung to me. When she seemed to have control again, I held her away from me and was glad to see that the glaze of shock was almost gone from her eyes.

"Yes, I'm all right, Rikardon," she said. Her voice was still shaky. "But—oh, look at this! I'm getting oil all over your tunic." She looked down at the messy rag, and the bowl of oil resting on the ruined table. She laughed a little. "Isn't that silly? All I could think of was fixing the table before Thanasset came home." She chuckled again, more loudly. "Isn't that silly?"

"Milda," I said, shaking her to forestall the hysterics that seemed imminent. "Where is Thanasset? What happened?"

She pulled herself together. "Thanasset left the house after lunch to spend some time at his office," she said. "He said not to expect him for dinner. I went out to do some shopping and visit Holla—she's an old friend—and when I came back, I found this awful mess.

"Rikardon, who would do a thing like this? That dinnerware has been in our family for six generations, and it's all . . . it's all . . ." She seemed to sense she was on the verge of hysteria again, and she shook herself. "Well, it's all broken, that's what. And it needs cleaning up. I'd better get started."

She put the rag down on the table and headed for the door into the midhall, but she paused there, reading my expression with characteristic accuracy.

"What are you thinking about, boy? Do you know who did this?"

Milda reminded me so much of Ricardo's grandmother, Maria Constanza. She was sweet and gentle and frail—and heaven help anyone who crossed her. It was built into me, from both Ricardo and Markasset, that I couldn't lie to Milda.

"Worfit's men did it," I said. Then I told her everything that had happened that day, beginning at Worfit's office. By the time I had finished, we were sitting down at the table and she was rubbing oil into the scars while I talked.

"It seems Worfit *has* found a safe way to get back at me. Or so he thinks. But if he believes that just because nobody was hurt . . ."

I stood up.

"Sit down," Milda said.

I sat down.

She put the rag aside, cupped her elbows in her hands, and leaned on the table. "If you've got any thought about riding Keeshah right down Worfit's throat, you forget them. That's just what he wants you to do. Think about it. Worfit knows he'll never find an assassin willing to come after you. Everybody knows about Keeshah. So he provokes you into an attack, and surrounds himself with enough men to handle *ten* sha'um. To defend their own lives, they'd kill you and Keeshah both."

We sat in silence for a few minutes, while I thought about what she'd said. She was right. If I hadn't been suffering from my own sort of shock at seeing Thanasset's beautiful things destroyed, I'd have seen it myself.

If I don't do anything, this will happen again. And maybe somebody will get hurt next time. I'll have to leave Keeshah here all the time, to protect the house. But how will I protect Milda and Thanasset when they're away from the house?

I was afraid to leave Raithskar for fear this would happen. But it looks like staying here will only provoke Worfit. . . .

"I'm going to Thagorn," I told Milda.

She nodded. "That seems the right choice to me, Rikardon. Worfit won't trouble Thanasset and me if you're not right here to get angry about it. And it does seem unfair of your dad—I mean, Thanasset," she corrected quickly. I reached over and squeezed her shoulder, and she covered my hand with her own for a moment, "It does seem unfair to put so much pressure on you right away, after everything you've already done for us.

"Don't you worry about this Captain business, either," she said. "It will work out to whatever is right for you."

"Milda, you . . . I'll miss you a lot."

"And we'll miss you, Rikardon. Shall I tell Thanasset about Worfit?"

"I guess you'd better, but please ask him not to take any action on his own. I'll leave quietly, tomorrow morning. Worfit will know I've gone. He might even think he's scared me off, and that will be enough for him."

"You won't leave without saying goodbye to Thanasset, will you?" she asked. "He would be very sad."

"Of course not. I promised to talk over the Supervisor's job with him before the Council meeting tomorrow. I'll have to do that in the morning, so that he can take my answer to the Council for me.

"Tonight . . . there's someone else I have to say goodbye to."

4

I had taken a quick bath and dressed with care in a suit I had admired on my first day in Raithskar. It was a thigh-length yellow tunic and a green, sleeveless surcoat embroidered in a matching yellow. Such color coordination was the mark of evening dress, since ordinary clothing was a jumble of bright colors. With brass-studded sandals and a heavy chain belt, I accepted Markasset's judgment that I was very well dressed. It didn't hurt my ego any when I passed a lady and drew a second look.

Illia's house was located northwest of the Square, halfway across the city from Thanasset's home. It was a modest house, with a smaller yard and grounds than Thanasset's had. But it, too, opened directly from the street with two doors, one into the house and one into the garden. Its midhall—a long, central room which divided the house—had walls faced with smooth plaster, spotlessly white. In this house, the sitting room to the right of the entrance door was not closed off with a wall, but formed an extension of the midhall. When Illia's mother answered the door, she led me into that parlor and we sat there for a while, exchanging slightly awkward small talk.

Her father, a big man with a lopsided grin, came home while I waited there. He worked for the city as a gardener; he said a quick hello, then excused himself to go and get cleaned up. Just after he left, Illia appeared on the stairs which faced the parlor.

Before I had touched Serkajon's sword, I had been plagued with a sort of double vision, especially regarding the Gandalaran people. To Ricardo, they had been ape-like creatures with prominent supraorbital ridges, slightly pug noses, and outsized canine teeth that resembled tusks. To Markasset, they had looked quite ordinary, like people I had grown up with and known all my life.

Regarding Illia specifically, Markasset remembered her as inordinately pretty, but he had found more value in her unquestioning trust in him than in her looks. In Thanasset's garden on the day I first came to Raithskar, Ricardo had recognized Illia's beauty while accepting its alienness.

It was *Rikardon* who looked at her now. The alienness was gone. She was so beautiful that I stood up and stared, speechless, as she came down the stairs.

Her head fur was a dark gold. It shone in the lamplight, looking so soft that I wanted to touch it. Her face was small and delicate, her mouth a gentle curve.

She was wearing a long, sleeveless shift of lightweight linen in a soft shade of green. Glass beads in a darker green decorated the low neckline and the belt which pulled the soft folds of the gown snug to her waist. The skirt was slit up the left side, almost to her hip, to allow walking freedom. There was a single fine chain of gold around her neck.

Somehow, I said goodbye to her mother, for I suddenly found myself outside, walking beside Illia in the direction of the restaurant district. There was a tense silence that I didn't like, and didn't quite know how to break.

"I thought we'd eat at the Moonrise," I suggested finally. It was a restaurant that Markasset's memory recommended.

"That sounds wonderful," she agreed. She hesitated a moment, then added: "They have a way of cooking glith steaks that is delicious."

"I remember," I said softly. She caught her breath sharply. I took her hand and made her stop walking, then drew her around to face me. "Illia, are you nervous about being out with me tonight?"

"I—yes, of course I am," she admitted. I thought she sounded relieved that she didn't have to pretend. "It's—well, it's very strange, knowing you and not knowing you."

"Please don't be afraid of me."

"I'm not. It's just . . ." She took a deep breath. "Do you remember . . . everything about Markasset?"

I thought about lying to her, but I decided she deserved at least honesty from me.

"I remember every moment you and Markasset spent together."

"Oh, dear."

She turned away abruptly, and we walked along again. But she didn't take her hand away, and this time the silence was more comfortable.

In a few minutes, she began to talk of ordinary things: the fruit she and her mother had been preparing for the drying oven that morning; her sewing projects; her work as a teacher in a school for young children. I realized that she wanted to deal with only the present, and not to contend with our "mutual" past or the uncertain future. That suited me perfectly, and I set myself to keep that tone in my end of the conversation.

It was one of the most enjoyable evenings I have ever spent. We had a wonderful dinner at the Moonrise, then went on to a dance hall, where we sat at a numbered table, sipping faen, until our table's number was called. Then we joined the other couples on the patterned dance floor and performed the stylized, intricate dances of Gandalara. There were about a hundred tables, and only twenty couples danced each dance, so we were able to rest well between sessions. Markasset had been a good and an energetic dancer, and I loved dancing with Illia.

There was one awkward moment when, after recognizing us, the band—a harp, two flutes, a clarinet-looking instrument, and bongos I might have bought in Santa Barbara—changed their schedule to play our "favorite" melody when we reached the dance floor. We studied the painted wooden tiles with great concentration while we danced, and burst out laughing as soon as we were seated again.

Just before dawn, we finally left the dance hall. As we walked back toward Illia's house, I tried to think of a way to tell her I was leaving.

"Zaddorn stopped by my house this evening," she said suddenly. "He told me that you've been asked to join the Council. He also said he wants you to work for him. Which will you do?"

"Neither one, I'm afraid. There are . . . circumstances Zaddorn doesn't know about. I'll be leaving Raithskar for a while."

Her hand gripped mine more tightly. "How soon?"

"Tomorrow."

"Did you know this when you came by this morning?"

"If I had known it then, I would have told you," I said.

"Yes. I believe that."

We walked together quietly, then, until we reached her home. She didn't take me to the house door, but led me through the gate into the back yard. I followed along with her, busy with my own thoughts, until I realized where we were going. Behind her father's bath-house and storage shed, there was a grassy area that was hidden from all the houses nearby, but was open to the sky. It was a very private place—and very special to Markasset.

I stopped; she stopped and turned to me. Her face and hair were pale, and her eyes reflected the glow of the moonsoaked clouds above us.

"You don't owe me this kind of goodbye, Illia," I said.

"Isn't it more of a greeting . . . Rikardon?"

Markasset's memory of his last night in Raithskar brought me tender images of Illia's body, its sweet eagerness, its beauty in the moonglow. If I had been Ricardo, in a human world, it would have been easy and natural to accept her invitation. Or if I had been entirely Gandalaran, a new boyfriend, I'd have had no compunction about being in a place she had once shared with Markasset.

But I was an alien personality, in a body which she had known intimately. I fought for a grasp of the ethics of the situation, even while my body and my emotions were responding to Illia's willingness.

I hesitated so long that she became embarrassed. "I thought . . . Don't I . . . I mean, don't you want to . . ."

"*Yes!*" I said quickly. "Oh, yes, I want to."

She came to me then, and put her arms around me. I could feel her fingers pressing into my back. The sight of her face, looking up at me with serious eyes, was too appealing to resist. I kissed her, tantalizing my tongue on the rounded tips of her large canine teeth. All thought was swept away in a surge of affection and gratitude, and arousal more intense than I had experienced in a long time.

She broke away from the embrace with a soft sound of contentment, and we walked to the grassy area Markasset remembered. The distant thunder of the Skarkel Falls settled over us as we lay down together.

When I kissed her goodbye at the back door of her house, she whispered: "I won't decide about—anything. Not until you come back, Rikardon."

Suddenly I was swept up in an "echo" from Ricardo's life. I saw Julie, young and loving, saying: *"I'll wait for you, Rick. No matter how long the war lasts, I'll wait for you."*

Julie hadn't been able to wait, and had paid a high price in guilt.

"Don't make me any promises, Illia," I whispered to the Gandalaran woman in my arms. "Do what seems best for you."

She kissed me again, briefly, then pushed herself away from me. "You're a very gentle man, Rikardon. I do care for you. Keep safe."

She went into the house, and I walked home under the colorful dawn sky. The first rays of sunlight, diffused by the cloud layer, marched by overhead in a parade of changing, blending color, deep red to pale yellow and all shades between.

I stepped quietly into Thanasset's house through the front door. I turned left to climb the stairs, but a sound from the sitting room made me look that way. Through the door opposite the stairs, I could see Thanasset. He was standing by one of the tall and narrow wood-latticed windows that lined the outside wall of the room. He had one foot propped on the low stone ledge that ran along under the windows.

There was something about the way he held himself, with his arms propped on his raised knee and his shoulders hunched up, that made me cross the midhall and pause at the sitting room door.

"Father?" I said. He turned away from the windows, surprise and relief plain on his face. "Are you well?"

"Come in and sit with me for a moment, Rikardon," he said, coming away from the window. "I need to talk with you before you leave."

"Then Milda told you about Worfit?" I asked as I sat in one of the wood-and-fabric armchairs scattered around the center of the room.

Thanasset looked thin and strained. The small scar beside his left eye seemed whiter, and there were lines of tension around his mouth.

"She told me what happened, yes," he said. "And she told me what you told her. I want to ask you, bluntly, if you told her the truth." He was leaning forward in his chair, intent upon my answer.

"Yes, it was the truth," I said, surprised by the question. "Worfit—"

He waved his hand impatiently, as though Worfit, who had threatened my life and damaged his home, were of no importance.

"Your reasons for going to Thagorn," he said. "To rest and take some time to think. Are these your only reasons?"

"Yes."

"But why Thagorn? Why not Omergol, or all the way to Chizan?"

I was thoroughly confused, and beginning to feel a little impatient, myself.

"Father, I don't have any idea what you're getting at. Why don't you ask for the information you really want?"

Thanasset sighed and leaned back in his chair. He closed his eyes for a moment, then suddenly stood up and began pacing around the room.

"Ever since we had that short talk yesterday, Rikardon, I've been worrying about this. When Milda said you planned to go to Thagorn, it seemed to confirm my guess." He stopped his pacing, and leaned on the back of a chair. "Are you taking it upon yourself to find the Ra'ira and bring it back?"

I couldn't help it. I laughed out loud.

"It's rather more likely," I told him, "that I'll swim up the

Skarkel Falls. Why would I have lied to you about my motives, if that were true?"

"Two men have died, already, because of their involvement with Gharlas," he said. "It was conceivable to me that you would want to protect me from worry for your safety. I viewed it as . . . considerate, rather than deceptive."

There are three men dead, I corrected him silently, sobered by the thought. *Hural and the man who killed Markasset, both of whom were Gharlas's accomplices, and the man I killed the last time I left Raithskar.* The worry lines were still present in Thanasset's face. *He doesn't just want the truth,* I realized. *He wants to be convinced that it's the truth.*

"I haven't had a chance, yet, to tell you about the Sharith. Let me tell you now, so that you'll really understand why I'm going to Thagorn."

He nodded and sat down, and I related everything that had happened to me in the stronghold of the Sharith. I told him about Dharak's strength, and Thymas's impatience. I described the valley, and the call of kinship I had felt when I had looked at it that night. I told him about the huge Hall, built to hold men riding sha'um. Last of all, I told him what Dharak had said about my future place with the Sharith.

"So I'm going back to Thagorn to tell Dharak exactly what I'm telling you now, Father. Zaddorn seems confident of finding Gharlas through his contacts with other peace officers. He's a good man, and I believe him. I have no intention of chasing Gharlas clear to Eddarta on my own."

Milda appeared at the doorway with a big bowl of fruit and two glasses of fresh, cool water. "Thought you might want some breakfast," she said. She stared pointedly at my clothes as she set the things down on a table within our easy reach, and asked: "Did you have a good time last night?"

I grinned at her. "None of your business."

She laughed and went out of the room. I was relieved to see Thanasset smiling, his face smooth again. "I hadn't noticed what you were wearing," he said. "It's obvious you haven't had any sleep at all. Do you still plan to leave today?"

I was already munching on a tart, thick-skinned fruit, and I had to sip some water and swallow before I could answer. "The sooner I leave, the sooner I'll feel that you and Milda are safe from Worfit. I'll bathe and change clothes and pack—I should be ready to go by noon. I'll be able to nap while I ride."

"Then you won't be going to the Council meeting, after all?" Thanasset asked.

I shook my head. "I'll write a note to Zaddorn, but I hope you'll take my answer to the Council in person."

"What *is* your answer?" He was suddenly tense again.

"Only that I can't decide right now. I'll be back in a moon, perhaps less time. Maybe if you explain that I have some business to complete before I can commit myself—?"

"Of course. I'm sure they will make the offer again, when you return. Though Ferrathyn will be disappointed not to see you before you leave. He has taken a great interest in you. Did you know that it was he who suggested creating a special post on the Council for you?"

"No, I didn't," I admitted. *Ferrathyn's a nice old guy,* I commented to myself. *It's too bad he and Zaddorn don't get along better. Power politics, I suppose. But it's no wonder Ferrathyn expected me to accept the position—I'm sure he set it up simply as a favor to me and Thanasset.*

"What about you, Father? You seemed really to want me to take the job of the thirteenth Supervisor."

"You haven't decided *not* to take it, have you?" he asked.

"No."

"Well then, since you've convinced me that all you want is a vacation, and you'll be coming back to us soon, I feel better about—well, about everything. We'll find a way to handle Worfit. And I hope I'll see a Supervisor-in-the-making when you return."

5

It surprised the hell out of me that I could ride right up to Thagorn's gate without being challenged. The explanation occurred to me as soon as I heard the voice bellowing from the top of the wall that filled the narrow opening to the valley.

"What in the name of Kä are you doing out of uniform outside the city gates? You'll serve a seven-day cleaning the bath-house for this!"

Of course, their sentries aren't looking for strangers on sha'um! Any who may have seen me probably thought the same thing this guy does—and they probably chuckled about the reception I'd get. Latrine detail, yet!

I shaded my eyes with my hand and looked up at the man leaning over the edge of the wall. He was wearing a round-topped uniform hat. Its wide brim cast a shadow over all of his face except his mouth and jaw. His angry grimace displayed one snaggled tusk that looked awfully familiar.

"Don't you think, Bareff," I asked mildly, "that you ought to let me join up before you start giving me penalty duty?"

"What?" He leaned over so far that I thought he might fall. Then: "I'll be a vlek's daddy. Rikardon?"

I copied the gesture he had used to introduce his sha'um to me, nearly two weeks ago. I leaned forward, and drew my right hand along the side of Keeshah's jaw.

"And Keeshah," I said. "Will you tell the Lieutenant that we're here?"

"Why, I'd be pleased right out of my senses to do that little thing for you, Rikardon," he said. "The Lieutenant won't be surprised, will he?"

I hid a smile. "No."

"Nobody tells me *nothing*," he grumbled. Before he turned away he grinned down at me. "But I'll swear to Zanek it's good to see you again. It's been downright dull around here since you left."

Keeshah moved restlessly as we waited in front of the gate. I had sensed a growing ambivalence in him as we had approached Thagorn. He was both eager and apprehensive about meeting the sha'um of the Riders.

We had made the trip from Raithskar in a week, without rushing. We had stayed overnight at the Refreshment House of Yafnaar, where Balgokh, the eldest of the family of desert-dwellers, had invited me to dine with the entire clan in an inner courtyard. Such invitations were rare, and I had accepted gladly.

In return for a wonderful meal, I had answered the questions that they were too polite to ask: about the theft of the Ra'ira, now common knowledge in broad terms, but full of rumor concerning the details; about my adventures in regaining my memory (I gave them an altered version of the truth, omitting the fact that it wasn't *my* memory that I had found); and about all I knew of the history of Serkajon, his sword, and the Sharith.

Balgokh had announced that Keddan, one of the three men who were with me when I woke up at Yafnaar, had settled a marriage contract, and his bride had already set out from Kanlyr, near Eddarta. I had presented Balgokh with a gift to express my appreciation for his help, and asked that it be earmarked for the new couple, to which he had agreed with pleasure. The gift had been one of Milda's embroidered hangings, depicting the sha'um which Thanasset had once ridden, and it had delighted Keddan.

From Yafnaar, I had gone to Omergol and hoisted a few with Grallen, the proprietor of the bar where I had unknowingly offended two Sharith, and found myself with a fight on my hands. Much later, those two men had brought me into Thagorn. Just now, one of them had gone to fetch Dharak, the Lieutenant.

During the few minutes that Keeshah and I stood there, I tried to ignore the heads bobbing up above the edge of the wall, and the whispers that ran along overhead.

They're figuring out who I am and wondering why I walked *into Thagorn last time*, I speculated. I wonder if everybody here knows about the Ra'ira, or if Dharak has managed to keep it quiet. Well, I guess I'll find out pretty soon, now . . .

The massive gate was swinging inward slowly. It opened to reveal Dharak, standing beside a rangy gray sha'um. He put his hand on the cat's neck and they started toward me.

He's walking out to meet me! I thought. *Uh-oh, I don't like the look of that. Dharak, please don't . . .*

"Markasset, son of the sons of Serkajon," he began, in his rich and resonant voice, "be welcome in Thagorn as the new Captain of the Sharith."

You did it! I groaned to myself, and closed my eyes for a moment. *Now what do I do?*

I knew what I couldn't do. I couldn't embarrass the old man by stamping my foot and shouting "no" out here in front of God and everybody. There had been a giant communal gasp from the Sharith who had gathered curiously around the gate. Dharak had pulled off the surprise of the century, and I could see, from the way his mouth was twitching at one corner, that he was enjoying the effect he had created. I couldn't spoil it. I had to go along, at least for now.

It seemed eminently unfair to have this man, who had led the Sharith for most of his life, standing down out of respect for a newcomer, so I said: "Ride with me, Dharak."

He smiled broadly. "It will be my pleasure, Captain." He mounted his sha'um, brought him alongside Keeshah, and touched his cat's jaw. "This is Doran," he said.

I returned the introduction. Then, side by side, Dharak and I rode through the gates of Thagorn. We followed the main avenue of the city, which ran straight out from the gate between a long line of barracks buildings on the right and, atop a rise some distance away, the Hall on the left. The way led directly to the widest bridge across the river. Before we reached that bridge, we turned left toward the only family residence on this side of the river: a big, rambling house, traditionally the home of the Lieutenant and his family.

I had to struggle to keep my eyes forward in good military fashion. The exhilaration of riding *with* someone made me lightheaded, but full of strength. I was intensely aware of the motion of Keeshah's body under me, of the rippling muscles of the sha'um beside me, of Dharak on his back. It was a fresh-air feeling, a sense of freedom and power. And of belonging.

I had known I wanted this, but I hadn't suspected the depth of the need.

To belong, I reminded myself, as I dropped to the ground in front of Dharak's house. I was trembling with reaction to the swelling pride my entry into Thagorn had stirred in me.

But not to lead. I'll tell Dharak the truth, first chance I get.

Keeshah had been nervous, so close to a strange sha'um, but he had held his place at my request. As soon as he and Doran were free of their riders, they separated and faced each other, their nostrils distended, their tails fluffing slightly.

Will you be all right? I asked Keeshah.

He didn't answer specifically, but he was radiating a don't-bother-me-right-now attitude. I knew I couldn't help him, so I resolved to mind my own business and let him do things his own way. After all, unless I was in danger, Keeshah never mixed into my relations with other people.

"Welcome back, my friend," Dharak said to me. "You couldn't have arrived at a better time. Come in the house. We have a lot to talk about."

We certainly do, I agreed grimly as I followed him through the door. His wife, Shola, gave me a warm greeting and led us into a small room, where two places were set and a rich stew was steaming in the bowls. She excused herself from joining us, on the grounds of having eaten earlier. I caught a meaningful glance between her and Dharak before she left, and I figured that he had asked for privacy.

"I have heard, of course, that Thanasset was cleared," Dharak said, after we had finished eating. He had explained to me, before I left last time, that the Sharith had a network of friends who provided Dharak with information about the "outside world"—via *maufa,* the fast-flying Gandalaran message birds, I presumed. "I'm glad of it. What are your plans now?"

"All I want, for the moment, is to rest here awhile and get to know you and your men better," I said. *Get it over with,* I told myself. "Dharak, I'm not your Captain. I don't *want* to be your Captain."

"I saw as much in the look on your face today," he admitted. "But I had good reasons for greeting you in that fashion, Markasset. The Sharith *need* a Captain right now. I managed to keep your identity to myself, but news of the Ra'ira's loss has created a serious problem here. A faction of young men—led, I'm sorry to say, by my son, Thymas—is very close to breaking discipline and riding out after Gharlas.

"That would be a terrible mistake for three reasons. First, outsiders have an unflattering opinion of the Sharith already. I doubt that a group of headstrong yougsters—and their sha'um—would improve it any. Second, I would have no choice but to forbid their return." His voice wavered a little.

And one of those in exile would be your son, I thought.

"It would cost us a third of our Riders," he said. He looked out of the window and sighed. "There were a thousand Riders when we settled here. Now there are less than a hundred.

"Last and most important," he continued more briskly, "they have little chance of success, and every opportunity to cloud the trail you'll be following."

"I—I'm not going after Gharlas, either. Partly for the same reason you've just given. Zaddorn is working on it through his Peace and Security contacts. I figure that, if I go tramping into the middle of things, it will make finding Gharlas that much harder for him."

The Lieutenant got up from his chair and walked over to a small window which overlooked the river. He stood there for a few seconds, then turned back to me.

I was struck, again, by the similarity between him and Thanasset. It wasn't physical; Dharak had a thicker, stronger body and a startling shock of snow-white head fur. But the window gesture, and now the look of uncertainty . . .

"I wish I knew more about the customs of Serkajon's house," he said. "Has Thanasset—"

The door burst open at that moment, and Thymas stomped in. He had his father's build, on a shorter and slimmer scale. He had pushed his sand-colored hat off his head to hang by its neckstring, and I could have sworn that his head fur, a little more yellow in tone than his father's, was bristling.

"I just got back from my patrol," he said to his father. "I heard what happened. How could you—" He caught sight of me, and whirled in my direction, his hand on the hilt of his sword.

"You *filth*," he spat at me. "You lied to us. You betrayed your own sha'um by riding others. And you betrayed a sacred vow by letting Gharlas get away!

"You're a coward and a liar, Markasset! I do not accept you as my Captain!" He drew his sword. "Agree to leave Thagorn *today*, and never return, and I will spare your life."

Ah, the perversity of human nature. Here I had just been ducking the Captaincy for all I was worth. Yet Thymas's accusation that I was *unfit* for it made me madder than hell.

Before Dharak could move a muscle, I was on my feet and around the table. Thymas crouched back, ready for a fight, but I had enough control to know that I didn't want that. The boy would be no real trouble for Markasset's swordsmanship, but Thymas was so angry that I might have to hurt him to put him out of action.

"*You* will be lucky to get out of this room with your head still attached, if you don't put that sword away *right now!*" I yelled. I took a step toward him; he backed up, still holding his sword at the ready. I had the offensive. He knew it, and didn't like it.

"How dare you dishonor your father by baring your sword

in his home?" I challenged him. "You are threatening your father's guest."

I pointed my finger at him for emphasis, and stepped forward again. He backed another step, and touched the wall with his heel. Dharak, who had been behind Thymas, had moved aside, and was watching us with concern.

"If you had come in here and *asked* for explanations, I'd have given them," I growled. "I'd have told you that I had to go back to Raithskar to save my father's life—would you have made a different choice? I'd have told you that Gharlas is going to Eddarta, and Zaddorn has people watching for him. I'd have told you that *I had Keeshah's permission to ride with Bareff and Liden*."

I saw his face register disbelief as I loomed over him. He placed the point of his sword against my chest, and I leaned into it until I could feel it pricking skin, and I knew he could feel my weight against his wrist.

"But since you have violated all the rules of common courtesy, I'm only going to give you one answer, plus a small warning, out of respect for Dharak.

"My name wasn't Rikardon *then*," I said, jabbing my finger at him, "but it is *now*. If you insist on fighting me, you'll be facing Rika, the steel sword of Serkajon!"

I backed off. Thymas was angry, humiliated, undecided.

"I'm just about out of patience," I said. "Do yourself a favor and get out of here."

The boy looked from me to Dharak, who wasn't offering him any support. Then he sheathed his sword. "If this weren't my father's house—" he muttered. Then he stormed out the door, and Dharak and I both sighed with relief.

"Do you see?" Dharak asked. "He is nearly uncontrollable."

"I hope *you* see that I wouldn't be much help in that department," I told him. "It was sheer luck that he wasn't just a little bit more angry. He had a perfect opportunity to kill me just now."

"Thymas may, very well, be past saving," Dharak said sadly. "But the others are not. They are restless and idealistic. They are concerned for the Ra'ira and want action.

"Well, the acquisition of a new Captain is action of a sort. Where they would defy me, they will accept your authority and remain here, content under your orders, at least for a while. By the time they get restless again, perhaps Zaddorn will have found the Ra'ira and there will be no more problem."

I sat down at the table and drained the last of the glass of faen.

"Then you agree that Zaddorn can do it without my help?" I asked. "Before Thymas burst in, I thought you were unsure. Weren't you going to ask me something?"

He smiled. "You have answered that question for me. If Thanasset gave you Serkajon's sword—well, I accept your judgment of how best to return the Ra'ira to Raithskar.

"We have had word that Tarani will arrive in a seven-day. Let me arrange for a formal ceremony that day, presenting the Riders to you. We'll have a banquet that evening, and Tarani will perform for us. It will be an occasion to remember, a respite from tension and disagreement. We could all use it.

"In the meantime, you can get to know us better, and have the relaxation you need. Afterward, you can go back to Raithskar, or anywhere you wish, and we will leave the recovery of the Ra'ira in your hands—and, through your choice, in Zaddorn's."

I thought about it while Dharak poured more faen from the ceramic pitcher that had been left on the table. The Lieutenant hadn't brought up how silly *he* would look, if I turned him down after he had acknowledged me as the Captain in public.

He seems to want me only for a figurehead, I thought. *I did lie to him that first time. He knew it, and he covered for me. I owe him for that. But this . . . something doesn't feel right.*

"What would happen at the ceremony?" I asked.

"I'd just say a few words to the assembled Sharith—everyone will be there, not just the Riders—and introduce you. From there, you can do what you wish." He lifted his glass to me. "Health."

"And wisdom," I answered the toast automatically. "There won't be an oath of allegiance, or anything?"

Dharak laughed, nearly choking on his drink. "Certainly there will be, Mar—I mean, Rikardon. *Our* allegiance to *you*. As to your reply, I've said that it's up to you. This is, after all, the first time such a ceremony has been necessary—or possible. Write the rest of it yourself."

Something was still bothering me. "Isn't this deceptive, Dharak? I mean, letting your people believe I'll get the Ra'ira back, when you know I have no plans in that direction at all? And binding them to me, but asking nothing *from* me?"

"My conscience is clear about this, my friend. Shall I tell you why?"

"I asked, didn't I?"

He leaned on the table and reached across it to put his hand on my wrist.

"We need no oath from you, Rikardon. You're already part of us. It's why you came back here. You felt it, yourself, as you rode in."

I sure felt something, I admitted to myself. *I'm feeling it now, a sense of . . . completeness. It scares me a little.*

"I felt it *about* you, the first time we met," Dharak continued. "Do you realize that it has been hundreds and hundreds of years since any man of Serkajon's descent set foot in Thagorn? And now it has happened in the wake of the Ra'ira falling into the possession of a madman. It is difficult not to see meaning in all of it. I believe that it is important, for you as well as for us, that we establish your position here.

"I know you think it's a waste of time, and that you will never have occasion to exercise the rights of command you'll be given. I even hope that you're right, for all our sakes."

"But you don't think so, do you?" I asked him.

"No, I don't." He sighed. "I'm getting old, Rikardon. These changes in the world I've always known frighten me. I'll admit that I want you formally named Captain as a precaution against a troubled future."

Why, all he's doing is buying insurance, I realized with a deep sense of relief. *If all hell breaks loose because of this Ra'ira thing, he doesn't want to be the only one holding the bag. Thymas won't be any help. In fact, Thymas might be the one to set it off, if he goes through with his screwy plan about chasing down Gharlas.*

If I agree to this, the harm Thymas can do will be reduced, because fewer men will follow him—according to Dharak's line of thinking. If Gharlas does slip through Zaddorn's net, reach Eddarta, and begin a war to re-establish the Kingdom with him at the head of it . . .

Sure, it would be a mess, and the Sharith would be the strongest weapon of opposition. Yet they've been sitting here in Thagorn, playing military games and living off "tribute" for so many generations, that attrition has cut them way down. They aren't the weapon they were once. I can see why Dharak wouldn't want the duty of leading them into battle.

So he's setting me up, and I'm damned if I can get mad about it. Especially since he has admitted it, openly. And for one other reason—nothing of this scenario is ever going to happen. Zaddorn will find Gharlas, get the Ra'ira back, and I can help Dharak by just minding my own business.

Where's the risk?

"All right," I said out loud. "I'll do it."

6

Without realizing it, I had acquired preconceptions about the lifestyle of the Sharith. Most of them, as usually happens, were wrong.

I had expected an organization like the military groups of which Ricardo had been a member—the Marines during World War II, and the Marine Reserves for many years afterward. The only similarity I could find, during the week I spent learning about the Sharith, was the chain-of-command principal, and the requirement that on-duty Riders always wear their tan, desert-ready uniforms.

The Riders weren't the only people who were given rank and assigned duties. The distribution of tasks was roughly like this:

The Riders were responsible for city security, surveillance, and "assessment of tribute." Certain unpleasant jobs—like cleaning the mire from the fine-mesh filters that covered the bath-house drains—were routinely assigned as punishment details.

The women of Thagorn handled the daily maintenance, including cooking, cleaning, and laundry. Wives did these chores for their own households, sometimes assisted by their youngest children or by the kids of a larger family. The older girls and unmarried women did the same things for the unmarried men.

The children were obligated to attand a school conducted by most of the adults on a rotation basis. It taught reading and writing, sewing and building skills, and the all-important history of the Sharith. Girls twelve and younger, and all boys up to age sixteen, worked in the grainfields in their off hours, and helped wherever they were needed.

There was a special category of children called "cubs." These were boys thirteen to sixteen who had returned from the Valley of the Sha'um with two-year-old cats, after spending a year, living on their own, in that valley. Their off-school time was spent in training with the Riders and in developing precision coordination with their sha'um.

Most surprising of all, to me, was the large number of men who were not Riders—about a third of the adult males. These men were the farmers, the masons, the carpenters, the millers. They were as well trained in fighting skills as any of the Riders. They spent part of their time as guards on the wall and could, if necessary, be carried into battle as second riders on sha'um.

They were treated with no less respect than the Riders. At age twelve, every boy had to make the choice of whether to risk a trip to the Valley of the Sha'um. If he stayed, he learned some other necessary skill, and he was never faulted for his choice. It went without saying that a boy who didn't want to go would have less chance of survival.

As it was, a fourth of the boys who went to the Valley never returned. I was sure that those losses had contributed to the declining size of the settlement.

The Riders were honored by everyone in Thagorn as the symbol and purpose of the Sharith. But men who did not ride were respected as contributors of important support functions.

A series of ranks existed within each group of the Sharith. The Riders were organized into four companies. Each company had a leader and sub-leaders, though the only title of rank belonged to the Lieutenant. Among the married women, rank corresponded, more or less, to the ranks of their husbands. Age was the general criterion for rank among the unmarried women, and among the children.

Dharak's wife, Shola, settled disagreements among wives, unmarried women, and older girls, in the same way that

Dharak held authority over the men. But his was the ultimate authority in every case. Even children who felt they had been given unjust punishment could appeal to him for an objective decision. He, and previous Lieutenants, had discouraged abuse of these rights of appeal by upholding all prior judgments unless a bias was obvious and the penalty was grossly unfair.

This is not to say that all was peace and order in Thagorn. By no means. The Sharith had their share of wild kids and irresponsible adults. There was just an organized, on-the-spot way of dealing with problems.

Which brings me around to Thymas.

Thymas was the youngest of Dharak's and Shola's four children, and he had been conceived almost at the end of Shola's fertility—she had been forty-two, Dharak forty-five, when the boy was born. Of the other three, two were daughters, both of them married and with their own children now. The fourth had been a boy. He had never returned from the Valley of the Sha'um.

I spent a lot of time talking with Dharak during that week, and I began to understand Thymas better. Sharith custom did not provide for the son of the Lieutenant *necessarily* to replace his father. But from the time he could talk, Thymas had been determined to make it so in his case. He had worked and trained hard, demanding a great deal of himself, his sha'um and anyone who was under his authority. At thirteen, he had taken the leadership position among the cubs—an unusual achievement—and held it for three years.

Dharak loved the boy, but thought him too much of a perfectionist. Thymas had won respect among the Riders, but not many friends. Still, he had done nothing wrong, so Dharak had given him the red sash of a future Lieutenant at the ceremony when he and three other sixteen-year-olds had been accepted into the Riders.

Thymas stayed out of my way throughout the week I spent in Thagorn, and I was just as glad. I joined the combat exercises, and worked myself to exhaustion. I was pleased that Markasset's training compared very well with the skills shown by the Sharith, but I knew that if Thymas had participated, the competition would have been much less friendly. I heard, from some of the men, that he was tough and fast, full of tricks in wrestling or sword work.

It's a good thing he backed down from that fight, I thought then. *He wouldn't have been the easy opponent I expected. There's going to have to be a showdown before that ceremony. But I won't worry until it happens.*

Keeshah and I rode on patrols, watched the cubs training, and occasionally accepted private lessons in mounted combat techniques, field procedures and orders, and other things a Rider learned as soon as he had a sha'um. Keeshah seemed to enjoy the training, too; he felt at home in Thagorn.

Two evenings of that week, I tried to get drunk with Bareff and Liden. The first occasion had been initiated by Bareff, who had grabbed a handful of the front of my tunic and pulled me nose-to-nose with his craggy face.

"When do I get some answers about what the filth has been going on?"

"Would right now be too soon?"

"Right now would be just fine," he said, and let me go. "Liden's got the barut poured."

Barut was a Gandalaran liquor, aromatic and powerful. Thanasset had introduced me to it. Along with water, the Fa'aldu produced it in their refreshment houses and charged a high price for it.

Bareff and Liden both lived in one of the barracks buildings with several other bachelors. There were ten buildings, each built to provide private-room accommodations for forty men. Three of the barracks were still in use as bachelor's quarters, with fifteen to twenty men in each one, so that the men had plenty of room to spread out.

Bareff had obtained permission to tear down a wall and build an interior connecting door so that, instead of one good-sized room, he had a huge parlor and an attached bedroom. There was a dining area in the center of the building, where he took his meals with the other residents. But he and Liden usually spent their evenings in Bareff's living room, playing *mondea*.

I joined them that evening. The explanations were quickly made, since I had no reason to tell them of Markasset's "memory loss." They didn't know that I had been on the caravan, under a different alias, before they attacked it. So the story they heard was of a Supervisor's son who wasn't sure how he'd be greeted in Thagorn, as the only non-Sharith

Rider in Gandalara. Bareff and Liden were suitably impressed, when I told them that Keeshah had allowed me to ride with them.

"I doubt that Poltar would have stood for it," Bareff said.

Liden shook his head. "I can't see how it would be, living off by yourself with no other Riders".

"Let's just say I'm glad to be here now," I said, and lifted my glass of barut. "Health."

"And wisdom," they echoed. We drained the tiny glasses, then Bareff broke out the *mondeana*, the dice-like playing pieces of the game.

There were six mondeana, cubes cut from some hard wood, with different shapes carved into each two-inch-square side. The carvings had been stained or dyed with different colors to emphasize their detail, and though the surfaces showed signs of wear, the colors were still bright. The figures were men, animals, birds, trees, an image of an oat-like grain, and a symbol I had seen on the map Thanasset had given me to guide me to Thagorn. The symbol represented a Refreshment House.

The rules of the game were complex and challenging, and I understood why Markasset had been fascinated by it. Each of the thirty-six figures had a different rank, and the total score of a throw depended not only on which sides turned up, but where they were positioned. The object of the game was not to achieve the highest score, but an exact one. The player had many choices to make, and there was at least as much skill as luck involved in winning a game.

I was surprised that Bareff and Liden didn't insist on betting. They explained, with elaborate modesty, that they wouldn't allow me to lose my money to a pair of pros.

My first impulse was to let Markasset take over as we played, thinking his experience with the game would make for faster, surer playing. Then I recalled his record of losses in Worfit's gaming houses, and decided I'd struggle through on my own. I had a good command of the rules, thanks to Markasset's memory, but I tried to learn the game's strategy from ground zero. By the end of the evening, I was winning an occasional round.

I've said that I *tried* to get drunk. Along about the fifth round of barut, I was feeling pleasantly relaxed and detached from the world. I accepted another glass to keep the high going, but found that I couldn't make myself drink it. Something inside was saying: *This is not good for you. Don't do it.*

I realized, at once, that this was another manifestation of the Gandalaran "inner awareness."

Gandalarans are highly tuned to their own body needs and rhythms. I always *knew,* within minutes, what time of day it was, and when the sun or moon would rise or set. Hural, the four-fingered man Dharak and I had questioned, had *known* that he would die, shortly, of his consumptive cough.

On the ride from Raithskar to Thagorn, I had begun to see a connection between inner awareness and the All-Mind. According to the explanation Thanasset had given me, all Gandalarans were linked, at least subconsciously, with all the experiences of thousands of years of other Gandalarans. It seemed to me that there might be an automatic search-and-report hookup. The body says to the All-Mind: *I feel this way,* or, *Light and temperature are like this.* The All-Mind then locates all identical feelings among its members and tabulates the events subsequent to the conditions described by the body. It comes up with: *You will hate yourself in the morning if you drink another glass of barut,* or, *In two hours and six minutes, it will be noon.* It's naming probabilities based on similar experiences. Given a large enough sample, it's most likely right, nearly all the time.

The inner awareness seemed to be a pretty good deal, in general. But it was a handicap for me, whenever I returned to the unanswerable puzzle about where Gandalara was located. It assured a viewpoint that was incontrovertibly subjective.

I knew that there was no place like Gandalara on the Earth as I had known it. I might have conceded the possibility of an undiscovered salt desert like the Kapiral, but you could never convince me that, even with the Earth's extensive cloud cover, our satellite surveillance could have missed the Great Wall.

The differences were acceptable. It was the similarities that caused me problems. I could tell by the movement of light across the cloud cover at night that this world had only one moon. There were human-like creatures and cat-like creatures, birds and insects and apes—all not quite the same as I had known them. How was it possible that such similar inhabitants had evolved on two different worlds?

I couldn't tell for sure without standing a human next to a Gandalaran, but I thought these people were about the same size as humans—perhaps a little shorter, on the average. Mostly, that judgment was based on the comparative size of the sha'um. Their musculature was thicker and more dense than that of the tiger, which the sha'um resembled in shape. That fitted in with what I knew of the square-cube law, that the mass of a thing increases cubically as the size is squared. The bigger the cat, the more need for muscle.

There was a further coincidence in the time-keeping methods of my two worlds. The Gandalaran year had three hundred and sixty-five days; it was composed of thirteen "moons" and a "year day"—which Raithskar celebrated as Commemoration Day. I would have regarded that as tentative proof that I was, indeed, still on Earth—except for the existence of inner awareness.

I *knew* how long a day was, but there was no way to measure it against Ricardo's subjective standards. The days and nights might be fifteen Earth hours long, or only three. How could I tell? And regarding this world's single moon—I had never seen it. The cloud cover had broken only once at night. I had seen a sky with no familiar constellations, but I hadn't seen the moon. Markasset didn't know what the phases of his moon looked like.

Gandalarans did have a concept of objects in the sky which gave off light, but their actual words for "sun" and "moon" meant "daylight" and "nightlight." I had developed the habit of translating automatically into my own, more familiar, terms.

I had begun doing that for distances, as well. Thanasset's map had shown distances in "days"—a day was the distance a man could walk in one day, allowing adequate time for food and rest. I computed a day to be twelve hours of walking at an average of two and a half miles per hour, or thirty miles.

I suppose it would have been easier, in the long run, if I had just learned to use Markasset's terminology. But Ricardo Carillo, a reasonably intelligent man who had learned to speak several languages with great fluency, had reached age of sixty, using the same set of measurements all his l. Through my frequent trips to Europe for conferences, and a conversion campaign in the United States, I had learned to live with metric measurements—but I had always needed to *think* about them in the terms of the English system. Markasset's memory was with me now, but Ricardo was doing most of the thinking.

What I thought, when I got that glass of barut close enough to drink, was: *I can still drink this, and suffer the consequences. But why should I?*

I put the glass down, shaking my head, and Bareff poured it back into the glass pitcher and put the stopper in. "Yeah, I've had enough, too," he said.

We played mondea for another hour or so, then I said good night and went to my own room, which was located in the same barracks. Dharak had wanted me to stay at his house, but I had refused as gently as possible, saying that I wasn't officially the Captain until after the ceremony. I wanted to be part of the group for a while.

I discovered that I *liked* being part of the group. As the day approached when I would be named Captain, my resistance began to increase again.

It had all sounded so simple when I had talked with Dharak. Take a title. Don't do anything with it. Whatever I was moved by "fate" to do, even if turned out to be doing nothing, that would be the right thing to do.

There had to be a catch. I knew it couldn't have been set up deliberately by Dharak. It was clear that he believed everything he had said to me. But the feeling persisted—*there was a catch*.

It was to escape that feeling that I suggested another session of mondea on the night before the ceremony. Privately, I had resolved to ignore my inner awareness and get blotto. It was an impulse as rare in Ricardo as it had been in Markasset, and it worried me. As I sipped my third glass of barut, it seemed to me that this kind of make-merry-now philosophy had been the basis for bachelor's parties in Ricardo's world. While I regarded that as a deep truth in my fuzzy state of mind, I failed to see the parallel until the fatal sixth glass was being poured.

Then it hit me.

Of course there was a catch.

I was the catch.

No matter what I said I wanted, no matter that nothing would be demanded of me—I couldn't go through that ceremony without being prepared to accept the responsibilities it conferred. I was none too sure what they were, or might be in the future, but I knew that if I didn't commit myself to them, totally and honestly, I would be doing the very thing Thymas had accused me of—betraying the Sharith.

With a sigh of resignation, I handed my filled glass back to Bareff. "I'd better quit now," I told him. "I'll need to be sharp for the ceremony tomorrow."

7

In the morning, I called Keeshah, and we ran up into the hills at the back of the valley. The ceremony had been scheduled for early afternoon, and I wanted some time alone before facing Dharak at lunchtime.

This slope, and the heavily wooded areas at the sides of the valley, were the hunting grounds of the sha'um. The Sharith raised herds of domestic glith, but were careful to repopulate the wild herds, when necessary. The sha'um hunted their own food, which kept them in shape and maintained their sense of freedom. Not that they were captive in any sense—they remained in Thagorn because their riders were here, and they wanted to be with them.

Keeshah picked his way carefully through the tangled brush of the hillside. Several times, his presence startled small groups of glith from their grazing. The glith were goat-sized animals with thin, graceful legs, and bilateral horns that came straight up from their skulls, then twisted slightly to point forward.

Their fur was dark and long. In the domestic herds, the fur was salvaged when the skins of slaughtered animals were tanned. It was too fine and smooth to be woven into yarn, but it served as filling for the sleeping mats.

Except when we had trained together, I had left Keeshah pretty much to himself. Any fears I'd had about his being accepted by the other sha'um had vanished immediately. There was plenty of room in the valley, and plenty of food.

And the other traditional source of conflict between male cats wasn't a problem.

To take my mind off the impending ceremony, I asked Keeshah a question I'd been wanting to ask ever since we arrived.

Don't you want a female sha'um, Keeshah?

I do not need one yet.

Markasset was twenty-three years old, so Keeshah was twelve. Markasset had known that sha'um had lifetimes as long or longer than those of men. It was conceivable that Keeshah would undergo something akin to puberty. His use of the image "yet" indicated it.

When will you need one?

I will know.

Oh, yes, I thought, *I'm sure you'll know.* To him, I said: **What will you do when you need one?**

Return to the Valley, he answered. **Females there.**

Shall I come with you?

No.

My stomach knotted up. I had to ask the next question.

Will you come back from the Valley?

I do not know.

With startling suddenness, Markasset's memory gave me an entire, tense year of his life, when Thanasset had waited for the return of his sha'um. Markasset had been ten at the time. When his father's sha'um had not returned by the end of the year, the boy had become determined to go to the Valley himself. For his own sake, yes—but partly to bring another sha'um into the household so that his father wouldn't be so lonely.

I wondered if Thanasset had known about the boy's generous impulse. It was almost certain that it hadn't borne the fruit Markasset had wanted. The sight of Markasset and Keeshah together would have brought Thanasset only pain, at first, then wistful memories.

Let's see, Thanasset was fifty-six now—*why, he's younger than I was when I left my other world. Yet with Markasset's perspectives, I've been calling him an old man. Ah, youth!* —which meant he had been forty-five when his sha'um had left him. The cat had been thirty-four years old.

That couldn't have been the first time his sha'um had gone to the Valley. Markasset's memory of that year includes such an air of expectancy—Thanasset thought the cat would be back. I wonder what happened to him? Killed by a rival for the same female, maybe? Or a love affair too potent to abandon?

A whimsical notion struck me. *Markasset went to the Valley only two years later. It's conceivable that Keeshah is the son of Thanasset's sha'um!*

It would be useless to ask Keeshah to verify that. To him, a sha'um's identity was an impression of appearance, odor, and voice. His communication with them was purely physical, a matter of gesture or attitude combined with vocal pitch.

Do you understand what is going to happen this afternoon? I asked Keeshah. **Do the others understand?**

It doesn't matter.

Well, I guess that told me, I thought, laughing to myself. *A Rider's only worth to a sha'um lies in his relationship to the big cat. And I think all the Riders would agree that it's a higher honor than any rank they might confer on one another.*

Let's get it done.

We turned back down the hill.

Dharak greeted me at his door with a glass of faen and a question: "Have you decided what your part of the ceremony will be?"

I gaped at him. "I haven't even thought about it," I admitted. "Something will occur to me when it's time."

We had a quiet homey lunch with Shola, then Dharak offered me the use of his private bath-house. When I returned to the guest room, I found that Dharak had replaced my "civilian" clothes with a Sharith uniform.

It consisted of trousers and long-sleeved tunic, both tan and made of a tightly-woven, soft linen. All the uniforms looked like this, but few were of such fine quality fabric. With the uniform was a beautiful pair of sueded leather boots which reached to my knees. On the outer sides of the boots, holes had been cut at small intervals. Groups of thin leather strips had been threaded through the holes, interlaced and knotted with one or more other of the groups, and then allowed to drape into a pointed fringe about four inches long. The knotting, besides being decorative, served to make the boot more rigid. The interior sides, which would press into a sha'um's flanks, were left bare and smooth.

As I was stamping into the second boot, Dharak knocked and came into the room. He beamed at me when he saw the boots on my feet.

"It's time they were worn again," he said.

"You're not going to tell me that *these* belonged to Serkajon, are you? They're brand new."

"They are copies of his boots, which we kept carefully for him, wrapped in oiled cloth, until they were barely recognizable, much less wearable. Since then, one of our people has crafted a new pair, whenever signs of spoiling appeared on the old ones. These were made only last year." He smiled slyly. "I see they fit you well."

"Yes, they fit," I said. "But they make me uncomfortable."

He frowned. "I have seen how much this troubles you, my friend. If you say so, I will cancel the ceremony."

Make yourself look the fool, and foul up all the plans you've made, based on my new position? I believe you would do that out of friendship, and I'm grateful. But I realized, last night, that it was too late to cancel, the day I agreed to it.

I stood up and gripped his shoulder. I tried to smile naturally. "You've convinced me that this is supposed to happen," I told him. "And I guess I'm ready."

"Not quite," he said. He had brought a bundle with him, and now he unwrapped it. He unfolded an embroidered sash much like the blue one he was wearing, only this one was a silky white, stiffened and decorated with silver threads. "This, too, is a duplicate," he explained as he helped me to arrange it around my waist in exactly the right way. Then he picked up Rika, which rested now in an ornamental scabbard, and held it out to me. "Your sword, Captain."

I reached for it, hesitated, then grinned and took it from him.

Keeshah and Doran were waiting outside Dharak's house. The Lieutenant and I mounted and rode, close together, up to the Hall. I could see that the rest of Thagorn was deserted; there weren't even any guards on the wall. The great, heavy gates were shut and barred, a visual symbol of the security of the valley.

The Hall was a huge, square building, two stories high, but empty of a second floor. I had crossed its vastness once, walking across its marble-tiled floor. I was no less awed by its size now, as I rode into it.

Enormous double doors in the center of the south wall opened as we approached them. They closed behind us, and the men who had manipulated them went to stand with the other non-Riders, who were waiting quietly in the western quarter of the Hall.

Dharak and I rode through an aisle formed by mounted Riders. They faced toward us until we had passed by, then turned toward the great marble block in the center of the floor, which was the Hall's speaking platform.

As we rode up to that platform and stepped down to it, I felt a familiar tightening in my chest. It was like the feeling Ricardo had experienced, whenever he had watched a Marine company doing close-order drill. The beauty of precision, the hours of training necessary, the sensation of unity—to these were added the grace and stength of the big cats and the very special pride of the Riders. Again I was swept up in that feeling of *belonging*.

As we turned to address the Riders, Dharak let out a small gasp of impatience. It wasn't hard to figure what was bothering him. The four companies of Riders were arranged in sharply dressed columns, three abreast. The companies were separated by wide aisles, and their leaders were out front. That is, three of the leaders were there, visible evidence of the chain of command. The fourth leader was missing.

So Thymas didn't want to come to the party? I thought. *I really don't mind—but Dharak does*.

The Lieutenant's face was grim, as he called the order to dismount. When the men were standing, the cats crouched down to the floor, each to his Rider's right. Dharak began speaking.

"Great changes have come upon Gandalara," he said. "For the first time since the fall of the Kingdom, the Ra'ira has left Raithskar. It is in the hands of one whose amibition makes him both unworthy and dangerous to the peace we are pledged to preserve. Because of this terrible threat, the long centuries of separation between us and our leader are now at an end."

He put his hand on my shoulder.

"This is Rikardon, the son of Thanasset of Raithskar, who is descended in direct line from our great Captain, Serkajon. I tell you, from my own knowledge, that he brings honor to the boots and the color of rank which he now wears. He carries Rika, the great sword of rakor which Serkajon carried during his lifetime."

Dharak's voice rose from just louder than normal, until he was shouting his last words.

"He *rides*!" the Lieutenant called out. "Honor Rikardon as our Captain!"

A tremendous sound surged upward from the men before me, and from the rest of the Sharith standing to the west of the platform. Stunned by the suddenness of the sound, it took me a few seconds to realize that they were shouting my name. When they repeated it twice, they quieted expectantly.

All right, smart guy, I told myself. *This is where you're supposed to wing it. Do something.*

I looked out over the people and sha'um on the floor around me. I tried to see a dwindling society, desperate to maintain its heritage and traditions against pressure from the outside world and against the erosion of inaction. But the pity associated with such a vision refused to come.

I saw the Sharith. Proud of their beginnings, satisfied with their lifestyle, confident that their use would come again to the world. Sure that I was the signal and the instrument of the world's need for what they had to offer.

I should say something about the Ra'ira, I thought. *I ought to lay the groundwork for Dharak's orders to sit still. But that—even that—seems unimportant now. Only one thing is important.*

I am the Captain of the Sharith.

Every one of these men, women, and children has pledged life and service to me today. I'm not sure I deserve it, but they've done it. And they *deserve more than a disappointing speech.*

I jumped down from the dais and called Keeshah to walk on the right side of me. We went up to the leader of the third company, which was the one closest to me. It was Liden. His sha'um, Cheral, stood up as Keeshah and I approached. "This is Keeshah," I introduced him formally. Then I offered my hand to Liden. "Thanks for your friendship, Liden. And for yours, Cheral."

As Liden grinned and accepted the handshake, I lifted my left hand, palm upward, to the cat. He dipped his head and touched my palm lightly with his muzzle. Liden copied my gesture, and Keeshah responded in the same way.

Smells good, Keeshah told me. **Like friend.**

I moved around Liden and walked up to the first rank of his company. The boy on its eastern edge, along the aisle I had ridden down, stood up straighter. His sha'um stood up.

"I am Raden," the boy said, then introduced his cat: "This is Borral."

Again I offered my hands to the Rider and his sha'um, and Keeshah greeted the man.

"Welcome, Captain," Raden said, as he gripped my hand. His gaze strayed to Keeshah at the touch of fur and whiskers to his left hand.

"I'm glad to be here, Raden and Borral," I said. Keeshah and I moved on.

It took time to greet each one of nearly a hundred Riders individually. Part of me was focused on the men and their sha'um, making an effort to store the names in my memory. Another part of my consciousness was congratulating me on finding precisely the right way to confirm my place with the Sharith.

The handshake wasn't a Gandalaran custom. I had used it out of Ricardo's habit, and out of an instinctive desire to verify the reality of the occasion by touching someone. The open-palm gesture had originated on my first arrival in Thagorn, when I had sought a way to express my thanks to Poltar and Cheral for carrying me as extra weight. Now it was giving Keeshah an opportunity to record the identities of the Riders by sight and smell, and the sha'um were receiving the same information about me.

Those sha'um were also receiving an influx of whatever emotion the Riders felt as I spoke to them. I suspected they shared what I was feeling, and projecting to Keeshah—a singing gladness and a sense of history changing at our fingertips.

When Keeshah and I had greeted all the Riders except Dharak—and the missing Thymas—we moved through the other members of the Sharith. Because I was aware of how long everyone had been standing here, I didn't ask names, but walked through the crowd rather quickly, greeting the people I did know, and saying hello in a general way. Keeshah followed me, the crowd moving back when necessary to let him pass, and he did greet everybody. He walked with his head bent, and skimmed his nose across the hands that were held out to him eagerly.

Finally, we returned to the center of the Hall. Dharak had stepped down from the platform, and was waiting beside Doran. His eyes were shining as he gripped my hand strongly, and lifted his left hand to Keeshah. He didn't say anything, and neither did I. I turned away and mounted Keeshah, then asked him to climb up to stand on the platform. I had a high, clear view of everyone in the Hall and all of them, from the sha'um to the smallest child, were watching me.

"You have done us great honor this day," I forced away the constriction in my throat, and tried to project my voice clearly. "Keeshah and I thank you.

"It is not yet time for the Sharith to ride out of Thagorn and back into the affairs of the world. I must leave you tomorrow—and I am sad to go—but Dharak will continue his excellent leadership in my absence. Show him the respect you would offer to me. I will return when there is need."

I guess that's ambiguous enough, I thought, with a twinge of guilt. *And long enough. I'll bet the little kids are really tired of all this standing.*

"I will try to be worthy of the friendship of the Sharith," I finished off, and I could hear my voice crack, revealing how deeply I had been moved by this ceremony.

Keeshah jumped down from the platform and started down the aisle of cats and men toward the double doors. Men ran around the Riders to get to the doors and open them, and I told Keeshah to go slowly, so they would have time to get there.

Behind me, Dharak shouted: "Rikardon and Keeshah!"

The cry was taken up all around me, and this time the men's voices were accompanied by the roaring of the sha'um. Keeshah and I moved through a horrendous, glorious noise, and I was overtaken by a fierce surge of joy.

Keeshah's feeling it, too! I reached for him, and we merged. *The sha'um are saluting him, not me. He can hear it in their voices.*

I am not the Captain of the Sharith.

We are.

Keeshah and I, together, rode out of the Hall into a world that was sharper and brighter than the one we had left.

8

"He has gone too far this time," Dharak was saying. "He will pay for his insult to you. I told him, specifically, that I required his presence, in spite of his uncertain feelings about you."

That's mild phrasing. Thymas hates my tusks.

We were standing, with Shola, in the main avenue, facing the gates which were now open. As soon as the wall guards had returned to their posts after the ceremony, they had reported the approach of the entertainment troupe, and we had come here to greet them. The rest of the Sharith lined the avenue, leaving a broad pathway from the gate to where we waited.

"It was part of his duty. That's exactly the way I stated it to him. It was his *duty* to be there to acclaim you the Captain."

I didn't particularly care whether Thymas accepted me or not. But I knew there was more at stake here than Dharak's pride. The Lieutenant had based his plans for controlling an incipient rebellion on my authority, and Thymas had already, indirectly, defied that authority. It couldn't be ignored.

"You are too angry, Dharak," I said, using the same quiet, intense tones Dharak was using, to keep from being overheard by those nearest us. "I will judge him."

Shola stepped between us. "Thank you, *Captain*," she said.

The Lieutenant turned to face the gate. "Perhaps Thymas won't come back to Thagorn," he said quietly. "Perhaps that would be best."

"Look—the acrobats!" Shola cried, with a forced show of excitement.

The first members of the troupe were, indeed, somersaulting and flipping through the somber gates of Thagorn. They were followed by a procession which reminded me delightfully of the circus parades I had seen when Ricardo had been a child. Jugglers tossed crockery around at dizzying speeds. Men and women strutted by in incredible and intricate costumes: one made up entirely of feathers, one of tiny bronze rings, another covered with tiny glass baubles, so that there was a continuous musical tinkling as the wearer walked by. Musicians were spaced throughout, to lend rhythm and continuity to this preview performance.

The entertainers moved down the line of Sharith to the shouts and laughter and applause of their audience. They stopped directly in front of us, performed a special piece of business, then moved off to our left. The last barracks building in from the gate had been set aside for them.

Some distance behind the entertainers came the support group—vleks and carts laden with costumes, props, and travel provisions. To make things less worrisome for the vlek handlers, all the sha'um had been asked to stay on the other side of the river while the caravan remained in Thagorn.

But between the entertainers and the rest of the caravan walked a tall woman, strikingly beautiful, dressed in a black robe, and carrying a restless white bird on her right shoulder. She moved with a stately grace, seeming to ignore the cheers of greeting which rose when she came through the gate. This was Tarani, the illusionist, and she walked with her hand upon the extended arm of a man.

The man was Thymas.

The two of them approached us without speaking. I couldn't help staring at the girl—she couldn't have been more than twenty years old, though her height and her air of assurance gave an impression of greater age. Most Gandalarans had light-colored head fur which turned darker through the years. But Tarani's pale, almost luminous face was crowned by head fur that was coal black. Her eyes were large and wide-set, so dark that they seemed solid enough to turn away the light before it entered. They stared back at me for a long moment before she spoke, and during that time, I began to be uncomfortable.

The strangest thing about it was that she was somehow familiar, but I couldn't quite touch the right memory . . .

Gharlas! it came to me. *He was tall, too, and his facial structure was similar—flatter cheekbones and less prominent supraorbital ridges. But that's not the real similarity.*

Markasset felt almost exactly this way when Gharlas stared

"It would be my pleasure," she said. But she didn't smile.

Thymas hadn't missed any of that. He flashed a look of pure hatred at me as he and Tarani turned toward the barracks.

The caravan, part of it already a good way inside the gate, began moving again, but nobody was much interested in watching a bunch of vleks plod along. I turned the bracelet around my wrist and stared in that direction, thinking. I did notice that the vlek handler in the first position of the caravan was the biggest man I had ever seen. Not just tall, but massively wide. He could have wrestled a vineh and won.

The crowd was scattering, the Riders going back to their duties, the children, free for the day, running after the troupe. Since only the Riders and their wives (or guests) would be present at the performance that evening, there would be a special daylight matinee for everyone else.

The women were on their way back to their cook-stoves Preparations had been going on all day for the banquet tha was scheduled for three hours ahead.

As soon as Shola had excused herself, and there was no on within earshot, Dharak started to fume again.

"Let it go," I pleaded. "Dharak, I want you to ask yours something. Are you angry on my behalf, because of the ins o me, or because it was your son who caused it?" I put hand on his shoulder. "Thymas is an adult, my friend. Y are no longer responsible for his actions. He pulled a smo *at him with that peculiar intensity. Thymas said that Tarani has the same kind of power. I believe him now.*

Thymas and Tarani stopped about two yards from us. Before Dharak or I could say anything, Tarani spoke in a low and vibrant voice that set my spine tingling.

"I am pleased to be here to help celebrate your accession, Captain," she said, "and I give you my thanks for sending my good friend Thymas to meet me, deliver the news, and escort me to your gates. In return for this gracious courtesy, may I offer you a small gift?"

Dharak was gritting his teeth, and I sympathized with him. Thymas knew very well we wouldn't air dirty linen in front of these outsiders by calling him down for not being at the ceremony. But if we didn't contradict Tarani's statement, the rest of the Sharith (at least, those who didn't know Thymas very well) would assume that I *had* issued the escort orders, and punishment at a later date would confuse the issue.

Very neat, Thymas, I thought. *You haven't said a word, so you are technically innocent of lying. She has called me "Captain," but you haven't.*

You don't know it, but you've done me a big favor. It would have been tricky, awarding punishment to the Lieutenant's son without seeming to be overly harsh or lenient. Dharak will hate me for this, but I'm going to let you get away with it. At least for now.

"I would welcome a gift from you, Tarani," I said. I could hear Dharak's teeth gritting again.

Thymas dropped his arm, and didn't try to hide his smile of triumph. Tarani's face registered no emotion at all. She put her right hand into a hidden pocket of the robe and lifted her left hand high over her head, palm opened flat to the sky. She brought her right hand up and dropped something into the open palm.

"Lonna, please deliver our gift to . . . the Captain."

Was that little hesitation a subtle gibe? I wondered. *To tell me she knows the score, and is on Thymas's side?*

The bird had taken flight when she lifted her hands. Its wingspan was surprisingly large. What I had thought to be an odd-looking tail had actually been the tips of its wings, folded over its back and crossed at the base of its tail.

This was a species of bird Markasset had never seen. As a

with unbelievable slowness. It
hovered at my chest level, watching me with a one-eyed star
that reminded me of its mistress, carrying something shin
gold in its beak.

I realized what it wanted, and held out my hand. It droppe
the gold thing into it, then returned to Tarani. Shola can
close and Dharak, for all his irritation with Thymas, look
over her shoulder curiously.

"It's a bracelet," I said, and held it up for them to see
did admire it. It was a soft chain made up of golden links
fine that, with five links abreast, the bracelet was only hal
inch wide.

I was surprised to hear a derisive sound from Dha
"Why, it's nothing but a chain of mud-beads!" he said. Th
in a lower voice: "Thymas, you are behind this. How
you arrange a public insult to Rikardon? You'll—"

At his first words, the bracelet had changed in my han
was, indeed, a string of tiny, brownish beads. But as I st
at it, I saw the glint of gold beneath them. I blinked.

"Dharak," I interrupted the Lieutenant. "You are fo
ting who gave this gift."

Tarani looked at me, and this time, I found her gaze
to bear. Slowly, she smiled. I swear, she out-dazzled th
bracelet.

"You have found the trick quickly, Captain." She
her hand. "Now see it truly."

raven of Ricardo's world was so black as to be iridescent in direct light, this bird was that white, almost silver. As we watched it fly upward, the sky's glow was visible through the delicate edges of the wing feathers. Against the gray-white of the clouds, it nearly disappeared.

It flew upward for a few seconds, turned, folded its wings back, and dived straight for Tarani. As it got closer, we could all see its head stretched for the least wind resistance, its sharp, downward-curved beak aimed for the girl's hand. At the last possible moment, the wings spread, the dive leveled out, and the bird breezed across us. Tarani lowered her hand to show that it was empty, and I started to breathe again.

That's quite a show, I conceded. *But if you think I'm going to give that sharp-nosed torpedo a target . . .*

It wasn't necessary. The bird had pulled up its high-speed flight and was coming back toward us, its wings beating the air [illegible] It flew right up to me and

Shola and Dharak oohed and ahed over the golden chain, Dharak less enthusiastically because of his accusation against Thymas.

"How does it open?" Shola asked.

"The clasp is hidden," Tarani said. "May I show you?"

"Please," I answered, holding it out toward her. She came to me. Over her shoulder, I saw Thymas scowling.

Tarani took the bracelet in long, tapered fingers, twisted the chain inside-out, and showed me the clever clasp mechanism. She opened it, then hesitated. I extended my left wrist, and she put the bracelet on it. For a moment, both her hands pressed the gold chain into the flesh of my arm.

"May this gift bring you only good fortune, Captain," she said, with a return of that queer intensity.

"Thank you, Tarani. I am looking forward to the performance tonight. Perhaps, after it is over, you will join our table for some refreshment?"

trick today. It's irritating, yes, but most of your people don't understand what happened. Unless he flaunts it—and we both know he's too smart to do that—it will remain a private itch, and nothing more.

"Tomorrow I'll be gone, and things will be back the way they were, except that Thymas will have more trouble getting support for his crazy schemes." I grinned. "At least, I hope so. That's what today was for, wasn't it?"

"It worked, too," Dharak said, clamping down on his angry mood. "You made a deep impression on us, Rikardon. Can you doubt, now, that it was right?"

"No," I said, then changed the subject. "Tell me about Tarani."

"I don't know much about her," he said. We started walking back toward his house. "She and her troupe showed up here one day—two years ago, now, and it was a smaller group—and she has been returning regularly since then."

"Do you pay her well?"

"Very well," he said, without hesitation. "And she earns it. You will see, tonight." He glanced at me from the corner of his eye. "You're thinking of Thymas? Does she come here because of him?" He shrugged. "That's a possibility. Thymas believes it."

"Don't you?"

"Thymas thinks she'll stay, one of these days."

"Marriage?" I suggested. Dharak only chuckled at my astonished reaction. "How did this get started between them?"

We had reached the house, and we settled down in armchairs which overlooked the opposite bank of the river. It was peaceful, with the sound of rushing water nearby and the conversation of sha'um in the distance.

I really will be sad to leave, I thought.

"It began the first time Tarani came here," Dharak said. "The troupe stayed for a few days. Our people so seldom see outsiders, and the members of the company were very . . . obliging, except for Tarani. Thymas had just been accepted into the Riders. The red sash made him eager for new challenges and, well . . ." The Lieutenant sighed. "Everyone else thought of the troupe's visit as a pleasant diversion. Thymas, of course, began immediately to make wedding plans."

She may have been his first girl, I was thinking. *It's a cinch he's scared everyone else away, and because she sees only him while she's here, he thinks she wants it that way.*

No wonder Thymas looked daggers at me this afternoon. Is an invitation to table taken to be an invitation to bed?

Did I mean it that way?

Dharak and I chatted away the rest of the daylight, then dressed for dinner and went down to the barracks building that had been converted into a huge meeting room. Tonight there were several tables, each twelve feet by four feet, set up around a large, waist-high platform that must have been carried in pieces on the vleks. It was supported by *lots* of thin wood strips, bracing apart three layers of frames.

Four tables stood parallel to one another along each short wall of the room, their ends toward the platform. Between the last pair, and directly in front of the platform, was another table. The best seats in the house.

Dharak and I were the last men to arrive, and everyone stood up as we entered, waited until we sat down, then resumed their noisy conversations. There were four chairs at that head table. Thymas was occupying the one at the end nearer the door.

He had stood up, too, but it was clear to everyone that the honor was meant for his father, only. I touched Dharak's arm, hoping he wouldn't make a scene. He didn't speak a word, but walked right by his son. I took the chair at the other end of the table, and Dharak sat next to me.

I guess Thymas means to make sure Tarani is well-chaperoned, I laughed to myself. *Well, he needn't worry. She's beautiful, but . . . there's something really disturbing about her. And I'm leaving tomorrow. I don't need any one-night stands that might generate a murder.*

But I will enjoy having that drink with her. She's a fascinating woman. Strange, but intriguing.

In a few minutes, the women arrived. They had finished preparing the food, and had taken some time to prepare themselves. Shola came to our table, dressed in a full-skirted gown of pale orange, wearing a necklace and headband of copper. She made a gracious comment about my new gift—still on my wrist—being finer than her own jewelry, then seated herself silently, tactfully, between her husband and her son.

The older girls served the meal, and it was a proper feast.

Roast glith, hundreds of small birds served whole, large bowls brimming with fruit, fresh-baked bread, and plenty of faen.

When the dishes had been cleared away, the lamps which had lit the tables were all moved to line the edges of the platform in a regular pattern. Three edges, that is. The fourth edge, farthest from the head table, was left open for the entrance of the players. The rearrangement left the stage brightly lit, and the rest of the room in shadow. The room grew quiet.

The dancers came first, creating complex patterns with the location and positions of their bodies, moving with stylized grace to the music of the harps and flute. The jugglers appeared next, with a really remarkable display of skill and timing. Some of the stunts were done with swords and knives, and I applauded wildly with the rest of the crowd.

It was a great show—well paced, with excitement balanced against beauty. I began to admire Tarani for her showmanship. She had assembled a talented group of people.

The illusionist herself appeared once, early on in the show, still wearing her black robe. It was instantly clear that this was not her spot, but the bird's. She asked it questions, which it answered in "yes" or "no" fashion, either spreading its wings or remaining still. There were math problems on the order of "Two plus two are five, right?" which the bird always answered correctly, catching every apparent trick. By the time that segment of the show was over, I was willing to grant that Lonna was a pretty smart bird, and I joined in the polite applause.

That must be the hit of the show in other towns, I thought. *But when you've lived with a sha'um inside your head, a clever bird isn't much of a novelty.*

After a long time of sitting in those un-padded, armless, wood-and-tile chairs, the troupe gave us a break, and we stretched and laughed and discussed the show.

After about ten minutes, I caught sight of Tarani, climbing the rear steps of the stage. There was a peculiar darkness hovering over center stage, and she walked into it without anyone taking notice of her.

It's one of her illusions. She's diverting everyone's attention until she gets into place.

This confirms what I've been thinking, ever since this

afternoon, I thought, touching the gold bracelet with the fingers of my right hand. *I'm not susceptible to her power.*

I leaned forward eagerly, making the table creak. She looked, for a brief instant, in my direction.

I'm going to enjoy this show.

9

Tarani threw her arms out wide. A yellowish powder fell from her hands, and the lamps flared up with a hissing noise. At that exact instant, the shroud of darkness vanished, and the crowd gasped, then applauded madly. I joined in, but I wasn't applauding the trick so much as the lady herself.

The long, shapeless black robe was gone. Tarani was wearing a shimmering blue gown she must have designed for herself. Certainly no other women I had ever seen could have worn it. Where most women's garments draped and flowed, clinging only incidentally, this was tailored to cling to her upper body and display curves which were more impressive for having been hidden away in the black robe.

A glittering band of blue circled her neck, supporting a tight bodice which left her arms bare. From her small waist, a full skirt flowed over her hips and nearly to the floor. The fabric was so soft that her legs were outlined at every step. A semi-circular white cape, fastened to her arms with jewelled bands at shoulders, elbows, and wrists, set off the blue of the gown. The cape also had a tall, stiff collar which stood up behind her head, creating a dramatic background for her black head fur.

I blinked twice.

None of that is illusion. That's all Tarani. No wonder Thymas is crazy for her.

Tarani stood perfectly still for a long moment. I became aware of a barely audible sound. It was her voice, humming a soft, deep-toned melody. The sound gave me the same thrill along my spine as I had felt when she first had spoken to us that afternoon.

She began to sway to her own music. Soon she was moving around the stage in an irregular pattern, approaching each lighted edge, then veering back. Her arms were held out from her sides a little way to silhouette her gown against the white of the cape. She seemed to glide without moving her feet. Only by blinking frequently could I detect the quick, tiny steps with which she moved.

That humming is hypnotic, I realized. *Is that all her power is, a talent for hypnosis? Or is this a bonus that makes her real talent more effective?*

She glided to the front of the stage, opposite our table, and she broke from her rigid posture to kneel before us. The music of her voice rose in pitch and increased its pace. She lifted her right arm above her head. In her left hand, she held a thin strip of wood; she extended it toward a lamp. The end of the wood caught, and she carried the tiny fire upward . . .

pressed it into her palm. Her right hand burst into flame. She clapped her hands together, and the left caught fire. She brought her hands down behind her head, and she wore a brilliant crown of flame.

She began to dance. Beautifully, rhythmically, moving always in time with the eerie melody . . .

. . .leaving streams of sparkling fire, lingering in the air behind her.

It was fascinating. I could shift my perception from the gorgeous illusion to the reality beneath it, where she carried three long strips of burning wood, one in each hand, and one mounted in the stiff collar of her cape. They burned so slowly that they must have been specially treated and prepared for her act.

And what an act. In either version, the dance was wonderful to watch. Tarani's tall body, its outlines plain against the cape's light background, moved continuously and with a grace that seemed effortless. When the illusion was in effect, she drew intricate and ever-changing patterns in the air with the trailing flames.

If Gandalarans could perspire, she'd be all over sweat by now, I thought. *Such energy! She doesn't even need the illusion to make this a great show. But look at her face—eyes nearly closed, expression rapt. She loves it. The dance trans-*

ports her. She'll never give this up to stay in Thagorn. Poor Thymas.

I did feel a real twinge of sympathy for the boy. And a surge of affection for Illia, who wanted a normal life and seemed to want me to be part of it. She might not be as glamorous, or as challenging a personality, as Tarani, but at that moment, I felt a warm appreciation for Illia's more simple charms.

It might have been because I was thinking of Illia—and, by association, Raithskar and Worfit—right then. Whatever the reason, when I heard the soft creak of leather behind me, I reacted instantly. If I had been as entranced by Tarani's performance as the rest of the audience, I would have missed hearing it.

And I would have died.

It was a near thing, anyway. As I toppled my chair into the open space between tables on my right, I saw the faint glint of lamplight on a dagger blade that plunged through the air, just where my heart would have been. I could barely see the man who held the dagger—he was bending over in reaction to his unresisted downward swing—and another man behind him. The huge bulk of the other man told me that I had seen him before. The vlek handler, in Tarani's caravan.

At the sound of the chair falling, the humming had stopped. Just as I rolled back on my shoulders and aimed a double-leg kick at the nearer, smaller man, the lights went out.

My feet connected with the side of the man's head, and I heard him fall. I rolled to the right, trying to put the table between myself and the big guy, but he was too fast. A huge hand grabbed my foot. I felt myself dragged across the floor like a rag doll, then another huge hand touched my face.

"Dharak! Assassins!" I yelled. I brought my arms up to deflect an expected blow. I kicked out with my feet, with little effect. Instead of hitting me, that hand closed on my throat, and the big man leaned on my neck.

A different darkness, full of spinning lights, began to close in on me. With an odd detachment, I wondered whether my larynx would collapse, or my neck crack, before I passed out from lack of air.

Not close enough to help! Keeshah's wail of frustration reached me, steadied the wheeling blackness. **Don't die,** he pleaded.

The pressure on my neck vanished suddenly, and I gulped in a painful, delicious draft of air. I opened my eyes to faint light. Some of the lamps had guttered back to life, not quite extinguished by whatever Tarani must have thrown at them. . . .

Keeshah, I'm all right. Find Tarani.

In the flickering light, Dharak had seen me struggling, and had thrown himself at the man-mountain. They had rolled together, and now it was Dharak who was pinned, his arms entangled with his attacker's. Over the milling confusion around us, I heard the sound of bone snapping, and a yell of pain. From outside, a scream of rage sounded from a sha'um—Doran.

"Father!" Thymas was yelling, as he ran around the far end of the table.

"There's another man, Thymas!" I croaked, my throat still aching. "He had a dagger. Get it!"

Thymas checked his forward rush, grabbed up one of the lamps, and dashed back around the table. I staggered up and got the big man around the neck, then lifted with all my strength. The man grunted and released Dharak, only to reach backward and grab my right leg. He pulled me off balance and we fell, the big man knocking my breath away as he landed on top of me.

Thymas ran up with the dagger. He glanced at his father, lying still on the floor, then turned toward us with the most savage expression I have ever seen on the face of a Gandalaran.

The knife blade sank into the man's side. Once. Twice. Three times. Blood ran out of the wounds, soaking my clothes as the man quit struggling.

I pushed myself out from under the corpse, fighting back a wave of nausea. "You didn't have to kill him!" I panted, then stopped short. Thymas still held the dagger, and he was ready to use it again . . . on me.

"He's a piece of filth!" the boy shouted in a strained voice. "And so are you. My father may be dead because he was trying to save your fleabitten life. And if he is," Thymas threatened, waving the dagger, "if Dharak is dead . . ." His voice choked off.

"I'm far from dead," said a weak voice. Behind Thymas, Dharak straightened out a leg. The boy whirled, and dropped to his knees beside his father. Blood still dripped from the dagger.

My knees went weak with relief, and I moved to lean on the table. *Thank God!* I prayed, sincerely. *Thank God Dharak didn't die for my sake. How did Worfit know where I would be? How could he arrange for this so quickly?*

In Thagorn, surrounded by sha'um and soldiers . . . I quit looking over my shoulder. Mistake. Worfit must have more connections than Zaddorn does. I'll have to settle with him, one way or another, when I get back to Raithskar.

But first, I want to be sure that nobody—but nobody—tries this and gets away with it.

"Bareff," I called, coming to my feet.

The banquet hall had been full of confusion for a while, with the sudden darkness and the sounds of a nearly invisible fight. It hadn't helped anything that Doran had squeezed through the human-sized door, and trampled a few people in the darkness, trying to get to Dharak. But now Dharak was calming the sha'um, stroking the cat's jaw with his right hand, while he talked to Thymas to allay his son's concern.

Old Snaggletooth had taken things in hand, and was creating some order out of the mess. He was beginning to get the dead lamps relighted when he heard my call. He came running.

"I heard you yelling," Bareff said, "but with the darkness . . ." In one quick glance, he took in the huge corpse, my bloody tunic, Dharak lying prone, Thymas and Doran beside him. "Great Zanek!" was all he said.

"The Lieutenant is alive," I assured him. "There's a man on the other side of the table. If he's alive, have him guarded. Round up the troupe and find out what they know about all this . . . and where Tarani is."

He opened his mouth, closed it again, nodded, and moved around the table. I went over to Dharak, but before I could speak to him, I heard the thud of a falling body, and Bareff yelled.

The man I had kicked was leaping over the table, which had miraculously remained upright through all the scuffling. I whirled to face the assassin, but he went past me to the edge of the stage, and caught up one of the lamps. He brought the faceted glass chimney down on the edge of the stage, knocking out the thick candle and breaking the glass down to a jagged shard.

He didn't try to kill me with it.

He drove it into his own stomach, and ripped it sideways.

Bareff had followed him over the table, and we stood side by side, watching the man die. "My fault," Bareff said gloomily. "I got too close . . . how could anybody *do* that to himself?"

Ritual suicide? I wondered. *The Japanese samurai used to do that routinely, if they failed at something, or were dishonored. But the Japanese believed there was another life on their earth waiting for them after death. The Gandalarans believe they'll live forever in the All-Mind. Same thing? Somehow, I wouldn't think so.*

Get hold of yourself, "Captain." This is no time to be studying comparative religion. Two men are dead, and Dharak injured, because of you.

"Bring Tarani," I told Bareff. Something he heard in my voice sent him sprinting for the door, shouting names and orders.

Keeshah, I called. **Have you seen her?**

Hmmm? came a lazy, contented thought.

For a few seconds, I stood there and swore at myself.

He's seen her, all right, I thought bitterly. *Why didn't I think to warn him about her? But she's been in Thagorn before, and has probably practiced on sha'um before, too. Keeshah might not have been able to resist, anyway.*

The thought made me feel a strange sadness. I suppose I had come to rely so completely on Keeshah that finding him vulnerable was a shock. But there was something else. I was vaguely disappointed in Tarani, too. She was so beautiful, so skilled . . .

And so treacherous. Something else in her like Gharlas. Maybe it's that power they both have. Political power was a corruptive influence in Ricardo's world, and that was only indirect influence. How much more potent direct mind control must be!

But she won't get away with this.

Keeshah, where are you?

Outside the gate, he answered, becoming more alert.

I groaned inwardly. **Come inside.**

Dharak had convinced Doran to go back outside the building, and Shola had taken charge of Dharak. She was working over his left arm, holding it gently, and wrapping it with a length of cloth. Lamps had been brought and arranged close to Dharak's head to give her more light, and Thymas had stood up to give her room. I knelt down at Dharak's right side, ignoring a look of hatred from Thymas. The Lieutenant was pale, but he smiled at me.

"Told you I was getting old," he said. "Bones brittle. What happened?"

I hesitated.

Shola spoke, without looking up. "The arm is broken in two places, Captain," she said. Her voice was carefully neutral. "Otherwise, he is well. I, too, want to know what happened."

He means: what happened to the assassins? She means: why was Dharak hurt, trying to protect me?

I answered Shola first. "There is a man in Raithskar—a dangerous man—who wants me dead. I thought I had left him behind. I never thought he would dare send anyone into the stronghold of the Sharith." I put my hand on Dharak's good shoulder. "My carelessness has cost you much, my friend," I said softly. "Forgive me."

He made a sound of impatience. "The assassins?"

"Two are dead. The one who hurt you was killed by your son. The other took his own life. I will be leaving shortly to go after the third one."

"You know who this third is?" he asked.

"Tarani."

"You're lying!" accused Thymas, who had edged closer to us.

Bareff's voice cut off whatever else Thymas would have said.

"Where's Rikardon?"

I called to him, and he ran up into the lamplight.

"Tarani is gone, Captain. We found the gates open, and eight members of the troupe wandering near it in a daze. They can't remember how they got there, and I don't think they're faking it. It looks like she forced them to open the gate for her." He shook his head. "I wouldn't have thought this of her."

"It isn't true!" Thymas said.

Had I felt a flash of sympathy for Thymas, earlier? It vanished now in a wave of annoyance.

"Thymas, she brought these killers here in her caravan, for

the one occasion when all the Riders would be unarmed. She put out the lights when all the trouble started. Now she has run away."

"These were vlek-handlers," he insisted stubbornly. "She hires new ones every trip. And for the lights—perhaps she *did* realize what was happening, and was trying to give you a better chance."

I resisted the impulse to laugh in his face. "Then why didn't she stick around for a while?"

"Because . . ." If I hadn't been so irritated, I might have admired his loyalty, as he groped for a plausible reason. "Because she knew we would think—I mean, *you* would think—that she knew those men were assassins. She's afraid."

"She needs to be," I said grimly, and turned back to the Lieutenant. "Dharak, I'm going."

"No," Thymas said. This time, he wasn't challenging me, but appealing to his father. "I am the one who must go. She won't be afraid of me. I can persuade her to return and explain everything."

"Of course she won't be afraid of you," I said. "She can probably make you believe that vleks climb trees."

"She never uses her power on me without my consent," he said angrily. "It is a matter of honor between us."

Just in time, I remembered how Thymas felt about Tarani, and I cut back the scornful reply I was ready to make. Instead, I said: "That may be true, Thymas. But she *can't* use her power against me. It doesn't work."

Complete silence greeted that announcement. I was touched again with the warmth I had felt in the Hall. Nobody doubted the truth of what I said. They were surprised, but if I had said it, was true.

"So I am the only logical one to go," I continued, "and the more time I waste here, the farther away she is getting."

"Go, then!" Thymas shouted. "And so will I. We will see who finds her first."

"Thymas!" Dharak said, in a ringing tone of command. His son turned to him quickly, out of long habit. Without looking at me, Dharak said: "Captain, have I your permission to rule on this request?"

That was a request? I wondered. Aloud, and with some uneasiness, I gave him permission.

Shola helped Dharak to sit up, and then to stand. His face

twisted with pain, but he was steady on his feet. She had finished binding his arm—not stiff and straight, as I would have done it, but with separate bindings on forearm and upper arm, and a sling supporting the bent arm.

"Thymas, in the presence of these Riders, offer your allegiance to our Captain." Dharak's voice rang out, releasing all the suppressed rage of a disappointed father. Shola flinched back from him, and it was a tossup who was more startled, Thymas or me.

"This isn't necessary right now," I said to Dharak.

"You gave me permission to handle this, Captain," he said coldly. "Now stay out of it."

I shut up. *Your son's not the only tricky one in your family*, I thought.

"*I will never call this man 'Captain'!*" came Thymas's predictable answer.

"Do you want to go after Tarani?" the Lieutenant asked.

"Yes, but—"

"I agree that she may be more willing to return if you are present," Dharak said. "So you may go *with* Rikardon and *assist* him. You will make public, here and now, your acceptance of him as Captain. And you will make another promise, personally to me as your father, that you will respect him properly, and *obey him in all things*."

Wow. "I prefer to travel alone." I said. They both ignored me.

"I refuse!" the boy said icily.

"Then you have two choices," Dharak said, his voice rolling out like an inexorable force. "Go . . . and never return to Thagorn." The watching people gasped. Shola lifted a hand to her mouth, bit into her clenched fist. "Or stay . . . give up the red sash, and ride with the cubs for the rest of your life." Another sound of amazement, then a waiting silence.

In the circle of the lamps, I could see Thymas's hands trembling. His face was ashen. I thought of all I had learned about him—his devotion to the traditions of the Sharith, his conviction that he would lead them one day. I thought, too, of what my coming had meant to him. As Captain, I had taken away the very thing he had aimed for all his life.

"Father—" Thymas began. Dharak interrupted, lashing the boy with his words.

"I remind you that these are official orders, backed by

authority delegated to me, in front of witnesses, by the man whom everyone else has accepted as Captain. You have been given three paths to follow. *Choose!*"

Thymas looked at me, and his hand clenched around the handle of the dagger he still held. Then, with a truly extraordinary display of self control, Thymas shrugged back his shoulders and made his face blank of all expression.

"Only one way may be ridden with honor," he said levelly, his gaze still fixed on me. "The son of Dharak can choose no other. You have the promise you asked for, Father.

"I am ready to leave immediately, Captain."

10

Bareff's investigation turned up the remains of an early dinner in Tarani's quarters. The Sharith girl who had served it was brought in, and she confirmed that whatever could be carried easily was gone from the tray. Nothing else had been touched.

One of the women dancers was asked to examine the dressing room. Scared and confused, she identified several articles of clothing that were missing, among them a pair of heavy walking boots.

"So she didn't just run off in a panic, wearing nothing but that impractical gown," I said to Bareff and Thymas, after the dancer had left the room. Thymas was glaring at me, daring me to gloat over being right. Whatever he had promised to Dharak, he couldn't hide his hatred of me. I tried to hide the fact that it bothered me.

"What about weapons?"

"All visible weapons were turned in when the troupe came through the gate," Bareff answered. "But if the assassin smuggled one in, Tarani could have done it, too. The dancer might not have known about it.

"She has that bird with her, too," Bareff continued. "It will warn her of being followed. I don't think you'll have much luck finding her in the dark, even while the moon is up.

She'll head either for Omergol or the Refreshment House at Relenor. We'll notify our friends in Omergol to watch for her—but the Fa'aldu at Relenor won't be any help."

"Then we'll search the trail to Relenor first," I decided. "She can't get very far in the dark, even with the bird to guide her. Thymas, we'll leave at dawn. Don't wear your uniform, and pack food and water for a seven-day, just in case."

As we rode through the gates the next morning, I was glad we hadn't rushed off the night before. I had bathed away the big man's blood, and slept for several hours. Thymas was stone-faced and formal in the presence of Dharak, but he looked rested. I hoped the night had brought him nearer to accepting the truth about Tarani.

He might be a pain in the kazoo, I thought, *but he's young, and he's had a series of shocks these past few weeks. That was a nasty trick of Dharak's, forcing Thymas to accept me in order to protect Tarani. But if Thymas could pull himself together last night the way he did, he ought to be able to handle everything, given enough time.*

We followed the road south that day, traveling slowly and watching the sky for sign of the bird. By nightfall, we were certain we had come farther than Tarani could have traveled since the end of the show. We moved away from the road, found an area free of brambles, ate a cold meal in silence, and stretched out to sleep. In the morning, we would ride back to Thagorn, and follow the caravan trail north toward Omergol.

Thymas seemed to fall asleep instantly. I stared up at the silver clouds for a while, remembering the fire dance.

It's obvious why her illusions don't work on me, I thought. *She is trained to affect Gandalaran minds. I have the brain of a native, but the mind, the cognitive faculty, of an alien. Perception—analysis of stimuli—is not as automatic for me. I require a second, conscious interpretation of data before the data is entirely assimilated.*

If Tarani can't manipulate me, maybe I'm immune to Gharlas, too.

Suddenly I was awake. An odd, scary feeling crept over me.

If I were the All-Mind, trying to preserve a world threatened by a single madman, what better way than to create his opposite? Someone who is insane in such a way as to cancel out the dangerous craziness?

In Gandalara, where the only two kinds of weather were hot and hotter, I felt a positive chill at that moment.

And wouldn't it be convenient if the new fool were in a position of power, at least potentially? Like a son of Serkajon's house, who logically could be named to the Captaincy of the Sharith, provided he didn't turn out feeble-minded?

Well, that lets me out, I laughed, trying to shake off the disturbing mood. *I must be feeble-minded to think of such a thing. First things first. Tomorrow we find Tarani.*

I had strange dreams, filled with the sound of Tarani's humming. When I woke, just after dawn, my eyes focused on the point of a sword, about four inches from my face.

There was a person, tall and slim, dressed in desert garb, on the other end of that sword. A headcloth was tied to cover her head and drape one corner down her back. But even without the distinctive dark head fur showing, I had no difficulty recognizing Tarani.

That's one way to find her. That's some weapon she smuggled into Thagorn. Or maybe she stole it from a house before she left. Looks like she knows how to use it, too. How the hell did she sneak in here . . . the humming! Stupid, the humming!

Out of the corner of my eye, I could see Thymas and his sha'um, both of them sound asleep. I reached for Keeshah with my mind, but he was out cold, too.

Tarani was staring down at me with those compelling and disturbing eyes. Her face and hands showed tiny scratches, evidence that she had fought her way through the choked brush, rather than follow the road. She held Rika, point to the ground, in her left hand.

She must have some effect on me, I decided, *or I would have felt her take the sword from my baldric.*

"May I sit up?" I asked.

She nodded and stepped back. I sat up and stretched my shoulders, moving slowly. "I have to . . ."

"Go ahead," she said in her low-pitched voice. "I'm not shy."

I stood up and turned my back on her, and did what I had to do. Then I turned around slowly. When I was almost facing her, I stepped forward and kicked out at the hand which held my sword. Her grip loosened, and Rika skidded away. She lunged at me, but I dived beneath her blade and rolled, coming to my feet with the satisfying weight of Serkajon's sword in my hands—just in time to block a vicious overhand cut.

Tarani recovered quickly, and swung her sword around in an arc to slice across my midsection. I blocked that, too, then feinted a lunge to drive her backward. She dodged around my sword, swinging low to keep me off balance.

Before she could set herself for another slash, I threw my weight against her, dropping Rika and grabbing her sword wrist as we fell.

She struggled against my grip with less strength than I had expected. We rolled a couple of times, crushing the tart-smelling ground cover, then I put my full weight on her to hold her down, and forced her to release her sword.

With no warning, no transition, I found myself lying across the meanest, ugliest female vineh Markasset had ever seen.

It was sudden enough, and effective enough, to make me jump with surprise. Then I caught the trick, and blinked away the ugly brute.

As Tarani's face re-formed, it took on an expression of despair. The dark eyes closed in defeat, and she whispered: "So it is true. I cannot make you see, as I can others."

I slid off of her to relieve her lungs of my weight, but I could still feel her chest moving against me as she took short, heavy breaths. Looking at her face more closely now, I could see hollows under her eyes. Creases of tension surrounded her mouth and lined her brow, crisscrossed by the tiny, blood-crusted scratches.

"How did you know?" I asked her.

"I sensed it when we met," she said. "And I heard you say so."

"But that was after you left . . . no, it was after we *found the gate open*. You just slipped back into the banquet hall and hid yourself in the crowd. Clever."

"Not clever. Necessary. That was the first time in years I have tried to make someone *do* instead of merely *see*. Eight at once—I had barely enough strength left to cast away sight."

"When did you leave Thagorn?"

"A few hours before dawn. I stayed in the banquet hall, ate all the food I had, then climbed the east wall of the valley."

That's where she got the scratches. I have to give her credit for making it through that wilderness.

"You heard what went on. You know Dharak was hurt."

She was silent for a moment. "Yes," she said finally. "And I witnessed Thymas's humiliation.

"That's why I have given Thymas sleep. I wanted the chance to convince you to let me go. Thymas would want to help, and he . . ."

"He might do more harm than good? You're probably right."

Speaking of Thymas, if he wakes up and finds us in this clinch, neither one of us will score many points with him.

I rolled away from her and stood up, picking up the swords. She sat up, a little shakily.

"Where is your bird?"

"Hunting. She knows where I am."

"When she shows up, you control her, or Keeshah will have her for breakfast. Clear?"

She nodded, her eyes bright.

"Now," I said, putting Rika away and tossing Tarani's sword to one side of the clearing, "I'll listen. No promises."

She sighed. "I had no choice in what I did, Captain. I know you won't believe it, but I was glad the Living Death failed. I—I'd have grieved for your death."

"And I'm sure I'd have appreciated it," I said. Her shoulders twitched. "The Living Death must be those assassins. Are there more where they came from?"

"There are many of them, yes, but your danger came from these two, only. Molik was paid for one attempt. Unless he is paid again, there will be no other."

I wonder how much Worfit thinks I'm worth, I thought bitterly.

"Who is this Molik?"

"A powerful roguelord. He owns most of Chizan, and charges outrageous trade fees from the caravans passing through. He runs all the gaming houses, and controls the water that comes into the city. But his most profitable operation is the Living Death.

"They are people who know they will die in a year or less. They come to him, and he sets them up to live extremely well for part of the time left to them. In return, they swear to do anything he asks of them, including suicide if they are in danger of capture.

"Most of them come from Eddarta's copper mines. I think Molik pays the mine guards to recruit for him."

Molik sounds like just the type of friend Worfit would have. That's not a bad setup, a crime ring that is completely untraceable to its leader.

I wonder if I can believe her. She's admitted she was in the banquet hall when that guy killed himself. She could be making this up out of whole cloth, to save her own skin.

"Are you one of them? The Living Death? You look healthy enough to me."

"Molik forced me to take two of his men into Thagorn," she said ignoring my sarcasm. "I have an uncle, Volitar. He is a glassmaker who lives in Dyskornis."

Markasset's none-too-certain geographical knowledge placed Dyskornis somewhere east of Chizan.

"He is my only living relative," she continued, and now her voice faltered. "He raised me. My parents died when I was very young. He is the only family I have, and I—he is very important to me."

She paused a moment, then went on in a business-like tone. "I was on my way to Thagorn for my regular visit. I had left Volitar in his workshop in Dyskornis. When I reached Chizan, Molik's men were waiting for me. They took me to Molik, and he said that the Living Death had Volitar and were bringing him to Chizan. At a signal from Molik, they would kill him."

"And you just accepted his word for that?" I asked.

"I am not that stupid," she retorted scornfully. "I sent Lonna to see, and she reported Volitar traveling south toward Inid, in the company of two men she had never seen before. It was not an idle threat. Molik had Volitar, and he would have killed him." Her voice sank to a whisper.

"I couldn't let Volitar die because of me. I agreed to bring the assassins to Thagorn."

"I never thought to hear that from you, Tarani," said Thymas. He picked himself up from the ground. "Until just now, I hoped there would be some other explanation."

I watched Tarani's face as she looked at Thymas. The eerie and powerful woman I had seen on stage vanished completely under the boy's punishing stare. She was a girl, sitting cross-legged on the ground, shamed and repentant and vulnerable . . .

She's a trained actress! I reminded myself sharply. *She may not be able to cast her illusions for me, but that doesn't restrain other, more common forms of deception.*

You must know it all, then, Thymas," she said softly. "I did not know that Rikardon would be in Thagron. When I accepted Molik's demand, I thought—" She swallowed hard. "I thought the assassins were meant for your father."

"What's that?" I broke in.

She stood up from the ground and faced me squarely, and once again she was Tarani the illusionist, with the great presence and aura of power. I was conscious of a sense of loss.

Don't be a fool, I warned myself sternly. *First, you don't trust her. Second, Thymas is hurting right now, but he still loves her. There's enough friction between you and him already. Third, you have a lovely lady waiting for you in Raithskar.*

So stick to business.

"Molik's instructions," Tarani was saying, "were to bring those two men into Thagorn and identify 'the leader of the Sharith.' I did think he meant Dharak—until Thymas told me about you."

"When did you leave Chizan?" I asked.

"Krydu twice ago."

Two weeks and two days ago. The same day I left Raithskar.

"I hadn't even reached Thagorn by that time," I told her.

"I knew that, from what Thymas said. But it seemed possible to me that Molik knew you *would* be there. I followed his instructions. I placed the two Living Death at the front of the caravan, and told them that . . ." Here she hesitated.

"That the man who got the gold bracelet was their target," I finished for her. She nodded. I began to do a slow burn. "Weren't you relieved to find out about me? It meant you didn't have to make things difficult with Thymas by getting his father killed. I can see the ethics of it—better to kill the stranger than someone you know."

By the time I finished, I was shouting. She drew herself up and shouted back at me. "You have no right to—"

"No right?" I interrupted. "You set me up for a pair of killers!"

"But I didn't want you dead! I only wanted my uncle to live."

"It was a fair trade, I suppose, his life for mine?"

"I didn't know about you!" she cried. "I was willing to trade *Dharak's* life for Volitar's. That should tell you how deeply I care about my uncle!"

"It's great that I could give you such a bargain. Kill me and get something for nothing, right?"

"*Yes*, that's right!" she screamed. Her eyes were blazing.

Thymas stepped between us, a look of alarm on his face. I turned away abruptly and left the camp.

I found Keeshah, and nudged him awake with my foot. He yawned and blinked up at me.

Some sentry you are! I fumed at him. **Tarani walked right past you into camp.**

Woman? No harm, he said.

No harm? I asked, outraged. **I woke up with a sword only inches from my nose!**

Woman hurt you? he asked, with little concern, since the answer was obvious.

No, but that's no thanks to you! I said angrily, and stomped back toward the camp. Keeshah's thought followed me.

Grumpy.

11

Grumpy? I was in a towering fury, and I didn't dare go back to camp in that mood. I turned aside, and pushed my way through the brush, getting some relief from the physical struggle.

Bad enough that she tried to knock me off, I thought angrily. *And that she was able to befuddle Keeshah on the night of the show. Now she seems to have enough pull with him to override my suspicions of her.*

He wasn't the least bit surprised when I told him she was here. He let *her come into the camp.*

I stopped where I was, with one hand lifting a ground-crawling branch of a dakathrenil tree. Ordinarily, I would trust Keeshah's instincts, but these were no ordinary circumstances. I felt jealous of Keeshah's trust in Tarani, and of her power to command that trust. I felt betrayed.

It's not Keeshah's fault, I reminded myself.

I pulled up the branch, walked past it, let it fall.

Ricardo always had tried to see every side of an argument before choosing sides. I resisted the impulse as long as I could, enjoying my sulk, but all too soon I was thinking: *She's right about one thing. No matter that I was the target. I'm not in any position to sit in judgment.*

I made much the same deal when I killed Worfit's man, getting out of Raithskar. His death, and Worfit's persecution, are the price I paid for saving Thanasset. Knowing that, would I change things now?

No.

So she fingered me for the killers, instead of Dharak? At the show, Dharak was completely under her spell. If they had attacked him, he'd be dead now. I don't want that on my conscience.

So what's really bothering me?

The way she did it, came the answer. *She put that bracelet on my wrist and pressed it there, and wished me good fortune of it. And when I asked her for that drink, she said: "It would be my pleasure." Would. Conditional. She meant: "If you're still alive by then."*

I really hate it that the warm touch of her hands on my skin was really the touch of death. One thing is clear. If I wouldn't let Dharak judge Thymas—or tried not to let him—because he was too personally involved, I'd better let him judge Tarani because I'm the one who can't think straight in this case.

She disturbs me.

I was still far from calm, but I wandered back toward camp. Thymas had brought out our supplies, and he and Tarani were sitting far apart, eating breakfast in an awkward, angry silence. I sat down and ate a piece of fruit and a chunk of bread, washing it down with water from one of the waterskins.

The bird showed up, and settled down on Tarani's ankle after she finished eating. Lonna was about the size of a large falcon, with the downward-hooked beak of a hawk. She made a soft, hollow sound of pleasure as Tarani stroked her back and the tips of her wings.

When I was nearly through with my meal, Tarani literally threw the bird away, casting it up into the air to let it spread its enormous wings and settle on a high branch. Tarani came to stand in front of me.

"I want to go back to Chizan, Captain. After I settle with Molik, and get Volitar out of danger, I will return to Thagorn to be judged for what I have done. You have my promise."

It was on my tongue to tell her what I thought her promise was worth, but somehow I couldn't say it.

"You failed your assignment. How can you save your uncle now?"

"It was one of the terms that Volitar would be released, no matter what the outcome."

"What if Molik refuses?" I asked.

"He is a businessman; he keeps his bargains," she said. Her fists clenched. "But if he refuses . . . I have learned, again, how to compel."

"Why didn't you just do that in the first place?"

One hand started beating her thigh; she didn't seem to be aware of the action. "Volitar would not have wished it," she said. "As long as I can remember, he has told me that every person deserves a measure of respect, and a fair chance to make his way in the world. He called my skills a special advantage, and said I had a special obligation to respect other people. It took me a long time to convince him that my entertainment illusions were harmless.

"No, he would not have wanted that kind of help, not even to save his life. He still won't want it, and I don't want to do it. That kind of control is a violation of those used, and a degradation of the user," she declared. "I would not have done it in Thagorn, if it hadn't been so important to misdirect you. But if there is no other way to free Volitar . . .

"May I go to Chizan?"

I stood up. "Dharak was the one hurt; he will be the one to judge. We'll go back to Thagorn."

Thymas had listened to all this in silence, and now he spoke up from his side of the clearing. "Let her go to Chizan first," he said. "I will go with her, to make sure she comes back to Thagorn when her business is finished."

"No!" Tarani said. "Captain, I must go alone, or Volitar will die—because of me!"

"Not because of you," I said. I began clearing away the fruit leavings. "From what you said, you are a victim, as well as your uncle. We'll go to Thagorn. If Dharak says you can go to Chizan, sha'um can carry you partway there to make up for the time you will have lost."

She didn't say anything, and in a few seconds, I looked up from my work to see her studying me. Her face, her posture, the way her tongue worried her right tusk—everything about her bespoke indecision. I straightened up.

"Thymas, go away," I said. "I'd like to speak to Tarani alone for a few minutes." I glanced at him. It took no special talent to know what he was thinking. "It's business, Thymas. I won't touch her." When he still didn't move, I added: "You have my word. Now do it."

"Tarani?" he said, still uncertain. I held back from reminding him that he had promised obedience, and waited for her answer.

"I will be safe, Thymas," she said. "Lonna will come to you when we are through talking."

Defeated and angry, he called to his sha'um, mounted him, and rode off.

When he was out of earshot, I said: "This isn't your first dealing with Molik, is it?"

The corners of her mouth lifted in a small, bitter smile. "You read people well, Captain."

I wish that were true, I thought. *The few intuitions I have about you conflict with the visible evidence. You tried to kill me. The last thing I should do is trust you. But I can't help it. I believe every word you've said.*

"Yes, I have known Molik for several years," she admitted. "Because of me, Volitar is in danger, Dharak was injured, and you were nearly killed."

She came closer to me. "I have said that when we met, I sensed that you were . . . different. There was also something almost familiar about you. I can't quite describe it. But I had the feeling that you wouldn't let death surprise you. I'm glad I was right."

I felt that, too—a strangeness mixed with a vague feeling of recognition. It's back, now. I feel . . . drawn to her.

We were standing so close that I seemed to be leaning toward her. It would be a short reach to—

Watch it! Watch it! I nearly panicked. *If she's not dangerous enough in herself, think about Thymas. You promised him hands off.*

As though the same reminder had crossed her mind, we each stepped back a pace, tripling the distance between us.

"You were telling me about Molik?" I prompted.

"Yes. I—Thank you for sending Thymas away." She sighed. "I've never talked to anyone else about this. I don't quite know where to start."

I gestured for her to sit down. She perched on a ground-hugging branch, and I plopped down in the soft-bladed ground cover. I felt more secure with half the clearing between us.

"My uncle sent me to a Recorder's school when I was a child," Tarani said. "I was the youngest there; I remember one of the teachers saying that Volitar had been very alert, to recognize my skill so quickly. I missed my uncle while I was at school, but I enjoyed the training. I went home fairly often, so that I was reasonably content.

"Until I turned fifteen. Then, all of a sudden, I felt . . . bored. I avoided classes, and went walking in the hills around the school. Nothing seemed challenging any more; I began to experiment with my skill. I found I could call wild animals to me.

"One day, terrified and excited all at once, I tried to call one of my teachers. She came. I learned, later, that her face had gone blank in the middle of a class, and she had walked away without a word. I know that when I saw her, I—I loathed myself. And I despised the power I had discovered. It was a violation of all that Volitar had taught me."

She shuddered with the memory.

"I left school that day. I wanted to go back to Volitar, to spend the rest of my life in his workshop, isolated from people. But I'd have had to give some explanation for returning in the middle of a school session. I couldn't lie to Volitar, and I was too ashamed to tell the truth. So I just wandered around the hills for a few days, eating what I could find.

"One night, there were four boys traveling along together. They saw me near the road. They chased me. They caught me, and held me down, and—" She took a breath, coughed, and then continued. "That is, they *tried* to.

"I made them see a female vineh."

Having had a brief encounter with that particular illusion, I could imagine the result. Total rout. But she had been only fifteen. It must have been rough for her.

"I wasn't hurt," she said, "but I was in shock for a while, I think. I came back to myself in a wild part of the hills. The first thing I saw was a bird, trapped in a thorn vine, and a *dralda* getting ready to attack it."

Markasset's memory wasn't much help here. He had heard of a dralda, but had never seen one. It was a small carnivore, something like a dog, from what I could tell.

"I soothed the bird, and frightened the dralda, by sending images," she said. "Of course, the bird was Lonna."

I heard the bird's odd call from somewhere above us, and I knew it had recognized its name.

"I lived in those hills for a while. Lonna shared her kills with me, when I needed meat; otherwise, there was wild fruit and rooted plants that I learned to eat. Lonna seemed to want to stay with me, and she was so smart, that the idea of performing with her came to me easily. I had kept track of the time, so that I know that I thought of it on the day after my sixteenth birthday.

"I told Lonna about my plan, and she agreed. She can understand a lot of words, and she can read the images I send. She has even learned to cast them, to a small extent. I've never seen another creature like her."

"Except sha'um," I said.

She leaned forward eagerly, diverted from her story for the moment. "Thymas has tried to tell me what it's like," she said. "But I'm sure I don't really know how a Rider feels."

"Let's stick to the subject right now," I said. "You had the idea for the show."

She settled back again, disappointed. "The entertainment you saw is very close to the vision I had that day," she said. "The first version was much smaller, of course, and I didn't have much experience on stage—but it was well-received in Chizan, and along the caravan trails.

"But before I could assemble even that tiny group, I needed money," she continued. "I never considered asking Volitar for it. He makes a comfortable living, but he works alone, producing small things. I knew he wouldn't have any money to lend me, even if he approved of the idea.

"So I went to the Refreshment House of Inid, and from there to Chizan. There was only one source of money in Chizan."

"You borrowed what you needed from Molik?" I guessed.

She looked at the scratched hands in her lap. "That's what I told Thymas, when he, too, asked me how I came to be involved with Molik," she said. "But the truth is, I *earned* that money."

I couldn't believe what I thought she meant. Prostitution was hardly unknown in Gandalara. It was a percentage of Worfit's business, and I supposed a crossroads like Chizan would have a booming red light district. But there wasn't as much demand for it, generally, as there had been in Ricardo's world.

This was another byproduct of the Gandalaran inner awareness. Women *knew* when they were vulnerable to pregnancy. At any other time, they made decisions based on their own desires. There seemed to be no venereal disease in this world, and without the threat of unwanted pregnancy, sexual activity was considered part of a normal life, even of very young people. A father would be more upset if his daughter *liked* an unapproved suitor than if she slept with him.

With that atmosphere of freedom prevalent, prostitutes served the strangers in town, or the men or women with tastes so bizarre they couldn't find willing partners. Sometimes a prostitute was especially good at something . . .

Holy jumping Harthim!

"But—" I stammered, unable to hide the shock I felt. "But a man in Molik's position could have all the women he wanted!"

Again, that bitter little smile. "With my skills, I could *be* all the women he ever wanted. I walked into his office and told him so, proved it, and agreed to stay with him for six moons, if he would finance the show at the end of that time."

You were sixteen years old! I was thinking. *And Markasset seems to think a Recorder's school is a pretty sedate and sheltered place. Something doesn't jibe here . . .*

She shrugged her shoulders, her thoughts running parallel to mine. "It seemed strange to me that I knew just what to do. I was—I hadn't been with a man before that time. I understood that it wasn't the most honorable way to earn money, but it seemed the only way to raise the quantity I needed in a fairly short time.

"Those six moons weren't unbearable. Molik is a presentable man, and he was always lavishly grateful . . . until the time was up. I discovered, much too late, that illusion in certain circumstances is dangerous. Molik had begun to be . . . needful."

Psychological addiction, I thought. *Not surprising.*

Tarani had picked up a waterskin, and was tossing it lightly between her hands.

"I will say Molik this much good—he honored our agreement," she said. "He let me go. But he has never stopped trying to find a way to possess me again."

"You may be right, and he will release your uncle—this time," I said. "But now that he's found the right lever, what makes you think that Volitar will ever be safe from him?"

One hand grabbed the half-empty waterskin and squeezed hard. "What makes you think he will live long, after he releases my uncle?"

I sat quietly, considering what she had said. Finally I asked: "Why have you told me all this?"

"To convince you to let me go. Alone. I thought, if I told you everything . . ."

"Is this everything?"

"Yes. I swear it. And now that I have told you so much, will you tell me one thing?"

"I don't know. You can ask."

"Molik gloated over the high fee he charged, to send his men into Thagorn. Why does someone hate you that much?"

"There's a certain roguelord in Raithskar," I said. "He and Molik would make a good pair. I killed one of his men—it was unavoidable. I have no idea how he knew that I would be in Thagorn. You left Chizan about the same time I left Raithskar. Even if Worfit's spies had overheard when I was going, and even if a maufa could make it to Chizan in one day—"

"Worfit?" she interrupted my speculation. "Who is Worfit?"

"The roguelord who wants to kill me," I explained, with exaggerated patience.

"But . . . I told you that Molik boasted in front of me. He even let slip the name of the man who paid him, and he was angry with himself for doing it. I'm sure that Worfit wasn't the name I heard."

Great day in the morning! I felt thoroughly exasperated. *I no more than get one thing figured out . . .*

"All right," I sighed. "Who did pay Molik to threaten Volitar to force Tarani to take hired killers into the house that Jack built?"

She blinked. "I beg your pardon?"

"*Who hired Molik?*"

"I've never heard of the man. But his name was Gharlas."

12

"*THYMAS!*"

I yelled it at the top of my voice, scaring Tarani into a quick retreat, and sending the bird fluttering up. The girl ordered: "Lonna, bring Thymas." The white bird circled a few turns, then took off westward.

"If it took that loaded caravan of yours two seven-days to get to Thagorn, we should be able to ride to Chizan from here in about a third of that time . . ."

I was talking to myself, mostly, as I tied together the packs I couldn't help thinking of as "saddlebags." A Rider held their joining rope across his thighs when he traveled, so that the heavy rope would not chafe his sha'um's back.

"My only chance to save Volitar is by facing Molik alone," Tarani cried. "If you come with me, you'll be killing Volitar!"

I kept working, ignoring her.

She came over to me and grabbed my arm. "If you don't care about Volitar, what about Thymas. What do you think it will do to him, to learn the truth about Molik?"

"Thymas claims to be an adult," I snapped, "though he doesn't show it much when he's around you. If you're so worried about shocking him, maybe you'd better tell him yourself, before Molik rubs it in his face.

"I am going to Chizan," I told her. "And you are going with me, because you are my key to Molik. If you want me to order Thymas to stay behind, I'll do that. I'm sure he'll be glad to ride back to Thagorn and leave us alone together."

I shrugged off her hands.

"Sure he will," I said. "Thymas will be behind us all the way. He'll disobey my orders, break his promise to his father, and effectively exile himself from Thagorn. He'll think it's worth it, too, if he can have you at that price.

"You can have a wonderful, wandering life together," I continued savagely. "And that should suit *you* just fine. You'll have a sha'um for the star of your show."

I had finished tying my packs, and Thymas's too. Looking around, I found the backpack Tarani had used. I picked it up and tossed it to her. "Thymas will be here in a minute," I said. "Get ready to go."

She caught the bag awkwardly, then threw it to the ground.

"No!" she yelled. Her hands were shaking, and her eyes were gleaming slits of black. Her lips were drawn back from her teeth, exposing the canine tusks.

"Put that travel bag on," I said. I kept my voice soft, but I was in no mood to accept interference, and I tried to make that clear to her.

"There is nothing *you* can do to force me," she said. "Without me, you'll never get close to Molik. That's not a threat—it's the truth."

Molik has her uncle, I thought. *And Thymas has her affection, or trust, or maybe even love. But I don't have any hold on her, is that it? I've already wasted the only thing that might have worked—the chance of telling Thymas about Molik.*

There's always physical force, I considered briefly. *But look at the way she's standing—like she expects something like that.*

First, I wouldn't give her the satisfaction of being predictable.

Second, she's got her strength back, and she's mad as hell, besides. It wouldn't be easy.

Third, neither Ricardo nor Markasset was the sort of man to bully people. Rikardon, Captain of the Sharith, isn't about to start.

"You want us tromping all over Chizan, looking for Molik?" I asked. "Maybe we won't find him. But he'll know we're there. He'll have plenty of time to give orders about Volitar."

"You are *despicable!*" she hissed. "You'd throw away the life of a good man like Volitar—"

"I don't even know Volitar," I said. "My interest is in finding Gharlas."

"And I don't give a fleabite about this Gharlas!" she shouted.

"What about Gharlas?" Thymas cried, as he slid off his sha'um's back.

I turned on him so fast that he flinched back.

"You have a positive talent for popping up at a critical moment," I snarled. "Now stay out of this."

To Tarani, I said: "Are you coming with us, or not?"

She thought for a moment, visibly calming down. "On condition that you'll see Volitar safe, before you chase this Gharlas," she said. "In return, I will do all I can to help you find him. Who is Gharlas, anyway?"

"A thief," I said. "He has—" I caught a look of warning from Thymas. His message was clear: the Ra'ira was Sharith business. Tarani didn't need the information, and I didn't need to antagonize Thymas any further. I recovered as best I could. "—tried to kill either Dharak or me. I have a condition, too. A dead Molik can't give us any answers about Gharlas."

"Molik will tell you what you want to know, before he dies. But Volitar's freedom is to be our first priority. Agreed?"

I sighed. "All right, Tarani, it's a deal. Now get ready to go."

She started to strap on her pack.

"Wait," I interrupted her. "Can your bird take a written message to Dharak?"

She nodded, dropped the bag again, and started digging in it. She brought out some thin strips of leather and a small glass bottle of ink wrapped in padded fabric. The cork stopper of the bottle had the three-inch handle of a brush pushed through it, and she used the brush to take down the few words I had to say to Dharak.

"Gharlas hired assassins. Going to Chizan in pursuit."

I signed the message, having less trouble than I expected with the many-lined Gandalaran characters. She tied the strip to Lonna's leg, then tossed her up into the air with one word of instruction. "Dharak."

He's going to read that and say, "I told you so." Why am I doing this? The trail will be two weeks old before we get there. It was the suddenness, I guess, the surprise. It's almost as though I were meant to . . .

I'm sounding like Dharak. I know why I'm doing this. Because I believe Tarani. Gharlas gave me an excuse to change my mind, and try to help her.

I called Keeshah, and looked around the camp to see if anything had been left. That was when I noticed that Thymas had untied his pack. He was shaking out a rope net, and laying it down on the ground. As I watched, he pulled a tightly rolled pad from the open pack, and began to spread it across the net.

The first time I had seen one of those things, Zaddorn had been rolled up in it like a rag doll. The nets were designed to carry supplies when the Riders wanted to move fast. They opened flat to a size of about six feet by four, and the short ends were tied off onto a series of bronze rings. Such nets would be loaded, the ropes at each corner threaded through the rings, then the ropes looped around a Rider's hips and fastened in a sliding-ring catch. Two Riders hauled one net, dividing the extra weight between their sha'um.

I remembered how Zaddorn had looked when he rolled out of that Sharith cargo net. His clothes had been worn through in places, and his skin abraded by the thick, rough rope.

"At least you're padding it for her," I said sarcastically. Tarani's worried gaze left the net to rest on me, but Thymas missed the point.

"I knew we would have to carry her back to Thagorn," he answered steadily, still unrolling the pad. "I planned to make her as comfortable as possible."

"You don't really propose to cart her all the way to Chizan in that thing, do you?" I asked him. "If she doesn't suffocate in the padding, she'll be too stiff to move!"

"She has to come with us," he said, looking puzzled.

"Of course, she has to come with us," I repeated impatiently, thinking: *We aren't communicating. Either he's missing something, or I am.* "But not like that. Let her ride."

Very slowly, his lips formed a single, silent question. *Ride?*

"No female sha'um has ever come out of the Valley," he said, looking around behind him, as though I had suddenly seen one appear.

"Ride with *you*," I said. I looked at his sha'um, a little

smaller and a darker gray than Keeshah, who had settled down at the edge of the clearing. "Ronar can carry you both."

"Ronar will not carry a woman," he said flatly.

Well, I wanted to get outside of Markasset's experience, I thought. *And here I am. Standing on the sensitive toes of an ancient Sharith custom. Maybe I should just let it go . . . no, I can't see making Tarani flop around in that contraption, if there is any other way.*

"Have you asked Ronar?" I said.

"Why don't you ask Tarani?" he suggested. "She knows that it is unseemly for a woman to—"

He was looking at Tarani.

"We discussed it only once, Thymas," she said hurriedly. "You were so positive that it couldn't be done, that I haven't mentioned it since. But a hundred times, I have wanted to ask—has any woman ever *tried?*"

"No Sharith woman would even think it!" he said.

"I may never be Sharith, if we don't get to Chizan," Tarani answered.

"The net will take you there," he said coldly. He took out another pad, began unrolling it. "You will be comfortable."

It's possible that male sha'um really won't accept female riders, I speculated. *Then, too, it's possible that, because the King's Guard was all male originally, it has simply "always been" this way.*

"Thymas." I tried to imitate Dharak's command tone.

The boy stopped his work and waited, his cheeks red with anger.

"Try, Thymas," I said. "It can cost us only a few minutes now, and it might save us from fooling with that net all the way."

Thymas threw down the pad, and walked over to Ronar. He mounted the sha'um and brought him over near Tarani. The cat settled down into a crouch, but his head was turned toward the girl, and his lips twitched back from his teeth.

"Sit behind me," Thymas ordered gruffly. "Be very still." His body and face were tense. He was fighting to control the sha'um.

Something tells me this may not have been a good idea . . .

Tarani approached the sha'um slowly. She put her hand on Thymas's arm, and was preparing to swing her leg over the cat's hips. I doubt she was even breathing. I wasn't.

With a headache-quality roar, Ronar surged up, scraped Thymas off against a tree, and started to advance on Tarani. Thymas was up instantly, panic in his eyes. It would do no good to try to control the sha'um physically. He had to do it with his will, and he was failing.

Tarani backed away from the creeping, snarling sha'um. She looked less frightened than Thymas did, and I guessed she was trying to calm Ronar with her power.

It wasn't working.

The cat charged.

It had happened so fast that I had not had time to absorb it. Now it was too late to do anything. I thought, with horror, that it would all be over in a matter of seconds.

A tan shape hurtled into the clearing and knocked aside the charging sha'um. A tangle of fur and claws and teeth wrestled back and forth on the ground in front of Tarani, making ear-splitting and terrifying sounds.

Keeshah! Enough! I ordered, when I came out of that shocked paralysis. To Thymas, I yelled: "Call Ronar, and *control him*."

We both ran over to the free-for-all, but stayed clear of the snarling cats. We struggled to separate them through their habit of obedience to us. It was Keeshah who rolled to his feet and backed off, his ears tight to his skull, the fur on his neck bristled into a mane, and his tail twice its normal size.

Ronar had gotten the worst of it. He was bleeding from deep scratches along his flank, and a hunk of flesh and fur had been scraped away behind one ear. But he wasn't ready to quit, yet. He feinted at Keeshah, and got a claws-out slap across the nose for his pains. He fell back, then, and Thymas regained control. I wasn't sure how long he could hold it.

"Tarani, take off that pack," I said. She obeyed me without question.

You saved her, Keeshah, I said, as I transferred some of the food from my saddlebags into Tarani's pack. **Will you carry her?**

He was panting heavily, watching the other sha'um.

You want her. I will carry her.

Thanks.

I strapped on the pack and, pulling it high on my shoulders, tightened the fasteners.

"You'll have to ride first position, Tarani," I said. "You saw where Thymas was sitting. Sit there and lie forward, tucking up your knees and holding Keeshah's shoulders."

Still watching Ronar, Keeshah crouched down. Even after a sha'um had nearly killed her, Tarani went up to Keeshah with no trace of fear. She lay on his back with her eyes closed. Keeshah waited calmly while I checked her position on both sides.

I settled on Keeshah's hindquarters and leaned forward across Tarani's back. Keeshah stood up, lifting both of us easily, and I asked him to turn so that I could see Thymas.

The boy was spluttering with outrage.

"We need to keep the sha'um apart for a few hours," I said, "so I'm going to ride ahead. How far is Relenor?" I asked Tarani. I could see one side of her face. Her eyes opened, but her expression reminded me of the way she had looked when she was dancing.

"A day and a half, walking," she answered.

"We'll meet you at the Refreshment House tonight, then," I told Thymas. "Bring my packs, too, after you get Ronar calmed down. And repack that cargo net.

"We may need it for something else."

13

"Two are here who request shelter and water," I called, as Tarani and I stood in front of Relenor's gateway, about an hour before nightfall.

Relenor sat in the middle of a wide valley that would narrow and climb until it became the Zantil Pass. The Refreshment House looked just like the one at Yafnaar, with the entire compound surrounded by a man-high wall made of whitish blocks of rock salt.

The only opening in that wall was covered by a strip of yellow cloth, to remind travelers that staying here meant obeying the laws of the Fa'aldu. The desert-dwellers were called by that word as a single group; it meant "bringers of water." The Refreshment Houses took individual names based on the first person to settle in each location.

"I am Lussim, Elder of Relenor," said the man who appeared in the gateway, when the cloth barrier was dropped. He was wearing the traditional long white robe. He was younger than Balgokh, but he carried the same air of authority the Yafnaar elder possessed. "No quarrel shall enter here," he said. "Put aside your weapons, and be welcome to any service we can provide."

He stood aside, and Tarani moved through the gateway, removing her baldric and placing the sheathed sword in the Elder's out-stretched hands. He turned and handed it to one of the two boys who had lowered the barrier cloth. While he was doing that, Tarani was speaking her own formula.

"I have a weapon which cannot be surrendered," she said. "I give you my oath that it shall not be used while Relenor shelters me."

"Your oath is accepted," Lussim replied, with a smile. "As always, it is a pleasure to see you, Tarani."

She stopped aside, and I moved in, holding out Serkajon's sword. "I am Rikardon, Respected Elder, and I must ask for food and water for my sha'um, as well as for myself."

He had been in the act of handing the sword to the kid when he heard my name. He pulled it back, held it gently before him as he spoke to me.

"I know the value of this sword, Rikardon, and I will guard it, myself, while you shelter here. In the name of my cousin Balgokh, you may enter Relenor only as the guest of the Fa'aldu."

I bowed slightly. "I am honored, Respected Elder. If you please, I will see to my sha'um before I enter."

Lussim signaled to the boys, who went running off, staring at me over their shoulders. One bounced against a wall before he found a door and disappeared.

There has been time, since I left Yafnaar, for a letter to get here, I was thinking, *even if it came with a caravan, instead of a bird. I wonder what Balgokh said about me.*

I untied Tarani's pack, slipped it off, and handed it to her. She looked tired. She had been running from us, and following us, for two days without sleep. "I'll wait for the supplies," I said. "Go ahead and get settled."

Lussim led Tarani off toward the line of cubicles on one

side of the crowded courtyard. There was an enormous stack of goods in one corner of the yard, and twenty or thirty vleks were stamping around nervously, their low-slung bellies nearly dusting the floor of the courtyard.

Stay downwind, Keeshah, I said. **Did Tarani ride well?**

Yes, he answered. He sounded almost as tired as Tarani had looked.

There will be fresh meat soon, I told him. **I hadn't realized how much of this trip would be uphill. Will you be able to carry us both over the mountains?**

Try. Let woman ride behind.

That made sense, putting the lighter person where the rider's weight had to be less evenly distributed, right over Keeshah's hips. I voted for it, too, because I had been very uncomfortable all day. Keeshah's movement had been bad enough while I was sitting nearly upright. But the inevitable movement of Tarani's body under mine had created a different kind of discomfort, and the continual need to think of other things.

Mostly, I had thought about Gharlas. Why had he hired those assassins? To kill Dharak? His power might have let him learn that Dharak didn't fulfill his agreement to kill everyone on that caravan. Revenge is always a good motive.

But what if I were the target? How had he known that I would be in Thagorn? More use of that power? He had hired Molik sometime after I had *decided* to go to Thagorn. Could he have known about that decision?

But why kill me? Because I had been the one to track down Hural and prove to Zaddorn that Gharlas has the Ra'ira?

What if he tried to read my mind, and couldn't do it? I wondered, as I waited for the boys to bring out meat for Keeshah. *Another motive enters the picture. Fear of the unpredictable, maybe the uncontrollable. But then he couldn't have known where I would be. Maybe he had Molik send assassins to Raithskar, too. Expensive insurance. Would peace of mind be worth it to him?*

The boys came back, lugging a haunch of glith and a large waterskin. They wouldn't let me take the things, but insisted on carrying them outside the gate for me. There were water troughs along the wall like the ones in the center of the yard—large semi-circular tiles, braced by a frame of salt blocks. The boy with the waterskin poured the smallest trough half full.

Keeshah came around a corner when I called him, and the boy next to me—I thought he was the younger of the two—staggered backward under his load of meat when he saw the cat. I grabbed hold of the glith to steady the boy.

Here's dinner, Keeshah, I said. **Try not to scare the kid to death.**

The boy hung on, wide-eyed and fascinated, as the big cat approached, and sank his teeth into the fresh meat. Tiny rivers of blood oozed out around Keeshah's tusks as he lifted the weight from the boy's hands. The blood dripped on the ground, as the sha'um carried his dinner to one of the empty troughs and set it down.

Thirsty, he told me. **Drink first.**

He came over to the water trough. I lifted a palmful of water for him to lap up. This was part of the tradition of Serkajon's house, that a sha'um would not feed or drink among men, unless his rider offered him his first taste.

The other boy was watching us. Looking at the boys closely, I was sure they were brothers.

What's fair for one . . .

Will you drink from the boy's hand, Keeshah?

Why? The thought was complaining; he wanted a drink, not a sip.

It would please me. And the boy would like it.

Yes.

"Your turn," I said to the boy, and waved him into my place by the trough. He turned pale and started to stammer, but I grabbed his shoulder and nudged him forward. "Go ahead. He won't hurt you."

He let the waterskin fall to the ground, and scooped up a double handful of water from the trough. He held it up to Keeshah's muzzle. I saw him shiver when the raspy tongue flicked across his hands. Then he stepped away, and Keeshah lowered his head to the trough.

"Keeshah thanks you for your service," I told the boys. "If you'll leave the water with me, I'll return what he doesn't drink."

I could see they wanted to stay, but they knew a dismissal when they heard one. They backed through the gate without a word, then ran across the yard again, chattering excitedly.

As I turned to watch them, I saw Lussim waiting beside the gate.

"That was generous of you, Rikardon," he said. "You have given them a precious memory. The Sharith patrols stop by here now and then, so that the boys have seen sha'um before. But not so closely. The Sharith are not . . . thoughtful, as you are."

The Sharith encourage everybody to see their cats as dangerous creatures. To them, a sha'um is also a weapon.

That's true. But I like it better, my way.

"I should tell you, Respected Elder—"

"My name, please," he requested.

"Since I was last at Yafnaar, Lussim, I have become part of the Sharith. Another Rider will be arriving soon."

"Tarani has told me that Thymas would join you."

"You know Thymas?"

"Slightly," he said, noncommittally. "Um . . . it was my intention to ask you to dine with us this evening."

You're wondering what the situation is among the three of us, aren't you? It's plain that you like Tarani, but if Thymas has to be included, you'd rather not offer the invitation.

"I am not required by courtesy to dine with Tarani and Thymas," I said, to get him off the hook. "In fact, I think they would prefer to take their meal alone. I would be very pleased to dine in the inner court."

"Oh."

"Is something wrong?"

"Well . . . Tarani . . . We're very crowded, as you can see. Tarani assured me that one room for the three of you . . ."

"It will be sufficient," I assured him. He gave me the dinner hour, identified our room, then went into the family buildings.

Keeshah had taken the glith haunch off somewhere. I poured out another portion of water and took the skin inside. Behind me, two different boys hauled up the cloth barrier.

The room we had been assigned was about fifteen feet square, with man-sized blocks along three walls. Plain pallets and folded blankets rested on each of the three beds. One corner was screened off by wood-framed tapestries to provide a private dressing area.

Tarani was sitting on one of the beds, letting her head rest against the wall, when I came in. She sat up straight when she saw me.

"Thymas is probably no more than an hour behind us," I said.

"I wanted the chance to talk to you, before he arrives."

"Oh?" I said. I unrolled the pallet of the bed opposite hers, bunched up the blanket for a pillow, and stretched out. "What about?"

"*About* Thymas. The scene you described this morning—Thymas traveling with me, Ronar performing—you said that would make me happy. Do you really believe that?"

"It shouldn't matter to you what I believe."

"Thymas is Sharith," she said stiffly. "You are the leader of the Sharith. Your opinion matters to us, naturally."

Thymas probably loves latrine detail a lot more than he cares about my opinion, I thought. *You're just worried that what I think will influence what he thinks. See previous thought, and quit worrying.*

But, for the record . . .

"I was impatient and angry when I said that," I told her. "I can't have watched you mount Keeshah and think that you would ever demean a sha'um in that way."

"Thank you," she said. The long, fine fingers of her hands were interlacing and pulling apart, twisting together and separating. She noticed them, closed her hands into fists, and dropped them into her lap.

"I am to marry Thymas," she announced suddenly.

I felt as though I had swallowed an iceberg.

"Does Dharak know this?" I asked.

"Not yet. Thymas brought his betrothal gift to my dressing room, just before the performance."

"Just before he found out you were involved in a plot to murder his father," I corrected. She winced.

"I offered to return the sword to Thymas today, while you were gone—" she began heatedly.

"Thymas gave you a *sword* for a betrothal gift?" I demanded.

"Yes, why not?" she flared back. "He has taught me sword work. I go through Chizan so often—he believes I need the protection."

Like a porcupine needs a shotgun, I thought. *Thymas knew she had that sword, and that she could use it. If she hadn't been so tired this morning . . .*

And he didn't say a word about it. Some cooperation.

"I see you still have the sword," I said drily. "After you told Thymas about *borrowing* money from Molik." I knew it was cruel, but there was a queer pain blocking my kindness channel. "You needn't worry about how he'll feel after he learns the truth. There are a lot of things Thymas lacks, but a sense of honor isn't one of them. He will keep his promise to marry you."

Her eyes blazed. "Will that be his only reason for the marriage, because it was promised?"

"Of course not," I answered. "By now, he probably needs you very much."

She sat up as though I had slapped her.

"Do let me know if Thymas wants a dose tonight," I went on, cringing away from my own nastiness. "I'll sleep in the yard."

She was on her feet, her fists clenched.

"If that is all you think Thymas wants of me, rest easy," she said, her low voice trembling. "I have sworn not to use my power in Relenor. I, too, keep my promises."

She left the room.

Should I go after her? She needs sleep more than I do.

She knows what she needs, I told myself gruffly. *And it's a little late for gallantry now.*

I turned to my left side, facing the wall, and tried to sleep. An hour later, I gave it up, and went into the yard to wash my face and hands before dinner. Water was too precious for bathing. At least, for the travelers. The Fa'aldu themselves lived a life of considerable comfort.

It had become dark, and lamps had been lit along the walls of the courtyard. Sitting on the ground under one of those lamps were Thymas and Tarani. I walked over there quietly; Tarani was sound asleep, with her head on the boy's shoulder. I had another unsettling glimpse of the girl within the powerful, hardened woman.

"Have you eaten?" I asked Thymas. He nodded, tightening his arm around Tarani's shoulders. "Do you know where our room is?" Another nod. "I will be with the Fa'aldu until late," I said. "Then I think it would be best for all of us if I slept outside. Do you need help to carry her in?"

"I need no help from you," he said shortly, keeping his voice low. Unspoken, the word "ever" hung between us for a moment. "Tarani told me about Molik. But she refused to tell me why she wouldn't go in the room while you were there. She didn't say it, but I'm sure she knew I would kill you, if I knew the reason."

The lamplight from above him gleamed off his forehead, but left his eyes invisible in the shadow of his brow ridge. I didn't need to see his eyes. My skin was sizzling under his gaze.

"For Dharak's sake," he said softly, "don't ever let me find out what you said—or did—to Tarani tonight."

14

Dinner was served for the twenty-odd Fa'aldu—and their only guest—after all of Relenor's visitors had been given their meals. The inner court was lit by the glow of two cookfires, and by several of the glass-and-candle lamps. All the food was put on the table, and everyone seated in order of age, except for me. Lussim and I sat side by side at one end of the wide, long table.

After dinner, I found myself the center of attention, and I started talking. The Fa'aldu never asked questions, but they were rapt listeners. I knew Balgokh had already told them about me, but I repeated the story I had given at Yafnaar, omitting any mention of Ricardo.

I continued the story from there, describing Thagorn and the lifestyle of the Sharith. The two boys who had served Keeshah were seated at the far end of the table. When I spoke of the ceremony that had made me Captain, I saw them straining forward to hear better.

Then I started lying.

"Tarani happened to mention to Thymas that she saw Gharlas in Chizan," I said. "When she found out we were looking for him, she offered to come with us. She has friends in Chizan who may help us trace him."

"Gharlas," Lussim said, shaking his head. "You know, of

course, that our oath of neutrality forbids our helping you to find Gharlas."

I nodded. Balgokh, too, had told me this.

"The Refreshment Houses owe their existence to the Kings," Lussim went on. "But Gharlas is a fool to think he can re-unite Gandalara. The desert has claimed too much land. The cities have moved to the Wall to get enough water to survive. If he offered to share Eddarta's water, he might have a chance. But from all I know of him, he will wish to conquer, not befriend, his neighbors."

"That's my guess, too," I said. "If I'm not being rude, may I ask about the history of the Refreshment Houses? You said they were established during the Kingdom . . ."

"During the time of Harralen, the third King. Until then, merchants had carried water to posts along the caravan routes, and sold it for extortionate prices. Travelers appealed to Harralen, and he sent an unarmed envoy into the desert beyond Chizan, to the place of the Fa'aldu. It was a daring risk for the man who came to us, but his courage impressed us. We were . . . barbarians."

Lussim picked up a fragment of tile, broken away from the table-top, and rolled the angular chunk between his fingers.

"We could bring the water, even then," he said, watching the movement of his hand. "But we didn't have much else. We guarded our water ferociously, and terrorized passing caravans, stealing whatever was left unguarded, sometimes attacking them."

No wonder you hesitated to ask Thymas to your table, I thought. *The tribute demanded by the Sharith reminds you of your own beginnings.*

"The envoy—a man named Stester—brought us Harralen's proposition. If we would settle along the caravan trails, and agree to trade water for goods at a reasonable rate, he would make such trade our exclusive monopoly. We would be asked to trade only what we did not need for ourselves, and never to turn away anyone truly in need.

"It was a difficult decision," Lussim continued. "The Fa'aldu had lived in that place for many generations. But in all that time we had been desperately poor, and never at peace. We accepted the King's offer, and his Guard drove off all the opportunists along the caravan trails—except in Chizan. Chizan was a city, not a collection of vleks with waterskins. Harralen was forced to be content with requiring reasonable prices for Chizan's water, a control long since forgotten.

"Relenor was the second Refreshment House to be established," he finished, with obvious pride.

"And the oldest one? Is it Yafnaar?" I asked.

"Oh, no, there was no need for Yafnaar until later," he answered, "when the Great Pleth had become much smaller. No, the first Refreshment House was at Inid, on the other side of the Korchi Mountains. Here, let me show you . . ."

He went through a door and came out again with a folded parchment. He brought a lamp close, and opened out a map.

It was about the same size as the one Thanasset had given me to help me find Thagorn. Like that one, this map had a solid black line to represent the Great Wall. It trailed across one long edge of the rectangle. The relative location of Thagorn, and a fragment of the Morkadahl Mountains, told me that this map would not fit edge-to-edge with the first one, and that the Great Wall made a turn southward, past the Morkadahls.

The central feature of this map section was the Korchi mountain range. With the Great Wall "north"—that is, placing the rectangle so that the side with the Great Wall shown on it was at the top—the Korchis filled most of the right-hand side of the map. They were roughly triangular, with one point meeting the Wall. There was a slim corridor shown near the bottom of the map, forming the base of the triangle. The mountains below that corridor didn't show a name; they might have been a continuation of the Korchi.

West of that corridor was Relenor. East of it was Inid. Smack in the middle of it, where it widened considerably, was Chizan. In that first glance, I noticed two other features. Dyskornis was north of Inid, halfway up the eastern edge of the Korchi triangle. And north of Relenor, on the western side of the mountain range, was an area marked "Well of Darkness."

What the . . .?

But Lussim was talking about the trail to Chizan, and I brought my attention back to him quickly. The Zantil Pass was a stretch about forty miles long (figured roughly from Lussim's description, and the estimated passage time shown on the map). It lay fifty miles from Relenor, and about a hundred from Chizan. There was another pass between Chizan and Inid, called the Zantro, and the distances were about the same in reverse.

"You'll find that the Zantro is the easier passage," Lussim said, "because, though it is a little higher, it is more level. The Zantil has high points here and here." He pointed to the beginning and end of the pass. "There is so much loose rock and blowing dust, that even the downslope is slow travel. Climbing back up, with the air so thin, is the hardest part of the journey."

It sounds as though the Zantil and Zantro are as high as the Khumbar Pass, which twelve-year-old Markasset had to cross on his way to the Valley of the Sha'um. Thanasset hadn't told the boy what to expect, but I suppose the Pass was an endurance test. Markasset toughed it through, and he learned. When he took Keeshah back across that, he went slow and easy, walking the sha'um across the worst part.

The Zantil has to be passable for sha'um, or Zanek could never have sent the Guard across to convince everybody on the other side to join the Kingdom. But it's a long trip, and Keeshah will be carrying two of us through most of it.

"Is there game along the way?" Lussim looked blank. "Wild glith, birds, meat for the sha'um?"

"Oh! I'm afraid I don't know that, Rikardon. I've never been through there myself, and the people who have given me this information didn't have that need." He stared thoughtfully at the map. "I have never heard anything to make me think it likely, though. From all accounts, there isn't much more than barren rock, most of the way. It would please us to send some live glith with you for your sha'um, if you wish it."

"That's a generous offer, Lussim, and I thank you for it," I answered slowly, thinking it over. "But just getting across the pass will be trouble enough, without trying to lead a herd of glith, half-crazed with fear of the sha'um."

I studied the map. *The pass itself will be the hardest part. We'll walk, of course. It will take us a day and a half to cross it, maybe longer. But we ought to make it to the pass in only a day, even cutting our speed in half to allow for Keeshah's extra load. Past the high crossing, it's all downhill. If we take enough meat with us to let the cats feed well, just before we enter the pass . . .*

"If I may trouble you for one fresh-killed glith," I said, "I think that will get us through. We'll need supplies for ourselves, as well—"

We discussed more details, and Lussim agreed to have everything ready for dawn the next day. He walked with me into the courtyard, expressing his thanks for my company through the evening. I stood thoughtfully for a minute, wondering if I'd be able to sleep outdoors. The ground would be comfortable enough, but the milling vleks were too stupid not to step on me.

Lussim cleared his throat. "It is late, Rikardon, and you might disturb your friends by retiring now. You are welcome to sleep in one of our family guest rooms."

"That would be very kind," I accepted his tactful offer. Then, because I felt he deserved some sort of explanation, I said awkwardly: "It has been only two days since Thymas and Tarani were betrothed."

Lussim raised his eyebrows, but said nothing. He conducted me to the guest room in the family quarters, wished me a pleasant sleep, then left me.

I didn't rest well. Tarani haunted my dreams. I saw her stalk out of our room, hurt and angry, as she had been that night. I watched her sleeping peacefully against Thymas's shoulder, her breath coming slowly, her face incredibly young.

I saw Tarani dance again, only this time the hanging darkness of her illusion didn't dissipate. It flowed behind her, and formed a human shape. A shadow woman danced on the heels of the real one.

I should have been pleased; I knew that no one else could see the shadow, or witness the dramatic pas de deux. But I was frightened, and all the more so because the shadow did nothing frightening. It just followed Tarani, clinging to her, and imitating her movements.

The dance reached the point at which the assassins had interrupted it in Thagorn, and I was almost relieved to see the knife descending. It seemed to explain that strange dread I had been feeling.

Just at that moment, the shadow-shape changed and solidified. It was a real person, a man. He continued to dance with Tarani; it should have been ludicrous, but it wasn't. He danced with a sinuous, sinister grace, and the same rapt expression Tarani wore, except that his eyes glittered with reflections of the trailing flame.

He had more purpose, and a higher pleasure, than the dance itself. I knew it. I was the only one who knew it. Tarani was in terrible danger.

I had a choice. I could save myself from the knife, or I could take the time to warn her, and let myself die. In the dream, the split second of the knife's descent slowed to give me time to think about it. I decided.

Just as the knife pierced my heart with an awful pain, I shouted: "*Tarani, look out! Gharlas is behind you!*"

I jumped awake, staring wildly into the darkness. I felt an anxious, puzzled query from Keeshah, and, automatically, I sent him a reassuring response. After a moment's disorientation, I recognized where I was, and that the terror I had just experienced had come from my own subconscious. It was nearly dawn, so I got up and began to dress. I shivered, as though I could shake off the lingering strangeness with physical action.

When I met Tarani and Thymas at the gateway, I saw that the bird had caught up with us again. Lonna stood on Tarani's shoulder, watching curiously as Thymas packed away the bread, salted meat, and fresh fruit that Lussim had ordered for us. A dead glith, blood still seeping from its cut throat, lay beside the gate.

"Did Lonna bring a message from Dharak?" I asked.

Tarani shook her head.

Thymas finished tying up my saddlebags, and hefted both his and mine over one shoulder. Tarani's pack, he handed to me. I took it, but gave it to Tarani.

"Keeshah has asked if you will ride second," I said. "You weigh less than I do."

She took the pack without comment, and began to fasten it on. The bird fluttered to the top of the wall and waited there.

Lussim came out to say goodbye. I was glad that he didn't congratulate Tarani and Thymas. I had wondered—too late, of course—whether I had any right to spread the news.

I shouldered the glith, which weighed about seventy pounds, and we carried our returned weapons out beyond the walls of Relenor. The sha'um came at our call, one around each corner of the enclosure.

The few scratches Keeshah had endured during the brief

fight the day before were clean, and almost hidden by his fur. Ronar's wounds shone black against his gray fur. His muzzle twitched into a snarl. He dropped into a fighting crouch, and Keeshah advanced on him slowly, tail lashing and ears laid back.

No more fighting! I commanded.

Tell the other one, Keeshah snapped back at me. But he stopped.

"Thymas—"

"I'm trying, fleabite it!" His jaw bulged as he clenched his teeth with the effort.

Ronar began to calm down, glancing from Thymas to Keeshah. At last, he relaxed a little, and let Thymas approach. The boy smoothed the standing fur on the cat's neck. When the sha'um's ears came forward, I started to breathe again.

"Let's get going," I said.

It's going to be a long trip to Chizan.

15

Ronar snarled at Keeshah, Thymas snarled at me, and Tarani moved and spoke, when necessary, as though she were animated stone. Most of her words were for Thymas, but she delivered them in the same disinterested monotone that she used the few times she addressed me. The only time I saw a flicker of life in her eyes was in the moment before she mounted Keeshah each time.

Tarani tried twice more to mount Ronar. I couldn't decide—was she showing courage, or merely dislike for her dependence on me? Thymas's sha'um was less violent in these refusals, but he made it clear that he would not accept her. So she rode with me in second place, and didn't complain of being tired, even when she could hardly stand up at the end of a ride.

Thymas suffered more, physically, than either Tarani or me. The Zantil Pass was easier than I had expected; I decided it had to be a lot lower than the Khumbar. Tarani had made the crossing many times. But Thymas had been able to reach the Valley of the Sha'um merely by following the eastern edge of the Morkadahls northward from Thagorn; he hadn't experienced the Khumbar. Apparently, the information network developed by the Sharith had made it unnecessary for Riders to cross the Chizan Passage for many generations. Tarani must have warned Thymas, but hearing about shortness of breath, and living with it, are two very different phenomena.

Emotionally, Thymas was a wreck. He knew Tarani was riding with me purely in the interest of faster travel, but the sight of her clinging to me upset him so badly he insisted on riding ahead of us. He was probably less jealous than angry with himself and Ronar for forcing the situation.

The timing of the trip worked out fairly close to my estimate. We camped just below the pass on the first night. The sha'um grumbled and growled, next morning, as they shared the glith that Thymas and Ronar had carried up. At dawn, we started the long walk across the Zantil Pass. We had run across two caravans the day before, one going toward Chizan and the other just out of the pass, headed for Relenor. But there was no traffic in the pass itself.

Lussim hadn't exaggerated. A sharp, hot wind screamed between the walls of the shallow chasm, blinding us with dust, and sucking the loose rock out from under our feet. We wore headscarves around our faces, and used spares to fashion protection for the sha'um. Lonna rode through the pass inside Tarani's tunic, to escape the dust.

We walked slowly, and rested frequently. Without needing any consultation, we didn't try to camp in the pass, but pushed on while there was moonlight. We staggered down the outside slope of the far ridge after twenty hours of grueling work.

As soon as we descended far enough to breathe more easily, we collapsed where we were, and slept through the next morning. The rest of that day, plus one more day, brought us to a landmark Tarani knew, a high column of rock striated in reds and browns and grays.

As soon as Tarani and I had dismounted, Keeshah flopped on the ground and lay there, panting heavily. I brought him some water. After he had licked some from my hand and rested a moment, he rolled into a crouch and drank from the bowl.

You've worked so hard, I told him.

I sat beside him and began to smooth his fur with my hands, brushing out dust, scratching the skin lightly. I noticed that his ribs were easier to find.

Can you make it to Chizan, with two of us riding?

How far? he asked.

I looked around for Tarani, and was startled to find her standing next to me, staring down at us. An expresion of concern vanished from her face, just as I turned my head.

"How far to Chizan from here?" I passed along Keeshah's question.

"One day more," Tarani answered. "Our supplies are almost gone, and Ronar carries much less weight now. Tomorrow, I will ride in the cargo net, so that Keeshah's burden will be less."

That was more than she had said, at any one time, since Relenor.

"I didn't ask—" I began.

"You should have."

She turned away to help Thymas assemble our simple meal, and I tried to ignore my rising anger.

Another day, I gave Keeshah his answer. **Tarani will ride in the net. Can you make it?**

Yes. Now sleep.

The sha'um rolled over on his side, pushing me away, and closed his eyes.

I got my dinner, and took it away from camp, out of sight of Thymas and Tarani. I had made this a habit on the trip, thinking to give them some semblance of privacy. Tonight I admitted that I had been doing it partly to get away from Tarani's eerie coldness. The woman still disturbed me.

And never more than right now. She had broken out of her silence—for what? To criticize the way I treated Keeshah.

If only she hadn't been right, I groaned. *Keeshah was so grateful. Why didn't I think of it myself?*

Because I've been responding to her cold-shoulder treatment with my own version of it. I never considered breaking the ice, not even to save Keeshah some hardship. That's a pretty sad state of affairs, when I let my own pride blind me to Keeshah's needs.

And when I consider the facts, whose fault is it that we're all under such strain? Sure, Tarani's doing it, but why? Because she informed the Captain of the Sharith of her impending marriage to Thymas—no more than her duty, as a future Sharith wife—and the Captain responded with a personal insult.

She's over-reacting, though, I thought. *There might be some justice in freezing me out, but it looks as if Thymas isn't any better off than I am.*

I had found a place where I could lean back against a sloping rock to eat my dinner, which was now finished. I was too comfortable to move, and so tired that I drifted off to sleep.

The landscape around me was silver and black when I woke up, and I heard Tarani humming.

What's she up to now? I wondered.

I got up and moved, as quietly as I could, around the pile of rocks which had screened me from the camp. To my right, I saw Thymas, sprawled out, sound asleep. Near him was Tarani's pack, bunched up and with a dent in it that might fit her head.

Five yards to my left, Tarani was kneeling at Keeshah's head, facing me, but looking down at the sha'um. And this was no bleak, stony stare, such as Thymas and I endured during the day. Her face and voice were vibrant with tenderness, affection and admiration.

I began to get angry. I couldn't tell whether I was jealous of Keeshah, receiving honest emotion from Tarani, or afraid that Tarani's power might be stronger than my bond with the sha'um. I just knew that it was important to disrupt that scene, to make Keeshah aware that Tarani's power was dangerous.

Keeshah, I called. I had to repeat his name several times before he answered me.

Yes. Slow and lazy.

Tarani is using her power on you, Keeshah. I don't know what she wants—

Wants to help, he interrupted. **Feels good. See?**

With no more warning than that, Keeshah melded his mind with mine. I felt relaxed, unworried. There was no tiredness or pain. No hunger. Only a great gathering sleepiness. I wanted that sleep. I longed for it . . .

I broke the bond with Keeshah, and wrenched myself awake—but not before my relaxing muscles had let me lean against the rockpile and dislodge some pebbles. Tarani looked up at the small sound, and the humming stopped. She showed a flash of recognition, then her face closed down again.

"Walk away from camp with me," I said, as she stood up. "If we're going to reach Chizan tomorrow, I need to know what to expect."

She nodded, stepped around Keeshah quietly, and followed me back down the narrow gulley where I had eaten and napped. I asked her questions about the city, and she answered them exactly, completely, but with no elaboration beyond a direct answer.

I listened to what she said, for it was true that I needed the information. But another part of me realized that the questions were only an excuse, a stall. I had seen a glimpse of the sensitive woman inside the shell. Now the barricade was unbearable, and as we walked along, I was searching for a way to break through it again.

If all else fails, tell the truth, I thought.

"Wait," I said suddenly, catching her arm to make her stop with me, nearly at the end of the gulley. We were some fifty yards from camp. Her arm tensed under my hand, and I felt the solid, elastic muscle of a dancer. I let go. The last thing I needed was to make her afraid of me.

"All I really wanted to say is . . . thank you for what you did for Keeshah. I thought, at first—well, I'm not very clear on exactly what I was thinking, but it wasn't flattering. I apologize for that."

"My power is good for something besides giving pleasure," she said shortly. "If you wanted to say this, why didn't you just say it, and let us both get some rest?"

Anger—at least, it's an emotion. Hallelujah.

"Habit," I said. "For some reason, it's easy to say things to you that I don't really mean."

Except for that first, direct glance across Keeshah, she hadn't looked up from the ground. Now she faced me, and the rage she had suppressed for four days blazed out of her dark eyes.

"For example?" she hissed.

I recoiled, bristling. Then I reminded myself that I had

invited this encounter. I had admitted to myself that she had a right to be angry. It was time I admitted it to her.

"I can't account for why I suggested that Thymas needs—that your illusions are—" I fumbled to a stop, tried again. "Thymas loves you. I find that easy to understand." *Very easy*. "But I confess to wondering . . ."

"Why I want to marry him?" she finished for me. "Isn't it possible that I return his love?" she demanded. "Does there have to be something else I might gain by marrying Thymas?"

I grabbed her shoulders, angry in spite of all my resolution. "Why do you always put the worst possible meaning to my words?" I growled. "I didn't say that. I didn't *mean* that."

She glanced down at my hands, then smiled up at me with a bitter wisdom much older than her years.

"Do you want me for yourself, then?"

I released her as though my hands had been scalded. I was horrified to hear myself saying: "You forget that your illusions don't work on me."

Her face went gray. She turned around and started back toward the camp, hugging her arms to her as though I had delivered a body blow.

I ran after her and caught her arm again. She stopped, but kept her face turned away from me. I took a deep breath, and ordered myself to keep control of my tongue.

"Of course I want you," I said quietly. "There's no man in the world who could get within touching distance of you, and not want you. But that has nothing to do with what I mean about you and Thymas.

"Sharith women live simply, with regulation and conformity and duty a daily part of their lives. They are trained to it from birth, and I'm not the one to find fault with it.

"But you wouldn't be able to stand living in Thagorn, Tarani. You're too strong, too complex, too skilled, too much an individual. Your power—that's extra. You don't need it to make you . . . special.

"I know I've said some vile things to you," I went on, relieved to be expressing all this at last. "It was reaction to—well, when I thought of you among the Sharith, I had this terrible feeling of something being wasted. I don't mean any insult to them, or to Thymas," I added, hurriedly. "And I see, now, that it's none of my business anyway. I have no right to judge you, or your choices. I'm just trying to explain . . .

"I'm sorry," I finished, and took my hand from her arm. She didn't move a muscle.

"That's finally, really, all I wanted to say," I told her after a moment. "Except that I won't try to interfere between you and Thymas again. And please think about this—we need to be a team, when we face Molik."

Still she stood there, immobile.

"It's time we got some rest, as you said."

Tarani walked away.

Did I get through to her? I wondered. *Or did I make things worse? At least I tried.*

I followed her into camp, stretched out on the ground near Keeshah, and fell asleep.

Nothing much was changed, the next morning. There was no more conversation than usual; we packed up and got ready to leave camp in about the same way we had done it every day.

But the tension was gone.

I saw Thymas glance at me, and then Tarani, and I knew he was wondering what he had missed during the night. He was subdued and thoughtful as he laid out the net and padding, and we rolled up Tarani in it like a long sack of grain.

Ronar and Keeshah crouched down at either end of the net. Thymas and I buckled on the end ropes and mounted. The sha'um stood up and sidled apart, until Tarani was clear of the ground; then we started forward.

I had made an easier trip, so far, than Thymas or Tarani. The boy had carried all the supplies in our four saddlebags, draped across his thighs. Tarani had worn her own pack, and suffered the discomfort of the second position. All I had been doing was hugging Keeshah. Now, since Thymas carried all the packs to relieve Keeshah of as much weight as possible, and since Tarani had volunteered to be hauled around in that net, I still had the easiest job. All I had to do was support half the girl's weight, and keep myself balanced on Keeshah.

I had ridden in several training sessions with the cargo net while we had stayed in Thagorn. But by the time Lonna sounded her hooting call—a signl pre-arranged to tell us when we were a mile or so from Chizan—every muscle in my body was cramped.

We turned aside from the trail, which was now well marked. The desolation of the pass had given way to a flattish, high-walled valley with its floor covered with growth. Not the fertile green of the Morkadahl hillsides, fed from rivers flowing down out of the mountains. And not quite the stubborn scrubby brush that clung to the dunes of the Kapiral Desert. There were humps of growth on the ground that waved feathery arms in all directions, some of them reaching higher than a trained dakathrenil tree. A hardy species of the narrow-leaved plant that filled the ecological niche of grass covered the ground between the great, fluffy domes. Its blade looked similar to the other "grass" I had seen, but its color was a sickly yellow-green.

We dropped Tarani in a clearing. While I fell off Keeshah, Thymas—hardened by years of training with loaded cargo nets—unrolled the girl. She emerged from the net on hands and knees, groaning with the effort of making her stiff muscles move. We hadn't stopped, except for brief rests to take care of compelling physical needs, and now it was midafternoon. She had been wrapped up in that contraption for almost nine hours.

The first thing she did was crawl over to Keeshah, who lay crouched beside me, and wrap her arms around his neck.

"I didn't know—" she said, her words muffled by the fur on his neck. "Oh, Keeshah, thank you for carrying me alone."

She pushed herself away from him, and sort of plopped down into a sitting position beside me.

"Does he understand?" she asked.

"Not the words," I said, without needing to ask him. "But the feeling. Yes, he understands."

"I owe you thanks, too, Rikardon," she said. "I give them now, and . . . and I ask that the hard words we have exchanged be forgotten."

"What hard words?" I asked. She responded to my smile with an honest-to-goodness dazzling Tarani smile.

It felt good.

But Thymas was glowering at us suspiciously. I got to my feet, and offered my hand to help Tarani up. She took it, but had so much trouble rising that Thymas rushed to help, too.

I untied my last waterskin, took a long sip, and poured the rest of the water into a bowl for Keeshah.

"There are enough supplies left for you two to have dinner," I said. "I'll go into Chizan and bring back some water and meat for the sha'um, and find us a place to stay. It will be safer if Tarani doesn't show up in the daylight."

Nobody tried to talk me out of it.

"Leave Chizan well before sunset," Tarani advised. "It is a vicious place, after dark. Lonna will watch for you, and guide you, if necessary."

"Thanks. See you in a couple of hours."

I set off at a trot, really glad of the way the exercise eased the pain in my legs.

16

Chizan was an education in Gandalaran profanity. Chizan might have inspired it. Most of the city was "fleabitten" in the literal sense.

The city had no wall, and no specific marketplace. Vleks stayed in pens near the inns where their handlers were staying. The outer streets of Chizan were littered with trickles and heaps of yellow crystal, left over from passing vleks. It was impossible to avoid stepping on them, and the crushed waste gave off a pungent odor that flavored the air.

You could tell the natives by the way they wore their headscarves—wrapped securely around their faces—and by their total silence out-of-doors.

I stopped one of these, took my scarf away from my face long enough to croak: "Water?" The man pointed to a tall building, set away from the rest of the town. I slapped his shoulder in thanks, and went over there.

The building itself was a single story; its entire upper floor was a water tank. The first floor had doorless openings at the short ends of the rectangle, and the inside looked like a tavern, with bars along both long walls. Along those same walls, on the outside of the building, were watering stalls for vleks.

Caravan masters came inside, paid for the water they needed, and were directed to take their vleks through stalls identified by numbers. The "bartender" then opened cocks, from inside the building, that filled each separate drinking bowl outside with the specified amount of water.

Men were served across the bars, at an exorbitant price per cup of water. But I didn't begrudge the four zaks six that I dug out of my pouch. After five days of allowing myself only a sip of water at a time, that drink of tepid liquid, served in a rough clay bowl, tasted delicious.

I filled two of my waterskins, and shoved my way out through the thirsty crowd to look for a place to stay. I really wanted a good night's sleep in a quiet, comfortable room, before we tried to tackle Molik.

No such luck.

I was carrying over four hundred zaks—what remained of the twelve hundred zaks Markasset had stolen from Thanasset, the morning he had left Raithskar with the ill-fated caravan. Thanasset had insisted I keep everything left over after I paid Worfit.

I kept one hand on my moneypouch as I walked through Chizan. It was immediately clear that we would need that money.

The Green Sha'um Inn in Omergol had charged me ten zaks for a night's rest in a private room. In Chizan, the medium fee was twenty zaks per person, for part of a room's floor that was crammed full with pallets laid head to foot. I got one entire room, after some haggling, for a hundred zaks. I watched the clerk's head fur jump with tiny brown bodies, and I resolved to sleep on the bare floor.

Next, I set out to find some food for the sha'um, and to do some exploring. Tarani had told me that Chizan consisted of three semi-circular layers. I was in the first of these, a district devoted to the maintenance and entertainment of the vlek handlers who traveled here from all points, and stayed until their money ran out.

I wandered through the second district, where there were residences and support businesses for the people who worked in Chizan, and better class inns (at much higher prices) for the caravan masters and more discriminating travelers.

Then, because I was running close to the deadline I had set myself for heading back to camp, I allowed myself only a quick stroll through the third, elite district: the rogueworld.

Here were restaurants, gaming houses, rented sex partners, and bathtubs. I walked through to the center of the city, where a large and luxurious gaming house overshadowed all other structures. In that building, in a well-guarded apartment, lived Molik.

Tarani said that Molik owns Chizan, down to the last stone of the last building. He can hire people to work here, give them a small percentage of the take, and let them set prices so high that they can make themselves a fortune. Then he probably acquires their fortunes through his gaming houses. Slick.

Tomorrow, Molik, I promised silently, *we'll have a long talk about hired killers and kidnapping. I'm looking forward to meeting you.*

I went back to the second district, and visited several meat shops, buying small to medium portions of glith in each one. It might have been an unnecessary precaution, but I was determined that Molik shouldn't have any idea that Tarani was back in Chizan until she told him herself.

A caravan master might buy bulk lots of fresh meat for his crew, but all the masters were known in these shops. For a single man to make such a purchase, or to march out of the city with a live glith on a leash, would be unusual. I was sure that anything unusual would be reported to Molik. If he couldn't make the connection between a lot of meat and a sha'um, sha'um and Sharith, Sharith and Tarani—then we were wasting our time worrying about the girl's uncle.

I made several trips to our room, leaving the small purchases in a corner cleared of the flea-infested pallets. When I had the equivalent of a glith—at four times its cost in Raithskar—I packed all the bundles in oiled canvas and stuffed them into Tarani's knapsack. Then I bought a couple of meat pies to eat on the way, and set out, glad indeed to leave Chizan behind me for a while.

I reached camp shortly after dark, my shoulders badly cramped from the weight of the meat. Lonna had appeared when I was ten minutes or so away from the clearing. I got the impression that the bird had been sent, not to guide me, but to warn Thymas and Tarani of my approach. They looked stubborn and unhappy.

Terrific. They finally start talking to each other, and the first thing they do is argue. Now who does that remind me of?

"See what you can do to make our bags look like Tarani's

travel bag," I said to Thymas, as I unwrapped a chunk of meat and tossed it toward the cats. Keeshah reached it first and crouched over it, snarling. Ronar backed off, his ears flat to his head. I tossed another chunk to him, then unpacked the rest of it.

"Tarani, it may be best if you ask Lonna to stay with the sha'um. If somebody spots her, Molik will know for sure you're back."

"Tarani will be staying, also," said Thymas.

I sighed. "Tarani?"

She stood up. "Lonna has her instructions, Captain. I am ready to go."

"Tarani is to be my wife, Captain," Thymas said, stressing the title just a little. "This is my decision to make. I demand that you order her to obey me."

I almost laughed out loud at the image of me ordering Tarani to do anything. But it wasn't laughable.

He was serious.

She was determined.

I was so tired of it all.

"I can't command Tarani's actions," I said, "and neither can you, until you're actually married." *If then,* I added silently. "Besides, we need her. I just got a look at the outside of the building where Molik is. I saw a lot of people going in. Nobody had to turn in their weapons. If Molik feels that secure, we'll have to fight an army to get to him without Tarani's help."

"But—"

"If you don't want to see her with Molik, then stay here," I snapped. "And if you come with us, you'd better keep quiet and follow orders—especially those regarding Molik."

"Tarani is—"

"Do you understand the terms, Thymas?"

"Yes, *Captain.*"

I grabbed my saddlebags out of his hands. The ropes had been re-tied to serve as a shoulder harness, and I arranged them as I walked away.

In a few minutes, I looked back to see Tarani following me and, some five paces behind her, Thymas.

He might not want to see Molik and Tarani together, I thought. *But neither does he want them to be together while he's not there.*

I've seen some jealousy in my time, but Thymas takes the prize. I can't see what's bothering him, since it's more than clear that Tarani despises Molik, and Thymas has everything she gave to Molik, plus a promise of marriage . . .

Oho.

Everything?

She told Thymas she had borrowed her grubstake from Molik. She didn't tell him the truth until she was forced to. And whenever I've mentioned the "pleasure illusions," Tarani has gone off like a firebomb. Embarrassment over the business arrangement may have been only part of it. Compulsion is degrading, she said. What about this other talent? The idea of using her power like that again probably disgusts her.

So of course she recoiled when I made that crack about Thymas being addicted to her illusions. And when I implied that the only thing about her worth wanting was that pleasure she hated to give . . .

I sucked in my breath.

How I hurt her. My God, how I hurt her.

She was sixteen when she went to Molik, and she admitted that she was a virgin then. The onset of sexuality, coupled with unusual control over how that sexuality is used—that makes the ordinary pain and problems of growing up look like a trip to Disneyland.

She would have been eighteen when she went to Thagorn for the first time. There probably hadn't been any men since Molik; anybody who knew Molik still wanted her wouldn't have dared to cross him. She probably identified sex with misuse of power—until she met a young man who had never heard of Molik, and was in the mood to celebrate a big day in his life.

I turned my thoughts away from what it must have been like for her, having her physical needs awakened early, and then repressed for so long.

Now I understand why Tarani consented to marry Thymas. She's grateful to him, maybe she really does love him. But beyond that, Thagorn must seem like a sanctuary to her, a place where Molik and his memories can never reach.

Or couldn't reach, until the roguelord kidnapped Volitar. Her uncle must really mean a lot to her, if she agreed to contaminate the one place she felt free of her past.

Poor kid. Her whole world has crashed around her, these

last three weeks. Her uncle is in danger, the show she went through hell to get is probably ruined, and Thymas knows about a time she wants to forget . . . .

Hoohoohoohoohoo.

I recalled the way Thymas and Tarani had acted, after spending the night together at Relenor. Tarani's stiffness, I had attributed to my own clumsiness—I winced again as I thought of what my words had done to her. But Thymas, too, had been gloomy and snappish and generally peeved about something.

Could Thymas have resented it, that she had never told him about that particular talent and given him a chance to choose for himself whether he wanted it? Could that hot-headed, jealous s.o.b. have been stupid enough to ask Tarani for a sample?

Man, we both clobbered her that night.

Of course, all this might be a total crock, resulting from an overactive imagination. But I doubt it. Ricardo Carillo used to be a shrewd judge of character. Besides, it all fits together too well. I'd bet my shirt that I'm right.

Which means that I'll have to watch Tarani and Thymas both, every minute we're with Molik—or he'll be dead before he can tell us anything about Gharlas.

Molik may be something unmentionable, but it was Gharlas who pulled the strings. Now, I may not be as convinced as Dharak that Gharlas is a world danger, but I'm sure as hell fed up with the way he messes into other people's lives. Thanasset could have been killed. Dharak, too. Not to mention yours truly. And now Tarani and Thymas . . .

Scratch that. I don't approve of the method, but I think that those two kids will be better off, in the long run, for knowing these things about one another. So you're off the hook for that one, Gharlas.

But only for that one.

17

Tarani was sure that Molik would be holding Volitar in one of the rich homes in the third district. Several of these were reserved for use by the Living Death, until their time ran out one way or another. I thought it might be possible for Tarani to reach into Molik's mind from a distance, and find out where Volitar was. But I didn't ask her to do that.

First, I guessed she would be so anxious about Volitar that she wouldn't think to get the information I wanted about Gharlas.

Second, Molik was no dummy. If he thought Tarani might be able to do that, he'd have arranged things so that he didn't know where her uncle was—only who to contact to find him.

Third, Molik was a living memory of something Tarani wanted to forget. I didn't know whether she could project a compulsion strong enough to kill him, but I didn't want to take the chance of tempting her.

So it was necessary for us to get close to Molik physically. It had taken a lot of heated discussion, the night before, to agree on a plan which would get all of us close to him with as little risk as possible.

Molik, like Worfit, kept dusk-to-dawn office hours. The last hour before sunrise was the slowest time for the never-closed rogueworld, and Tarani, Thymas, and I had chosen that time to come to Molik's gaming house, the Lonely Caravan. I was standing beside a mondea table in the second-floor salon, not ten feet from Molik's office door. Two uglies were guarding it. I was losing what remained of my bankroll, and trying to look cheerful about it.

Thymas came running up the stairs. He paused at the wide doorway, looked over the people in the room, then came straight for me. He panted as he ran up, making a good show of excitement.

"Lakad!" he said. "Remember that show we saw in Dyskornis—the girl who lit her hands on fire while she danced? Well—" he paused and took a breath. Out of the corner of my eye, I could see the two guards listening, almost leaning toward us. "Well, I could swear I just saw her downstairs. I went over to talk to her, but she saw me coming and moved off into the crowd. You remember her, Lakad. What was her name?"

I pretended to search my memory. "Tarra? Torelli?"

"Tarani!" Thymas crowed, the loudness of his voice quite in keeping with the act he was putting on.

One of the guards knocked on the door.

"Yes, that's it," I agreed. "Great show. Wouldn't mind seeing it again. Is she performing in Chizan?"

"Let's go ask her," Thymas urged. "I'm sure she's still down there somewhere, wearing a desert rig with yellow tunic and trousers. With two of us, we ought to find her."

The door had opened a crack. One man was talking into it; the other was saying something now and then out of the corner of his mouth. He was watching us closely.

"Later, maybe," I said. "Right now, I'm more interested in getting my money back from this table."

"Losing, are you? How much have you dropped so far?"

The guard lost interest.

"A hundred zaks," I told Thymas, keeping up the act. "Here, why don't you try your luck for a while. Mind if I just watch for a round or two?" I asked the table attendant, who indicated it would be all right. Thymas took the dice, and I tried to watch the door and the table at the same time.

When a man came out of the office and headed for the stairs with one of the guards in tow, I began to breathe again. We had counted on Molik wanting to see for himself.

As the round ended, Thymas gave up his bet with a shrug.

"That's all I can afford to lose," I told the attendant. "See you next trip."

"Health and wisdom to you, sir," the man said.

Thymas and I strolled slowly toward the stairway, idly watching the tables, waiting . . .

Someone in the far corner said: "Why, these mondeana are made of gold!"

"Let me see those," said a voice which had to be an attendant's.

"Fleabite you," came the response. "I'm taking these with

me for a souvenir. Some repayment for all I've lost in this filthy place."

"Those are the property of—"

"Let him have 'em. He's right about this place. Hey, are they really gold?"

"Yeah, they just changed . . ."

"Maybe I'll take some, too . . ."

It was in character for us to stop to watch the incipient riot. When the door guard, along with the other heavies stationed around the wall of the salon, headed toward the trouble, Thymas and I made a dash—to the door, and through it.

Thymas flattened himself to the wall on the hinge side of the door. I knelt on the far side of the big desk. Behind me was the door into Molik's living suite.

We waited for five long, tense minutes before the outer door opened. Tarani lurched through it as though she had been pushed from behind. Molik sauntered in, holding Tarani's sword and baldric. He swung the door shut behind him, and turned to fasten the bar-and-pin lock.

He froze when he saw Thymas. By then, I was behind him. I got one hand over his mouth, and the other arm locked around his throat, before he could recover.

"I'm going to let you go, and you're going to talk to us quietly and tell us what we want to know. If you call for help, you'll be dead before it gets here. Understood?"

If he hadn't sensed that I could kill him with my bare hands—Ricardo's combat training, as well as Markasset's wrestling skill—he would have been convinced by the point of Thymas's sword, which was pricking his chest. My hand felt the movement as he tried to nod agreement.

I released him slowly, staying ready to grab again if he started to yell. The first thing he said was: "Somebody will die for letting this happen."

He turned around, and I stepped back, trying to get a good look at him. He was about my size, but slimmer. He had the look of a man who had once been tough, but lately had gone soft—at least, physically. His head fur was a pale brown. His eyes were set deeply, wide apart under jutting supraorbital ridges, and his mouth was a thin line, never quite still.

Tarani had called him "presentable," and I approved her choice of words. A smile, a spark of laughter in the eyes—

these might have made him handsome. But they weren't there.

Molik looked me over with the same close attention a bird pays a worm.

"Who are you?" he asked. "What do you want to know?"

"We're Tarani's friends," I answered sharply. "We want the location of Volitar, plus instructions from you to free him—with no tricks. And we want to know where Gharlas is."

Molik's gaze shifted to Tarani, who was standing behind me and to my right, leaning against the desk. When he looked at her, there was something in his eyes. It wasn't laughter.

"Volitar is a matter to be settled between the two of us, my love," he said, caressing her with his voice.

"Thymas," I cautioned the boy, as I saw his face darken.

"Why have you brought outsiders into our small quarrel?" Molik continued. He had a soft, smooth voice.

"Be glad they are here, Molik," Tarani said. "If I had come alone, I'd have killed you by now, and taken my chances of finding Volitar alive."

"Oh, why so violent, darling?" he asked. His lipcorners twitched upward in a mockery of a smile. "We have been . . . many beautiful things to one another. Why spoil that memory now?"

Thymas made a choked sound. Molik heard it, and stepped aside so that he could see Thymas as well as me.

"I see this one has enjoyed you," he sneered. "Well, I don't mind having shared you for a while, my dear, now that you've come back . . . to . . . to . . ."

Molik's voice shrank to a whisper, then faded altogether. His eyes strained open and his mouth began to work frantically. He wasn't trying to talk—he was trying to breathe. He fell to his knees.

"Tarani!" I cried, whirling. She stood in a fighting crouch, her fists and jaw clenched. She was focused entirely upon Molik, who was crawling toward her, lifting a hand in supplication. She backed away, hatred almost tangible in the air around her.

"Stop it, Tarani!" I ordered.

"Let her do it," cried Thymas. "Let her kill the fleason."

"He hasn't told us anything, yet!" I said.

Tarani had backed up against the connecting door to Molik's apartment, and Molik was clawing weakly at her legs. His face had a bluish cast; he couldn't last much longer.

I dragged him out of the way, stood in front of Tarani, and slapped her hard across the face. Her head snapped aside, and I heard a huge, raspy gulping sound from Molik as her concentration broke. Tarani's face came front again, and that look of hatred focused on me. I began to feel a constriction in my throat. I grabbed the girl's shoulders and shook her, and the pressure at my throat relaxed.

Tarani stared at me, and slowly sanity returned to her dark eyes. She put her hands over her face, sat down in one of the big armchairs, and curled up into a small, shaking ball.

Molik was still on the floor, but he was beginning to breathe almost normally again. I grabbed his fancy tunic near his throat and hauled him up into a chair. Then I knelt beside him so that our eyes were almost level.

"Answers," I said.

"I don't know," he whispered. He stopped, coughed, and started again, speaking in a high, strained tone. "I don't know where either of them are."

He saw what I thought of that answer, so he hurried on.

"It's the truth, I tell you. When I arranged things with Tarani, two of my men were on their way here with Volitar. They didn't show up on time, so I sent out a search group. They found the two men in the Zantro Pass—dead. There was no sign of the old man."

"Are you telling me that you don't *have* Volitar any more?"

He nodded, swallowing. "He's not in Chizan—I would know if he had made it here."

"What about Gharlas? Where was he headed?"

"I'd tell you if I knew. That creepy-eyed—I swear I don't know where he is. He left Chizan the day after he paid for Tarani's job."

"Did he know Tarani would be involved?"

"Of course not," he said, his voice regaining its smoothness. "My clients pay for results, not methods. In this case, I would accept a commission only for an attempt, since the odds were so high against success. What happened, anyway?"

"Your killers missed their target, whichever one it was," I said. "Were they after Dharak, or me?"

"I'll ask again: who are you?"

"Rikardon is my name."

Molik's eyes narrowed, and he pulled himself into a straighter sitting position. "If I had known it was you Gharlas wanted, I might have charged him less. The reward Worfit is offering for your tusks would have made up the difference nicely."

"Am I the one he wanted?"

"Are you the 'leader of the Sharith'?" Molik retorted. "Those are the words Gharlas used, and I passed them on to Tarani."

So I still don't know which one of us Gharlas wanted dead.

I went over to Tarani. When I touched her shoulder, she jumped slightly, then uncurled. Her face was calm but strained; her eyes were clear.

"I heard what he said about Volitar," she said.

"Can we believe him?" I asked her.

"I—I don't know, Rikardon."

"Well, can't you . . . uh, reach into his mind, and find out whether he's telling the truth?"

"That's preposterous," she said flatly. "What made you think I could do that?"

"Oh—just a guess."

Maybe Tarani's power wasn't as much like Gharlas's as we had thought. The idea was oddly comforting.

Tarani stood up and followed me over to Molik. He flinched back from her, but the gleam of lust was even stronger in his eyes.

Thymas saw it, too. He lifted his sword.

"Thymas, wait," I said. The sword stopped, ready for a cross-cut that would slice through Molik's neck.

The roguelord looked fully into Thymas's face, and saw his death there.

"Have you told us the truth, Molik?" I asked.

"Yes. I swear it's the truth."

"Then we don't need him any more," Thymas growled.

"We don't need to kill him, either," I said. "You know the plan—knock him out so that we can get away from Chizan."

"And you know I never liked that plan," Thymas retorted. "He can send word to Dyskornis to stop us."

"Molik," I said, and the frightened eyes turned to me. "Will you guarantee to leave us—and Volitar—alone, in exchange for your life? Will you stop harrassing Tarani?"

"Yes. Anything."

"You expect a roguelord to keep his word?" Thymas asked. He lifted the sword slightly.

"He will keep it," Tarani said softly. "I know him that well. And our association is over now. Forever. Isn't that right, Molik?"

The fear faded from Molik's eyes, and was replaced with something new as he looked at Tarani. Tenderness.

"I regret it," he said. "But I do accept it. Goodbye, Tarani."

"This fleason has come between us!" Thymas exploded at the girl. "You told me you hated him. You wanted him dead. Prove it now. Say to kill him, and I'll do it. Say Molik's death," he challenged her. "For us, Tarani."

"Rikardon . . ." Tarani said uncertainly.

Years of hating him, and hating what she did for him, I thought to myself.

"I'll step aside, Tarani. The decision is yours."

There was a full minute of silence. Molik seemed frozen in his chair, his gaze locked to the girl's face. Then Tarani said: "Let him live."

Molik slumped back.

Thymas let out an angry roar . . . and swung his sword.

Molik's headless trunk slid down into the blood-soaked chair.

I grabbed Thymas's sword wrist and squeezed until I felt the bones grinding together. The sword fell to the carpeted floor. Then I buried both my hands in the boy's tunic and shoved him hard against the wall.

"If you weren't Dharak's son, I'd tie you to that corpse and leave you for the Living Death to find. Now, we are going to continue with the plan as scheduled. After we're safely out of Chizan, we'll ride for Inid and see if we can trace Volitar from there. And if you so much as blink when I've told you not to, I'll cut off your ears and feed them to you. Got that?"

Thymas swallowed, and nodded.

I looked over my shoulder at Tarani, who had one hand pressed over her mouth. She looked ready to go into shock. "Do you know where Molik keeps his cash?" I asked. She nodded numbly. "We'll need some traveling money."

She went over to a corner of the room and began to fiddle with the stones in a section of the wall.

I turned back to Thymas. "Tell Ronar to come to the outskirts of the city, grab the first vlek or glith he sees, and eat it. We'll meet the sha'um an hour or so out, toward the Zantro Pass."

I let Thymas go as Tarani came up with a small, heavy, brass chest. We took a handful of coins each.

"Are you all right?" I asked Tarani. "Can you manage the illusions?"

"Yes. Let's please . . ."

I wanted out of that blood-stinking room, myself. I opened the door and called in both the guards. They saw me, and heard me, as Molik—until they lay unconscious on the floor. Then Thymas, Tarani, and I walked out of Molik's office.

Everyone in the salon saw Molik, the girl he had taken to his office a few minutes earlier, and one of the guards. We even got a salute from the Living Death beside the stairway. On the first floor, I ordered two men to watch Molik's door, saying that I had assigned the others elsewhere.

It wouldn't be too long before they got to wondering why Molik had gone out during his habitual sleeping hours. But it was the best we could do, and we had to hope for an hour's grace, at least.

Outside, it was growing light. As soon as we were out of range of the gaming house, Tarani let the illusions fade, and we scattered, each of us to find water and food for ourselves. In our room, half an hour later, we packed our supplies, then checked out of the inn.

Less than two hours after we'd left Molik's office, Tarani and I were astride Keeshah, riding beside Thymas toward the Zantro Pass. I was glad enough that the boy hadn't spoken a word to either one of us; I was still seething over Molik's death. I didn't want to think of the chaos Chizan would be in in a few hours.

Tarani's hands rested on my shoulders. Every now and then, they tightened for a few seconds, then let go.

She didn't want him dead, I thought. *But he's gone, now, for good. His memory can't hurt her any more, unless she lets it.*

18

"It is not our habit to speak of one traveler to another," said the Elder of Inid. He was standing in Inid's gate, stiff with the affront to his ethics.

"Respected Elder Nerral," I said, moving Tarani aside, "I am called Rikardon. I hope that, in respect for my friendship with Balgokh, you will allow this one exception. The man we seek is Tarani's uncle, and he has been in serious danger. Tarani is eager to know if he is well. Please tell us if he has been here."

At the sound of my name, the man had thawed. I reminded myself to thank Balgokh, sometime, for the good press.

"In that case, I would help you if I could, but the truth is, no one named Volitar has come through this refreshment house." He shrugged. "I'm sorry if that is unplesant news."

Tarani made a soft sound. Thymas started to put his arms around her, but she stepped away from him.

"It may not be bad news," I said suddenly. "Molik's men would have planned things so they wouldn't have to stop here—or maybe only one of them came in, and got water for all three of them. If Volitar got away and was running, he couldn't have been sure of not being followed. Probably he would have given a false name—to protect his life, Respected Elder."

"But how can I know, then, whether he has been here?" Nerral asked. "In the past three seven-days, I have seen a hundred men traveling alone. He could be any of those."

"Tarani, can you show him what Volitar looks like?"

"Yes, of course," she said. "With your permission, Respected Elder?" She pointed at Thymas. "If you look closely, you will see my uncle, Volitar . . ."

I tried to see the illusion, too. I'm sure it was not as solid and real-looking as it was for Nerral, but I was able to see it. Volitar was a small man with brown head fur that almost seemed reddish. He had lines of tension around his eyes, but his mouth seemed ready to smile. His hands were finely molded, with strong fingers. The entire image gave me an impression of neatness and precision.

"Why, yes, I have seen that man," Nerral said happily, as the illusion faded. "But he wasn't traveling alone, not any of the three times he has been through here."

"Who was with him the last time?" I asked.

Simultaneously, Tarani was saying: "Was he all right? How did he look?"

"Uh—" the Elder began, confused. "I should say he was all right," he said then. "At least, he wasn't injured in any way, though he seemed . . . distant, preoccupied. In fact, it was his companion who introduced him. The name he was given was Shandor, I believe. Yes, Shandor."

"And his companion?" I asked, exchanging a look of total bewilderment with Tarani.

"His companion I know well," Nerral said, with the neutral tone I had begun to recognize as passive disapproval among the Fa'aldu. "It was the caravan master, Gharlas."

Tarani started to say something, but I put a hand on her arm and squeezed. "You say the man you know as Shandor had been here twice before? Was Gharlas with him then?" Nerral nodded. "How long ago?"

"Oh, it has been moons," he said, "since I last saw him—though Gharlas, of course, comes through here regularly. I'm sorry I can't give you a more precise answer, but I would say it has been over a year ago, and then his visits were two or three moons apart, as I remember."

With my hand still tight on Tarani's arm, I thanked Nerral, and went through the formal request for shelter for the night. Again, I was asked to be the guest of the Fa'aldu, but this time I protested. We had two sha'um to feed, I said, as well as ourselves. I admitted we had nothing to trade, but would he not bend the rules far enough to accept coin payment, only this once?

Tarani broke away from me at that point. "We do have something to trade," she said, and slipped her travel bag off her shoulders. She rummaged in it for a moment, and brought out the beautiful gown she had worn on stage at Thagorn. Nerral caught his breath as the soft blue fabric spread out in the breeze, and sunlight glinted from the hundreds of tiny beads which decorated the collar and armbands.

"The dress will be useless to your women as it is," Tarani said. "But the fabric is fine quality and these beads—" she ran her thumb across the glittering surface of one of the armbands "—were made for me by Volitar, after he finally accepted the idea of the show." Abruptly, she extended the dress toward Nerral. "Take it, please," she urged. "I will not need it again."

The elder's hands enfolded the soft stuff carefully. " This is part of your life, Tarani. I thank you, and I hope that the giving of it brings you good fortune. Come in, and be welcome, all of you."

We gave him our swords, and a boy led Thymas and Tarani away, while I made arrangements for meat and water to be left outside the wall for the sha'um.

It's all right to start without me this time, Keeshah. I need to talk to Tarani.

Inid was twice the size of Relenor and twice as crowded, a fact I might have predicted by the number of caravans traipsing across the Zantro Pass. We had been able to buy meat for the sha'um out of one of the supply herds.

There was no question of private rooms at Inid. Tarani and Thymas and I would be sharing again. I hoped we'd all make it through the night alive.

As I approached our room, I could hear voices through the door. I hesitated with my hand on the latch. I told myself that it might be best not to interrupt. Nobody wants to admit to a desire to eavesdrop.

"—Gharlas?" I caught the end of Thymas's question.

"I don't know any Gharlas," Tarani said. "I told you, I heard his name for the first time in Molik's office, after he had taken Volitar."

"In his office?" the boy sneered. "Not in his bedroom? I saw the way he looked at you—that was not a passion two years dead.

"And you lied to me," Thymas went on. "First you had 'borrowed money from him.' Then he had 'taken advantage of you.' You 'hated him.' Hate? A Sharith kills his enemies, Tarani. You spared Molik when you had the chance to see him dead."

"Don't think that was an easy decision, Thymas," Tarani

retorted. "I did hate him—enough to kill him, myself, if Rikardon hadn't stopped me.

"In that moment when my word could destroy him, I had to see things clearly. Molik did nothing except agree to a business deal. He was weak, and that was unfortunate. But I have been blaming myself for his weakness, then blaming him for my guilt. I was making him more important than he was. His passion was fresh, yes—because he knew he still had a hold on me.

"When I faced Molik's death, I finally put him where he belonged—in the past. You were wrong to kill him, Thymas. I am free of him now. To let him live, wanting me, and knowing I was out of reach—that would have been a more severe punishment."

"A Sharith kills his enemies," Thymas repeated.

"I am not Sharith," Tarani said. "I won't be going back to Thagorn with you, Thymas."

I caught my breath and held it. *You fool, go away,* I told myself. *This is none of your business, remember?* I didn't move.

Thymas's voice was hard. "We'll talk about this after we have your uncle safe again. You're upset now, because I killed Molik in spite of what you said."

"We have been playing Molik's game without realizing it," Tarani said. "In Thagorn you wanted to see—and I let you see—only the part of Tarani which might fit into the Sharith life. I didn't deceive you deliberately. I told myself that it was what I wanted, too. I was trying to run from a past that I, myself, was keeping alive.

"I have great respect for the Riders and the women of the Sharith, Thymas, but I don't belong there.

"If you don't believe me, ask Ronar."

"Ronar? But he doesn't hate you, Tarani," Thymas said. "He only . . . doesn't want you . . . to ride." His voice slowed, stopped.

The silence stretched out until I was about ready to go in, just to end it. Then Tarani said gently: "You understand now, don't you? Ronar doesn't accept me because *you* can't accept me. Not the whole person. Not the real Tarani."

"I think I'm beginning to understand," Thymas said angrily. "Someone has come between us, all right, but it wasn't Molik. Keeshah lets 'the real Tarani' ride. So Rikardon—"

I'd heard enough; I opened the door. Both of them looked at me when I entered the room. I didn't bother pretending that I hadn't heard anything.

"Thymas, for once in your life, listen to what somebody says," I ordered. "Tarani rides with me because she can't ride with you. It's that simple.

"Now, Tarani, what, in the name of Zanek, is Volitar doing with Gharlas?"

"That's what I want to know, Captain," she said. "Who is Gharlas? Is Volitar still in danger?"

"Gharlas stole—"

"Tarani is not Sharith!" Thymas interrupted.

"You sit down and keep quiet, Thymas." The boy's face clouded, and he headed for the door. "Do as I say!" He stopped, considered, then walked back to sit sullenly on one of the blockbeds.

"Gharlas stole a gemstone called the Ra'ira from Raithskar," I resumed the story. "Have you heard of it?"

"Only that it is beautiful, and highly regarded by the rulers of the city."

"The Council of Supervisors," I supplied. "The Ra'ira is a symbol, historically, of the right to rule. Gharlas is convinced that he can re-create the Kingdom and rule it from Eddarta, with that stone as proof that he is the rightful King."

"He sounds mad," Tarani said. "And dangerous."

"Very dangerous. He has the same kind of power you do, Tarani, but without your conscience. What did Nerral's description of Volitar remind you of?"

She saw it immediately. "Compulsion?" She shivered. "It would be necessary, to involve him in something dishonest. Volitar has a high sense of honor. The compulsion—it must be terrible for him." She shuddered. "But what use can Volitar be to Gharlas?"

"Just what does Volitar do?" I asked. "I mean, what kind of glass objects does he make?"

"You saw the beads on my gown," she said. "He delights in fine work like that, and he has won a reputation for brilliant, precise colors in his glass. Sometimes, for his own amusement, he creates glass pieces that look exactly like gemstones . . ."

Her voice trailed off.

"What does the Ra'ira look like?"

"It's an unfaceted blue stone about this big," I said, shaping it with my hands. "The color seems to darken toward the center, and there is a suggestion of a crystalline pattern as you look through it."

"I have seen something like that," she said. "Wait, let me think this through—" She paced around the room for a few seconds, then began talking as though she were explaining something to herself.

"The nervousness I've thought to be a sign of age—could it have meant that he was frightened of someone? That's been going on for two years now, at least. And I knew he took a trip, but he didn't mention going to Raithskar with anyone."

"He went to Raithskar? A year ago?" I demanded.

She stopped pacing. "Yes, he left with no warning at all. I found a note from him on one of my visits to his workshop. There were other incidents this past year. I always send Lonna ahead with a message for Volitar, when I know I'll be in Dyskornis by nightfall. Three times, he sent a return message saying not to come see him, he was too busy. Two of those times, I respected his wishes, though it was very unusual, and it worried me. The third time, I decided to go anyway.

"As I arrived at the workshop, I saw someone leaving hurriedly. I got only a glimpse of him, but he was standing in the light of the doorway for a second or two. What does Gharlas look like?"

"Tall," I said, pulling out Markasset's memory. "His features are a lot like yours, actually, except his eyes are set closer. There is an intensity about him—"

"What color is his head fur?" Tarani asked.

"I've no idea," I answered. "I've never seen him when he wasn't wearing desert headcovering. Thymas? Do you know?"

"Dark," muttered Thymas. "His head fur is almost as dark as Tarani's."

Tarani was nodding. "Yes, that fits the man I saw. I remember noticing the head fur particularly, since it is so uncommon. To be sure . . . Thymas, look at Rikardon, and see the man who was running from Volitar's workshop."

I felt nothing as Tarani cast the illusion, but Thymas's eyes widened. "Yes, that is Gharlas."

"Volitar was beside himself when he saw me," Tarani continued her story. "He wouldn't calm down until I assured him that the man could not have seen me well enough to recognize me again. Then he refused to say anything else.

"He also covered up something hastily when I walked in and surprised him," she added. "It looked like the blue gem you've described."

I felt as though I had lost my step on a treadmill. "How long ago was this?" I asked.

"Three moons ago, more or less."

"Then it couldn't have been the Ra'ira itself," I mused. "And if it was a duplicate—that was long before the theft. Why didn't Gharlas take the thing with him, and use it to replace the real one? It might have given him some extra time."

"Perhaps it wasn't a good enough copy?" Tarani suggested. "I still don't understand how Volitar could have gotten involved in this. He couldn't have made a duplicate—if that's what it was I saw—under compulsion. A compelled person surrenders will and initiative, and all creative thought. Any artistic effort would fail."

"Let's get down to the big question," I said. "Where are Gharlas and Volitar right now?"

"I've sent Lonna to Dyskornis," Tarani answered. "It is an easy trip for her from here, since she doesn't have to cross the mountains. She will be back by morning."

"If Volitar is in Dyskornis, we'll go there tomorrow," I decided. "If he isn't, we'll assume that Gharlas—for whatever reason—rescued him from Molik's men in order to take him to Eddarta. We'll head in that direction.

"Either way, Tarani, we'll find Volitar and ask *him* what the Kingdom has been going on."

19

In the morning, Lonna was back. Tarani spent a few minutes in silent communication with the bird, then turned grimly to Thymas and me.

"Volitar is at his workshop in Dyskornis," she announced.

"Gharlas is there, too. Lonna's images . . . Gharlas wants some information from my uncle."

He's torturing the old man, I translated. *Can't he use his power to find out whatever he wants to know?*

We walked to the gateway with Nerral, accepted the return of our weapons, and said goodbye. Ronar and Keeshah were waiting for us, not too close together. Ronar was edgy and threatening, Keeshah quietly suspicious.

Tarani said our sha'um reveal how we feel about her. They certainly speak for the way Thymas and I feel about each other, too.

"Keeshah looks so thin," Tarani said. "Should I not ride in the net again?"

"Let me ask him, first." I did, and he assured me that he was feeling strong and fit.

Not much exercise in the city, he explained. **Running feels good. Even with two.**

"He says he's fine," I told Tarani.

I didn't mention that I didn't want to trust her to the cargo net. I wasn't sure I could count on close cooperation between the sha'um today. Thymas was quiet. I couldn't read his mood.

"Let's go," I said.

Molik may not have been much help regarding Gharlas or Volitar, but that tidbit about Worfit's reward for me was invaluable. I hadn't wanted Molik's death, but I had to admit that I was breathing easier because of it. If he had decided to break his word, one message to Dyskornis would have had every rogue in the city waiting for us; we'd have had to fight our way to Volitar's workshop.

That kind of reception was still a possibility. There was a lot of traffic on the trail between Dyskornis and Inid, and almost every caravan carried a cage or two of maufa. In the interest of not being recognized, we traveled across country, at some distance from the trail.

Coming down the steep slope from the Zantro Pass toward Inid, we had been treated with a view of a desert more vast than the Kapiral, but the point of the Korchi triangle had blocked our view northward. As we rode toward Dyskornis, the countryside changed dramatically.

Most of the morning was spent in that desert, which crawled right up to the barren foothills of the Korchi. There wasn't much to see—salty emptiness off to our right, and the mountains to our left. I fell to wondering about the map I had seen at Relenor.

That map showed the Great Wall 'way north of us, I thought. *But the Korchis are so high that their tops are masked in cloud. From out in the desert, wouldn't these steeply climbing foothills look just like a wall? The mountains south of the Kapiral desert—they must be the same range that form the south wall of the Chizan passage, and they could all be part of the Korchi—were like this, too. They got so tall, so suddenly, that they'd look like a wall from a distance.*

It's a wonder I didn't head in the wrong direction when I woke up in the desert. But I seem to remember only one wall . . . I'll bet that was Markasset's inner awareness taking care of me.

Gandalaran maps are just for reference about distance and direction. They show how to get from here to there. The cartographers must merely draw that line to represent the Great Wall, and trust to the All-Mind to help anybody relying on a map to be able to distinguish a mountain range from the wall.

The desert, which seemed even hotter than the Kapiral, ended at last by changing into a Gandalaran version of the American southwest. Short, woody bushes dotted the landscape at first, then were joined by small plants, some of them flowering, which resembled some of the friendlier cacti of Ricardo's world.

All we need now are a prairie dog and a coyote, I thought. *Here we are, the cowboy riding his trusty steed to rescue the little lady's poor old uncle from the villain. Beside him is his trusty sidekick . . .*

Oh, no, I thought, chuckling to myself. *The day I hear any variation of "kemo sabe" from Thymas, I'll eat my baldric.*

But—hold on there, maybe I've got the characters reversed. Maybe I ought to practice saying: "Oh, Cisco!"

With that pale head fur of his, we could even call Thymas the white hat and Gharlas the black hat . . .

Get hold of yourself, Rikardon.

We made a brief stop for lunch. After the desert, which had seemed oppressively hot and close after the high country we had just crossed, a drink of water was most welcome for all of us. We were soon on our way again, and in no more than two hours, the edge of the "sage" country, as I had come to call it, blended into the first forest I had seen, outside of the Valley of the Sha'um.

The trees weren't the giants that grew in Keeshah's native territory, but they were tall enough for us to ride beneath them. They seemed to be a greener variety of the sage scrub, and their open branches cast a lacy shade that we all appreciated—until the sun set. Then it was so dark that even the sha'um, with their better night vision, had to slow considerably. I called a halt.

"There ought to be something in this forest the sha'um can eat," I said, sliding down off Keeshah's back and reaching up to catch Tarani's shadowy form. "We'll walk awhile, and let them hunt. Can Lonna guide us?" I asked Tarani.

The answer came from the bird herself, who called to us from a tree branch a few yards ahead. We left Ronar and Keeshah to their own devices, and began to walk through the darkness, hands linked to prevent one of us getting separated.

I led the way, my free arm out in front of me to brush aside low branches, and Thymas brought up the rear. Tarani's hand held tightly to mine. There were sounds all around us—birds and insects and small animals—and sometimes it was hard to tell which call was Lonna's. If I started moving in the wrong direction, Lonna would come diving through the branches to scold me.

No one had suggested that we just camp until morning. Each of us had special reasons for wanting to get to Dyskornis as fast as possible. Tarani feared for her uncle's life. Thymas was anxious to get to Gharlas and, no doubt, to be free of his association with me. I—well, I wanted answers.

I felt as though my decision to leave Raithskar had bought me a ticket on a roller coaster ride through an endless maze. And the fellow who had pulled the starting lever was Gharlas.

We had walked for about five hours, and the strain was telling on all of us, when we stepped out into brightness. We were in a field of the bush-trees, all of them small enough to step over.

"It is a yearling lot," Tarani explained. "The glassmakers have set aside much of the forest around the city as fuel for their furnaces. They harvest only the full-grown lots, and replant them as they are used."

"How long does it take a lot to reach full growth?" I asked, starting out across the field.

"Less than ten years," she answered, following. We had released our holds on one another when we had come into the light. Thymas trudged along behind Tarani, lost in thought and paying little attention to us.

I thought about the European glassmakers. In his study of languages, Ricardo had become familiar with bits and pieces of history, and he had always been impressed with the skill, knowledge and physical endurance of the glassblowers.

I seem to recall that some glassworks had to move because they used up all the fuel in one area. I guess the Gandalaran glassmakers have had time to learn that lesson. Then, too, I doubt that they have the same methods, or the same need for high production. Most of the table service I've seen here is ceramic.

I tried to remember where I had seen glass used. *Barut is always served in those tiny glasses. It's always kept in glass decanters, too, come to think of it. Probably eats through anything else.*

I've drunk faen from glasses, and out of earthenware mugs, depending on the surroundings.

A lot of Raithskar's buildings—including Markasset's house—had glass windows. But they were all lattice style, as I recall, small glass shapes mounted in frames of thin wood strips. The frames were fastened together to make the large windows.

Let's see—oh, the lamps, with their faceted chimneys. Glass beads as jewelry and as decoration on clothes, including Tarani's costume. And, unless we're going down another blind alley, at least one imitation gemstone.

But all these things are fairly small—though the decanters and lamp chimneys probably take an enormous amount of skill. In Ricardo's world, a glassblower used a long iron tube. That would hardly be practical here, with iron so scarce.

To pass the time, I asked Tarani about her uncle's work. She said, at first, that she didn't know much about it, but memories surfaced as we talked. Putting her information together with my earthly memories of the glassmaking process gave me an understanding of Volitar's profession.

The glass furnace of Gandalara were double-walled cylinders made of ceramic bricks. They were built first, on level ground cut away from hillsides, then buildings were erected around them. The down-slope side of each workshop was supported by fill rock, mortared together with rock salt. A corridor was left open in this foundation that was just wider than the diameter of the furnace, so that the hillside could be hollowed out for the fire bowl.

This was a replaceable unit made of sun-hardened clay, fitted to the bottom of the furnace and supported by the repacked soil. If it cracked, it could be cooled and removed, and a new one put in. Tarani said that they usually lasted through at least one work season, and it had become the practice to replace them every year.

The glassmakers spent part of each year accumulating the supplies they needed, another part producing the raw glass pieces, and the rest of the time applying artistic finishing details.

"Don't they split up that work?" I asked, "with one person gathering material, another doing the basic article, and yet another doing the finishing?"

"Sometimes, but not often," Tarani said. "The finished piece depends upon the beginning materials. Every glassmaker is trained in all phases of the work before he is allowed to sell his creations."

"Creations" is the right word, too, I thought. *The glass recipe is a touchy thing; the glass can be too brittle, the color can go haywire. If one man starts with silica sand and winds up with a lamp chimney, that is creation indeed.*

Sand is no problem in Gandalara; there are at least two entire deserts of it. But what else goes into glass? Something to help the sand melt. They probably retrieve the ashes from the fire-bowl for part of that. And they'd need lime—limestone caves, chalk deposits. I seem to have the impression that the "Great Pleth" was on the other side of the Korchi Mountains, but I might be wrong. Probably it would have left a layer of lime in old seashells—

If Gandalara has or had shellfish. Quit thinking in earth terms.

"It must have taken Volitar a long time to learn his craft," I commented. We had crossed almost all of the yearling lot, and were approaching a taller section of the trees.

"Less time than most," she said, "but he worked hard to learn. Old Kardin used to joke about Volitar trying to squeeze every ounce of knowledge from him before he died."

"Kardin?"

"The glassmaker who trained Volitar. He died when I was ten years old. I remember him saying that Volitar had learned more, and faster, than any glassmaker's son. It's very rare, you know," she said proudly, "for anyone not connected with a glass family to be awarded an apprenticeship. And it's almost unknown for a full-grown man to be accepted for training."

"You mean, Volitar hasn't always been, or wanted to be, a glassmaker?"

"No. He came to Dyskornis when I was born, to care for me. He has never spoken of his life before then. It was always his way to say that I . . . was . . . his life." Suddenly she was choking up. I put my arm around her shoulders to guide her to the edge of the taller trees.

"Thymas," I called softly. He was ten paces or so behind us, veering off to the right. He looked over at the sound of my voice, then came toward us when I motioned to him.

"We've got to get some rest, or we'll be useless to Volitar. Make Tarani comfortable, and stay with her. I'm going to ride ahead a little way to see what's coming. I'll be back in a few minutes."

Thymas put his arm around Tarani as I removed mine, and she turned to his embrace. I walked away, calling Keeshah, who popped out of the half-grown forest ahead of us. I mounted and rode away, glancing back to see them still where I had left them.

She's had that bottled up inside her ever since Molik first told her Volitar was in danger, I thought. *And she is bone-tired. We all are. She needs the kind of comfort a stranger can't give. Thymas, please do it right. Just be there for her now.*

I had intended to do exactly what I had told Thymas—ride ahead far enough to give Tarani the time she needed to break down and pull herself together again. But I found, on moving out of that next lot of trees, that I had reached Dyskornis.

More or less.

The city, surrounded by the traditional wall, sat atop a hill about half a mile away. Coming toward me down the slope of that hill was another small town, a hundred buildings or so sprawled out with no particular design. It was brightly lit and humming with activity; the trees had screened us from the noise of it. Some distance from the buildings themselves, there was a huge corral that was three-quarters full of vleks.

This must be the transient section of Dyskornis, I decided. _Look how dark and somber the actual city is by comparison. Probably the city fathers are trying to exclude the rowdy element from the city. I wonder how many city fathers are out here, whooping it up?_

I wouldn't mind a glass of faen right now, myself. It would give Tarani and Thymas a little more time. I might learn something about Gharlas or Volitar or . . .

Quit kidding yourself. You want a glass of faen.

Wait here, Keeshah, I ordered, as I dismounted.

Don't go, the sha'um urged me, causing me to turn around and stare into his gray-flecked eyes.

Don't tell me you can see the future, I teased him. *_What will happen if I go?_*

*_Serious,_' he scolded me. *_Place smells bad._*

I laughed.

You didn't get very close to Chizan, or you wouldn't say that about Dyskornis. Don't worry, I added, scratching behind his left ear. *_I'll be careful. One glass of faen, and I'll be back before you know I'm gone._*

I walked toward the nearest row of buildings, and I felt my skin creep with much the same feeling Keeshah had tried to describe. There was a tension in the air here that had been absent in Chizan. For all his faults, Molik had kept an iron-handed order in his city. In these outskirts of Dyskornis, the high spirits were uncontrolled, the complaining loud, and the competition fierce.

I walked down the street, looking for a quiet bar tucked into a corner somewhere. It was soon evident that I wouldn't find one unconnected to a gaming room. Because I really hadn't planned to be long—and because that feeling of standing near a stack of dynamite wouldn't go away—I finally just turned into the next door I found open.

It was a place called Pemor's, and it was so crowded that I almost changed my mind again.

Get your faen and go back to Keeshah, I told myself.

I pushed my way up to the bar and yelled my order to one of the two busy bartenders. While I was waiting for it to arrive, I felt my left elbow jostled. I looked down to see a short, slender man reaching to pick up his glass of faen. He smiled, shouted something I couldn't hear, and took his glass out of the mob. My order arrived, and I reached for my money pouch to pay for it.

There were only the leather thongs which had fastened it to my moneybelt. The dangling ends had been sliced through cleanly.

I saw the little guy, just getting through the door into the street. I started after him, yelling for somebody to stop him, but the bartender's big hand claimed my right forearm and wouldn't let go.

"You owe me nine zaks, stranger. No credit."

"Somebody just stole my pouch!" I yelled at him, struggling to free my arm. "He'll get away, if you don't let me go."

"I've heard that before," the man said drily, and gave a twisting nod of his head.

Uh-oh, he's calling in the bouncers, I thought. *Probably the thief gives all of them a cut. I'd better count Molik's money well lost, and concentrate on getting the hell out of here.*

I jerked my arm out of the man's hold, and the force of my movement sent my elbow into my neighbor's ribs.

"Hey! Watch it!" he complained—but I was already trying to push my way to the door.

Through the crowd, I caught glimpses of two heavyweights converging on the doorway. It was going to be close.

I made it through the door with only seconds to spare. And there, across the street, stood the little man who had taken my pouch. He was counting.

The two bouncers had followed me out. I should have run for it, but my temper got the better of me, and I launched myself at the thief. He looked up at a call from one of the uglies, dropped the coins back in the pouch, and whipped out a thin-bladed dagger. I swerved my charge far enough to get room to draw my sword.

"You drop that pouch, and you can keep your life," I said. He looked at the sword, then my face. He dropped the pouch and ran off down the street.

I whirled to face the two bouncers. By this time, one had his sword out, and the other was holding a big, sharp knife. Behind them, the gaming room was emptying into the street. I heard bets being made. The odds weren't in my favor.

Coming, Keeshah told me.

Not down the main street, I ordered, as I blocked the sword and dodged the knife. **Don't let them see you. But make some noise.**

Noise, I had asked for? Keeshah started with a roar of anger, and ended with a climbing wail of frustration. He must have been just outside the light at the end of the street where I was standing, because that hair-lifting sound bounced between the buildings, froze every person in place, turned every head toward its invisible source. By the time they shook off the eeriness of it and turned back to me, I had snatched up my pouch and was long gone.

I slipped through the darker streets toward the edge of town. Keeshah met me, and we wasted no time in putting distance between us and Dyskornis.

The next time you give me advice, Keeshah, I promise I'll take it.

20

Thymas stepped out of the shadows as I was getting down from Keeshah's back. He was holding a drawn sword. The trees couldn't have blocked off Keeshah's cry.

"What happened?" he asked.

"I found Dyskornis," I answered shortly. "How is Tarani?"

"She's asleep. She's very worried about her uncle."

"So am I. People who help Gharlas don't live very long. The two men who helped him steal the Ra'ira are both dead."

"Two men?" Thymas said. "Who beside Hural?"

Wups. Thymas doesn't know that Markasset got himself beaned out in the desert by the other henchie, who was then killed by Keeshah. The end result of all that was my arrival—something else Thymas doesn't know about.

This is beginning to be a hassle, trying to remember what I've told to whom.

"Thanasset said there were two men," I said. "I suppose the other was killed in the caravan raid—which was what Gharlas planned for Hural, too."

I thought that sounded pretty glib, but I had hesitated a heartbeat too long.

"You're lying about something," Thymas accused. "Just the way you lied to my father, the first time you came to Thagorn. How did you force Dharak to name you Captain?"

"It was Dharak's idea in the first place, if you want to know," I said. "Just like it was his idea to send you moping along with me. You and Ronar have been more trouble than help."

"I have kept my promise. Except for Molik. A Sharith—"

"Kills his enemies, I know," I finished for him. "You broke your promise before we left Thagorn. Why didn't you tell me you had given Tarani a sword, that very afternoon?"

"You asked Bareff about weapons," he said. "If you had asked me, I would have told you."

This was getting us nowhere.

"After we find Volitar . . ." I didn't have to finish.

"I look forward to it," Thymas said, keeping his tense voice low, out of consideration of Tarani's sleep.

"Right now, we need some rest, too."

He nodded, and we found ourselves grassy spots to sleep.

We were all awake again by dawn, and we ate a light breakfast. We hurried into Dyskornis, leaving the sha'um to prowl restlessly through the forest, and Lonna to fend for herself.

We had to walk right down the street I had visited the night before in order to get to the main gate of the city. Tarani and Thymas wore their headscarves tied desert fashion, but I wrapped my scarf around my face like a Chizan native. Tarani was in the lead, walking at a brisk pace, her head thrust forward.

We moved through the main area of the city fairly fast, crossing one of the many bridges across the Nisa River. Then we turned toward a series of small hills with odd-looking buildings, set well apart from one another. The road climbed steadily up the steep slopes. Its surface was imbedded with stones, and the grassy areas on either side were crisscrossed with wheel ruts.

Tarani was nearly running up one of the ramps which connected the level sections of the road. I caught up with her and held her back. I could almost smell her fear.

"Which place is Volitar's?" I asked.

"That one," she said, pointing to our left. "The second in the next row of workshops."

"All right, now, hang on to your good sense," I said. "Where are the doors?"

The building was only half workshop, Tarani explained. An open porch ran around five sides of the hexagonal building, and on that porch were bins which held raw materials. Each side of the workshop had a door onto that porch, because the shops were designed to allow five glassmakers to share the furnace in each one.

The house was a two-story structure. Its upper floor had an outside entrance from the hillside, as well as a door which connected to the workshop through its sixth side. The lower floor was built against the mortared stone which surrounded the fire-bowl corridor and served as foundation for the hexagonal workshop and porch. A door led into the house from the lower slope of the hillside.

"Kardin had the workshop all to himself, so he lived in the house year-round, instead of only when the furnace was burning," Tarani said. "We lived with him until he died, then Volitar took it over."

"I'll go in the top floor of the house. Thymas, try the lower level. Tarani, you get into the workshop. Be careful."

We went uphill to the crossroad and followed the stone-paved road that ran in front of all the workshops on that level. We ran as quickly as we could, keeping to the shelter of the nearer workshop for as long as possible. In a few minutes, we were all in position.

My door was locked from the inside. It had a lattice-glass window; I broke one of the panes, reached through to move the bar, and went into the house with my sword ready.

I was in a big room that seemed to serve as bedroom, parlor, and office. Except for the sparse furniture, it was empty. A noise made me turn toward the corner on my right, and Thymas jumped out of the stairwell. We headed for the door on my left, which had to open into the workshop.

I opened it a crack, first, and looked in. The door straight across the room opened on a porch rail and a view of the workshop we had passed. Tarani was on her knees near the furnace, frantically removing a gag from the mouth of an old man.

I'll be damned. He's alive! Wonder how long he's been tied up like that. . . .

"Tarani!" the man gasped in a cracking voice, the instant his mouth was free. "Get out of here! Leave Dyskornis. Gharlas must not find you here!"

I stepped through the door. "Gharlas is still in Dyskornis?"

Volitar twisted around at the sound of my voice. He looked like the image Tarani had cast of him, except that he was even thinner, and his intelligent, thoughtful face had changed shape. There wasn't a square inch of it that wasn't bruised and swollen. It looked as though his nose might be broken.

"You," the sick old man gasped, squirming so that Tarani couldn't get hold of the ropes which tied him. "Leave me, and take Tarani out of here. I beg it of you. If you have any spark of kindness . . ."

"We'll go, Uncle," Tarani said. "But not without you. Now hold still." She drew her sword, and sliced through the rope that bound his wrists behind his back. Volitar's arms flopped apart, uncontrolled. His hands were bloated and bluish. Tarani made a whining sound, and put the sword through the bonds around her uncle's ankles.

Volitar was still looking at me and Thymas, who had followed me into the room. "I can't travel," he said. "Please, I ask it for her sake—take her out of here. Force her to go, if you must, but do it, I beg you. Gharlas may return any minute!"

Tarani had Volitar's legs free, but it was evident that they were no more useful than his arms. "Help me," she said, trying to lift him by herself. I hesitated.

"He said Gharlas might be here soon—" I began.

Thymas dashed past me, and he and Tarani got a still-protesting Volitar on his feet, slung between them. "You're so worried about promises!" Thymas snarled. "You gave your word to see Volitar safe."

"I only meant—"

A tall, thin shape filled the open doorway behind Tarani, Thymas and Volitar.

"—that we ought to watch for him," I finished, reaching for Rika. Thymas released Volitar and drew his sword, spinning around into a fighting crouch. Volitar's dead weight crashed to the floor, pulling Tarani with it.

Thymas crowed with triumph, and aimed a deadly thrust at

Gharlas, who was still a mere silhouette against the outdoor brightness.

Gharlas didn't move.

After one forward step, neither did Thymas.

He stood frozen in position, except for the bewildered widening of his eyes. I tried to charge across the room, but I couldn't even take a step. I was saying "go" to my muscles, but someone else, more imperatively, was saying "stop."

Is this compulsion? I wondered. *What happened to my theory about Gharlas's power not working on me? Wait a minute—I can still think; I'm not the zombie Tarani described. There must be some way . . .*

While I was working to break the compulsion—and to stay calm—I watched Gharlas.

He walked into the room. He was very tall; he topped me by a good six or seven inches. Markasset remembered him wearing a desert headscarf, but his head was bare now, showing the dark head fur. It was longer than usual, and it lay back smoothly, making a thick, dark frame for his narrow face.

The intensity of his close-set gaze hadn't changed, except for one thing. The gleam of fanaticism was no longer hidden. It shone out of his eyes, his face, his bearing, that this man was not quite sane.

He stood over Volitar and Tarani, looking down at them.

"You must be the niece Volitar has been hiding all these years," he said in a soft, silky-smooth voice. Tarani was picking herself up from the floor. The old man had been knocked out in the fall; he made a moaning sound, and Tarani turned to him, still on her knees.

"How do you do, my dear?" Gharlas continued. "Your name, please?"

She didn't answer him, and his lips twitched into a smile.

"At a later time, you will speak when I ask you a question, my dear. Indeed, you will. For now, however, do tend to your uncle. I need him alive for a while yet. As for your friends," he said, strolling over to the statue that was Thymas, "I can't say much for your taste. This one is opinionated and tactless. The other one—ah, the other one . . ."

He walked over to stand in front of me, and stared down into my face. My eyes could turn to watch him, but my voice was mute. Inside, I was screaming and straining against the holding spell:

"You," he said softly, almost affectionately, "have been an endless trouble to me. If you hadn't first lied to me about your name, then come snooping after me when I left the caravan, Yolim would have lived a little longer. Not much, to be sure, but long enough to do another service I had planned for him.

"If you hadn't found Hural in Thagorn, Zaddorn would still be circling around Thanasset instead of looking for me. I don't know how you found your way here, my double-minded friend, but killing you *permanently* will be a high pleasure."

Double-minded? That's the key! Think about Ricardo. Remember things that have no connection to Gandalara. The Marines. Oceans. Sailing, swimming, diving off a board into cold, clear water . . .

I moved my hand! Did Gharlas notice? No, he's turning back to Tarani and Volitar. All right, now, keep it up. Playing tennis, riding horses, snow skiing. Driving a car. Electricity . . .

"I see Volitar is awake," Gharlas said. "Now, my dear, you will answer a question for me."

Volitar said: "Don't tell him—aachkk-k-k." His eyes went wide, and his hand came up to his throat in a wide, floppy arc.

"We don't want to be interrupted, do we?" purred Gharlas. "I can keep him from talking. I can keep him from breathing. Do you understand?"

"I understand," Tarani said, and I thought of Molik. "What do you want?"

"A simple thing. Such a simple thing, to cause so much pain," he said, spreading his hands. "Somewhere in this house and workshop, your uncle has a special hiding place. He has been . . . *insufferably* stubborn about telling me where it is." Gharlas's voice wavered a little with frustration.

He wouldn't even let you draw it from his mind! I translated gleefully. *Good for you, Volitar. Good for you!*

I had been straining against the paralysis, wearing at it the way I'd work against a physical bond. Tense and release. Tense and release. Knowing that Volitar had resisted Gharlas's power for two weeks or more was such encouragement that my entire right arm moved, lowering the sword about four inches.

Gharlas still had his back to me, but Tarani had seen the jerky movement.

"I think that is a poor show of gratitude to the man who rescued him from two very unpleasant men. He has also refused to tell me why they were holding him prisoner, though that is unimportant. I was merely curious. But I am most serious about finding your uncle's hiding place. Where is it?"

"I will tell you," Tarani answered. She made no attempt to hide the contempt in her voice. "If you will first tell me what this is all about. What have you forced Volitar to do?"

While she was talking, I felt . . . something.

It's Tarani! I realized. *She's stalling Gharlas, and trying to help me break free.*

Now I was applying constant pressure against the constraint. I worked alone as Ricardo, and when I tired, Markasset and Tarani took over. It was weakening, we were gaining. It was slow work, but that was an advantage in itself. Gharlas didn't seem to take any notice of the step-by-step erosion of his control.

"Do not think you can set terms for me," Gharlas told Tarani, but he was more amused than angry. "I will answer your questions, purely for the vexation to Volitar, who has tried so desperately to shelter you from the truth."

The old man got agitated, tried to talk, tried to move. Tarani pulled him back to the floor so that his head rested on her knees. Gharlas had his back to me. But I knew he was smiling.

I wanted to kill him.

"Your uncle, my dear, *belongs* to no less a personage than the High Lord of Eddarta himself, Pylomel." He sneered the name. "Volitar was a gemcutter, highly skilled. I wouldn't demean his work, not I, who have so profited by it! After Volitar disappeared from Eddarta—he had some foolish notion that he, and not his landpatron, should be paid for the work he did—nothing was heard of him until I saw him, quite by accident, selling his glass beads in the Dyskornis marketplace.

"Ah, how well I remember Pylomel's fury at the loss of Volitar," Gharlas chuckled, a nasty sound. "He raged more over that, even, than over missing his latest, most beautiful, and least loving bride-to-be, who disappeared around the same time. It was appropriate, as it turned out; the woman came back, but the gemcutter was lost for good. The High Lord's frustration was a keen delight to watch."

Gharlas began to pace slowly around the room, but I noticed that he was careful to keep Tarani and her uncle in his line of sight. He walked over to one of the tile-topped worktables located around the walls, between the porch doors. He picked up a small, truncated pyramid made of clay—it looked like a mold for a barut glass, which could be broken out of the cooled glass and discarded. He turned it around and around with his fingers as he talked.

"Naturally, Pylomel would be delighted to find Volitar after all this time. But I owe him nothing!" Gharlas suddenly shouted. He threw the mold to the floor; it shattered with a snapping sound. He paused to recover his bland, patronizing manner, and then continued. "I spoke too hastily, my dear. I do owe Pylomel something—repayment for his arrogance. Thanks to your uncle, that debt is nearly repaid.

"Through the years of Volitar's service, Pylomel collected a magnificent array of jewelry. I called upon Volitar, who had learned this new skill of coloring and forming glass, to duplicate some of the stones he had cut for Pylomel. Where his memory failed him, I put into his mind a picture of the finished pieces, as I had last seen them. Volitar did this for me, because he did not care to return to Eddarta to face Pylomel's anger. I learned much later—only a few moons ago, in fact, after I caught the barest glimpse of you, my dear—that Volitar had another reason for his cooperation. He didn't want his lovely niece to learn that he was merely pretending to be a free artisan."

He began his pacing again. Tarani watched him, but I felt her power in my mind, working against Gharlas.

"I took Volitar's glass duplicates to another, um, friend of mine, who—again, with the help of my images—reproduced the correct setting. In cheaper materials, of course." He chuckled drily. "The finished pieces were perfect copies to the casual glance, and the jewelry is rarely displayed. Pylomel hoards his wealth jealously.

"Long ago, I found the vault he believes to be impregnable. I have visited that vault on almost every trip to Eddarta, since I relocated Volitar, and each time, I have left it a wealthier man. In Raithskar, or Omergol, or even here in Dyskornis, such fine jewelry commands a rich price."

He walked by Thymas, who was still lunging stiffly. The sight amused Gharlas, and he laughed out loud. "And how is your traitorous father, Thymas?" he asked. "In poor health, I hope? I must remember to let you live long enough to tell me if Molik did his job properly."

While his attention was distracted, Tarani looked directly at me. Slowly, I nodded my head, and she flashed a quick smile of satisfaction. She looked down at Volitar again, as Gharlas came toward her. I was in his line of vision, so I kept perfectly still. Internally, I was doing the hardest work I could remember ever doing. I was nearly free.

"Your uncle has given me much, my dear. A great deal of profit from the sale of the replaced jewelry. A great deal of private satisfaction. And, indirectly, a great deal of knowledge."

Gharlas took a bundle of cloth out of a pouch tied to his belt. He began unfolding layers of cloth.

"On one of my visits to Pylomel's vault, I found a book that is intended for reading by the High Lords only. It spoke of the Kings of Gandalara, their history, their power. It revealed the secret of that power." His voice shook with emotion. "And now I possess that secret."

He held his hand low, to show Tarani what he had unwrapped. Resting on the palm of his hand was the Ra'ira.

21

"Is it not beautiful?" Gharlas asked, stroking the blue gem. "But small. So small, to have so much importance.

"Veytoth was the first King to write about this. It is called the Ra'ira. It was sent to the Kings from Raithskar, where it had been found in their rakor mines. Veytoth was practical. When he became King, he inquired about breaking the pretty bauble into jewelry-sized pieces. But his gemcutters warned that, if it could be cut at all, the lines within it indicated that it might shatter.

In time Veytoth grew fond of it, and kept it near him. He quickly learned that in its presence, his mindpower—the thoughts of people who were days away from him, were made clear. People around him obeyed his wishes, as well as his spoken orders.

"It was then that the Kings began to breed for the mindpower, a custom continued to this day in Eddarta." His hand closed around the blue stone, and began to tremble. "The High Lord of Eddarta must be a child of Harthim's descent, the product of a legal union between the last High Lord and a woman of the family of a Lord. If none of those children have the mindpower, the children of the High Lord's siblings may be considered—*provided they are the products of a legal union.*"

He was shouting again, staring at the ceramic curved-brick furnace, but not seeing it.

"I am cousin to Pylomel," he said, "his father's sister's son. And I have the mindpower. *I have it!* When we were tested, as children, even then my skill was greater than Pylomel's, and it has grown even more these past few years. Now Pylomel is puny by comparison.

"But am I Eddarta's High Lord? No. Those self-righteous fleasons declared me ineligible, beause my mother loved a servant. She had only one opportunity to lie with him, and she took it, knowing she would conceive from the union. I have despised her for that, yes, despised my own creation. But no longer.

"I *am* a bastard!" he shouted, shaking his fist in the air. "But I am also the new, the next, *King of Gandalara!*"

He seemed to recall where he was, then, and spent a moment calming down. Tarani chanced a quick glance at me, and I shook my head slightly. I was free now, but a little dazed by what I had been hearing.

Why didn't Thanasset tell me? Because I told him I wasn't going to get involved with this crackpot. I convinced him that I just wanted a vacation to think about the Council's offer . . .

The Council! Of course, the true nature of the Ra'ira has to be top secret, available to confirmed Supervisors only. What was it Thanasset said? "You may need information Markasset didn't have." He meant about the Ra'ira. He wanted me to join the Council so he could tell me the truth.

"But I am wandering from my purpose," Gharlas said, his voice oily again.

He changes so quickly. There's not a doubt in the world that he's as nutty as an almond grove. Let's get the timing just right . . .

"The Lords have grown soft and self-satisfied, resting in comfort in Eddarta. There hasn't been a High Lord for generations who has suggested seriously a plan to re-establish the Kingdom. When I found that book, I knew that it was my destiny to possess the Ra'ira and rule Gandalara.

"So I came to your uncle and persuaded him to make a duplicate. We went together to Raithskar, to view the stone on Commemoration Day, which honors that despicable traitor, Serkajon.

"I came to pick up the duplicate a few moons ago—that was the evening we nearly met, my dear—and found that Volitar had constructed *two* copies. They were slightly different from one another, but even at close viewing, either would have passed for the real gem. To those who do not know its special quality, that is. And those fools in Raithskar are sworn never to use it—how could they discover that the real Ra'ira had been replaced?

"I chose one of the copies, and took it to Raithskar. By fortuitous accident, I lost that duplicate before I could complete my original plan. It was only then that I realized the folly I had been about to commit.

"It must be clear to everyone in Gandalara that I, and only I, have the Ra'ira. As before, no one shall know its true power, but it has a strength and a charm of its own. It carries its own feeling of history, of grandeur. Some people will follow me, simply because I have it.

"So there must be no one else who *might* have the stone," he said. He leaned toward Tarani. "I needn't worry about the copy I lost in Raithskar. It was disguised as a clod of dirt; the street sweepers probably gathered it up and dumped it outside the city that very day, and it is well buried by now.

"But I want the other duplicate," he said, getting to the point at last. "And you will tell me where it is. Now."

Gently, Tarani laid her uncle's head on the floor. He flopped his arms and kicked his legs weakly in protest. To comfort him, she kissed his bruised forehead. She stood up and moved around Volitar. Gharlas fell back to give her room. He was just outside my sword range.

"Yes," said Tarani. "Now!"

I lunged forward, aiming for Gharlas's back. But he had caught something—a change in Tarani's expression, perhaps, or even her thought. An instant before I lunged, and Tarani reached for her sword, Gharlas threw himself sideways and down to the floor. He rolled over Volitar and came face up with the old man in front of him as a shield. He was pressing the blade of a knife against Volitar's throat.

"You are a most uncooperative man," he said scornfully. "How interesting that you can break my command. Must be that doubleness of yours."

"Let Volitar go," Tarani said. "I'll give you your filthy copy. Let him go!"

She was standing to one side, her sword shaking in her hand. I was looking right down at Volitar's face. He closed his eyes for a moment. Then he opened them, looked at me, and said four words. In the confusion, Gharlas hadn't maintained his silence control on Volitar.

"Take care of Tarani," the old man said. Then, his arms and legs still nearly useless, he bucked his body violently upward, driving the knife blade deep into the bruised flesh of his throat.

Tarani screamed.

I lifted my sword for an overhand slash. Gharlas was trying to scramble out from under Volitar's body, and I had a flash vision of the way Molik's head had bounced when it fell off the lifeless trunk of the roguelord. The face changed to Gharlas's narrow features.

Off with his head, I thought, amazed at the savagery of my hate. *Off with the sonofabitch's head*.

I put all my strength into that deathstroke—but a sword came out of nowhere to block it, and Gharlas slipped out of reach.

Furious and frustrated, I jumped back to get room to fight this new threat. My stomach started to churn when I saw what it was. Thymas was coming after me, his face contorted with self-disgust. Gharlas was controlling him; it probably amused him to see Thymas's reaction to what he was being forced to do. The boy's face was a pathetic plea for help—but how could I help him?

It was all I could do to stay alive.

Dharak hadn't exaggerated his son's fighting skills. He must have been a little slower, a little clumsier, than usual, moving under the control of another man's mind. But he was still a strong and cunning fighter.

I backed away from him, blocking when I had to, trying desperately to think of a way to avoid hurting him and still save my own skin.

I couldn't find one. I had to fight back.

I aimed a two-handed swing to his midsection. He blocked it, slid his blade across mine, and brought his sword down hard, slashing at my left shoulder. I ran out from under it; he changed it to a diagonal cut at my legs. I dodged his blade, and managed to score a cut across his left forearm. I backed away, facing him, waiting.

I tripped over Volitar, and landed flat on my back. The wind was knocked out of me, and my vision blurred for a moment. When it cleared, Thymas had kicked away Rika and was standing over me, arms and sword raised in almost the same position I had held over Gharlas.

Thymas didn't move. His face was a mask of sickness and fury.

I lifted my head and looked around. Across the room, Tarani was standing stiffly, awkwardly. Gharlas was beside her. He grinned, and came toward me, holding Tarani's sword. He stopped beside the furnace and lifted a square ceramic tile out of the floor. He dropped Tarani's sword into a hole; we could hear it sliding into the firebowl underneath the furnace.

Keeshah! I called.

Coming, Keeshah answered, impatient and anxious. **City big. Can't smell.**

I'll show you, I said, and we merged for an instant, into that closeness that required no images for complete communication. **Do you know it now?**

Yes, Coming.

Bring Ronar.

His reply was the equivalent of a snort of derision, as if to say that Ronar could find his own way; Keeshah didn't have time to fool with him right now.

I broke the contact, which had taken only a few seconds, to find Gharlas standing over me, still grinning.

"Well, my dear," he said, over his shoulder, "now that you are safely tied down, I wonder if this meddling fool means as much to you as your uncle. I offer the same trade—his life for the duplicate Ra'ira. I think I'll let you speak, so that you may agree."

"You'll kill us all, anyway, you bastard," she said.

Gharlas's face turned dark, and a pulse beat visibly at his temple. He strode over to her, struck her across the face. She glared at him, her limbs frozen awkwardly.

"Bastard," she said softly.

He hit her again, so hard that I winced. Her headscarf was knocked loose; it twisted so that its trailing edge fell across her right shoulder.

What the hell is she doing? Did Volitar's suicide send her over the edge? Or . . . could she be stalling Gharlas again?

I looked at Thymas. There was a fierce light, joy or fury, shining in his eyes.

She's leaving herself trapped, and helping Thymas break Gharlas's control. The girl has courage. It will be tougher with Thymas, but she's had practice now, and she's madder.

"There is more than one way to die," Gharlas hissed at Tarani. "Volitar's death will look easy, compared to this one, I promise you. Now, *where is that duplicate?*"

She hesitated just long enough to irritate him into lifting his hand again, then she spoke out in a hurry. "Under the workbench behind Thymas. Where the table joins the wall, there is a loose tile with a compartment behind it."

"Show me," he said, and grabbed her arm. She walked with him, jerkily, toward the table. As she passed me, she looked down. Again, I nodded. There was no smile in reply this time, only a grim determination.

She knelt on the floor and crawled under the worktable. Gharlas bent down to see what she was doing. Thymas gave a violent start, then grinned savagely and turned toward Gharlas, lifting his sword for a killing blow.

Either Gharlas had heard something, or he had sensed the abrupt break of his control. Before Thymas was halfway turned, Gharlas surged up from his bent-over position. His knife was in his hand, and he drove it to the hilt into the boy's side. He released the knife to catch Thymas's sword hand as the boy struggled to bring the sword to its target. Then Thymas's face went blank suddenly, and he sagged to his knees. He fell over and lay still on the floor.

Gharlas held the sword and stood over me, his face growing dark with rage.

"Is this more of your doing?" he accused me. "For yourself, I could see it. But for this one—how—?"

"I am the one who did that, Gharlas," Tarani said. As she stood up, the edge of the worktable caught her loosened headscarf and pulled it clear off. Ever since we had come into the workshop, she had been kneeling, crouching, fighting. Now she raised herself to her full height, and gathered around her the regal bearing she had worn at our first meeting. The dark head fur was startling, revealed so suddenly, and Gharlas stepped back a pace in surprise.

"My name is Tarani," she said. Strength seemed to reverberate in the low voice. "I see now why Volitar so hated the misuse of power. You will pay for what you did to him, Gharlas!"

Seeing them face to face this way pointed up the similarities between them: their height and general slimness, the unusual head fur, the glow behind their eyes. Gharlas seemed to see it, too, for he fell back further, and his face went pale.

"You look like—your name—*Tarani?* Where have I heard it—the illusionist!" he gasped. "The dancer who can cast images!"

"Do you think only Eddartans can carry power?" she challenged. She stepped forward, following him, but aiming her steps toward Rika, which had skidded toward the furnace, and lay across another of the fuel doors in the floor.

"But you—" He stopped suddenly. He cringed—physically cringed—away from Tarani. "Great Zanek, *you're her daughter*. I thought Volitar was trying to hide his past from his niece. But he was hiding *you* from *me*. He knew I'd see the resemblance at once.

"The old fool succeeded, too, may his tusks rot! Not until this very moment did I connect Tarani the illusionist with his phantom 'niece.' "

A derisive laugh exploded from him, and was quickly choked off. "And I thought *I* had played a fine trick on Pylomel. I give Volitar credit. *I* never thought to hide the child of the High Lord's promised wife!"

He had been backing toward the workshop door that opened

directly out on the road. Thymas's sword was in his right hand; his left hand clutched the pouch that held the Ra'ira. Tarani had moved within reaching range of Rika. Gharlas was facing the girl, now, with a shaky confidence. He spared a glance for me, but looked quickly back at Tarani.

"You will both have to die," he said matter-of-factly. "But not today. We will settle this another time."

He dashed out the door.

I threw myself across the floor and caught up Rika, even as Tarani was reaching for it. She struggled with me until I said, "Keeshah." She understood, and let go.

I saw her kneel beside Thymas, as I went out the door.

Keeshah, how close are you?

Almost there.

As I came outside, I saw Gharlas running around the hexagonal stone foundation of the workshop, heading down the slope. I ran after him, with too little caution. I skidded and fell in the slick grass. I grabbed the stone wall and hauled myself to my feet, slipping and swearing.

Out of the corner of my eye, I saw a flash of color at the left hand edge of the wall.

Gharlas—waiting for me! I thought. I tried frantically to get my balance, but the slope was steep and uneven, and my feet kept striking it wrong. A figure ran out, away from the wall, and behind me.

There was a sharp, piercing pain in my back, just above my right shoulder blade. A knife. It pulled out, struck again.

I let myself fall and slide down the steep slope. I skidded to a halt, a few feet past the lower edge of the workshop. I pulled myself up on one knee and brought Rika around to face Gharlas.

It wasn't Gharlas.

It was the little man who had tried to steal my money pouch the night before.

Rikardon?

Don't let Gharlas get away, Keeshah, I ordered. **No matter what happens to me. Understand?**

Yes.

The thief skidded to a stop a safe distance away from my sword point. He grinned at me.

"Handsome sword," he said. "Even in the poor street

lighting, I could tell it wasn't bronze. Only one sword in the world made of rakor. Only one man who'd have it."

He was moving back and forth in front of me, the knife ready in his hand. I kept the sword between us, fighting the weakness creeping into my bones.

If I pass out, he'll kill me. Why is this happening now, of all times? Damn you and your reward, Worfit! In the back of my mind, I could picture Gharlas walking away, without a care in the world. *No—Keeshah will get him.*

"Thought you'd be safe, hiding inside your headscarf?" the thief sneered, lunging in on my left side. I slashed at him; he ducked and retreated. "I wasn't looking at faces," he said, moving back and forth again. "I was watching for that sword. When I saw you with Tarani, I knew where you'd be—I only needed to wait for you."

He moved in close on the right, and I made the sword follow him. I had to hold it with both hands, now.

He moved further right; I twisted to face him. Then, suddenly, he leaped to the left and lunged in past my guard. As though I were watching a slow-motion film, I saw the dagger drawn back in the man's fist, ready to gut-stab me.

Something white flashed in front of the man, and he screamed. He brought his free hand up to his face, but not before I had seen the livid, bleeding wound that crossed his face diagonally, exposing bone at cheek, nose, and chin.

Lonna pulled up her dive, flew back to attack the man with claws and bloody beak. The gentle, hooting call was silent now; she uttered a piercing shriek as her claws sank into the man's forearm. He dropped the knife.

I staggered up and followed the struggling pair. "Lonna, enough," I said. My voice was barely a whisper, but the bird understood. She disengaged, flew upward, hovered over us, beating her wings slowly in the air.

I fell forward, driving Rika straight through the man's midsection. I landed on the grass and rolled a few feet downhill, leaving wet red spots where I passed.

What's happened to Gharlas? I wondered urgently. *Where is he?*

I propped myself up on my left elbow, and forced my vision to focus as I searched the downslope for his running form. I spotted him, running across the grassy field between this row of workshops and the next one. He hadn't reached the road yet.

Coming up that road were two large-size cats, one on the heels of the other, both of them making riotous noise. I felt such a sweeping relief that I could spare the energy for a small chuckle at the confusion the sha'um must have left behind them in the congested downtown area of the city.

But the next minute, I wasn't laughing.

Ronar was *chasing* Keeshah. Mad with rage and grief, lacking even Thymas's insincere control, Ronar was giving free rein to his old grudge against my sha'um. He didn't care about Gharlas. Considering how suddenly Thymas had been wounded, and how quickly he had lost consciousness, it was possible that Ronar didn't even know about Gharlas. To Ronar's perception, the last danger Thymas had faced might have been me. That would amplify his fury toward Keeshah.

Keeshah angled away from the road toward Gharlas, who skidded and scrambled on the hillside, trying to stop his headlong run. When Keeshah was barely thirty feet from the terrified man—three strides for the huge cat—Ronar made a tremendous leap, and landed half across Keeshah's back. His claws caught Keeshah's side and back, and his teeth sank into Keeshah's tan haunch.

I felt it.

Keeshah roared with pain, dragged Ronar a few steps toward Gharlas, then couldn't stand it any more. He threw himself over on the ground and brought his hindclaws up under Ronar's belly. Ronar let go his hold and backed away. Keeshah leaped to his feet, and the two cats circled warily, heads down, teeth bared, neck fur flared. They grumbled and challenged, the terrible sound of their voices floating out across the city and drawing a crowd of people up the hill.

Gharlas edged around the angry sha'um, moving downhill again. I saw him go with a despairing acceptance. Keeshah's fighting instincts had been roused by Ronar and he needed them, undistracted, to defend himself against the other sha'um.

The world started to wheel slowly through my blurry eyesight. I remembered what Gharlas had said, and I believed it. One day, it would be settled. There would be another chance.

I began to yield to the faintness; my supporting arm slipped out from under me. I lay on the ground and watched as the sha'um closed again, teeth and claws of each cat finding targets in the other animal. I heard the angry roaring dimly.

I reached out for Keeshah's mind, gently. I didn't want to distract him, but I needed to speak to him before I lost consciousness.

I will not die, I told him. **And Thymas may not be dead. For his sake, spare Ronar if you can. But oh, God, please take care of yourself. Please . . .**

22

In the instant I was awake, I was running with Keeshah. His mind held me with him, as he slipped through the shadows of a tall orchard, then broke free into the bright daylight of a yearling lot. He ran right over the young trees; they scratched at his belly.

I didn't try to think. I accepted Keeshah's joyous welcome, and let myself share his strength and contentment. It was a gentle awakening. Sharing those first moments with the sha'um was a cushion from reality. At first I thought we were back in Raithskar, returning to the city from our picnic. Gradually, I sorted out what had happened. I became aware of the pain in my right shoulder, and of the stinging of Keeshah's many wounds—along his flanks, across his back, most painfully across his chest—as he stretched his muscles in the run.

What happened, Keeshah? I asked finally. **Is Ronar alive?**

Yes.

And Thymas?

Him, too.

What about Gharlas?

Gone, Keeshah told me with some embarrassment. **Sorry.**

It's not your fault. You tried. Were you hurt badly?

Could I run? he snorted. **Stupid.**

I laughed out loud, ignoring the pain in my shoulder.

"That's a welcome sound," Tarani said. I opened my eyes

to see her kneeling at my right side, smiling gently, sadly. One side of her face was a dark bruise.

"Tarani, I'm so sorry about Volitar," I said.

"We did our best to save him," she said, shrugging. "If only he had told me the truth long ago!"

Say that once for me, too, I thought. *If only Thanasset had told me what the Ra'ira is. Or Dharak. Surely Serkajon had to tell his Lieutenant about the stone's powers, in order to persuade him to abandon the Kingdom. If Serkajon's boot design has been passed through all these generations, surely such an important secret . . .*

Dharak was trying to decide whether to tell me, that first day, I realized. *Just before Thymas burst into the room. Then he found out that Thanasset had given me Serkajon's sword, and he assumed that Thanasset had told me everything.*

Two near misses. Such near misses. Oh, well.

I brought my mind back to the present.

"Volitar did his best for you, too," I said to Tarani. "He was a remarkable man. I wish I'd had a chance to get to know him."

"Yes, you would have liked each other," she said. She made a choking sound, and turned her face away.

"How long have I been unconscious?" I asked, changing the subject with little subtlety. My inner awareness told me it was morning, but I couldn't be sure *which* morning.

"Only a day." She faced me, composed again. "I cleaned and wrapped your wounds, but I couldn't tell how bad they were. I—"

There were deep creases across her brow, and shadows under her eyes. "You've been worried about me. And Thymas," I added. "How is he?"

"Hurt badly, I think," she said. "He hasn't awakened, yet."

I lifted my head and looked around. We were in the upper room of Volitar's residence. Thymas lay on a pallet not far from me. His skin was pale and waxy. He didn't look at all good.

"How did you get me up here?" I asked.

"Keeshah helped. I wouldn't let anyone touch you, after that man tried to kill you. Keeshah has stayed nearby most of the time; you are safe here."

"You sent Lonna to me," I said. "She saved my life."

"Fair payment," she said, awkwardly, "of a debt long overdue."

"At Inid, you told Thymas you had put Molik in the past, where he belonged. The incident in Thagorn belongs there, too." I brought my left hand across my body and opened it to her. "Agreed?"

She caught my fingers tightly with both her hands and smiled shakily. "Agreed." She let me go, and my hand dropped to my chest. Its weakness surprised me.

I must have lost a lot of blood.

"Do you think you could eat something?" she asked, noticing my sudden alarm.

"Now that you mention it, I think I could eat a lot of something."

She brought me a thin rafel, and helped me to sit up and lean against the wall. A folded pallet protected my injured shoulder. My right arm was useless, my left hand weak and awkward. I didn't object when she offered to manage the fork-tined spoon for me. The rafel was hot and filling; I had to quit after only a few bites. I felt stronger, but very tired.

"Keeshah said he didn't kill Ronar," I said, as Tarani helped me to lie down again. "I'd expect him to be howling to get to Thymas."

"He was doing that, last night," she said. "He was in a lot of pain, I'm sure. I tried to help him clean the deeper wounds, but he wouldn't let me near him. I think he might have attacked me again, if Keeshah hadn't been right there with me.

"This morning, he was gone."

"Couldn't you have just put him to sleep," I asked, "and fixed him up, whether he liked it or not?"

"A sha'um?" She actually laughed. It was a rich, deep sound. I liked it. "A sha'um won't do anything he doesn't want to do."

"But—Keeshah in Thagorn—Ronar and Keeshah both, the morning you came into our camp—"

"And when Ronar tried to kill me? How effective was my power then? I had shocked Thymas by wanting to ride, and Ronar had stopped trusting me. So I was helpless against him."

I stared at her, thinking about it.

Is she saying that if a rider is susceptible to her power, so is his sha'um? I wondered. *No, that doesn't work. I'm immune, but she can charm Keeshah. And her illusions worked for Thymas, even when Ronar continued to be unmanageable.*

She said "trust." Certainly Thymas's devotion had a large dent in it, after Tarani and I rode off together, but his trust didn't get damaged until we reached Chizan. How does that apply to Keeshah, though? After the performance in Thagorn, I really thought that Tarani was in Worfit's pay. Didn't I?

Keeshah, Tarani says her power doesn't work on you unless you want it to. Is that true?

Yes.

Why did you let her put you to sleep in Thagorn?

You said to find her. I found her. Sleep felt good.

I counted to ten, slowly. Could he really have taken my instructions that literally?

I thought she was a criminal! I insisted.

No, you didn't.

I started to argue, but stopped myself. The day of our picnic, Keeshah had read my feelings on a deeper level than I could reach consciously.

What* did *I think of her? I asked him.

You knew her. You wanted her.

So he had sensed what I had felt on meeting Tarani, that strange feeling of recognition and immediate interest. Probably those had been no more than her resemblance to Gharlas and my fascination with her power—but they had been sincere at the time.

But—after the assassination attempt—

Did I trust her, Keeshah?

Yes.

I accepted it. I had kept reminding myself not to believe her, while she was telling me about Volitar and Molik. I had never once taken my own advice.

I sighed, and smiled at Tarani, who had watched me steadily through the few seconds my conversation with Keeshah had taken.

"I think I understand," I said.

"Good. Because I believe you're like the sha'um. My power will work if you let it. You'll need deep rest to heal properly. Will you let me give you sleep?"

Thymas will be awake soon, I thought. *That is, if he's going to wake up at all. It will be easier for her, if there is only one of us to care for at a time. I remember how Keeshah felt—so peaceful.*

"I'll try," I told her. I closed my eyes.

The humming started, and I focused all my attention on it. The tones vibrated through my body, draining the tension from the muscles, pulling away the pain, slowing my mind.

My body was heavy, relaxed, peaceful. My mind floated in blankness, listening. There was almost a melody to the sounds Tarani was making. If I listened closely, I would be able to find it, remember it. I searched for the melody . . . searched for it . . . searched. . . .

The first sensation to greet me, when I woke up this time, was intense hunger. I sat up, amazed that my shoulder flexed easily, though it twinged mightily.

Tarani had her back to me. She was giving Thymas small spoonfuls of soup.

"Hey!" I said. "Welcome back to the living!"

Tarani jumped at the sound of my voice, splashing soup on Thymas's bare chest. His middle was wrapped in bandages.

"Good morning," Tarani said, laughing and mopping up the mess. "Hungry?"

"Starving," I said. "But I can wait."

Thymas turned his head toward me. There was color in his skin again. There were also deep lines around his mouth, and a shadow in his eyes.

'I'm glad you're still with us," I said gently, sobered by his pain. "How is Ronar?"

He took a shallow, careful breath. "Hurt, but healing," he panted. "Like me." Suddenly he burst out: "Why aren't we dead? Because of us, Gharlas got away!" His shoulders had come off the pallet, but they fell back now, and his arms folded across the bandage. He closed his eyes, and suffered in silence.

When his breathing became even again, I said: "Thymas, listen to me." He opened his eyes. "Nothing that has happened can be changed now. Don't agonize over it. Concentrate on getting back your strength."

His eyelids flickered, then closed. Tarani put her hand on his forehead, hummed a single tone, and he was sleeping deeply.

Tarani fed me, helped me take care of some necessary

functions (and put down a fresh pallet, hanging the old one out on the porch to air), then put me back to sleep.

I was able to get up and around on my own the next morning. After Tarani had tended to Thymas, I insisted that she get some rest, herself. She curled up in the corner and slept for the rest of the day. I was glad to see, when she got up, that the hollow look around her eyes was gone. She woke up Thymas to give him some dinner; I helped her lift him and put down a fresh pallet.

Two days later, the three of us walked down the hill to the nearest public bath-house. Dyskornis wasn't like Raithskar, with water supplied through pipelines and tanks to every house. Water had to be delivered in velk-drawn carts, and nobody in Dyskornis would come near Volitar's house. We—and Keeshah—were major celebrities. There was usually a small crowd of curious people, looking up at the workshop from a safe distance down the hill.

Tarani had walked into town once to get water and supplies, and again to arrange for her uncle's cremation. But she had been anxious about us, and in a hurry to get back. Now we made the trip together, moving at a pace comfortable for Thymas, who still hurt a lot. We were glad of the fresh air, and of the prospect of being clean again. It surprised me to think that it had been more than two weeks since we had left Thagorn, but it seemed a much longer time since I had last bathed.

Free, at last, of the dust we had carried out of the Zantil Pass, we walked back up the hill. Keeshah, who had planted himself conspicuously outside the bath-house, ran across the fields around us, rolling in the grassy plants and jumping around like a kitten. His wounds were no more than dark, thin lines. Tarani's skill had helped all of us to heal ourselves much faster than usual.

All at once, Keeshah stiffened up, and his neck fur began to rise.

Rònar was limping toward us across the field. He was skinny and bedraggled.

I had put Thymas's right arm across my shoulders to help support him, when he had admitted to being tired. Now he pushed me away and moved out, slowly, on his own.

Stay back, Keeshah, I warned.

Tarani and I watched as Thymas went out to meet Ronar.

The boy's pale golden head fur stood out sharply against the cat's blood-darkened shoulder as he hugged his sha'um. Then they walked together toward Keeshah, who crouched defensively.

Steady. Wait and see what they want.

Thymas stopped and stood unsupported, weaving slightly, while Ronar moved closer to the other sha'um. Ronar stopped about three yards from Keeshah, and looked back at Thymas. Then he took two more steps forward, and lowered himself stiffly to the ground. He flopped over on his side, and stretched out his neck, exposing his throat to Keeshah.

"No!" Tarani gasped.

But Keeshah didn't close in for the kill. He lifted his head, and sounded a high-pitched roar of triumph, an acceptance of Ronar's surrender.

Thymas collapsed to the ground. Tarani and I rushed over to him. He hadn't passed out; he'd just lost the strength in his legs.

"Keeshah would have killed Gharlas," Thymas gasped, as we reached him, "if Ronar hadn't interfered. My sha'um hated yours, because I hated you . . . Captain. I never kept the spirit of my promise to Dharak. And now I have let the Ra'ira escape."

I couldn't stand the misery in his face, his voice.

"Not for long, Thymas," I said. "We'll be going after him, as soon as you're well."

"As soon as I—but he has four days' head start already!" Thymas protested. "You and Keeshah are healed—go after him now, before he gets away again!"

"Here, look at the sha'um," I said, lifting his shoulders from the ground. Ronar had rolled up into a crouch, and Keeshah was licking a nasty-looking wound just behind the other sha'um's head, where Ronar couldn't possibly reach. "We're a team, Thymas. When we go after Gharlas, we'll go together."

23

After Tarani and I had helped Thymas back up the hill, and he was resting, Tarani put Ronar to sleep in the shade beside the workshop. She came back in, and found me sitting at one of the work tables, working with brush and parchment.

"What are you doing?"

"Writing letters," I said. "When I left Raithskar, I had planned to be back by now. There are people there who will worry."

"Family?" she asked.

My mind was still on the letter, so I answered absently: "Yes, Markasset's father and aunt."

"Thymas told me that *you* were Markasset, before your name was changed."

Oops.

I looked up at her. She was standing with her arms folded over her chest, her hip braced against the table. She was looking at me speculatively.

" 'Double-minded'?" she said. "I think I've suspected it all along. You're a Visitor, aren't you?"

I had a strong urge to tell her the absolute truth, to explain to *someone* that I was alien to this world. But I checked it.

"Yes," I said. "And, before you ask, you've never heard of me. I'm *not* Serkajon."

She laughed, and again I thought how much I enjoyed the sound of her laughter. "I was thinking exactly that," she admitted.

"My being a Visitor—does it bother you?"

She sobered, and looked at me directly with those expressive, dark eyes. "It's why we're here right now, isn't it?"

I sighed. "I can't help but think so, Tarani. A moon ago, I was making plans to settle down in Raithskar, and let Zaddorn—the Chief of Peace and Security—take care of Gharlas. Then things started happening.

"First, I was running from Worfit. Then I was chasing you.

Then I was trying to help Volitar. But all of it led me to one place—this workshop, face to face with Gharlas. It just seems that I was meant to find out what the Ra'ira is, and how dangerous it can be. Gharlas will turn the world upside down, if I don't stop him."

"If you don't stop him," she repeated thoughtfully. "You—because you can resist his power, even as it is increased by the Ra'ira. Thymas—he is part of it, too, I sense that. And me, Rikardon. You have been led to me, because I am a weapon of opposition. I will be coming with you, won't I?"

I held out my hand, and Tarani placed hers in it, briefly. "I didn't feel I could speak for you, Tarani, but I hoped you would want it this way. We won this battle, by virtue of surprise. He must have learned about me through the Ra'ira's thought-reading power, but he didn't see the significance of my 'doubleness" until we tested one another. He won't underestimate me again. And he still has every reason to want that duplicate stone—

"It *is* here, isn't it?"

She jumped slightly, startled.

"I don't know. This is the first time I've been back in the workshop since I took Volitar out . . . just a minute." She went to her knees on the floor, and crawled under the table.

"The hiding place is exactly where you told Gharlas it was?" I asked.

"Surely," she said, her voice sounding odd through the wood and tile of the tabletop. "I was afraid he would know it, if I lied." I heard something scrape, then Tarani backed out from under the table and sat on the floor. In her hands, she held a brass-hinged wooden box.

"Volitar told me where this was, many years ago,' Tarani said. "He wanted me to know about it, in case of sudden death, but I've never seen what is in it. I suppose, now, that he was in constant fear of being recognized and killed or, worse, sent back to Eddarta."

I tried not to sound impatient. "Open it."

She did. She lifted out a gorgeous blue stone.

"If I didn't know that wasn't real . . ." I said, extending my hand. Tarani put the large, irregular, blue chunk of glass on my palm. I held the thing up to the light, looked through it. The interior flaws were there, the color was perfect—as well as I could remember it.

"I don't know much about glassmaking," I said, "but I do know this must have taken hours and hours of work. Layers of glass, heated and cooled unevenly to make stress lines, reheated so the next layer would bond without a mark—"

"You do know a lot about glassmaking," Tarani said. "Look, here is one that failed."

She held up another glass piece, the same size and shape as the one I held. But in hers, the blue color was visible faintly, deep down in the center. The outside of the copy was crazed, all different colors spreading around the surface in random distribution.

"Why, there is something else in here," she said, setting the damaged copy on the floor. "A pouch, and—it looks like an old letter."

She opened the pouch, and poured coins out into her hand. She drew a startled breath at their quantity. Some of them spilled over, rolled and bounced on the floor. I picked one up that had come to rest near my foot. It was a gold twenty-dozak piece.

"How could he have saved all this?" she wondered. "He never seemed to sell more than he needed to, to keep us going."

"It looks to me like he's had these awhile," I said, holding out the coin to her. "This is an Eddartan coin, graced with a picture of Gharlas's pal, Pylomel." The face was sensuous and arrogant, with some resemblance to Gharlas. "Maybe the letter—?"

She poured the coins back into the pouch, spilling some more. But she didn't bother picking them up; she was opening the folded parchment carefully. She made a soft sound, then began reading aloud, hesitating now and then over the faded ink.

" 'I have only a moment, and I must take this chance to let you know that I am well. Pylomel was angry when his informants brought me back to Eddarta, but I have convinced him that my going was the whim, soon regretted, of a headstrong girl. It suits his self-esteen to believe that only my pride has kept me from him. There has been a public reconciliation between our families. He and I are to marry in three days.

" 'I have accepted my fate, and so must you, dear one. I will not try to escape again, for then even dense Pylomel would guess the truth—that I was not alone when I ran away the first time. I cannot leave, and you must not return; the secret, cherished knowledge that you and Tarani are free of this hateful life is all that makes the prospect of my imminent "marriage" bearable. The High Lord must never suspect—*never*—that I bore a child during the blessed year we spent together.

" 'Let Tarani believe that her parents are both dead, darling. Though it will hurt you to say it, it will quiet her questions.

" 'My body is lost to you, but not my love. That will be yours always. Zefra.' "

She folded the parchment again, pressed it to her chest, and closed her eyes. "He was my father," she said after a moment. "Not my uncle. My father."

"That's the way it looks," I said. "I guess this changes things a little."

Her eyes opened. "What do you mean?"

"Well, the letter," I said, waving my hand at the parchment. "All that punishment Volitar took from Gharlas before we got here—he wasn't hiding a chunk of glass, Tarani, he was hiding that letter."

"Yes, I see that," she said impatiently. "He was protecting me from Gharlas. But I don't understand—"

"He was protecting *Zefra*. Assuming she's still alive, what do you suppose Pylomel would do, if he found out she's been deceiving him for twenty years?"

She worried her right tusk with her tongue as she thought about it. "You're trying to tell me that I should stay away from Eddarta to keep my mother safe? But Gharlas *does* know about me, Rikardon. She's already in danger."

"Not as much as if you took your look-alike face back home, Pylomel can't be too fond of Gharlas; he'd be a fool to accept such an accusation without proof."

"And I'd be all the proof he needed," she concluded. She picked up the scattered coins and sat quietly for a moment, letting them sift through her fingers and rattle into the box. Suddenly she dumped them all in, set the parchment on top of them, and clapped the lid down. "There's something you've overlooked," she said, getting to her feet. "Two things, in fact."

"I'm listening."

"First, Volitar's death. Gharlas had seen me; Volitar must

have known the truth would occur to him—sooner or later, with or without the confirmation of the letter. The cause he had protected with his body, with his . . . pain . . . was already lost. Why did he kill himself?"

I started to say something, but she cut me off, answering her own question. She had begun pacing about, thinking out loud as she walked.

"I've told you what Volitar taught me, what he *believed* with all his being—that no man has a right to impose his will on another person. When Gharlas had him pinned down as a shield against your sword, Volitar was a tool being used to control us—to control me. He destroyed himself, rather than be used that way. He might have done the same thing when Molik's men took him, if he had realized what was happening.

"He must have hated it that thought of our safety kept my mother in Eddarta—but for my sake, he accepted her choice. Now Gharlas has the capability of using me against her, and her against me. *If* she is still alive, which we don't know for sure. I have no more liking for being someone else's weapon than Volitar had, Rikardon. And I'm tired of my family being used against me. I want to find my mother if I can, and free her from Pylomel, if I can."

She paused, and turned toward me.

"The other thing you've overlooked is something we've just discussed. I'm part of your team. I'm going with you, Rikardon."

I felt the return of the sensation I'd had, the night it had occurred to me that I might be immune to Gharlas's power. It didn't frighten me, now. I welcomed it, drew it in, let it fill me.

I had told Thanasset in my letter—in cautious terms—that I had discovered what he had wanted to tell me. He would know what was happening, and he'd tell Ferrathyn and Zaddorn to look for other job applicants. I'd have to write a letter to Illia, too, and tell her to stop waiting. I'd do it partly because, though I had this need to try to stop Gharlas, I didn't have any intuition of what the outcome would be.

But partly, I would tell Illia goodbye because I knew I had turned a corner in this new life of mine. A tranquil, domestic scene in Raithskar just wasn't in my future. I was headed in the opposite direction.

"You and I and Thymas," I agreed softly. "And Keeshah and Ronar and Lonna. We'll go all the way to Eddarta, if necessary."

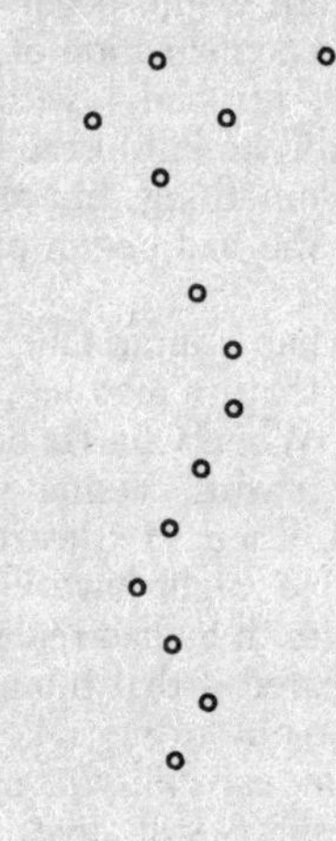

End PROCEEDINGS:

INPUT SESSION TWO

—I can go no further, Recorder.

—We will separate our minds from the All-Mind . . . and I shall withdraw my mind from yours. . . . You seem to be in pain.

—My right shoulder hurts.

—That is the lingering memory of your stab wounds. It is regretful that you must suffer through every injury again.

—But I may relive the joys, as well. It is a good balance. I found the Recording easier, this time. But I am tired.

—We will continue later. Rest now. Sleep. . . .

The Bronze of Eddarta

PRELIMINARY PROCEEDINGS:

INPUT SESSION THREE

—Ah, it is you. Is it time to begin once more?

—If it suits you, Recorder.

—And your shoulder?

—The pain of the remembered wound has faded, as you said it would. I feel quite well again, and ready to continue.

—Then be comfortable, and we will prepare by reviewing the material you have already given to the All-Mind.

You spoke of the uniting of two lives, one nearly ended, one barely begun. You were Ricardo Carillo, in a world outside the Walls of Gandalara. You saw a fireball, which you call a meteor, and after an undetermined period of unconsciousness, you awoke in Gandalara, sharing the body—and some of the memories—of a young man named Markasset.

—And sharing his telepathic bond with a member of Gandalara's intelligent feline species, a sha'um.

—Markasset's father, Thanasset, was implicated in the theft of a political treasure, a jewel called the Ra'ira.

—At first, I wanted only to prove that Thanasset—a man I liked and respected as soon as I met him—was innocent. Later, however, I accepted the task of recovering the gem and returning it to its protected place in Raithskar.

—A duty you shouldered reluctantly.

—That's a little unfair, Recorder. I had no idea, at first, that the Ra'ira was anything more than an ordinary, if uncommonly valuable, gemstone. In Ricardo's world, such beautiful jewels had often been surrounded with a mystique of charm or danger. I assumed that the Ra'ira had attracted a connection with the transfer of political power.

—I meant no implication of blame. I Record; I do not judge.

—And I must apologize for my short temper. The fact is, I suppose, that I blame myself. Perhaps if I hadn't spent so much time trying to avoid responsibility for the Ra'ira . . .

—Such speculation is useless to the All-Mind.

—Of course it is. Again, my apologies.

—In any case, when you discovered the true nature of the Ra'ira, you didn't hesitate to commit yourself to its recovery.

—By then, I felt I had no choice. Only a few people knew how dangerous the Ra'ira could be. It was a telepathic tool, a transmitter which could amplify the native mind-talent of a Gandalaran. The ancient Kings had used the Ra'ira to keep absolute control over Gandalara.

—You shiver. Are you cold?

—The image of the old Kingdom makes me shudder. Ricardo had some experience with societies in which expressing an opinion that disagreed with governmental precepts could send an individual into confinement, or worse. The concept of watching every word you say is appalling enough, but under the corrupt Kings, your very thoughts could betray disloyalty or discontent. I hadn't quite believed Thanasset when he told me that the slaves, sent as tribute to the last Kings, never rebelled against their lot. Once I understood about the Ra'ira, I could see how fearful they must have been . . . how demoralized . . . how utterly without hope.

—You said you felt you had no choice but to pursue the Ra'ira. Was it because of your sympathy for the ancient slaves?

—Yes, and because somebody had to do it. Thymas and Tarani and I were convinced that we had been brought together for the purpose of opposing Gharlas's insane plan to reconstruct the Kingdom. If he tried, we were sure he would succeed only in creating a civil war that would destroy and demoralize Gandalara. We weren't sure we could stop him—but we knew we had to try to return the Ra'ira to the protective custody of the Council of Supervisors in Raithskar.

—Are you ready to continue the Record?

—I am ready, Recorder.

—Then make your mind one with mine, as I have made mine one with the All-Mind . . .

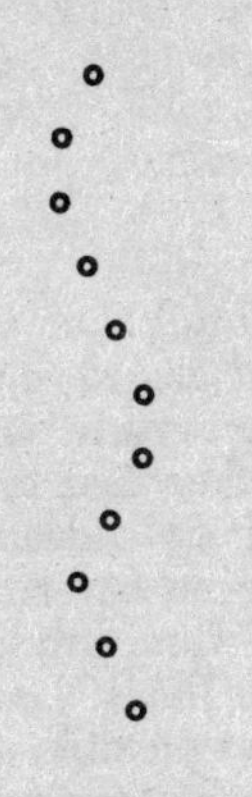

WE BEGIN!

1

I was on my way back to Volitar's old workshop. I had been to the market area of the city to "mail" some letters and buy a map. Both letters were already on their way to Raithskar—one by caravan, the other tied to the leg of a *maufa,* the fast-flying message bird of Gandalara.

Caravans could move no faster than their *vleks,* the goat-size pack animals that were only slightly more stupid than stubborn. It would take Illia's "Dear Jane" letter nearly fifty days to reach her. It was possible—not likely, but possible—that I could be back in Raithskar with the Ra'ira before she got that letter, and I approved of that idea.

Illia had loved Markasset, and his memory of that relationship made Illia very special to me. I felt I owed it to her to tell her, in person, that I couldn't just settle into the ordinary domestic life she and Markasset might have shared.

It was also possible that I wouldn't get back to Raithskar alive. That's why I had written the letter—it was better than letting her believe that I hadn't thought of her at all after our sweet farewell.

Thanasset would receive his letter in only a few days, the bird-handler had assured me. His maufa wouldn't take it directly to Raithskar, because he couldn't direct a bird to a place where he, himself, had never been. His maufa would take the message to another *maufel* in Chizan, who would send it with one of his own birds.

I had watched, fascinated, while the old man had held the small gray-green bird in front of his face. He had laid his forefinger against its white bill, and stared into one bright eye for a few seconds before flinging it up into the air. I watched the bird fly, the thin strip of leather trailing after it, until it was out of sight.

That's another kind of mind skill, I realized. *Like a Recorder's conscious link with the collective memory of the All-*

lind. Like a Rider's telepathic bond with his sha'um. Those kills are—well, not common. But accepted, at least.

It's the "mindpower," the ability to influence another peron's mind, that's scary. Tarani has it, and it scares her. harlas has it, and HE scares ME. I have some resistance to is power because I'm "double-minded," and it's non-andalaran Ricardo who controls Markasset's body and memries. But even I'm not immune to it. The sooner we take harlas out of action, the better.

The letter to Thanasset told him, in guarded terms, what I 'as doing. He was one of the Supervisors, and he knew what ne Ra'ira was. He had tried to get me appointed to the Council so that I could be told the truth. My message to him 'as, essentially: "I understand. I'll bring it back."

When the bird had finally disappeared, I had gone to everal letterers, looking for a map that would tell me where ddarta was. Markasset had only the vaguest notion, which idn't surprise me. His interests had been more physical than cholarly—a trait which had saved "our" life more than once.

I was delighted to find a map which showed *all* of Gandalara, nd with that important piece of parchment folded and tucked ito my belt, I started the climb back to Tarani and Thymas.

Dyskornis sprawled across the feet of the rising hills which ipported three tiers of glassmaking workshops, built out 'om steep slopes so as to make annual replacement of the reakable firebowls under the glass kilns practical. Further own the hill, a smaller, noisier city catered to the trade of 'ansients. Beyond that lay marked lots planted with the ard-wooded trees that provided glassmakers with heat durig one work season, and ash for the glass mix in the next.

Following the road, I walked between open fields with ieir grasslike ground cover. A writhing shape of tan, bright gainst the green, caught my eye—Keeshah, rolling in the lossy field.

Come here, and I'll scratch that itch for you, I invited im.

He rolled once more, then stood up from the greenery. He 'as more than ten yards away from me, but I could see the lint of his tusks as his lips pulled back from a huge yawn. He ame toward me slowly, and I left the road to meet him alfway. I was fascinated by the ripple of muscle across his road chest, which was almost on the same level as my shoulder. When we met, I reached under the massive wedge of his head to scratch his chest first.

Feels good, he told me. He laid his bulk on the ground and rolled half over.

Hey, I thought it was your back that itched, I thought though I put both hands to work, combing torn plants out of the thick, pale fur on the sha'um's belly.

Itch everywhere, he complained. **Don't like this place.**

When we leave, Keeshah, we'll be on the road for a long time. How are your wounds doing?

Following the directions of my hands and mind, he rolled over to his stomach and crouched patiently while I searched through his fur for the remnants of the scratches and gouges he had taken during his fight with the other sha'um. They were no more than faint lines in the newly healed skin.

I was surprised, but in the next instant I reminded myself that Tarani's gift of healing sleep had shortened my own recovery by at least half. I flexed my right shoulder; all that remained of the double stab wound was a twinge, and even that seemed noticeably less sharp than it had yesterday.

A far-off rumbling sound washed down the hillside to us, and Keeshah and I both looked up toward Volitar's workshop. Standing half in, half out of the downslope shade was Thymas's sha'um, Ronar. He looked in our direction for a moment, then paced into the light, paused, turned, and paced back into shadow.

Was that comment directed at us? I asked Keeshah.

No.

His mind closed down around that answer, as it always did when he discussed the other sha'um—or, for that matter, the sha'um's master. I scratched idly where Keeshah liked it the most, just at the base of his neck, while I watched the other cat pacing.

As far as I had learned in Gandalara, the direct mind-to-mind communication which Keeshah and I shared was a unique bond between a sha'um and his Rider. I had talked with Tarani about her link with the huge white bird who had been with her for four years. It was a limited kind of communication, consisting only of images, and requiring intense concentration. It also seemed hard for the maufel to give his instructions to his bird. Keeshah and I maintained a constant, nearly subconscious link. Intense emotions, especially fear or anger, flowed readily along that link. Conversation required a conscious decision, but not much effort.

Among themselves, sha'um used vocal and physical signals, and except for rare people like Tarani and Gharlas, the Gandalarans had to depend on voice and attitude. But Riders had a special . . . well, sometimes it might be considered a handicap. No matter what a man pretended, or really wanted to believe, his true feelings were mirrored in the action of his sha'um.

Tarani had been the one to tell me that. Ronar had refused to allow her to ride him, but Keeshah had accepted her as second rider without hesitation. She had pointed out that their behavior reflected our attitudes, and there was no denying the truth of it.

Thymas, entrenched in the male-militarist traditions of the Sharith, had been scandalized by the idea. Both Markasset and Ricardo had grown up free of Sharith tradition, so Rikardon's decision was based only on consideration of Tarani's comfort. Her alternative to riding one of the sha'um had been swinging and bouncing between the huge cats in a cargo net.

So I tried, now, to read what Ronar could tell me about Thymas. The boy had told me he was impatient to get going, in spite of the fact that he and Ronar were only partially healed. I had been hearing his words as false bravado, but in watching Ronar, I realized that he really was feeling restless and confined.

And what, I wondered, *is Keeshah saying about the way I feel? Am I—*

Bored, came Keeshah's complaint, as if in answer. I laughed. He raised up on his forelegs a little, and swung his head suddenly, catching me in the side and knocking me into an ungainly somersault.

"Hey—mmph!" I yelled. I came upright spitting greenery and skidding down the slope. Before I could get good purchase, I felt a whack on my shoulders, and I was tumbling again. I yelped once more when my injured shoulder caught all my weight. I let my body relax; one last roll, and I slid to a halt, facedown.

I lay there, keeping both mind and body as still as I could. I couldn't hear Keeshah approach, but I could feel his breath on my neck when his anxious thought reached me.

Rikardon?

It was as though time had turned back, and I lay upon salty sand, instead of the fragrant grassy stuff in which my face was buried. Keeshah had called me Markasset then . . .

I had meant to "play dead" as a joke on Keeshah. By the time I realized how cruel that was, I couldn't give up the ruse because I was caught up in a memory, immoblized by it.

It wasn't *my* memory. It was Keeshah's.

I felt the torrent of his anguish as Markasset died, felt in my own throat Keeshah's scream of grief, in my own hands and feet the pull of the killer's flesh against his razor claws. I grieved for the emptiness in his mind. I ached for the touch of hand on fur.

I felt his need to run, to roar, to speak to his own kind, in his own way, of the lost kinship. And I felt the other need, the strange one, the unbidden knowing. The need to *wait*.

I felt his wonder when he sensed new life within the dead shell of his friend. I felt his caution, his hesitation, his awareness that this new person would perish without his help.

In Keeshah's persona, I accepted responsibility for myself.

In Keeshah's memory, I touched the stranger's mind—my own—and found it strong and clear, but needful.

As Keeshah, I accepted Ricardo.

I *was* Keeshah, and every muscle thrilled with the joy of the bond with my new friend, with a fierce pride in our partnership . . .

Suddenly, I was back in the present, nearly overcome by the unexpected sharing of Keeshah's intimate memory, totally ashamed of having frightened him.

I rolled over, and Keeshah snapped his head back in surprise.

Keeshah, I rushed into the apology, **I'm sorry. I'm not really hurt—hey! What the! . . .**

It never crossed my mind to be afraid of Keeshah, even though my own reaction to that sort of joke would have been anger. But I wasn't prepared for his surge of gladness. He was so happy that I wasn't hurt that he forgot I *could* be. A sha'um's idea of mischief . . .

When I dragged myself through the door of the two-story house attached to Volitar's workshop, Thymas and Tarani both stared at me in amazement. I looked down at my clothes. Blue tunic and tan trousers, even my leather boots, carried ground-in green and brown stains. I felt an itch behind my ear, slapped an unbeautiful insectish creature to the floor, and stepped on it.

"Keeshah was bored," I said.

2

I wasn't expecting a roar of laughter, but I had hoped for a smile or two. Tarani tried to oblige, but the shape of humor didn't rest well in her tense face. I glanced at Thymas, sitting sullenly on his pallet, pretending to mend a cargo net that was perfectly whole, and I understood how she felt. She had been alone with Thymas most of the day, and the boy's self-loathing was a tangible, oppressive burden to anyone around him.

"I saw Ronar moving around," I said. "How is he feeling, Thymas?"

"He is nearly healed," the boy said. He threw down the net and stood up with nearly his old grace. If I hadn't been watching for it, I never would have seen the flash of pain in his eyes as he stretched the muscles around the still-mending wound in his side. "We are ready to travel."

Now, everybody in the room knew that was an out-and-out lie. Ronar had lain low for days after his fight with Keeshah, before he came forward to offer my sha'um his undefended throat. That gesture of surrender was partially Thymas's idea—a reflection of the boy's guilt feelings—but it could never have happened if Ronar hadn't been badly injured and demoralized, himself. Tarani had used her hypnotic/psychic skills to help him, but Thymas's sha'um had slept only one night under her spell. The body healed itself faster in that restful sleep, but it still needed a minimum of time to do the job. Ronar was hardly "ready to travel"—at least, not at the grueling pace we had kept since leaving Thagorn.

But I said: "Good. We'll leave in the morning, then."

I walked over to the dining table, unfolded the map which I had, fortunately, lost during Keeshah's first assault, and later retrieved. I ignored Tarani's questioning look, and spread the parchment out on the table.

"The Walls of the World." I had wondered about that term, while I was still only Ricardo. When I had acquired Markasset's memories, I had also, inevitably, acquired his viewpoints. At every opportunity, I made a conscious effort to step aside from them, but lately there hadn't been much opportunity. I'd been worrying too hard about staying alive to think much about Markasset's complacent acceptance of the limits of his world.

Now, in a two-dimensional image of Gandalara, the edges of the "world" were clearly marked.

As in the fragmented maps I *had* seen, a thick, dark line winding its way across one long edge of the map represented the Great Wall. Gandalaran charting conventions placed the Great Wall at the top of the map. Though I was sure the Wall didn't run truly east-west, it did mark the northern edge of Gandalara, so Ricardo was fairly comfortable with using such a map.

The southern border was marked off into sections. At the left edge of the map was a feature with the intriguing name of Valley of Mists. From it, the Wall of Mist ran eastward below the Kapiral Desert toward the Morkadahl Mountains, where it merged into the unnamed mountain range which butted up against the Korchis to form the Chizan Passage. East of the Zantro Pass, one of the two high crossings that enclosed Chizan, the southern wall was divided into three sections. The Rising Wall began at Inid, the Refreshment House at the foot of the slope leading down from the Zantro. It approached a plateau isolated from the walls, and became the Desert Wall. Further east, it was known as the River Wall.

I put the index finger of my right hand on a spot marked in the middle of the River Wall. "This is Eddarta," I explained to Thymas and Tarani, who were looking over my shoulders. I hooked a chair out with my foot, and sat down to give them a clearer view.

"And Dyskornis is here." Tarani touched the map.

Thymas studied the area between our markings. "Gharlas will take the quickest route," he said. "Tarani—which way?"

Without hesitation, Tarani said: "South." She moved her finger as she talked. "The main caravan route to Eddarta follows the line of Refreshment Houses. Inid. Haddat. Kanlyr. Iribos. You have said that Gharlas was a caravan master—that is the way he must have traveled before."

The shortest way home is the way you know best, I thought. *She's probably right.*

Thymas was peering at the map closely, muttering to himself. "Five days to Inid, another five to Haddat. He's four days ahead, but with the sha'um . . ." He tilted his head. "We should catch up with him midway between Haddat and Kanlyr."

"Correction," I said. "We *would* catch up with him—*if* he went that way, which I think is likely, and *if* we followed him, which we aren't going to do."

"Not follow—"

I held up a hand to cut off Thymas's explosion. "Use your head. There's nothing in that direction but Refreshment Houses. Tarani, you tell us—what is the southern route like?"

"The way from Inid to Kanlyr lies in a trench between dry hills. I have gone no further, but that far, at least, it is a miserable trip." She smiled a little wistfully. "That's why my troupe did so well through there; the caravans were desperate for some distraction from the journey."

I nodded, thinking that Gharlas had traveled the main caravan route regularly between Eddarta and Raithskar, yet had never seen Tarani, who had entertained caravans with her dancing and illusions. The odds against his missing her had to be enormous.

But there's no doubting it—he was astonished when he finally put it together that Volitar's phantom "niece" *was the illusionist he had heard so much about.*

Call it destiny, I thought. *Call it fate. Call it scrambled eggs, if you like. But Gharalas wasn't meant to know about Tarani until we all met here in Dyskornis.*

"Right," I said. "So we're going to follow the Great Wall—" I traced the northern route with my finger. "—past all these little towns.

"The reasons we are going to do it this way," I said, forestalling something else Thymas started to say, "are threefold.

"First, there are towns and rivers north of us, which means

that the countryside is more hospitable, and it's likely the sha'um can hunt for their meals along the way.

"Second, Gharlas is crazy, but not foolish. He'll expect us to follow him. There's no telling what sort of traps he'll leave along the way.

"Third, I hope he *won't* expect us to be waiting for him in Eddarta when he gets there."

"You mean you're going to let him reach his home territory?" Thymas demanded.

I sighed. *Why is it that the only time he sounds like himself, is when he's arguing with me?*

It was Tarani who answered the boy. "You're forgetting that Gharlas is more than just an Eddartan, Thymas. He's a caravan master. He probably knows every vlek-handler from here to Eddarta. If they do not already owe him service, he can buy them. And those he cannot buy, he can . . . command."

I glanced at Thymas, but he wouldn't meet my eyes.

He's remembering that he nearly killed me, while Gharlas controlled him.

"We're already in his home territory," Tarani continued, in the vibrant voice that contained its own kind of command. She sat down and leaned over the map. "I agree with Rikardon's plan, but that has little weight." She placed her hands flat on the map and lifted her head to look directly at the pale-haired boy. "It does not matter that you *disagree*, Thymas. We will *both* do whatever Rikardon suggests."

Uh-oh.

I waited for the explosion, but it never came—at least, not from Thymas. He squared his shoulders, stared at his boots, and said: "Yes, I see what you mean. I've done enough damage."

I slammed my hand on the table—Tarani snatched her fingers out of the way just in time—and stood up.

"I've had all I can take of your simpering self-importance, Thymas."

Thymas gasped. "But I—"

"You *think* you keep apologizing, but you know what you're really doing? You're trying to take credit, all by yourself, for letting Gharlas get away. *Your* mistakes were the serious ones. *Your* mistakes were the avoidable ones. If *you* had done things right . . .

"You want to talk about stupid mistakes? What idiot, who knew there was a price on his head, went into the rogueworld and flashed Serkajon's sword, so that every thief and assassin in Dykornis knew who he was?" I stabbed my thumb at my chest. "This one, that's who. *You* didn't let Gharlas get away, Thymas. *We* did. Even Tarani. She could have sent Lonna after Gharlas, but instead she chose to send the bird to help me. If the only important thing is to stop Gharlas, she made the wrong choice.

"She did succeed in saving my life. Maybe you think that *was* the wrong choice!"

"Rikardon!" Tarani's shout cut me off in mid-harangue. I was leaning across the corner of the table, forcing Thymas to back away from me. I straightened up.

"You once told me," she said more gently, "that it is easy for you to say insincere things."

Ouch, I thought. *Touché*.

Thymas tried to read the silent message that passed from Tarani to me, and he was beginning to look angry.

Is that what I'm trying to do? I asked myself. *Provoke him into being as nasty as he used to be? God forbid*.

"Sorry," I said. I rubbed my hand over the short, dark blond fur on my head, searching for the right words—and sending a small shower of dirt onto the map. "I'm only trying to say that we're a team, and that none of us can take credit or blame alone, from here on out.

"Tarani is right about this—a team needs a leader. For reasons that mystify me, I'm it.

"You're right about something else—there is *nothing* more important than getting the Ra'ira away from Gharlas.

"Trust is the key to teamwork, Thymas. You and Tarani have to trust me to give the right orders, and I have to trust you to follow them. Not because you promised your father to obey me."

Which is yet to happen, I thought. *Wups, "Captain"—could be you need some lessons in trust, yourself*.

"Especially not because," I continued, "you feel you've proved yourself unworthy of command." He flinched a little at that, and I knew I had touched a nerve. "We can't afford your self-pity.

"I'm the first to admit that you and I aren't the best of

friends, Thymas, but we *have* fought the same enemy. And we've ridden together."

A muscle along Thymas's jaw tensed and relaxed.

This "boy" is going to be the next Lieutenant of the Sharith, I thought. *He takes that duty very seriously. It's time I showed him that I take HIM seriously.*

"Tarani's power and your sword, Thymas. If I'd had a choice, I couldn't have selected two stronger weapons to use against Gharlas. But an unwilling weapon is more hazard than help. Convince me that I'll have your cooperation—not obedience, mind you, but *cooperation*—or stay behind."

I stopped, wondering if I'd said enough, or too much. The boy was thinking about it; that was a good sign. He leaned heavily on the back of the chair in front of him, looking at me, considering. When he spoke, the meek, whining tone was absent from his voice for the first time since the fight with Gharlas. If I'd done nothing else, I'd taken his mind off his guilt.

" 'Trust.' 'Cooperation.' 'Sincerity.' " He quoted the words skeptically. "Here's some sincerity, Rikardon. I don't like you. I don't trust you. And I *still* don't understand why Dharak made you Captain."

Your resentment is showing, Thymas, I thought, *but this isn't like your usual fit of temper. It is possible—barely possible—that we're finally beginning to communicate with one another?*

"Dharak was worried that you were going to lead the young Riders after Gharlas," I said. "He thought that if he made me Captain, and *I* told them to stay put, they'd listen. He does believe that I'm *supposed* to be the Captain. But what he really wanted was to avoid the split-up of the Sharith." I let that sink in, then I said: "Dharak still leads the Riders. So will you, when your time arrives."

Thymas was quiet for a moment. "Convince *me* of something," he said at last. "Convince me that you're the one who is supposed to lead this 'team.' And while you're at it, tell me what the filth you've been hiding all this time. Show me the same kind of trust you say you want from me."

I heard Tarani's intake of breath, but I didn't give her a chance to say anything.

"That's fair, Thymas, and I wish I could give you clear, objective reasons for it. I can't. It's just something I feel.

There is something which I *have* been concealing—not for lack of trust, but because I didn't think your knowing it would be useful to either one of us. I'm a . . . Visitor. Markasset was killed by one of Gharlas's accomplices. I arrived a few hours later."

I saw a look of revelation cross Thymas's face, and I was sure that I was about to be accused, once more, of being a reincarnation of Serkajon. Because Markasset was descended from the man who had destroyed the corrupt Kingdom, and because I had been given his unique steel sword, that seemed to be the standard conclusion people jumped to when they found out I was a Gandalaran personality returned from the All-Mind.

Of course, that's not what I was, but I had let the few who knew about me believe it, because the concept was acceptable to them. No one in Gandalara knew the truth about where this "Visitor" had come from.

Ricardo had been cruising the Mediterranean Ocean—a concept in itself unacceptable to the desert-familiar Gandalarans—in the company of the lovely young Antonia Alderuccio when the fireball had somehow transported Ricardo to the Kapiral Desert, Markasset,and Keeshah. That star-covered night, and Antonia, were secret memories that came often to my dreams.

It turned out that I was wrong about what Thymas was thinking.

"That's why Gharlas called you 'double-minded!' " he cried. "Is that why you could break—? . . . Oh."

I didn't say anything while he mulled it over, all his thoughts turned inward. When his eyes refocused, he said: "All right. You've convinced me. Now, what proof will you accept that I'll follow orders?"

"All I need is your word, Thymas, freely given."

3

I was on the slope below the workshop, walking back from the bath-house, when the sudden Gandalaran night overtook me. Although no starlight could penetrate the cloud cover, the diffused moonlight gave a ghostly glow to the large features around me—the road, the fields, the outlines of the workshops. A brighter patch of light marked the upstairs window of Volitar's old living quarters, and I aimed my steps in that direction.

As I neared the downhill entrance of the house, I heard the sound of Tarani's humming, and I was able to separate her from the other dark shapes. Ronar was stretched out on the ground, lying on his side. Tarani was kneeling behind him, touching the ugly, infected gash on the back of his neck with one hand. Her other hand was stroking his head slowly, smoothing the fur between his tapered ears.

While I stood there watching, the cat's labored breathing slowed and softened; his limbs moved slightly as the muscles relaxed into Tarani's hypnotic sleep.

I could resist or accept Tarani's powers. This one I had accepted, benefited from, and enjoyed. It had become harder to resist, and right then I had to shake my head to keep from falling under the spell of her rich, compelling voice.

When Tarani had finished, she stood up and came over to me. She touched my arm and led me away from the house so our voices wouldn't disturb the sleeping cat.

"It would be hypocritical of me, now," she said, "to question your decision, Rikardon. But I am concerned for Ronar and Thymas. You must know that they really aren't ready to travel."

"Tell me something," I said. "Was it easier to put Thymas and Ronar to sleep tonight?"

"Yes," she answered, after thinking about it for a minute. "Yes, it was."

"Staying here was tearing Thymas apart inside, Tarani. He

wanted us to get going, but didn't want to be left behind. His sense of duty was in conflict with his desires. And that was another source of guilt for him.

"Sitting still is hard for a man like Thymas. That inner turmoil had to be interfering with your healing. Now that he knows we're all going to *do* something—and now that he and I know where we stand—I'm hoping he'll mend faster."

She laughed and shook her head as she took two quick steps forward. The window's light cast a golden sheen on her fine-boned, pale face as she turned toward me.

"Why is it, Rikardon," she said, "that I have the mind-gift, yet you read people more clearly than I?"

She was not speaking of telepathy. She meant what Ricardo would call intuition, or empathy, and what Markasset would define as a strong link with the All-Mind: an ability to compare an individual's actions and attitudes to a wide spectrum of experiences, and to define his motivation.

If Markasset had such a link, it was entirely subconscious in Rikardon. But Ricardo hadn't lived for sixty years without learning something about people. Gandalarans weren't human, physically—their body and facial construction differed slightly from *Homo sapiens*—but their mental and emotional patterns were very human.

"Perhaps it's because I'm older, Tarani."

"You're referring to your . . . other lifetime?"

"Yes."

"What was it like?"

I shrugged. "Ordinary." I felt the usual twinge at the deception; I let her assume that we shared the same heritage. "I was something of a scholar, something of a fighter."

I was grateful that she didn't pursue her curiosity. She merely nodded. "I expect it was the second one that lets you see what Thymas is feeling."

"I . . . can appreciate something else he feels," I said. *What the hell am I doing?* I asked myself.

"The sha'um," I stammered lamely, and too late.

"Don't back away from it, Rikardon," she said quietly. "You and I—we need to 'know where we stand', too."

She was right, of course. And in the lamplight—in any light—she was beautiful. Even Ricardo would have appreciated Tarani's slim, dancer's body, the high-cheekboned face. She shared the patrician looks of the Lords of Eddarta, which were closer to human facial features. The wide tusks that took the place of canine teeth were there, still, but the supraorbital ridge was less pronounced, the face more narrow. Her unusual dark head fur and the glow of power in her eyes set off her striking appearance—even now, with refracted candlelight wavering across her face.

"Before I walked into Thymas's life, he had everything, Tarani. The respect of the Riders, a guarantee of the future he had aimed for all his life, a woman he hoped to marry. I'm not responsible for the upheaval he has lived through in these past weeks, but I am associated with it.

"He and I made a start, this afternoon, toward—well, not friendship. Call it noncompetition. If I were to . . . say certain things to you right now, that balance would be destroyed."

Her back stiffened. "You seem to know so well what Thymas feels," she said. "Assuming that I am no more than a prize for a footrace, does he think he can still compete for me?"

"You know I didn't mean it that way. Thymas has an abundance of pride. I think he's accepted the fact that the woman he loved was only one dimension of the complex Tarani he's getting to know now. But he knows—more importantly, you and I know—that, within the limits of the personality you showed him, you really did love Thymas.

"Maybe you still do."

"Yes," she admitted, and her stiff posture relaxed. "At least, I still care for him insofar that I would not wish him any further hurt. I do see your point. It is one thing that I have turned away from him. It would be quite another if I turned to you. It would disturb him and disrupt the healing process."

"And we need Thymas healthy when we meet Gharlas," I agreed.

She shook her head. "Your concern goes deeper than that," she said. "I can read that much, at least. In spite of all the trouble he has been to you, in your own way, you care for Thymas, too."

"I said we have ridden together. You know Thymas, and the Sharith."

"A bond of loyalty," she said. Abruptly, she took a couple of paces, then came back.

"I confess that I feel drawn to you, Rikardon. It may be no more than curiosity. It may be a kinship created by what we are trying to do. It may be gratitude for your compassion toward Thymas, and Volitar. Whatever is causing it, the attraction is there, and it is better that we recognize and control it.

"I think you and I must 'stand' apart, for now."

She walked away, leaving me feeling uncertain as to whether something had been settled . . . or begun.

The next morning, Tarani and I walked downhill to the market area of the city, and bought the few supplies we thought we would need. We were still Molik's guests, though the coins Tarani had grabbed out of his lockbox after Thymas had killed the roguelord were dwindling fast. I had been wishing that we could buy some extra clothes to take along, but it looked as though we couldn't quite afford it.

Tarani was holding the parcels which contained bread and dried meat. When she saw me counting, she said: "You are welcome to use Volitar's money."

I pulled the drawstrings of the pouch and tucked it into my belt. Then I picked up my parcels—fruit and the roast fowl we would eat on the first night—and led her away from the market stall.

"Thank you, Tarani," I said, "but I don't think that's wise. Why didn't your uncle—"

"My *father*," she corrected me, with sudden sharpness.

"Why didn't Volitar spend them?" I asked, after a second or two. "You said yourself, he never lived more than comfortably."

"They are Eddartan coins," she said. "Perhaps they were a memento of . . ."

Her voice trailed off, and I knew she was thinking about the mother she had never met. It was a romantic notion, that Volitar had kept that wealth secret, in memory of Zefra. It seemed to be a romantic story, what we knew of it. I knew Tarani believed she would meet her mother in Eddarta. I hoped, for Tarani's sake, that such a meeting would live up to her expectations.

"Volitar showed his love for Zefra in much more concrete ways, Tarani. I think he held on to those coins because spending them would be dangerous."

"But I have seen many Eddartan coins in Dyskornis, Rikardon."

"Gold twenty-*dozak* pieces? Bearing Pylomel's likeness?" I asked.

"I haven't seen many of the gold pieces, but . . . no, now that I think of it, I don't think I've ever seen coins like the ones we found with Zefra's letter. Do you think Volitar was afraid he could be traced here, if he spent the coins?"

I nodded.

"Then what shall *we* do with them?"

"Take them with us."

We were still in the marketplace, and just then I spotted a stall with leather goods and tanned, uncut skins.

"Here, hold these a minute," I said, and walked over to the leather dealer, who was seated under an awning supported by thin poles. On the ground around him were his wares. The worked goods—boots, belts, baldrics, vlek harnesses—were displayed on colored cloths. The skins—taken from *glith*, the deer-size food animal—were laid out in long lines, overlapped slightly so that a portion of each skin was visible. I walked around, bending over to look at the skins. When I found what I wanted, I sat down.

The dealer, who hadn't said a word (although he'd kept a wary eye on me), suddenly came to life.

"Yes, sir, how may I serve you this morning?"

I touched the glith skin I'd selected, asked him the price, and we started haggling.

"Sorry I took so long," I said, when I got back to Tarani with my new purchase. I took some of the bundles back, and we started walking northward, heading back to Volitar's shop. Tarani took the skin, which the dealer had rolled and tied, and looked it over skeptically.

"This is ugly," she said finally. "Thin and discolored—surely you could have afforded a better one. What are you going to do with it?"

At that moment, we were moving through the shopping crowd. "That's going to give me something to do along the way," I said. "Let's hurry, shall we? If we don't get back soon, Thymas is liable to leave without us."

She laughed at that, and I took pleasure in the sound of her laughter.

But I hadn't been far wrong. Thymas was waiting, with

Ronar, at the downhill entrance to the living quarters attached to Volitar's shop. He had our saddlebags and backpacks laid out on the ground, open and ready for packing.

"Half the day is gone," he complained, reaching for the food parcels. "Is this all we're taking?"

"Put the food in the backpack, Thymas. You can put this—" I handed him the leather. "—in your bags with the cargo net. Tarani, if you don't mind, may we take some of Volitar's clothes along? And will you bring down the things in Volitar's chest?"

She paused at the door. "All of them?"

"Yes, the duplicate Ra'ira, too. Gharlas wanted it badly enough to kill Volitar for it. That makes it valuable to us." When she had gone in, I turned to Thymas.

"How are you doing—and tell me the truth."

He started to say something, stopped, and began again. "I still have some pain," he admitted.

Probably hurt you more to say that, *than your side hurts you,* I thought.

"Ronar will be suffering for a while, yet, too. To start out, Keeshah will carry Tarani and me, and the heavy supplies. You and Ronar can have both sets of sidebags, with the lighter stuff in them. We have three days of supplies here, and we're going to take all that time to get to the nearest town—Krasa, I think it is. We'll restock there. We'll stop when I say so. Agreed?"

"I've already agreed," he snapped. "How long before we'll reach Eddarta?"

"I figure it at around eighteen days—we should be a full seven-day ahead of Gharlas."

"And what then?" he demanded.

"I don't know yet," I said. "We have eighteen days to think about it. The more we rest, at the beginning, the greater our strength will be when we get there."

Thymas concentrated on his packing for a few seconds, then sat back and rubbed his hands across his trousers in a rare display of nervousness. But his voice was steady as he said: "A second rider is a strain for a sha'um during a long trip. When Ronar is feeling stronger, Tarani can ride with me half the time." He paused. "If she wants to." He paused again. "*Will* she want to?"

Tarani came out, carrying Volitar's chest in her hands, several tunics and trousers over one arm.

"Ask her, when the time comes," I said. "Now, let's get packed and on our way."

4

The map showed Krasa to be a little over six man-days—I figured a man-day to be around thirty miles—away from Dyskornis. In good health and at top speed, a sha'um could cover the same distance in a third of a man's walking time, but I had meant what I said to Thymas. We took it easy, rising after dawn, camping well before night, and taking long rests for the midday meal. Tarani put Thymas and Ronar to sleep each night; Tarani, Keeshah, and I shared the watch.

I might have relied on Keesah's more efficient senses to alert us to any danger, but I felt more comfortable with a self-involved security plan.

You might say I was feeling paranoid.

Thanks to our noisy encounter with Gharlas and the greedy thief who had tried to kill me, the entire rogueworld of Dyskornis knew who I was. Worfit's reward for my death, and the acquisition of Serkajon's steel sword, were strong incentives for someone to follow us.

I was looking for danger up ahead, too. I believed we were doing the right thing, or we wouldn't be doing it. But the possibility that Gharlas *knew* what we were doing was a constant worry, no matter how often I told myself that worrying wouldn't solve anything.

Direct telepathy between Gandalarans was nearly unknown—but Gharlas said that the Ra'ira granted that power. I had to believe him. He'd said he had learned about the locked room where the Ra'ira was kept by reading Thanasset's mind. He had known about Rikardon without being told—I assumed that he had tried to read Markasset and had sensed the change.

I was fairly sure that he *couldn't* read me, or Tarani. She had proved in Dyskornis that her power could resist his. But that didn't let out the possibility of his being able to locate us, merely by the difference of our mind-patterns, or whatever. And it didn't protect us from Gharlas reading Thymas, who was more susceptible than either one of us.

So, useless as it was, I worried that Gharlas had traps laid for us ahead.

But I didn't waste my time worrying. By the time we reached Krasa, I had cut strips from the thin piece of leather to fashion a belt. I worked the coins into the long pocket one at a time; when no more would fit, we buried the rest of them.

I was wearing that fortune in gold around my waist when I walked into Krasa to renew our supplies. The weight was a burden at first, but it gave me a feeling of satisfaction, that I had devised a way to conceal those coins. I wasn't entirely sure why I felt it necessary to take them to Eddarta, but I hadn't questioned the impulse.

We had left green, hilly forests behind in Eddarta, and spent nearly two days in what I can only describe as scrub brush—not quite desert, but close. As we neared Krasa, the growth had turned green again, and I was walking through a lightly overgrown forest. There were wild *dakathrenil* here, the curly-trunked trees which, near Raithskar, were trained to an umbrella shape slightly taller than a man. Left to themselves, these wild ones sprawled on the ground like woody vines.

There were other kinds of trees here, too, and a variety of vines and flowers that I couldn't identify. I felt a familiar frustration over Markasset's disinterest in anything besides fighting, gambling, and Illia. This was a beautiful area, no less dramatic because it stood close in the shadow of the Great Wall.

I had already learned that the Great Wall was more or less a convention of Gandalaran thinking. Behind Raithskar, there was actually a *wall*—a sheer escarpment that vanished into overcast sky. Here, however, there were merely impassable mountains, and those not noticeably steeper than the Korchis west of Dyskornis. Yet these mountains were considered to be a continuation of Raithskar's barrier, and the Korchis a range of mountains.

I was learning to accept those conventions, just as I had

accepted the physical aspects of my situation. My body wasn't human—*Homo sapiens* would have been desiccated in hours by the intense desert heat that I hardly noticed anymore. I could accept the fact that I would probably never find out *how* Ricardo had been transferred to this world. But there was one mystery that returned to plague me again and again: Where *was* Gandalara?

I took so many things for granted in Gandalara that I often wondered why I couldn't just let *this* mystery lie, why the question circled around at the back of my mind and popped up at idle moments. I supposed it was this world's physical character, and its intriguing similarities to, and differences from, Ricardo's earth.

The evolution of such similar species on two different worlds seemed impossible. It was coincidental, too, that Gandalara had a single moon and a twenty-eight-day lunar cycle. Yet Gandalara had too high levels of salt in its soil, and too little access to iron. And there was definitely *no* physical feature like the Great Wall anywhere in Ricardo's world.

Today I resolutely set aside the puzzle, so that I could enjoy my walk through the woods.

I heard a hooting call, and looked up to see Lonna, Tarani's bird companion, flying overhead. She swooped down and settled carefully on my shoulder, her big wings folding so that their tips crossed at the base of her tail. She was heavy, but I didn't mind—in fact, I was pleased that she had chosen me for company. I stroked the feathers on her breast as I walked, and she made a sound that was both mournful and contented.

You don't mind if I make a friend of Lonna, do you, Keeshah? I asked.

Girl is my friend, he pointed out, reminding me of a best-forgotten period of unrecognized jealousy. **Bird, too.**

Lonna left me when Krasa came into sight through the trees. It was a small town, built mostly of wood and baked clay—the sort of place where you're a stranger until your family has lived there for three generations.

I had all the supplies I planned to buy, and was leaving a bakery with fresh meat pastries, when someone behind me called my name.

"Rikardon?"

The voice wasn't familiar; the man it belonged to was walking toward me. He was short but stocky, with prominent supraorbital ridges, not much nose, and a whole lot of scars on his arms and face.

I had heard no threat in his voice, but I turned around and kept my hand near my sword as I answered.

"I am Rikardon. May I ask who you are?"

The scarred face creased into a smile. "You can ask me, or anyone in Krasa, son. My name is Ligor, and I'm what passes for the Chief of Peace and Security in this city. I have a message for you—from Zaddorn. And some free advice—from me. Join me for a drink?"

"Sure. How about that place on the corner?"

"Good choice," he said, and we moved along the packed-dirt surface of the street toward what Ricardo would have called a diner. It served light meals that could be eaten on the premises or taken outside, provided you left a deposit on the dishes. It also served *faen*, the Gandalaran equivalent of beer, as did almost every restaurant.

It was just past midday, and there was a late-lunch crowd keeping the help busy. The number of people surprised me, and I resolved never to judge a town by its appearance again. Krasa looked to be a pretty lively place.

Ligor caught the eye of one of the workers behind the service counter, and two earthenware mugs of faen appeared on a table at the back of the room, even before we could work our way through to it.

I was impressed.

"Zaddorn doesn't even know I'm in Krasa—yet," I said, thinking of the message I had sent from Dyskornis. Thanasset would tell Zaddorn where I was, so that he wouldn't be expecting me any day, to fill the job he had offered me.

"True," Ligor said. He opened a pouch at his belt, and took out a fragile-looking letter. The thin paper had been folded umpteen times, obviously in order to be suitable for a maufa to carry it. "Read this," Ligor said. "Easier than my telling you."

I unfolded it, and leaned toward the window to get more light on the angular Gandalaran characters.

> *Ligor, old friend, I need your help. A caravan master named Gharlas stole something important, something you'll recognize if you see it. He's a dangerous man, and it's imperative that he be stopped*

before he reaches Eddarta. I doubt that he'll come by your way, but if you hear anything at all of his movements, please let me know.

There's another person you might encounter, a fellow named Rikardon. You'll recognize him, too—you knew him as Markasset. He left Raithskar today, and he may be following Gharlas. If you see him, trust him and help him all you can. And tell him, for me, that he's got the job, like it or not. I'm telling all my contacts to give him full cooperation.

Terrific, I thought. *Now I'm a deputy sheriff.*

"So this is the message," I said. "Now what's the advice?"

"Just this, son. Don't rely on any of that help he promised. Zaddorn doesn't know anything about this side of the world."

"How do you know Zaddorn? And—I'm sorry, but I don't remember you."

"Not much reason you should. It was always Zaddorn tagging after me, not the Supervisor's son." He took a sip of his faen. "I used to have Zaddorn's job."

"He mentioned he took office just after Ferrathyn succeeded Bromer as Chief Supervisor."

"Yeah. Ferrathyn fired me."

I searched Markasset's memory for Raithskarian law. "He couldn't do that himself, could he?"

"No, it was all proper, with unanimous approval of the Council. But it was Ferrathyn who started it. I bear no grudge, mind you—it wasn't just because the old man and I didn't get on well, though that was for sure true. Mostly it was because I didn't fit the Peace and Security image the Council wanted for Raithskar. I did my job, but I didn't do it . . ."

He struggled to find the right word, and I provided one that seemed to fit: "Gracefully."

He laughed and slapped the table. "That's it, exactly."

"I didn't mean—"

"Don't worry about it, son. I know what I am, and what I'm not. Graceful, I'm not. I've got a lot of blunt edges. Zaddorn's a good man, keen as a sword. He cuts cleanly what I'd bruise to death.

"But, to get back to that free advice, he's got his limitations, too. One is, he trusts too much."

"*Zaddorn?*"

"Oh, not people in general. Nobody works in our business without getting to be naturally suspicious of everybody. But he thinks every Peace Officer is respected, and has the kind of authority he has, with the Council to back him up."

"And you're telling me he's wrong?"

Ligor lifted his empty mug, and the same waiter appeared to refill both our drinks. The crowd was thinning out, and we could converse more comfortably.

"I'm telling you just that. He has his little list of Peace and Security Officers, and he writes to them, and he expects them all to be as conscientious and powerful as he is. He's got a security force of better than two hundred men. How many men you think I got working for me?"

I didn't have to think hard; he'd already telegraphed the answer. "None," I said, and he nodded.

"And I'm one of the good guys, the ones who try. Zaddorn's other 'contacts'— some of them have moved, or they're dead. Some of them might try to stop Gharlas, all right. They've got their own 'contacts' that can sell any . . . *important* thing they might find on his body."

"Say it straight, Ligor," I said, a little impatiently.

"All right. What Zaddorn did, with letters like this," he tapped the parchment I still held in my hand, "is warn the whole countryside that you're on your way to Eddarta. Stay away from those Peace and Security people. If they cooperate with anybody, it will be Worfit."

"The reward." In a flash vision, I saw the bloody face of the man who had tried to kill me for that same reward. I remembered the resistance against my sword as its blade passed through his body. I closed my eyes to block the vision.

After a moment, Ligor said: "You still going?"

"To Eddarta? Yes." I drained my mug, stood up, and reached for my pouch. He put his hand out to stop me.

"No, you're my guest, son. Free food and faen are part of my wages. I don't often stand host; there aren't many folk around that I'd care to drink with. Zaddorn is one. Now there are two." He stood up, slapped my arm, and gripped it for a moment. "Stay alive, boy. I'm looking forward to our next drink together."

5

I'm not paranoid, I thought. *Everybody really* is *out to get me*.

It was the second morning after my talk with Ligor. We were camped within walking range of Grevor, and Thymas had just now left, on his way into town. I wouldn't say his exit had been graceful. "Snarly" might describe it better.

"What is *wrong* with him?" Tarani demanded. She was standing in the middle of the clearing, staring after the boy. "His body gets better, and his temper gets worse. Surely he knows the walk will help him." She put her hands on her hips and looked speculatively at me. "You know, don't you? What *is* wrong?"

I shrugged. "He didn't believe a word I said."

"It made perfect sense to me," she said. "I think you are right about Gharlas—if he left traps for us, I would be his main target. And your friend in Krasa warned you that every town has been alerted to watch for you. So Thymas is the only one left who can get supplies. How can he not agree with that reasoning?"

"I didn't say that he didn't see the logic of the arguments," I answered. "He wouldn't have gone at all, in that case. What I mean is, he doesn't believe that any of that covers the real reason why I wanted him to go into town this time."

"Then what *does* he think?" she asked.

Can she really not know? I wondered. *Sometimes she's twenty, going on forty-five, and other times she's so naive . . .*

"That I wanted to be alone with you."

"That's ridiculous," she snorted. "You *are* alone with me, every night. There's nothing much that can wake him, once he's in the healing sleep."

"Maybe that's what's bothering him," I said.

She stared at me in confusion for the space of a heartbeat, then blushed clear up to her widow's peak of dark, silky headfur. "Perhaps," she said, sounding dangerous, "we should have a talk, the three of us, when Thymas returns."

"Ordinarily, I'd say that was a good idea. But not this time. His jealousy is only part of what's causing his mood, Tarani. The main thing is that he isn't *in control* of any aspect of this situation. He can't make his body heal any faster. He agreed to take my orders, but he doesn't much like doing it. He hates seeing you ride with me, but he knows you have to until Ronar gets stronger. And he can't hurry that along, either."

Tarani's arms dropped to her sides, and her eyes snapped wide open. "You mean that he will *let* me ride with him? That Ronar will accept me?"

"He said as much, before we left Dyskornis. I believe him. But he did seem to have some doubt as to whether you'd want to ride with him."

"Want to? Of course I do." She stopped, then fumbled on. "I mean—Keeshah could use the rest."

I smiled, and said: "Don't back away from it, Tarani."

She recognized the quote, and suddenly started to laugh. "All right, then, we shall be honest with one another. How will you feel, when I ride with Thymas?"

I sighed. "Jealous," I admitted. She laughed again, then sobered when I threw her question back to her: "How will you feel?"

She thought about it before she answered. "Proud that Thymas would accept me. Pleased for him, that he could make such a major change in his thinking. And I suppose I would feel . . . close to him. Do you understand?"

"I think so," I said.

It's ironic, really, I thought, *that Thymas is jealous of me. Riding may involve a lot of physical contact, but with me, it can only stimulate Tarani's imagination. With him, it will bring back memories. That gives him an edge I can't hope to overcome.*

Keeshah, I called. **Feel like going for a run?**

Both? he asked.

No, just me.

He came out of the forest, shaking his head as an ear brushed against a low branch. Tarani went to him and stroked the fur along his cheek. He put up with it for only a few seconds before pulling away and crouching to let me mount.

I thought for a moment that Tarani felt insulted. Then she smiled, and I decided I must have been mistaken.

"I can see that I'm not the one you want to yourself, Rikardon."

I sat down on Keeshah's back, and he stood up. "I'll be back soon," I promised. "Keeshah's itching for a run; that's all."

She said: "I understand."

I lay forward and grabbed the fur on either side of the cat's wide shoulders, and I tucked up my legs so that my feet rested just in front of his haunches. It felt strange, riding without the warm weight of Tarani's body across my back.

She can come too, Keeshah told me, sensing, as usual, the undercurrent of my feelings for Tarani.

I don't want her this time, I said, and hoped he would accept it. **Do you?**

No. Tired of walking. Want to RUN.

And he did.

At first, we crashed through trees and jumped over tangled brush, but it wasn't long before we were out in the near-desert that lurked at the edge of every watered area along the Great Wall. Then I reached out for Keeshah's mind, and we were one entity, pounding across the grayish sand on the sha'um's enormous paws.

The rhythm of his movement was as much a part of me as my own pulse. He felt the wind sweeping at me, and the way his fur felt against my cheek. It was a raw and natural and savage pleasure, the joy we shared when we ran together like this. When we returned to camp—much later than I had planned—we were both exhausted and exhilarated.

I hugged the big cat good-bye some distance from camp, and walked the rest of the way. I felt more relaxed than I had since the days I had spent in Thagorn, getting to know the Sharith lifestyle. Lonna greeted me, and I shouted a "hello" back at her.

Thymas had returned from Grevor, with fresh food for dinner. That—and the fact that he looked as though his walk had done him good—completed the good feeling that the run had kindled in me. After dinner, we discussed travel plans.

"The old couple who ran the meat shop said that there's a colony of vineh between here and Sulis," Thymas said.

"Wild ones?" I asked.

"Are there any other kind?"

Tarani's question was serious, and I realized that neither she nor Thymas had ever been to Raithskar. So I told them about the vineh who swept streets and paved roads and did other, fairly simple jobs under the supervision of their handlers. Tarani and Thymas looked skeptical.

"Why would I lie about it?" I asked.

"It's just that I can't imagine a trainable vineh," Thymas said. "Have you ever seen a wild one?"

"Not really," I answered, thinking of the scuffle I had witnessed in the streets of Raithskar, where a handler had almost gotten mauled by three of the curly haired, apish creatures. "What are they like?"

"Just hope you don't find out," Thymas said. "They said that this colony has a live-and-let-live attitude, *if* travelers stick to the road while they're crossing vineh territory. Anyplace off the road is a battle zone."

There was a problem with traveling the road. We were trying to keep the sha'um out of sight, and we didn't know how well traveled the road between Sulis and Grevor was. Thymas said that vineh denned in caves, so we decided to swing out south of the road and avoid their territory altogether.

It turned out to be pretty rough country, with lots of ground-hugging bushes that hid the actual contours of the land. But for this day only, I agreed to hurry. I glanced at Thymas and Ronar now and then, and was glad to see that they were handling the pace pretty well. In fact, I was looking back at them when the vineh attacked.

There were at least twenty of them, clawing their way out of an overgrown ravine and coming straight for us. There weren't any young ones, either; these were adult males, taller than a Gandalaran, at least as strong, with no sense of reason to which we might appeal.

They were out to get us.

In Ricardo's world, a mounted man had an advantage over infantry in that he could strike from above. But in Ricardo's world, the cavalry wasn't riding sha'um.

I can recall a second or two of the wildest ride I've ever had, as Keeshah roared his challenge, leaped forward, and slashed and snapped at the nearest four vineh. Then Tarani and I were left behind, rolling on the ground.

A vineh thudded down on top of me, his hands pulling at

my head and shoulder to get room for his underslung jaw to close on my throat. I curled up, got my knees under his hips, and pushed. I couldn't throw him off, but I managed to lift him enough to get my hands around his throat. His neck was so thick, the muscles so strong, that for a minute I was afraid I couldn't hurt him at all. Then my right thumb found a soft spot and dug in.

The beast made a strangling sound and grabbed my arms to stop the choking. I heaved with my legs; we rolled a couple of times, and I came out on top. Using the vineh's throat as a pivot, I jumped up and brought both knees down on his chest. I felt a rib crack, and the beast's eyes went glassy.

I drew my dagger and finished him, just as a hairy arm grabbed me around the throat and jerked, nearly twisting my head off. The pain and lack of air canceled out my eyesight, and I saw the swirling, undefined colors of unconsciousness closing in on me.

The pressure was released suddenly, and I could breathe. When my vision cleared, I saw Tarani pulling her sword out of a vineh's back. I got Rika up in time to stop another one from attacking her from behind.

"Where's Thymas?" I gasped.

"Over there." She tossed her head, then whirled to face a vineh who was trying to rush her from the side.

I looked in the direction she had indicated. Thymas had backed into the rocks, so that he stood in a shallow passage, and a frontal attack was the only kind possible. With sword and dagger, he was managing to hold off three vineh, but he was leaning to his right, to protect his wounded side, and his face was already gray with fatigue.

"*Rikardon*!" Tarani warned me. I ducked down and caught the running vineh across the middle with my shoulder. I intended to flip him over my back, but he was too heavy and my balance wasn't perfect, so we went down together, grappling. But I had knocked the wind from him; he didn't fight me as I used my dagger. Tarani guarded me as I stood up, and we discovered that we were alone among the fighting. Except for the three vineh keeping Thymas at bay, the rest of them were in two great snarling and snapping crowds roiling around the sha'um.

Keeshah was holding his own, whirling so quickly that the vineh were forced to keep their distance. But Ronar was slower, and the vineh were applying their favorite trick of attacking from behind. Even as we stood there, we saw four vineh converge on the cat's flanks. Ronar screamed in rage as teeth sank into his hindquarters, and he rolled over to get his hind claws into play.

Immediately, all ten or twelve vineh jumped the cat, trying to immobilize him with the sheer weight of their bodies. Tarani and I ran to help, leaping across the ring of dead beasts to harry the outer layer of Ronar's attackers. The vineh were so frenzied with the prospect of victory over the sha'um that they didn't notice us until we had killed two apiece. Then they turned and rushed us. Through the forest of curly haired bodies, I saw Ronar stagger to his feet. Clearly, he was close to exhaustion, but he lashed out at the nearest vineh, opening claw-gashes three inches deep across the beast's back.

Tarani and I tried to retreat, but the tangle of bodies provided unstable, blood-slick footing, and within seconds, we were surrounded.

It wasn't the first time I had reason to be grateful for the Gandalaran body I had "inherited." Young and fit, Markasset had been an expert swordsman, and his reflexes took over in times of physical danger. But I know I'd never have survived, that day, without Tarani to guard my back.

That's one I owe you, Thymas, I thought. *Thanks for teaching this woman to fight.*

With Ronar's help, we reduced our attack ground to five vineh. But Serkajon's sword was getting heavier by the minute, and my hands didn't want to hold on to it. Tarani seemed in as poor a shape as I felt; her clothes were bloody, her movements slowing.

The vineh who faced us now had been at the outer edge of the fighting, and were nearly fresh. They started closing in on us, and I knew we were in trouble. Worse, *they* knew it.

But Keeshah sensed it, too. He clawed his way through the three or four still dogging him, and launched himself, four sets of claws ready, at the group coming after us.

Once Keeshah, Tarani, and I were working together, it penetrated to the remaining vineh that they weren't winning.

It took long enough, I thought, as the seven or eight survivors scrambled back into the ravine. *We've been fighting for at least a year.*

I wanted to lie down and sleep, but there were other things to do first. I found Thymas in the rock niche where we had seen him fighting. He was hunched over and nearly unconscious.

"I think he's all right," I called to Tarani. "Scratched up pretty badly, but alive."

I hauled him up to his feet and put his arm around my shoulders. Tarani was trying to tend to Ronar, who was bleeding badly but too much in pain and shock to let her touch him. Thymas couldn't help control him—in fact, his dazed state was probably communicating itself to Ronar.

Keeshah, he has to lie down, or Tarani can't help him.

Keeshah's neck fur was still bristling from the excitement of the fight. Thymas's sha'um bristled and snarled in an automatic defense reflex when mine closed in, but couldn't offer much resistance. Keeshah wrestled Ronar to the ground and lay across his shoulders to keep him still while Tarani cleaned the deepest gashes on the cat's flanks.

I lowered Thymas to the ground and tended him as best I could. He was coming around by the time Tarani got up from Ronar and came over to us.

When Keeshah moved off of him, Ronar rolled up into a crouch and lay there panting. Keeshah cleaned himself—his wounds were mere scratches—and then worked his raspy tongue across the fur on Ronar's back, licking away the dirt and blood. He was careful not to disturb the ointment Tarani had applied to Ronar's flanks.

"We need to rest for a couple of days," I said, watching the sha'um. "But not here. Thymas, can Ronar walk?"

He closed his eyes for a moment, speaking to the great cat. "Yes. But not far." His hand, pitifully weak, closed on my arm. "This time, Rikardon, you don't have a choice. You have to leave us behind."

"You may be right, Thymas," I said, reluctantly. "But we still have a safety margin for beating Gharlas to Eddarta. We can afford a couple of slow days. If we *do* have to go on without you, at least we can leave you in a more hospitable place."

6

He didn't have the energy to argue. In fact, he'd been pushing his own and Ronar's reserves to keep up with the morning's fast pace. Now man and sha'um both were drained, physically and psychologically.

Ronar could barely walk; there was no question of Thymas riding him. I considered asking Keeshah to carry the Sharith boy, so that Tarani and I could keep our swords ready for another attack, but rejected the idea before it really took shape. Keeshah might not have objected—but it would have been a mortal blow to Ronar's pride, which was already down for the count. So Tarani and I traded off supporting Thymas while we all three walked, nervously, eastward toward Sulis. Keeshah circled warily around us and Lonna kept a lookout from the sky.

Thymas's informant had said the vineh lived "between Grevor and Sulis," so we couldn't be sure of being safe until we had actually reached the next town.

We didn't find it before nightfall. We took a brief rest, and Tarani asked Lonna to locate the town for us.

The bird reported that Sulis was close, and the way was fairly clear, so we dragged our weary bodies up once again and plodded on. We stopped just outside the city to find a concealed place for the sha'um to rest. Weary as she was, Tarani took the time to hum Ronar to sleep.

I will guard, and hunt, Keeshah told me. **This one will have meat at dawn; then I will rest.**

Good, Keeshah, I said. *We will all rest for a day, at least.**

Privately I thought: *They've come a long way—from fighting one another to taking care of each other.* I looked down at Thymas. Tarani's sleep spell had unintentionally zapped him, too. *But then,* I thought, pulling Thymas up from the ground and getting my shoulders under him, *Thymas and I are making the same kind of progress.*

I groaned as I lifted him. He wasn't as tall as Tarani, who was nearly eye-to-eye with me, but every inch of him was solid, hard-packed muscle. Thymas was a hefty chunk.

"Can you manage him alone?" Tarani asked, steadying me as I staggered a little.

"For a while, anyway," I grunted.

If Sulis had been one step further away, I wouldn't have made it. As it was, I stumbled into an inn and dumped Thymas on the registration table. The startled clerk didn't have to ask what had happened to us, but he was plainly curious about how we had survived an encounter with vineh.

"We *won't* survive, if we don't get some rest," Tarani said. "Will you help us take our friend to our room?"

"One room for the three of you?" the clerk asked, then seemed to realize that the question might be offensive. "That is—"

"*Yes*, one room for the three of us," Tarani said. "Please hurry."

It cost us the rest of our non-Eddartan cash, but that was the best night's sleep I ever had.

I didn't move until nearly noon the next day, and even though I was stiff and sore, thanks to the vineh and the strain of carrying Thymas, I woke up feeling confident.

Tarani and Thymas were still sleeping. I slid a single gold coin from my belt and went out of the room quietly. We'd need to eat, sometime between Sulis and Eddarta, and the Eddartan coins were now our only choice. We'd have to risk their being identified. I went in search of a moneychanger.

The man I found had never seen a coin exactly like it, and offered the opinion that it had been stamped to commemorate some occasion. But he shrugged and said: "Gold is gold, no matter whose face it wears." After he had taken his commission for changing the twenty-*dozak* piece, I had two hundred and thirty-eight *zaks*, in assorted coin sizes, available for spending. It was enough, easily, to manage the rest of the trip—depending on what I decided to do with Thymas.

He was going to have to stay behind and follow later; that much was clear. The exertion of the fight with the vineh had pushed both him and Ronar back to "square one", in terms of their recovering stamina and spirit.

Keeshah had to come with me, or our plan of laying some

kind of trap in Eddarta before Gharlas got there would be useless. But Tarani—did *she* have to come with me?

I mulled over the possible choices as I sat in the inn's dining room, sipping faen.

One, she could come with me, and leave Thymas to follow whenever he and Ronar could travel. Would Thymas wait until they were recovered? Or would he be just as heedlessly anxious to get going as he had been in Dyskornis, and arrive in Eddarta too weak to be any help at all? Worse than that, would he let his depression convince him that he might as well not follow at all?

Two, Tarani could stay with Thymas, so that he and Ronar would heal faster. Ronar would travel more slowly, carrying double, but they would be able to leave sooner.

I hate it, I thought, *but the second choice makes more sense. Are there any reasons why Tarani* shouldn't *stay behind with Thymas? Real reasons, that is—not jealous ones.*

There *was* one reason. Zefra.

I had considered Tarani's plan to find her mother as secondary to our need to find the Ra'ira. But if we could find Zefra, it was possible that she could *help* us against Gharlas.

If *Tarani* asked her.

I paid for my drink, and went upstairs to tell Tarani and Thymas what I had decided.

They didn't question it—Thymas would stay; Tarani would go. The only argument I got was, predictably, from Thymas.

"You will lose time if you move me elsewhere," he protested. "There is game here for Ronar, and I can rest here just as well as anywhere else. Pay the clerk for a few days of room and board, and go!"

"I *will not* leave you here, Thymas," I said. "You need experienced care, and a lot of rest. If you stayed here, you'd be on your guard all the time. We'll take you to a Refreshment House; you'll be safe with the Fa'aldu." I spread out the map, studied it for a moment, then tapped it with my finger. "Stomestad."

"Too far," Thymas snapped. "You'd lose three days, poking along at our speed."

"It would be straight across desert," Tarani mused. "A rough trip."

"We can stand a few days of desert travel," I said. "And Stomestad lies along the most direct route to Eddarta from here. Even if Tarani and I can't make up the lost time, we should still be able to reach Eddarta before Gharlas gets there. We'll go to Stomestad."

I was expecting desert, but not *that* desert. It made the Kapiral, with its stubborn, ground-hugging dry bushes, seem like paradise. *Nothing* grew in that wasteland. The air felt superheated, and the sand was so fine that we had to wrap our faces to keep from inhaling salty particles drifting in the air like dust motes.

By the time I realized what we were getting into, it was the middle of our second day, and too late to turn back. We adopted the travel pattern I had learned from Zaddorn: move for three hours, rest for one, the three of us hugging the shadows of the sha'um. Healthy sha'um could have run the trip from Sulis to Stomestad in two and a half days. It took us five days and nights of miserable tramping before we arrived at the symbolic canvas barrier of Stomestad.

It was mid-afternoon, and the sand shifted under our feet as we stood there, croaking the ritual request for shelter. Vasklar, Respected Elder of the Refreshment House, granted our request and ordered that the symbolic canvas barrier be lowered to admit us. He stared at us in shock for a moment, then hurried his people to help us.

The Refreshment House of Stomestad was the largest I had yet seen. It was enclosed in the same way as all the others I had visited, with a head-high wall of large bricks of rock salt. The interior compound, where the extended family group of desert dwellers lived, seemed much larger than those I had seen at Yafnaar and Relenor.

The Fa'aldu provided most travelers with sparing accommodations—mere cubicles with sleeping ledges and plain pallets. The small rooms opened directly on the enclosed courtyard where, on any given night, there might be twenty to a hundred vleks stamping and bawling. Travelers were also given water and cooked food, all in trade for some kind of goods—food products, fabric, crafted articles.

Across the long, rectangular court were doorways which opened into the family residence area.

I was one of the few travelers ever invited into the Fa'aldu homes—a privilege for which I often thanked Balgokh, the Elder at Yafnaar, who had been Ricardo's first source of information in Gandalara. Balgokh didn't know the truth about me; he believed that Markasset had awakened in the desert without his memory, and had later regained it. He had taken a fatherly pride in my possession of Serkajon's sword, and had accepted, without question, Thanasset's decision to implement the old custom of changing a son's name when he has proved himself ready to carry the family's sword.

It was part of the obligation of the Fa'aldu, assumed during the time of the Kingdom, to assist anyone in need in the desert. But I thought that Balgokh had helped me willingly, because he had sensed something of my difference from other Gandalarans. So I had returned to Yafnaar to give him a resolution to the mystery I had started. Balgokh had appreciated that gesture so much that he had sent word to all the Refreshment Houses, asking that I be honored as a fellow Fa'aldu.

And, as a side effect, making me into a legend.

When we surrendered our weapons and gave our names, the whole family came out to help.

The respect of the Stomestad Fa'aldu embarrassed me, but I didn't hesitate to take advantage of it. Fa'aldu children dusted us off with stiff-bristled brushes, and gave us a little water. Then Tarani took Thymas into a cubicle to tend him, while I arranged for meat and water for the sha'um, and had a talk with Vasklar.

Thymas's wounds, though deeper and nastier looking than the bruises and scratches Tarani and I had suffered, had been reduced to thin scabs after the two nights he spent in Sulis under Tarani's healing sleep, but the trek across the desert had reopened some of the worse ones. The salty grit that covered us from head to foot had crusted in the bloody scars, even though we had used some of our precious water to clean them whenever we rested. The edges of the opened wounds looked swollen and inflamed, even after they had been cleansed.

I went into Thymas's cubicle just as Tarani was using the last of her supply of soothing ointment on Thymas's nastiest gash. It started beneath his right ear, and slid down his neck and across the right side of his chest. She was sitting on the sleeping ledge with her back to me, blocking sight of Thymas's face, but I could see most of his body. She left her hands on his chest after she finished, moving them in small circles, massaging lightly. He said something too softly for me to hear it, and she laughed.

"I need to talk to Thymas for a minute," I said. She jumped, then stood up and left the room, turning back once to smile at the boy.

"I guess you know that Ronar is doing pretty well," I said, sitting down where Tarani had been. I could feel her warmth in the thin padding of the pallet, even on the surface of the huge block of rock salt beneath it. Thymas watched me warily, waiting. "Tarani's ointment matted his fur over those really bad cuts, and kept out the dust. They're starting to heal. I want you to stay here until you both feel *fit* to travel—got that?"

The boy nodded, and winced with the pain the motion cost him.

"Tarani will help you and Ronar sleep tonight—that should give you a good start on getting well. Vasklar will take good care of you, and he will give you whatever provisions you need when you're ready to go. Wait until Ronar can travel full speed, and ride directly for Eddarta."

"Where will you be?" he asked.

"Tarani and Keeshah and I will leave in the morning for the Refreshment House of Iribos. Vasklar gave me the name of one of the Fa'aldu there who can tell us about Eddarta. When we have some kind of a plan, Tarani will send Lonna to you with the details. If you need to contact us, send Lonna back—she'll be able to find Tarani, no matter where we are."

"All right," he sighed, and closed his eyes. There were creases of weariness radiating from their corners.

"One more thing, and I'll let you get some rest," I said.

He opened his eyes and looked at me again. I didn't have a clue as to what he was thinking.

"I'm going to leave Serkajon's sword here, where it will be safe, and where it can't identify me. I'll take yours in its place."

He didn't say anything, and after a second or two, I stood up.

"See you in Eddarta," I said, and went out into the courtyard.

I had supper with Vasklar's family, but Tarani had declined their invitation, pleading fatigue. The Refreshment House wasn't crowded, so Vasklar had given each of us a separate sleeping room. As I crossed the lamp-lit courtyard, I noticed light around the edges of the tapestry hanging which served as a door to Thymas's room.

Tarani said she was going to eat, put Thymas to sleep, and then get some sleep, herself, I remembered. *It's late—she probably left the lamp burning by accident.*

I stepped to the door and pulled aside the curtain. Tarani was seated in the same place; I couldn't see her face, or Thymas's. But as I watched, too startled to move, his hand touched her arm and moved along it slowly until he was holding her shoulder. She leaned forward, and both of his arms embraced her.

I dropped the curtain and moved away quietly.

7

"We're here," I said to Tarani, who had been struggling along stubbornly against her weariness, staring at the ground. We had left Keeshah where desert and the far end of a branch of the Tashal River merged to form a treacherous salt bog. For two days, we had walked through farmland. With every step, I had been forced to revise my impression of the size of Eddarta. A city which needed this much produce to feed its people must include a sizable collection of individuals.

Tarani's head lifted, and together we stared at the huge, strange city. Following the directions we had been given, we were approaching from the northwest along a well-traveled road that bordered the westernmost branch of the river. After many intersections, this road would lead us into the city—or, rather into *part* of the city.

There were two Eddartas. The original, older city sprawled on the lower slopes of the River Wall and drifted out toward the fields in strings and clumps of tiny buildings. Several branches of the Tashal flowed and rushed through the city itself, and the largest streets followed along beside them. All those wide boulevards merged into a paved avenue that led uphill to the second Eddarta.

This was a stone-walled enclosure entirely separate from

what I had already begun to think of as "lower" Eddarta. Its only links to the bigger town were the steep avenue and a single branch of the Tashal which meandered along the upper city's level, but tumbled in sparkling cataracts above and below it. The lower rapids came straight down the hill, beside the entry avenue.

"I didn't expect it to be so large," Tarani said, after a moment.

"Neither did I," I admitted. "But remember, we already know where to find the people we want to see."

"Inside those walls," Tarani said. There was no awe, or fear, just the statement. I knew she was thinking about her mother, but she said: "Do you think we have arrived before Gharlas?"

"Unless he learned how to fly these past three days, we're at least two days ahead of him. But just in case . . . do you think you can disguise us until we're safely in Yoman's shop? He said that guards are along the roads to check people going *out*, but if Gharlas sent word ahead . . ."

"I can do it," she said. "Before we approach the guards, we will need to move off the road, out of sight, for a moment. Then stay very close to me; it will be harder if we are separated."

A quarter of an hour later, the road turned to follow a branch of the river. Its banks were lined with tall, reedy plants, and Tarani stepped into the concealment they offered. I waited a moment, then followed her. We stepped out together.

When I looked at Tarani, I could see the illusion she cast for herself—the pale-haired, rounded body of Rassa. I could see Tarani through it, as though the image of Rassa were only a transparent hologram, but I was sure that everyone else who looked directly at Tarani, would see only Rassa. I assumed that I would pass for Yoman.

We had met those two people at the Refreshment House of Iribos, after explaining what we needed to the person Vasklar had named. I had been astonished to learn that our Iribos contact and Vasklar were both involved in providing an escape route for Eddartan slaves. It was strictly in violation of the nointerference rules of the Fa'aldu, but I had commended their courage.

Yoman and Rassa weren't slaves, but craftsmen—clothing

designers, specifically. They were "free" to work for pay, as long as they turned over a high percentage of their profit to the Lord who owned the property on which their shop was located.

It appealed strongly to Tarani that they had tired of their life in Eddarta, and decided to escape from it, much as Volitar had escaped years ago. How they had known whom to contact in Iribos was a mystery, but arrangements had been made for them to be "registered" with a caravan leaving the following day. Pylomel had informants everywhere, it seemed, who were on the lookout for unattached people who might be wanted in Eddarta. Such informants undoubtedly had been responsible for Zefra's identification in Dyskornis.

We had found it necessary to reveal Tarani's skill at illusion. After our contact recovered from the shock, the two Eddartans had been brought to us. They represented an opportunity to enter Eddarta without question. Tarani and I would have a place to stay, and real identities to conceal us.

Yoman, who was as tall as I, middle-aged, with a touch of softness around his stomach, had assured me that their short absence could be explained easily as a trip to visit an ill relative, should anyone inquire. He had given us that, and other, information in response to our questions, and he had volunteered little else.

Rassa, his daughter, had said nothing at all. She was a physical type that Tarani could imitate easily. As tall as Tarani, she had the same smooth brow and delicate planes at cheek and jaw. It was obvious that the two women shared some genes. But where Tarani's headfur was black and silky, Rassa's was thick and golden. Body curves at breast and hip were more pronounced in Rassa, and she walked with an unconscious sensuality that wasn't damaged at all by her haunting beauty.

Yoman and Rassa had become our key to Eddarta, and we had sent Lonna to Thymas with instructions to look for us at Yoman's tailor shop when he reached Eddarta. But I was uneasy as we walked within Tarani's illusion. I couldn't rid myself of the feeling that the merchant had been holding something back, that he had been running from Eddarta for a reason more specific than weariness of his lifestyle.

I didn't want to be recognized as Rikardon. But I was

halfway expecting some hassle when I was recognized as Yoman.

That danger didn't materialize, much to my relief. A couple of people said hello, but in the crowded streets, with folks hurrying to get home before dark, there wasn't time to do much more than wave and smile. By the time we located Yoman's shop, staggered through the doors and closed them behind us, I was a bundle of exposed nerves.

"Who is it? Who is there?" The quavering voice came from a man at the top of a flight of stairs that ended just to our right. He was silhouetted against a small window which let in some light from the street lamps below. He was a small man, and looked frail. He was wearing only a pair of trousers, tied with drawstrings at waist and ankles, and I could see the outline of his ribs.

I squeezed Tarani's hand. "He can't see us. Can you give me Yoman's voice?" I whispered. She returned the pressure, and I cleared my throat loudly.

"Who am I? Yoman, that's who! Now who are you, in my shop this time of night?"

"Yoman?" the voice whined. "Yoman, it is Bress, your good friend! Wait, I'll get a lamp . . ."

Bress. Yoman mentioned him—another fabric merchant.

"Bress!" I bellowed. "I need no lamp to see what is going on here! I am gone a few days, and you move in to take over my shop!" I started up the stairs, stomping heavily. The skinny old man whimpered with fright.

"No, I moved in here to *protect* your shop, Yoman! I didn't know where you had gone—someone else might have—"

I was near the top of the stairs, drawing Tarani up right behind me. The old man was holding a lamp base and struggling with a scissor-shaped sparker.

"No one else needed to," I yelled, causing the little guy to drop the bronze platform onto the hallway table. The fall jarred the glass chimney, which had been set aside, off balance; it toppled, rolled off the table, and made a nerve-jangling noise as it shattered. Bress jumped two feet into the air and completely lost his nerve.

"Please, Yoman, I meant no harm. You went away and left no word, you know how small my shop is, we have been friends, I didn't want them to think it was abandoned—"

"Out!" I said. I grabbed one thin arm and propelled the

man toward the stairs, turning Tarani behind me to keep her hidden. "And be thankful you still have your head. Rassa and I have traveled a long, hard way this day. Anything you moved *in*, you can move *out* tomorrow."

The little man dived halfway down the stairs, clutched at the railing to save himself, and stumbled the rest of the way. At the door, he paused to look up. I could barely see him.

"Rassa is with you?" he said in surprise. "But I thought surely . . ." I took the first step down, and he hurriedly opened the door. "No matter, Yoman, it's none of my affair. But—I do mean this, my friend—I *am* glad you've come to your senses. All we heard were rumors, remember." He ducked out the door.

I wonder what he meant by that? I thought, as I turned back to Tarani—just in time to see her start to fall.

"Tarani!" I whispered, as I caught her under her arms and tried, clumsily, to disentangle her from the backpack. She was limp against my chest, a dead weight that was almost too much for me to handle.

The illusions did it, I told myself. *On top of all that physical exertion, the psychic strain was too much. Why the hell didn't she tell me? Damn it, if she's pushed herself too far . . .*

I finally freed the backpack and dropped it to the floor. She had slipped down until she was nearly on her knees, and I was badly off balance. I was beginning to worry that I'd topple over backward and drag us both down the stairs, when she moved a little and clutched at my waist. I helped her as she pulled herself to her feet.

"Sorry," she murmured, still half-dazed. "I'll be all right soon—"

"A good night's sleep won't hurt you any," I said gruffly, as I lifted her in my arms. "Let's see if we can find Rassa's bedroom."

Cradled against my chest, Tarani's weight was manageable. It was relief, not fear of dropping her, that made my arms hold her so tightly.

I knelt down and laid her on the fluffy pallet in the smaller of the two bedrooms.

She propped herself on one elbow as I sat down beside her. There were two windows in this room, open to the night. The faint starlight, and stray beams from street lamps, gave us enough light to see each other. Her face, always delicate, looked fragile in the gray light.

"Why didn't you warn me that the illusions of Yoman and Rassa would cost you so dearly?"

"I didn't know," she said. "I've never tried to sustain an illusion for such a long period of time."

"Or for someone else?" I asked.

"Yes, that was a factor, too."

"You could have told me, when you felt the strain," I said, trying not to sound like I was accusing her.

"In Dyskornis, you said we had to be able to depend on one another, Rikardon. I had said I could hold the illusion; I had to see it through."

She only did what I'd have done, myself, I admitted. *Except that I couldn't have done it at all. Which is why she's here, isn't it? She's right—I can't preach teamwork and then tell one of the players not to do her part.*

"I can't argue with that," I said, and started to get up. Her free hand caught my arm and I paused, kneeling very close to her.

"Rikardon, your caring . . . it touches me deeply."

I felt the world shifting and changing around me.

The image of Tarani and Thymas together had burned itself in my memory, and I saw it again now, but with a different perspective. Then, and on the following nights, the remembered scene had seemed confirmation of Tarani's continuing affection for Thymas, and I had kept myself a scrupulous distance from the girl, especially in my thoughts as we rode together.

But there was no mistaking the invitation in her voice and posture, and another scene rose vividly in memory—the evening we had talked in Dyskornis and, in the most cautious of language, admitted the attraction we felt for one another. The scene in Stomestad was driven out of my memory. Tarani was with me, here and now, and emotions too powerful to be called "affection" were at work in both of us.

I leaned across the few inches which separated us, and kissed her. I meant it as a message of reassurance and of closeness. But in the next moment we were clinging tightly to one another, swept up in passion and physical need. The abruptness and intensity of those feelings disturbed me, and I pulled myself away from her.

She didn't say anything, but her dark eyes were glowing in that reflective way that sometimes had, and her chest rose and fell in quick, sharp breaths.

"It's been a rough trip," I said, taking deep, deliberate breaths, "and we both need some rest. Sleep well, Tarani."

I saw her thinking about it, wondering whether to press the issue. To my relief, she let it pass. She opened the light, woven blanket and shook it out over herself. As she lay back, she said, in a soft, carefully neutral voice: "Goodnight, Rikardon."

8

I was tired, too. By rights, I should have snuggled into Yoman's bed and slept the night through. Instead, I escaped into the streets of Eddarta.

Here, again, I had a reasonable excuse. I knew little about Eddartan customs, and there's no better way to get information than to buy a few rounds of drinks in a friendly bar. I had planned to go out for a while, anyway, if only to make some discreet inquiries about Gharlas, and his standing among the Lords. I figured to be safe with my own face. It was my sword which identified me to the rogueworld, and Rika was safe with Thymas. In any case, Eddarta's rogueworld was pretty tame—the *organized* thieves lived on the hill.

But the true reason I left was because of Tarani.

In Gandalara, where there was no venereal disease, and birth control was a matter of a woman saying no when her inner awareness warned her she was fertile, intimacy between a consenting couple was considered to be their own business.

If Tarani had been an ordinary Ganadalaran woman, I wouldn't have hesitated. If I had just met her, I wouldn't have hesitated.

But I knew Tarani's extraordinary history, and our relationship had an uncertain history of its own.

We had met in Thagorn, when Tarani identified me as the

target for a pair of killers traveling with her show. I had felt, and she had later admitted, a sense of recognition in that first meeting. In light of our later adventures, I attributed it to a sort of premonition of our joining forces against Gharlas.

Tarani's involvement in the assassination attempt had come through her association with Molik, the leader of Chizan's rogueworld. At sixteen, still a virgin, she had offered him a deal—her body, and her illusions, in exchange for the capital to create her traveling show.

At eighteen, free of Molik's attentions but not of his memory, she had taken refuge from his unwholesome need of her—a need she felt she had created—in Thymas's devotion.

At twenty, only a few weeks ago, she had finally found peace. Given the opportunity to destroy Molik, she had learned that only her guilt tied her to him. When her anger turned to pity, she was truly free.

But that was the *only* thing she had gained, these past few weeks. She had given up the show she had gone through hell to get. She had relinquished the security of her promised marriage to Thymas. She had found her "uncle," only to watch him die, and then discover that he was the father she had never known.

I had seen Tarani regal and strong, the very air around her throbbing with power. I had seen her young and helpless, suffering from my own thoughtless words. She had endured grueling physical demands with the stoic acceptance of a trained soldier. She had survived an emotional crisis that no twenty-year-old girl should be expected to face, and she had come through it sane, hurt but healing. I felt such admiration for her, such tenderness. Her strength of character awed me. Her vulnerability was a warm glow that nestled, trusting, in my thoughts and feelings.

Markasset, with the overriding passion of the young, saw Tarani's response as an indication of her need for emotional comfort. Ricardo, a man still subject to physical need but with a lifetime of wisdom to control it, wanted to give us both time to *understand* the source and destiny of those intense feelings.

I went from bar to bar, pretending to drink a lot of faen. Even while part of my mind was analyzing the information I gleaned from conversation and eavesdropping, I felt my thoughts circling profitlessly around the problem of Tarani.

I weighed responsibility against desire. I tried to decide whether her need was for me, or for anyone—for intimacy, or for assurance that there was more of value in Tarani than her beauty and admitted sexual experience.

In the end, only one thought came to me clearly, as I finished off what would be my final mug of faen:

I'm in love with Tarani. God help us both. I don't want to hurt her.

It was nearly midnight when I returned to Yoman's shop. The door creaked, the stairs groaned. I paused beside Rassa's bedroom door and listened, hoping with one last desperate, pass-the-buck impulse that I hadn't wakened Tarani.

And hoping that I had.

"I'm awake," her voice seemed to answer my thought.

I opened the door and stepped into the room. In the dim light, two things stood out. First, she was sitting up, with her back against the wall and the blanket tucked up under her bare arms. Second, her clothes were folded neatly on the ledge beneath the windowsill.

I wasn't aware of any conscious decision. But in less than a second I was across the room, kneeling beside her, taking her in my arms.

Nothing had ever felt so good, not in two lifetimes. She rose to meet me, and the blanket fell aside unheeded. I scrambled out of my tunic, barely aware of her hands helping me. I pulled her close again, holding her carefully, like the treasure she was, and I felt the steady muscles of her dancer's body tremble with eagerness. The touch of her skin on mine made me dizzy with need. Her tongue caressed my tusks as we kissed, sending tendrils of pleasure down my spine.

I felt such joy that I couldn't contain it, couldn't express it. I was transported by the wonder of her body, consenting to be separated from it only for the sake of learning it, by sight and by touch. When I was free of the rest of my clothing, I lay beside her and held her again, wanting to pull her inside my skin, to be entirely and completely one with her.

It was a time of peace, a pause, a lingering. A time of stretched sensitivity, of slow ecstasy. We kissed gently, silent acknowledgment that what we felt for one another was more than bodily need. But the kiss caught fire, and left us breathless and urgent. Tarani lay back, and I rose above her. Her eyes closed in anticipation . . .

"Oh, Ricardo," she whispered.

It was a word Tarani had never heard, couldn't know, would be unable to guess.

The world seemed to freeze around me.

She opened her eyes when she felt the tension thrum through my body. Her hands, caressing my back, grew still.

"What—what did you say, just then?" I panted.

"Say? I only said your name."

"Say it again," I urged.

Doubt flickered in her eyes, and the warm space of air between our bodies seemed to cool. She did what I asked, and said: "Rikardon."

And we both knew it was over.

I drew away from her, and she slid backward to sit up again. She pulled the blanket across her body with a self-consciousness that hurt me like a slap in the face. "It's Molik, isn't it?" she said. Her voice was deadly calm. "You can't bear to be with me because of what I—"

"No!" I nearly shouted the word, appalled that she could put such an interpretation on what had happened. "No, Tarani." More gently.

I took her hand; it lay unresisting, unresponsive, across my fingers.

"Thymas, then?" she said, bitterness creeping in, stinging me.

"Tarani, you have to believe what I'm about to say." She was silent, looking somewhere off to my left. "My . . . failure is in no way your fault. Thymas and Molik have no place in what you and I share. I feel—and you *must* know it, too—that what we wanted tonight *will* happen someday. But not tonight. I'm not sure I understand why, myself. I only know—"

I stopped, lost in misery.

She looked at me then, and I almost wished she would turn away again. The dim light from the window fell across her face. Deep lines etched the smooth skin on her forehead and cheeks.

"I'm frightened, Rikardon," she said, hurriedly, as though she were speaking a dangerous secret.

"Of me?" I asked, surprised and horrified.

"Of whatever is telling you that we cannot . . . that it is not yet time. Of whatever has brought us together, but will not let us *be* together.

"What we are doing, fighting Gharlas, I know it is *right*, Rikardon. But I do not know how it will end. You seem to see things more clearly. Can you tell me that we will *get* the Ra'ira back? That we will both live through what we must do? Can you tell me that there will *be* a 'someday' for us?"

"No, I don't have those answers, Tarani."

Her eyes blazed. "Then *defy* that 'whatever' for once! There may not *be* another chance for us, Rikardon. Give us this moment, at least."

I looked at her. Loving her. Wanting her. And I said: "I can't, Tarani. I'm sorry."

The lines in her face vanished, leaving her skin as pale and smooth as marble. "Please go now," she whispered.

I gathered up my clothes and walked to the door, feeling naked and foolish and miserable, and for the second time in one night, I escaped.

This time my refuge was Yoman's bedroom. When the Gandalaran dawn spread its glowing colors across the cloud-covered sky, I was still sitting and staring, thinking and wondering.

Things that had never made sense fell into place during that watchful night. The mutual recognition Tarani and I had felt, on meeting for the first time. The unusual sophistication of a sixteen-year-old virgin. The abrupt onset of confusion and restlessness that had drawn Tarani from her Recorder training.

The last time I had heard the word Tarani had spoken tonight, I had been Ricardo Carillo, engaged in a harmless and delightful flirtation with Antonia Alderuccio on the deck of a ship, in the middle of the Mediterranean Ocean. The Italian girl had noticed the increasing brightness of a "star", and I had not had time to tell her that I believed it was a meteor. I recall feeling a sense of injustice, as I lost consciousness, that someone as young and beautiful as Antonia had to die so uselessly.

Like me, Antonia had been reborn in Gandalara.

Unlike me, she had been delivered into a host body with a living, vital personality.

I had speculated that, if Markasset had been alive, his familiarity with his body and his surroundings would have given his personality natural control. The period of confusion Tarani had suffered may have been a struggle for control between Tarani and Antonia.

They both won, I thought, watching the early folk moving through the streets of Eddarta. *Tarani is usually in control—and she doesn't seem to have any conscious awareness of Antonia. But grown-up, adult Antonia, accustomed to wealth and wise in the ways of the wealthy, used Tarani's power to handle Molik.*

I remembered Antonia. The way she had laughed. The way she had looked at an old man and seen, not his age, but his experience, the depth and the value of it.

She couldn't have meant the girl harm, I decided. *She was probably only trying to help her get the money she wanted. And she couldn't have been closely integrated into Tarani's personality, or she'd have seen the girl's naiveté, and backed off.*

But there's no doubt she's there, I thought, *and because of her, Tarani's been through the wringer. That horror may be part of whatever is going on here, part of our "destiny."* I slammed my fist on my leg, taking a savage pleasure in the pain it caused. *But it's a hell of a rotten thing to do to a sixteen-year-old girl!*

I heard Tarani stirring in Rassa's room, and I remembered the coldness that had crept over me when I heard Antonia speak through Tarani. It hadn't been fear, or even surprise. How often had I thought that Tarani seemed always to be two different women, one powerful, one helpless?

No, what I had felt in that moment was indecision.

I loved . . . Tarani?

Or Antonia?

9

By the time Tarani had dressed, I had gone out and returned with breakfast. I found her leafing through a series of parchment pages tied at one edge with twine.

"Yoman's ledger," she explained, setting it aside to accept the fruit and bread.

There was a moment of hesitation as her fingers brushed mine, but that was the only sign of what had happened the night before.

Apparently, she's decided on a "business as usual" attitude. Good idea, I approved. *For one thing, we're running short of time.*

"Anything interesting?" I asked.

"He seemed to do a thriving business, even if most of the profit went to Pylomel."

"Pylomel? The *High Lord* is Yoman's landpatron?"

"It surprised me, too," she said. "Why did Yoman not tell us? He knew we wanted information about the High Lord."

"I don't know, but it just adds to the funny feeling I've had all along about Yoman—he was running from something. I feel sure of it."

"Well, it was not poor business, and from the way that fool last night acted, Yoman still has every right to run this shop. But he did not run it alone," she said. "He purchased the fabric and made men's clothes, but Rassa had established herself as a seamstress and designer of women's clothes. I found several commissions for her—from Zefra."

So that's why she's not upset with me this morning, I thought, feeling strangely disappointed. *Finding a way to see her mother is so important that she's forgotten . . .*

You idiot! I scolded myself. *Give the girl what happiness you can, while there's time. And keep your mind on business, OK?*

"Before we go any further with that, Tarani, let me go over what I found out during my drinking tour last night. I think I have a better picture of how Eddarta works, now. Yoman—well, maybe we just didn't know the right questions to ask when we talked to him."

It took me a long time to get back around to Zefra, but Tarani listened patiently, knowing that the more we understood about Eddarta in general, the better our chances of accomplishing *both* things we had come for.

There was no kitchen in Yoman's house, not even shelves where fruit, bread, or Gandalaran liquor, faen or *barut*, could be kept on hand, because Yoman was not a cook or baker. Everyone in Eddarta had a specific trade, and since the Lords took a share of everyone's trade, everyone's trade had to be necessary.

Farmers grew grain, therefore, but could not grind or cook it. Herders sold their glith to slaughterhouses, gave a portion of their profit to the landpatron, then bought table meat from the meat vendor—who passed along a share of *his* profit to *his* landpatron. Tradesmen like Yoman could occasionally benefit directly from their own services—he and Rassa could make their own clothes, for instance—but he had to consider the fabric as wasted inventory.

When the landpatron system had first been mentioned, I had thought of the feudal system of medieval Europe in Ricardo's world. It was a reasonable comparison, since the Lords of Eddarta did own virtually all the land in a huge region in and around the city.

Harthim and six noble families had arrived in Eddarta after their flight from Kä with the greatest, least resistable power—the treasury of the Kingdom. The Eddartans had enjoyed an easy life, with water plentiful and the general level of wealth higher here than anywhere else in Gandalara. The last King had brought an example of an even higher standard of luxury and had taught the Eddartans to crave it, and one by one they had sold their independence for it. When the self-styled Lords had owned Eddarta, they had begun taxing it, winning a hundred-fold return on their initial investments.

The descendent of these seven families lived on in the upper city, called Lord City by the Eddartans. The eldest of each family usually became its Lord. The High Lord, as Gharlas had informed us, was chosen from the descendents of Harthim—his *legitimate* descendents, which left Gharlas hanging loose on the wrong side of the blanket—and was the individual who displayed the strongest mind-power in some sort of test.

I hadn't been able to find an exact date for the building of Lord City, but I suspected that it had been built soon after Harthim's arrival, to protect the Kä refugees from those Eddartans who were discontented with the transition from free enterprise to thinly disguised monopoly. I did learn that each of the seven families had an area of its own inside those massive walls, and that all those areas were linked through what Ricardo would have called a palace. It was a government building called Lord Hall, and it contained meeting rooms, an audience hall, a Council Chamber which had extra-special official significance and, according to the eager gossip of my drinking companions, the hidden entryway to the fabled treasure vault.

"Gharlas it well known here in the lower city," I told Tarani. "Apparently, he's played up his hatred for Pylomel to the point where he's sort of a 'regular guy' to the common folk. Word is that Pylomel isn't fond of him, either, but family rules require that he give Gharlas a place to stay when he's in town."

"Then Gharlas lives in Pylomel's home?"

"If you could call it that. The family areas inside Lord City are huge, with a lot of separate dwellings. Pylomel has probably given Gharlas the cheapest quarters he could manage."

Tarani worried one tusk with her tongue. "Do you remember what Gharlas said about Pylomel's treasure?"

"You mean the secret way he's found into the vault?"

"If we could find the vault, we could reach Gharlas secertly," Tarani said. "Perhaps," she suggested, "if Zefra knows how to enter the vault . . ."

I laughed. Tarani's face darkened, and I touched her arm in apology.

"That's the hard way," I said. "At least, I think it is. Our first step has to be to find Zefra and get the two of you together. We can't do much until we know for sure whether she can—or will—help us against Gharlas."

"She will help if she can," Tarani said.

Take this part easy, I warned myself.

"Tarani, please remember that you don't *know* Zefra yet. The woman who wrote that letter to Volitar lived twenty years ago. This Zefra may not be the same person. For one thing, she's been married to the High Lord all this time."

"You are saying that we should not trust her," Tarani said. "Then why bother to seek her out?"

Her bitterness hurt me. I wanted to put my arms around her, but the scene of the night before told me I had no right to offer her comfort now.

"I believe she *will* want to help us," I said. "But I'm not allowing myself to rely on her help until we know for sure."

That wasn't quite true. The fact of the matter was, everything I had learned about Lord City made me realize that we *needed* some kind of inside help, and I had no idea where else to find it.

"All I'm really saying," I continued, "is that we should be cautious, even with Zefra. We can't tell her the real reason we're here."

She was silent for a few seconds. "I see the wisdom in what you say, Rikardon. I will not speak to Zefra of the Ra'ira. She will help us because Gharlas killed Volitar."

She set down her platter of fruit rinds and picked up the ledger again, the deliberateness of her movements revealing her tension.

"But there is a problem," she added. "These records show appointments in Lord City only at the request of the buyer."

"Something else I learned last night—there's going to be some kind of fancy ceremony in a few days, and Lord City is really stirred up about it. Do you see a recent commission from Zefra?"

She examined the book. "No. There was an appointment scheduled two seven-days ago, but there is no notation of it having been kept. Yoman and Rassa must have left before then." She looked up at me and smiled. "You are thinking that the High Lord's wife should have a new dress for this occasion?" I nodded. "But *she* will have to send for Rassa. How will she know—?"

"I'll tell her," I said. "It seems that each Lord has his own private guard. Whether that's traditional, or a defense against assassination by the next in line or another Lord, I don't know. But I should be able to get inside Lord City to talk to somebody about hiring on."

Her head tilted to one side. "That would leave you the entire city to search. Could Yoman and Rassa not simply present themselves at the gate with—say, a *gift* for Zefra or Pylomel?" Tarani suggested.

"They might. Do we *have* such a gift, or could you make one in less than a day?"

She shook her head.

"No, I didn't think so, and if my calculations are right, Gharlas will be here tomorrow or the next day. It's important that we get inside that city before he arrives.

"I'm going up this morning to try to get a job as one of Pylomel's mercenaries. That will get me into the right area. I'll just have to bet on having a chance to talk to Zefra, and I'll ask her to send for you."

"I could come with you, Rikardon. If I projected the image of a man—"

"You need to conserve your strength, Tarani." I remembered how she had looked just after we arrived in Yoman's shop—washed-out, haggard.

She remembered, too. She nodded, reluctantly. "What if the guards are watching for you?" she asked.

"They won't be. That's one thing I'm pretty sure of. Gharlas has no army of his own, and Pylomel wouldn't do him any favors."

I hoped I was right. As I stood up I felt the surge of tension and alertness that made Markasset the excellent fighter he was.

"The sooner we get free of Yoman and Rassa, the better I'll like it," I said. "I'll go up to the gate. You just sit tight, and don't open the shop. If customers come by, make the excuse that you've just returned from a long journey, and Yoman is still recuperating. Promise them you'll be open tomorrow. If we aren't both inside Lord City by tomorrow, we may have to take up tailoring for a living."

She stared at me, then smiled a little, and finally chuckled, shaking her head. "There is surely no other like you in Gandalara," she said. "This seems less a plan than merely the start of one—but it does seem to be our only choice. I will spend the day selecting fabric samples to take with me when I receive Zefra's summons."

"The one major hitch to this plan," I said, "is that I may have to *take* that guard job, and I might get stuck inside the city. If I *don't* return tonight, and you don't hear from Zefra tomorrow, don't panic. Just sit tight, play Rassa, and cover for Yoman. If you haven't heard from me or Zefra by the time Thymas gets here, make whatever plans seem right. You'll have to find another way to get inside, but I'll be watching for you, and trying to get a line on Gharlas."

She stood up, and for a second or two I thought—hoped—she would cross the few paces between us and let me hold her once more before we went our separate ways. But if that had been her impulse, she controlled it by stepping backward and hugging the ledger to her chest.

"Be cautious at every step, Rikardon," she said. "Eddarta is an unhappy place, and full of treachery. I feel it."

"Thank you for the warning," I said.

"I give it for my own sake," she said. "You . . . are important to me."

A foolish happiness washed over me. I had thought I'd destroyed whatever feelings Tarani was beginning to have for me. But those few simple words, spoken from all the way across the room, were a promise of another chance.

"As you are, to me," I said, and left the room.

I nearly ran down the stairs and out into the street. Then I paused to take a few deep breaths, and began to walk toward the boulevard that would take me up the hill to Lord City.

10

It's a little-known fact of life that, now and then, the odds *have* to turn in your favor. It might have been the warm feeling I carried away from Tarani, or it might have been the adrenaline surge of finally, after all this time, reaching the point of action—but I felt good about that short-notice plan as I climbed the zigzag avenue toward Lord City. I had a feeling things were going to work out right, for a change.

It was still pretty early in the day, and I walked up with a column of burdened wagons, dragged along by unhappy vleks. I looked back once or twice and was impressed, again, by the advantage the walled city would have in battle. This place had been built by frightened men hundreds of generations ago, and they had legalized and bequeathed their paranoia to its present occupants.

It seemed odd that any such unbalanced system could have survived for so long, but Gandalara was a world that changed slowly. Innovations had been made—the Gandalarans had a remarkably efficient economy and a respectable technology, hampered as they were by their lack of elemental iron. But they had an extra weight entrenching the natural conservatism of people who always feel the tentative balance of their survival. The All-Mind.

It wasn't just the "older generation" who set up the rules in Gandalara. It was the memory and experience of all previous generations—and that was a tough opponent to beat down. Gandalarans had struck a compromise between the need for change and the need for stability. Trades were family property, passed along from one generation to the next, so that improvements in irrigation techniques or the sand/ash mixture for glass were preserved each step of the way. Eddarta was the first place I had been in which each person was so strictly limited to his own trade; it reduced prideful occupations to the status of assembly-line construction.

Eddarta had another unique quality—the people of Eddarta used their river for transport of cargo and only cargo. There wasn't even a Gandalaran word to imply a *person* floating on water. Tarani and I had seen miles and miles of thick rope stretched along the riverbanks on our way toward the city. Vleks were tied to that line, and small, shallow-draft barges were tied to the vleks and hauled along. There was usually one person on the riverbank with a rear guiderope, and sometimes two or three other people with poles to keep the barge from beaching itself in the reedy growth along the banks.

The traveled areas of the river had their banks trimmed of the whitish reeds that grew taller than men, and the reed harvest served the secondary function of providing building material for the rafts. Bundles of reeds were cut, then bound tightly together. The open ends of the reeds were sealed somehow to create a long, floating log. Several logs, lashed together, made a raft.

We had seen such rafts hauling stuff upstream and controlling speed downstream—only on the smoothest, slowest stretches of water. A few yards of rapids called for wagon transport beside the river until the current calmed down again.

A series of those rafts operated on the branch of the Tashal which flowed through Lord City. I saw two stone archways as I approached the high walls. One admitted only people; the other admitted cargo. The wagons which had toiled up the slope were unloaded onto rafts, and the goods were taken inside by Lord City boatmen, who were dealing with faster current, here, than I had seen out in the country—the cataracts above and below the city kept the water moving pretty fast. To counteract the speed of the current, the Lord City boatmen had contrived a pretty complicated two-bank system.

One vlek team did the primary work of hauling, while the team on the opposite bank kept the raft aligned properly. Both banks had two levels of pathways, so that while one set of vleks hauled a raft upstream on the higher paths, another set provided brakes for a raft going downstream. The downstream rafts were pulled toward the opposite bank, and the ropes were given plenty of slack. It looked to be a pretty tricky proposition, keeping the upstream raft from fouling itself on the downstream ropes—but I watched the operation go smoothly a couple of times.

"You got business here?" A voice at my elbow called me away from watching the river. I turned around to face a huge man with leather straps crisscrossing his bare chest. Bronze discs studded the leather. He was wearing desert-style trousers instead of a leather breechclout, but his muscles and stance and attitude reminded Ricardo of a badly researched movie about Roman gladiators.

I put a smile on my face. "I hope so," I said. "I'm just in from Chizan. A fellow I met in a bar last night said the High Lord might be in need of another sword. I could use the job."

The man looked me up and down. He was a brawny type, with very prominent supraorbital ridges, a low-slung jaw, and hair on his knuckles.

"Experience?" he snapped.

"Four years as a caravan guard, saw some action with the Sharith before the master gave in and paid the toll."

The guard snorted. "Them turncoats."

The subjects adopt the masters' politics, I thought. *The original Eddartans had no reason to hate the Sharith*.

Or did they? After all, the Sharith more or less drove Harthim into settling here, which hasn't done them much good.

Hey, pay attention! I ordered myself. *Is he giving you advice?*

That's exactly what he was doing. I reached back into my short-term memory and recovered the words I had missed. "All the Lords are hiring," he had said. He went on: "But the High Guard has the best pay and—" He smirked. On that face, it wasn't a pretty sight. "—and the best extra benefits."

"Sounds great," I said. "What's the catch?"

The big man roared out a laugh, then slapped me on the back so hard that I staggered away from him. "You're a wise one, you are. You gotta pass a test to land a job on the High Guard."

"What kind of test?" I asked, bracing myself for a fight.

He saw me tense up, and laughed again. "You got the right idea, friend, but the wrong man." He pointed to his chest with his thumb. "I'm Sendar. The man you need to see is Obilin. And I'll give you this much warning—don't judge him by his size. Or," he added, sobering up, "by his smile."

"Well, I'm grateful for your advice, Sendar," I said. "I'm Lakad." It was an alias I had used so often that it felt natural now. "Where will I find Obilin?"

Sendar took my sword—it was the first time I'd been really glad that I'd left Rika behind—and said I could pick it up on my way out, if I wouldn't be staying. He gave me explicit directions on how to find Pylomel's guardhouse, and warned me to announce my presence quickly.

Here was the luck I had felt was waiting for me as I climbed the hill. It just so happened that Pylomel's guardhouse was located close to the High Lord's garden, a favorite place for the lady of the house to walk, of a morning. Sendar warned me that sneaking around the garden was an easy way to get killed.

I thanked him again.

"One more thing," he added. "I've got gate duty all day. I'll expect to see you come back through here, or to find you in the barracks tonight. If you're not one place or the other, I'll know you lied to me. And anybody who lies to me don't live long."

"A-huh," I said. "Well, see you later, Sendar." I didn't feel the confidence I was trying to project, but I fooled the guard. He laughed and slapped me on my way.

I had wondered why the complicated river transport was necessary. I discovered the reason as I stepped through the stone archway and into Lord City. Except for the river animals, vleks weren't permitted inside the walls. The cargo was unloaded and delivered by an endless chain of slaves. Not *servants,* who could be categorized as people who practiced their trades—cooking, cleaning—in the exclusive employ of one individual or household. These were *slaves*—thin, dejected creatures whose only value seemed to be that they were cleaner and quieter and more cooperative than vleks.

I had known that slaves were used in Eddarta, particularly in the copper mines and the bronze foundries. Theoretically, they were criminals who were sentenced to a period of service. But Dharak had talked about *selling* slaves to the Eddartans as if it were a routine thing, so I assumed that there were less "official" ways of obtaining the muscle needed to mine copper.

I had felt a distant sort of sympathy for Eddarta's slaves, but I wasn't prepared for the shock of actually seeing such people. Somehow it seemed more deplorable for the Eddartans to use slaves for immediate, private service than to employ them for broad economic gain in the copper mines. In the shock of seeing slavery close up, I realized how unfair that distinction was. *Any* use of men and women as slaves was totally undefendable.

I didn't dare let my outrage show, so I turned my face away and aimed my steps in the direction of the large central building. It stood some five hundred yards away from the water, and looked to be two stories or more. It was octagonal, with one face opening on the stone-paved avenue which led through the entryway, and one face fronting each of the seven walkways.

Columns composed of shallow marble blocks, carved to stack smoothly, supported canvas awnings stretched across wooden frames. The awnings shaded the area around Lord Hall, giving an effect much like the columned porticoes of Ricardo's ancient Rome, and extended to provide shade for the seven walkways which radiated from Lord Hall, each one joining the entrances to the Hall with the entrances to one of the seven family areas.

Sendar had said that Pylomel's living area was the largest in the city, and was located to my right. The walkway which joined it to Lord Hall led across pontoon bridge; a channel had been diverted from the river itself to run through Pylomel's much-prized garden.

There was no denying that Lord City was beautiful. The segments of territory between the radiating walkways had been landscaped with meticulous care, and these mini-gardens boasted a variety of trees and bushes, as well as flowering plants I hadn't seen anywhere else. The overall impression was one of lushness and wealth—undoubtedly the object of the careful arrangements.

The lovely garden areas proved an obstacle to me, however, for they implied that it was mandatory for visitors to keep their feet on the pavement. Even though I was standing nearer to the entrance of Pylomel's area than to Lord Hall, I had to follow the avenue up to the immense building, then turn back toward the river along the walkway.

Sendar had said, and it was readily confirmed, that the entrance to every family area led into the courtyard bounded on either side by wings of the guardhouse. As I walked carefully across the pontoon bridge, I could see two men on duty at the arched stone entrance to Pylomel's area. The courtyard was visible through the archway. Beyond it, a pathway branched immediately. From what Sendar had told me, I assumed that the left-hand branch led into the garden, and the right one led around to the front entrance of the huge building that had to be Pylomel's home.

The luck I was feeling was still with me. The attention of the outer guard was directed to the unloading platform. The weight of one raft's load had been poorly distributed, the men unloading it hadn't noticed until too late, and it looked as though load and workmen all were going for a swim very shortly.

I stepped into the shrubbery and moved quietly to my left. A low stone wall running from the guardhouse back to the river was a token marking of the boundary of Pylomel's personal domain; high brush just inside that wall provided privacy for his garden. I heard a step, and crouched behind a bush just in time to avoid being seen by a guard patrolling that short stretch of wall.

Just then, a sound I had attributed to the river came

clear—another guard at the water's edge, drinking. I crouched back out of sight as he walked into view. He stood beside the wall, midway from the guardhouse to the river.

Two guards, one stationary, one patrolling, I thought, and spent a few seconds swearing under my breath.

There's no way to get into that garden without taking out one of those guards, which would kill my little play-act about wanting work.

I sat tight and thought about it for a while. I could try for the guard job, and hope to have the opportunity to contact Zefra later. I could turn around and leave right now, and tell Sendar I'd changed my mind about the job, once I saw Obilin. But both courses would result in delays we *couldn't* afford.

Something made me decide to chance it—a whiff of fragrance that was subtly nonfloral. Perfume.

The use of perfume was rare in Gandalara, but it seemed to be, socially, the exclusive property of wealthy women. I *knew,* so surely that I'd have bet my tusks, that I had come at the right time. Zefra was walking in Pylomel's garden.

I summoned all the patience I could, and waited my chance to move. Little by little, while the guard's attention was fixed somewhere, I crept closer to the wall, keeping to the cover of the larger bushes. I had my big chance when I heard the hollering and splashing from the river as the poorly balanced load finally knocked a couple of the workers into the river. Both guards moved toward the guardhouse to get a clearer view of what was going on. I ran for the wall, slid over it, and made my way on my belly, slowly, through the tangled growth at the base of the privacy hedge.

The garden was truly beautiful. The channel which brought the river water formed a series of tiny streams and ponds, and every kind of plant Markasset had ever seen—plus a few species that were new to him—was represented in the garden. But I didn't have the time, or the inclination, to admire the botanical genius of Pylomel's gardener.

Zefra was there.

11

She wasn't alone. There were guards *inside* the garden, and though they stood at a respectful distance, I got the distinct impression that they weren't so much protecting Zefra as keeping her under surveillance.

She was walking along the pathways slowly, bending to examine flowers, meandering in my direction. I eased myself to my feet, but stayed hidden in the hedge, waiting. If she kept on going, she would walk right by me . . .

She stopped to examine a flower on the bush next to me. I was stunned by her close resemblance to Tarani. Her body carried a few extra pounds for her twenty extra years, but the fine shape of her face, the lustrous black of her headfur, even the graceful way she used her hands—I could see Tarani clearly within the frame of her mother.

I hope she has Tarani's coolness, too, I thought. *I don't have time to do this gently*.

"Volitar is dead," I whispered. Her hand, cupping the flower, tightened to crush it. "Tarani is in Eddarta. Send for Rassa, the dressmaker. Your daughter will come to you instead."

"*She must not be seen in this place*," Zefra whispered fiercely.

"She will be seen only as Rassa," I said.

The woman gasped, and her composure almost deserted her. To cover her sudden motion, she moved past me and began to examine a different flower.

"Then Tarani has learned to use her mind-gift," she said. "Who are you, and why have you brought Tarani into danger?"

I refrained from asking her why she assumed that *I* had done the bringing. Instead, I answered: "I'm a friend, Zefra. Tarani and I have an important job to do. We need your help. She'll explain when she sees you."

"And if I refuse?" she asked. But her eyes were closed, and her hands were trembling. I didn't say anything, and after a moment, she sighed deeply. "I will do it. Tell me your name."

"Rikardon."

"If my daughter suffers harm from this, Rikardon, I will not rest until your heart has been fed to Pylomel's dralda."

She cried out suddenly, and put her finger to her lips as though a thorn had stuck her. She turned and hurried out of the garden, and the guards watched her go.

So they didn't see me slide back across the wall.

The outside guard was returning from the ruckus at the river. He was, in fact, less than ten feet away from me. He was saying something over his shoulder to another guard, so that his head was turned.

There was nowhere I could go in a hurry, so I stood up and walked toward him. "Excuse me?"

He jumped. When he landed again, his sword was in his hand.

This guy's no slouch, I thought. *And Sendar—I wouldn't care to take him on. Pylomel's got some good-quality heavies on his side.*

"Where in the name of Harthim did you come from?" he asked, looking around. The wall into the garden was the closest concealment; I saw his eyes narrow with suspicion.

"Are you Obilin?" I asked him, to distract his attention from the garden. It worked. He looked at me as though I should be stepped on.

"No," he grunted. "Who are you?"

"Name's Lakad," I said. "Fellow named Sendar, at the gate, said I should talk to Obilin about joining the High Lord's guard."

"He must have given you directions, too," the man said. "You're pretty far from the main path."

"Yeah, he warned me about that," I said. I tried to grin companionably, but I'm sure the effect wasn't very convincing. "I just got sidetracked by these trees—I've never seen any like this."

Half-true, I thought.

"They're pretty rare, all right," the man said, straightening his shoulders and puffing out his chest as if he personally had planted every one of those trees.

"But listen," he added gruffly, "don't wander around until you've signed up—otherwise you won't live to meet Obilin."

"If you'll tell me where he is, I'll go straight over there now," I said sincerely.

"I'll show you," he said, grabbing my arm and dragging me toward the walkway and the entrance to the guardhouse. I dug in my heels; he stopped and looked at me in surprise.

Not used to folks who don't jump when you say so? I wondered. *Well, I'm not going to start my career as a fifth columnist by being pushed around.*

"I can walk very well alone, thanks," I said, and pulled my arm out of his grasp. There was a visible pulse at his temple as he considered contesting the point, then he shrugged and waved me ahead of him.

Up to this point, I'd had some choices left. I could have gone back out the gate, sent Tarani in to see her mother alone, and made further plans after their meeting. *If* Tarani weren't spotted. *If* Tarani didn't just decide to stay with the mother she had never met before. *If* one of the hundred other possible complications that would keep me chewing my nails didn't actually happen.

Unappealing as it was, the choice had been feasible up to the time I was buttonholed next to the forbidden garden. As I walked through the brick-faced archway and turned left into the common room of the guardhouse, I knew I was committed to our plan, sketchy as it was. The next step was to get myself hired on, which would involve, if I had understood Sendar correctly, a competitive test of my fighting skills. In other words (in *Ricardo's* words), a brawl.

The stone walls of the rectangular room were topped by a high, flat ceiling made of unfinished wood. There were several long tables and benches, and padded stone shelves around the edges of the room which seemed to serve as lounging seats. A game of *mondea* was in progress at one table—it had the same persistence among Gandalara's military-style folk that poker had in Ricardo's world.

"Watch him," my escort growled to the players, then left by a door which led off to the right, and which he closed behind him.

The four players looked up at me briefly. Appearances aren't everything, I know. But from the look of those scarred, slack-jawed faces, I'd have bet there wasn't an ounce of charm among them.

I smiled. "I'm not going anywhere," I said. "And I'd rather watch you. Who's winning?"

"Me," growled the biggest man, who was missing one ear and several teeth. "You can watch. Quietly."

I nodded, and moved closer. It was a fast game, with rules that were slightly different from those I had learned from Bareff and Liden during my short stay with the Sharith. I became so completely absorbed in the action of the *mondeana*, the dicelike playing pieces, that I was surprised by a light touch on my shoulder.

I turned around to face a very small man, while the clatter and hooting at and around the dice table crashed into absolute silence.

"I'm Obilin," the little man said. Then he hit me in the stomach.

It was a sharp, high-powered jab of surprising power. He delivered it with his left hand, and I saw his right get ready to swing at my head as I doubled over. I let my knees fold, so that I dropped clear to the floor, moving faster than he expected. Then I swung my body to my left, catching Obilin's midriff on my shoulder, and heaved myself upright again, sending the little man flying into the air. While I took short, quick breaths to try to get back my wind, I watched Obilin right himself in the air and come down on his feet.

Chairs scraped away from the table behind me, and I heard the clinking as the coins and mondeana were gathered up hastily.

"Wouldn't you rather do this outside?" I suggested. "Not much room to move around in here."

The smile was still there, and I heard a soft, whispery laugh that made my skin crawl.

"Good," he said. "No questions. No complaints. Immediate grasp of the situation. Very good, Lakad.

"But, to answer your question, no, we'll stay here. A fighter has to be aware of his surroundings, as well as his opponent, don't you agree?"

One minute he was standing quite still, nearly ten feet away from me. Suddenly he was on top of the table next to me, a kick heading for my chin.

I ducked aside, grabbed for the moving leg, missed it, grabbed for his balance leg, but it was already gone. He was on the floor on the other side of the table, bouncing.

You certainly are a fast mother, Obilin, I thought at him, as I hit the floor to dodge his two-fisted dive across the table. *And smooth,* I added, as I watched him somersault down the narrow aisle between tables and come up on his feet, facing me. *How can you judge distances so well?*

The answer occurred to me almost immediately.

Because you're not distracted by defending yourself, that's how. You stage these fights in here to keep your opponent a safe distance away from you. Your game is all offense, Obilin, I realized. *Let's see what happens when you're cornered.*

The other men in the room were reclining on the benches against the walls. If I'd had time, I would have been surprised that they weren't calling bets back and forth, or encouraging one of us. But they were quiet, and I noticed that only long enough to be glad for the chance to give my complete attention to Obilin.

He came at me again, aiming his right arm and using the inertia of his self-propelled body to add weight to the intended blow. I stepped aside with the intention of snagging him and pinning him down—but he had anticipated me. His right hand missed me, but his left hand came up out of nowhere and slammed the side of my head, and sent me reeling. I let myself go loose, and I groped for support from a nearby table, lowering myself to the bench. Obilin closed in, the smile unchanged on his face, his short stature towering over me where I sat. Then he made his first mistake.

He grabbed my head with both hands, to steady it as a target for his knee. I let him begin the knee jab, but then I snapped my head up, grabbed that upraised leg, and yanked with all my strength. Obilin was *very* quick; I felt his body register the danger the moment I touched his leg, and he tried to brace himself to resist. But that hard pull brought him down, with his legs scissored around the bench. I had time to deliver one sharp, backhanded blow before he slipped away from me, rolled, and stood up.

The smile still looked the same. It still scared me.

"Well done, Lakad," he said. "You impress me. Still, the true test of a fighter is in his sword work, wouldn't you say?" He held out his hand, and someone slid a sword, hilt-first, across the nearest table to me. I left it there.

"Well, Lakad?" he said, gesturing at the sword.

Suddenly, I wanted to laugh. *Didn't I watch this scene in a pirate movie with Burt Lancaster?* I wondered, a little hysterically. Then I looked at Obilin's face, and a new thought chilled me. That smile was genuine, and reflected real pleasure, real anticipation.

I stopped being scared, and started to dislike Obilin. A lot.

I picked up the sword, just in time to block his first blow. He was fast, but not really strong. As long as I could anticipate him, and get a block up in time, he couldn't touch me. But the very speed of his attack kept me backing away, and on the defensive.

Same game plan, I realized. *All offense.* I realized something else, looking into the small man's grinning face. *The way to get hired on around here isn't to beat this guy. If I win, he'll hate me. On the other hand, if I lose badly, he'll have no reason to hire me. I need to show some capability, and then lose. And somehow, in the process, stay alive.*

That last seemed to be the hardest part, because there was no doubt that Obilin was sincerely trying to kill me. If I *gave* him an opening . . .

I had backed up against a table, and suddenly the chance I needed was there. He brought in a low slash and, instead of blocking it, I jumped the blade and scrambled up on the table. On my knees, I had the advantage of extra striking room in a downward swing, and for an instant, Obilin was defending himself against the overhead attack.

Then he did what I expected; he grabbed a leg of the table and heaved, to knock me off balance. I fell off, banging my shoulder on the stone-paved floor, and when I stopped rolling, I felt a sword point against my throat.

The smile was still there. "You're hired," he said, and put away his sword.

12

I spent the next couple of hours getting acquainted with the area and with the rules, courtesy of a wrinkled old man who seemed to be a butler-type person for the barracks. He issued me a sword—to be used until Sendar came off duty and returned my own (Thymas's)—and delivered all his information in a bored monotone, eyes and voice aimed into the air above my left shoulder.

My quarters were surprisingly comfortable—one large room, divided into sleeping and visiting areas. The duty roster was complicated, but not hard to live with. A series of shifts (six hours on, six off) for three days, then one full day off. Meals were served in a community room, except on your day off. Then, if you requested it, a woman would serve your dinner in your rooms, and stay with you through the night.

So that's what Sendar meant by the "extra benefits" to be had by working for Pylomel.

"The High Lord is very generous," I said to the old man, whose name was Willon. "Who do I ask for this extra service?"

"The High Lord ain't got much to do with it," Willon said, looking straight at me, finally. "You ask *me* when you're ready."

"Ah-huh. And how much do I pay *you*?" I asked.

"Not a zak," he said. I must have let my skepticism show, because he got defensive. "Oh, I get paid, all right—a portion of what they get. And *before you ask*, you don't pay them, either. The Guard has a friend who really appreciates the work we do."

Suddenly, it all made sense. "Would this friend's name be Gharlas?"

The old man peered at me suspiciously. "How'd you know that?"

I shrugged. "I may have just come into town, Willon, but I know how to keep my ears open. And, *before you* ask, my mouth is shut."

"Good," he said, with an emphatic nod, and the matter was closed . "You'll be on the supper shift this evening, so you best take a short rest."

I did, in fact, lie down on the fluffy pallet for a few minutes. But I was too restless to sleep.

So far, I had been able to control the execution of our plan, at least to some extent. I had been very lucky, too—I was well aware of that. But I had been the one taking action, and I had felt a sense of confidence, knowing that success or failure were, for the moment, entirely my responsibility.

Now it was different. The next step was Tarani's play. I felt a different kind of confidence in her, a sureness that she would do whatever was necessary. But not being able to *see* what she did was like an unreachable itch.

Finally, I went into the common room. I watched the mondea game for a little while, sat in for a few rounds. But I kept feeling more and more restless, and finally had to excuse myself and walk around. I found myself in the court between the barracks and the "back door" of Pylomel's home.

Tarani/Rassa was coming through the entryway, followed by two slaves who were loaded down with bolts of cloth.

She gave me a strained smile, and I grinned back in relief. She was totally unsurprised to find me waiting for her.

So that's what a mild compulsion feels like! I thought. *That paralysis Gharlas laid on us in Dyskornis must have been something different—a blocking, rather than a forcing. But he was able to compel Thymas,* I remembered, and shivered in sympathy for what the boy must have suffered. *I'm glad that kind of power scares Tarani.*

I felt another mental nudge, and moved out into the courtyard so that my path intersected Tarani's. Her hand caught my arm, and I fell into step beside her while I watched a shadowy, semitransparent version of myself move past and out of the way. I pulled my arm through her fingers until I could hold her hand, and I squeezed it, hoping the pressure would give her some reassurance.

She was trembling, but I was at a loss to guess whether it was the strain of the illusion—two illusions, now that I was "invisible"—apprehension about the situation, or anticipation of meeting her mother. I kept close to her, exactly beside her, hoping that I was minimizing the effort she needed to keep the illusions intact.

Instead of following the well-marked pathway which led to the front door of the huge house, Tarani and I followed an extension of the courtyard to a small door in the back of the building—the servant or merchant entrance. As we approached the doorway, the guard stepped aside to let a small man come out into the court. I had no difficulty recognizing Obilin. He grinned widely when he saw Rassa, and deliberately took a stance which blocked the entry.

"So you've made the wise choice, after all, Rassa?"

Tarani stopped, and her hand tightened in mine.

"The only choice I have made is to obey the summons of Zefra, who has asked me to design a gown for her for the Celebration Dance. Please, let me pass by."

"Why, of course, dear dressmaker," he said, stepping to our right and waving the entourage through with an elaborate bow. But his grin never faded, and as Tarani passed him, one lightning-quick hand closed on her arm. He leaned close to her and whispered: "But you don't think, for a minute, that you will leave here again before the High Lord gets what he wants, do you?"

"My concern now is what the lady Zefra wants. Release me."

He did, and it was a good thing. There have been few times in my life when I wanted so badly to hit somebody. But I realized, as Tarani and I walked carefully through the doorway into the High Lord's home, that it wasn't Obilin I wanted to hit.

I finally pinned down the source of the uneasiness that had plagued me since Tarani and I had assumed the identities of Rassa and Yoman. I had had the feeling that both of them had been running away from something specific. Now it seemed so simple that I wondered why I hadn't figured it out before now.

The talk I had heard last night had been full of complaints against the High Lord's habit of appropriating any woman among his landservants who caught his fancy. It was only a now-and-then sort of thing, apparently, or resistance to it would have been more cohesive. But the women never returned to their homes.

Rassa had met with Zefra frequently, so that Pylomel would have had many opportunities to see her and be attracted by her unusual beauty. There had been some warning of his interest, and Yoman had made the choice to leave his entire life behind, in order to save his daughter from that fate. Yoman didn't tell us that Pylomel was his landpatron—perhaps he feared we would guess the situation and back out on the plan which promised him and his daughter a better chance of escape.

So Yoman had sacrificed two strangers for his daughter's safety. Try as I might, though, I couldn't blame him. The face I *really* wanted to smash was Pylomel's.

Inside the entryway, Tarani pulled me aside and gestured to the two slaves to go ahead of us. They went, walking with a quiet acceptance of their burdens which seemed less stoic than merely resigned. Tarani sighed softly as we started to follow them. I looked at her, and I put my arm around her for support while we walked through a labyrinth of hallways.

I feel like a white rat, I thought, hopelessly trying to keep track of the twists and turns in the route we covered. It seemed as though every High Lord since Harthim had added his own shape and taste to the building. I had a vague sense of remaining near the garden side of the house, and I was sure that we were on the second floor, but I also knew it would be hopeless to find our way out again without help.

I hope Zefra is on our side, I thought.

Finally, the slaves slowed and stopped. Tarani straightened up, and only our hands touched as we passed the slaves to stand in front of a large double door. There was a guard on either side of the door; I felt naked and exposed, and I thought: *If Tarani's illusions can hide me when I'm face-to-face with these guys, they can do anything*.

A young girl answered Tarani's knock.

"I am Rassa," Tarani told her. "I am to create a gown for the lady Zefra."

"She awaits you," the girl said in a shy but formal voice, and opened both doors to admit "Rassa" and the goods-bearing slaves. I entered beside her; Tarani's hand was clutching mine so hard that I worried about something breaking.

We were in a small, rectangular sitting room that had doors in both narrow halls. A stone ledge ran along the bottom of one long wall, and was padded with embroidered cushions that matched those in the three free-standing chairs. A ledge along the other doorless wall was left bare, and it was there that the slaves placed the bolts of cloth under Tarani's direction. When the cloth was properly displayed, and the slaves had left, the girl spoke again.

"The lady Zefra asked me to bring you her greetings, Rassa. She will be with you shortly. In the meantime, I have another errand to perform. With your permission . . ."

The girl bowed and left through the entry door. Tarani sighed and relaxed as the illusions vanished; I caught her and lowered her into one of the chairs. No sooner was she seated, however, than the inner door opened and Zefra came in. Clearly, she had been waiting for the slave-girl to leave us alone.

Tarani looked around toward the door as she heard it open, and she stared for a long time while Zefra stood, as if turned to stone, and stared back. I was kneeling beside Tarani, but I might as well have been still invisible. I must have responded subconsciously to their exclusion of me, for by the time Zefra moved, I was on the other side of the room, pressing my back against the double door.

Tarani was still shaky from the strain of holding the illusions so long, but she stood up as Zefra approached her. The older woman's hands reached out to frame the girl's face for another long, searching look, and then Zefra moved closer and placed her cheek against Tarani's. Suddenly they were holding one another, gasping softly and rocking back and forth.

Right smack in the middle of it, someone knocked on the door behind me, so heavily that the vibrations sent me staggering toward the women. A voice boomed through the closed doors: "OPEN FOR THE HIGH LORD."

I ran for the inner doors, grabbing Tarani's hand as I passed. "He wants Rassa," I whispered, dragging Tarani toward the door.

Zefra caught the girl's hand and hauled the other way, stopping me. "Then he must find her here," she said. "I know you're weary, daughter," she whispered, touching Tarani's face again, "but you must keep Rassa's illusion a bit longer."

"Rikardon—" Tarani started to say.

"He *can* hide in my apartment," Zefra said. "You need only keep Rassa's illusion. *Can you do it?*"

Tarani nodded.

"You—" she said to me. "Go through the door. Tarani will be safe—you must trust me."

"OPEN FOR THE HIGH LORD!" the voice boomed again. I dived through the open door and pulled it nearly shut behind me. Then I drew my sword and waited with my ear to the door. I trusted Zefra because the woman I had met matched the woman I had imagined from her letter. But Pylomel was an unknown quantity.

I heard some quick movements in the room, then Zefra opened the door. "Why did you not open on the first summons, wife?" said a voice I disliked instantly. It was whiny and carried a sarcastic, affected petulance.

"Your pardon, Pylomel," Zefra said coolly, "but I was disrobed. My dressmaker is here, as you see. She was measuring me for a new gown for the Celebration Dance."

"And would it be so inappropriate for a husband to see his wife disrobed?" said the nasty voice again.

"Not at all. But would my husband like his announcer to see me in such a state?"

I heard a bass-tone chuckle that was quickly choked off. It solved the puzzle of how one voice could both whine and command so convincingly.

"Obilin informed me that your dressmaker had arrived," Pylomel said, obviously deciding that it was time to get to the point. "It is she I have come to see, not you, lady. Rassa, my beautiful girl, come with me."

"She will stay here," Zefra said, her voice still quite calm.

"By sending her here, her father has granted me certain . . . privileges, lady. I'm sure you understand."

Zefra made a tight, sharp sound that might have been a laugh. "I understand quite well, Lord. I have no quarrel with your pleasures. But the Celebration Dance is only two days away, and Rassa must make a gown for me. She will stay here in this apartment until the gown is complete to my satisfaction. Then you may have her."

"And when, dear lady," said Pylomel, "did you decide to attend the dance? The last time we discussed it, you denied your son the honor of your presence on this important occasion."

"I have thought better of it," Zefra said, and her voice took on a different tone, almost humble. "Indomel is my only child, after all. And now that I have acceded to your wishes, Lord, will you punish me by depriving me of the only dressmaker I trust to prepare my gown in the time left?"

A moment's silence. My hand tightened on the hilt of the sword, while I strained and waited to hear Pylomel's next words.

"Very well," he said at last. "She may stay—with this understanding. On the night of the celebration, after the dance, she will come to me." He laughed. "Perhaps that is appropriate, after all. It is a high occasion, and we will continue our celebration through the night. Is that not so, Rassa?

"Why, girl, you're trembling. Let me comfort you a moment."

I gritted my teeth, and told myself: *Zefra knows what she's doing, and Tarani isn't being hurt*. But as the silence stretched on, it changed to: *If he doesn't take his hands off her* . . .

"Better now, dear girl?" Pylomel's voice said, and he was answered by an indistinct murmur. "Then it is settled, Zefra. She will stay here until after the Celebration Dance—and it is your duty to see she remains. Is that clear?"

"Perfectly, Lord. Now, may we get on with the measuring? Time is very short."

"Certainly. And I will inform our son of your change of heart. Doubtless he will be overcome with joy."

The minute I heard the doors close, I ran out into the room and took Tarani into my arms. She sagged against me and shuddered.

13

"Did you see him?" Tarani asked. "Rikardon, I've never met anyone so . . . repulsive." She pulled away from me and faced Zefra. "Mother, how could you stand to be here . . . *with him* . . . all these years?

"I had to be with him only a short time, dear," she answered, and turned away abruptly. Her voice came softly, bitterly, over her shoulder. "Only until I produced an heir." She seemed to shake herself, then began to pace about the room as she talked. "Since Indomel's birth, Pylomel has left me quite alone. I have even been spared the need to appear at official functions—though he did request my presence at the Celebration Dance."

"I've heard something of the celebration," I said. "But I don't understand what the occasion is."

"Indomel will be designated the next High Lord," Zefra said. "Oh, he won't have the position until Pylomel dies, but I wouldn't put it past the little fleason to assassinate his father, first chance he gets."

"You said Indomel is your son!" Tarani cried, shocked.

"The son of my body, Tarani. But Pylomel took him away *hours* after his birth, and he's trained him to be as devious and decadent and . . . I hate him almost as much as I hate Pylomel."

Tarani and I were both a little stunned at the violence of the outburst, but in the next moment, Zefra's voice was tender once again.

"You, my darling, are the daughter of my spirit as well as my body."

"Mother," Tarani said impulsively, "you must come with us when we leave Eddarta. You've no reason to stay here any longer, not to protect me or—Volitar."

"Yes, your young man told me that he is gone," Zefra said sadly, and once more mother and daughter embraced.

I didn't ask Tarani how she planned to get her mother out of there. Tarani's world and Zefra's world had been entirely separate until bare moments ago, yet the two women, so much alike physically, had formed an immediate affection for one another. I knew that if it were possible, Zefra would leave Eddarta with us. I could no more willingly leave her behind than I could leave Tarani.

But other things had to come first.

"Gharlas killed Volitar," I said, and Zefra and Tarani drew apart. "And he stole something which belongs to Tarani. That's why we've come—to get it back."

"Gharlas? Why would he kill Volitar?"

Tarani spoke, then, telling then Zefra about Gharlas. How he had blackmailed Volitar into duplicating gemstones, so that Gharlas could replace the treasures in Pylomel's vault, using the secret entrance Gharlas had found. How Volitar had fought to the last to protect Tarani from him. How we had confronted Gharlas in the workshop, and Tarani's display of power had proved her heritage.

"He knows who I am, Mother, and he could use that against you. Even if he hadn't killed Volitar, the threat to you would give me enough reason to be here."

I was startled when I got a good look at Zefra's face. There was sadness in it, and an odd glow that made me uneasy. I didn't know if it meant she was a little unbalanced—hardly an unreasonable occurrence, considering the peculiar life she lived—or if that light was anticipation of revenge on Gharlas.

"There are few here who would regret Gharlas's death," she said. "But he isn't in the city, as far as I know."

"He's on his way," I said. "Tomorrow—the day after at the latest—he'll be here. We need your help to know where to find him."

Zefra smiled, and the odd light went away. "He is easily found; he lives in the last house, the one nearest the wall. Also the smallest." She laughed. "What sweet justice that the old passageway really does exist."

"You know about it?" Tarani asked. "Can we use it to get into his house unobserved?"

"No, child, for if it truly is Troman's Way, it connects only with the Council Chamber in the Lord Hall. There have always been rumors of its existence. Troman was a High Lord of an elder age, who believed in the semblance of discretion. He installed a succession of young women in that small house, and visited them while he was, supposedly, inspecting the treasure vault."

"Wasn't he afraid that the women would steal from him?" I asked.

"Indeed, he was. That's why he concealed the house entry so cleverly that none of the girls ever found it—or the many residents who have searched for it since. When he died, the secret died, which was just as well. There has never been a High Lord since Troman who bothered to conceal his . . . pleasures. It has been so long, now, that it's generally believed that Troman's Way was only a rumor."

"Well, if we can't use it, then it's not important," I said. "This Celebration Dance—will Gharlas be there?"

"If he has arrived by then, certainly. Attendance is mandatory." She smiled, and the strange light was back. "For everyone but me, that is."

"Then we'll plan to search the house that night."

"And if it isn't in the house?" Tarani asked.

"Then he'll have it on his person. We can wait for him to come back."

"Meanwhile," Zefra said, "I must do something about a new gown. Pylomel is nothing if not observant; if I wear an old gown, he will recognize it."

Tarani laughed—a beautiful sound. "Oh, that's not a problem, Mother. I *can* sew. Come and choose a fabric."

We spent the night and the next day in Zefra's apartment. At first, Tarani did most of the talking, her fingers busy with the soft, pale fabric which Zefra had chosen. I could hear the love and admiration in her voice when she talked of Volitar—his care of her, the things he believed in, his patience and skill as he mastered his new trade. Tarani spoke more diffidently of the Recorder's school which she had attended until age sixteen.

"Yes, I knew you had a strong mindpower the day you were born, Tarani, and I warned Volitar to watch for it to emerge."

"How did you know, so soon?" Tarani asked.

Zefra didn't answer immediately. "Even as an infant," she said at last, "your resemblance to me was apparent. I have a strong mind-gift, and it seemed possible that you would inherit that quality, also." She smiled. "You are very skilled at illusion, daughter. Did the Recorders teach you that?"

"No," Tarani said, and the skin of her cheeks seemed to shrink in on the bone structure.

She's trying to decide whether to tell Zefra about Molik, I realized. *Surely Zefra, of all people, would understand her drive and determination to get what she wanted—at any cost. But Tarani's still not comfortable with the memory.*

Even as those thoughts were flashing through my mind, Tarani had made her decision, and was speaking. "I worked for a while as a seamstress," she lied, "and when I had enough money, I organized an entertainment troupe."

She continued the story from there, and managed to tell it without mentioning Molik or his assassins. She dwelled mostly on the acts in the show, including her own. Once Zefra turned to me—the first time she addressed me directly—and asked me if I had seen the show. Tarani busied herself with her sewing, and I knew she was remembering that her performance had been a diversion, so that Molik's assassins would have a chance to kill me.

Is she afraid I'll tell the truth? I wondered, feeling a little hurt at her lack of trust. *Well, I will*.

"I have seen Tarani dance, Zefra," I answered. "There is nothing in this world more lovely."

"And how did you meet my daughter, Rikardon? Why are you helping her in her quest for revenge against Gharlas?"

"It is my quest, too," I said, then hesitated, searching for a plausible reason for my involvement.

But Zefra smiled and nodded, reached out to press my hand with her own for a moment. "You needn't try to hide the obvious, Rikardon. I have seen the love you share. Remember that I have known that kind of love, as well. I'm very glad that Tarani is not alone."

I didn't dare look at Tarani, and I noticed that she was quick to change the subject.

"Tell me about Volitar," Tarani pleaded. "What happened when you left Eddarta?"

Zefra sighed and shivered, but she remained silent for a moment that became more awkward as the silence continued. Finally, Tarani prompted her gently: "Mother?"

"You must be a little patient with me, child," Zefra said. "For eighteen years I have used every power at my command to keep hidden the story you have asked to hear."

"If it is too painful to remember now, Mother—"

"No, Tarani, I want you to know . . . about Volitar. But the story begins two years before I met him, when I was a child of Ruthanan—my birth family's name—and attending my first Gathering, an event which is held yearly to commemorate the safe arrival of the Seven Families in Eddarta. Attendance at the Gathering is not mandatory, but absences are noticed. Besides, there is much business done at the Gathering, where all Families are, for a time, equal.

"Some of that business concerns the children. Everyone who reached sixteen years of age during the previous year appears at the Gathering. In a year such as this, when the next High Lord attends the Gathering, it becomes a Celebration Dance, and the confirmation ceremony is performed on the following day.

"For most of the children, it is the first time they have

been seen by members of the other Families. It is here that the bargaining begins."

"Bargaining?" I asked. "For what?"

"For marriages," Zefra answered shortly. "It is required that everyone marry someone from another Family. One isn't obligated to marry at all, of course, but—again—failure to marry is regarded as suspicious, since it is everyone's duty to assure the continuance of the mind-gift."

Gharlas said that they were "breeding for the mind-gift," I remembered. *Somehow, I didn't expect such a formalized, highest-bidder sort of situation.*

"But mindpower wasn't all there is to be gained," Zefra went on bitterly. "A property trade usually goes along with a marrige bond, and the Lords look upon the Family children as marketable items."

"But after all these years, how can any individual claim to be from only one Family?" I asked.

"In every marriage, the woman—and her children—become members of the husband's Family: No, that's wrong," she amended. "They become the *property* of that Family, at least since Pylomel became High Lord, which happened two years after my first Gathering. He 'reformed' the property system by assigning all patronages held by Family members to the Family as a whole, and giving the Lords the power to assign rightful portions of their income to each household in the Family."

"Could he do that," Tarani asked, "without the *consent* of the other Lords?"

Zefra laughed. "My dear, he had no trouble winning their consent. In the first place, the system did need some kind of reforming. Originally the Families had been granted patronages that were localized—one farming area, one city area—and they had been assigned to the Family units living at that time. But after years of subdivision to heirs, and trading for beneficial marriages, it took ten full-time clerks to keep track of who was entitled to what revenue within each Family.

"In the second place, Pylomel was quick to recognize that the other Lords shared his greedy temperament, and would see the opportunity for control as an opportunity for profit.

"In the third place," Zefra continued, "Pylomel included, as part of the agreement, that the High Lord would have the right to monitor each Lord's dispersal of patronage funds, and would be the final judge in any Family dispute. In this way, he gave the Families some promise of protection against greed, while unofficially assuring the Lords that he would support their decisions completely."

Zefra shook her head. "No, Pylomel had no trouble convincing the Lords to his 'reform proposal.' But to give them credit, they hadn't had the chance to know Pylomel by then. He was the youngest High Lord ever to take office! Did you know that? Some say, now, and very softly, that he arranged his father's death. But at eighteen, he had an impressive knowledge of the details of the system, and of the personalities of the individual Lords. What would have taken the old High Lord days of discussion and argument to settle, Pylomel could accomplish with only a few words."

I exchanged glances with Tarani. "Compulsion?" I asked. "Was he using his mindpower to convince them?"

Zefra nodded her head in a mock bow. "Very good, Rikardon. But you must remember that you are acquainted with someone with a strong mind-gift. We of the Seven Families, although the concept is never far from us, have rarely seen so powerful a mind as Pylomel's."

Suddenly I was very worried. "Gharlas said he was denied the accession because of his illegitimacy," I said, "but that he 'tested' *higher* than Pylomel."

14

"That's quite true," Zefra said. "Pylomel admitted to me that he showed only enough of his power during the final testing to assure that he would win the succession. And he was well aware of the effect it had on Gharlas; to this day he still laughs about it."

No wonder Gharlas hates Pylomel's tusks, I thought, feeling a kind of sympathy for the man, with full recognition of how ironic my reaction was. But something didn't make sense.

"Everything I've heard about Pylomel leads me to think he

would have wanted to boast about his strength," I said. "He seems to enjoy controlling people. Why did he hide the extent of his power?"

"In that," Zefra said, "he had an excellent example from the previous generation. The mind-gift has been reappearing, ever more strongly, in recent times. Pylomel's father faced a High Lord candidate who showed a startling gift, and had no hesitation about using it. You must understand that all the official testing is done in private—the children don't see the performance of the other candidates. Well, *this* boy's power frightened the Lords. The story goes that he could read, as well as control, minds—the most rare of all mind-gifts. The Lords agreed to tamper with the test results, to keep the boy from gaining power.

"When they announced that Horinad, Pylomel's father, was to be the next High Lord, the boy understood immediately that he had been cheated. He stood up in the room where all the candidates waited for the results, denounced the Lords, and laid a suicide compulsion on all of them. Three were dead by the time the boy could be knocked unconscious."

"What happened to him?" Tarani asked.

"The remaining Lords had him killed, of course. So you see, Pylomel knew better than to frighten the Lords too early with the strength of his mind. He waited until he had the political power to support it, and he used it most subtly, until he began to believe that he is invulnerable."

"What are the tests like?" The question came from Tarani, but I was curious about the answer, too.

"There are two sets of tests," Zefra said. "The early one is given to all children, not just those who may be eligible to become High Lord."

"To the girls, as well?" I asked.

"Yes, certainly, to the girls," Zefra answered bitterly. "The mother-buyers have to know how much power we have to offer as breeding stock." Then she laughed. "Not that it does them much good. The girls learn about the system, early on, and regularly cheat on those tests."

"How can you show more power than you have?" Tarani wondered.

I answered her. "Not more—less. Am I right, Zefra?"

"Exactly right again, Rikardon. What mindpower we do have, is our only protection; we prefer to keep it a secret.

"To answer your question, Tarani, those tests are very like the ones you probably had at Recorder's school. Throwing mondeana and calling the results before they settle. Identifying shapes held out of sight. That sort of thing."

Like the star/circle/wavy-line cards used in ESP research in Ricardo's world, I thought. *But they don't consider that kind of sensitivity, which would seem to be very common, to be the same thing as direct thought reading. Maybe that's because of the probability factor. The Gandalarans may think that the right answer about the cards or the mondeana comes through the comparison/computation link with the All-Mind, rather than as a message from the mind of another person. While actual understanding of another's thoughts . . .*

Hello. There's a new idea. If the All-Mind consists of the memories or personalities (depending on your viewpoint) of all past individuals, are living individuals part of it? Or can they just "talk" to it, in varying degrees, on a conscious or subconscious level?

That would put direct thought reading or control between living people in a wholly different category. And even here in Eddarta, where they claim to value mind-gifts, that power scares them. Maybe that should be: especially *here in Eddarta, where the Lords know it can happen, and can threaten their own political power.*

"The second test is more complex, but basically the same skills, I think," Zefra was saying. "The first set is given at age twelve, the second at age fifteen—only to High Lord candidates. There is a third and final test given to the next High Lord as part of the ceremony which names him successor. He must read the Bronze."

She said that as if "the Bronze" were some kind of sacred document, I thought. *Yet, as far as I know, the Gandalarans don't believe in any sort of God. They think they understand the All-Mind, and everyone has access to it.*

Oh, well, I'm still a stranger here, as I am reminded every day.

"But I have strayed far from the story I was telling," Zefra continued. "Pylomel instituted his 'reform' for only one reason—to get me for his wife. I know that sounds immodest, but it is true, and it should tell you to what extent he will go to achieve his slightest wish.

"I met him on the night of my first Gathering. He was eighteen, and the designated successor. I have said that my own gift is fairly strong—I sensed the corruption of his personality, and could hardly bear to have him near me, even for the time required for a single dance. I knew how he felt about me, of course. Ill with fear and repulsion, I left the celebration early.

"I waited up for my father, and ran to meet him when he came home. He held me tightly as he spoke of the bargaining that Pylomel's father had initiated.

" 'I've always promised you that your marriage would have your own consent, Zefra,' he told me. 'Since I couldn't find you to discuss it, I compromised. I told them that I would not consider you marriageable until you were eighteen. But, daughter, it is an honor to be sought by the next High Lord. Would such a match have your consent?'

"I told him the truth then—that I would rather die than let Pylomel touch me. And he promised me that Pylomel would not have me—not if it cost my father his fortune.

"Two years later, Pylomel's father was dead, and Pylomel was High Lord. He approached my father again, about a month before my eighteenth birthday, and was again refused. The next day, I found my father assassinated in his bed."

Zefra's voice had become soft and fragile as she had talked of her own father. Now she shook herself and continued in a stronger voice.

"It is our custom that, if a marriage bond is not confirmed before a girl turns eighteen, she is free to make her own choice. I had seen Pylomel a few times—at obligatory social functions, in chance meetings—and he knew that I would never come to him willingly. I think now that it was only my repeated refusals which kept him so determined to have me. My father's brother had the power to make such a bond, but after I told him the whole story, he, too, refused Pylomel's offer.

"That's when Pylomel invented his brilliant 'reform', which gave the Lord the right to manipulate matters of property. The day before I was eighteen, *I* was still 'property', and my Lord traded me for three grain farms and a butchery."

We were silent a moment, Tarani and I feeling the tragedy of the young girl whose life was completely out of her control.

"Is that when you ran away?" Tarani asked at last.

"Soon afterward," Zefra said. "Pylomel insisted that I be given quarters in his home—these very rooms, in fact—until the wedding celebration could be held. He . . . visited me, one evening, asking . . .

"I was unwise. Not content with a simple refusal, I let my hatred of him show, saying that I would perform that duty only when it was legally necessary.

"Of course, he was furious—and determined to break me down, one way or another. The way he chose was humilation. He ordered that a commemorative coin be issued for our wedding, but that it display only *his* face. He decreed that each of his landservants would, out of the joy of the occasion, purchase one of those coins at twice its value. Then he sent *me* into Eddarta's streets to 'sell' the coins. He succeeded this far—" She clenched her fists, and a tremor ran along her arms. *"I was humiliated!"*

Zefra became aware of her tension, and made a visible effort to relax, taking several deep breaths before she continued.

"I had rid myself of three quarters of the coins when I came to Volitar's shop. As always, I left the guards outside the shop and went in alone. There was something special about Volitar, who was nearly as old as my own father. I had seen a lot of grief and resignation in far younger men, but in Volitar I saw a spark of defiance. It seemed the most natural thing in the world to tell him . . . everything. Without another word, without once looking backward, he took my hand and led me out the rear door of his shop, then out of Eddarta."

She smiled, and there was a softness in her face we hadn't seen before. "At first, I didn't love Volitar. We both understood that we had chosen to do something together that we had been too frightened to try while we were alone. We took pleasure in being together, and in being free, even though the trip was a hard one for us. It was so ironic—I still had Pylomel's gold coins, but we didn't dare spend them, for fear of being traced.

"But once we were in Dyskornis, and he had found a means to support us, and I began to believe, really *believe* that we might get away with it—then my gratitude to Volitar changed to love. When you were born, Tarani, I thought there could never be two people more happy than Volitar and I. Even when Pylomel's agents found me, I could be happy that I was alone, and that they didn't know about Volitar and . . . about you, dear. I let Pylomel believe that he had won what he wanted—that I had hated the outside world, but I had been too proud to return on my own. He was satisfied, and I was content. I gave him my body, but kept my mind closed to him—I have that much power."

"Didn't that make trouble for you?" I asked.

"On the contrary," Zefra answered, "Pylomel is so sure of his own power that he doesn't suspect mine. We discussed his power only once, but I remember what he said. 'I don't read thoughts,' he told me. 'But I can sense a person's attitude. I know when I'm being lied to,' he said, not realizing that I was lying to him at that very moment. I think that he doesn't realize he *can't* sense anything from me, but his unknowing reliance on *only* my words and actions makes him nervous around me. As I said, he has left me to myself since Indomel's birth."

"Yet he has kept you here," Tarani said, "in fine state."

"Do you think he would put me aside for another wife?" Zefra asked. "No. An agreeable, undemanding wife affords him a shelter under which he can pursue his other interests. And Indomel is my son—to get rid of me without declaring the boy illegitimate, he would have to kill me. Pylomel still takes some pleasure in my imprisonment, and in what it represents—the memory of his hardest-won victory. Or so he thinks.

"But surely that's enough about me. I was asking, too, where you and Rikardon met, Tarani."

"In Thagorn," Tarani said. "My troupe was performing—"

"*Thagorn?*" Zefra demanded, startling Tarani into missing a stitch. "Isn't that the city where those traitors, the Sharith, live?"

"Traitors?" Tarani repeated.

"Yes, traitors! It was because of them that Harthim had to leave the golden halls of Kä and bring the Seven Families here to Eddarta!"

To say that Tarani and I were surprised by Zefra's challenge would be to understate our reaction—then, or in the next moment, when Zefra laughed, showing some embarrassment.

"But how foolish of me to judge them today by what they did generations ago! One has trouble seeing any kinship between Harthim's enlightened leadership and Pylomel's self-serving, greedy manipulation of the Seven Families. Why should one expect the Sharith to remain the enemies of the Kingdom, or ask them to bear that ancient blame?"

"Enlightened leadership"? I thought, incredulously. *I guess it does depend on your viewpoint. But I wonder if that was Volitar's opinion, too, of the last King.*

"So," Zefra continued, "you were saying that you met this young man while your troupe was performing in Thagorn?"

I answered her: "I was visiting a friend in Thagorn when Tarani's show was to be given. My friend invited me to attend, and introduced us after the dance was over. As I was ready, by then, to continue my journey to Dyskornis, Tarani invited me to travel with her caravan, for reasons of safety. We were friends by the time we reached Dyskornis, and I went with her to meet Volitar. We found him being tortured by Gharlas—the rest you know."

"This thing which Gharlas has—what is it?" Zefra asked.

Tarani looked at me, and I happened to move my hand across my home-made leather belt. I grabbed the belt and the idea at the same time.

"Volitar still had all the gold coins," I told Zefra. "Gharlas stole them. Even if they were only ordinary coins, Tarani would be entitled to recover them. Now that we know what they mean, however . . ."

"Yes," Zefra agreed. "Yes, you must get them back. I will do all I can to help you."

15

Tarani stayed with Zefra nearly every moment on that day. I was occasionally exiled to an inner room, as meals were delivered, or as Zefra received or sent messages. Thono, the young girl who had let us into the apartment the day before, came and went a few times in the morning, and arrived again in the afternoon with the news we wanted to hear: Gharlas was in Eddarta.

I didn't have a chance to speak to Tarani alone until that night. Zefra had wished us goodnight, and we were in the room which Tarani's mother had given us to share—without asking our approval of the arrangement. The night before, we had been too exhausted by tension to be bothered by the awkwardness of the situation; we had merely pulled the side-by-side pallets a little way apart, and slept.

Tonight I was thinking: *We spent night after night in the desert, alone, and never felt this tension. What is it about being in a* room *together that gives a situation sexual overtones?*

Quit fooling yourself, I told myself then. *In the desert, our feelings for one another were hidden. Now they're out in the open—so obvious, in fact, that Zefra read them easily. How was she to know that Tarani and I haven't yet expressed those feelings in the traditional way? The tension won't dissipate until we do.*

It was Tarani who broke the uncomfortable silence. "Thank you, Rikardon, for—" She laughed a little. "—for lying to my mother."

"What you want her to know is your own affair, Tarani," I said. "I have the feeling she isn't telling you everything, either."

Tarani looked hurt, and worried. "Yes, I have had the same thought. Rikardon, I do not understand why it should be this way. I thought I had come to terms with the memory of Molik, yet I found I could not tell Zefra about him. Why not?"

Maybe Antonia wouldn't let you, I thought. *I think she was right.*

"For the same reason you didn't tell Zefra about the Ra'ira, Tarani. You don't know her that well, yet. You may be as closely related as two people can get, but that doesn't mean that both of you will automatically accept each other without judgment. I saw how shocked you were when Zefra reacted against the Sharith."

She began to pace slowly around the room. "I have asked her more than once to come with us when we leave, but she has never given me a definite answer. She always turns the discussion to another topic." She faced me, held her arms out in question. "Do *you* think she wants to come with us?"

"I can't answer for her, Tarani. But if she wants to come, we'll do everything we can to take her with us."

"Thank you," she said, and the tension intensified. She seemed to be waiting for something. For me.

I wanted her with an aching need, but the question was still there: Which woman did I want? The sensitive young girl who was, even now, undergoing the emotional upheaval of the first meeting with her mother? Or the worldly woman, not much older in years, but rich in experience and knowledge of people?

I opened my arms, and she came into them. I held the body that belonged to two different women, and gave a silent prayer for patience and wisdom.

After a moment, Tarani barely whispered: "It isn't time yet, is it?"

I pressed the slim, supple body even closer to me, then released her . . . them. I hoped she heard my regret as I said: "Goodnight, Tarani."

I blew out the candle in the lamp, and we settled in to sleep. I simply lay down in my clothes, but I heard movement and rustling that told me Tarani was taking off the dress she had borrowed from Rassa's wardrobe. The sound soothed me, rather than excited me. It was such a natural thing to do, and so completely a sign of trust, that it brought back the feeling of uninvolved companionship we had shared in the desert. The ache abated, and I was able to sleep.

My rest was fitful, and in the many wakeful moments of the night, I blamed the inactivity of the previous day. After our routine of hard physical activity, the enforced idleness had all my muscles complaining of disuse.

But Tarani's day had been more strenuous—hurrying to finish the gown, talking to Zefra, switching Rassa's illusion on and off—and the rhythm of her breathing spoke of a deep, restful sleep.

So it was I, and not Tarani, who heard the tapping and scratching in the early hours of the morning. I got up, followed the sound, and opened the latticed windows that faced the garden. A heavy object struck me in the chest, and I staggered backward, trying to support the weight so that it wouldn't fall.

It flapped and hooted and butted at my chest. "Lonna!" I

whispered. "Yes, I'm glad to see you, too. Now hush, or you'll wake Tarani."

Finally I held the large bird cradled in my arm, and stroked her back and the tips of her long wings. She twisted her neck until the downward hook at the end of her beak dug affectionately into my shoulder, then just enjoyed the attention.

She didn't have a message tied to her anywhere. The bird had a surprisingly large vocabulary of words she could understand, but I didn't feel like playing "twenty questions" at that time of the morning—especially since Tarani's limited psychic link with Lonna could retrieve any message easily, once she woke up.

Tarani did awaken at first light, and nearly scared me to death by sitting straight up in bed and calling out: "Lonna!" I had been sitting with my back against the wall, half-dozing with the bird resting in my lap. The bird jumped away from me, wings flapping, with such force that I was sent sprawling to one side. When I righted myself, I saw Tarani, naked from the waist up, trying to hug Lonna while laughing at the bird's happy antics.

I turned my face away, filled with a need that had nothing to do with Tarani. I wanted to be with Keeshah, so badly that I could feel his fur in the palms of my hands. I reached out to him mentally, and thrilled to feel his joy at the contact.

When together? he asked me.

Tonight, with any luck, I told him. **Wait until after dark, then come as close to the city as you can. When we leave, we'll be in a hurry.**

Keeshah must have sensed what I wasn't saying: *If we get out of here alive.*

I will help! came his determined thought.

There is nothing you can do, Keeshah, I told him. **Strength won't win this round. It will all be easier for me, if I know you're waiting.**

I will wait, he agreed reluctantly, then amended it: **For a time.**

I want a promise from you, Keeshah—one that will not be easy to keep.

What? he asked, the feeling of suspicion clear in his thought.

**If I am killed, I want you to take Tarani to safety. Let*

*that be your first duty, even above avenging my death. Do you agree?**

There was a short silence, just the quiet awareness of our link. Then, with little warning, Keeshah's mind swept into mine, forming the close, intensely personal contact we had shared before. He withdrew nearly as quickly, leaving me a little breathless, but in that moment of contact, he had learned what he wanted to know—that my request wasn't just a whim, or a mere favor to Tarani, but that her life was infinitely precious to me.

I will do it, he promised. **But don't die.**

I laughed out loud. **Thank you, Keeshah. I'll try my best.**

I broke the contact to find Tarani dressed, holding Lonna, and smiling at me. "Keeshah?" she asked.

I nodded. "He'll be waiting outside the city for us tonight."

"So will Ronar," she said. "Thymas sent Lonna to tell us that he's in Eddarta."

It was comforting to know that Thymas was here. Tarani and I discussed procedure, and decided that it was important for us to remain hidden until time to act; we didn't dare risk a meeting with Thymas. So we sent a message with Lonna:

> *We are in the Inner City, will move quietly against G tonight. Wait near city gate, be ready to distract guard. May be late, T will tell you when.*
> *R.*

While Tarani worked furiously on the gown, Zefra and I conferred about the layout of the Harthim section, and the best way to get to Gharlas's house unseen. She sketched as much of the house's floorplan as she could remember. When we had discussed everything she or I thought might be helpful to us tonight, I sat back from the table we were using and said: "Tarani wants you to come with us, Zefra, but you won't say yes or no. Don't you think she deserves an answer?"

Tarani, who was seated on the window ledge, working by the window, let the pale yellow dress settle into her lap.

"There will be so many people at the dance, Mother," she said. "It will be easy for you to slip away. I'll let you know when."

A *light compulsion,* I thought. *That's what she'll use on*

Thymas, too. It's not as efficient as a walkie-talkie, but it makes a pretty useful signal device.

Zefra sighed, and closed her eyes for a moment. "Tarani, I cannot say how much it has meant to me, seeing you grown, hearing that Volitar loved me to the last, and respected my wishes for you." She got up and walked over to the window, sat beside Tarani, and took her hands. "It would be wonderful if we could be together for the rest of our lives, daughter. But why must I go with you? Couldn't you stay here with me?"

"But Mother, you've said that it would enrage Pylomel if he ever learned you have deceived him all these years! It would be dangerous for both of us, if I stayed."

"No one need know you are here," Zefra said quietly.

Tarani stared at her mother. "You mean that I should stay in these rooms with you, and hide whenever someone comes in? I couldn't live like that, Mother, not like a hunted animal . . ."

Her voice died as Zefra's point hit home.

"I did live like that once," Zefra said. "It takes a special kind of strength, Tarani, and I have used all I had. I am comfortable here, and I have more influence in Lord City than it seems I do. Just by being here, I am proof that Pylomel has his limits. The Lords sometimes ask my advice on important issues, and I give them what guidance I can on how best to deal with the High Lord."

She stood up and came over to me. "Take the coins back from Gharlas," she told me. "Take Tarani and the gold far from here, and—mind this, now—have the gold melted and recast. If any one of those coins turns up outside Eddarta, it will be noticed.

"Even deducting the cost of the metallurgy service," she said, "you will have a small fortune. I hope and trust that you—" Her voice broke; she had to clear her throat before she could go on. "—that you and Tarani will have a happy, peaceful life together."

Tarani let the dress fall to the floor as she rushed over and threw her arms around her mother. They clung to one another, talking at the same time, sharing the misery of the parting that seemed so close now. It was another of those times when I was merely a spectator, and again I withdrew from them as a purely automatic reaction. Before I knew it, I was alone, standing at our bedroom window, looking out over the garden.

Tarani came in a few minutes later and said: "She asked me to call her away from the dance tonight, anyway, so that we can say good-bye one more time. I said I would do it—I hope that's all right."

"Of course it is, Tarani. Let's take a few seconds and go over what she told me about the house where Gharlas will be staying . . ."

16

The room we had first entered was merely a wide hallway with chairs. It led into a large, private sitting room which connected with several other rooms, including a tiled balcony where meals were served. We were in the private sitting room now, and Tarani was adjusting a fold of the gown while Zefra admired herself in a polished-brass mirror.

"It's lovely," Zefra said, "truly lovely. Rassa herself could have done no better."

A knock sounded on the outer door, and before any of us could react, we heard it open. I made a dash for the bedroom door and pushed it nearly shut after me, just as the inner door opened and I heard a booted step strike the tile which floored the private sitting room.

"Obilin!" Zefra said. "How dare you enter my apartment without permission?"

"I have a higher permission, lady," said the small man's voice, heavy and insolent. "I am to escort your dressmaker to her new apartment."

"My bargain with the High Lord specified that Rassa would be available to him *after* the Celebration Dance," Zefra argued.

"And *his* bargain—as he explained it to me, lady—was that you would keep the dressmaker until your gown was completed. Which it is. And quite lovely, too, if I may say it.

"The High Lord sent me to assure Rassa's safe arrival in her new quarters."

Zefra put on a good show of fuming and fussing. "Does he think I would go back on my word? You may return to him, Obilin, and assure him that Rassa will be awaiting him after the dance. *I* will see to it, as I promised."

"Sorry," Obilin said, and I could almost hear him grinning. "There is a complication—an intruder."

"What?"

"A man named Lakad hired on as a guardsman two days ago, and then disappeared. We have no idea where he is, but he may still be in the area. The Guard has been alerted to watch for him, but the High Lord thinks it wise that all . . . ladies . . . should be . . ."

His voice trailed off like the noise in a toy as its batteries finally give up. The short fur on the back of my neck lifted as I heard Zefra speak. Her voice was like a whip of ice.

She said: "Obilin, you have done as the High Lord commanded. Rassa is in the apartment prepared for her, awaiting Pylomel. What's more, you, yourself, located the intruder, and killed him. You will call off the watch. Do you understand all that?"

"Yes." A murmur.

"Then return to Pylomel. When you see him, you will act and think normally. You will remember what I have told you as if it truly happened, and you will not remember that I spoke to you at all. You came here, collected Rassa with no trouble, and delivered her as ordered. Go now."

I came out of the bedroom as Obilin reached the outer door of the entrance room; he had gone through the inner door without bothering to close it after himself. He was moving slowly, just as you'd imagine someone would move, under the control of anther mind. I went through the formal sitting room to close the outside door, then returned, closing the inner door as I came through it.

I couldn't read Tarani's face, but Zefra's was openly triumphant. "Now you see what I have hidden from Pylomel all these years. My mind-gift is as strong as his—even stronger, in some ways. Tonight, when he goes to Rassa drunk and lustful, and finds an empty apartment, I will send him into unconsciousness and give him a memory of all he wanted to experience. And he will never guess the truth."

"It's time for us to go," I said, taking Tarani's hand and

pulling her toward the doorway. "We need to be in position to see Gharlas leave the house."

Zefra moved to Tarani and hugged her. "Be careful, darling. And remember to call me—I must see you one more time before you leave."

"I won't forget, Mother," Tarani said.

As we had planned, Zefra called the two guards inside, on the pretext of moving a heavy piece of furniture. Tarani and I, cloaked by her illusion, stepped out into the main house and left the apartment which had been our home for the past two and a half days.

We moved cautiously through the twisting hallways. Twice, it was necessary for Tarani to conceal us through illusion, as guards or servants walked by. Though it seemed a long trip, it was no more than five minutes before we stepped out into the fragrant garden. Only then could we talk about what we had seen.

"She *enjoyed* setting that compulsion, Rikardon," Tarani whispered, shuddering. "What would Volitar have thought, seeing her like that? How could this have happened to the woman who ran away from exactly that kind of power?"

"Tarani—" I began, but she hadn't really stopped talking. She gripped my arms.

"Please, Rikardon, you read people better than I do. I cannot leave her unless I understand how this . . . corruption could have happened to her."

"All right," I said, drawing her into the concealing shadow of the wall of the house. The sun hadn't set yet, but brilliant hues of red and orange had claimed the sky.

"Here's what I think," I told Tarani. "First, Zefra had a strong gift to begin with; she admitted she used it when she and Volitar escaped. Second, she's been virtually a prisoner for sixteen years, and her power was the only thing that gave her some control of her circumstances. Not to mention a touch of revenge against Pylomel, who created the prison for her.

"And third, the use of power is addictive, Tarani. Zefra's has become almost second nature—she has used it on me twice."

"On *you?*" she demanded. "When? Why did you not tell me?"

"Because I didn't realize it until she showed us how strong

she is. Twice, when you and she were together, I was suddenly somewhere else, with no memory of how I got there. She probably didn't even know she was doing it."

She thought for a moment, while I kept a nervous watch for wandering guards. I didn't feel we really had time for this discussion, but I knew Tarani was right—until she had it settled in her mind, she wouldn't be able to concentrate fully on Gharlas.

Finally she sighed and said: "She wants us to think she will stay behind to help the Lords against Pylomel. But that is not the true reason, is it?"

"For what it's worth, Tarani, I think she really believes what Volitar taught you—that it is wrong to control another person's life or mind. She sees herself as defending Volitar's viewpoint."

"But she *has* to see it that way, does she not?" Tarani said bitterly. "To justify using the methods that Volitar despised." She shook herself sharply. "As you said, Rikardon, Zefra and I are strangers to one another. I cannot stand in judgment of her—she accepted this life of horror for my sake. But now . . . I feel less grief for leaving her. She and her power belong here, where the only people who can be hurt are those who inflict hurt."

I sensed a change in mood, the shrugging off of her sadness. "So now—the Ra'ira."

It was night by the time we slipped into a brushy area in front of Gharlas's house, which stood far back in the Harthim area, close to the outer wall of the city. Zefra's information had been invaluable in finding it; many of the homes looked alike in the dimness beyond the lamp-lit walkway. The timing, too, was perfect; we had been waiting less than ten minutes before Gharlas came out of the double entry doors and passed us, walking toward the Family entrance.

He was wearing dark clothes—a soft tunic and loose trousers, covered by an embroidered, hip-length vest cinched at the waist with a dark-jeweled belt. The dark colors accentuated his extreme height and paleness. When he walked between the marble pillars which supported the lamps, he seemed to be only a floating face and hands.

Tarani tensed as he passed us, and her hand went to the sword she had smuggled into Lord City inside a bolt of fabric. We were both dressed to travel, in tunic and desert-style trousers that tied at waist and ankle to keep out the salty dust. I kept my hand on my sword, too, and wished that it were Rika. I realized that part of my gladness to have Thymas close by was the prospect of getting Serkajon's steel sword back into my hands.

When Gharlas was out of sight, Tarani and I went around to the back of his house and slipped inside. *Good thing doors aren't locked in Lord City,* I thought. *I guess that's because everybody's so busy milking their landservants that they don't have time to steal from one another. Except Gharlas, that is.*

We lit some lamps, glad the house was in a secluded location. We were in a kitchen area—long unused, by the look of it, which was a relief. I had wondered about servants. If he had any, they didn't seem to be around.

We did a quick search of the exposed shelves and the reachable cabinets, then moved through a double doorway into a dining area. Another cursory search, and we passed into a sitting room that was really a huge hallway. Like the midhall in Raithskarian architecture, this one huge room ran the full length of the house, right down its center. Matching, marble-topped tables stood at strategic points. Only two lamps had been left burning, so that the entire room was very dimly lit. There was very little furniture—a chair or two—to cover up the intricate geometric pattern of the floor tiles.

We were standing in a short hallway that led to the kitchen/dining area through which we had just come. Hulking darknesses at intervals on either side of the room seemed to be hallways that led from this main room to other living areas of the house. Between those entry areas, the walls were covered with thick tapestries, their scenes concealed from us by the dim light.

Pretty fancy, I thought. *Just what I would have expected from Gharlas. But spooky, with those flickering lamps. The place gives me the willies.*

Our plan was logical: first, make sure the Ra'ira wasn't in the house; next wait for Gharlas to return. Neither Tarani nor I seriously believed that Gharlas would let the jewel out of his possession for an instant, but we had to consider the possibility, if only because it was so unlikely.

But all the logic in the world isn't worth one good, gut-seizing hunch.

"This is too easy," I told Tarani, fighting the panic that was suddenly clutching at me. "Let's get out of here, right now."

"So soon, my friends? Why, you've only just arrived."

There it was—one hunch full-grown into one dangerous situation. Gharlas had appeared from behind the tapestry that hung beside the big, doubled front doors.

17

Tarani drew her sword and started for him, but I grabbed her.

"Bastard," she snarled at Gharlas.

In a world where women *knew* when they could be made pregnant, the word was a weighty curse, and maligned the mother as well as the child. In our last encounter with Gharlas, Tarani had used the epithet to distract him, but he wasn't going to be baited this time. His long, lean form seemed to ripple and he smiled as the word ran around the room in whispering echoes. Gharlas's smile wasn't the sort of thing you wanted to remember in the middle of the night. It creased his face and never touched the cold light that shimmered behind his eyes.

"Welcome to Eddarta, dear friends," he said. "It will be most beneficial to your future health if you will put down your swords. *Now!*"

Out of the dark hallways stepped swords with lots of husky muscle attached. It looked like Gharlas had selected the biggest and meanest of Pylomel's Guard.

So this is the payoff for all those "extra benefits", I thought. I recognized one of the men. Worse, he recognized me.

"You should have told me this was the guy, Gharlas," he said, stepping toward us from the hallway directly opposite the one we were blocking. "I caught a lot of grief for letting him into the city. It's gonna be a pleasure to kill him."

"*Stop, Sendar!*" Gharlas shouted. The big man did stop, but didn't quit leering at me like I was somebody's dinner.

"Death is very close to you right now, my friends," Gharlas said, his voice oily. "You know what I want. Give it to me."

I could almost feel the duplicate Ra'ira grow warm in the pouch hanging from my gold-lined belt. It was the real reason Gharlas had killed Volitar. Not everyone knew about the Ra'ira's special qualities, but nearly everyone did know it as a symbol of the Kingdom. In the process of forging a glass duplicate for the gem, Volitar had made *two* replicas. Gharlas had taken one of them to Raithskar with the intention of replacing the real one, and had later seen his accidental loss of the phony jewel as a blessing. He had realized that there must be no question, when the time came for him to reveal himself as King, that he did possess the only true Ra'ira. The existence of the second duplicate, the glass bauble I carried in my pouch, had taken him to Dyskornis. Volitar, having hidden it with his other greatest treasure, the letter from Zefra, had died without revealing either.

I glanced at Tarani, and saw the same determination on her face that I myself felt. We had come too many miles to back down now. Either we would leave here with the Ra'ira, or . . .

"How did you know we were going to be here?" I asked Gharlas. I was stalling for time, and he knew it. But he thought he was in control, and he had already shown us a tendency to boast. Not a modest guy, our Gharlas.

"Simple deduction," Gharlas said. "Hardly worth mentioning. The first thing I heard, when I arrived, was the rumor of an intruder calling himself Lakad. If you were here, so was she—and I knew what you wanted. *My* exceptional mind didn't have to guess when you would try to get it. I invited my friends here tonight, pretended to leave, and returned by the front door while you were scratching for lamps in the kitchen."

Markasset used that alias when Gharlas hired him to guard the caravan. Stupid. STUPID! I scolded myself. *But there's no help for that stupidity now.* I concentrated, tried to remember of our encounter in Dyskornis, searched for a weakness. Then I had it. His weakness was the same as his strength. The Ra'ira.

"I see that the female companionship you've been providing to the guards was money well spent," I said. "Got them to do the messy, dangerous work for you, haven't you? I see you prefer muscle to brains—otherwise Sendar wouldn't be here."

"Shut up," warned Sendar. "Gharlas, you want me to make him quiet?"

"That might be *just* what Gharlas wants, Sendar. Because he may be just a little bit worried that I'll tell you what this is all about. You see, he stole a jewel from Raithskar called—"

"*KILL HIM!*" Gharlas shouted, and Sendar leaped forward, his sword descending in a two-handed arc that would have split me in two—*if* I'd stood still.

But I had ducked around Sendar, and was running straight for Gharlas, scattering or jumping over furniture as it got in my way. Out of the corner of my eye, I saw Tarani slash at the big man's back, as his unresisted blow sent his swordtip clanging against the tile flooring. I was too busy to see more than that, because two other guards rushed out to intercept me before I could reach Gharlas.

These two were used to working as a team; one aimed high, the other low. I blocked the sword aimed for my head, jumped, and aimed a kick at the head of the guy swinging the lower blade. He flinched backward and missed his aim.

I heard footsteps behind me, and did some quick calculations. Six hallways opened into that room, and there had been a man in all but the one we had come through. That meant there were at least five guards—maybe more. Even if Tarani were calling Thymas in as reinforcement . . .

It doesn't look hopeful for the good guys, I thought.

I will help. Keeshah's thought struck me an instant before his mind merged with mine.

The Gandalaran who had been Markasset was a strong and skillful fighter. In the first, awkward days of my residence in his body, Markasset's trained reflexes had saved me more than once. But there had been an occasion, like this one, where the odds were against me and Keeshah had been unable to join the fight physically. He had saved me then, as he was trying to do now, by lending me some of his abilities.

The effect of Keeshah's help was a drastic reduction of my reaction time. I had no greater strength and, in fact, no quicker reactions. What I had was the giant cat's *alertness* to sound, scent, and sight clues that were beyond Markasset's normal ability to interpret quickly. Keeshah's mind accepted the stimuli of *my* surroundings, as perceived by *my* senses.

Because of the close joining of our minds, as soon as he interpreted, I had the knowledge necessary to guide my reactions.

So I knew, from the slightly differing odors, that there were only five men in the room. These two were trying to keep me away from Gharlas. From the sounds behind me, I could tell that Tarani was fighting Sendar, and the other two men were coming after me.

They don't know it yet, I thought fiercely, *but they just made a BAD choice.*

That was another thing Keeshah gave me. Spirit. When we were together in this special way, we *loved* a good fight.

I gauged the distance of the men behind me, and waited to hear the intake of breath that signaled a blow was about to be delivered. Then I whirled and ducked between them, running toward Tarani, and leaving them to scramble out of the way of their own swords.

That's your second mistake, guys, I thought, as I saw Tarani bring the big man down by slashing into his thigh, and then finish him. *You underestimated the lady.*

I turned to make a stand against the four guards, but Gharlas was smarter than that. "Go after the girl, you fools!"

Tarani was on her way to join me, but two of the guards broke past me to block her.

Damn you, Gharlas! I thought. *You think I'll leave myself vulnerable in order to protect Tarani. What you don't know is, she's worth any two men in a fight.*

But as my opponents and I circled and feinted, I caught glimpses of Tarani's struggle. It seemed more desperate than mine—I saw a couple of last-minute blocking moves that just barely saved her life.

What's going on? I wondered. *It's almost as though she can't control her own muscles . . .*

"Gharlas, you *bastard,*" I yelled, as the truth struck home. He was using his mindpower to slow her down.

In Dyskornis, Tarani had proved that she could break through Gharlas's paralyzing control, given time. Part of her resistance came from her own mindpower, but I knew now that she could resist, partly, for the same reason I could—the non-Gandalaran portion of her mind was less susceptible.

Pressed as she was with immediate physical threat, she couldn't afford the concentration necessary to block Gharlas's power entirely. The paralysis trick had surprised us last time; this time, her natural resistance kept her moving, and the weight of his power kept her fractionally, dangerously slower than she needed to be. It might have had the same effect on me, but he had chosen Tarani for his target. First because, of the two of us, she was the weaker fighter. Second because he was counting on Tarani's predicament distracting me from my own problems.

It was working.

I snapped back into focus in time to knock aside a thrust aimed at my throat, but I was too late to dodge the other man's wild, hopeful slash, and the point of his blade cut a short gash on the left side of my chest.

The burning pain helped me to concentrate; I told myself I couldn't help Tarani until I got rid of these two.

Under the onslaught of these two men, I had been backing toward one of the long side walls, and I had about two feet to go before I wouldn't have room to breathe, much less fight.

Do something, I told myself, remembering one of Ricardo's favorite mottoes, *even if it's wrong*.

Getting myself pinned had lost me most of the advantages of Keeshah's help, but the eager, feisty presence of his mind in mine gave me a different kind of help—inspiration.

I took a deep breath and offered my best imitation of the roar of an angry sha'um.

Everybody paused for a second or two, startled by the unexpected noise. Everybody, that is, except me. I took a quick step backward, dropped my sword, clenched both hands in the fabric of the ceiling-high tapestry that covered the wall, and yanked the heavy stitchery down. As it came loose, I spun around and sent it sailing at the two guards who, recovered from their moment of surprise, were barely two paces away from me.

The weight of the thing sent them staggering; one corner flipped up to block their vision, and another whipped around behind them. I grabbed up my sword again as one of the guys tripped and fell. The other one was so busy trying not to get dragged down with him that he didn't see me coming. In another few seconds, both of them were out of action.

I jumped over them and ran to help Tarani, who was being pressed into the corner furthest from Gharlas by her two guards. She was fighting grimly, with sword and mind; every muscle of her face and body seemed wire-tight. I roared as I ran and one guard, distracted, looked around. Tarani thrust her sword through the left side of his chest. His eyes went blank, still staring at me, as he collapsed to the floor.

The pull on her sword sent Tarani to her knees, and the last guard closed in on her. I was one jump away from him, my sword raised and ready—and Gharlas turned his power on me.

My body completed the running step that had been in progress, but instead of striking the blow I planned, I skidded past Tarani and the guard without having time to swing my sword. I slammed heavily into the wall. The impact sent the sword flying from my sluggish hand. I turned around, and pushed away from the wall toward the fighting pair. It was like trying to swim through treacle, and inside I was screaming in frustration.

Tarani let go of the hilt of her sword to reach up with both hands; she grabbed the man's sword wrist and hung on. He wasn't as big as Sendar had been, but big enough. He couldn't pry Tarani's clutching fingers away from his wrist, so he pulled his body sharply from side to side, dragging Tarani along the floor.

She stayed with him, her body trailing his sword arm with a violent, jerking motion, until he swung the hilt of his sword at her head. She turned her face aside at the last minute, but the bronze hilt clipped her temple and she went down like a rag doll.

The guard looked around at Gharlas.

"Kill her," Gharlas said.

18

The fighting red haze of a sha'um's rage shot through me, burning away Gharlas's control.

In Dyskornis, Tarani had helped me fight that power. Given time now, I could have broken free on my own. But with a sword already descending toward Tarani's slender throat, I surrendered to Keeshah the control I denied Gharlas.

I seemed to be only a spectator, as my body lunged for the guard. I caught the man's throat in my hands and dragged him away from Tarani. He turned the edge of his sword against my back, but before it more than touched me, I threw him to the floor. I pinned his forearm with my knee and shifted my weight to that knee, slowly increasing the pressure on his arm.

His body bucked and heaved. His left hand beat against my arms, clawed out at my face. I leaned on neck and arm. The blows became so weak that I barely felt them.

I was delighted when his right hand opened to release the hilt of the sword.

I laughed out loud when I felt bones break under my knee.

I shook the throat I held, and the head wobbled back and forth.

Keeshah left me, and I was empty. I pulled my hands away from the dead neck. My fingers left blackening indentations in the man's flesh. The sight of them appalled me, but reminded me of the reason this man was dead.

I half-walked, half-crawled back to Tarani and put a shaking hand against the fair, unmarked throat. When I felt her pulse, mine started to move again.

I stood up and turned toward the big double entry doors. Gharlas was still there. His smile had become a grimace, and there was no mistaking the message of hatred that flowed from his glowing eyes.

"She's alive, Gharlas," I said, picking up the sword Tarani's would-be killer had used. "Your power won't work on me, and all your hired muscle is dead. In Dyskornis you said we would settle things 'another time'—*now*, Gharlas. Just you and I. We'll settle it now. I will leave this room with the Ra'ira."

I started down the middle of the long room, kicking aside the debris of broken furniture. Miraculously, the two tables which held the lamps were still intact.

Gharlas waited for me, his hand resting on the hilt of his sword. When I was a third of the way across the room, he cried: "*Stop!*"

There was a ring of confidence in his voice. Suspicion made me pause.

"You say 'you and I'," he sneered, "as if we were equals." He took a step closer, and the lamplight from the table nearest him sent wavering shadows from his supraorbital ridges leaping up across his brow. "But you're forgetting who I will be."

" 'King of Gandalara'?" I mocked him. "You're a fool, Gharlas. You can't even hope to rule Eddarta, much less all the cities and towns scattered around the Walls. What are you planning to do, mind-control all the Lords?"

"Such crudeness is unnecessary," he answered. "Pylomel's influence rests with his fortune—when the Lords discover it is worthless, that *I* have the wealth he pretended to have, and that *I* have the loyalty of the Harthim guards, I will be acclaimed High Lord."

He might be right, at that, I thought. *Political rules in this city, though they make a show of being traditional, seem to be largely a matter of convenience.*

"What about Indomel? He won't let you take over without a struggle."

"I see you have learned a lot about Eddarta since you arrived," Gharlas said. "Until my plans are ready, I will allow Indomel to act as High Lord—under my control."

"All day, every day? Even with the Ra'ira, do you really believe you can do that?"

"All I need, at first, is subtle control at key moments, and the ability to know what the boy is thinking—those things the Ra'ira can give me easily. But if brute, total control is necessary? That, too, is within my power. For example . . ."

The door beside Gharlas opened, and Thymas walked in.

"You remember this young man, don't you?" Gharlas said. "Without Tarani to help him, he is completely mine. How delightfully ironic that you gave him Serkajon's sword for 'safekeeping.' I look forward to having that sword—after he kills you with it."

Thymas came toward me, the steel sword held lightly in front of him. I shifted my weight to face him. I didn't back away.

"When we decided to follow you, Gharlas," I said, keeping my eye on the slim, muscular boy approaching me slowly, "we all knew the odds, and agreed that the stakes were worth any risk. Thymas knows that I won't hesitate to kill him to get to you."

Thymas stopped, about ten feet away from me. His body reflected the struggle inside his mind. Muscles stood out on the sides of his neck, throwing into bright relief the ugly scar left by the vineh. A vein at his temple pulsed in a slow, heavy rhythm that seemed to symbolize the boy's determined resistance to Gharlas's power. His arms and hands trembled with the effort to break free of that terrible compulsion.

"He wants it that way, Gharlas," I said, still watching Thymas and feeling a fierce pride in the boy. He was fighting with everything he had, fighting so hard that I could *feel* the strain. "If the only way he can help me get to you is by dying, then Thymas will make it easy for me to kill him. He'll slow down at a crucial moment, leave openings in his defense."

I glanced at Gharlas, and was jolted by what I saw. His eyes widened, his breath started coming faster, and the smooth line of his jaw bunched out as he clenched his teeth. Thymas took another step forward—stiffly.

Come on, Thymas! I thought, excitement growing in me. *If there's one thing you are, it's stubborn. Don't let go! Don't give in!*

"You see?" I gloated. "All you've done is bought a little time, Gharlas. You picked on the wrong man. You can't use Thymas as a weapon again: *he won't let you*.

"You want ironic? You sent assassins to kill Dharak, and they attacked me by mistake—and both of us were the wrong targets. For you, *Thymas* is the most dangerous man of the Sharith."

I heard two sounds simultaneously, then. One was a moan from Gharlas, the other was a word whispered by Thymas: "Sharith."

"He's weakening, Thymas," I encouraged the boy. "You can break him! Keep trying!"

Thymas and I were together now. I fought Gharlas with words of encouragement, and the boy's entire body was quivering with the intense strain of what he was trying to do. We both knew that if he couldn't break free of Gharlas's control, one of us would have to kill the other.

"Sharith . . ." Thymas gasped, more loudly this time.

"Sharith . . . *kill their enemies!*" He jerked forward, as though he had been pressing against a physical barrier that had just given way.

Thymas gave a yell of triumph, and we whirled toward

Gharlas. He had turned his back to us, and seemed to be dancing, stepping quickly from one tile to another in a rhythmic pattern.

Has he flipped out for good? I wondered. Then it dawned on me.

"The secret passageway!" I shouted, and stated running. Thymas was right beside me, but we were already too late. Gharlas pressed on a section of the wall; it moved back to reveal the top steps of a narrow stairway leading downward to our right. One of the lamps stood on the table right beside him. He caught up the light and vanished down the stairway, leaving us in near-darkness. The wall section started moving back into place, unnervingly silently.

We reached the door an instant before it came flush with the rest of the wall. It pushed back on its bronze tracks easily enough, though it was heavy.

"Hold it while I get a lamp," I told Thymas. "If it closes, it'll lock, and we'll never figure out the sequence of tiles to push to open it again."

He leaned against the tall slab of wall, but demanded: "Is Tarani all right? Where is she?"

"There were five guards waiting for us," I said, as I got back with a lamp and an extra sword. "Tarani got knocked out in the fight, but I'm pretty sure she's all right. We'll brace this door open, so she'll know where we went."

We squeezed together on the few inches of landing inside the wall, and let the door begin to slide past us. I held the spare sword at waist level until the hilt was firmly caught. Then we started down the stairs, single file.

Like everything in Gandalara, Troman's Way was well constructed. Long, narrow slabs of marble lined the walls and supported similar ceiling slabs. The floor of the passageway looked like cobblestone, set directly into the earth to allow for both a dry walking surface and a means of draining off the moisture that seeped through the marble joinings.

The place stank abominably; the walls and rocks were covered with a growth like mildew that seemed to shrink away from our lamp as we passed by.

We tried to hurry, but we couldn't run across those slick rocks. The direction seemed right to take us under Lord Hall, but it was hopeless to try to estimate the distance we were covering. It seemed like hours before the passage ended in a narrow stairway, much like the first one, leading upward.

The door at the top was closed, but there wasn't any sort of lock that we could see. Cautiously, our swords ready, Thymas and I pressed our shoulders against it; it gave way easily.

We stepped sideways from behind the door, pushing aside a heavy tapestry. We were in the High Lord's treasure vault, which seemed to be L-shaped. We were facing straight down the long leg of the L, with the shorter branch leading off to our right.

Marble shelves stair-stepped up both long walls of the long wing, leaving a narrow walkway toward the end of the room, which was invisible past our circle of lamplight. A richly textured fabric was draped across the shelves, and against its dark background shone a dizzying array of gems, jewelry, and coins.

I glanced at the floor and noticed that it had tiles similar to that in Gharlas's house—just as I heard the soft whisper of the door as it moved back into place.

I whirled around and snatched at the tapestry, and discovered that we had come out through a section of a massive, wall-long woven scene. I fumbled around the shape of the receding door, but by the time I found the edge of the section, the door had closed and relocked.

"You can't get it open." It was Gharlas's voice, coming from the end of the shorter wing of the room. Our lamp cast enough light for us to see all the way to the far wall. Gharlas wasn't visible. I felt my skin begin to get restless.

"Throw down your swords, and I may let you live," the disembodied voice said.

Where the hell did he get all that confidence again? I wondered. *He was running scared when Thymas broke through; what could he have found here?* . . .

"Pretty clever, Gharlas," I said. "What better place to hide the Ra'ira than in Pylomel's own vault."

"You're remarkably quick, Rikardon, I must grant you that. Yes, I chose to face you without the Ra'ira for two reasons. First, it was an excellent test of how close one must be to the gem to utilize its special powers—closer, obviously, than from here to the pitiful quarters Pylomel assigned to me. Second, I was slightly concerned that the girl's mind-gift might also be able to work through the Ra'ira. Now that she is no longer involved, I have no further hesitation. *Do as I say: put down your swords!*"

"Show yourself, you cowardly bastard!" Thymas shouted. "Come out and face—*acchh* . . ."

His voice choked off, and he clutched at his throat with his free hand. I knew what he was feeling; my windpipe was closing more slowly, with a pressure that made me feel some pity for the big man Keeshah and I had strangled.

This was a stronger force than I had felt before. I could resist it more effectively than Thymas, but I wasn't immune to it. I would die of asphyxiation more slowly; that was all.

I never really believed we could lose, I realized, as I gasped for breath. *I felt so strong, with Thymas and Tarani on my side. I figured I might get killed, but not all three of us. But—damn it!—Gharlas is winning! There must be something more we can do, SOMETHING!*

With the onset of the attack, a light had appeared near the end of the short passage. Now Gharlas stepped out from around a hidden corner, carrying his freshly lit lamp in one hand. The Ra'ira rested on the palm of his other hand.

19

The lamplight penetrated the smooth surface of the gem, sparkled along the faint lines that marked its strange internal structure, then jumped out at us again. Gharlas's hand was bathed in blue light, his face lit from below with the pale edges of that reflecting glow. He walked toward us, insane, insufferable satisfaction on his face.

Keeshah! I called. **Can you help me again?**

I will try, he promised. I could sense that he had been running, and that he had reached the outskirts of the city. He was tired, fatigued by the frustration of not being with me, and on the brink of desperation because he could sense my doubt. We had broken Gharlas's power once this way, and I had yet to see Gharlas make the same mistake twice.

Not yet, I told Keeshah, and I deliberately slowed my

breathing. Panic was the last thing I needed. **He needs to be closer. I'll tell you when.**

But Gharlas stopped when he was only halfway down the room. Stopped, smiled, and pushed harder with his mind. Thymas dropped Rika and fell to his knees; I knew he had only seconds more to live.

The door behind the tapestry pushed open with a slight, but audible sound. Gharlas's attention wavered for an instant.

NOW, KEESHAH! I signaled, and the sha'um's consciousness surged into my mind like a muscle flexing against a binding. Gharlas reeled backward, and Thymas started taking deep breaths.

The man with the Ra'ira stared at us in astonishment. It didn't take telepathy to guess that he was suffering through the same revelation I had faced moments before. He knew he'd lost.

He threw his lamp to the floor; the glass chimney shattered, and the candle nearly went out.

Keeshah started to withdraw from me, but I held on for an instant. There were no words to the message we shared—only gratitude and joy. The exhilaration that comes only after a close brush with death, or after nearly losing a loved one. And I realized, belatedly, that in merging with me, Keeshah had endangered his own life. He would not have withdrawn until it was over, win or lose. It was conceivable that, so closely linked with me, the great cat would have died with me.

Together soon? Keeshah asked, when the link had faded.

Just as soon as possible, I promised, then returned my attention to Gharlas.

I was too slow. Thymas had been a single breath away from passing out, but he had reacted immediately when Gharlas let go. Gharlas, sprawled at Thymas's feet, was aboslutely still. When I reached them, Thymas was using Gharlas's sleeve to clean the blood from Rika's blade. He was still gasping, trying to catch his breath.

Thymas bent over, then straightened and held the Ra'ira and the lamp base. He turned the gem over, examining it near the candle flame. Then he pushed it toward me. "Here, take it," he said gruffly. I hung the lamp I carried on a bronze hook, and held out my hand. Thymas let the blue stone drop into my palm, just as we heard Tarani's voice.

"Thymas?" it said, sounding muffled. "Is that you? Where are you?"

We looked back to see the tapestry bulging around the door. The far edge of it flapped, and Tarani appeared at its edge. She looked around cautiously, and her face lit up when she saw us. She put her lamp down and came running the length of the room.

"Thymas," she cried, and threw her arms around him. "I'm so glad to see you!"

He hugged her joyfully, lifting her off her feet to whirl her around. There wasn't much space, so I moved out of the way. A cold, dead weight was hanging in my chest. To take my mind off of it, I busied myself trying to identify a familiar, whispering sound.

"The door!" I shouted. "Don't let it lock again!" I dashed to the tapestry and for the second, frustrating time, failed to block the door.

"What's the matter?" Tarani asked.

"What's the matter?" I raged, whirling on her. "We can't get out of this fleabitten place, that's what's the matter!"

"Rikardon," she said, coming down the room toward me. The light behind her showed the lines of her body through the loose-fitting desert tunic and trousers. "Are you all right?"

"You're the one we need to worry about," I said, grabbing her arm to turn her around so that her disturbing outline didn't show. I held her chin up and examined the bruise on the left side of her face. She flinched away from my probing fingers, and seemed about to say something.

"There's another door here," Thymas called. "Gharlas was trying to get out." He dragged the long body back around the corner where Gharlas had first appeared, then came back. Tarani and I met him at the doorway. "There's another treasure room over there, just like the one we were in, and just as full."

"Zefra said this door will open into the Council Chamber," I said, running my hand along the surface of the door. It was wooden, and not quite smooth. "Unfortunately, I forgot to ask her for a floorplan of Lord Hall. We might come out smack in the middle of the Celebration Dance.

"Tarani," I said, without looking at her, "do you think you could manage a three-way illusion to cover us, until we get out of the Hall?"

"I will do what I have to do," she answered.

"Maybe this will help," I said, and put the Ra'ira in her hand. For a moment, she looked as though she wanted to drop it, but then she closed her fingers around the blue gem.

"Ready?" I asked. They nodded.

We leaned on the door.

It didn't budge.

We tried again, pushing harder, and this time it moved a fraction of an inch. Sideways.

Suddenly the small depressions in the surface of the door made sense. We each gripped and pulled to the right. It moved—slowly at first, then so quickly that it slid to the end of its bronze runners with a determined clang that sounded as loud as a gunshot.

We moved through the large opening, tensed for another fight, but all we found was the empty Council Chamber. We were on a raised area at one end of a room which seemed to be about as long as the treasure rooms, but more than twice as wide. The one chair on the dais faced a rectangular table that did a fair job of filling up the room.

There were seven other chairs. Six were identical to the one near us—carved from wood, their backs and armrests adorned with etched metal plates—but they rested on the floor, a level below what could only be the High Lord's chair. There were three of these on each side of the table. The seventh chair was little more than a stool at the far end of the room.

The door started sliding shut. It was bigger than the opening through which we had stepped. It was nearly six feet wide and as tall as the nine-foot ceiling. Made of layers of wood laminated together, it was four inches thick. And if that weren't enough, covering it on this side was a thin sheet of bronze, decorated with a lot of tiny geometric designs.

I don't know how the Eddartans rigged that one-way spring system. The door was so well balanced that one man could open it. Thymas and I both put our weight and muscle against it, trying to *keep* it open. But it was determined to close, and we had to snatch our hands away at the last second to keep our fingers whole.

"Now what?" Thymas asked.

"Same plan," I said. I pointed to the far side of the room. "Different door."

"Wait," Tarani said. "Zefra must be nearby. Let me call her in here, Rikardon. She can tell us what to expect and I—I can say good-bye. I promised her," she added, a little defensively.

Thymas said: "Let's get *out* of here."

"And I promised *you,*" I reminded Tarani. "Do it. But keep it short." She nodded, then sank into one of the chairs and leaned back, holding the Ra'ira in her lap. She closed her eyes for a second, then said: "She's coming."

Using her power is getting easier for her, I thought. *That's another reason to get her out of here.*

I started pacing. Thymas started looking at the figures on the bronze face of the door, and Tarani just sat there, waiting.

I was at a loss to explain the sense of urgency I felt. A number of explanations occurred to me, all of them plausible, none of them precisely right.

Now that we had the Ra'ira, I was eager to get it away from Eddarta.

Knowing I was probably surrounded by the Eddartan "nobility" made me itchy.

Certainly, I was looking forward to hugging Keeshah.

Where are you now? I asked him.

In the city. Smells. Can't find you.

We're up on the hill, but you wait there. We'll be down soon. Has anybody seen you?

In answer, he sent me a flash of what he was seeing: a crowd of people, carrying torches, following him at a respectful distance. I saw something else that made me glad—Ronar was with him.

Nobody bothers us, Keeshah said. I would have laughed at the understatement, but my nerves were too jumpy. I was half-afraid I'd get hysterical.

A soft click warned us that the entry door was opening. Zefra slipped through, and let it swing shut behind her. "So Troman's Way *does* exist!" she said. "Gharlas?"

"Dead," I said.

"Good. You . . . recovered what you came for?"

Thymas gave a small start. "We found the gold, yes," I said, and out of the corner of my eye, I saw Thymas relax. Zefra noticed him. "May I present Thymas, of the Sharith? Thymas, this is the lady Zefra, Tarani's mother."

Thymas was prepared to greet her respectfully, but Zefra

merely glanced at him, nodded coolly, and started to walk past him. But she stopped, abruptly, near his left arm, and swung on him in a fury.

"You *dare* to bring that vile thing before the Bronze?" she demanded, and reached out as if to snatch up Rika's gleaming blade where it hung free of Thymas's baldric. "It was a symbol of trust between King and Guard, until the Guard turned its blade against the Kingdom. What *insolence* to bring it here!"

Tarani grabbed her mother's shoulders and pulled Zefra away from Thymas, who had jumped back with his hand on Rika's hilt.

So much for not judging the Sharith, I thought.

"How dare *you* insult our friend?" Tarani demanded of Zefra, yanking her around. "You speak of the distant past, Mother. That sword has no meaning here except that it has saved our lives."

Confronted by her daughter's anger, Zefra blazed up. "No meaning, you say? The *distant* past? You are mistaken, Tarani. The past is here in this room. As the Bronze is the symbol of the Kingdom, so is that sword the symbol of its destruction!" Zefra had shaken loose from Tarani and climbed to the dais. She touched the massive piece of decorated metal, almost reverently.

"This is the Bronze. It was created here in Eddarta, at the command of one of the early Kings. It was installed in Kä, to be the final test for one who would be High Lord. Harthim brought the Bronze back to Eddarta, and mounted it as you see it here. No one, other than the Lords and High Lord candidates, has ever seen it before."

She turned around and fixed her gaze on Tarani. The peculiar intensity I had seen before had returned to her face, and I thought that even Tarani saw it now, and was a little frightened.

"I was wrong to attack your friend, Tarani. There is meaning in his presence here with you. It is a signal that you can command the loyalty that Harthim lost.

"A message lies hidden on the Bronze, daughter. The very mind-gifted can read the message, because the All-Mind knows what it says. The mindpower has weakened in us through the generations since Harthim, and most of the message has been lost. I have heard that only the first few words are still readable."

Zefra went to Tarani and put her hands on the girl's shoulders, turned her to face the huge, patterned door. "But you can read it, Tarani. I know it. Read the message of the Bronze," Zefra breathed to her daughter.

My skin crawled.

"There is nothing here but meaningless decoration," Thymas said.

"There *is* a message!" Zefra cried. "This is the old writing. The message was imprinted first, then other markings were added to make all the characters look like the master figure. Those who have the power, whose link with the All-Mind is strongest, can see the original inscription."

"We don't have time for this," I said.

Tarani's back stiffened. "I think this is little enough to grant in return for all the help Zefra has given us."

I controlled my impatience, and nodded assent. Thymas moved restlessly away from the wall Tarani was going to "read"

Now that Zefra had explained the markings. I found some knowledge of the "old writing" in Markasset's memory.

Gandalaran characters were made up of lines joined in precise angles or crossing one another. Modern writing employed brush and ink on paper, and considerations of speed and appearance had allowed the development of curves and longer lines in writing style. But the original characters were based on the "master figure" Zefra had mentioned: eight short, straight lines, radiating from a common center at precise forty-five-degree angles from one another. Every character was made up of *some* of those lines.

I looked at the Bronze, and all I could see was the master figure, repeated over and over again. All the tiny marks were imprinted to exactly the same depth, were exactly the right length—the vertical and horizontal markings slightly longer than the intermediate lines.

But Tarani looked at that wall full of nonsense and started to read out loud. At first she read slowly, hesitating over every word. Then she began to read with more confidence.

I stared at her in amazement, and I noticed that she had the Ra'ira, hidden inside her clenched hand. Whether that was helping her, or her own native power was doing the trick, I couldn't have said. Zefra watched her daughter with a look of rapture as she and Thymas and I listened to Tarani's voice speaking a message from the distant past.

20

I greet thee in the name of the new Kingdom.

From chaos have we created order.
From strife have we enabled peace.
From greed have we encouraged sharing.

Not I alone, but the Sharith have done this.
Not we alone, but the Ra'ira has done this.

THESE ARE THE WEAPONS
OF WHICH I GIVE THEE CHARGE
AND WARNING:

The Sharith are our visible strength—

Offer them respect; . . .
Be ever worthy of their loyalty.

The Ra'ira is our secret wisdom—

Seek out the discontented;
Give them answer, not penalty.

THIS IS THE TASK I GIVE THEE
AS FIRST DUTY:

As you read the scholar's meaning
Within the craftsman's skill,
So read within yourself
Your commitment

To guide
To lead
To learn
To protect

If you lack a high need
To improve life for all men,
Then turn aside now,
For you would fail the Kingdom.

I greet thee in the name of the new Kingdom,
And I charge thee: care for it well.

I am Zanek,
King of Gandalara

I was totally stunned. Not just by the fact that Tarani had read the thing. Not even by the nobility of its message. The signature was what got to me.

Zanek? Zanek had the Ra'ira when he created the Kingdom? But Thanasset said the stone had been sent to Kä when the corrupt Kings began to demand tribute, which was ages *after Zanek's day. Maybe Thanasset, and the other Supervisors, prefer to think that the Ra'ira was used only during the bad times, so they can justify keeping it in Raithskar.*

I don't know the answers. But I do know that there is no more relationship between Zanek and Pylomel than between me and a vineh. That foolish gem belongs in Raithskar, where Pylomel and his kind can't get to it.

Zefra had Tarani—who seemed a little dazed by what she had read—by her shoulders, and was shaking her lightly. "You see? Yours is the strongest mindpower in generations, Tarani. You are meant to be High Lord. It is why you came here."

Tarani pulled out of her stupor to push away her mother's arms. "So that we can rule your way, instead of Pylomel's? Mother, were you not listening? Zanek warned that the power of the Ra'ira could be used well or badly. He was a good man; I could sense that from the message. But there are few like him in the world today." Her voice trembled. "Volitar was one. I thought you might be another, but I see I was wrong.

No matter what you say you want, Mother, you are not much different from Pylomel."

Zefra gasped, and hauled back her hand, and slapped Tarani. The girl accepted the blow, and faced her mother again.

"I offer you my thanks, Mother," she said. "For your protection of me all these years and, now, for giving me proof of the rightness of our duty. We *must* get the Ra'ira back to Raithskar, where it can be protected."

"*Tarani!*" I said sharply. Her intake of breath told me she realized her mistake, but the damage was already done.

"You *have* the Ra'ira?" Zefra whispered, and began to plead. "Think of it, child. You could be High Lord. The changes you could make. The good you could do. The things that Volitar believed in—you can make them real! If you have no other ambition, merely keeping Indomel from becoming High Lord would be a thing worth doing."

A new voice, high-pitched and full of sarcasm, sounded from behind us. "What a loving thing to say, Mother."

We whirled around to see a handsome boy, tall and dark-furred, close the entryway door. He walked through the room as if he owned it, and stopped a couple of paces away from the women. Thymas and I were both on the other side of the table, with our hands on our swords. But he made no move toward the jeweled dagger that complemented his rich clothing—a floor-length tunic of green covered by a heavier, sleeveless tunic in a deeper tone of green. He just looked Tarani up and down in an appraising, insulting way.

"I grant you that this lovely creature is talented," he said. "I felt the compulsion she sent to you. I didn't understand what it was, until I saw you sneaking into the Council Chamber—where you have no business being.

"I caught the door before it quite closed, and I heard almost everything, but I'll be glad if you'll confirm a few things. For instance, I gather that Gharlas is dead?"

"Yes," Zefra said.

"I should be grateful for that, I suppose. My father is many ways a fool, but never so seriously as when he permitted Gharlas to win the favor of the Guard. My first act, as High Lord, was to be the destruction of Gharlas—an unnecessary task, now."

He walked slowly beside the table, letting one long-fingered hand caress the back of one of the huge chairs.

"I heard another name that sounds vaguely familiar," he said. "Volitar?"

"He was my father," Tarani said. "A good man. Gharlas killed him."

I wondered what she thought of the self-possessed boy who faced her. She showed no affection or revulsion, merely wariness.

"Ah, I remember, now—the jeweler who disappeared before I was born, around the same time as my mother's infamous escapade. Or should I say 'our mother,' since it appears you are my half sister?"

"No," Zefra said, with a fierceness that made the boy retreat a step. "How often I have longed to say this to you, Indomel. Tarani is your *true* sister, your elder, the rightful candidate for High Lord."

"What are you saying?" Tarani demanded.

"*Pylomel* is your father," Zefra said. "The night he visited me, the night before I left Eddarta—he *compelled* me to lie with him, and how I hated him for it. I didn't have the power, then, to resist him completely, but I managed one small defiance—I hid it from him that I was fertile, and that I had conceived.

"But I told Volitar the truth, that I carried a child with a great gift—I could already sense it, Tarani. I feared to raise you in Lord City, for Pylomel would have taken you from me. Volitar understood. He took me away. He loved you like his own daughter."

"I *am* his daughter!" Tarani cried. "Everything I am, Volitar gave me. I refuse to accept that—that filthy old man as my father!"

Indomel laughed with genuine humor, but the sound of it was sour.

"An apt description, sister, and a wise choice. We who are in this room believe that you are my full and true sister, but should you claim that before the Lords, you would find it difficult to prove. All you have is the word of a woman who has been locked away, by choice, for many years, and who is generally spoken of as eccentric, if not actually insane." He smiled. "A reputation I have encouraged at every opportunity, dear Mother. You see—Tarani, is it?—our lack of affection for one another is entirely mutual."

Tarani's neutrality vanished. "You are a monster," she said.

"Yes," he said agreeably. "And I have power that not even our dear mother suspects."

Suddenly, there was pain. Not the concentrated hurting that Gharlas had inflicted, but a general, intense pain. It struck. Thymas, Tarani, and I flinched, gasping. It receded.

Indomel was smiling.

I really hate this, I thought. *Aren't we ever going to get out of this bizarre place?*

"I can use a less . . . exotic form of compulsion, as well. Your friends look formidable, Tarani, but could they defeat the entire Guard? No, I think not."

"She is your *sister,* Indomel!" Zefra cried.

"So you say, Mother, and so I must believe. Because of that, and because this is the eve of a great day for me, I am feeling generous. Tarani and her friends may leave here alive—on condition that they never return to Eddarta, and that they leave the Ra'ira with me."

"Do not take us for fools, Indomel," Tarani said. "We have not come this far to give up now."

"I am not often generous, sister, as you should have learned by now, if only from Zefra's teaching. Why don't you consult with your friends? I can't imagine two healthy young men sharing the company of such a delightful creature without becoming totally devoted to her. How do they feel about your being the first to die?"

Tarani jerked convulsively, then doubled over, moaning in pain, and Indomel sighed. "You may have a strong gift, Tarani, but it is limited by your kindness. I have no such restraint on mine." He waved his hand, as if in dismissal. "I have nothing to fear from you."

"Then let her go!" I shouted, running around the table to put my arms around the girl. Thymas was right behind me.

"Stop hurting her," he growled, "or I will cut your hands off and feed them to you."

Indomel, self-assured as he had seemed until then, took a step backward before Thymas's ferocity. Then he straightened his shoulders and spoke with some bravado: "I will stop when I have the Ra'ira."

Tarani gasped: "No!"

I stared at Indomel, projecting my hatred. I hoped that, if his power could penetrate my "double-mindedness", the strong emotion would mask my plans.

"It isn't worth Tarani's life, Thymas," I said. I opened the pouch at my belt and pulled out the duplicate we had brought from Volitar's workshop, that Gharlas had wanted so desperately to possess.

Indomel's long, thin fingers took the glass piece from my hand. He turned it over once, looking at it carefully; then Tarani stood up, free of pain. She kept one hand clenched around the real Ra'ira; the other hand reached for mine and pressed it tightly.

"The Ra'ira," Indomel breathed, looking through the blue "stone" toward the light. He was trying to seem only politely interested, but his breathing had quickened. He was beginning to see the implications of what he *thought* he had.

"There have always been legends, of course, that this beautiful bauble had some power of its own. How I shall enjoy learning the truth of it.

"How did it come to be in Eddarta?" he asked.

"Gharlas stole it from Raithskar," I answered shortly. "You said you would let us go."

"Oh, yes, certainly. Go on. I'm sure my dear sister can provide you concealment as you move through the celebration. You may wish to pause a moment, and have a dance or two. What are you waiting for? Go on." His eyes never left the blue stone as he waved us past him.

We moved down the room toward the entry door. Tarani turned back to her mother. "Zefra?" she said uncertainly. "Please . . ."

"I will stay," Zefra said. "I—regret striking you, Tarani. I heard Volitar's words in your voice, and they shamed me. But I cannot change now, daughter. Go carefully . . . and be safe."

Tarani waved her hand slightly, then pulled herself around to face the chamber door. Music and laughter greeted us as we opened it. A short corridor lay before us. Beyond the open entryway we could see the food-serving area of the party, a chaotic collection of tables and servants.

Without bodies blocking sight of our actions from the Council Chamber I took the Ra'ira from Tarani's unresisting hand, and put it in my pouch. We sheathed our swords and joined hands.

"Ready?" Tarani asked.

Thymas and I nodded, and the three of us stepped out into the Celebration Dance.

21

The door moved behind us, and we heard the muffled sounds of a struggle. We jumped back into the concealment of the hallway and whirled around.

Indomel was pressing back against the stone wall, fury and amazement plain in his face. His mouth opened and closed, but made no sound.

Zefra stood near him, not touching him. She was glowing with triumph. "He planned to betray you to the Guard," she said, then smiled grimly. "But I have power that not even my dear son suspects. I can control him—for a time. With your help, Tarani, *we* could control him—always. Perhaps he is right, and you could not be acclaimed High Lord. But we could use *Indomel* himself, Tarani, to bring about the changes we know are right. I ask you again: stay."

Tarani hesitated.

I thought, again, how much the two women resembled one another. Height, facial structure, bearing—it was uncanny. Could I blame Tarani for feeling the call of a common heritage that was so plainly visible to all of us?

What will I do if she wants to stay? I wondered. *It's her choice. Please, Tarani . . .*

She said, softly and sadly: "No."

Zefra sighed, and I started to breathe again.

"Then go quickly, daughter," Zefra said, and opened her hands to show us what she held. "I will keep the Ra'ira." She watched us warily, prepared for some argument.

"Keep it, then," Tarani said. "But don't rely upon it, Mother—remember that the Kingdom fell, without it.

"Thymas. Rikardon."

The commanding tone of her voice hid the grief I knew Tarani must be feeling. Deceiving Zefra was *necessary*. Using her power to help us get away was *necessary*. Leaving her was *necessary*.

But the only thing that made it *possible* for Tarani was the glimpse she had been granted of her mother's desire for actual power. There was no stronger argument for securing the true Ra'ira than the way Zefra, who knew the corruptive influence of power better than most, coveted that harmless piece of blue glass.

So we turned away and started once more across the dance floor. I felt Tarani's hand trembling, and I knew she was close to collapse. Possibly for that reason, she had assumed the familiar semblance of Rassa, and given me the look of Yoman. Thymas she had not changed physically, but she had given him, as well as us, clothing appropriate to the occasion.

We moved around the tables slowly, only pretending to be surveying the selection of refreshments. Ahead of us was the door which led to the main avenue of the city—and to the entry gate. To our left and right, the ballroom flowed around the Council Chamber that was the core of Lord Hall. People milled and danced, laughed and talked. And one particularly large group had planted itself directly in front of the door we were heading for.

Is it possible to die of impatience? I wondered, as Tarani shifted our path into an arc which would swing around the knot of people. *I'm going to jump right out of my skin, any minute now.*

The group of people was in a constant state of change, with individuals leaving, joining, or working their way through. Just as our arc began to swing back toward the doorway—it was barely twenty paces away, now—someone broke away and stepped right in front of us.

It was Pylomel.

"Doubtless you have forgotten our appointment for later this evening," he said softly. "Lovely Rassa. I look forward to it now, more than ever." He reached up to stroke the golden hair he thought he saw—and Tarani wasn't up to coping with a tactile illusion. As his hand touched her hair, the entire illusion vanished.

I reached for my sword, but Pylomel didn't raise the alarm. His mouth sagged open, his eyes grew large, and he sank to his knees, holding onto Tarani for support. She pushed him away, shuddering.

People looked around, just as Pylomel fell over. When they saw the hilt of Thymas's dagger protruding from the High Lord's chest, just under his rib cage, somebody screamed.

We drew our swords and headed for the door, three deadly points on our triangle. Nobody near us was going to be a problem—there was a lot of yelling, and a general and uniform scramble to get out of the way. I was surprised at the contempt I felt as I thought: *They're so used to having everything done for them—including their fighting.*

Trouble is, I thought in the next second, *they've got people to do it.*

There were four guards in the doorway, waiting for us to get clear of the crowd.

Thymas and I attacked, leaving Tarani to keep the mob at bay. Apparently Gharlas had appropriated the best fighters for his own plans, because these four were rookies. In seconds, they were all dead or badly damaged, and the three of us ran out into the avenue.

Lamps had been placed on platforms along the main avenue. We had a clear view to the city entrance. The river, with a line of rafts tied up by its bank, was barely visible, though we could hear its rushing murmur clearly above the clamor coming from Lord Hall.

We ran like hell along that lighted pathway, then skidded to a halt, not a hundred yards from the gate. Where I had expected two guards, maybe four, there were twenty. And they had heard the ruckus. They were ready for us.

Tarani groaned, and Thymas swore: "By the Nine! Is there no escape from this fleabitten place? Not even the sha'um could fight these odds!"

Damn Eddarta and its blasted Celebration Dance, I thought. *And its blasted hired muscle. These guys know it'll be their skins if we get away. Thymas is right, we're trapped. Unless—*

This was a Gandalaran situation, and suddenly I was thinking like Ricardo, who saw *two* gateways into—and out of—the city. "Come on," I said, and dragged Tarani toward the line of tied rafts. Thymas followed. The guards set up a yell and started running down the avenue.

I let go of Tarani's hand and jumped from the bank onto one of the rafts. It wobbled in the water; I dropped to my knees to steady it for Tarani's arrival.

But Tarani and Thymas were standing on the bank, staring at me in confusion.

"What are you doing?" Thymas demanded. "There aren't

any vleks, and anyway they would be too slow—what are you *doing?*"

"Shut up and get out here!" I ordered.

Tarani dropped to all fours and crawled out to me with teeth-gritting slowness. I put my arms around her and could almost feel her terror through her skin.

She knows what's going on, I thought. *But she came anyway.*

Thymas was still on the bank, and he had figured it out, too. "That's crazy!" he said. "You'll kill us all!"

Two lines held the raft against the shore. I slashed one, and the raft swung out toward the current, Tarani and I balancing precariously on our knees. "You want *them* to kill you?" I asked. He looked over his shoulder at the oncoming guards, fifteen yards and closing. Then he turned back and took a deep breath.

"No, don't jump!" I warned, too late. He landed on the tied corner of the raft. "Grab him!" I told Tarani, and sliced through the last line.

By some miracle, Thymas didn't send us all into the river. "On your stomachs," I yelled. "Spread your weight on the surface of the raft." Daggers and swords flew overhead as the raft drifted away from shore. A couple of the guards, either braver or more desperate, ventured out into the water after us, but retreated when it got too deep to walk.

I didn't have any trouble getting Thymas and Tarani to hang on to the ropes that lashed the reeds into logs, and tied the logs together. They were terrified, and probably seasick, as the rudderless raft spun slowly toward the arch that marked the edge of Lord City.

The guards were running along the bank, arguing about what to do. Some of them were laughing at us; others were just plainly amazed. There seemed to be no question at all in their minds that we were totally, thoroughly crazy.

Things floated in Gandalara. Pontoon bridges. Rafts steadied by vlek power. *People* drank water, bathed in it, used it to irrigate crops. They did *not* float on it. It simply wasn't part of the Gandalaran lifestyle.

No wonder Tarani and Thymas were scared to death. I felt some of their fear, myself—but Ricardo's logic put a hammerlock on Markasset's traditionalism.

"Listen," I warned the others, "when we hit the rapids,

we're going to get wet. *Don't let go!* Even if the raft breaks up, pieces of it will float."

The raft was through the archway, moving more or less straight and faster, now, toward the brink of the cataract. Tarani looked up, whimpered, and pressed her face back into the reeds. Thymas looked up, too, and watched grimly as the blackness of the empty Gandalaran sky seemed to rush toward us. A roar of falling water drifted up from the hidden slope of the hill.

"*HANG ON!*" I screamed, as the raft tipped sickeningly forward.

The raft plunged down the hillside, crashing against rocks, dipping and bucking like a thing alive and trying its best to get rid of us. It didn't matter that it was too dark to see; all our senses were concentrated on breathing, when we had the opportunity, and clinging to that bundle of reeds.

The raft took one deep dive, and when it bobbed to the surface, it took us a few seconds to realize that we were level again. I looked up to see lights and the straight lines of the edges of buildings ahead of us.

I lifted myself cautiously to my hands and knees, to make sure. We were at the inner edge of Eddarta. "Tarani, Thymas," I urged, "take a look. We made it."

Just then, the raft hit a hidden crosscurrent and spun wildly. My knees slipped, and I wound up half in, half out of the water, my weight canting the surface of the raft at a crazy angle.

"Rikardon!" Tarani cried, and started to come after me.

"Stay there!" I ordered.

We had drifted into the city itself, now, and there was a crowd of people, carrying torches, on the riverbank. I wasn't sure how they knew we were here, or what they thought of us, but the immediate problem didn't relate to them at all. As far as I could see, we were spinning slowly, and not making much speed downstream.

All right, smart guy, I thought to myself. *How the hell are you going to get this thing back to ground? Didn't think about that, did you?*

My hands were stiff and chafed, and I was beginning to swear at the weight of the gold around my waist—but when I thought of it, the solution occurred to me.

"Thymas!" I called. "When I move, you move along the

opposite edge, to keep us balanced. Tarani, you stay put. Understand?"

They both nodded, and Thymas released each hand in turn, working out the stiffness in preparation of moving around.

I was hanging off the raft from its side, so that water was striking abreast of the reed log. I started pulling myself along the log by its lashings; Thymas crept along the far edge in the other direction. It was tricky, turning the corner, but worth it—with my body weighing down the log ends, the current channeled itself along the ridges, and the spinning motion stopped. When I had worked my way into the center of that edge, we started moving downriver with some speed.

Only now there was a new problem. I couldn't get back up on the raft. The lashings which held the logs together were too close to the end of the raft to give me any leverage, and the next set which could provide a handhold was too far away to reach. All I could do was hang on.

Rikardon? The thought struck my mind, and I realized that it had been repeated before—I had been too busy surviving to recognize it. The small mystery of how the crowd of people had spotted us in the dark was solved, too—they were following the sha'um.

Keeshah! I called. **Follow the raft down the river.**

"Tarani, untie the middle lashing of the raft. Don't cut it unless you have to."

She started working at it with one hand and got nowhere. Thymas readjusted his position, and their two hands, together, loosened one knot. It was slow going, and I was beginning to wonder if my arms would hold out—but at last they had a good length of the sturdy, woven rope free.

Thymas—who, of course, was aware of the sha'um—had already seen what I had in mind. He pulled Tarani down to his end of the raft, tipping me out of the water for a moment, then moved nearly to the middle and stood up cautiously. He tied one end of the rope to another lashing, then threw the other end toward the bank. It fell far short, and he dragged the rope back, talking to himself.

"I'll try to guide us closer to shore," I shouted at him. "Tell me when you think we're close enough for the rope to reach." I strained my aching arms and pretended I really was a rudder, holding my body rigid with the legs pulled up at an angle. I could feel the difference in the water pressure against my body.

I'll be damned! It's working! I thought, and suddenly I had new energy.

Even that second wind was gone, by the time Thymas called to say it was time. I took a deep breath, let go with one hand, and dragged along underwater, fumbling with the fastening on my homemade belt. Finally it was free, and I spent my last bit of energy swinging the long, heavy thing up to the deck of the raft.

Thymas grabbed it, tied it to the rope, and threw it at the shore, nearly all in one motion. None too soon, either, because without that belt I made a rotten rudder. We were already moving toward the center of current again.

I craned to see the shore, and was surprised that we had left most of the city behind. The crowd of torches was still there, the huge shapes of the sha'um clearly silhouetted. There was a roar of noise from the nearly invisible people.

I had told Keeshah what we were doing, and I assumed Thymas had told Ronar. I saw the belt arc through the torchlight, and heard it slap into the ground and slither toward the river as we moved away from the bank. Keeshah went after it, pawing at it like a kitten chasing a string—and then he had it in his teeth.

He dug his claws into the muddy shore and yanked—and Thymas pitched head over heels into the water. He surfaced near the raft; I grabbed him and held him up until he was able to get a grip on the lashings.

The sha'um hauled us in leapfrog fashion, one pulling until the other had a jaw grip on the rope closer to the bank, then circling around while the other pulled.

When we scrambled to shore, we didn't take time to say hello. Thymas caught up the weighted belt, cut it free of the rope, then leaped on Ronar's back. I mounted Keeshah, and Tarani swung on behind me. The half-circle of torches opened where we aimed.

Wet, Keeshah complained, then carried us out into the night beyond Eddarta.

22

For more than two hours we ran through the pale moonlight. We passed through grainfields that looked like thick black carpet. We pounded through pastures, scattering grayish shapes—terrified vlek and glith.

I pressed my face into Keeshah's fur and didn't think of anything at all, for a while, except the exhilaration of riding again. There was an open, flowing contact between my mind and Keeshah's that was like a mental hug. There was little deception possible in our relationship; we each knew how glad the other was that we were together again.

Gradually my awareness expanded to include the others who were with us. Thymas and Ronar were a single, moving shadow off to my left, and Tarani was a warm pressure against my back. A hooting call from above told me that Lonna was nearby. For a breathless moment, I felt the bonds which tied me to each of them.

They were different—less intense, less intimate—than the special touching Keeshah and I could share. But I felt them.

It was an amorphous feeling, and very brief, like a glimpse into the heart of a brilliant diamond when, just for a second or two, you can *almost* perceive the structure of the faceting. You can *almost* understand—not the crisp angles and cool planes of the stone, but the *art* of the gemcutter who chose them and executed them.

It went beyond simply a sense of shared destiny—the team spirit of which I had spoken in Dyskornis.

It went beyond gratitude that each of them had saved my life.

It went beyond pride that, together, we had accomplished what we had set out to do—that we were carrying the Ra'ira back to Raithskar.

Team spirit, gratitude, pride. None of them quite identified what I felt, yet they were all part of it. I reached for the truth with all my intuition, but the moment passed too quickly.

I felt my failure to understand as a piercing, cold ache, an inconsolable sense of loss.

I sought comfort in the steady rhythm of Keeshah's movement. After awhile, the stinging sadness eased, and I slept.

I woke when Keeshah's rhythm changed. **What?* I muttered sleepily to the sha'um.

Other one stops, Keeshah told me.

I came fully awake in a hurry. Tarani's weight stirred slightly as I moved, and I thought: *Could she be asleep, riding second? She must be utterly exhausted.* And she *hasn't recently recovered from Thymas's injuries . . .*

I suffered a twinge of pure panic as I opened my eyes. We seemed to be in a narrow corridor with walls so tall that I couldn't see over them from my present eye-level, which was Keeshah's shoulder height. I thought that we had gotten turned around, and were back in Eddarta.

"Thymas!" I called, sitting up. Tarani, startled into wakefulness, put her arms around my chest to steady herself.

"What's wrong?" she asked. Her cheek pressed my shoulder for a moment, then lifted. "Where are we?"

I felt foolish as the disorientation faded. Sitting up had brought my line of vision above the obstructions beside us, and I could see that the "walls" of the corridor were lattice frames covered with leafy growth. We were on a farm, in a Gandalaran version of a berry patch. The frames were about ten feet long, and stood in rows about six feet apart.

Thymas's head popped up, two rows away and some thirty feet behind us. "Here," he said. "What's the matter?"

"Nothing," I said. "I was asleep—"

"You woke suddenly. When you didn't see me, you assumed that I had fallen behind, *once more,* isn't that right?"

He said it with a bristling finality that dared me to contradict him. I could see him well enough in the pale moonlight to read sullenness in the shape of his mouth, resentment in the set of his shoulders.

I tried to count to ten. I got all the way to two.

"Sure, that's right," I agreed. "You're our weak link, Thymas. You and Ronar. Of course I have to look out for you all the time." I could find no trace in myself of the gentle kinship I had sensed earlier. "I was so afraid you'd just quit on us that I gave you Serkajon's sword to bring to Eddarta. You might fail *us*, I reasoned, but you'd never shirk your fleabitten Sharith duty!"

"Rikardon!" Tarani shouted, pulling at my shoulders. "You will regret what you have said. Be silent now."

Thymas looked grim. He was walking Ronar along the row of frames, coming opposite Keeshah.

"I've coddled this fool with my silence long enough," I said. "Now I'll say what he's wanted to hear—that he's been a stone around our necks ever since we left Thagorn. He lied to his father when he promised to obey me. His *actions* have sometimes been obedient, but his *thoughts* never have. Twice, Gharlas has used him to try to kill me. I can't help but think there was a predisposition in that direction before Gharlas took a hand."

Thymas was facing me, now, across the top of the barrier. He was deadly calm. "You're right about that last, Rikardon. Let's get out of this field, and settle it. I'll even give you back Serkajon's ever-precious sword."

"I don't want to kill you, Thymas—for Dharak's sake. And I don't need Rika to loosen your tusks."

Keeshah and Ronar leaped away, running down the parallel rows to the end of the field. Tarani was beating on my shoulders, shouting something I refused to hear.

When we reached an open meadow, I slid off Keeshah's back, knocking away Tarani's clutching hands. Thymas landed on the ground at the same time, berries showering out from the cupped hem of his tunic.

I threw myself at him.

He ducked my swinging fist, and tripped me. I went down and rolled; his stomping foot hit the grassy stuff instead of my throat. He was on me again as I got to my feet. I let my balance shift backward, flipping him over my head as we fell. I jumped for him, landing on the ground as he rolled out from under just in time. He got to his feet and swung a kick at my ribs that connected with breath-stopping power.

I caught the leg, pulled him off balance, crawled up his body, felt the satisfaction of my fist slamming into his jaw.

Suddenly, there were three of us on the ground, wrestling. Tarani had thrust herself between us and was pushing us apart, taking some of our blows and delivering a few of her own in the process.

"Stop it!" she was yelling. "For Zanek's sake, will you two fleasons *stop it*!"

It was as though I were waking from a dream. The meadow was gray and silver in the moonlight. I could sense the vine-frames looming behind me. I could *see* Keeshah and Ronar, facing each other across us, their thickened tails and standing neckfur clearly revealed in silhouette against the grayish sky.

I sat on the ground, looking at Tarani, and remembered the sting of her hand across my face. Thymas, too, seemed stunned by the girl's fury.

"Fools!" she was raging. "Both of you—*fools*! Will you do to yourselves what Gharlas could not?" She stood up, making a sound of contempt. "If I thought Keeshah would carry me alone, I would take the Ra'ira and go. Indomel would be delighted, I'm sure, to find you fighting each other."

"Indomel?" Thymas echoed. "But Zefra was controlling him."

"Believing that her power was increased by the Ra'ira," I said. "That extra strength won't last long. Then they *will* send out pursuit."

"If I were in his place, I'd let us go quietly," Thymas said. "He thinks *he* has the Ra'ira—if we were caught, we could tell others."

"He is obligated to avenge the death of his father," I said. "He will make a show, at least, of pursuing us. And if he finds us, you can bet we won't have much chance to do any talking."

Thymas stared at me for so long that I wondered if his mind had slipped away. Then Tarani said: "Of course—you did not know that the man you killed was Pylomel."

"The High Lord?" Thymas said, still trying to understand. He surged to his feet, went to Tarani and touched her arms. "Your *father*, Tarani . . . I didn't know, I swear by the first King."

The girl jerked herself away from him. "*Volitar* was my true father," she snapped. "The sha'um can outrun any pursuit Indomel may send," she said. "Shall we go on?"

"Not together," Thymas said. He pulled Rika out of his baldric, and turned to face me. The blade shone softly in the moonglow.

What little refreshment I had gained from my nap on

Keeshah's back had been drained away by our brief, explosive struggle. Where I wasn't actually cut or bruised, I ached with weariness. The desperate strength that had kept me going through the fight with Gharlas and the riotous trip down the Tashal was utterly used up. I knew, and the boy knew, and Tarani knew, that if Thymas wanted to kill me, he could.

He grabbed the long steel blade, and offered me the hilt of Serkajon's sword.

"I knew why you gave me this at Stomestad," he said angrily. "Am I a cub, to be tricked and teased into doing what I promised? Take it back, and free me from this 'team'. You have the Ra'ira. Our purpose is finished."

Numbly, I reached out and accepted the sword. The hilt felt cool and *right* in my hand, and I realized how much I had missed having Rika with me. I pulled myself to my feet, drew the sword I carried, and offered it hilt-first to the boy.

"I had to surrender your sword to a Lord City guard, Thymas," I said. "Take this one, for now. When I return to Raithskar, and our purpose is *really* finished, I'll replace it with the best sword I can find. Something worthy of the next Lieutenant."

Thymas lifted the bronze blade, and slipped it through his baldric.

"I never meant to let you think you weren't trusted or important," I said. "We'd have failed without you. I saw what it cost you to throw off Gharlas's control."

And to overcome your conditioning about water, I thought. *It took guts to jump out to that raft. Only I can't say that without explaining why I wasn't horrified by the very concept of floating on a river*.

"I can't say it's always been a pleasure, Thymas, but riding with you and Ronar has been an honor. I owe you a life-debt many times over. If you ever need someone to guard you . . ."

Hesitantly, I held out my hand.

Thymas had seen me use the handshake, before, as a parting or greeting gesture. He gripped my hand with a warmth that surprised me. It must have surprised him, too; he seemed embarrassed as he spoke.

"We share that life-debt, Rikardon," he said. "I respect your sword, and I've learned to respect your leadership. I can't yet call you a friend, as Dharak does. But I do call you Captain."

It was the last thing I expected to hear from Thymas. I was too stunned to speak. I walked over to Ronar, and offered my left hand, palm up. He dipped his head, and the stiff/softness of whiskers and fur grazed my palm. I reached up to stroke the fur along his cheek. That was a liberty usually permitted only to a sha'um's rider, and I was pleased that Ronar allowed it.

I discovered that my voice was working again. "It has been good, riding with you," I told the sha'um, then turned back to Thymas.

He and Tarani were locked in a close embrace, kissing. I stared in shock, too tired to be embarrassed, in too much physical pain to feel the inner hurting. Much.

When they pulled apart, I said: "Go with him if you want to, Tarani."

"Why would you think she wants to come with me?" Thymas asked, his chin hooked over Tarani's arm, which still rested on his shoulder.

I made an indefinite gesture to indicate their present physical arrangement. "Why wouldn't I?"

"Because she *loves* you," he said. "She told me so in Stomestad."

Before I could hold it back, I stammered: "But—but I *saw* you, the night before we left . . ."

Tarani dropped her arms and stepped around Thymas. "You *saw* us?" she demanded.

"Accidentally," I hurried to say. "I was walking by the room—"

"Is that why you—?" She stopped herself abruptly, with a glance at Thymas. I couldn't tell in the dim light, but I thought she was blushing.

"No," I said. "I told you, Thymas had nothing to do with that."

"With what?" Thymas asked, plainly bewildered. When neither one of us answered, he shrugged. "Well, Captain, what you *saw* in Stomestad was a good-bye to what Tarani and I once shared. I had fewer regrets than I expected; Tarani had changed, and you and she seemed to belong together. We promised friendship, but our love isn't forgotten. Do you begrudge me a farewell kiss?"

"It may not be farewell," Tarani said, looking at me. "Rikardon suggested I go with you. Perhaps he wants it that way."

A sound startled us all. Thymas was laughing. It was the first time I had heard his laugh; it was a full, hearty noise that cracked through the tension in the air. He walked to Ronar and mounted, still laughing. As the sha'um stood up, he said: "Maybe if I leave you two alone, you can start talking to each other. And that's one conversation I'm not sorry to miss." He took a deep breath. "I think I understand you better, now, Rikardon. You're still the strangest man I've ever met—and you and Tarani are well matched. You'll both be welcome in Thagorn at any time."

"Thank you, Thymas," I said, and pulled my attention away from Tarani. "Give Dharak my best regards."

"I will," he promised. He waved a hand to me, and then to Tarani.

Even after Ronar's running figure had disappeared, I stood still, staring off into the distance, not the least surprised that I already missed the boy. Tarani's hand on my shoulder drew me back to the present.

I turned and held her closely, gently.

Go soon? Keeshah asked.

"Keeshah is restless," I said, still holding Tarani. "We do have some talking to do . . . can it wait?"

I felt her head moving against my shoulder as she nodded. Keeshah crouched, and we mounted, Tarani riding second, as usual. There was special meaning to the weight of her body against my back.

Take us home to Raithskar, I told Keeshah, and let myself really relax.

It's a little-known fact of life, I thought sleepily, *that, now and then, the odds* have *to turn in your favor.*

END PROCEEDINGS: INPUT SESSION THREE

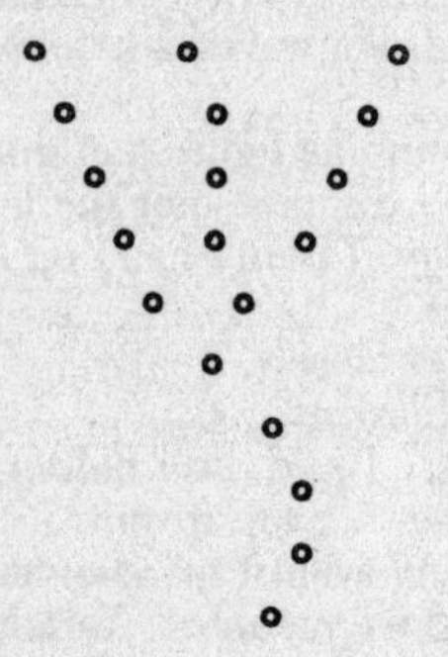

—I shall withdraw our minds from the All-Mind . . . and mine from yours . . . Is the Record now complete?

—This portion of it is complete, yes.

—Will you wish to Record again?

—Someday the full accounting must be made to the All-Mind. But, as you promised, the Recording process is fatiguing. I must rest before I can begin the next portion. May I call upon you again, Recorder?

—At any time. I am at your service.

About the Authors

VICKI ANN HEYDRON met RANDALL GARRETT in 1975. In 1978, they were married, and also began planning the Gandalara Cycle. A broad outline for the entire Cycle had been completed, and a draft of *The Steel of Raithskar* nearly finished, when Randall suffered serious and permanent injury. Working from their outline, Vicki has completed the Cycle. Of all seven books, Vicki feels that *The River Wall* is most uniquely hers. The other titles in the Cycle are *The Glass of Dyskornis*, *The Bronze of Eddarta*, *The Well of Darkness*, *The Search for Kä*, and *Return to Eddarta*.

Vicki lives in Austin, Texas, and is currently working on *Bloodright*, an occult novel, and *Castle of Judgment*, a futuristic mystery.